PENGUIN BOOKS

STRIP THE WILLOW

Sybil Marshall was born in 1913 and grew up in East Anglia. A villager all her life, she witnessed the breakdown of the old way of life in a rural community following the sudden growth of mechanized farming and the post-war period attitude to sexual morality. Having been a village schoolteacher, at the age of forty-seven she went to Cambridge University to read English. She became a Lecturer in Education at Sheffield University and subsequently Reader in Primary Education at the University of Sussex. In 1965 she devised Granada Television's popular programme *Picture Box*, and continued to act as adviser and to write the Teacher's Handbook until 1989.

As well as works on education, Sybil Marshall has written non-fiction books recording life in her native fens in their pre-war isolation, including *Fenland Chronicle*, *The Silver New Nothing* and *A Pride of Tigers* (Penguin, 1995). She also won the Angel Prize for Literature for *Everyman's Book of English Folk Tales*. Her first novel, the bestselling *A Nest of Magpies*, was written when she was eighty years old, and was followed by *Sharp through the Hawthorn* and *Strip the Willow*, all of which are published by Penguin.

Dr Sybil Marshall lives in Ely, Cambridgeshire, with her husband, Ewart Oakeshott, FSA.

Strip the Willow

Sybil Marshall

PENGUIN BOOKS

PENGUIN BOOKS

Published by the Penguin Group
Penguin Books Ltd, 27 Wrights Lane, London W8 5TZ, England
Penguin Books USA Inc., 375 Hudson Street, New York, New York 10014, USA
Penguin Books Australia Ltd, Ringwood, Victoria, Australia
Penguin Books Canada Ltd, 10 Alcorn Avenue, Toronto, Ontario, Canada M4V 3B2
Penguin Books (NZ) Ltd, 182–190 Wairau Road, Auckland 10, New Zealand

Penguin Books Ltd, Registered Offices: Harmondsworth, Middlesex, England

Frist published in Great Britain by Michael Joseph 1996
Published in Penguin Books 1997
1 3 5 7 9 10 8 6 4 2

Printed in England by Clays Ltd, St Ives plc

In gratitude
I dedicate this book
to three men who in their different ways
made possible the trilogy.
They are:
Robert McCrum,
who gave me new belief in myself, and Hope;
Bill Everett, F.R.C.S.,
who gave me a new lease of life, and Time;
and
my husband, Ewart Oakeshott,
who gave me new horizons, and Love.

Yesterday Returneth Not

I

Something on the grass verge ahead of her had moved before disappearing again into the cover of the tall stems of dried cow-parsley and yarrow near the roadside hedge. The movement had alerted Frances Catherwood that she was doing it again – day-dreaming at the wheel of her car. It was a dangerous habit that might one day get her into serious trouble. She had absolutely no recollection of anything after leaving the built-up outskirts of Swithinford, yet here she was already halfway home, on the open stretch of road just the Swithinford side of the Franksbridge Hotel and the Sports Centre.

She slowed the car to a walking pace at once. There was no other traffic in view; no harm had been done.

Still travelling very slowly, she kept a sharp watch in case whatever it had been should change its mind again and bolt across the road and under her wheels. She thought it had been too big to be rabbit or bird, and might have been a dog. The last thing she wanted to do was to spoil her day by killing an animal, let alone someone else's pet. Nor could she just drive on and leave an injured animal in pain. She stopped near the place she had seen the movement, and scanned the grass verge. Common sense advised a certain amount of caution in approaching a strange dog, especially one that might already be injured. She would have to sit there for a few minutes till she saw it again – if she did.

She couldn't let it delay her too long because she was already much later than she had said she would be, and she didn't want to make William anxious about her. It was a reversal of their usual roles for him to be at home waiting for her, but this year the Michaelmas Term at William's college had already begun without its Professor of Medieval History because at last he had been granted a whole year of long-awaited sabbatical leave.

Fran wasn't in the least averse to sitting where she was and thinking about him for a few minutes. A broad smile crossed her face as she remembered how she had left him – in the large room that served them as both breakfast-room and library, sorting out a huge pile of books to take into his study to begin 'work'. She wondered if he was as well aware as she was that with term still less than a week old, all he was really doing was making an apologetic gesture towards his own conscience for not being in his room as the head of his department. He was demonstrating to himself (and her) that he honestly did have every intention of setting about the bit of obscure medieval reasearch for which his sabbatical year had officially been granted, but – as St Augustine said on the question of chastity – not yet.

She probably knew him better than he knew himself, and vice versa, because they were so much part of each other that they often shared each other's thoughts. She guessed that she would find when she got home that he hadn't been doing academic research, but delving into the intriguing mystery of the extraordinary house at Castle Hill Farm and the even greater puzzle of the isolated, unusual and fascinating little church that stood so close to it – that is, if his thoughts had been turned towards anything other than the pleasure of being able to do just as he liked as the hours passed. Well, she didn't care what he did with his unaccustomed leisure as long as it made him happy, because when he was happy, she was happy too.

She gave herself another broad smile in her driving mirror, this time thinking how well Mark Twain had understood human nature. The whitewashing of Aunt Polly's fence in *The Adventures of Tom Sawyer* so accurately described most people's state of mind with regard to any task staring them in the face. What one had to do was work: what one did to please oneself was pleasure.

And she had no right to laugh at William about it, either. She hadn't been exactly panting to get back to her own desk to start on her next commission, which was to write another full-length play for the TV screen. She was usually very good at getting down to anything she had agreed to do, but as she kept telling herself lately, there really was no urgency. It occurred to her that one reason for her reluctance to begin on it was the knowledge that whatever her fertile imagination could concoct would hardly rival the real-life drama they had lived through in the last twelve months.

Maybe they were now heading for a less eventful period – though she doubted it. Experience had taught her that, in contradiction to popular belief, a small remote village was about the last place you were likely to find peace and quietness. People accustomed to life in towns had very little understanding of how deeply rooted the ways of rural communities were. The smaller the community, the more commotion every event caused, however small and insignificant in its own right. A bumble-bee trapped inside a window pane can't be ignored, though the same bee flying free is hardly noticed. In Old Swithinford, everybody knew everybody else's business, often irritatingly so; but 'business' in this sense did not mean facts and figures, bank balances or bankruptcies. It was mainly concerned with such everyday things as births and deaths and marriages – and, in the past two or three years, with how well those who had been born and brought up there were getting along with the newcomers in their midst. Friends and neighbours were expected to listen to each other, though they might not always agree, and though in many cases the good-neighbourliness amounted to little more than nosiness.

Fran and William understood the system, having known the village and many people in it since childhood. They knew that the old way of life must be changed, like everything else, by 'envious and calumniating time', and grudgingly agreed that not all change was for the worse; nevertheless they resented those who wanted everything altered overnight in the name of 'progress'. Fran's smile was a little cynical when she remembered what men like Arnold Bailey meant by 'progress'.

The October sun was already slanting westwards in the great expanse of the East Anglian sky, and deepening in colour to a rich golden amber that brought out a glowing response from the yellowing leaves on the lime trees and enhanced the brilliance of the autumn-tinted larches against their dark background in the conifer stands that had been left on what had once been the old de ffranksbridge estate. Just where she sat waiting, low hedges allowed her a view of open farmland on both sides. Though most of it had been ploughed, there were enough fields of stubble, some still dotted with bales of straw, to give the picture both colour and texture. Berried hedgerows framed the garnered fields and presented a prospect of past plenty and future promise. Surely it was in October, not January, that the old year came to an end and a new one began? Academia had at least got that right!

Her eyes caught another movement among the dried relics of such wild flowers as had escaped the local council's ritual murder of them in May. Concentrating her gaze on the spot she saw what she had been waiting for, though hardly what she had been expecting. Among the tall pale stalks she had a brief glimpse of a small head so covered with coppery curls that at first she thought it was a fox. She sat still until it appeared again for an instant, disappeared as suddenly, and popped up again and then down again like a ball being patted by some invisible hand. When its owner at last succeeded in remaining upright for long enough, she saw a little boy standing completely naked among the screening kex. He was sturdy and chubby, with no definable waistline. His little pot-belly showed that he couldn't be much more than three. A Renaissance Cupid fallen out of some celestial picture-frame? What other explanation could there possibly be?

He swayed, and sat down again rather abruptly. Fran's pleasurable wonder gave way to maternal instinct, because he looked only too vulnerably human, and so close to nettles hiding in the grip among the kexes. She went to solve the mystery, and came upon him sitting at the very edge of the slope down into the narrow ditch, struggling valiantly to find his way into a pair of washed-out khaki shorts.

'Hello,' she said, bending down to help him. He didn't reply, but stood up to make it easier for her, his face puckered with concentrated effort to stand on one leg and insert the other into the top of the shorts she was now holding open for him. He wobbled and almost fell, but clutched at her shoulder and clung there trustingly till the shorts were more or less in place. Then he turned an angelic face up towards her and said, 'Thank you vewy much,' in so grave a tone and with such cultured aplomb that she began to distrust her senses again. He released his hold on her and had taken only a few stumbling steps through the matted grass-bents before the shorts lowered themselves again round his ankles and tripped him up. She was quick enough to grab him before he rolled into the grip among clumps of dark-green, seeding and extremely venomous nettles. She pulled up the shorts yet again.

'They seem to be a bit too big for you,' she said, watching them begin another descent over the rotund little abdomen. Even after she had yanked them up as high as she could get them, which was almost under his armpits, the bottoms of the legs came down well below his knees.

'Yes,' he said, 'that's why they falled off. I 'spect they're Basher's.'

He clutched at them with both hands and began to turn away. She was enchanted by his Cupid-like charm and delighted by his apparently un-shakeable sang-froid in such a predicament. She didn't want to let him go.

'Wait a minute,' she said. 'You stand still and hold them up while I go across to my car and see if I have a safety-pin in my handbag. Then you can tell me all about yourself.'

He nodded acquiescence, and waited patiently till she came back and pinned a large pleat in the waistband of the shorts. 'Now,' she said, 'my name is Frances Catherwood. What's yours?'

'Tanner Petwie. Jasper Petwie, weally, I fi – *th*ink.'

'And who is Basher, then? And why have you got his shorts on?'

'My big bruvver who fumps – *th*umps me. He fumped me this morning and pushed me out of bed. So I got dressed and runned away. I 'spect I just got the wong shorts. I didn't have any bweakfast, and I'm hungwy. I fink I'll go home now.'

Fran was doing her best to sort out this information. Unless he was making it up, it appeared that he had left home before anybody else in the household was up, and had been out alone, without food, all day. Hadn't anybody missed him, or tried to find him? He couldn't have wandered

6

very far. His speech was not that of a 'traveller', nor that of the ordinary indigenous village child. Besides, the effort he made, when he remembered, to turn his baby 'f' sounds to 'th' ones meant that somebody was trying to correct him.

'Where do you live?' she asked.

He turned and looked all round him, and for the first time he wore a troubled expression, from which she gathered that he was lost.

'Over there,' he said, waving an arm vaguely towards the fields behind him. Then he suddenly became quite communicative, as if any sort of information he could add to what she had asked might be useful.

'We all live over there – me and Basher and Emmy and Ammy and Topy and Saffy. And Jade. And the baby. His name's Aggie. And Daddy.' Then as a kind of afterthought, he added, 'And Mummy.'

Naturally. There had to be both Mummy and Daddy for a brood like that. All the same, she got the impression that Daddy was of more consequence than Mummy.

Fran gave him her hand and looked around her, trying to figure out what 'over there' might mean. She must have been up and down that road at least a hundred times in the three years since she had returned to Old Swithinford to buy and restore for her own occupation Benedict's, the old house that had once been her grandfather Wagstaffe's, but she realized now that she had never given a great deal of attention to her surroundings. She had probably often been lost in a sort of day-dream, or, perhaps, had been giving all her attention to William, if he had been at the wheel. After all, he was a major part of the dream. She had not expected to find the childhood playmate who had become her adolescent sweetheart and, as it had turned out, the greatest love of her life thrown in with the deal for the house.

She dragged her thoughts back to the present. 'Over there' must mean somewhere along the narrow side-road which joined the Swithinford road roughly opposite where her car still stood. The light of a reasonable conjecture broke. While her house was being made habitable, she had been forced to live as a paying guest in the hotchpotch of between-the-wars housing to which the Post Office authorities had allocated the grand name of Swithinford Bridges, but which to everybody else was known as Hen Street. During that period, there had been a typically rural storm-in-a-tea-cup about a right of way to some very isolated cottages which lay behind Hen Street. It was just possible that Tanner/Jasper/Cupid came from one of those cottages, though Fran could have sworn she had heard that they had been condemned since.

When she looked down at the child again, she saw that the corners of his mouth were turning down and quivering, and she was afraid that he was going to cry. She squatted to bring her face level with his. 'If I take you home in my car, can you show me the way?' she asked.

'Will you weally? I'm so hungwy. I finded some blackbewwies, but they weren't nice.'

She looked at her watch. 'Is there a telephone in your house?' she asked.

He nodded, looking troubled. 'We mustn't touch it. It's Daddy's. Basher does, and says it was me.'

'I expect Daddy would let me use it if I take you home,' she said. 'So come on. Let's go.'

He took her hand and smiled up at her in evident relief. She had to fight down the impulse to pick him up and cuddle him, but experience had taught her that it was always wise to offer friendship to children and animals in small doses.

They were on the way towards her car together when she heard the screech of brakes, and turning her head saw that in the entrance to the side-road was a battered car of extreme age and doubtful pedigree. Emerging from it was a tall, gaunt man in workman's clothing, whose bare head at a distance was as white as William's. A second glance showed her that his face, his hair and his garments were all of the same greyish-white tone, even his boots. She had to cling to the little boy's hand to prevent him from bolting across the road towards the man, who was, it seemed, shouting at her.

'Madam!' he roared. 'Will you kindly explain what you were about to do with my son?'

The stance, the accent and the tone were such as in any other circumstances she would have sworn were those of a high-ranking officer of the Brigade of Guards. Yet there he stood, looking like a quarryman, bawling across the width of the road at her and as far as she could deduce, he was not only claiming to be Cupid's father but insinuating that she was about to abduct the cherub.

She was drawing herself up to deliver a cold, dignified and cutting reply when the entire situation turned a somersault in her mind and showed her its unbelievably ludicrous underbelly. She let go of the child's hand to fish for a handkerchief, which she pressed against her mouth to prevent the bubble of ready mirth that lived in her throat from escaping, but it was too late. The man was now standing at her side, no doubt having concluded that he had been in the nick of time to rescue his son from the clutches of an escaped lunatic.

'Please excuse me,' she gurgled, 'but this is ridiculous! I'll explain as soon as ever I can' – and turning away from him she leaned on her own car, almost stifling herself in her effort to compose herself before attempting to speak again.

She turned back at last to face him, meeting a pair of intelligent hazel eyes in which there was more than an answering twinkle. She saw that her laughter had infected him, and that they were both having to make stupendous efforts to behave reasonably. Then they spoke at the same instant, stopped with their mouths open, and the battle was lost. They laughed in unison, though only for a moment. He was checked by a paroxysm of coughing over which he seemed to have no control, and which killed instantly her desire to laugh. He coughed until he was exhausted and she was frightened for him, as she noticed that his face under its coating of white dust had turned greenish-grey, and that beads of sweat were standing out on his forehead and across his top lip. He tried gaspingly to apologize, but she stopped him.

'Get your breath back,' she said. 'You must have inhaled some of that dust. You are Mr Petrie, of course, and Jasper's father. I'm Frances Catherwood, and I live in Old Swithinford. I found Jasper in difficulty because he couldn't keep his brother's shorts on, and I was just about to try to deliver him back home – if he could show me the way. But I was a bit worried, because he told me he had run away early this morning without having anything to eat, and had tried picking blackberries which didn't taste right. I only hope they were blackberries!'

She had gone on talking to give him time to recover. Colour was returning to his cheeks. He bowed, and held out his hand. 'Peter Petrie,' he said. Then he squatted down by the child. 'Tanner,' he said, gently but in a voice that immediately explained to her the child's own cultivated speech, 'how many times have I told you that blackberries are the fairies' food, and that you must never eat them unless there is a grown-up with you to ask the fairies if they mind? Did you swallow them?'

'No. I spitted them out.'

The man looked up at Fran, relieved, before turning back to Jasper. 'Where have you been all day? And why did you run away? I didn't know until I stopped work for a cup of tea, and Emmy told me. I came to look for you straight away.'

Jasper explained. The man's face clouded. 'I thought so. Emmy said Basher's shorts had disappeared, and he'd had to stop in bed till Ammy had got him some washed and dried. That served him right, didn't it?'

He stopped and looked up at Fran again, a slight flush colouring his rather haggard face, as if he owed her some sort of explanation that he wasn't really prepared to give. She noticed that the bout of coughing had dislodged a lot of the white dust, and that under it his face was as bony as the rest of his body was thin. She sensed his embarrassment, and she didn't want him to start to cough again.

'Why do you call him Tanner, when he's got such a nice name as Jasper?' she asked, to give him time to collect himself.

He smiled at her, letting her know that he appreciated her tact. 'I suppose because he was the sixth. The older ones started calling him Sixer, then Sixpence, then Tanner. That stuck.'

'So now there are seven. Are they all like Jasper?'

This time his smile was rueful. 'Eight. There's another between Tanner and the baby.'

'Whom Jasper says is called Aggie.'

'Short for Agate. With luck, he'll be the last.' He held out his hand to her. 'I apologize for shouting at you, Mrs Catherwood. Thank you for taking care of Tanner. I'm so glad to have met you in the flesh, because of course we have heard of you. I wonder if you would like to come down and see my conversion of the cottages when it is completed – if it ever is.'

That explained the coating of plaster, as she now knew it to be. 'I – we – should love to,' she said. The warmth of her voice told him that she meant it. They bade each other goodbye with mutual courtesy, and he stood bareheaded till her car began to move again.

The sun was going down and the East Anglian sky about to produce one of its spectacular sunsets, always at their best in October. She didn't want to miss a minute of it, but she wanted to get home as fast as she could to tell William about her afternoon's adventure.

Mr Petrie had never once mentioned his wife, though Jasper had very vaguely referred to 'Mummy'. Could it be that she was ill after the birth of Aggie, leaving him with all eight children, including the baby, to cope with alone? No wonder he looked so gaunt and ill himself! She would make it her business to find out about the Petrie family and see if there was anything at all she could do. Not now, though. She wanted to share that sky with William.

2

She was surprised that he had not heard her car on the gravel and come to let her in. The heavy old door opening made a lot of noise, but that didn't bring him to her side, either. She stood for a moment listening, but no sound from anywhere indicated that he was aware of her arrival home. If he had gone out, whatever the reason, he would certainly have left her a note. She went to look for it on her own desk, then tried his desk and the kitchen table before going into the beautiful sitting-room which was the holy of holies of their life together. She breathed a sigh of relief.

The sky was now a riot of colour, and though the house faced south, the room's two long windows were catching enough of it to bathe every-thing in a glow of rosy light. William was stretched out in his chair on one side of the fire with his long legs crossed at the ankles, fast asleep. His head had fallen sideways, and his shapely long-fingered hands clasped a book to his chest. He very rarely dozed off in daylight, so perhaps she had been unjust to him, and he had been hard at work in her absence.

She went to stand over him, thinking how deceptive his head of white hair was. He didn't look his fifty-two years, any more than she felt her own half-century when he was by her side. Sitting gingerly on his chair-arm, though reluctant to wake him, she stroked his head and kissed the tip of his nose.

The book flew across the room as she was grabbed and pulled down on to his lap, her legs waving in the air above the chair-arm. She wound her hands into his thick hair to stabilize herself, and hung on. He loosened her fingers and held her down till he had kissed her and she had stopped struggling.

'You idiot!' she said. 'You play possum better than anybody else I've ever known. I honestly thought you were sleeping the sleep of the just, worn out with honest labour.'

'Sleeping the sleep of the deserted husband, worn out with doubt and anxiety, more like,' he said. 'Where on earth have you been for so long? I guessed you had sneaked off to Monastery Farm without me, so I de-cided to teach you a lesson.'

She shook her head.

'No, I know,' he said. 'I rang Monica. She said she hadn't seen you. But if it wasn't your new grandchildren keeping you, who was it?'

'*Our* new grandchildren,' she corrected him. When he didn't answer she changed the subject. It was still a rather sensitive one.

'Who kept me? You'd never guess in a month of Sundays, as Sophie would say.'

'Male or female?' he asked.

'Oh, decidedly male,' she said. 'I know because I had to help him put his trousers on.'

'I knew I should never have let you out by yourself,' he answered resignedly. 'Whose head have I got to go and knock off now?'

'Cupid's,' she said. 'Let me get up and I'll tell you all. But I'm dying for a cup of tea, so let's go and see what Sophie has left for us.' He kissed her again, and did his best to help her off his lap.

'You certainly are no lightweight – er – in any respect,' he said.

'And you,' she said, 'would take a prize for quick-thinking. Most men wouldn't have got out of that gaffe so cleverly.'

'I like you as you are. Besides loving you to distraction.' They went together to the kitchen.

Sophie, their childhood playmate who had never married and was now their housekeeper (much to the satisfaction of all parties), had left their tea on a tray, complete with a batch of scones filled with strawberry jam and cream.

'No wonder you can't lift me,' Fran said ruefully, as she took one and launched into her tale.

'Mm,' said William. 'Peter Petrie, looking like a stonemason covered in dust and with a son called Jasper? Too good to be true! Too much like Miss Bunn the Baker's daughter. He was either having you on or you are having me on.'

'No – truly. There's another child called Jade – male or female I couldn't guess – and a baby named Agate. You know how silly people can be about naming children when they get an idea like that. I wouldn't have said he was at all that sort, though. Too – nice, as well as too cultured, I would have thought. Too sensible.'

He raised one still-dark eyebrow at her. 'With eight young children? Did you find out what the other five are called?'

She tried to remember. 'Tanner mentioned an Emmy and an Ammy and a Topie and a Saffie. With Basher, that makes eight.'

'Emerald and Amethyst and Topaz and Sapphire. His wife's idea. Not all cultured middle-aged men have wives to match, do they? I wonder what Basher's baptismal name is.' He reached for another scone.

'Pumice, probably,' she answered promptly. His spluttering laughter caused the scone he had just bitten into to explode into a sticky shower of jam and whipped cream. He was still chuckling as he returned from the sink after cleaning himself up. Fran was a constant source of delight to him.

She was following her own train of thought. 'We must ask Sophie if she knows anything about them. I think they must have been there for quite a while, because he spoke as if his conversion of the cottages was on the way to being finished. How come that we've never heard anything about them till now?'

'Too much else going on. It's been a pretty hectic summer, one way or another.'

She nodded. 'Yes, I suppose that's it. Everybody seemed to have problems, and we got involved in most of them. I remember thinking once that we were like the pectin in jam, the agent that made the rest jell. And then all of a sudden it was harvest, and in spite of all the new-fangled machinery and whatnot, there was only one thing in anybody's head – getting their own harvest in while the weather held. It has always been like that. Until the harvest's in, there's a sort of limbo of "time out" when all that matters is the passing day.'

'That's how it ought to be always,' William answered. 'Yesterday is already history, and tomorrow never comes. You don't have to be reck-lessly hedonistic to make the most of every day as it passes. I used to try never to think about yesterday, and I was always thinking ahead – because I hadn't much reason for thinking that any day was special for me. Now every day is. It's like harvest all the time. But I know what you mean. Every farm in harvest time was a separate unit turned in on itself and its own affairs.'

She acknowledged his admission of his present happiness with her by reaching across and putting her hand in his. 'And this year,' she said, 'we were as turned in on our own affairs as any farmer, waiting for Monica to have her baby. If I had known she was going to have twins . . .'

'You would have been twice as anxious, my precious old Puritan! You worried yourself because you expected it to start up all the talk about you and me again. Being you, you would have thought that two babies instead of one meant twice as much sin to be expiated. Am I not right?'

She laughed. 'Possibly. I did expect a back-wash about us. We could hardly expect village folk like Thirzah Bates to take "twins born out of wedlock" to my son's girlfriend in their stride, especially as she's still a new-comer and he a married man. Once upon a time the whole lot of us would have been "run out of five parishes" – to quote Sophie again.'

William replied in a more serious vein than she had expected. 'You know you really do have Puritanical streaks in you, my darling,' he said. 'They bob up every now and then and get between you and your common sense. Finding out who the father of Monica's child was didn't double the scandal. It halved it. Monica is out of the ken of people like Thirzah, and to some of them her father is still the big bad wolf who came huffing and puffing quite literally threatening to blow their houses down. But Roland is in a different category. Deep-dyed sinner as they may think him, he is still a Wagstaffe of Benedict's by blood if not by name. That makes him one of them – and it makes them feel safer from real outsiders like Arnold Bailey to have new shoots springing up from old roots. What frightens them is the possibility of having all their old roots dug up and thrown away. That's why they still went on accepting us even when their new Rector openly branded us adulterers with whom he would have nothing to do. But in any case they have no option but to come to terms with the twentieth century, and perhaps we helped them to do it. If it had ever come to a showdown between the seventh commandment in the abstract and you and me in the flesh, we should have won the day. We both "belong". And if they have been shaking their heads in this last two or three weeks about Roland and Monica, we haven't known. Why worry about it now?'

'I'm not, really,' she replied. 'I wasn't philosophizing – I was only remarking that for about three weeks we've hardly given a thought to anything or anybody but ourselves, as if we had pulled up the drawbridge and lowered the portcullis.'

'Yes. I've been thinking the same. What I've been looking into today means I must soon go up to Castle Hill again, so I gave Bob a ring. He wasn't himself – he was all shy and embarrassed with me, like he used to be when we first knew him. I think something's wrong up there.'

She was all immediate concern. 'Oh William! He's the very one we ought not to have neglected! It's because of the tenancy of the farm, I'll bet. He's so vulnerable – he wouldn't ask, and he must have thought we had forgotten him and had simply left him to it! It's nearly Michaelmas and he's got to make a decision about the farm. He knows that if he doesn't buy it as the sitting tenant, there's another bidder waiting . . . ten to one it's Arnold Bailey. Bob said he couldn't raise the money, even by selling his fen farm, which he doesn't want to do anyway. But he'll feel that he's let us all down if Arnold Bailey gets his claws on Castle Hill and covers it with another ticky-tacky estate like he's doing at Lane's End. Is that the trouble?'

'He didn't say so. I got the impression that it was something more personal worrying him. I hope to high heaven that lousy wife of his hasn't turned up again.'

'Oh, darling, I do feel guilty. Can't we go up now, straight away, to put things right with Bob?'

'No, I said we would try to go up tomorrow.' He went round the table to her. 'Come on, sweetheart. Stop worrying. Don't try to solve the equation till you've got the data. After I'd rung Bob, I rang round some others as well. I felt guilty, too, but as far as I could tell the village hasn't gone absolutely to the dogs without us. Let's go and sit more comfortably, and I'll tell you all I found out.'

'It managed perfectly well without us for more than twenty years,' she said. 'I shall be surprised if they've missed us any more than we've missed them. Anybody other than Bob, that is.'

They went back to the sitting-room, drew the curtains and made up the fire. She sat down in her chair, with Cat on her knee, and William on the floor at her feet.

'Well? Where did you start?' she asked.

'With Jess, of course, out of duty. She was at work, and on the defensive as soon as she knew it was me. Feeling guilty herself, I think. Said she really hadn't had time to get down to visit Monica because since the day the twins were born she's hardly seen Eric, and as his personal assistant she has simply had to stand in for him morning, noon and night.' He paused, and looked up at Fran. 'I might have believed her if she hadn't added that she couldn't see that it mattered whether she went or not, because Greg had been there often enough to count for both of them.'

Fran made no comment. She knew how much he hated to criticize Jess, who was his half-sister and her first cousin. Their three-fold relationship had been difficult even in childhood and, since they had all returned to Old Swithinford, far from easy. There had been coolness amounting to real rows between the two women at first, but these had simmered down under the influence of William and Greg, Jess's husband. In fact, there had been during the last year a warm, close friendship – until lately when Jess had been begun putting out prickles like a frightened hedgehog again.

'I wonder what's the matter with her this time,' William said. 'She knows perfectly well now that her nasty suspicions were false, and that the man responsible for Monica's babies is your son and not her husband.'

'She's only being honest,' Fran said soothingly. 'She's said often enough that she has never been one to drool over babies. I expect it just makes her mad that her boss is showing his feelings so much about his new grandchildren. Greg's as soft as cart-grease and can't help wearing his heart on his sleeve, bless him. He can be as sentimental as he likes as long as it's her he's being sentimental about. It irritates her if he shows that he cares at all about anybody else. And even you are showing more interest in the twins than she expected you would. That must be the last straw to her, though to me . . .' – she leaned down to him and cradled his head against her knee – 'it makes it absolutely perfect. Don't let Jess spoil it for us. She'll come round if we leave her alone. What next?'

'Elyot and Beth. Of course, they think we are the only ones who know that Beth is pregnant, but if the whole village hasn't read the signs by now I'll eat my hat. They might as well hang out a banner. Greg couldn't show his heart on his sleeve any more obviously than Elyot. One may be an artist and the other a retired naval officer, but . . . well, I don't know that I blame him. Maybe in his shoes I'd be the same. Beth tried to keep her feet on the ground, and reported that her father will be leaving at the end of November, but Elyot . . .!'

'The Colonel's lady and Judy O'Grady are sisters under their skins,' quoted Fran. 'I expect men are much the same, really. Didn't George Eliot say something of the sort – to the effect that there was no denying women were queer creatures, because God Almighty had made them to match the men?'

'I can't contradict you,' he said. 'I guess you and George Eliot are both right. Beth's news about the Rector made me ring George Bridgefoot while I was at it. I thought he sounded a bit subdued – but maybe he's worried in case they don't get a replacement for the Rector this time. It would break George's heart if Old Swithinford had to be held in plural with the new church at Swithinford. He said he would like to come up and talk to us. So I asked if all the family were all right, and he said they were, but he did have a problem he would like to discuss with somebody other than them. I hope that doesn't mean he's ill.'

'Not he,' said Fran confidently. 'He's like an oak tree. He may be felled in a gale or struck by lightning, but he won't die of anything but old age. His roots are too deep. People like George and Sophie seem indestructible to me. I suppose because their sort have always been here. They are the core – no, the *soul* of the village. If they weren't here, or people just like them, it would be dead. One can't imagine it without them.'

He nodded, understanding. He got up. 'Drink? Same as usual?'

'Let's go and have our supper soon,' she said. 'I am glad we're in touch with some of them again, though I shan't stop worrying about Bob till we've seen him tomorrow. And as soon as Sophie comes in the morning, we'll find out about Cupid's family.'

He held out a hand to help her out of her deep armchair. 'I don't think you ought to tell Sophie you helped a strange male to put his trousers on,' he said. 'She isn't quite up to taking that yet, emancipated though she is compared with her sister. I really can't imagine Sophie swooning, but there's always a first time.'

Fran giggled. 'She might very well have done three years ago,' she agreed. 'What a sight that would have been!

'As falls on Mount Avernus
The thunder-stricken oak.'

His laughter rang through the house as he threw his arms round her. 'Three times in five minutes,' he said. 'The first time you fail to find an apt quotation on the spot, it'll be me who'll imitate the thunder-stricken oak!' He was still chuckling when they sat down to eat.

3

Fran often averred that she thought in her sleep. She was one of those lucky people who are wide awake the moment their eyes are open, with the windmills of their minds already going round. Her thoughts were instantly so clear that she often felt they must be simply a continuation of what she had been thinking while asleep. She never minded waking early, to lie comfortably beside a still supine William, and go on thinking.

She raised herself gently on her elbow, so as to be able to see out of the window and judge the time from the light instead of rousing him by reaching for her bedside clock. The garden was still wrapped in diaphanous veils of morning mist. The sun was up, somewhere low in the sky, but hadn't yet got warmth enough to clear her view of the far side of the garden. She could see the outline of the nearly bare arms of the copper beech, but the dark, graceful mass of the huge wellingtonias at the front was still no more than a shadowy presence looming through silvery pearl light. It was the first misty autumn morning there had been – not at all surprising after the long sunny day yesterday; and even as she watched, the outline of the tall conifers grew more and more distinct, almost as if they were walking towards her. It was going to be another warm, bright day.

She lay flat on her back and began to think, somehow catching hold of the tail of what had been in her mind when she first roused. They were reconnected with their friends again, and to some extent with normal routine. It was rather like the first morning back home after a holiday. However enjoyable a holiday has been, coming home again to familiar surroundings and circumstances is a pleasure in itself. Fran had no illusions with regard to the way Time passing changed everything. They were bound to find today that there had been changes they didn't yet know about.

William's round of phone calls yesterday had sorted their acquaintances neatly into 'family' and 'friends' – except that last year's extraordinary happenings had mixed those two categories together. The Choppen family, who had been unwanted 'intruders' so short a time ago, were now inextricably mixed with 'family', and 'old friends' – meaning those who were indigenous to the village – were already tangled with the 'new'. The Bridgefoots, for example, were linked with Bob Bellamy at Castle Hill because Brian Bridgefoot had a son and Bob Bellamy a daughter.

Her mind switched to the birth of twins to her son's — her son's what? Girlfriend? Ugh! Lover? One always thought of a 'lover' as the male half of a couple — though 'lovers' in the plural had lately been filched from standard English to signify any two people, even of the same sex, in a sexual relationship. Monica and Roland could be 'lovers', or Roland be Monica's 'lover', but to call Monica Roland's 'lover' meant only that she loved him, not necessarily that she was his sexual partner. Mistress? Too old-fashioned, and tainted with the hypocrisy of the nineteenth century. Common-law wife? No! Because whatever Monica was to Roland, she was to William, and she refused utterly to think of herself as his 'common' anything. There was nothing whatsoever 'common' in any sense about their relationship.

She turned over gently to look at him, loving every curve of his long, sensitive face and remarking yet again how strange it was that his eye-brows were still as black as they had always been, in spite of his gleaming white hair. Her mind ran over the other words the English language offered her. Paramour? She decided that she would rather be William's paramour than anything else she had so far thought of. She wanted to snuggle down close to him, but that would wake him, and she didn't want to rob him of any sleep. So she still sat up on her elbow, looking down on him. His paramour. The other half of him, as he was of her. She gazed down at him now, wondering how she had ever managed without him in the long years since the outbreak of war had separated them. What on earth did it matter now that she wasn't his legal wife? She was utterly content to go on being his paramour — if that was the word for it — as long as she lived.

He roused, stretched, opened his eyes and saw her, and said, '"Leman", my darling. Medieval, but right.' Then he sat up, rubbed his eyes and said, 'I must have been dreaming. Whatever am I talking about?'

'Reading my mind again,' she said. 'I was trying to think of the right word to describe what I am to you, or Monica to Roland.'

He reached for her and made available to her the hollow of his shoul-der where she loved to put her head. 'I can't answer for Roland,' he said. 'But there's no word in any language that can describe what you are to me. Except "mine".'

'I had decided on "paramour",' she said. 'But as usual, you're right. "Leman" is English, and lovely.'

'"Par amour" has a lot to be said for it,' he said. 'I haven't got to get up early to go to work this morning.'

'Maybe not — but don't get ideas. It's nearly eight. We must get up *now*.'

She took her head off his shoulder and sat up. He pulled her back again to kiss her. 'I'm sure a true leman never had so hard a heart,' he said. He kissed her again, and she responded, but he let her go. She made a hasty escape to the bathroom, and they didn't meet again till he put coffee and toast before her at the kitchen table. They were still sitting there together when Sophie arrived.

Sophie represented another strand of friendship. She was indigenous, a villager from a family that had been there for as many centuries as the church registers recorded. Sophie and her sister Thirzah Bates were ana-chronisms in post-war society. They clung with a sort of defiant despera-tion to the past in matters of appearance, speech, custom, tradition and morals, though Sophie's devotion to Fran and William was gradually changing her outlook. The relationship between her and them was, as William the historian had once remarked, valuable in its own right as a museum piece, because it demonstrated, in full working order, the mech-anism of the interdependence that had once been essential between the various layers of society in a remote and isolated community.

She was a little late, and consequently flushed with hurrying. Fran picked up at once that she was either worried or put out. She went through her usual routine of donning a spotless apron over her clean overall. William had stood up at her entrance, and pulled out a chair for her. 'Coffee or tea?' he asked. She looked at him gratefully. 'There ain't nothing as I should like better 'n a good strong cup o' tea,' she answered. He went to put the kettle on, and Fran looked enquiringly at her.

If asked, Sophie would have said she worked *for* 'them two up at Benedict's'. It would have been nearer the truth to say she worked *with* them. In the three years since first Fran and then William had returned to the old house, sad and momentous events had overtaken Sophie, includ-ing the death of her childhood sweetheart, Jelly, the very week he had plucked up courage to ask her to marry him; and it was to them as her childhood friends that she had turned for support, not as her employers. They had not failed her then, and in return she had stood loyally by them when it had become common knowledge that they were 'living in sin' as man and wife. For their sakes she had defied her dogmatic and autocratic elder sister, Thirzah, and yielded up to her love for them her lifelong obedience to the Victorian code of morality to which until then she had adhered to the letter.

In age she came neatly between William and Fran, but there any resem-blance ended. She was taller than Fran, and where Fran tended to run to unfashionable curvaceousness, Sophie was solidly 'well made', with muscles developed by a lifetime of physically hard work.

Fran sometimes wondered where on earth Sophie and Thirzah still managed to buy the black woollen stockings and laced-up ankle-boots they wore on weekdays, even in summer, though on Sundays they ran to grey lisle stockings and low laced-up shoes. In her Sunday best, Sophie was a handsome, dignified woman. Though with her still dark hair parted in the middle and her rosy face shining with soap and water, she resembled nothing so much as an old-fashioned wooden Dutch doll, there was nothing in the least wooden about her head or her heart.

Her emancipation from the code of morality that tied her to the past had been a slow and difficult process. One of its tenets had been that an unmarried woman should not know, or at least should pretend not to know, anything whatsoever of the mysteries of sex. Until she had made her stand against Thirzah by continuing to work for her friends in their adulterous relationship, she had been expected to keep her thoughts, and her tongue, as virginal as her body. Now, though she would rarely of her own accord introduce such a subject, it was possible for the two women to hold a conversation on the everyday affairs of the village, including those relating to sexual behaviour. As Fran said, Time changed everything, even Sophie.

William set down the teapot, and Fran poured out a cup and handed it to Sophie. William sat down again, and the smile Sophie bestowed on him assured Fran that she dared now ask what was wrong.

'I 'ad to goo round to see Thirz' afore I could come to work,' Sophie answered. 'She were took bad again last night. You know as our Het's been having 'sterricks a lot lately. Well, I keep out of it as much as I can, but Thirz' 'ad to goo up to Hen Street to Het last night, and there were such a to-do there as it give 'er another of her bad turns. Dan thought 'e might hev to send for the doctor to 'er. But she's up and about again this morning, though I can't say as I like the look of 'er much.'

Hetty was Sophie's youngest sister, and it was tacitly agreed between Fran and Sophie that Hetty was, and always had been, 'a bit short up top'.

'What's the trouble?' Fran asked. 'With Thirzah, I mean.'

'It's a pain as ketches 'er across 'er middle an' then spreads round her chest till she can't 'ardly breathe. This is the third time she's 'ad it, and it were worse last night than it 'ad been the first two times. She says as it's only wind and there ain't nothing the matter with 'er as a good dose o' sody-bicarb don't cure, but Dan'el said she had three teaspoonsful o' sody last night and it didn't do no good at all. But she soon felt better after she went to bed and laid still.'

'She ought to see a doctor,' William interposed.

Sophie nodded. 'Dan says he'll send for the doctor do she get it again. But it's to be 'oped there won't be no more do's like there were up Hen Street last night to upset 'er.'

She didn't seem disposed to offer any further information, though Fran was longing to hear what it could have been to throw stolid Thirzah into what sounded ominously like a mild heart attack. She knew Sophie too well to ask outright, but suspected that Sophie was just as anxious to tell as she to know. She decided to approach the matter by a devious route.

'Don't go for a minute, Sophie,' she said. 'I want to ask you about something,' and proceeded to give Sophie a severely edited version of her meeting with Mr Petrie.

'Oh, *them*,' replied Sophie, in a tone that told Fran a good deal. 'They come this way summer afore last with that gang o' ragamuffins as camped down Danesum till the council turned 'em off. Them hooligans as goo about from place to place living in old buses and suchlike. What-d'-yer-call-ums.'

'Hippies?' suggested William.

'Ah, tha's right. Only that lot didn't go when all the others did. They stopped in one o'them old condemned cottages 'cos the woman were like to 'ave a child any minute. That lot as you're talking about never went away, and is still there.'

'Mr Petrie told me he was doing the cottages up,' Fran said. 'Who do they belong to?'

'Tha's a bit of a myst'ry, like. They stand in a little pingle right up where Prior's Lode runs into the river. It's only about three acre all told, with water three sides of it and the road on the other. Them cottages stand facing the road, with their backs to the field, and the Grift runs on the other side of it. It ain't no good to nobody, 'cos it's like a h'island in winter if we get a lot o' rain. And as far as I know it ain't never been ploughed up, 'cos it's all 'umps and bumps. Jack Bartrum all'us claimed as it were part of 'is farm, but it couldn't ha' been, else why didn't that Choppen buy it with the rest?'

'What's the Grift?' asked William. 'And what did you call the place?'

'The Grift's a little ol' brook as runs into Prior's Lode, and the field's called Danesum.'

William was intrigued. 'A grift's a holding,' he said. 'And I'd like to bet that Danesum is a corruption of "Dane's Holme". Dane's Island. The humps might even be barrows – burial places, because they could have brought the dead up the river to it by boat. You tread on history wherever you go round here!'

'Don't you everywhere?' Fran didn't want Sophie to wander off the subject of either the Petrie family or the 'goings-on' in Hetty's house. William took the hint, and left the two women to it.

'That man you met yist'day's very like doing what 'e can to keep the roof over them child'en without asking nobody,' Sophie went on, having made sure that William really had gone. 'There's such a hussle of 'em – enough to make up a schooltreat, was what Ned said – though they ain't all his'n. The man's, I mean, not Ned's.'

She need hardly have bothered with that bit of information. Ned was Fran's gardener, a wiry sixty-year-old widower whose morals were as rigid as Sophie's own.

Sophie dropped her voice. 'It's one o' them there mixed fam'lies, you know, like liquorice allsorts – every one of 'em by a different father, so they say. Joe's seen and spoke to the man. He says the child'en wander down that ol' right o' way into Hen Street and the man comes down in a car and rounds 'em up. They don't goo to school nowhere, but Joe says they're very well be'aved.'

William opened the door and put his head round to remind Fran that she had to be ready to go out soon after ten.

'We've been so busy that we haven't seen much of our friends lately,' Fran told Sophie. 'So we thought we'd walk round to call on some of them this morning. Would it be a good idea if we had a cold lunch?'

Relief showed so plainly on Sophie's face that Fran was puzzled. When she answered there was deep satisfaction in her voice, too. 'Ah! That'll be for the best all round,' she said.

Fran awaited explanation, and was given it. 'Thirz' wanted me to goo up Hen Street today and set with Hetty, seeing as she ain't well enough to walk that far 'erself, in case Het ain't got over last night. I never said as I would, 'cos till I'd seen you I didn't know what your plans might be, seeing as 'e ain't got to goo to work, like. If you hev a cold dinner you'll want a 'ot meal tonight, but I can't be 'ere a-cooking for you and up there looking after Het an' all, can I? So Joe'll hev to deal with 'er by 'isself, seeing as 'e is 'er 'usband.'

'Whatever's the matter with Hetty that Joe can't deal with anyway?' asked Fran, wanting to hear the tale but afraid to prompt too loudly. Sophie was slow to reply, and Fran guessed that she was weighing up her desire to tell against her family duty to keep any dissension quiet.

'It's Joe as is giving 'er the 'sterricks this time,' said Sophie. 'An' all on account o' that Bailey as is starting to build all them nasty little 'ouses on Lane's End Farm. It appears as these 'ere developers reckon to sell the 'ouses afore they're built. I'm never 'eard 'o that afore, selling places as ain't there yet. But he's got a chap as is a 'ouse hagent to set up and sell 'em for 'im. 'E's a-gooing to hev a hoffice somewhere soon, only Bailey's set 'is 'eart on getting 'is own great fancy 'ouse built as fast as 'e can, on the spot where the Lane's End farmhouse were when poor Tom and Cynthia Fairey lived there, and all the Faireys afore them.'

'Bailey?' interrupted Fran in tones of horror. 'Do you mean he's going to *live* here?'

She meant in Old Swithinford, because Lane's End Farm and Hen Street were both in the parish, though well away from the church after which it had been named.

'I did tell you so, soon as I knowed,' said Sophie a bit huffily. 'Only you hadn't got no ears for nothing till them babies had been born. So I stopped bothering to tell you anythink else.'

Fran apologized, wondering how on earth she could have forgotten if she had been told, because of the effect Bailey's presence always so close to him might have on her friend Bob Bellamy, and the decision he was having to make. Bailey's behaviour to Bob had been diabolical, and had created a very nasty situation between the two men. That Bailey intended to live near him might account for his strange mood when William had spoken to him yesterday. She looked back at Sophie, who was waiting to be given her attention again.

'And it's that there estate-agent chap what's a-coming atween Hetty and Joe. See, Joe 'appened to meet 'im one night outside Het's 'ouse, and the chap asked 'im if 'e knowed anybody as would be likely to take 'im in as a lodger till 'e got his own place set up. Well, you know what Joe is – do anybody a good turn. Joe says outright as they'd got a spare bedroom as was never used now their Wend' lives in America, and if 'e liked to go and look at it there and then, 'e could. So by that, 'e started to lodge there, and Het liked 'im well enough. Though Thirz' and me didn't like her to come down to taking lodgers, we was both of the opinion as heving a bit more to do, like, wouldn't be no bad thing for her.'

Sophie paused, as if to acknowledge to some Invisible Presence her share of the guilt.

'And your silly Hetty's got too fond of him.'

'Lawks, no! It's Joe 'as got too fond of 'im. Come right atween Het and her 'usband, this Daffy Pugh 'as.'

Fran told herself that she couldn't be hearing aright. She would have sworn that emancipated as Sophie had recently become, she had never in her whole life heard of such a thing as male homosexuality. Let alone be sitting the other side of the table discussing it with her! She quailed at the thought of having to answer any questions Sophie in her innocence might put to her.

'Poor Hetty!' she said.

'Well, that's as maybe,' Sophie answered, prim-mouthed. 'You know 'ow crazed she is about that place as she calls a church, even though it were that man who played at being a parson there as got our Wend' into 'er trouble. While she goos and kneels down in such a place as that, I can't see as she's got much right to find fault wi' Joe if 'e chooses to goo to another new religion. Serves 'er right, in a way.'

Fran was floundering.

'Religion?' she asked. 'What's it got to do with religion?'

'I'm telling you as fast as I can,' Sophie said. 'This 'ere Daffy Pugh's a Welshman as were brought up chapel. But a little while ago 'e went to London to 'ear some American chap preach, and 'e got saved. So 'e gets settled in Joe and Het's 'ouse, and knows as Het still goes to church, but Joe don't go nowheer. Won't have nothing to do with no church nor no parsons, since Wend's do. So this Daffy sets about saving Joe, and bringing 'im back to God, like. 'E said they didn't need no church to pray in, 'cos any wheer would do. And 'e went down on 'is knees there and there, b' the side o' the kitchen table, and started to pray as Joe might be brought back to the fold. And Joe broke down, and said 'e wanted to be saved – and down on 'is knees 'e goes, an' all. Well, I ain't got nothing against that! But it appears as Het took ag'in Daffy from that minute.

'This Daffy's got Joe under 'is thumb proper now about what a wicked sinner 'e's been, and every night soon as they're 'ome and 'ad a wash they get on their knees and pray a side o' the table while Het's trying to get their supper – and if you ask me I should say that's enough to give any woman the 'sterricks, let alone one like our Het. Then after supper they read the Bible together, and sometimes hev a lot of other folks in as well, or else they go out to a meeting in somebody else's 'ouse. Het told Thirz' as by last weekend she 'ardly knowed 'er own 'usband!

'Well, night afore last, Het goes into 'sterricks, and orders Daffy out of the 'ouse. But Joe said as Daffy could stop 'cos it wasn't 'er 'ouse, it was his'n. So yist'day Het comes and begs to Thirz' to goo and square Joe up, and by that, she went.

'Seems she told Joe straight that it were 'is duty to put Het first, and tell the lodger as 'e'd 'ave to goo. You know what Thirz' is like when she starts ordering folks about. But Joe turned on 'er! Like a mad bull 'e was, she said. And then Daffy come in, and 'e wanted 'is say. And what with Het a-crying and Joe a-bawling, and that Daffy trying to insterfere, Thirz' didn't know what to do for the best. So she says per'aps they 'ad all better pray for guidance, same as we all'us have done. And Thirz' orders Het down by the table o' one side, while Daffy and Joe goo down on their knees o' the other side. And then both lots start to pray out loud. But all at once Het squealed like a pig being stuck and clawed the poker up and tried to 'it Joe with it. Thirz' went 'ome to fetch Dan'el to 'elp 'er. But 'urrying brought her pain on, and she couldn't goo back. Tha's why she wants me to go – to find out what 'appened after she come away.'

Troubled though she was, there was a gleam in Sophie's eye and a twist on her mouth that Fran could not but be aware of. Sophie caught her eye, and gave voice to what she was thinking. 'Tha's the first time in my whull life as I'm ever knowed anybody to get the better o' Thirz' at *praying*,' she said.

Fran was in grave difficulty. Her sense of the ridiculous was a great liability to her at moments like this. She doubled her fists till her nails dug into her palms, and held them squeezed between her clenched knees to stop herself from showing any expression that might hurt Sophie. She pushed her shaking shoulders back against her chair, and somehow managed to keep control of her face. Sophie was expecting some sort of rejoinder from her, but Fran was beyond trying to speak.

'I don't know what I ought to do,' Sophie went on at last. 'As I see it, nobody 'adn't ought to come between man and wife, and Thirz' 'adn't got no more right to do that than Daffy 'ad. And if she couldn't get the better of 'im, whatever did she think as I could do?'

'My dear Sophie, what she should have done in the first place. Minded her own business, and let Hetty and Joe sort themselves out. Fran, darling, there's Monica on the telephone, wanting to speak to you.' Fran got up and ran, and William sat down in the chair she had vacated. Fran knew that the telephone had not rung, and that William had been listening and had rescued her deliberately. So did Sophie. She looked up with anything but a solemn face at William and said, 'I don't wonder she 'ad to go away and laugh. I'm sure I should if it was anybody else but my own fam'ly acting like they was. I kept thinking all the while as Thirz' was telling me this morning that it must ha' been just like that bit in the Bible about Elijah and the prophets o' Baal. "Call 'Im louder! Per'aps 'E sleepeth!"'

Seeing William smile, she smiled herself, and then became serious again immediately. 'I promised Mam when she were dying as I'd all'us do what I could to take care o' Hetty,' she said. 'And so I all'us shall. I can pray as well as Thirz' or that there Daffy Welshman, and I know as it ain't all'us them as prays longest nor loudest as get their prayers answered. For one thing, I were a-praying as I come this morning for some sort of excuse so as I needn't goo up to Hen Street, by myself, and as soon as I got 'ere Fran says she wants a cold dinner as means I shall have to stop to cook your supper. So my prayers was answered, wasn't they?'

William allowed himself to chuckle, and Sophie joined in. 'We are too late now, I think, to walk all the way to Castle Hill, so we'll take the car. We want to call and have coffee with Monica, and pay our respects to young William Gregory and Miss Annette Frances Wagstaffe.'

He had heard Fran come back, and knew that she stood behind his chair, watching Sophie's face. They both saw the words that William had spoken hit Sophie, and then sink in. All else forgotten, Sophie's grey eyes were gazing wide open, first at one of them and then at the other.

'Wagstaffe?' she said. '*Wagstaffe?* 'Ow do you make that out?' Fran pulled up a chair beside her, and explained that Monica had changed her name to Wagstaffe. Sophie's gloom melted 'like dew against the sun', her shining face clearing and beaming satisfaction over everything in sight. Tears of joy were standing in her beautiful eyes, but she forbade them to fall.

'There's times,' she said, 'when it seems to me as 'Im Above takes more notice o' the still small voice of a little bit o' common sense than 'E does of a whull Sunday full o' folks in churches and chapels a-bellering prayers to see who can shout loudest. I ain't never prayed out loud as I know of for there to be Wagstaffes back in this 'ouse one day – but then, 'E knows the prayers in our secret 'earts, don't 'E? And tha's somethink I 'ave all'us hoped for.' She got up, and began to bustle about her work.

4

The noise that greeted their ears on opening the door into the sitting-room of the restored Tudor house which Monica shared with her father was not a duet from two infant voices, as might have been expected, but that of a vacuum cleaner being vigorously wielded by Eric Choppen. He switched it off and greeted them as the friends they had become – even before his and Fran's mutual grandchildren had been conceived.

'Where's your cap and apron?' Fran asked. 'Wait till I tell Sophie! Never will she believe me that I caught "that Mr Choppen who tried to turn her out of house and home" doing the housework! How are the mighty fallen!'

Eric laughed. 'Don't tease me too much about my defeat at the hands of your Sophie, Fran,' he said, leading her to a chair and putting a coffee table beside her. 'One of these days I'll make it up to her. I'll present her with a token of my esteem. She taught me a lesson. I would have said I had enough sense never to underrate an opponent till I met her. I had been used to dealing with men – but tackle a God-fearing maiden lady who knows her rights as well as she knows her Bible on her own home territory and see how you get on! I learned from her that if I wanted to get on in Old Swithinford, I had to have people like her on my side. Sit down, William – move that pile of nappies. I hadn't quite got round to them.'

Fran surveyed the scene with a huge grin on her face. Two years ago the academic and the businessman would have been like oil and water in each other's presence, the Professor courteously polite but reserved, the entrepreneur a little too self-assured and assertive. Now, they were two men sharing the camaraderie of those who had been through the war and survived; friends and neighbours who liked each other's company; and partners in the new joint stockholding of Monica's twins. Fran feasted her eyes on them. Eric, the forceful leader of the syndicate which had threatened the old village, transformed it, and in doing so had preserved it, was winding up the cable of the vacuum cleaner, while Dr William Burbage was sitting clutching to his midriff a huge pile of babies' nappies. Who would have thought it possible?

'Here's Monica with the coffee,' Eric said, not bothering to put the cleaner away. 'Here, give me those.' William was struggling to stand up at Monica's entrance, a bit hampered by the load of terry towelling on his knees. Eric grabbed it and looked round for a flat surface, eventually plonking it on top of the radiogram, and William went to kiss Monica. Fran also greeted her warmly, and she began to pass round the coffee.

'Sorry we're in such a mess,' she said, 'but we haven't found a workable new routine yet. This is supposed to be Dad's part of the house, but I'm afraid the demarcation lines are a bit blurred at the moment. And if you're wondering where Roland is, he's gone to York to see his father-in-law and his old firm. Sir Manfred rang last night and wanted to see him rather urgently. Might be good news about Roland moving his job.'

'Where are they?' asked Fran, meaning the babies.

Monica pulled a face. 'Not be disturbed until feeding time at 11 a.m. By order of the Gorgon – Nurse Conway. Having such a dignified presence around doesn't half show up my domestic incompetence, as well as my slapdash lifestyle. In fact, it's quite clear that she disapproves strongly of everything about all of us except Dad. She's got her eye on him as a distinctly eligible widower whose immortal soul is at risk if he isn't removed pronto from this den of sinners. Her morals are as well starched as her uniform. She hardly lets any of us see the babies except at feeding time – and is affronted if I don't cover myself with a sheet or something, in case Roland or Dad should see what I'm doing. I suppose she does know how babies are conceived? I sometimes wonder. We tried getting her to sit with us, but if she deigns to do so she leaves coyly at feeding time, and tries mashing Dad if she's left alone with him. It's really rather pathetic.'

Eric snorted. 'I assure you I'm not in any danger,' he told William. 'The time may come when I may need a housekeeper, but in these promiscuous days where could I find a woman under eighty willing to leave it at that? Women like Nurse Conway I can deal with, though. It's those I have to work with that faze me. Purposeful and attractive women who aren't satisfied with their lot in life.'

'Not Jess?' asked William, more seriously than the conversation so far had seemed to warrant. Eric, answering William's tone rather than the question, became serious himself.

'You know as well as I do that there's only one man who matters in that way in Jess's life,' he said. 'She hates him having to be away such a lot on business now, even though he's been made a partner and is on to a good thing. She's a marvellous PA – she's coped splendidly without me for the last three weeks, but . . .'

He hesitated, and then went on. William, after all, was Jess's half-brother. 'She's not being herself. She's got some grievance that's making her miserable and bitchy, and she's far too thick with Anne Rushlake for my peace of mind. I can't help feeling that they are too different to be quite such buddies as they are now. Jess lives on her emotions. Anne keeps hers under cover. She wants somebody to cling to – and at the moment she's intent on making that somebody Jess. That's what worries me. Anne puts on a brisk, woman-of-the-world exterior, but that's a lot of hoo-ey. It isn't like Jess to be taken in by it, and I can't help wondering what Greg thinks about Anne always being there when he's at home. Or why Jess wants her. Look out, Monica – the Conway woman approaches with one of her charges in each arm and a face that would turn milk sour – caused, I imagine, by William's presence. He can't claim either my real right or Roland's doubtful one to have seen you uncovered below your neckline before.'

The stout middle-aged 'monthly nurse' held out one of the babies to Monica, preparing to stand by with the other herself to make sure that everything was done according to her rules. Monica gave Fran a wicked look, took the baby, and handed it on to William. Then she proceeded to pull off her 'top' and push her slip and bra down to her waist.

'Thank you, Nurse,' she said sweetly to the scandalized woman, taking the other child from her. 'That will be all. As you see, we're having a lovely family party. I'll bring them back to you when I'm ready.' The insulted nurse retreated.

'That was naughty of me, I know,' Monica said, 'but I'll put it right when I see her again. I don't want her to leave in a huff just yet.'

It was surprising how quickly time passed in such uneventful domesticity. 'Golly!' said Fran suddenly. 'We promised to be up at Castle Hill by midday. We're late as it is, so we must go. Come on, William.'

William kissed the top of the baby's head and put him into his mother's arms, stooping to kiss her as well. 'Thanks for everything, Monica,' he said.

'Bring 'em up to us tomorrow, so that I get a turn,' Fran said. 'If Roland has any news he wants us to know, he'll be willing to come as well – and Sophie can't wait to see two young Wagstaffes back under Benedict's roof again, so come before she goes home. She thinks we ought to have brought her here to see them, as soon as they were born.'

'She doesn't know that we have been living under martial law,' Eric said. 'Can I come too, and bring her my token of reconciliation?'

'Depends what you have in mind,' countered Fran, eyeing him suspiciously. 'Don't make it anything whatsoever personal. So no Chanel No 5 – she'd regard that as a pointed insult. Anything useless but expensive would smack to her of patronage.'

'Would this do? I intended it for you,' he said, 'but I'm not sure it won't do more good to give it to Sophie. See what you think.' It was a framed photograph of Roland holding a day-old baby in each arm. 'All Wagstaffes,' Eric said.

'You couldn't possibly do better,' Fran replied.

5

Castle Hill was not really part of Old Swithinford at all, except for postal convenience, though it could be reached only by one gravelled road that led from the outskirts of the village proper. There were a lot of other overgrown muddy or grassy tracks that met and crossed each other up to the hill, such as it was, that gave the place its name, and to the strange little church that stood right on the highest point. Close to the church was the farmhouse where Bob Bellamy lived; a very strange construction, part medieval, part pseudo-Gothic Victorian.

William had been intrigued by it from the first. The living-room of the house was of such gigantic proportions as to make no sense at all, especially as the ceiling rose to a truncated pyramid two storeys high, and one wall, facing up the hill, was filled with huge clear-glass windows set close together, as in Early English style. They gave a magnificent view of the church and the wood beside it, which was edged by a row of huge elms, laden with the abandoned nests of what had until last year been a lively rookery. The grotesque house suggested a historical mystery, and to William's surprise and delight, he had found its occupant as curious about it as he was himself. It was the basis of an almost instant bond of friendship between them.

The site was perfect, the view from those windows astounding, and inside that vast fantastic room, there was an unmistakable aura ... which Fran was not at all sure at first that she liked. Bob's many cats neutralized her slight uneasiness in the room. They would not have been so purringly comfortable if the aura was a sinister one. Apart from his animals, Bob was living there alone when they had first met him.

Except for – as he had been forced by events to disclose to them – the ghosts. It was the ghosts that had provided an excuse for his wife to leave him, and eventually to seek divorce, and the ghosts which had given his daughter-in-law the lever with which to prise his son away from him.

Bob had a daughter who had spent most of her life away at boarding school because, though she was the apple of her father's eye, her mother had never wanted her and had showed positive antipathy towards her from the time of her birth. So as soon as she was old enough, her father had removed her out of her jealous mother's reach and left her there in safety. Now that her mother was no longer there, she had come home last Christmas, only to step, or literally to fall, into the dramatic events of the last year.

She had been thrown from her horse at the feet of young Charles Bridgefoot, son and heir of Old Swithinford's top farming family. From that moment it had been the stuff of high romance – but the course of their young love had not run at all smoothly. At this time, Charlie (short for Charlotte) had just gone up to Cambridge to follow her ambition to become a vet.

The friendship William and Fran had formed with Bob Bellamy was warm and close, in spite of him being something of an outsider among the rest of the farming community. He was an extraordinary man with extraordinary gifts who had taken them to his heart as readily as they had taken him. He was of different origins, and possessed of strange powers inherited, William guessed, from pagan Celtic ancestors. For example, he believed wholly in the ghosts of which he spoke: he 'knew' things often before they actually happened. William cast him as a throw-back to a tribal shaman whose sixth sense could be trusted.

He had also, as Fran commented, a kind of poetic magic about him born of his kinship with the natural world and the elements. It showed in all sorts of ways; in his love of beauty, for example, in his natural ability to make music and paint pictures, though he was entirely untaught in both skills. He 'heired it', he said, from his forebears. And to Fran it mattered a lot that what he had 'heired' included being a born dancer.

She said he was the only man she had ever met who could rival William on a dance floor.

Dancing had been Fran's passion in those heady dancing days just before the war, and was still something absolutely essential to her well-being. When she had met William again, she had been almost over-whelmed to discover that one thing she had not previously known about him was that he responded to rhythm and dance exactly as she did herself. Given any chance to dance, anywhere, any time, they took it, feeling that they only had one pulse and one pair of feet between them. Non-dancers had no conception of the ecstasy it gave both of them to move in such perfect harmony together. Bob's expertise on the dance floor was a mixed blessing to William. It put a keener edge on the jealousy he felt towards any man who was able to offer Fran the one thing that he could not – marriage. But he knew in this case it was childishly silly, and it certainly made no difference to the friendship.

It had come as a surprise to them to find how low Bob was in the pecking order of the village hierarchy. The main reason appeared to be that he did not own the land he farmed, and was therefore 'only a tenant farmer'. That he was a 'fen tiger' who did in fact own a sizeable holding in the fen, which he farmed as well as Castle Hill, placed him in a sort of social no-man's-land where he could not be categorized as fish, flesh, fowl, or good red-herring. His friendship with William and Fran had raised his esteem a little till his divorce from the wife whose lifestyle was notorious had pulled him down again. It made him the butt of scandalous tongues.

William and Fran were distressed at the personal insults he had had to endure, particularly the insinuation that his beautiful, clever, and highly educated daughter was not good enough to marry into the Bridgefoot family, though the boy who wanted her would have laid down his life for her rather than face life without her. But for Charlie, Bob would not have cared much when he received notification from the Bursar of the Cambridge college which owned Castle Hill Farm that they intended to sell it when his five-year-lease on it ran out. For her sake, he would have done his best to buy it, so that she could remain near to the boy who loved her. The attitude of Charles Bridgefoot's father towards his son's courtship of her, however, was bringing out in Bob the stubborn independent pride that is a tribal characteristic of true fenmen. There was little incentive for him to stay, and he had more or less made up his mind to return alone to his native fen when Fate played the court card she had been keeping up her sleeve.

It concerned Jane Hadley, the enigmatic character who had appeared in the village twenty years previously with a baby in her arms to take up the post of housekeeper for the worst boor of a smallholder in the district, a man for whom even the poorest and the neediest of the women who knew him would have been wary of working. They had eyed her with suspicion from the start, and she had remained 'a mystery woman' to them. She had 'kept herself to herself' though they had had no trouble in putting two and two together with regard to her child. They resented her aloofness as well as her cultured voice and demeanour, and had wasted no sympathy on her when her employer had died and she had become a peripatetic 'daily'. Nor when her handsome and gifted son had been the victim of a road accident that had left him in a deep coma, and her a penniless, helpless outcast. When she had disappeared, their attitude had been that she had got what she had asked for, with her stuck-up ways, and could expect no sympathy from them.

Only Bob Bellamy, who had found her in the little church near his lonely farmhouse, and Fran and William, from whom he had sought advice, knew how he had saved her life and her reputation by letting it be known that she had taken a job as his housekeeper, till such time as her son's condition should force her to make other arrangements. Then harvest had started, and the birth of Monica's twins had caused even Fran and William to lose touch with Castle Hill and its inmates. Much had happened in the interval.

For one thing, Bob had not known that when Jane had been *in extremis*, she had appealed to the wealthy diplomat father whom she had disgraced and had had no contact with for twenty years. He had not responded. It had been at that point that her courage had broken at last, and Bob had rescued her. Her advent into his life just at that time had given Bob the one thing most likely to help him over his own troubles, something to lavish care and attention on, till her father had surfaced after all, with extraordinary results.

From the moment he had looked down on the boy in his hospital bed, Jane's father had taken charge. Nick should be transferred to the care of the most eminent brain surgeon in London, and Jane was invited to live with him in his luxurious service flat close to the clinic where her son would be a patient.

Jane told him that there were reasons why she could not accept his offer of a home with him. She owed her rescuer too much to leave him alone again, whatever her father held out to her. It was the wise cosmopolitan man who told her what her true reason was; that it was not just gratitude that prevented her from leaving Bob, but love.

She had known him to be right, and was afraid. She argued that if or when Bob discovered her true origins, there was no hope that her love for him could ever be returned. Bob had that strange mixture of humility and pride that would never aspire to a woman so much his social superior as she was, however much he might want her. But she would not leave him, just in case.

But when harvest was past and Nick on the mend, she had been filled with new hope, and had promised her father that somehow she would break down her humble host's proud reticence. His answering gage to her had been that if she found new belief in herself and enough courage to make the running so far as to propose marriage to Bob, and succeed, Castle Hill Farm should be the wedding present he would give them.

Jane had persuaded Bob to take her 'down the fen', and its magic had worked on them both. There, with flower-filled water at her feet reflecting the huge sky above, surrounded by the intoxicating peace and smell of the fens, she had found out what it really meant to be loved. Everything was perfect, except for one thing. Bob wanted her, not her father's wealth or position. He would not countenance any such proposal as her father's offer of the farm as a wedding present. On that point she had not been able to move him. He would not explain to her why, or the real reason that prevented him from letting his incredible dream come true.

So when William had rung to ask if they might pay a visit to Castle Hill next day, her hopes began to rise. Fran was just the ally she needed. Of all that had happened since the birth of Monica's babies, the two from Benedict's were in total ignorance. She persuaded Bob that they must be told everything, and to her great relief, he had agreed.

She had to decide whether to greet them as a *ci-devant* charwoman, or in her own right as her wealthy and distinguished father's daughter. Well, the sooner they knew the truth, the better. She dressed herself with care, and made up her face with expensive make-up. Emboldened by what her mirror showed her, she smiled at her own reflection as she brushed her thick bobbed hair till it crackled and shone. Three weeks of knowing that Bob loved her had done far more than her father's cheque at Harrod's to produce that happy image.

Whatever Bob decided, she wasn't going to leave him now. Not even if it meant she had to go back to charring. The only piece of jewellery she possessed was a gold chain that had once been her mother's. She put it on, feeling the precious relic touching her skin like a talisman, and, filled with new joy and confidence, she took one last look at herself in the mirror, pulled back her shoulders, and as Jane Hadley-Gordon, with luck soon to be Mrs Bob Bellamy, she went proudly down the stairs to receive her guests.

She met Bob as he came down the main stairs after 'tidying himself up'. All he had done, in fact, was to take off his wellington boots and put on some shoes, and change his old working jacket for a pullover, though he had had a wash and brushed back his thick, crisp hair till the slight waviness showed in it. She could read his intention as plainly as if he had written it out for her. *'I am what I am, and nothing else. A tenant farmer and a working man. Nobody can make a gentleman of me, not even you.'*

She looked up at him and blocked his way at the bottom of the stairs. He looked her over, approved, knew that she understood his motive in being only himself, and took her into his arms.

'That's what we have to face,' he said. 'Nobody can make a lady of you, because you're one already. That's the difference between us.'

'There isn't any difference between us,' she said. 'You forget that I've been a working woman for the last twenty years, a charwoman. That's why I'm not going to lose the chance of being a farmer's wife, if I can help it. Of course, I can't do anything about it if the farmer concerned won't have me.'

He tightened his arms round her and kissed her, gently at first and then with pent-up passion that made her gasp for breath. Since their day down the fen, when surprise and incredible delight had robbed him temporarily of his natural humility and shyness, he had held himself on a very tight rein. On that evening under a full harvest moon and a huge sky 'clifted with stars', as he had said, he had proved himself to be the sort of lover she had always dreamed of. She had expected that back at Castle Hill the space in her big double bed would be filled by more than a couple of cats – but he had never once in the last three weeks made any attempt to repeat the ecstatic experience. Starved of love as she had been for so long, she had been terribly disappointed at first, afraid that she might have been too willing, and thrust upon him a situation he was not prepared for. But when it became clear to her that he was still taking nothing for granted, she cooled her own impatience.

He had kissed and caressed her, making her feel loved and needed, pulling her on to his knee and telling her of the sort of things he had in mind if and when . . . but never again had he allowed himself to introduce a note of passion. Now, as they clung to each other on the bottom of the stairs in the stolen moment before their guests arrived, she got an inkling that he was protecting her. Perhaps there were subtle reasons that she hadn't properly understood.

Take Fran and William. Whatever *they* did, they would not lose the respect they had in part inherited and in part earned in their own right by being the sort of people they were. But Bob was not in the same class as they were, or that of the Bridgefoots or even the Giffords; and as for herself . . . She had been in the village for twenty years till now a domestic sometimes driven to work in the fields, at best only a charwoman with a grown-up son but no husband. Bob was defending their future standing in the community with the only weapon against scandalous tongues that they possessed: the knowledge that they were *not* yet living together.

He was sure what he was about. The lovemaking out on the river bank would not be repeated until she had a wedding ring on her finger. As the future Mrs Bellamy her reputation as his wife meant more to him than any immediate sexual gratification.

So what about that one time he had not resisted? That was his second reason for not letting her tempt him again. If marriage between them were for any reason not possible, his possession of her absolutely just that once would forever be to him what a vision is to a saint. He had said as much to her, but she hadn't understood then the deep significance of it.

'I've never seen you look so grand before, my beauty,' he said. 'Listen, shall you mind if I take William for a walk up to the church where I can talk to him by myself? I mean, if I leave you and Fran here together?'

Mind? It was what she had been praying for, but hadn't dared to suggest. She needed Fran to help her beat down his silly misgivings. If he thought that William might see his point of view, he could just possibly be right – but what did chance did two poor men stand against Jane Hadley-Gordon and Frances Catherwood in cahoots together?

'Here they are,' she said. 'They're your friends, and they have no idea yet of what has been happening to us. You go and meet them and bring them in. We'll play it all by ear.'

6

They sat at ease in front of the hearth with drinks in their hands, Jane hovering in the background until the formalities were over. Fran looked round her, thinking that even such vast dimensions could be made homely by a few touches like those flower arrangements, and the absence from the beautiful old hearth of rows of old saucers full of cat food. Jane must have banished the cats' meals to the kitchen; the cats themselves were still in evidence on the hearthrug or sunning themselves on the window-sill. But there was something else that was different in the room . . . she could feel it.

Bob possessed a genuine sixth sense, but Fran had something akin to it. She called it her 'overdrive gear', because once she went into it all her wits became sharper and her perception more finely tuned. She went into her overdrive now, and sensed something in the air, something in Bob and Jane themselves – in each singly, but much more telling when they were together. She was not really surprised.

Fran took in Jane's smart appearance, her make-up, the new shoes, the cared-for hands – and her face; the glow about Jane came from inside. She stole a glance at Bob, and her guess was confirmed. So that could be why Bob had sounded embarrassed when talking to William, and why William had got the impression that the cause of it was 'something personal'. How splendid!

'Come and sit down, Jane,' she said. 'I want to ask you all about Nick.'

'Hold hard a minute, Fran,' Bob interposed. 'I hope you ain't in too much of a hurry, 'cos there's such a lot to tell you and a lot more that I want advice about. But it's past dockey time a'ready – so what about yours? I reckon it's going to take most of the afternoon.'

'Our lunch won't spoil,' Fran assured him. 'We were only going to have something cold, because Sophie's cooking tonight.'

'That's lucky,' said Jane coolly, suddenly emerging from the shadows as a competent hostess. 'I've got soup and sandwiches all prepared, just in case. Will that be OK for you, Bob?'

'Anything you say'll do for me, my duck,' he answered, twinkling. 'I'm only a working man, remember.'

'You told me only yesterday that you hadn't much work to do,' Jane answered serenely.

'No – well – that's the truth. This dry weather has got us well forr'ard down the fen with getting potatoes and sugar-beet up – and it's no use me doing much more here till I know whether I'm farming for leaving or not in this next year. That's one o' the things I want to talk to you about.'

William nodded. He was about to say that that was what they had surmised when Jane cut him short. 'Professor Burbage,' she said, 'would you be kind enough to take that poor miserable working-man fen-tiger as far as the church and back to blow some of the cobwebs out of his head before we eat? Lunch will be ready in half an hour. If Mrs Catherwood doesn't mind, I should like a chance to talk to her.'

There was no answer from anyone. Then William spoke. 'Professor Burbage?' he said, looking around and performing his trick of lifting one eyebrow and lowering the other simultaneously. 'Oh, you mean *me*! The professor's off duty for a whole year. I'm only William.' He crossed over to Jane, held out his hand, and when she took it, pulled her towards him and kissed her. 'And my wife's name is Fran.'

('Bless him,' thought Fran. 'He's guessed the state of things between them as easily as I have. So what's amiss, I wonder?')

Jane shooed the two men out, before saying to Fran, 'I wanted them out of the way. But I'd better just put the soup on. I don't really know how or where to start.'

Fran smiled at her. 'No need to tell me the most important thing,' she said. 'I can't tell you how glad I am for both of you. You look a different woman.'

Jane blushed, but kept her head held high. 'I'm afraid that's the difficulty,' she said. 'One of the things I have to tell you. I *am* a different woman – at least, rather different from the one you have known previously, and who was so grateful to you for finding me work.'

'And now you are Bob's new wife?'

'No! Well, er – yes. But not yet – that isn't what I meant. Because I am my real self again, my father's daughter. He and I have found each other again, and I just can't believe how happy I am.'

To Fran's tremendous surprise, the woman who had taken the news of her only child's near fatal accident with no more than a stiffening of her back and a tightening of her mouth burst into tears. Fran was at her side in one movement, and Jane clung to her till a wet and wobbly smile reflected Fran's own. To Fran, Jane had spelled out a lifetime's *Angst* in about half a minute. Fran could have told Jane the outline of her own life story up the moment when a passing van had put a period to it.

'My dear Jane,' she said, 'you don't credit us – any of us – with much sense if you believed we ever thought you had been reared in Dr Barnardo's and stole Nick from a pram outside a fish-and-chip shop.'

She had the pleasure of hearing Jane laugh, a deep contralto laugh with genuine amusement in it, and remembered that she had never heard Jane laugh at all before. What an immensity of sadness lay behind that fact.

Jane gave Fran a brief outline of her youth till her mother's death in Khartoum, and its sad outcome when she was twenty. The advent of Nick.

'I hadn't seen or heard from Father since then till this summer. That was because we had both totally misunderstood each other . . . perhaps we hadn't been together enough when I was small. I had to appeal to him for help when I thought Nick was dying and he came to find me.

'I think I was too young to understand just what my mother had meant to him, and how lonely he was. If only I had turned to him then . . . but another thing I didn't understand at all at that time was his capacity for loving. He seemed to me always to wear his public face – I suppose a high-ranking diplomat is schooled to do just that. I thought only of how I had disgraced him, and that he would never want to see me again. He thought only of how he had failed me, and that I never wanted to see him again. Now we both feel guilty, and want to make it up to each other.'

Fran could bear no more. 'Oh Jane, don't go on! If only we had known . . .'

'It was better that nobody did, I think. What hurt me most was that I had only Nick to love, and I had always known that sooner or later he would leave me – for some other woman if for no other reason. Then that silly accident happened. Have you ever heard of such a serious accident having so stupid a cause before? One loose bolt on the side of a van. I thought that must be my final punishment, but –' She flung her arms wide in a gesture that seemed to take in the whole world. 'How wrong can you be? Just look what it has brought me! Love again. Three men now where I had only one! I think I had forgotten what love was, until Nick's accident. I had confused it with possession, of Nick.'

Fran nodded. 'Love's got so many faces,' she said. 'Most of us think we know it all as soon as we've found the sexual element in it. But we don't. It takes us all our lives to find out all the rest it has to offer.'

'You speak like an expert on the subject – but then, you are, aren't you?'

'I've learned what I know by experience. Now I get frightened, because I feel I have no right to so much of it. Much more than I deserve.'

'Nonsense!' said Jane. 'You get it because you give it. Why do you suppose Bob loves you as he does? But I've only really just found it. The obverse side of it, too – that people suffer because they haven't got anybody to absorb all the love they want to give. Like my poor Effendi, after my mother died and I had left him. Like Bob, till I crashed in amongst his dogs and cats and injured birds. But now, if only Bob will be sensible, we shall all have each other. I can let Effendi do whatever he wants, though we both know that we can't erase the last twenty years altogether. We can't get back all the years of love we've wasted. But I can offer him a belated substitute. I'm not going to lose Nick now, but I am going to give the biggest share of him away, to Effendi. Nick'll have a doting grandfather, and Effendi what he always wanted, a grandson. They'll have each other, and Bob and me. We shall have each other, and both of them – if only Bob will see sense! But it all depends on him. That's why I've told you. I need your help, now, today. Bob will listen to you. Do you mind me involving you?'

She had gone tense again, and was standing in agitation beside Fran's chair. Fran instinctively put out a hand to her, and to her surprise, Jane clasped and held it. Fran was conscious of great relief. The Jane Hadley she had known till now had shrunk away from any ordinary contact as if all humanity was leprous.

'Tell me quickly what the trouble is, and what you want me to do,' she said.

'Ssh! Too late. They're here. Just back me up.'

7

While they ate the simple meal Jane had prepared, talk was general. Fran answered questions about her enlarged family, Jane about her son's progress in hospital, William about what he was going to do with his leave, and Bob about Charlie going up to Cambridge.

'How does Charles feel about it?' Fran asked Bob.

'The same as any youngster would, as head over heels in love as he is,' Bob said. 'Cambridge is too full of other young men! But he knows he doesn't have to watch her. The sooner she starts, the sooner it will be over and she'll marry him. They're happy enough. So could we be, if . . .' He looked across at Jane, who coloured slightly and began to clear up the dishes.

Fran looked enquiringly at William, wondering how much Bob had told him. She raised her eyebrows at him, and he shook his head almost imperceptibly. He hadn't been told; but Bob's last remark was surely a leading one? She sent William a silent message to take the plunge and ask.

'Come and sit down again, Jane,' William said, standing behind her chair till she had sunk back rather shyly into the circle. 'We should have to be blind and deaf not to know what's changed since we last saw you. We're getting to be old hands at matchmaking, you know. Have we guessed right?'

They needed no other answer than the look on both faces. Fran leapt to her feet to hug Bob, while William played the chivalrous courtier to Jane.

'There's no need to explain to us that Jane is not exactly what she has been trying to pretend she was all these years. We weren't blind then, either, but we know how to mind our own business. So why "if", Bob? And what did you mean about "farming for leaving"?'

Bob got up and went round to the back of Jane's chair. He bent and kissed the top of her head. It was, Fran guessed, an apology in advance, in case anything he said might hurt her.

'There's things none of you understand,' he said. 'And it ain't myself I'm thinking about. It's Jane. She knows she can have me and everything

I've got – my life into the bargain if that's what she wants, and if it would make her happy. But will it? How long for? What if I have to take her back to live on my farm in the fen? Listen to her talking – and then listen to me. Look at her – and then at me. I wasn't good enough for Charlie's mother, who was only a farm-labourer's daughter. What have I got to offer Jane?'

'Yourself,' put in Jane. 'That's all I want or need.'

'So you think now,' he replied. 'But what about when your posh father's had a dekko at me and seen what he's got for a son-in-law? And what about Nick? What's *he* going to think? Is he going to break your heart, my beauty, by being ashamed of you because of me? If you are ever going to have to choose between Nick and me, do it now.'

Fran's wrought-up senses heard the catch in his throat. Again she put out a hand to touch Jane, giving her a coded message to play what Bob was saying down and keep her courage up. It heartened Jane. She couldn't get used to having friends so literally at hand.

'You needn't worry about Nick,' she said. 'He isn't used to luxury any more than I am. Money isn't a problem any longer, but caring's a very different thing. He doesn't know about anything, yet.'

'You haven't told us much, either. Why don't you start at the beginning?' William suggested. Jane made it plain that she was leaving that to Bob.

He went back to sit down, and was at once besieged by two cats. He was searching for words as he pulled their ears. 'Well – it turns out as Jane's father is a real Somebody: posh as they come and wealthier than most. She hasn't told me – 'cos I wouldn't let her – why they haven't had anything to do with each other for the last twenty years. But he's glad to have her back again, and wants to do all he can for her, and for Nick. A lot more than I could have done, or can ever do. I ain't going to spoil any o' that for her 'cos she thinks she owes me anything. I know what she's been through better than most.'

'Effendi knows what I want,' Jane said, serenely. 'It's you who won't believe me, not him. Go on. Tell Fran and William the rest.'

When Bob didn't answer she went on. 'My father knows all about Bob, because I told him. He knows all Bob's done for me, and' – her head came up – 'how much I love him. I've explained to my father as well as I know how about the farm and the decision Bob has to make. His idea is to buy it himself and give it to us as a wedding present. Bob won't listen. He says he won't come between me and Effendi and Nick. That's just what he will do, if he goes on being so silly. Because where he goes, I'm going with him, married or not. He loves this farm – you know he does. So do I, and I always shall, because this is where he found me, and where

I found him. But if what he wants is to go back to the fen again, he's only got to say so. I'll go with him. I don't understand why he – we – can't accept the wedding present my father wants to give us. But I get the impression that Bob thinks it would disgrace him for ever.'

William, sympathizing with both, felt unable to decide what advice, if any, he dared offer. While he hesitated, and Fran wisely kept silence, Bob spoke again.

'It's what you mean by a wedding present,' he said. 'There's a difference between a rolling-pin and a wooden spoon tied up in a dishcloth, and a two-hundred acre farm.' He stood up, so as to be able to face them all. 'And I may be only an old fen tiger with no proper education, but that don't stop me from being able to think for myself. I don't intend to be beholden for the rest of my life to a man as I don't know, and who'll very like despise me soon as he hears me speak – and Jane as well, for marrying such as me. Seems to me as he'd all'us wish that she'd give it a bit more time, and waited to find herself a husband to match her and suit him. But that ain't all!

'He may be a proud man – I don't know 'cos as I said, I ain't seen him yet – but then so am I! There's an old saying that a fenman's all'us got his pride when everything else has gone. We heir it. As far back as Roman times, and them old ancient Britons as wouldn't give in to 'em. They hid in the fens, and they had to marry into the tribe 'cos that were all the choice they had. So they never got changed much, and that's what makes us as we are. They had to be independent, and they were proud to be different. *So am I!*

'Owning the land I farm here in Old Swithinford wouldn't change me. I shall be proud and independent and obstinate, 'cos wherever I live I shall still be the old fen tiger I am till the day o' my death. That's the bit of me not even you'll be able to change, my pretty, though you can do whatever else you like with me. *I can't help it.*'

It was a long speech for him to make, and he sat down suddenly, after a beseeching look towards Jane. She looked at Fran despairingly.

'My father may not understand that yet, but he will. Bob just won't believe me. I love them both. I know how hurt Effendi will be. He feels guilty at what was all my fault, and wants to make up for the past. Bob won't let him, because of this idiotic "old fen pride", as he calls it. As if nobody but a fenman knows what pride is!'

She sat down and actually glowered at Bob, as an alternative to throwing herself into his arms and kissing him to wipe the anguished look off his face.

'And why,' asked William in a very matter-of-fact tone, 'have these two proud men never met each other?'

It was Fran who answered him, since neither of the two principals seemed capable of doing so. 'Because this silly argument started before they ever had a chance, I suppose,' she said. 'Am I right?'

Bob nodded, looking sheepish, and buried his face in his hands. Jane's mouth quivered.

'Well,' said Fran briskly, 'that's the place to start. A meeting must be arranged as soon as ever possible, because it seems that "time is of the essence", as the lawyers say. How soon do you think your father could make it, Jane? And where? I don't want to seem to be interfering, but I don't think you ought to expect Bob to go to London.'

'Nor would it be fair to ask Jane's father to come here,' put in William, 'on Bob's own territory, as it were. Fair's fair. What we need is a bit of good old English compromise, so that they meet on neutral ground.'

'I think my father's so anxious to do all he can that he'll come when and where we ask him to,' said Jane, looking much more hopeful. 'I suggest the day after tomorrow. At the hotel?'

William looked dubious. 'It would be very public,' he said. 'And again, if I may say so, a bit unfair to Bob. May I make a suggestion? What are friends for? Couldn't we give them all lunch, Fran, and then leave them to it? It would break the ice between them much easier if someone else is there at the beginning of the meeting.'

Jane was looking pleadingly at Bob, who was maintaining a rather glum, unwilling silence.

William glanced at Fran, got an appreciative nod, and went to Jane to hold out his hand to help her out of her chair. He took advantage of the moment to raise his eyebrows at Fran with a slight inclination towards Bob, and received in return what he knew to be her agreement to what it was he had in mind.

'Off you go straight away to ring your father, Jane,' he said. 'Have you got a phone that's a bit more private than this one in here?'

'In Bob's bedroom,' she said, hesitating slightly.

'That's fine. Suppose I come as far as the landing, so that I can be go-between if Bob needs to be consulted? Or if you need any information I could supply?'

Jane relaxed visibly. A supporter at hand was exactly what she needed at that moment.

Fran gave William what was almost a wink. She knew precisely what he was up to. He wanted to leave her alone to deal with Bob.

'I do think William's got the right idea,' she said. 'Bob can't possibly say he's not on neutral ground at Benedict's. It has been in his dreams since he was a little boy. It's the place where all his best dreams begin. The very best place to turn a day-dream into a reality.'

Bob had raised his head like a startled colt, but by that time the door was already closing behind Jane and William.

Fran moved close to Bob, in case she needed to touch him. She looked quizzically down on him. 'That shook you, didn't it, you silly, self-effacing stubborn old fen-tiger?' she asked. 'What's happened to your sixth sense? Don't tell me it's warning you! Hasn't it been yelling at you ever since you picked Jane up in the church that your dreams were beginning to come true? You've been shutting your ears and refusing to listen! Is it truly because of your pride? Honestly?'

He didn't reply. She stood up and faced him, blazing with indignation.

'How dare you even mention the question of pride to a woman like Jane? Compared with her, you don't know what pride is. Bragging about independence inherited from a race of savages who had no option but to be independent to a woman who at twenty chose independence in circumstances worse than anything your old Ancient Britons ever had to face, because she was alone. With nothing – nothing at all – to support her but her pride. And you pretend to love her! After all she's been through, and it's in your power to make her happy, you'd sacrifice her to your pride? Tell that to the Marines. You're just plain scared, Bob Bellamy.'

There was still no reply. Fran changed her tactics.

'Bob,' she said, 'there was a time when I was in just such a state as you're in now. Old Mary Budd took me to task, just as I'm making you face up to things. She told me what I've just told you, and she was right. You're afraid that it may not work out. So was I. But as she said, how can you know till you try?'

He was shaking, and she was sorry to have to hit him so hard, but she had to go on. 'I'm sorry, Bob, truly, and I ought to have known without William's help that of course you had to meet Jane's father in our house. William was just being practical, but I should have seen that it might make a difference if you were to meet in the room you dreamed about so often before you had ever been inside it. It has to have some special significance to you. Bob, don't you *know* that if you meet there, everything will be all right?'

He still didn't answer her. She tried once more. 'Mary told me that I had to stop trying to do for myself what the gods were willing to do for me. Now I'm telling you the same. Leave it to the gods, and Benedict's.'

'Same thing,' said Bob, looking up at her at last. 'Listen – here they come.'

'All set up,' said William, putting his thumbs up. 'I'm going to meet him at Cambridge. And Fran, darling, we really ought to go to give Sophie warning that she's got to prepare lunch for visitors two days running.'

Jane and Bob, arms round each other, watched them off.

'You seem to have done a bit of softening up,' William said.

'I had to hit him hard,' Fran answered. 'Thank you for giving me the chance.'

William smiled. 'Send him a bill, like the plumber sent the Professor of Physics,' he said.

'Tell me.'

'The professor's hot-water tank developed a dent, so he sent for the plumber. All the plumber did was to clout the tank with a hammer, and send a bill for £50. The professor protested, of course, and insisted that the plumber sent him a more reasonable bill, which he did. It said "To hitting the tank, £5. To knowing where to hit it, £50. Total, £55." I knew quite well who could hit that particular tank best.'

She detected a slight dryness in his tone. Even now, he couldn't help it. She hugged his arm and rubbed her face against his sleeve. 'I wish I knew that plumber,' she said. 'I would ask him where to hit my professor to get the dent out of him!'

8

Before reaching home they decided that they must tell Sophie what was afoot. With regard to the next day, Fran had no qualms. In Sophie's eyes, all the visitors except Eric Choppen were 'fam'ly', and she held out against him only to save face with her sisters. Sophie had so far never seen the twins. In their anxiety about Roland's illicit involvement with Monica, they had withheld knowledge from Sophie until she had put two and two together, drawn her own conclusions, and let them know she had been hurt by their not taking her into their confidence.

'It's going to be very difficult for Jane, isn't it?' Fran said to William. 'It would have been so much easier for both of them if they had gone right away and started afresh. She's been around here too long as a domestic cleaner with a fatherless son – though some must have guessed that she was a dark horse out of a very good stable who didn't mix because she had a secret to keep. There will be plenty said now! Especially as it's Bob she's marrying. In their eyes he doesn't quite make the grade either. He knows what a barrage of talk they'll have to face till the topic wears itself out. That may account for some of his reluctance to stay on at Castle

Hill. If they'd gone down the fen, no one there would have known anything about her.'

William agreed. Some people wouldn't be able to hide their envy, but he thought that there would be many more whose main difficulty would be embarrassment – not knowing how to behave towards Jane now. 'I don't think we need worry ourselves much about Sophie,' he said, 'as long as she knows all about it first. It will be people like Brian Bridgefoot who'll be difficult. The Bridgefoots are top dogs among the farmers, and Brian's let it go to his head a bit – he won't like Bob suddenly popping up in the same league, having already taken his stand against his son marrying Bob's daughter. Funny how things happen! This is an example of the old "cautionary" tales about being careful how you spent your three wishes. Like "The Monkey's Paw". Brian's first wish was for his son to marry the daughter of "a somebody" and his second that that somebody should be well-to-do. The boy falls in love with the daughter of an uneducated fen tenant farmer, who picks up a ragged pauper with a damaged reputation. Then, hey presto – she turns into a princess whose father is willing to give her husband half his kingdom. So where does that leave Brian? Does he have enough sense to retract his first wishes, or does he use his last wish for the youngsters to live happily ever after?

'My guess is that he would rather his first wishes had never been granted at all than have to face the fact that Cinderella's bastard to whom he has been able to play "the rich man" all these years may now inherit such wealth as Charles can never hope for. It's a real test of character, and one can't help feeling a bit sorry for Brian. He'll either have to be seen eating humble pie, or be at odds with his father and his son. I can't see it making an iota of difference to his father – except that George'll be glad for everybody's sake, specially for Charles's and Charlie's. I don't think George knows what envy is.'

They were inside the house by now, and Sophie came to meet them. She had heard the last bit of their conversation. 'If it's George Bridgefoot you're talking about,' she said, 'I reckon you ain't far out, though as far as I know 'e ain't got no reason for being jealous o' nobody. 'E 's been up 'ere this afternoon to see you, but I 'ad to tell 'im as I didn't know 'ow long you'd be, so 'e didn't wait. If it's all right with you, I'll just make your tea and then slip round to see 'ow Thirz' is afore I get your supper.'

'Put the tea in the kitchen and we'll come and have it with you,' Fran said. 'We've got things to tell you.'

Sophie took the news of next day's invasion for lunch in her stride – she liked nothing better than cooking a good meal for hearty eaters. She showed how pleased she was that the babies were going to be brought

45

especially to show her – though her sniff added that it was not before time.

Then William launched into the tale of what had happened at Castle Hill. Sophie was very quiet as she listened with bowed head, looking down at her hands clasped in her lap.

'I'm afraid they'll find things difficult till people get used to the idea,' William said.

She looked up at him with her grey eyes wide and unblinking. 'God works in a mysterious way, 'Is wonders to perform,' she said. 'I can't 'elp wondering why 'E chose to take my Jelly away from me like 'E did and give Jane 'Adley 'er son and 'er father back and a good 'usband into the bargain. But there, it ain't for us to question what 'Im Above chooses to do. I'm sure as I'm real glad for 'er sake, 'cos if any woman ever 'ad a 'ard life till now, she 'as.'

'I'm afraid we've asked them all to come here to lunch the day after tomorrow,' Fran said. 'We hadn't time to ask you first. Can you manage that? Jane's father is coming as well – William's going to meet him at Cambridge. I'm sorry, Sophie – it isn't really fair on you, but it was either here or at the hotel, and you know how shy Mr Bellamy is. Do you mind?'

Sophie knew exactly what she was being asked – did she mind cooking and waiting on Jane? There was never any beating about the bush with Sophie. She answered what Fran had asked, though the words had not been spoken.

'You ought to know me well enough b'now to know as I shall do anything as you ask me to as is within the bounds o' reason. I never would ha' waited on some as you never should ha' got so thick with. Do, as I remember you never did ask me to. So I know as you won't ask me to do nothing as I shouldn't be willing to do for your sakes anyway. Besides, I'm got no fault to find with 'er. And if I don't get off now afore the butcher's shop closes, none of 'em get anything to eat neither the one day nor the other. Can I tell Thirz'?'

'I'm afraid not. Nor anybody else, until we are sure that Bob's daughter and Charles know,' said William. 'We shall have to keep it a secret between the three of us.'

Fran smiled at William's cunning. That 'three of us' would have sealed Sophie's lips through medieval torture.

She was hovering in the hall next day when the cars disgorged their passengers – Roland and Monica each carrying a baby in a carry-cot, and Eric with a large basket in which were two bottles of champagne, a heap of clean nappies and a flat gift-wrapped parcel.

'I feel as if I've been let out of prison,' Monica said. 'The Gorgon isn't watching me. I can do what I like with "her" babies! There they are – wake 'em up if you want to.'

Fran called to Sophie to come, and offered her a chair. Then she put one of the babies into Sophie's arms. Speechless, Sophie just sat and gazed. Fran watched her undoing the shawl that enveloped young William, and holding him up to her face. A sudden silence fell like a vacuum into which Fran's thoughts and feelings rushed till they nearly overwhelmed her again. It was almost a 'holy' moment, filled to overflowing with Love, and Sophie in the role of the Madonna.

'Let me hold the other one for a minute,' Sophie was saying. Fran exhanged babies with her and handed the boy to William. The spell was broken and the talk flowed on.

'Take her now,' Sophie said. 'If I don't goo and get on there'll be no dinner for anybody.'

When lunch was finished, Eric went to fetch the champagne, and took the opportunity of asking Sophie to leave what she was doing and come with him to drink a toast he was about to propose. She actually smiled at him as she dried her hands and followed.

'To all the Wagstaffes,' he said, raising his glass. Fran noticed that only Eric and William drank. She couldn't, obviously, because the toast had been meant to include her, and Monica and the babies. Why not Roland?

Eric was speaking. 'I think Roland has something to tell you,' he said.

Roland got to his feet. 'I went up to Yorkshire yesterday. I'm joining a new firm in Cambridge from the first of next month – Smith, Akehurst and Wagstaffe. I'm the Wagstaffe.'

Nobody spoke, so he had to go on. 'You see, I've known for months now that Sue's case is hopeless. She's getting more and more mentally unstable, and now needs constant care. At her own request, she's gone into a nursing home run by nuns. She has become a Roman Catholic, and wants to stay where she is. What it means is that there can be no further question of ever asking her to divorce me. I could, of course, put in a petition for desertion, but I shan't. Nobody's asking me to. But Monica and I want a home and a firm base for all our family to start out from and come back to when they want. These two are already Wagstaffes by name, and by blood, like I am. So – I hope you won't mind, Mum – but in order to give us all a new start I have simply turned my names round, and I am now, quite legally, Roland Catherwood Wagstaffe. As soon as I can possibly find us a suitable house, we shall start our lives afresh as a whole family of Wagstaffes. So let's all drink to the future.'

In the ensuing mêlée, Eric managed to move close to Sophie's side, and turned all his charm on her, while the rest, pretending not to notice, watched it work. He presented her with the flat parcel, and asked her to accept it.

'Open it,' somebody said. Glad to get rid of her glass, because she hated all wine except her own sweet homemade variety, and thought champagne only fit for pig-swill, she blushingly complied and found the photograph. Sophie was overcome, both by the gift and the giver. Like all Kezia's family, she kept a special word for such special occasions.

'Thanks,' she said.

9

George Bridgefoot had been disappointed at not finding anyone but Sophie at Benedict's. He was niggled and uneasy about a lot of little things that together amounted to a worry that had somehow got under his skin in a way he wasn't used to. All he had wanted was somebody outside his family to talk to, and he had decided on Fran and William because, besides his deep personal affection for them, he had a considerable respect for their grasp on village matters as a whole, and could rely on intelligence backed by common sense.

Two days later, he felt an even greater need for a chat with them. It was the evening of the day they had spent at full stretch dealing with the meeting between Bob Bellamy and his prospective father-in-law, but, of course, of that George knew nothing – though Bob Bellamy and his grandson's connection with Castle Hill had been brought by pure chance to the top of his heap of worries.

He sat in his old Windsor chair between the fireplace and the table of the kitchen of the Old Glebe farmhouse, with his pipe in his mouth. The pipe was empty, and though his tin of tobacco and his box of matches lay within his reach on the corner of the table, he made no move to fill it. His long legs were stretched out because just lately he had found it hurt his hip too much to put his stockinged feet up on the table, as he had been in the habit of doing after supper for most of his married life. He was nearing seventy, and his joints had begun to remind him of it, even when lying in bed. But that wasn't what was making him ill at ease. He was philosophical enough by nature to accept that if you lived long enough to be old, you had to expect some discomforts. He had no grumbles on that score, because apart from joints that were getting a bit stiff, he was still hale and hearty, and as willing to count his many blessings as he had always been. He enjoyed his after-supper pipe when his mind was wholly at ease, but at present it wasn't. Whichever way he turned his thoughts, they led him back to the same problem. Sooner or later – probably sooner – he had to make à decision, and then act on it. The end of another farming year was in sight, and he had to decide whether or not the time had come for him to hand over to his son, Brian. If he did, he would be the first Bridgefoot ever to give up before, as George said, 'they planted him in the churchyard'. But things were different now – and so was Brian. That was the real core of his worry.

He looked across at his wife, who had fallen asleep in her armchair the other side of the grate, as she so often did these days when she had finished washing up the supper dishes. Bless her – let her sleep. She would go along with whatever he decided, whether or not she thought it wise. He hadn't broached the subject to her at all, yet, which was strange in itself, because from the very first day of his marriage to Molly he had talked everything over with her; but he had good reason for keeping to himself what was in his mind now. He had been hoping that the things that were worrying him at present would right themselves, that there was no sense in worrying her. But they hadn't righted themselves. Instead, they were getting worse, and every day there seemed to be more of them. He now had some reason for being uneasy in his mind about all his nearest and dearest except perhaps Lucy, his youngest.

Molly had been 'at him' for days to do something about the broken chain in the downstairs lavatory. She had chuntered so much that morning that he had gone down to the village to buy a new length at Kenneth Bean's Do-It-Yourself shop. Kid had a good deal of business acumen, but was handicapped by his wife, Beryl, who ran the shop. She was a woman of very meagre intelligence, though well endowed with the crafty cunning that so often replaces it in the somewhat simple-minded. Moreover, her voluble tongue, activated by inquisitiveness and an envious nature, was a by-word among her peers, who knew her well enough to believe only about a tenth of what she said. Others, like George, declared that she needed a gob-stopper, and laughed, more amused by her inventiveness than hurt by her fabrications. But like everything else, the circumstances surrounding her had changed. Her presence in the shop in the middle of the village, where she operated a scandal exchange with any willing customer, had made her dangerous, because what she didn't know, she invented.

As George drew up in front of the shop that day, he saw at once that there had been large alterations to it since the last time he had passed by. One of its two large plate-glass windows, which usually contained a display of wallpaper and paint, now bore all the usual signs connected with a house agent, including a placard behind the glass informing the public that 'D. PUGH, ESTATE AGENT AND VALUER' was within and at their service to sell them the wonderful new homes being erected on 'the Lane's End estate'.

When he opened the door between the two plate-glass windows, he saw that a flimsy partition had been erected between the two halves of the shop to provide Mr Pugh with privacy. In the partition was a wooden door, on the other side of which Beryl Bean was talking to her new tenant. She stood, as she herself would have said, 'with the door in her hand', which meant that she still had her hand on the knob, leaving a chink two or three inches open, and through which her strident voice was quite audible.

He made the shop bell tinkle, and stood waiting to be served. He could not help hearing what it was she was imparting to Mr Pugh, whom George had already placed in his mind as one of Bailey's entourage: a scavenger of custom and a jackal located centrally to sniff out for his master any other land that could be devoured for development.

What Beryl was in fact regaling Pugh with was her belief that Castle Hill was indeed very likely to fall into Bailey's hands. She and her Ken got to know the truth about such things, she told him, dropping her voice a fraction, on account of Ken always being out and about, and her always being in the shop where she 'was told' things. The news was that Bob Bellamy couldn't raise the cash needed, so it was now only a matter of time before the farm came on to the open market.

George felt that he was eavesdropping, and tinkled the bell again, but Beryl could not bring herself to cut her tale short for the sake of selling a box of matches. So she ignored her customer.

'It's no wonder the Bridgefoots are upset about young Charles getting tangled up with that queer gel of Bellamy's,' she said, her voice coming through the half-closed door as clearly as if she were speaking direct to George. ''Specially Charles's father, Brian. He's going to put a stop to it, once and for all. I do know that's the truth, because my Ken heard him say so, with his own ears, at Mr Bailey's. Ken's doing business with Mr Bailey now, and when he went to see him the other day, Brian Bridgefoot and Vic Gifford, as is his brother-in-law, was both there in his office. If he gets hold of Castle Hill, seems they are going in with him, like – at least, that's what Ken thinks. You being Bailey's man'll know all about it a'ready, I dare say. There ain't no flies on Brian Bridgefoot, nor yet on Vic Gifford. They know which side their bread's buttered on, you mark my words.'

George waited no longer. He left quietly so as not to draw attention to himself, and went home very troubled to try to sift out the grain of truth he felt sure that there must be somewhere in Beryl's bushel of chaff. Brian must have been opening his mouth too wide somewhere in public.

George liked Bob Bellamy. As far as he was concerned, it didn't matter a tinker's cuss that Bob was a newcomer, a fen tiger and only a tenant farmer. While as for his daughter, Charlie . . . she was exactly the sort of girl he would have chosen for his only grandson, if Charles hadn't been sensible enough to choose her for himself anyway.

That she loved Charles for himself, and not for what he could offer her, was plain for all to see; but it had been made plainer still by her determination to go on with her own ambition to become a vet. She had agreed, at the boy's pleading, to a formal engagement when at his next birthday he would be twenty-one and come into the money George had already settled on him.

George felt a stab of enormous understanding and sympathy for Charles, who was young and healthy and strong and normal, with the means to marry as soon as he liked, but who still had to be kept waiting for a girl like Charlie who loved him and wanted him as much as he wanted her. But that was what she had decreed.

Charlie loved George, and often talked to him about things concerning herself and Charles. She had told him she wanted time to prove herself 'good enough' for the boy. Because of her mother being what she was, she felt that she had to earn Charles's respect – which really meant that she had to prove to all the Bridgefoot family, especially Brian, that she didn't take after her mother. That being the case, George would have staked his life that, even in these permissive days, and when Charles did marry her, she would still be as fresh as a daisy for him. That pleased George. He had strong feelings about the modern attitude towards sex, though he had been forced to modify them a bit lately – but he still thought there was a lot to be said for a bit of proper courting. It was something very few youngsters had much experience of nowadays. George and the rest of the family were quite content with Charles's choice. The fly in the ointment was Brian. Whatever it was that had 'come over him' in the last year had made him so different that they hardly knew him. They were all suffering from his tantrums, and getting fed up with it. Not that they loved him any less. They just didn't like the sort of 'modern' man he had become – and 'they' included Brian's wife and son. George sighed. He had seen his son's wife that very morning, and heard about the quarrel there had been last night between Charles and his father, about Charlie.

'The truth of the matter is,' said Rosemary, 'that Brian's been kidding himself all along that once Charlie had gone up to Cambridge, that would be the end of it. You know he's never thought she was good enough. He really let himself go to Charles about it last night! Went on at him about how much better he could have done for himself than the daughter of a tenant farmer who wouldn't even be that much longer, and whose mother as everybody knew was no better than a whore. Not that there was a lot to choose between her mother and her father, he said, from what he had heard about the way Bob was carrying on with Jane Hadley.'

Then Charles had lost his temper, and it had nearly come to blows – with Brian yelling that he'd break his son's bloody neck rather than let a foot of Bridgefoot land go to a son Charles would never be able to be sure was his own. Rosemary had cried at that point. 'I couldn't stand it, Grandad, and I let fly at Brian. So we had the worst row we've ever had, and this morning nobody's speaking to anybody else. But it won't do any good. Brian will never give in, now.'

George had parted from her very heavy-hearted, because he knew that she had been right. That had been before he had eavesdropped in the shop.

He shifted his position in his chair to try to ease the pain in his hip. It didn't make things any easier for him that even his own body was hinting to him that it was time to act if he truly intended to. It was a big decision, though, and in making it he had to think of everybody, himself and Molly included. And be fair to the others. Brian was his only son, but not his only child.

Could he really contemplate retiring, under those conditions? Give up the reins and the management of the farm to the man his son had become? Put his daughters and his grandchildren more or less under Brian's thumb? Break Charles's and Charlie's hearts? See Charlie's father chased out, and Castle Hill covered with another of Bailey's terrible estates? With his own son a party to all of it? Not if there was a single thing he could do or say to prevent it!

He got up. He couldn't wait. He would go up to Benedict's again, here and now, before he broke down and poured all his misgivings out to his wife. 'Mother,' he said. 'I'm going down to see the Rector, and then up to Benedict's to talk to them about the best way of arranging the presentation to him before he leaves. I shan't be any longer than I can help.'

'Fill your pipe,' she said. 'They won't care if you smoke. I don't know what it is you're maunching about, but whatever it is a breath of Benedict's company'll do you good.'

His face broke into the first smile of the day as he closed the door behind him. He never had been able to hide much from Molly.

I O

William had gone to take Jane's father back to Cambridge station. Fran was alone, feeling absolutely worn out. She had slept badly the night before. Wholly satisfied with the visit of their family from Monastery Farm, William had been asleep almost as soon as his head touched the pillow; but Fran had tossed and turned in vague apprehension, though what the cause of it was she could not identify, except that it concerned Eric.

The October moon, by long tradition called 'the hunters' moon', was full, sailing serenely above the wellingtonias. By its light she looked down on William's sleeping face. Already, after so short a time of being free from work, it seemed to her that he looked relaxed, younger, handsomer and more adorable than ever. How terrible it would be if the time ever came when the moonlight showed her only an empty space again where he ought to be.

That was it! She was worrying because of something Eric had said, that he had to be careful about the women he worked with. Why? Monica had said she could swear that he had very little if any use for women in a sexual context. But loneliness was a powerful force, and Eric was going to be lonely after Roland had taken Monica and the children away. Loneliness might make a man like Eric, with a virile man's normal needs, do silly things, such as – ? Such as making a pass at the enchanting, chameleon-like personality of her cousin and his PA, Jess Taliaferro? Whose husband, Greg, was so often away for days at a time now, leaving Jess lonely too.

Her worry had crystallized. Until recently, she could have sworn on her own life that nothing but death itself could ever part that couple; but it was no good deluding oneself. The cracks in their relationship had already begun to show. Was Jess's sudden close friendship with her second-in-command Anne Rushlake anything to do with it?

Anne was a bit of an enigma. She took pains to present herself as a tough woman-of-the-world, though she also exhibited traits more usually associated with strait-laced maiden ladies. The glimpses she occasionally offered Fran of her unshackled life in wartime London assorted oddly with the sanitized aroma of antiseptic that quite literally followed her wherever she went. But Anne wasn't her problem. A possible rift between Jess and Greg was. She longed for it to be morning, so that she could set her thoughts before William and they could discuss her fears together. She had wanted so much for William's year of sabbatical leave to be a lot less fraught than the last year had been, and allow them both to go contentedly along with their work and each other. Not that such a thing could ever be expected in the closed community an old-fashioned village was. As Sophie's mother was always saying, 'If it ain't one thing, it's another.'

Fran turned over again, wider awake than ever. 'Drat it,' she said, half aloud. Kezia, Sophie's mother, would have been right. If there was nothing else for her and William and their friends to worry about, there was the threat of that horrible Bailey and his predatory designs on their peace and quiet. She consigned him and his development plans to the depths of the bottomless pit.

Over breakfast she told William what a bad night she'd had, and why. He teased her about the way she always rushed to meet trouble halfway, and not being able to distinguish between real threats and those raised by her fertile imagination 'in the dead waste and middle of the night'.

'We've got a long day ahead of us,' he said. 'Let's get through today before we begin to worry about tomorrow. Be fair! I didn't expect, when as Sophie would put it I "took up" with my stepcousin, that I was letting myself in for a lifetime of solving agony-aunt sort of problems. Men aren't cut out for it. You have an absolute genius for entangling yourself in other people's affairs. Why should we consider ourselves responsible for Greg? Or what we are going to have on our plates this lunchtime? We can't get out of it now, I know, but how did we ever get ourselves into it? Because, my precious, anybody with a problem of any sort just makes a beeline for you. You draw them like a magnet draws iron-filings.'

Her face informed him that his too-light response was not what she had hoped for, and he was immediately contrite. He stretched his hand across the table to her, and made her look back at him eye to eye.

'And I'm one of the iron filings, as helpless against the pull of you as anybody else. Where you go, I follow. What you do, I do, too. Even as far as landing myself with a day as full of stress and strain as this promises to be.'

She squeezed the hand still holding hers. 'Then you'd better get on with your breakfast. You have to be at Cambridge in exactly two hours from now. You'll need all your diplomacy to cope with him, so don't waste any more of it on me. You know as well as I do that I can't help it. And who was it suggested the meeting should be here, anyway? You. So it really isn't any good you starting to worry about it now. The only thing we can be sure of is what we propose to offer the great man for lunch.

There may not be any answer to their problems, though I think I got through to Bob. You will have time in the car to brief Jane's father a little about what to expect. Apart from that, we can't do better than to be ourselves and play it by ear.'

He agreed, and set off. She remained where she was, waiting for Sophie. She was still a bit anxious about Sophie's first encounter with Jane. If Jane in her embarrassment showed any sign of 'stand-offishness', or if Sophie let her feeling of the unfairness of life show, it could get the whole day off to a bad start. On such tiny things do great events depend.

Today's encounters involved so many others besides the principals. There was Jane's son, Nick, and Bob's daughter, Charlie, and because of her, the Bridgefoot family – and so *ad infinitum*. Fran was wishing she had kept out of it all. She should have let the gods get on with their game of human spillikins, and not made this first move.

William was beset by much more mundane problems. It was only when he was well on his way that he realized no one had given him any brief. What, he wondered, had Jane's father been told? Having had to switch his attention back to the family yesterday, he had quite forgotten to ask what arrangements had been made for him and his passenger to recognize each other. The one thing he guessed he could be sure of was that Jane would have told her father to look out for a tall man with white hair. In fact, she hadn't said anything so helpful. Her father's swift and willing reaction to her request had quite undone her. She hadn't yet got used to taking him or his love for her for granted. She'd been struggling with the lump in her throat, and had merely informed him very briefly that some friends of Bob's were giving them hospitality to prevent them having to meet in a public place, and that 'William' would be waiting for him at Cambridge station. She had shied away from warning him of Bob's obstinate rejection of his magnanimous offer. Diplomatically he had asked no questions, and it hadn't occurred to him to ask who or what 'William' was. He had been accustomed for a long time to uniformed chauffeurs in limousines. He expected 'William' to be the proprietor of Old Swithinford's local one-man taxi-service.

William placed himself at the exit in the middle of the long platform and watched the train from Liverpool Street disgorge its passengers. A lot of students – of the sort he knew only too well; mostly a dishevelled crew, blearily unwashed, male and female alike wearing jeans deliberately whitened with splashes of bleach and boiled till they were too tight either for comfort or hygiene. There were also some old colleagues legitimately on their way to lectures, some day-trip shoppers and one conspicuous 'city gent'. He was tall and upright, about the right age and obviously expecting to be met. William's heart sank. The man coming towards the exit was wearing a bowler hat and carrying an umbrella. What hope was there of any real understanding between such cultured urbanity and Bob's dogged pretence of rural simplicity?

He stepped forward. 'Mr Gordon?'

The man inclined his head. William swallowed his misgivings and deliberately turned on his charm. He held out his hand and said, 'William Burbage – Jane's friend and at your service.'

They were being swept through the narrow door from the platform to the concourse by a tide of elbows, shoulders and backpacks and in such confusion and noise that both instinctively stepped aside and waited for the impatient young to pass. It gave them the moment's respite they both needed to collect their composure.

Mr Gordon was holding out his hand, his face a study of incredulity. 'Not *the* William Burbage?' he said. 'Professor William Burbage, the historian? My dear man, what a pleasure it is to meet you! But – I'm sorry, I simply don't understand.'

'I'll explain in the car,' William said, leading the way. 'We're neighbours of Bob Bellamy's. I thought Jane might have explained. Here we are.'

'May I get rid of this impedimenta?' The umbrella and the bowler were tossed, with the briefcase, into the back seat of the car. 'I had to go to my office to sign some urgent correspondence before I caught the train, and had no time to change. Will it matter, Dr Burbage?'

There was such genuine concern in his voice that William was quite touched. Without the 'impedimenta', he saw a man with a face so like Jane's and so reminiscent of Nick that he was able to put himself in a flash into the difficult situation his passenger was facing.

He turned and held out his hand again. 'My name's William,' he said.

'Nicholas.' This time the handshake was warm and meant a lot.

'All that will matter to Jane is that you don't overawe Bob,' William said. 'We'll leave your impedimenta in the car.'

'Tell me about him.'

William did as well as he could, without pre-empting the business of the day, keeping it all very general. He felt that he could not, in all fairness to both sides, do what Gordon was asking of him, and make it personal. In the end he said, 'Jane loves him. Isn't that recommendation enough? And he loves her. If he's a bit difficult today, it will be because he's trying to protect her, and prevent her, and you, from doing anything either of you may regret later.'

'You know the whole story?'

'We live here. That's almost enough of an answer in itself, though so far it hasn't become village gossip. Castle Hill Farm lies outside the village proper. We happened to go up there at the crucial moment.'

'Do you like him? Bellamy, I mean?'

They had reached Old Swithinford, and were just about to turn into the avenue of trees across the 'front cluss', at the end of which Benedict's Suffolk-pink colourwash glowed like a smile of welcome. The sight of it helped. William was now very conscious of the importance of the personal answer he had to make to the directly personal question. He searched himself and his feelings towards Bob as if he might have been in the confessional. Then slowly he shook his head.

'No,' he said. 'To answer you as openly as you ask, and for the same reason as you ask, I have to give you as honest an answer as I possibly can. It wouldn't be true to say I like the man. It isn't a strong enough word for the sum of my feelings towards him. I love him. As my wi – as my Fran does. For all the same reasons as Jane does. As I hope you will. He's a very unusual man. Come and meet him.'

I I

Sophie had found Fran still sitting, and immediately asked what was the matter. She brought into the kitchen with her an air of stability and serenity that was balm to Fran's taut nerves.

'I'm worried. I think I may have bitten off more than I can chew.'

Sophie went through her usual arrival procedure before answering. 'Folks as don't know one another afore'and usually mix well enough, seems to me, once they get their feet under a table,' she said. 'I reckon as we can give 'em a meal good enough to keep 'em busy till they get used to each other, can't we? Bellamy and that posh chap from London, I mean. Tha's what you're fretting about, ain't it?'

Fran nodded. She saw that Sophie understood the nature of the difficulties almost as well as she did herself. 'They haven't a single thing in common that I can think of,' Fran said miserably.

'No more hadn't 'im and Bellamy to start off' (when Sophie said ''im' it meant William).

Oh, blessed common sense! Fran cheered up. 'I suppose they do have Jane in common. But I hate having to be hostess to a bunch of strangers.'

'Bellamy ain't no stranger 'ere. More ain't Jane 'Adley, if it comes to that. Why are they coming 'ere instead o' Castle 'Ill? But that ain't no business o' mine. Wheer am I got to set the table?'

'In the dining-room,' Fran answered. Sophie 'chuntered,' a sure sign that she really approved. She'd got her work cut out, she said, to have what Fran had asked for ready in time. Had 'he' said as she had to get the best glasses out and polish 'em, or use the ordinary ones? Was Fran expecting one pair of hands to serve the coffee as well as make an apple-and-blackberry pie *and* a Sussex pond pudding as ought to ha' been a-steaming half a hour a'ready – and so on and so on, all of which reassured Fran.

She felt much better, though when at last Bob and Jane drove up, her doubts about the crucial meeting between Jane and Sophie returned. She let the visitors in herself, and led them into the sitting-room, watching Bob's pleasure in being in his 'dream' room again.

Jane had never been farther than the kitchen at Benedict's before, and was immediately appreciative of her surroundings. She was flushed and nervous, but today, as Fran could see, she was making no concessions to Bob's display of 'bumpkin' humility. On the contrary, she had dressed to show her father that whomever she proposed to marry, she had been born his daughter, and had not forgotten the fact. She wore a woollen suit of such classic elegance that Fran had a momentary twinge of envy of the figure that could give its lines such grace. Jane said, 'Oh Fran, what a beautiful room!' and turned to Bob to acknowledge that it was as he had said. Fran relaxed.

'Would you like some coffee, or would you rather wait till William and Jane's father get here for stronger drinks?' she asked. 'Or both?'

'I'm made coffee a'ready,' said Sophie from the door. 'I just come to see if you wanted it.' She was looking towards Fran, but her smile swept round the room to include Jane and Bob.

Fran tensed, now that the moment had come. Jane put down her handbag and gloves on the occasional table by the chair Fran was offering to her, and said, 'May I come and help you? I'm more used to getting the coffee than being waited on.'

She didn't stop for either Fran or Sophie to consent. Sophie gave her such a broad smile that Fran felt dizzy with relief. Once in the kitchen, Sophie said, 'You can't do nothing in that frock. It's all ready, any 'ow.' She looked Jane straight in the eye, and said, 'She's told me what it's all about. It's like that tale as Miss Budd used to tell us in school, about 'ow the kitchenmaid was really a princess all the while. And I 'ope as every-body'll live 'appy ever after, same as in them fairy-tales. Now, who's gooing to carry this 'ere coffee in? Me or you?'

'You take the coffee-pot and I'll bring the rest,' Jane said. She wanted to throw her arms round Sophie and thank her, but knew that any show of feeling would be interpreted as condescension. They marched side by side back to the sitting-room just as William's car was seen coming down under the trees.

As William tooted his Morse code 'F' arrival signal to Fran, it was the seasoned diplomat who was nervous. He had been steeling himself to accept whatever circumstances he found in Old Swithinford if by doing so he could make the daughter so long estranged from him happy. He hadn't realized how much he loved her till they had found each other again. He had wanted her to live with him, but she'd made it clear that she would be much more at ease now in the country than in the town, and in the home of an ordinary uneducated farmer than among his too well-off, too educated, too polished circle of friends.

If he wanted to keep in touch with her now, he had told himself, he would have to learn the ways of East Anglian rural society, as in the past he had had to be briefed about the customs and traditions of so many different countries overseas.

Now that his chauffeur and host had turned out to be who and what he was, and the house they had drawn up to so large, so old and so utterly full of charm and beauty, he was for the moment completely disorientated.

'William,' he said. 'Will you give me a minute to collect myself?'

'I'm going to put the car away, so stay where you are,' William replied. 'They'll have seen us arrive, so we can take our time.'

As they strolled towards the front door, it opened, and Jane stood there. She moved forward to greet her father, while William, satisfied, walked on.

Hovering just inside the door were Fran and Bob. Bob's arm was around Fran's waist, and William guessed that she had had to drag him to the door. That in fact he needed her support to keep him waiting there. So William stepped inside, gave Fran a quick kiss, and wound his arm round her on the other side. The three of them just filled the wide old doorway as the other two came towards them.

('The old country-dance pattern again,' said Fran's internal voice. 'It never fails.')

'Fran,' said Jane, 'may I present my father? And Effendi – this is Bob.' By the time the stranger had bowed over Fran's hand and turned towards Bellamy, William had drawn Fran aside, leaving Jane within Bob's encircling arm. The handshake was performed in silence, each man searching the face of the other.

'This is wonderful,' said Mr Gordon, his smile encompassing the scene entire – the house in its country setting, the great welcoming door, and two couples standing four-square to face the outside world. Fran could almost read his mind as they moved aside to welcome him in. As far as

Jane and Bob themselves were concerned, the battle was already over. What happened about the farm was a separate issue.

'Do come in,' Fran said. There followed a rather strained silence, which Sophie's voice, raised to reach them from the kitchen door, broke into.

'That there coffee ain't fit to drink b' now,' she said from the shadows. 'So I'm a-gooing to make some fresh. An' I'm set the best glasses out for you, William, but I ain't took no bottles in. I don't know nothing about such things.'

She was gone, leaving a totally bewildered Londoner looking into four faces as amused as his was bemused. As the kitchen door shut behind Sophie, they all broke into relieved and welcoming chuckles.

'So now you know,' said Jane.

I 2

The astonished raising of Gordon's eyebrows was too much for the delicate balance of Fran's sense of humour, especially as she was already keyed up with emotional tension. She strove valiantly against her desire to laugh till the bubble stuck in her throat and nearly choked her – and she had to give way. Sophie had sweetened the atmosphere, just as a wrong word from any of them could have curdled it. With the other four on Christian-name terms already, Jane's father had become 'Effendi' to Fran and William, though Bob avoided addressing him by name at all. All was well as they moved into the dining-room.

Mr Gordon had already encountered enough surprises to rob him of much of his suave politeness, but he was still having some difficulty in believing the evidence of his senses. One glance at Bob had been enough to show him that Jane's love for her rescuer was not due to gratitude; nor was it a clever solution to the dilemma she faced in being so suddenly metamorphosed. It could have been that she had seen a marriage half-way between her origins and her former status as a charwoman as a convenient stepping-stone. Mr Gordon looked again at Bob, this time seeing him through Jane's eyes. Though 'farmer' was written all over him, there was no question but that whatever else he was, he was an attractive man.

Nor had Mr Gordon quite recovered from finding himself so unexpectedly in such sophisticated company and socially up-market surroundings.

He had been rapidly adjusting his preconceptions of rural society when Sophie's use of William's first name jolted him again. (It had surprised Fran and William a bit. Very rarely did she use her childhood privilege and let their 'given names' slip out, and then only when she was in distress. Fran could not help but think that this time it had been deliberate. It had certainly been helpful to Bob, both as leveller and ice-breaker.)

Sophie had been right, too, about good food being a great social asset. Mr Gordon was not accustomed to home cooking, either in kind or quantity. Meals to him were more often than not merely a way of arranging a convenient venue for an important meeting. He had almost forgotten what the enjoyment of food for its own sake was; but he began to appreciate this meal in its own right as 'something else'. Beef not smothered by sauce to disguise its tastelessness; Yorkshire pudding with crisp brown crust at the bottom, an airy range of browned hillocks over the top, and soft succulence between; fresh vegetables locally grown.

Fran raised the lid of a vegetable dish to disclose an orange-coloured island in a sea of pink-tinted cream. He had been about to refuse because he didn't know what he was being offered, but just in time caught Jane's eye, and had raised his eyebrows in interrogation.

'Swede,' Jane said. 'What Bob feeds his pigs on.'

Caught absolutely off-guard, Bob said, 'Hold hard, my duck! Don't pretend you don't know the difference between a mangel and a swede! Mangels are beetroots big enough to feed stock on, but swedes are turnips.'

'I was only teasing Effendi,' she said. 'He knows nearly everything there is to know about the rest of the world, but doesn't recognize an English vegetable when he sees one. He'd have believed me that we ate the same as the pigs.'

'But turnip isn't that colour,' her father protested. 'It's white.'

'Try it,' Fran urged, proffering a very small taster on the end of a fork so close to his mouth that he had no option but to open it and taste. They all watched him with amusement investigating with his taste-buds the orange flesh, mashed almost to a purée with thick Jersey cream, and spiced with pepper and an elusive flavour of . . . nutmeg? Whatever it was, it was delicious, and he held out his plate for a proper helping. He was finding this unknown territory more and more to his liking. The degree of informality about everything made him feel like a prisoner loosed suddenly from bonds worn so long that he had forgotten them till they fell off. He caught Jane's eye again. This time it was merrily approving, and she winked.

With something like shock he came to the conclusion that it was not Bob who was being tested, but himself. He thought he had probably done well enough to pass so far, and was astonished to discover how much he cared.

'Trial by turnip,' said William, reading his thoughts. 'Our rural equivalent to trial-by-combat.'

Sophie gathered up the cleared plates and appeared again with a pie, which she placed in front of William, and a steamed pudding that was plonked down by Fran.

Mr Gordon watched with genuine curiosity as Fran sliced through the basin-shaped crust with a silver wide-bladed server, and allowed the gush of thick, sweet gooey sauce to flow out. A delicious aroma reached his nostrils and almost made his mouth water as she squeezed the last drop of juice out of the whole lemon that sat there in the middle of the sauce, before putting it aside and handing the first wedge-shaped serving to Jane, accompanied by a bowl of thick cream.

'I haven't tasted a suet pudding since I left school,' he said. 'Suet roll with half a dozen currants in it. We used to call it "dead baby". I hated it.'

'That ain't suet,' said Sophie from behind him. 'Though I don't see nothing wrong wi' suet, myself. We was all brought up on the suet puddings as my mother used to make for Mr Wagstaffe, only Fran and William and me and my sisters used to have to eat up what was left in the kitchen.'

After that he dared not refuse the pudding, and was glad he hadn't, especially as Fran flashed him a swift glance of gratitude on Sophie's behalf.

'Countryfolk needed that sort of grub in days gone by,' Bob said, taking them all by surprise by joining in the conversation and forgetting to be shy. 'Things were different, then, when men had to be out all day, plodding up and down a field behind a plough and a team of horses. You see, the hours were so long. They'd be out baiting their horses for an hour or more afore having a slice o' bread and dripping for breakfast, and then they'd only get a thumb-bit for their dockey, so by unyoking time they'd be nearly starving – but they'd still got to see to their horses first before going in for their main meal. They didn't expect meat – except perhaps for a tiny bit of fat salt pork in an onion dumpling – so it was the pudden that they looked forrard to to fill them up. Just plain suet roll with vinegar and brown sugar to help it down. Only it wasn't suet the pudden was made of. Suet comes from cattle, and farm-labourers' wages didn't run to beef. Puddens were made with home-made lard – while it lasted. If it ran out before the next back-yard pig was big enough to kill, all they got was a water-walloper made with nothing but flour and water. I'm talking about the fens, of course. I don't know what it was like on the highland then, but there were bad times everywhere for farmers till the second war changed everything.'

They kept him talking, while both pudding and pie disappeared. They plied him with questions, delighting in his knowledge as well as his easy flow of words. He told tales in broad fen dialect, miming to demonstrate, for example, what a 'thumb-bit' was and how it was dealt with. Fran was thinking that he could not have been more effective if he had been a barrister conducting his own defence in court. Jane was almost speechless with relief and pleasure, never having believed that he could be so free in company. She decided that she still had a lot to find out about him. With reluctance William reminded them how time was flying. They had to get down to business.

The conversation stopped as if hit by a bullet, and an air of restrained foreboding seemed to descend on everyone except Gordon, who couldn't remember the last time he had enjoyed himself so much. He liked his son-in-law to be; he could hardly hope for anything more than that Jane should now get her wish as soon as it could be arranged.

Sophie came to clear the table and to ask Fran where they would like coffee served. She took a swift decision. 'Here, please Sophie. We have some business to discuss, so we'll use this as a board-room table.' Sophie knew what she was being told – to close the door behind herself and not to interrupt again.

It was then that things began to go wrong.

Sophie went round behind Fran and whispered, 'I shall have to leave the washing-up. Dan'el catched Ned on 'is way back after dinner to tell me to goo as quick as I could to Thirz'. She's took bad again.' She went, looking worried, and the warmth of the gathering seemed to leave with her.

Gordon was the only one who had no reason to fear the next stage of the proceedings. Fran and Jane could only hope that Bob might have had second thoughts or that meeting Jane's father might have changed his mind.

Fran had hoped that she might have persuaded Bob to compromise for Jane's sake, but she saw by the stiffening of his back and the firm set of his mouth that he was not prepared to. What they were up against was a clash of cultures. How could anyone expect those two men to understand each other?

Gordon was not aware of the tension building up. He looked round expectantly at the suddenly silent table. 'So I presume that all we have to do now is to plan a wedding?' he said.

Fran winced, and Jane drew in a great breath. Taking Bob for granted was the worst mistake he could have made.

'No!' said Bob. 'There's a lot o' things first as none of you understand. We can't plan nothing till I've had my say.'

The pause that followed was barely noticeable, measured by the standard units of time; yet it held in suspension an incredible aggregate of emotion. Fran's mind was racing as she watched Jane. She had turned papery white, then found the stony mask she had for so long in the past used to cover her feelings, and for a moment she put it on. But it was too fragile for this occasion, and crumpled. She lowered her head, and tears began to slide down her cheeks and drip silently on to the tablecloth. It was the silence, particularly of those falling tears, that gave Fran such pain, as if her heart were being squeezed by a huge, ruthless hand.

This was happening in her house – hers and William's – and they were both helpless to do anything to stop it. Why didn't somebody speak, and end this dreadful suspense?

It was Bob who did. He reached across the table to touch Jane. 'Don't, my beauty. I can't bear it,' he said, hiding his face briefly with his handkerchief.

Gordon, stunned and bewildered by the dramatic change, looked from one to the other for enlightenment. What until then had been so civilized became chaotically disjointed, and he lost his bearings. He was disappointed, disbelieving and confused; he was out of his depth, fighting for some sort of logic in a world that appeared to have none.

Two or three voices began to explain. He was pulled this way and that by conflicting versions of the same story, catching here and there words that made sense, only for them to be contradicted by other words that to him meant nothing.

There was Jane's voice, pitched high above the others because of the misery in it, berating somebody for spoiling everything for the sake of his 'pig-headed pride'. Did she mean him, and if so, why? No – because Fran was defending Bob, so it must be him Jane meant. Fran was looking at Bob so appealingly that one might have thought it was her fragile bubble of dreams his words had so unaccountably burst. He looked for help toward William, but even William the courteous appeared for the moment to have lost control.

It was William, however, whose calm voice restored them to something like order, apologizing to his guest and asking the others to be quiet so that he be allowed to tell as much as he understood of the situation in his own way.

'Explain what?' Mr Gordon asked.

Bob put up a hand and stroked Jane's head, trying to dry her tears, but she pushed his hand away, sobbing out that she wasn't one of his cats. She was only the woman he loved but was too proud to marry.

Fran flinched. What interpretation could her father be expected to put on that? It had been made plain that Jane's past was no secret to any of them. That was the worst of words. They could so easily be misinterpreted. Yet now they were the only things that could put matters right – and it was William who was using them.

'Jane's got a point, there, Bob,' he said, wisely giving Bob no chance to reply.

His measured voice calmed Fran. It was having its effect on the others, too. She watched the play of strong emotion on the face of the man trained to show none, and saw there as William went on not the anger she had feared, but the dawn of understanding. She saw Bob's arm creep round Jane's shoulders, and his lips murmur into her ear. She knew what he had said as well as if she had heard it. He had laid his pride at Jane's feet. Their faces touched, and remained together. If Bob's pride had been so fragile an obstacle, whatever had they all got themselves so worked up about?

Jane's father folded his hands together on the table and looked at each of the other four in turn, but it was to Fran he spoke.

'Forgive me,' he said. 'The fault was entirely mine; I can only apologize.' He turned towards Bob.

'Mr Bellamy,' he said, 'I beg you to believe that all I want is for Jane to be happy. I offered to you what I thought might make up to her for what she has suffered in the past – thinking I could never forgive her for damaging my pride. Now she is suffering again because it seems that I have wounded yours – but by God, man, yours is a different sort of pride, and the only sort worth having!'

He brought his clenched fist down on the table, his face now without a trace of diplomatic urbanity, but only that of a man showing his feelings.

'You didn't tell her so, but what you must have thought was that I was trying to *sell* her to you – to get her off my hands, as it were, at any cost – and I don't wonder you considered it an insult. To both of you. That's what made you mad, wasn't it? You couldn't have been more wrong, you know. I love her – more than she can believe. But so do you.' He held out his hand. 'I won't sell her to any man on earth, but I hope you'll let me *give* her to you? You will make me a very proud man again if you do.'

He was unable to go on, and though their hands met, Bob was just as incapable of answering. Jane had turned her face into Bob's shirt and he was holding it there with his free hand as if he would never again let her out of his reach. William got up and went to supply Fran with his own clean handkerchief. He was the only one standing.

'Let's adjourn,' he said, like a chairman bringing a meeting to order. 'We'll reassemble in half an hour's time to plan that wedding.'

Again, it was Bob who put a damper on their hopes. 'Not so fast, William,' he said. 'We ain't out o' the wood yet, but the other side of it ain't too bad. Jane knows that my old fen's got magic in it for us, like Benedict's got for you and Fran. Don't you, my beauty?'

They watched the coloured tide flow into Jane's cheeks, making her the beauty her lover had called her. He pulled Jane up and kissed her, as if staking a claim that nobody thereafter should question. William and Fran decided they were *de trop*. They left Jane with arms round both her men.

On the other side of the door William and Fran stopped to fold their arms about each other, too. It was just as well they took their chance in the hall. When they opened the kitchen door, they found Ned at the sink doing the washing up.

'One o' that tribe o' children from up Danesum brought a note for you,' Ned said. 'It were than young helion as is all'us ready with a mouthful o' filthy language. I'd wash his mouth out wi' carbolic, if he were mine.'

She slit the envelope. The note was folded round a freshly laundered handkerchief she recognized as her own. She reminded herself that she mustn't forget her promise to Mr Petrie. But she had other more urgent things to attend to at the present moment. She tucked the note into her pocket unread, and enlisted the help of both William and Ned to help her prepare tea.

Back in the sitting-room, they left it to Bob to put his case. He went straight to the logistics of it, not referring again to the personal reason for him refusing Jane's father's offer. Fran found herself wondering if Vic Gifford, or even Brian Bridgefoot, would have had the sensitivity to realize how much it would have demeaned Jane for him to have accepted such a gift, or the strength of character to refuse so large an amount of money on those grounds.

The bursar of the college which owned Castle Hill Farm had been putting some pressure on Bob to make his decision. Once it had become common knowledge that the farm was for sale, several offers had been made. The only reason for selling being to raise cash needed urgently for other projects, they naturally wanted the highest price they could get. Two developers, prepared to go on outbidding each other, were raising the stakes all the time. But the terms of their agreement with Bob obliged them to offer him first refusal – at its value as agricultural land – which bore little if any relation to what it was worth as building land if developers could get planning permission.

As had been pointed out to him, homes were still very badly needed to replace those demolished in the war, and new towns were the 'in' thing.

Swithinford had already been designated as a 'new town'. Rural District Planners would raise few objections to development of land which could be regarded, if they so wanted, to be within the bounds of Swithinford. Small-holders with no more than fifty or sixty acres were rapidly being seduced by offers of anything up to half-a-million pounds. Old established farmers and larger landowners, on the other hand, would not budge whatever they were offered. The result was that any land suitable for development, especially if like Castle Hill it had never had a particularly good record as agricultural land, had a very high premium on it. In fact – but there Bob paused.

'They've got me cornered, whichever way I look at it,' he said. 'There's nothing in my tenancy agreement to say they have to renew it, so I've only got another year before they could turn me out. I never thought about them deciding to sell it. I was doing well enough down the fen, and there was always that to go back to. But then, I didn't expect anything to turn out as it has.'

'Bailey is bidding for it, I suppose,' Fran said, helping him out.

'Not yet, as far as I can make out. He's too crafty for that. He's waiting till whoever the other bidders are reach their limit, and then he'll step in with one that just overtops them – when they've done all the research into its prospects and proved to him for nothing that it's worth his gamble. But he wouldn't be building himself a house first and aiming to live here if he didn't think he had more than the Lane's End estate already in his pocket. He knows very well a'ready as he won't have trouble getting planning permission. We know the sort of man he is.'

'So who else is it bidding?' she asked, hardly daring to frame the question.

'Not Manor Farms, if that's what you're worried about. Though rather than let that bloody Bailey see me off, I'll go up to see Eric Choppen and Elyot Franks to beg them to think about it. We know them, now. I know what Bailey is.'

'Have you no rights at all? Would it do any good for me to go personally to see the bursar? I know him well enough.'

'No, William. You keep out of it. If it was your own college that owned it, you'd be on the other side. I reckon you're thinking about tenancy rights. They don't apply to me. I wasn't keen on coming here in the first place, and only agreed to give my son a chance. So we took it on a five-year lease – not automatically renewable – to see how we got on on the highland. In the end it was me that loved the place and the rookery and the church, and him and his wife that wouldn't stop with the ghosts. Now there's all the friends I've made, as well. But—' Again he paused.

He turned to Gordon. 'Jane told me you'd already bought it, but you see I knew that couldn't really be the case. For one thing because until I notify them officially that I'm not buying it, they can't sell. I guessed that what you'd done was to instruct your solicitors to outbid anybody else. So I had to give Jane some reason why I wouldn't let you, because of my real reason, that you were the only one clart enough to see through. But, as I say, nobody but me *can* buy it at its farming price, now or when my five years is up. I couldn't let you be done down and buy it at developers' price just to let me go on farming it, could I?'

(*No, of course he couldn't. Fran could hear Beryl Bean's interpretation of it, if ever the truth got out. 'Get rid of shop-soiled goods at any price. Even if you have to pay somebody to cart 'em out o' your road.'*)

'Now, 'cos time's running out, they're trying another tack. They're trying the old dodge of offering to pay me to get out, at so much per acre. There's nothing new in that. They've upped the bribe twice already.'

He turned to Jane. 'So now it's up to you, my pretty. We should still have my fen farm and a lot of money in the bank, but nothing else. No rookery. No oxlip wood. No peace for the ghosts. No church for William and me to play with. No memories for Elyot and Beth. Or for us – of the night I found you there. Don't leave it all to me!'

William was looking down at Fran. 'Fran and I were discussing it this morning,' he said. 'I was worried, afraid that we might be "interfering in matters which we do not understand". Fran said that if we played it by ear, we might still find some simple solution we'd all overlooked. It's occurred to me that she could be right. So let me get this clear, Bob. If you can raise the money, you get first choice of buying it at farming price. Right?'

Bob nodded. 'But I can't raise the money. Even if I sold my fen farm, I'd have to take out a huge mortgage. Castle Hill ain't in good enough heart yet to make much money, though it soon could be. But I still have to help Charlie, while she's at Cambridge, and I daren't take the risk. I would if I could, partly for your sakes. We shan't be here to watch the wood come down and Bailey's brick boxes go up, but you will. Though there's nothing we can do about it.'

'Don't be too sure,' said William. 'There's a lot of others besides us who don't want Bailey's boxes on Castle Hill. You said a minute ago that you'd go to Manor Farms Ltd as a last resort. You meant, of course, as a firm of developers you could trust to do better than Bailey. But Eric and Elyot are your friends, and ours, Bob. If somehow between us we could raise a private loan for you – a private mortgage, as it were – would that work?'

'It would be no business of anybody's where I got the money from to buy it,' Bob said. 'But I know too much about such arrangements. I'd rather lose the farm than my friends. Thanks, all the same. And there's Jane to be thought of, don't forget. I shouldn't want her to have to feel beholden to them as'll be her friends from now on, like you and Elyot and Beth Franks and Choppen family, the very ones she used to work for. It'll be bad enough for her, at least for a little while, in any case. There don't seem to be a way out that won't be. What I'm afraid of is that one day she'll regret that it was me that found her in the church.'

There was a long, uneasy silence. Bob's intuition had once again put its finger on a sore spot. They were startled at the sound of Gordon's voice, raised, as it were, in a sort of triumph.

'Fran *was* right! What am I here for? To sort out how I could help. Bob won't accept a gift from me – but I refuse to give up the privilege of being my son-in-law's banker! He can either pay me a reduced interest rate, if he insists, or take me in as a sleeping partner. As long as it remains in his name. Can anybody see any snags in that proposal?'

William stood up, wearing what Fran called his 'grin' – a broad smile with a glint of amusement in his eyes. They all apparently expected him to answer for Bob who wasn't exactly giving his attention to anything but Jane.

'No, none,' he said, 'except what a lot of bloody fools we've all been not to see till now the solution that was staring us in the face. We will now move on to the next item on the agenda. We've still got a wedding to arrange, and a train to catch.'

13

In the event, the next item on the agenda had proved to be so long and of such complexity that Gordon had missed two trains before he and William had finally set off to get him back to London.

It ought to have been simple enough. When and where was the wedding to take place? When was no trouble – the answer to that was 'as soon as possible'. Where proved to be much more difficult. It had to be a civil ceremony, because Bob was divorced.

'London, then,' Mr Gordon offered. 'With a reception as large or as small as you wish at one of the best hotels close to Caxton Hall.'

Fran sensed a reluctance in Jane to agree to this, and could only put it down to her knowledge of Bob's rural shyness. But Jane seemed to be wanting to communicate secretly with her father, and Fran surmised that there was some other obstacle of which only the two of them were aware. Fran was definitely puzzled. Mr Gordon let his suggestion hang heavily in the air, and said no more.

Cambridge, then, suggested William.

'No,' said Jane, loud and clear. Astounded, they all turned towards her. She who had until then been quietly acquiescent suddenly took the floor. She had, she said, a lot to say. Would they please all now listen to her?

She wanted their wedding kept secret. Somewhat stunned, they wanted to know why.

Because, she said, she hadn't lived as an outsider in a village for twenty years without learning a lot about village life. She and Bob were both still 'outsiders'.

'But Jane, it's practically impossible to keep any secret in a village!' William expostulated. 'You know it is. How on earth do you expect to keep this one? For one thing, there are all sorts of business ramifications. Is it really worth the bother?'

'Oh, can't even you understand?' she said. 'Imagine what sort of talk there will be! We don't want to have to go on being outsiders.'

She went on, fluently and eloquently, her voice betraying some of the pent-up emotion it had been so carefully schooled to hide from everybody till now.

How could they expect the village folk, among whom she had lived in such obscurity and poverty for so long, to accept her in her new persona 'just like that'? She and Bob were not Cinderella and Prince Charming in a Christmas pantomime. No fairy godmother was going to wave a magic wand and make it easy for her to be changed overnight from what she had been – a pauper with an illegitimate child – to a farmer's wife on visiting terms with such as William and Fran or Elyot and Beth Franks. Perhaps there were a few who might see it as romantic, and pretend they had seen it coming, but it was much more likely that the majority would feel affronted by her previous secrecy about herself, and resent having wasted any sympathy on her; or as an alternative, declare that what she was pretending to be now 'was only another pack of lies'.

As she saw it, she said, she and Bob would have to *earn* their right to their new status in the village, and that was going to take time. 'Sneaking off and getting ourselves married one morning in a register office in Cambridge would be asking for trouble. It would leak out somehow and then the fat would be in the fire. We might as well get ourselves into the *News of the World*. Every scrap of scandal there has ever been about me and Nick would be dragged up and raked over, and of course within hours I should have been the whole cause of Bob's divorce. We couldn't expect – and shouldn't get – the same interest and support that Elyot Franks and Beth Marriner got. That *was* a romantic affair, and there was nothing in their past for anybody to seize on and blow up into scandal. And – if you don't mind me saying so, Fran, your son's blatant affair with Monica Choppen was different again. They were young – and aren't all young people these days deliberately flouting respectability? Besides, Roland's your son, and therefore "one of them". Their age and your name let them get away with it. We're not youngsters, and we don't "belong". Besides, it's too much to expect anybody, let alone people like the real scandalmongers, to be magnanimous third time round.

'And that,' she added, speaking directly to her father, 'is what Bob was making all the fuss about. If he had accepted the Cinderella ending – as we all apparently expected him to – we should never have lived it down. He knew that, and was trying to protect me without hurting you. I didn't realize it myself until this afternoon. So why should we let anyone know anything? Look! They know that Bob has taken me on as his house-keeper. That's the truth. They whisper behind our backs that I sleep with him. That isn't the truth, incidentally – but it soon will be. I've been keeping my identity and everything else a secret here for over twenty years already – and it hasn't been easy. I had to learn how much gossip can hurt, and try never to show it, for Nick's sake. Why can't I have a bit of my own back, now?

'Let them wonder how Bob has managed to defeat Bailey! Let them wonder where he got the money from. And why people like William and Fran or the Franks or even the Choppens will have us over their door-steps! I want Mr and Mrs Bellamy to take their proper places without a lot of talk. I want to start afresh.'

She looked proudly around the circle, and Fran felt a moment of awe, as if she were watching someone being reborn.

'Until now I couldn't be sure there was going to be any wedding. I couldn't believe it – especially when Bob began to make difficulties. But there is going to be a wedding. My wedding, and the only one I shall ever have, to the only man I shall ever want. Isn't it my privilege to say what sort of wedding I want? Well – I want a secret one! I want to gloat over it. Please! I haven't had much to gloat about before!'

Bob was looking at her with such delight and admiration that it almost made the others laugh to see him, but Fran read doubt, even trouble, in his face as well.

'As far as I'm concerned you can do just as you like, my pretty,' he said. 'But, as William said, I don't know how we shall ever manage to keep it quiet. It'll be like trying to fill a horse-trough with a 'tater-riddle. What do you mean by "secret"? Not tell Charlie and Nick? Your son and my daughter? That wouldn't be fair. If Charlie knows, it means Charles Bridgefoot as well – but it would spoil everything if they weren't there, wouldn't it?'

'Of course we shall tell Charlie, and Charles.'

'And Nick?' William asked gently, having noticed the omission.

Reaching her hand across the table to her father Jane said, 'Tell them, Effendi, please. I can't.' They waited, tense, till he found his voice.

'I'm afraid the latest news of Nick isn't very good. There are – complications. His memory is affected. He has no recall of anything whatsoever before the accident. Apparently it isn't all that unusual after head injury or trauma. Sometimes the lost memory returns, more or less in a flash, even after years – so we mustn't give up hope. But he has to start learning *people* all over again, because he recognizes no one. That's what makes it so hard for Jane. He remembers nothing of all those years when all they had to live for was each other. It is his personal memories, those concerned with his emotions, that seem to have been wiped out. It will be hardest on those who knew him and loved him when he was a child. He won't recognize them, and they are bound to be hurt – Charles, for instance. We think that we ought not to put him – or them – to the test yet.'

Fran sought William's hand for comfort, but all attention was centred on Bob. He had gathered Jane into his arms, saying nothing. His face had taken on an intense, expressionless calm, and his head was cocked a little to one side, as if he were listening. Jane shivered, and the movement restored Bob to himself again.

'Nick'll be all right again one day,' he said. 'But we shall have to get married without him, for Charles's sake. Have it your own way, my pretty. Whatever you say.'

Fran had goose-pimples, because only she was fully aware that for those few seconds of silence Bob had been consulting his sixth sense, seeing both past and future. He was confident about relying on it again, now that he had been accepted wholly for what he was. After a minute or two, talk flowed on again.

'London, then,' said Mr Gordon. 'Will you leave all the arrangements to me? We may rely on you two to be present, I hope – and your daughter, Bob, and her Charles. Nobody else.'

'If Jane wants us, of course we'll be there,' Fran said. 'But I'm afraid I've already told Sophie, though you can take my word for it that she won't say a word – except perhaps in her prayers.'

Jane smiled. 'I thought by what she said to me that she knew.'

Gordon was becoming very practical again. 'I must see my solicitors tomorrow, to make sure the money is available when you want it, Bob.'

'It's me as has got to get a move on,' Bob answered. 'But I've still got a year of my lease left, so we shan't want the money for a goodish while, thanks all the same. I can't believe any of it. It's all too good to be true.'

He excused himself hastily. Jane was clasped in her father's arms, and both had abandoned all reserve. William and Fran left them to themselves.

A little later, they saw a very happy couple off to Castle Hill; then William went to fetch his car round to the front door.

Nicholas Hadley-Gordon was standing in the doorway with Fran, holding both her hands and trying to express his gratitude. He was not accustomed to dealing with emotions as strong as those he had felt all this afternoon. Fran understood his dilemma. That was her great gift.

She let go of his hands, put her arms round his neck, and kissed him. William, driving up, found her clasped in Gordon's arms, their faces close together. He got out of the driving seat and went round to open the door of the passenger seat, handed Gordon his bowler hat, his briefcase and his umbrella, saluted briskly and said, 'Your car, Excellency.'

The things were hurled again to the back seat as Gordon found and wrung William's hand, and then turned back to kiss Fran again, standing for a moment to take in the beauty of the scene, the rosy warmth of the lovely old house, and the twilit sky in which stars were just beginning to twinkle.

'If Jane can't believe all this,' he said, 'how do you think I feel?'

14

That evening, when Fran found it was George at the door, she wasn't as pleased to see him as she usually was. But George was George, however tired she was. Fran offered George William's chair, facing her. 'I've just made myself a cup of tea,' she said. 'Will you join me, or would you like something stronger? William won't be in for at least another hour and a half.'

George lowered himself stiffly into the chair and said, 'Tea, please. A cup of tea with you by yourself is more than I dared hope for.'

She had noticed his limp and the way his right leg was stretched out before him, and as she gave him the tea, she studied his face. She had never seen him look his age before. She knew instinctively, though, that it wasn't stiff joints that were causing the ravaged look on his face. She squared her shoulders, and prepared to give him all her attention. She made tea hot and strong, and just how he liked it. He said so, and they settled down, at ease with each other.

'It's been quite a day,' she said. 'We've had visitors, and Sophie had to desert me to go to Thirzah. She ought to have the doctor. Thirzah's "turns" sound very much like minor heart attacks.'

'I've told Daniel so,' he said, 'but you know what Thirz' is. She's afraid the doctor will tell her she's got to stop in bed, and as far as I know, she's never spent a day in bed in her life. Nor Dan'el neither, for that matter. They don't make 'em like him and Thirzah no more. She's worried about letting them two at the Old Rectory down, 'specially now. Is there any truth in the rumour that there's going to be a baby there?'

'It's supposed to be a secret,' Fran said, laughing. 'For a bit longer, anyway. So don't tell anybody that I confirmed it, will you?'

'Nothing's a secret here now, since Kid Bean set up that shop,' he said, rather bitterly. 'It's what I heard there today as got me to such a pitch as I had to talk to somebody. Beryl was gabbing to that Pugh about a lot of things – including our Brian. Didn't know I was there!' He paused, and sipped his tea.

'"The love of money is the root of all evil,"' he said. 'That's what's the matter with Brian, and Vic . . . My son and my son-in-law. They both want me out of the way. That's the top and bottom of it. I had made my mind up to give up next Lady Day, and let Brian take over, but I can't do it, Fran. I can't do it! Brian's changed so as I hardly know him. He ain't really interested in farming. All he wants is money. And he's up to something I don't know about.

'Thick as thieves with Vic as well now, though he never used to have a good word to say for him. So what are they up to? Some hanky-panky with that Arnold Bailey!

'Well, they won't sell any Bridgefoot land for development while I'm alive. But once I'm gone . . . any land as ain't the very best agricultural land will go to such as Bailey, like Lane's End has. Castle Hill'll be next, from what I hear.

'And then there's Charles. If I could just turn the whole lot over to him, I should live the rest o' my life and die happy. But you can see I can't do that. I've got to be fair to them all. Whatever I do, I shall be wrong for somebody. It can't all go to Brian just because he happens to be a man, like it would have done once. He wouldn't pass it down to Charles. He'd sell it to the first as offered him half a million for it. He's at loggerheads with Charles all the while anyway, mostly about Charlie Bellamy. I reckon it would kill Charles if Charlie broke it off now. But Brian's doing everything he can think of to make her. I don't know as I ought to tell you this, but . . .'

Out came the tale of his visit to the shop, and all that he had heard there.

Fran was in a serious dilemma. She couldn't tell him what she knew about Castle Hill, and she couldn't *not* tell him. He wanted her to make up his mind for him, but the connection between the Bridgefoots and the Bellamys made it impossible for her to say anything. On the other hand, she couldn't let him down when he was in such distress. She'd have to tell him something. She couldn't escape.

She got up, and went to get George a glass of whisky, while she tried to think the matter through. He simply had no idea of what the true situation was. Nor could she even guess how Brian would take the news – of who and what Jane was, and Bob's and Charlie's connections with her – when he did hear it. If he had truly become involved, either personally or businesswise, with Bailey, there could never be reconciliation between him and Bob Bellamy. And that lovely young couple, Charles and Charlie, could be torn apart – like Romeo and Juliet. She stood by the drinks hardly knowing in her abstraction what she was doing, and trying to peer into the future. Why had an appalling *arriviste* like Bailey had to choose to come here to spoil things? Old Swithinford and its community life mattered enormously to her, though perhaps if she had only ever seen it from a worm's eye view, as Jane had, she wouldn't care so much.

But Jane wanting to get her own back on scandalous tongues by secrecy wasn't going to help in this present crisis. There would be a Bailey faction, and a Bellamy faction, with George and his family in the middle.

They had feared what Eric Choppen could do when he had first appeared, though in the end it hadn't been all that bad. Bailey was far worse. He was real poison in their cup, and it was already beginning to work. It would affect everybody, in the course of time.

She was feeling the poison herself, already: Hetty's sterricks and Thirzah's attacks might rob her of Sophie. Benedict's without Sophie?

> 'Untune that string,
> And, hark what discord follows.'

Oh! Drat Shakespeare. Poking his nose in with an opinion he hadn't been invited to give – but how right he always was. For the moment, all she had to make her mind up about was what to say to George.

She pulled up a chair close to him and handed him the whisky. Grateful, he took a sip.

'I thought after all as has happened lately as I'd learnt enough sense to see as we'd got to go along with the times we live in. But this development as'll end up by all the land round here being under houses, especially if Bailey gets his way over Bellamy, and us being all part of Swithinford,

I just can't stomach. It ain't right! What will you and William do, if all you can see out o' them windows are rows and rows of houses between you and the church? Will the church still be there? Folks won't want churches! They don't want 'em now. I can't see Brian being a churchwarden after me, as I used to expect. I might just as well give in, and give up.'

He looked so forlorn that he made up her mind. She had to tell him as much as she dared. 'Don't be silly,' she said. 'We can't have yesterday back, however much we may regret it. We can't stop change coming, either, but we can perhaps slow it down. If you'd come to me last week I should have advised you to let Brian take over, soon. I can see why his generation feels as they do. People live so much longer now that if the old ones won't hand over before they die, the next generation never get a chance. I think I would have said, last week, that it was time Brian did show you what he could do if you'd let him. But if Brian truly is in cahoots with Bailey, it's a very different matter. And I know things now that I didn't know last week.

'There's a lot of bad blood between Bailey and Bob Bellamy already. Oh dear! If only I could tell you what I know – but I have given my word that I won't tell anybody anything.

'George, if I just say that what I know is good news for Charlie and Charles, will you believe me? And promise me that you will keep even that much to yourself, and not even tell Molly? Even if it means that you have to stand by and watch Brian making a bigger fool of himself than you think he already is? He may have backed the wrong horse, in spite of what Beryl Bean said.'

He nodded. 'I don't want to worry Molly,' he said. 'He's her son as well as mine, but what she don't know she won't grieve over.'

'Then I shall tell you that I know, for certain, that Bob Bellamy is going to buy Castle Hill Farm. I can't tell you any more details. But if you want my advice tonight, I'd say leave your decision just one more year. A lot can happen in a year.'

'Not all good, though, I'll be bound. As long as Charles and Charlie are all right, I'll put up with anything else,' he said.

'I daresay the course of their love won't run any smoother than any other people's,' she said, 'but at least you can be sure it's true love.'

He smiled at that, and heaved himself out of the chair. 'You always say the right thing,' he said. 'You've made me feel better, anyhow. I'll hold my tongue about Bellamy, don't you worry.'

He kissed her, and limped to the door. The first signs of age in him wrung her heart.

She went, weary in body and low in spirit, to the kitchen to prepare something for William's supper.

15

She made cold beef sandwiches and popped the remains of a half-eaten apple pie into the warming oven. While waiting for William she made herself another cup of coffee and sat down with it at the kitchen table, her thoughts like a blue-bottle zigzagging from one topic to another, agitating her to no purpose.

How right she had been only a few days ago when she had told herself that the last place anyone with any sense went to for a quiet life was a village! Which reminded her that she had completely forgotten the note in her pocket.

She fished for it and opened it. The sheet of white paper was cheap, but the writing was in black ink, executed in a strong but almost perfect calligraphic italic hand.

Dear Mrs Catherwood,

Tanner found the enclosed handkerchief after you had driven off, so we presume it must be yours. I had some difficulty getting it away from Tanner, who wanted to keep it because it belonged to the 'lovely lady'. He can't wait till he sees you again, and I am using him and the handkerchief as an excuse to remind you of your promise to come and see the conversion of the cottages into a house. It is now finished as far as I can do it, and I'm afraid my family may have to move on somewhere else sooner than I had thought. I need to sell the house as soon as I possibly can. To state it bluntly, there are reasons why I can't cope just at present with what is now becoming an urgent matter.

That I can bring myself to ask your help is a measure of my anxiety. The fact is that just at present I am out of action, and as my telephone is also out of order I am completely cut off. May I hope to see you one afternoon soon?

I realize how presumptuous this is. Please forgive me.

Yours, apologetically,
Peter Petrie.

P.S. Of course I do not expect you to enter into the lion's den without an escort.

So his cough had not been due to inhaling plaster. The man was ill, and in desperate straits to have had to take such a step to get help. Everything about the letter confirmed her first guess that he was not one of the usual type of 'flower people'. She spread the letter on the table, smoothed it out, and left it there for William to read. She hoped he would agree to go with her – and here, thank goodness, he was, home at last. He sounded a Morse-code F on his hooter as he passed the door on his way to put the car in the garage, but for once she felt simply too tired to go and pull the door open for him. She was still sitting at the table when he came in.

He looked tired, too, and though he kissed her as he passed her to sit down opposite her, there was something in his manner that disturbed her. His homecoming tonight was not the joyous occasion they usually made of it. As she made him coffee and apologized for the makeshift supper, she tried to guess what was causing his mood of polite detachment. For some reason – unless the coldness and controlled irritability were directed straight at her – she usually found these occasional bouts of courteous and cultured remoteness more amusing than upsetting. Often, when he got round to telling her what triviality had been the cause of it, they would both end up laughing. There didn't seem to be much hope of that tonight. Whatever could have upset him?

She conjectured that it must have been something that Nicholas Gordon had said, in which case he was just being silly. If he wasn't going to bother to tell her, she certainly wasn't going to bother to ask. She'd had as long and tiring a day as he had, even if he had had to make two trips to Cambridge and back. Better to try to ignore his mood altogether.

She told him of George Bridgefoot's visit, doing her utmost to be her natural self in spite of his unresponsiveness. She enlarged on her troubled thoughts about the Bridgefoot–Bellamy split widening, and her feelings of irritation with Jane for doing anything to exacerbate it. Not, she said, that she could blame Jane, especially after the disclosure of the truth about Nick's condition.

'You will run to meet trouble,' was all he said.

She felt rebuffed and disturbed by his tone. Doing her best to keep the conversation on an even keel, she confessed to him that she was feeling a considerable amount of guilt because she had had to break her word not to say anything about Bob buying his farm. 'I had to do what I could to comfort poor old George,' she said. 'But I hate having to keep secrets anyway. And people will tell them to me.'

'You shouldn't ask for what you don't want,' he said. 'I think you rather enjoy being an agony aunt. You just turn on the charm till people tell you their life stories, and want to put their heads in your lap and cry. Then you complain because they do.'

She was really hurt, now. She was silent, seeking to make every excuse for him that she could think of, including the fact that there was some truth in what he said. Besides, as he had said only this morning, her lame ducks inevitably became his as well. And she did know how worried he got about her when she showed any signs of fatigue or strain – as she was doing now.

But he seemed to be suggesting that it was all an act that she put on, and that her concern for other people was not genuine. He knew better than that! What she had said at breakfast time was quite true: she couldn't help it.

Offended, she made no move to defend herself whatever he chose to think. She simply could not face an argument with him tonight. It was too dangerous. On the rare occasions when they did quarrel, the result was usually an earthquake high on the Richter scale, not a mere tremor. She dared not risk it.

She got up and went to the sink, turning her back on him so that he should not see her face. He made no move to help her wash up.

She made a resolution that this time, whatever it cost her, she would not allow William to make her angry enough to cause a quarrel. His cold voice behind her almost undid the resolution as soon as it was formed.

'I suppose you did leave this letter here for me to read?'

'Yes, of course. I told you how dreadfully he coughed. I'm afraid he may be seriously ill.'

'I'm afraid he's just a charlatan well-versed in picking out a soft touch. He dares to load his troubles on you, on the grounds of one chance encounter. You won't do anything about it, of course.'

She swung round. 'I should never forgive, myself if it was a genuine cry for help that I could give, and didn't. At least I have to find out. So I shall do what he asks. You can come with me. Then you can judge for yourself.'

He made no reply. She went to him, and laid her face on the top of his white head. 'Let's leave it till the morning,' she said. 'We are both tired out.'

They went about their usual preparations for bed in a most unaccustomed silence, though it was at least an hour earlier than their usual time. Fran still felt a storm in the air, and hoped to shelter from it by getting to sleep before the rumblings turned to thunder and lightning.

Once in bed, William lay on his back and stared at the ceiling in the rosy glow of her bedside lamp. She lingered in the bathroom, to give him time to get drowsy. She took a bath instead of her usual shower, looked for and found a slightly warmer nightdress against the autumn coolness (as well as William's cold detachment from her) and, finally, as usual gave herself a squirt of perfume. Two squirts in fact. An extra one tonight for luck.

As far as she was aware, she had done nothing whatsoever to cause this withdrawal from her, except to stick up for her principles in the matter of Peter Petrie. But he had come back from Cambridge sulking – if that's what it was – before he had read Petrie's letter. So what was it she was being punished for?

'All right, Dr Burbage,' she said to herself, jutting out a chin he wasn't even looking at. 'Do your best. Be Richard the Lionheart and I'll be Saladin. You'll find me a silk cushion that your sword won't make any impression on.'

She climbed into bed and lay for a moment, thinking how much the bath had refreshed her. She was glad, after all, to find him still awake. She didn't want the sun to go down with this coldness between them. She sat up on her elbow, and leaned over him. He closed his eyes, opened them to glance at her, and then resolutely shut them again. Not, though, before she had glimpsed the misery in them. She stroked his hair, and smoothed out the frown across his forehead, lowering herself gently closer and closer to him.

His nostrils quivered as they picked up the perfume. She always smelt like that, fresh and sweet and wholesome. Since he had bought her the perfume himself, he knew it was an extremely expensive and sophisticated French one, but it didn't seem to him that sort now. It only served to emphasize her essential Englishness, reminding him of the scent of the old garden at Benedict's in Grandfather's time, when in summer the arches over the steps to the rose garden hung heavy with the blooms of 'Gloire de Dijon' and 'Maréchal Niel' roses. Her hair fell over his face as she kissed the tip of his nose, and then his mouth, before tucking her head on to what she called her 'bit of paradise', the hollow of his shoulder. He moved almost involuntarily to make it available to her. Then she said, 'And now, my darling, please tell me why my William went to Cambridge, and that morally disapproving Dr William Burbage came back.'

He couldn't speak, but his arms closed round her, drawing her face close to his. Tears ran down between their cheeks.

'I can't stand it, Fran. I know it isn't your fault – I know you don't put on charm just to attract other men – but the result's the same. And the whole bloody world we live in is full of men who are all free to offer you what I can't. Every new man we meet is either a bachelor or a divorcé or a widower. I go round the corner of the house to fetch the car in my role as your consort, and come back to find myself only the chauffeur appointed to take your latest conquest to the station. There you were – in the arms of the most eligible unmarried man yet! He's obviously fallen flat at your feet, like they all do. He sang your praises all the way to Cambridge, and I had plenty of time to think on the way back by myself.

'This isn't just silly jealousy, Fran. It's common sense combined with guilt. How can I continue to stand in your way of a marriage with a man like that? It just isn't fair on you. And all because I won't – no, can't – bring myself to break a promise I made to a pretty, silly, empty-headed maneater when I was still just a kid, in spite of my RAF wings! Why don't you throw me out now? You will one day. There's no reason why you shouldn't. And I feel such a cad, to expect you to go on taking all the flak of the sort Jane was talking about. I don't worry about it until something happens, as it did today, to remind me that I may be living in a fools' paradise after all. Then I can't take it. Like now.'

He pulled away, as if to get out of the bed. She held him fast, resolved to bend his will to hers. It wouldn't really take much doing, providing she kept herself from reacting too hastily to anything he might say or accuse her of.

'I'm so afraid, Fran. So insecure. I'm only your live-in lover, and I want to be your husband. I want to be able to shout to the world that you are mine and mine only. I'm so proud of you, just because other men do find you so attractive, till I remember that I have no more right than they have to call you mine. You could throw me over and go to one of them at any minute. After all, what am I but your lodger?'

He pulled himself out of her arms, and turned his back on her. She felt quite helpless to ease his pain. What can anyone do when a child drops a brick on his own toe or shuts his fingers in the car door?

She didn't feel anything missing in their 'marriage', at all, but then, she was 'free'. She understood, perhaps wholly for the first time, why it meant so much to him. She didn't feel vulnerable. Once she had committed herself to him, she didn't worry. He did. That streak of jealousy which had appeared now and then in the past, and which she had thought the only flaw that she had ever found in him, was caused by the insecurity he had just made plain to her. Her heart ached to put it right, but it was the one thing that she was powerless to alter.

He turned again, suddenly, holding himself where he could look down on her. 'I get so frightened, Fran. I couldn't live without you now. Have you any idea what you still mean to me?'

'Yes,' she said simply. 'Exactly the same as you mean to me.

'Light of my eyes to me. Half of my soul.'

She watched the eyes looking down into hers change their expression from pain to a flicker of amusement as he recognized yet another quotation, and then to a yearning tenderness that melted her every other emotion into her love for him. He breathed a deep sigh, closing his eyes, and when he opened them they were bright with a gleam that had in it no hint of diffidence or insecurity.

'May the god of Love one day give me the absolute right to do this,' he said, covering her with kisses and blocking out from her sight and her thoughts everything in the world but himself.

16

Fran could hear William whistling downstairs. He never had the faintest idea what he was whistling, and she had long ago given up trying to gauge his mood from the sound. She had been caught out too many times in the past, expecting a gloomy greeting after his rendering of Chopin's 'Funeral March' only for it to be changed to a spirited rendering of a medieval song (with vocal interludes), or 'The Irish Washerwoman' before she reached the kitchen. This morning she recognized a Brandenburg Concerto which broke off abruptly when the toaster popped up the toast – and though the whistling was resumed, it had turned into 'Lillibullero' before he saw her. That he was whistling at all told her that he had completely forgotten his forebodings of last night, and she greeted him with a huge smile. He hastily set down the coffee-pot and the toast rack to greet her, whistling till perforce he had to stop in order to kiss her.

There wasn't much wrong between them this morning. The relief made them both light-headed as well as light-hearted. They sat down to breakfast laughing, acting as if they were no more than half their chronological age. Petrie's letter still lay open on the middle of the table.

'What do you propose to do?' William asked. 'I don't need to tell you that I withdraw everything I said last night, do I?'

'No more than I need to tell you that I want your advice,' she replied. 'I still think it's genuine. A man in a tight spot driven into doing something he hated doing. It comes through the way he has couched the letter. Will you come with me to see him, today?'

'I'd go and see Old Nick himself today if you asked me to,' he said. 'When shall we go?'

'This very afternoon. His object, I think, is for me to persuade Roland to go and have a look, but what he needs is a valuer, surely? I don't like the sound of our new Mr Pugh very much. From what George said last night, he sounds every bit as foul as Sophie painted him.'

'Here is Sophie, now,' William said. 'She may have more information about him, after seeing Thirzah.'

Fran had forgotten the possibility of Sophie's possible dereliction, and waited uneasily till she appeared already clad in her clean overall with her apron tied over it. She had come to work.

Fran asked at once about Thirzah, and Sophie sat down to tell them her tale.

'Just the same as afore,' she said, 'only worse. All on account o' that Daffy Pugh and 'is goings-on again.' She paused to take a tiny sip of the very hot coffee William had set before her. 'Tell us while your coffee cools,' he suggested. She smiled on him in a way that set Fran's fears at rest. Sophie was herself, at any rate, prepared to enjoy the telling of her tale.

'Night afore last, there's a knock on Thirz's door, and when Dan'el opened it, there stood Hetty's Joe and that there Welshman. And according to Thirz', afore Dan'el could open 'is mouth, this 'ere Pugh 'olds up 'is 'and, like this 'ere, and says, "Brother, are you saved?"

'Well, Dan'el were so took aback, especially as it were Joe, as is 'is own brother-in-law, standing there with that Daffy, as 'e just didn't know what to say.

'"Saved?" he says. "Joe knows as well as I do I'm been a-saving with the Co-op since the first week I ever went to work. So if it's a shilling-a-week insurance you're a-selling, you're come to the wrong 'ouse."

'Then Daffy got 'is foot over the doorstep and said, "Nothing o' the sort, Mr Bates. Is your *soul* saved?"

'"Blowed if I know," Dan'el says. "I'm a Christian and a churchman, as Joe can't deny. Tha's as much as I can tell you. If you want to know more'n that, you'd better ask 'Im Above. Though for the life o' me I can't see what it's got to do with you."

'"I witness for the Lord, and I preach for souls. Every man's soul is my business. I shall ask for the Lord's blessing on you. We shall all pray together for your soul to be saved."

'And with that he pushes past Dan'el and gets inside, with Joe follering after 'im like some poor dumb animal what hadn't got no will of its own. Well, b' that time Thirz' were nearly busting wi' temper. Dan'el told me that when he looked round at 'er, she were standing up, nearly choking 'erself, and as red in the face as if she'd been b'iled. Then she clutched at 'er chest, and fell down. Joe pulled Daffy outside again, and Dan'el shut it and bolted the door after 'em.

'Thirz' soon come to, after Dan 'ad picked 'er up and set 'er in 'er own chair. But she were that savage, and put 'erself out wi' Dan'el for ever letting 'em get inside at all, that the pain come on again, worse than ever, till 'e managed to get 'er to bed. Then yist'day morning Dan went to work but went 'ome again to say George said she'd got to 'ave the doctor. Well, you know Thirz'. Do, she'll only ever hev 'er own way. So she says as it's me she wants. Seeing as she weren't well enough 'erself to goo and square Joe up like, I should hev to this time. She give me 'er orders to goo there and then. I daren't upset 'er, and I were wondering whatever I should do when I 'eard the back door open and in comes Dr Henderson. Seems George 'ad telephoned 'im without telling even Dan'el.

'So it were just as well I were there, 'cos he examined 'er all over, like, and told 'er straight as she'll hev a stroke if she keeps on getting 'erself into such takings. 'E said as she were a lot too fat, and 'ad better take a couple o' weeks off work to calm 'erself down, and goo on a diet. Told 'er that to lose a couple o' stone would be better for 'er 'eart and 'er blood pressure than any medicine as 'e could give 'er.

'She were that put out at him coming so near to telling 'er as it were all 'er own fault as I thought she'd have another turn there and then. I daren't leave 'er by 'erself. Tha's why I didn't come back.

'But I ain't going to see Joe. What he does is 'is own business, though I do wonder at 'im, 'cos 'e is b' nature such a kind and peaceable man. I never knowed 'im to lose 'is temper with Het nor nobody else till Wend' had that child. Nobody would ever 'ave believed Joe could be took like 'e is now.'

Fran was torn between amusement at Sophie's tale, and pity for all concerned. She said, gently, 'You mustn't blame Joe too much. He's had a lot to put up with, lately. It broke his heart when Wendy had the baby. He had good reason not to want to go near that church again, but perhaps he's been feeling guilty. I think this Mr Pugh may be good for Joe. Maybe he's been wanting somebody to help him.'

''E could ha' gone to the Rector, couldn't he?'

It was William who answered her. 'If it had been the old Rector, yes. But it wasn't. Don't forget what the Bible says. "In my Father's house are many mansions." Joe's perhaps found the key to one of them through Pugh. But, Sophie, you really mustn't interfere. And if you want my honest opinion, I think that in the long run this may be a good thing for everybody. If Thirzah can't go to Hetty and you won't, she'll have to pull herself together and stop having hysterics. She would have done years ago if she didn't know she could always get what she wanted that way. She's not half so simple as she pretends to be. And another thing – your mother's been dead twenty years now, and there's no sense in you being bound by a death-bed oath to her, either. That's how Thirzah's always kept her hand over you. It will do Thirzah a lot of good for somebody to stand up to her, as well. My advice is to do what you can for Thirzah while she's in bed, and let all the rest just die down. It's nothing to do with you or anybody else what Joe does. You keep out of it.'

Both Fran and Sophie were looking at him with surprise – Fran because he was saying just what she had wanted to say for a long time, and Sophie as if he might have been the Delphic oracle. It wasn't often that he was so outspoken. She had told her tale hoping for a bit of advice, and she had got it, in no uncertain terms. She looked entirely satisfied and answered him with the glint of battle in her eye.

'It's a pity as you and Fran weren't here to help me stand up against 'em a long while ago,' she said. 'I shan't be at Thirz's beck and call no more. Thanks.' She got up and went resolutely to her duties.

Fran was looking at William with amusement. 'Well Merlin,' she said, 'let's just hope your powers of divination are as good this afternoon.'

William had certainly put himself back in charge. They set out after an early lunch, left the car at the top of the side road, and walked.

'It's going to be a hard winter, if the berries are anything to go by,' Fran said. 'Just look at the hawthorn. And that tree in the hedge. That's rowan, isn't it?'

'Yes, though rowans are scarce round here. I expect that's survived because it happened to grow in the hedge. Farmers don't exactly encourage trees on arable land. Probably self-sown, so there must be another somewhere fairly close. It may even be a descendant from one planted in the dark ages. From one generation to the next, just like people.'

They reached a point where the lane became much narrower, and the hedges on each side of it were no longer trimmed to keep them from growing wild. Brambles had encroached till they almost filled the lane with their patchworked leaves of brilliant green, scarlet, deep crimson, purple and gold. Above the brambles, a pale grey veiling of old man's beard draped itself over the thorn, though taller saplings of hazel stood out over above the rest, still flying little pennants of dying yellow.

Nature didn't let the summer go out without giving warning that it was only taking a bit of a rest, signalling that autumn shouldn't be regarded as 'the beginning of the end'. Fran hugged that thought to herself, drawing an analogy with William's white head, which was certainly no warning of waning virility or senescence.

The lane took a sudden turn, and there, at the end of it, was the house that had been four tumbledown cottages. It stood thirty yards or so from the lane, fronting it across a wild garden, in the middle of which was a fine rowan tree so absolutely laden with bright berries that it was visually startling against the contrast of gleaming white new plaster; a big house, now, four windows wide and with another part, almost as roomy, in a T-shape at the back. Farther back still, across another wild garden in which old-fashioned apple trees like Blenheim Orange pippins and russets still bore a few golden globes of fruit too high to be reached from the ground, was another detached building that had once been, as Fran could see, both a granary and a dovecote. This had not been included in the restoration, and showed ragged and dishevelled against its bright, spruced-up relation.

As soon as they approached the rickety gate in the front hedge, they were greeted by a girl in her teens holding a toddler by the hand. She was clean and tidy, though thinly dressed and barefooted, with long hair caught into a rubber band at the nape of her neck. She was surprisingly self-possessed.

'Hello,' said Fran. 'Is Mr Petrie at home?'

'Hello,' said the girl, pulling the gate open with her free hand. 'Are you Mrs Catherwood? I'm Emmy. It was my turn to look after Aggy and Jade, so Daddy asked me to look out for you in case you came today.' Her voice had the same gloss of culture as Petrie's own, and little Tanner's. 'Will you please go in?'

They moved towards the door, which opened of its own accord as they got to it, and a solemn little face under a crop of glowing copper curls peeped shyly round from the inside.

Fran beamed her sunniest smile at the child. 'Hello, Jasper,' she said. 'May we come in?' He had forgotten his duty as keeper of the door in his pleasure at seeing her again, and his face broke into the angelic smile that had first captivated her. He still did not open the door, but with only his head in view, surveyed William with a long, searching look.

'Open the door, Tanner,' ordered Emmy, 'and then come with me.'

The child pulled the door open, admitted both of them, and then slammed it quick. He was already holding Fran's hand before Emmy could open the door again.

'Go away,' he told her, prepared, as Fran could see, to put up a fight if he should be dragged from her. A dreadful bout of coughing from a nearby room reached Fran's ears.

'Leave Jasper with me,' she said to the girl. 'We mustn't let him disturb your father. Is he ill?'

The girl nodded. 'He said I was to tell you to go in to him, and then I had to take the little ones away. Ammy is looking after all the others out in the field.'

'I'll look after Tanner,' Fran said, and made towards the door from which the hollow cough was coming. She waited till it stopped, and then gently pushed open the door.

He lay on a narrow single bed, which was the only article of furniture in the room other than a small deal table on which was a telephone and a directory, a few sheets of paper and some writing materials. A deal kitchen chair beside the bed supported a mug of water, and on its back hung a towel. The floor, the window and the walls were bare. The man was covered only by a washed-out old patchwork coverlet, above which his flushed and haggard face was bright with welcome.

He looked up at William, who introduced himself, and then without being asked, set the mug of water on the floor, put the towel on the table, and set the chair for Fran close by the bedside.

Then he turned to Tanner. 'Jasper,' he said, 'I came with Mrs Catherwood really because I wanted to see the funny humpy-bumpy field at the back of your house. If your Daddy doesn't mind, will you show it to me?'

The child stood gravely in front of William, looking up the tall length of him to study his face. Then he looked toward his father, who nodded. He took William's hand, and they went out, leaving Petrie and Fran together.

'It was good of you to come so quickly,' he said at last. 'I hope you didn't have to drag Dr Burbage here to protect you.' An impish twinkle lurked for a moment in the hazel eyes. 'Thank him for me. He deserves you.'

'I guessed you were ill,' she said, 'but I wasn't prepared to find you like this. Have you had the doctor?'

'No. He can't do me any good. I'm not just ill – I'm dying. That's why I had to appeal to somebody before it was too late. Maybe I'll go on for another six months or so, but that's about the limit. So I have no time to waste. I rather overdid things trying to get the house in good enough shape to sell. To provide for the others when I'm no longer about.'

Fran was shocked into silence, so he went on talking. 'You haven't seen it yet, I know, but if I'd had time to finish what I'd planned, it would have been a nice family house. Now, I can't and don't expect a rush of offers for it, because there's still such a lot left to be done. Besides, it's too big for most folks, and very lonely. My only hope is to sell it somehow, very cheap. I need to raise enough capital to ensure shelter of some sort for the children. Enough to buy a good-sized and reliable Dormobile, and the best camping equipment to be had.'

She was aghast. 'They couldn't live like that,' she said.

'It's more than they were born to,' he answered.

'But it wouldn't be allowed. The council would take them into care. Haven't you any family who will see to it that they are housed and looked after?'

'They have a mother. She coped with them before I came on the scene with no such luxury as a Dormobile or proper camping facilities will provide.'

Fran was embarrassedly out of her depth.

'I'm sorry,' he said. 'I have no right to involve you. The least I can do now is to explain the situation, and what drove me to beg you to get help for me. I may never be able to get up again – though I guess I shall last round to the spring. After that, it will depend on their mother. She isn't my wife.' He stated it abruptly in as flat a tone as he had used when bluntly confronting her with the fact that he was dying.

('Any more than I'm William's,' she thought. 'But he doesn't know that. He expects me to be shocked, no doubt.')

'But they are your children? You called Jasper your son,' she said.

'So he is – the only one I fathered. That doesn't make me any less responsible for them all. Though it's Jasper I'm most worried about, when the time comes.'

'But . . .' She coloured and was unable to frame her question.

He smiled, with a sort of rueful resignation, and helped her out. 'You're wondering about the two who are younger than Jasper?' He shrugged. 'Your guess is as good as mine. They aren't mine. Their mother – Crystal – has strong views about such things. She's an extreme example of the modern "freedom" culture: a sort of social anarchist who thinks that rules or conventions of any kind spell tyranny. Marriage is tantamount to slavery, and pregnancy as the price of sexual freedom a nasty trick Mother Nature plays on women.'

'But in these days . . . ?'

'When you're drugged up to the eyeballs, contraceptive precautions might as well not exist,' he said. 'And primitive abortions under a hedge somewhere are apt to be dangerous. The group helps to cope with those born into it – but it doesn't give them much chance for a decent future. Crystal is an intellectual middle-class drop-out with a kink in her conception of life. You may meet her before you go. There's no telling.'

Fran hoped not. His way of presenting her with bald facts and leaving her to fill in everything between them was most disconcerting. There was a wry cynicism in his voice, almost inviting her to show her surprise and distaste at the turn the conversation had taken. He attempted to raise himself up, and set himself coughing again. When he had recovered, he said, rather breathlessly, 'Go on, Mrs Catherwood. Say what you're thinking! Why don't you ask me what I'm doing in a set-up like this? I shall have to tell you, sooner or later, if you are willing to try to help me.'

'What is it that you think I can do?' she asked, helplessly.

'You mean why did I pick on you?' he said. 'Because you have a son who's an architect. I would appreciate his advice – on business terms. I'm not an architect. I need to know what to do next to make the place saleable. And time is short.'

'Of course I'll ask him,' she said, 'and I shall be very surprised if he refuses, busy with his own concerns as he is. But I'd rather get you a doctor.'

'That's an old music-hall joke. I happen to be a doctor – well, as near as makes no difference. I dropped out just before qualifying.'

'Why?' she said, bluntly. The answer, no doubt, was because of the woman he had referred to as Crystal.

His face broke into a grin. 'Wrong, Mrs Catherwood. Just sheer rebellion. Not part of the anti-authority mood in general. A private rebellion. I left when I did because I had to be alone to sort myself out. I suppose I was having some sort of nervous breakdown. I couldn't bear people near me. The hospital I was supposed to be working in terrified me. I just walked out one day, and kept walking. I wanted to disappear. I was already twenty-seven, so nobody could force me to go back. If anybody asked my name, I just said "Peter". A rolling stone.

'It was easy enough, because there were so many drop-outs just then. Hippy groups everywhere absorbed a lot of them. A man by himself was different. People let him alone. It was the gangs of hippies that upset ordinary folks, because they didn't conform to what country people understood.

'Crystal was – is, I suppose – one of them. Once into a university, she repudiated everything her wealthy middle-class family stood for, and experimented with alcohol and drugs, and sex, and became pregnant. So she and the boy concerned both dropped out. He stayed with her only long enough to see the child born and then went back home to start again. She didn't try. She liked the life and the freedom it gave her. She isn't the sort to be long without a man attached. When I came across her she'd been living with some fellow in an old bus, in the Elan Valley, and already had five children. Not all his, of course. The police turned them off the land where they were camped looking for mushrooms. The man took the bus and left her with nothing but a bit of camping gear and an old pram. I'd guess she was stoned when he drove off.'

Fran interrupted. 'Where were you, then?'

'Oh yes, me. Not part of that scene at all.' He lay very still for a few minutes, with his eyes closed. Fran wondered if he were tiring himself too much. He was looking backwards, she thought, and his handsome, mobile face was very expressive. When he opened his eyes to look at her he was wearing that rather rueful smile of his again.

'I guess Dr Burbage has been warning you not to be too credulous,' he said. 'I don't blame him. But in fact, I'm not exactly a beggar, cooking up a tale to elicit your sympathy or your largesse. I can pay for your son's services.'

She felt ashamed, and begged him to go on.

He did so rather apologetically. 'I'm the youngest son of four in a military family. My father had a high rank, and two of my brothers went up the ladder fast in a very posh regiment. I rebelled against following the family tradition. I wanted to do medicine, and said so. Father wouldn't agree, so it dragged on till I had to do my National Service. That experience decided me absolutely to go my own way. So I did, only to chuck it in the end.

'I was still based at home when Father came back. The world wasn't big enough for both of us. I found out what my mother had always had to put up with. He might as well have been a stallion at stud. He started his old tricks as soon as he was back in London, and she just couldn't take any more. She died of cancer, actually – but broken hearts don't help. It was when she died that I just gave up. I'd walked out before I knew that she'd left me everything she had. A small lump sum, invested, and an annuity she had bought for me when she knew she was dying. She wanted to make sure I could be free of my father and brothers. The only one that took after her.

'I felt as rich as Croesus, and free for the first time ever. I decided I would never use the brute's name again, or have anything more to do with my family. I ran away – or at least, walked. I had to keep on the move. I just roamed about, wherever my fancy took me, free as the wind, for several years.'

There was another bout of coughing, but he seemed more able to control it this time. His face was flushed, and Fran was wishing William would come back to rescue her. Petrie was an adept at reading her expression.

'Sorry,' he said. 'Can you bear to hear the rest?' She nodded.

'I'd been walking through Wales and from Devil's Bridge struck the Mountain Road to Rhyader. It was getting dark, and I knew I couldn't reach Rhyader before midnight, so I decided to sleep out. There was a ruined cottage in sight that I made for, but before I got there I heard children crying – well, screaming and moaning. The beam of my torch showed me that I'd walked into a nightmare.

'Crystal was there, lying asleep among nettles and docks on the ground with her hair spread out all round her. One look was enough. She was stoned to the world, but the children were ill, in pain and a frightful mess into the bargain. I deduced they had been so hungry that they had poisoned themselves by eating anything they could find. The baby was in an old pram – I thought at first he was dead. The others, all girls, were vomiting and writhing on the floor among the nettles, and relapsing into unconsciousness between bouts.

'Can you imagine it? I had no light but my torch. It was too late for other traffic to be on that lonely road, even if I could have induced anybody to stop. I couldn't leave to go and get help. I honestly think they would have died but for my medical training. By daylight they were all still alive, just about. As soon as I could see I cleaned them up with water from the stream, and began to get some fluid down them, made from spring water and the condensed milk I had in my pack. It was still far too early for passing traffic.

'When their mother came to, I fed her as well. She was anything but grateful to find all her offspring alive. She has never said so, but I think she had expected, and perhaps half-hoped, to find them all dead. I was in a dreadful quandary. I wasn't a crazy youngster. I was a man getting on in age with a medical training. I had to see it through. If I left, and reported to the police when I got to Rhyader, there would have been an inquiry, which even for me must have been an unsavoury experience. The mother would have been on charges of possessing drugs and of criminal neglect of her children.

'I hadn't saved their lives to condemn them to some awful children's home.' There was a pause. 'They were such nice little kids. Emmy was four and Ammy not quite three, and the twins about eighteen months old. The baby – the only boy – was no more than three months. If I kept quiet and looked after them till they were fit to travel again, nobody need ever know. So as soon as I could leave them, I went to buy provisions and extra camping gear. Maybe I'd been lonelier than I thought. I had acquired a ready-made family and a new problem.

'I couldn't bring myself to leave those girls to grow up in a hippy camp with a mother like that. I wondered about her. She's very beautiful, in a pre-Raphaelite way, and intelligent enough except for this "freedom of the individual" obsession. She might not be gone too far for rehabilitation.

'I offered her a bargain. I would set us all up with transport and proper camping gear, and provide food and clothes, on condition that she gave up drugs and let me look after the children, at least until I could get them all back to civilization in a healthy enough condition for her to apply for social service help, without any risk of them being taken from her into care.

'She refused. She would be bound by no rules. I could do as I pleased with the girls, but she was keeping the boy. Probably as a bargaining counter if she ever met his father again.'

There was another pause. For once Fran's previous experience provided her with no guidelines at all.

At last he went on. 'Men come in as many varieties as women, I suppose. Most men would have had enough sense to get out at that point.

I couldn't. When they were well enough, we moved on together. After three days the oldest were calling me Daddy, though there was nothing at all between me and their mother – but I suppose in the end that was inevitable. My annuity just kept us going as long as we had no overheads. Sometimes she would take off, leaving the children with me, and be gone for weeks. Then one morning, she was gone for good, taking only the baby with her. I accepted my responsibility for the four girls, and we went on roaming. I was happy again. I presumed she had rejoined the hippy group, and found herself another man. She had taken all the children's allowance books, so she wouldn't starve.

'She turned up out of the blue again one morning and demanded that I should restore her children to her. It was an ultimatum. I either took her and the boy – on her terms – or she took my family. She won.

'She said she had kicked the drug habit, more or less, and had started painting, things she could sell at country shows and so on, now and again. So we went on together. And in the course of time Jasper was born. My son.

'That had a very sobering effect on me. I wasn't going to let *him* grow up in a group of hippies! We were going to put down roots, somewhere, somehow. The answer was to use my nest egg to buy some ruinous cottage, and restore it with my own labour. To Crystal a permanent home meant bondage, so she left again, but came back later – pregnant, of course. The group she had been with were making for this field, which apparently had no known owner. I came too – you will understand that Jasper had sealed her hold on me absolutely – and here stood exactly what I had been looking for. We squatted here till the baby was born, and I traced the owner – long dead, but his heirs were willing to sell.

'Then I began to be ill. A bolt from the blue that none of us had bargained for. So whatever we had had in the way of a partnership broke up. She still comes and goes as she likes, and squats in what is now my property, that old granary in the garden. She's had yet another child since then, no more mine than any of them other than Tanner, but she added him to my family because the oldest girls are now capable of looking after him as well as me and the rest.

'Now I'm back to square one.' He paused, and turned so that he could look directly at her. 'Mrs Catherwood, I have lung cancer. I know too much about it to entertain any hope. My annuity dies with me. I spent all my lump sum buying this property. What is going to happen to my family? They are her children. She has the legal right to them, though I did insist on giving my own real name as the father of Jasper when I went to register his birth. I care about them all, though most about him.'

He turned his face away from her, and hid it under the coverlet.

Fran longed to reach out to him, to touch him, to comfort him, but knew she dared not. His plight was hopeless, and he had made it clear that he accepted that awful truth. Too much sympathy would undermine the courage he had so far displayed. She controlled her voice with a tremendous effort.

'My son is not a valuer, Mr Petrie,' she said. 'I'm sure he'll do his best to help with advice, but you need an estate agent and valuer first of all, don't you? Did you know that there is one in Old Swithinford, now? Would you like us to call on our way back to ask him to come up to see you?'

He turned back to face her. 'I couldn't ask for more,' he said.

William tapped at the door and came in. He was accompanied by the whole troupe of children, who all stopped politely outside the door.

'The Pied Piper,' Fran said, smiling down on the sick man. 'I've never seen him play that part before.'

'I've enjoyed myself,' William retorted. 'I've been giving a history lesson – and been treated to some of Ammy's griddle-cakes.'

He rearranged the room just as it had been when they had first entered it, his keen eyes missing nothing of the expression on Fran's face or on Petrie's.

He held his hand out to the man on the bed, and stood back for Fran to say goodbye. She held Petrie's hand between her own, unable to find the right words.

William said them for her. 'Come on, sweetheart, we mustn't tire Mr Petrie a minute longer, now.'

Fran squeezed the hand she held, and turned away.

William paused at the bedroom door. 'We'll be back,' he said.

They recounted to each other the gist of their visit as they walked back to the car. 'I was supposed to go to look over the house,' Fran said. 'But all I saw was one bedroom.'

'I was taken on a tour of inspection,' William said. 'It could be a wonderful place. But then we went out into the field, and I truly forgot what we'd gone for. I was fascinated by finding exactly what I had imagined when Sophie was telling us about it. I'm certain now that those tumuli are burial mounds. I hope the new owner, whoever he is, won't just bring bulldozers in to level the field. I wanted to say that to Petrie, but as we came back towards the house, we were waylaid by what I thought was a ghost from the past. I suppose it was Mrs Petrie.'

'Do describe her,' Fran said.

'I don't know that I'm capable,' he answered. 'She came sort of floating out of that old granary in what looked like an Indian sari with another bit of bright green velvet pinned together with safety pins to make a tunic over it. And her hair, more or less the same colour as Cupid's, hung over the top of that. Well below her waist, perfectly straight and floating wild. One of the older girls introduced her as "Mummy" – and I got the impression that she'd been watching us, so as to make her exit from her "studio" at exactly the right moment. She had stood some terrible modern "abstract" outside the door, on which I was forced to comment. You know how much I love modern art.'

> 'Will you walk into my parlour?
> Said the spider to the fly,'

said Fran, grinning at him. 'That's the effect she has on men, apparently.'

'Exactly – but it's no laughing matter, really. She's getting drugs from somewhere. I know that look in the eye. She speaks like a duchess, but her mind was as floaty as her hair. I think she'd pinned that queer outfit together while we were out in the field. Her hands were still covered in paint and her neck was far from clean.' It was his turn to grin at her. 'She showed plenty of it.'

He strode along in silence for a hundred yards or so, getting in front of Fran. Then he turned and waited for her. 'I apologize again for everything I said yesterday,' he said. 'You were absolutely right. Somebody's got to help them.'

She was so relieved that she could hardly speak. 'I promised him we would call on the way home and ask the new estate agent to go up and see him,' she confessed.

He made no demur, and they drew up outside the DIY shop just as Mr Pugh was locking up his side of it for the night. William got out of the car to speak to him, while Fran made the most of her first view of 'Daffy'. He was not in the least as she had imagined him. He was no more than thirty-five, she guessed, of middle height and fairly thick set. His complexion was rather healthily ruddy, and his hair almost blond. He had smoothed it down from a side parting, but it was springy and had a tendency to stand up whatever he did with it. He wore large round tortoiseshell spectacles, which tended to give him an owlish air of gravity.

William opened the car door to get back in. Mr Pugh moved with him, so Fran could hear his voice distinctly.

'I will certainly go up to see him sometime tomorrow,' he said. 'I'm sorry I can't go at once, but my priority is to get to the other side of the county by six-thirty to witness for the Lord.'

William let in the clutch without commenting. Fran sat silently by his side until the pink-washed walls of Benedict's came in sight.

'Well!' she said, wonderingly. 'I suppose there must be a limit to one's credulity somewhere. I think mine has been reached.'

He looked down at her, lifting one eyebrow and lowering the other. 'Really? Mine hasn't. I can't think it ever will be while you still exist. Let us now enter our own temple with thanksgiving and witness for our own lares by eating of whatever offerings to them Sophie has prepared for us. I don't know about you, but I'm starving.'

As October slid gently towards November, the mornings grew foggier and the nights colder. The clocks went back, and though the middle of the days was often bright and warm, log fires roared in the sitting-room at Benedict's from lunchtime onwards. Leaves still hung doggedly to the trees, though any breeze brought a few sailing gently down.

'Waiting for the first real frosty night,' Ned said, wheeling a barrow of logs up to the kitchen door.

'And then a bit of a gale,' Sophie agreed. 'Come the first Sunday after Guy Fawkes, they'll all be gone. It all'us seems to be good weather the first week of November, to let the trees stop as they are as long as ever they can afore going to sleep for the winter.'

Ned agreed. 'Just like child'en putting bedtime off,' he said.

'Tha's right. Jus' waiting, as you might say,' Sophie said, helping him pack the logs into the log box.

Fran, listening to the conversation, thought that summed things up. She and William were 'jus' waiting' to start work, but somehow they never got to it. So many events were blowing towards them in the wind.

Bob Bellamy's wedding to Jane had been fixed for the third Saturday in November. Jane had gone to stay with her father to establish her residential qualifications, and so far not a word had been leaked in the village. Jane had told Fran that they had considered it safer not to tell even Bob's daughter and her sweetheart till it was absolutely necessary for them to know.

Fran worried that it indicated that Jane was afraid of Charlie's reaction. William said she had much more important things to bother about. Peter Petrie and his problems, for example. Roland had been to see him, and William did what he could to help without giving offence. He was not at all optimistic that Petrie would ever be well enough to do what was needed to ensure a quick sale, let alone a good one. Fran was grateful to William for sharing that particular load of anxiety with her. It was all very well to be enjoined to love thy neighbour, but when, as in this case, there was damn all you could actually *do*, all you could do was wait.

Roland was having to wait for the house he had bought in Cambridge to be vacated. Fran was secretly pleased, because it meant a Christmas with all her family close at hand. She said nothing more to William about her uneasiness regarding Greg's ever more frequent absences. He would only have accused her of running to meet trouble.

The Rector's farewell sermon was fixed for the last Sunday in November, with the presentation to him at a social gathering in the old schoolroom on the following Saturday, which happened to be Fran's birthday. There was no news yet of a replacement for the Rector. It was one more burden on old George Bridgefoot's back, because almost all the church's business depended on him in the end. She heard a good deal about that from Sophie, who still gave daily reports on Thirzah's health, to which Fran listened willingly, mainly because she couldn't bear to miss Sophie's graphic reports of Thirzah's obdurate battle of wills with old Dr Henderson.

Like most other truly rural folk, she revered the medical profession in the same way as she did the clergy. Both callings had a mystique inherited from ages past. One had power of life and death over people's mortal bodies, the other over their immortal souls. Thirzah paid tribute to the mystique, but in this case, not to the individual who held office. He was too much of a 'hordinary man' for her liking. Besides, as she had been heard to say many times, she 'didn't hold with running to the doctor with every little ache or pain'. She relied on folk medicine learned from her mother, and planted her stolid feet in the footsteps of her forebears, like the trusting page following Good King Wenceslas.

'Thirz' don't 'old with this craze for dieting, no more than I do,' Sophie said. 'And she told the doctor so, to 'is face. "If 'Im Above had wanted me to be a beanpole like the Rector's daughter," she says, "'e'd ha' made me like that. I eat the same as my 'usband does," she says. "Do it don't make 'im fat, why should it make me?"

'She said as 'e told her it was because everybody 'ad something inside 'em what regulated such things. She said she could swear 'e said it were something made o' metal, though she weren't fool enough to believe that. She tried to remember what it were called, so's I could ask you, 'cos I've never 'eard of such a thing afore, neither. Now I'm forgot – wait a minute – metal – metal – metal abolism. That's it! He reckoned Dan'el's metal abolism works better than hers does.'

'And how is Hetty getting along without her?' Fran asked.

'I don't go near 'er, and she don't come near us, but I do see Joe now and then. That Daffy Pugh lodges with Beryl Bean now, though Joe still goes about with 'im, but Het don't seem to care about that. It were heving 'im all'us praying under 'er feet as she couldn't stand.'

'I've met Mr Pugh,' Fran said. 'I must say I was rather surprised. He seemed to take his religion very seriously.'

'Ah?' said Sophie, quite unruffled. 'Joe told me as 'ow it was you and 'im as sent Daffy up to see that fam'ly o' vagabonds up Danesum. And Joe went with 'im, same as 'e goos everywhere else. They goo up there a lot, now. The man seems to ha' took to Joe, like.'

'Mr Petrie wants Mr Pugh to try to sell his house,' explained Fran, trying not to let Sophie's disapproving tone irritate her.

'I reckon as 'e'll goo on wanting a tidy while,' Sophie said. 'It ain't everybody as would want to goo and live in a hout-o'-the-way 'ole like that, standing all by itself in that ghashly old field. There's some as say them big old 'umps there are graves. Not as I mind graves as is put decent into the churchyard or a cimmetary, but Miss Budd told us as the folks as might be buried there wasn't Christians. They had gods o' their own, according to 'er. And I've 'eard Mam tell tales o' folks as 'ave seen blue lights rising out o' them places. Christian ghosts is all very well, but you wouldn't catch me spending no nights there.'

The telephone rang, and Fran went to her study to answer it, glad to get away while she could keep a straight face.

17

Charles Bridgefoot's father, Brian, had had very high hopes that Charles would marry into the 'landowning' rather than the farming community, thereby giving him – and the Bridgefoots in general – the little bit of social cachet he could not yet claim. He averred, loudly, to anyone who would listen (and most loudly of all to his wife) that the local hierarchy nowadays was constructed on the basis of wealth. He knew it wasn't wholly the truth, and his wife just laughed at him. Why had he been so 'chuffed' when his youngest sister had married a doctor who was the son of a famous surgeon with a knighthood? That *had* put them up a notch or two, as she had told him when, last year, they had been invited to Benedict's to help celebrate Fran's birthday. He had been irritated by this metaphorical 'touching of the cap' to anybody. Who were such as Fran and William, these days? What did it matter now that once, time out of mind, their grandfather had been the 'old squire'? Or that Commander Franks, who had come to live in the restored Old Rectory, was the only heir to be found to the aristocratic de ffranksbridge estate? As long as one had enough money, he said, one could climb by its tendrils to whatever social position one wanted.

The Bridgefoots were by no means short of money, and Charles was a very handsome and presentable young man. There had been no reason against Brian indulging in a daydream of his son uniting their moderate financial standing with that of the largest local landowner – until he had met Charlie Bellamy.

She might be the most enchanting girl in the world, as clever and well educated as she was beautiful, but she didn't make the grade Brian had set up for Charles. She was the daughter of an absolute nobody – a complete outsider from the neighbouring fens, who didn't even own the land he farmed. And, of course, of his wife, a woman who by all accounts was little better than a prostitute.

Brian was furious at his son's obsession with the girl. *He would not have it!* He would show the bloody young idiot, and his senile old fool of a father, who it was that made such decisions in the Bridgefoot family. It might upset the sentimental womenfolk, such as his wife and his mother, who already loved Charlie for herself, and it might cause Charles distress for a little while. But the boy would thank him in the end. There was nothing, he judged, that would mend a broken heart quicker than the promise of more money and a lot of local prestige.

The events of last summer had not been in his favour, and he had been forced by them to bide his time before showing his hand. But time was on his side. Turning all the Bridgefoot farms into a company had been effected at Brian's instigation some years ago, though much against George's inclination. He had only agreed on condition that he remained in absolute control until such time as he chose to give up. Brian had confidently expected that to be when Charles reached his majority. Now he wasn't sure.

The boy had proved deaf to all argument and all hints as to his girl's unworthiness to become a Bridgefoot. If he didn't marry Charlie, he said, he would never marry anybody and that would be the end of the Bridge-foot name, if not of the family.

Brian had found, to his relief and pleasure, a most unexpected ally in Charlie herself. She was offended. She would not marry into any family that considered that she was not good enough for them, and said so. She would *not* give Charles up to please anybody but herself, but there were other ways. She would see to it that they would be glad to accept her, for herself and for what she was, wholly, before she consented to marry him.

Before he had appeared in her sights last Boxing morning, she had had every intention of attempting to get a place at a French or German university, using her proficiency in languages to help her realize her ambition to become a vet. She returned to that plan – except that, completely self-assured, she had applied and obtained a place at Cambridge, so as to remain near to Charles. She was not yet quite nineteen. It wouldn't hurt Charles, who was himself barely twenty-one, to wait at least the three years it would take her to get a first degree.

Charles had begged and pleaded, but she was adamant. She had compromised enough by going to Cambridge, where he could see her often; and to soften the blow a bit more, she had agreed to a formal engagement, to be announced at the party his mother and grandmother were already planning for his birthday on New Year's Eve.

So Charlie had 'gone up', and both were finding the separation harder than they had ever expected. Charlie had only found out for the first time recently what it really meant to have a family, and to be loved, by her father and by Charles. She was also somewhat disillusioned by her fellow students.

She was completely aware of her own identity. She had no illusions about her humble origins, or delusions about what her mother was. She was her father's daughter, content to be herself.

In this she found herself a misfit among her peers, who were mostly so intent on following the fashionable trend of ironing out all social differences that it was difficult to see them as individuals. To her there seemed to be nothing but a flat colourless uniformity, in which their clothes expressed their personalities.

She was drawn towards none in particular; it was not in her nature to conform to such an uninteresting degree of nothingness, and in consequence she was the one who became isolated.

Charles suffered in a different way. Brian twitted him all the time about what 'his' girl was up to with all those male students, and he simply could not help reacting to that. He was tortured by jealousy, believing all those Charlie now lived and worked among to be his superiors, because he was 'only a farmer'.

When they had cottoned on to the fact that the bronzed blond curly giant with the nearly-new car was her 'regular' they were curious, and asked her who he was. She astonished them by telling the truth very pointedly. 'The son of a local farmer, who is going to marry the daughter of another local farmer. Me, in fact. Both of us just nobodies, with nothing to hide, or to be ashamed of . . . Nothing at all in our background but honest folk who till the soil for a living. Just good examples of the sort of people you all try so hard to pretend to be.'

They didn't believe her, of course, but after that exchange she held her head a little higher and didn't bother to hide her contempt of those who dare not let their parents drive the new white Jaguar within ten miles of the Senate House. All it did was to make her look forward to Charles's visits more.

Charles didn't know how he was ever going to endure three years of waiting for her. To sit with her in the car down some dark country lane was a kind of exquisite torture he inflicted on himself – and on her – twice every week. To hold her in his arms, and stroke her face with gentle fingertips which of their own accord seemed to wander downwards towards the beautiful little hillocks of her breasts, showed both of them the flames of the volcano they pretended wasn't there. When his lips found hers and he felt her responding, he had to fight with an Apollyon of desire within himself. But she turned her head away, and said, 'No, Charles, please don't! Don't make it harder for me than it is already. I love you so much.'

He was stunned at such moments as those, as if he had never truly believed she could love him enough to feel the same as he did. She was wanting him wholly, letting him know but pleading with him not to take advantage of his knowledge. He couldn't promise himself that he could. Didn't all young folk these days 'have sex' with each other in the same way that they had a snack when they were hungry? It was all very well for Grandad to say 'Keep something to look forward to', but why should they be different? She had promised to marry him, and they would be engaged to each other at Christmas, but would they still feel the same about each other after three years – *three years* – of this misery?

How long, in any case, did this all-consuming desire for sex last? Nobody had ever talked to him about that, not even Grandad. He consoled himself by thinking about William, who was over fifty and obviously still 'in love' in that sort of way; and of Elyot Franks, who had been even older when he had married the Rector's daughter. He obviously wasn't beyond it. Rumour had it that Mrs Franks was expecting a baby.

Charlie said that what she wanted was that they should still be as much in love with each other when they were as old as William and Fran still were. He agreed with her in that – if it wasn't for all this waiting. But he would be with her again on Friday.

It was understood that at this time of the year he would often have to work on Saturdays and Sundays, though that went against his grandfather's principles. She used her weekends to keep up her language practice, and they settled down to a pattern of regular dates on Tuesdays and Fridays, which kept them constantly in touch and avoided disappointments or frustrating phone calls. If there was any sort of emergency, she could always get him on the telephone at home.

When the next Friday came, she was there waiting where he always picked her up, but he felt at once that something was wrong.

As he kissed her as she closed the car door, she said, 'Where have you been since Tuesday? I've been trying to call you. Three times on

Wednesday, and four on Thursday. Your Dad never knew where you were, and your Mum could only guess you might be at your Grandad's or at Castle Hill. I know you haven't been there. Dad wrote asking us to meet him here tonight for a meal, because he had a lot to tell me – well, both of us. Jane will be with him – and something's up. That's why I wanted to ask you to come early. I'm worried – I can't help thinking it may be something about Nick. I wanted to warn you, just in case. But you weren't there when I needed you, and I felt so lonely —' She was trying not to cry.

He was agonized by her distress, and almost choked by his own flaming anger. He knew quite well what had happened. They were parked in a main street, but he didn't let that bother him. He took her in his arms, and said, 'Kiss me!' demonstrating how it should be done. 'Now think. Tell me exactly when and at what time you rang me. Wherever I was, I was thinking about you. Lonely? You can't know what it means, compared with me! And it's only one month, yet, out of three years. But if the first time you can't get me on the phone it means you think I'm out chasing some other girl . . .' Words failed him.

'Why didn't you try to get me, then, when you knew I wanted to speak to you? Don't tell me. I know. They didn't tell you I'd rung, did they? Your Dad was barely civil to me, and your Mum dreadfully embarrassed. Why am I suddenly taboo again? Why am I not allowed even to speak to you on the phone, though we're supposed to be more or less engaged to be married? Or is that all off?'

She was magnificent in her anger, though her lips were quivering. His only desire was to take away the hurt.

'They didn't tell me, and I didn't know. Dad's made himself an office in what used to be Aunt Esther's sitting-room, and moved the phone down there. He says he has ordered extensions, but I wonder. He's up to something he doesn't want us to know. Mum is allowed to take messages, but I'll bet she's under Dad's orders not to say if you ring. Poor Mum. It isn't her fault.'

Charlie pulled herself away from him. 'So we're back again to where we were before. He's made up his mind, this time, to choke me off for good. I'm simply not good enough for him. And if my guess is right, it's my mother at the bottom of it all – and that's something we can't alter. So I'd better quit. It's no good, Charles. They'll never let us be happy. I know they won't care about me, but how on earth can they do it to you? Charles, my darling, I don't know what it is my Dad has got to tell us, but I guess that it's that he has got to go back down the fen. And if that is it, I shall give up my course here, and go with him to look after him. Right out of your life for ever. Your Dad will never be satisfied till they make you give me up, or the other way round. We've got to face it.'

Charles ground his teeth. 'If you give up your course for any reason, it will be to marry me. I shall be twenty-one at New Year, and then they can't stop me doing as I like. Don't forget that Grandad is still the boss. He's on our side. Nobody can make me give you up, as long as you still love me and want to marry me. Are you sure you still do? And always will? Because I'm going to have this out with them. If I have to move out from home afterwards, I will. Don't cry! I'm going to drive on to somewhere less public than this.'

The pub's car park was much more to his liking. She was still crying. He felt her tears running into his mouth as he kissed her, melting all resolve except his need to comfort her. She made no protest as he slipped his hand under her jacket and let it rest over her breast, where he had for so long yearned for it to be. He could feel her heart pounding in rhythm with his own. It was a long and lovely moment, which had quite the opposite effect on him from what might have been expected. He was filled with a sort of holy awe that such soul-satisfying ecstasy could ever be. He would wait for more than that for ever, if that was how it had to be. But when he tried to take his hand away, she caught it, and held it there. She had stopped crying, and when at last she spoke, he could hear the smile in her voice.

'Do you realize, Charles, that if you don't marry me, in thirty years time I shall be a very rare species – a genuine virgin old maid? Like Sophie Wainwright.'

His distress for himself and her, and his raging white-hot anger against his father alike, died down to manageable proportions.

'I don't actually have to marry you to prevent such an awful catastrophe, do I?' he countered. 'You've always said you wanted to be like those two at Benedict's, but they aren't married. You've given me a weapon against my Dad! If that's the way he'd rather have it, I don't care. We needn't wait three years for that, either, if they drive us to it. But the reins are still in your hands, my lambkin. I can wait for ever as long as you still love me, and want me.' He kissed her again. 'Let's go in and see what it is your father has to tell us. Ready?'

She didn't move out of his arms, but held him for one more long, clinging moment. 'Ready? Yes, ready for anything, now that we are together again. I have been trying to face up to what life would be without you. As soon as you had left me on Tuesday, I was sure something out of the ordinary was going to happen, and was so miserable because as I couldn't get you I'd convinced myself it must be something bad. Now you're here with me again, I'm pretty sure it's something good. Let's go and find out.'

Half an hour later, the two dazed youngsters had been put into the picture with regard to Bob and Jane. When the first shock had worn off, Charlie's first reaction was that if there was a woman who could make her father happy, he had found the right one. He would never be lonely again. She got up and went round the table to kiss him, and then turned to Jane. The warmth of Jane's response almost overwhelmed her.

They turned to less emotional matters. Charles and Charlie were asked to keep what they had been told secret for the time being. Only William and Fran were already in the know.

The young couple sat in their car till Bob and Jane had driven off, still stunned and wrung out by the emotions they had been through that evening. They were both absolutely satisfied now just to be able to sit and hold each other.

Charles felt that a good fairy had granted him every wish he could ever think of to ask for except one. He wanted to see his father's face when he got his come-uppance about Bob and Jane — but that was the sort of pleasure that would improve with keeping.

'I suppose I must take you back to your convent, Sophie?' he said. 'Much as I don't want to!'

She was silent for so long that he was afraid he had offended her; but when at last she spoke it was from a well of such deep emotion that it seemed she had had to wait for any reply suitable to rise. Her reply sent Charles into a peal of laughter, happier than he had felt for a very long time.

'*Sacré bleu!*' she said, exactly as she had done on the morning that he had first met her, and his whole young manhood had rushed out to claim this jewel for his very own.

18

On his way home, Charles felt just as he had done on his first day at his grammar school, when a big bully from the top of the school had seized him, turned him upside down and shaken him until everything in his pockets had fallen out and was scattered on the ground all round him. For a few seconds, he had viewed the world upside down, and had been separated from all the little things that made it familiar to him.

What he had thought was his world, until the events of this evening, was certainly upside down now. He found it very difficult to orientate himself in the circumstances of Bob's and Jane's disclosures. The only fixed and stable thing in this new whirling world was the conviction of Charlie's love for him. Remembering her response to his fingers round her breast, he closed his eyes and hit the grass verge with a bump that stalled the car and brought him back to reality. He pulled back on to the road, and switched off the engine, to sit for a while and think things out clearly. He had better take stock of his position all round before he faced his father again.

He had proof, now, that his father was absolutely serious in his attempt to part him from Charlie. It could not be simply that he didn't approve of her, personally, as a daughter-in-law or the mother of future Bridgefoots. The blatant truth stared him in the face, though even now he didn't want to believe it. It had to be something to do with money – and whatever the mysterious 'business' it was with Uncle Vic that Grandad had been so worried about lately. What it meant was that his father was quite willing to sacrifice his son's – and his parents' – future happiness to his own wishes and his greed for money.

That Charlie had been made the scapegoat in all this pointed to the fact that whatever Brian's plans were, they had some connection with Bob and Castle Hill Farm. All the rumours Charles had heard but refused to believe suddenly fell into place. Uncle Vic had boasted about his friendship and 'business links' with Arnold Bailey. Charles had taken it all with a pinch of salt, knowing his Uncle Vic, and finding how little he really knew now of Uncle Vic's daughter, his cousin Pansy, who was very friendly, too much so for Charles's liking, with Arnold Bailey's son, Darren. He had to make allowances for Pansy, though. She had been in love with his friend Robert, who had died last Easter, and had been sent away by her father to a riding school 'to make her forget him'.

She had come back different, hard and brassy – Uncle Vic's daughter all over. She belonged to the same show-off, horsey set as Bailey and his friends. The tales she had told him of what went on at the parties the Baileys gave and to which she went regularly shocked everything in him, young as he was; but then he was old-fashioned. He found himself wondering just how worried about Pansy Aunt Marjorie and her twin sister Poppy were. Poppy was a very different character.

Bailey's business interests were all concerned with development. Bailey and Bob Bellamy had already crossed swords before, man to man; light now dawned on Charles that Bailey had very good business reasons for wanting Bob out of Castle Hill. It was next on Bailey's list for 'development'. And Uncle Vic and his own father were mixed up in it. His father's hope that Charlie would throw him over for a fellow under-graduate began to make bitter sense. The talk of an engagement between his only son and Bellamy's daughter could only queer his pitch badly as far as Bailey was concerned. The nastiness he had lately shown to Charles himself might be due in some part to a guilty conscience. In this last week, though, he had shown that he would stop at nothing to part Charles from Charlie, or in other words to break the Bridgefoot–Bellamy connection. The business must be hotting up.

Anger welled up in Charles till it was like a pain in his throat. *That* was why there had been as yet no plans for his birthday and engagement party! He had wondered why his mother and his Granny and Aunt Marjorie weren't by now up to their eyes in planning it. They had obviously been given orders to leave it a bit, in case Charlie threw him over for somebody new. Charles found it impossible to believe that his mother went along willingly with his father in this, but – poor Mum! She was torn between them.

Until the last year or two, his parents had been such a happy couple. He had noticed the difference, just lately. His mother, who had always been so easy-going, so loving and so willing to give in to anything his father had wanted, had begun to show that if he pushed her too far, she had enough mettle to stand up to her husband. Now he knew why.

But – Bob was not going to have to give up Castle Farm to anybody! He, Charles Bridgefoot, was not going to marry a penniless nobody. Let his father put that in his pipe and smoke it!

There would be difficulties in the next week or two. He would have to find reasons for working on Saturdays, because he had promised Charlie he would go with her to buy her outfit for the wedding, and then there was the Saturday of the wedding itself. And what was he expected to wear?

In all the excitement, nobody had given any details about anything. So he would have to find out. The obvious person to ask was Bob himself. Jane, as he remembered, was off to London tomorrow morning, so Bob would be alone. Charles decided to take tomorrow off and go to see him, as well as his Grandad, just to make sure that everything was all right there. Nothing would ever shake his belief that Grandad would always be on his side – and with a shock like a douche of cold water, he understood that that was exactly the sort of situation they might now have to face: a great family bust-up that would leave them split into two camps.

He wanted to go home and challenge his father, there and then; to force him to consider what he was likely to do to them all by throwing in his lot with people so alien to them and their way of life. But he had gained wisdom, as well as knowledge, by sitting there alone so long in the dark. For everybody's sake, he had to play it cool. He had to be his own man, in his own way, and not let his father either ride over him or lure him into pointless arguments. Brian might still treat him as a boy, but he had to act like the responsible adult he was. An honest one, too, like Grandad, not a get-rich-quick boor like Uncle Vic or a devious bully such as his father had become.

He was horrified when he looked at his watch and found how late it was. It occurred to him that his father would by this time have suspected him of spending the night with Charlie and locked him out. The thought would have made him angry yesterday; now it only made him want to laugh. It was Brian who, when it suited him, still lived in the Middle Ages. He would either break in or climb in or sleep in an outhouse or even knock Grandad up – but he wouldn't be answerable to his father ever again. All the cards were in his hands, this time, and he would play them as well as he knew how, to the best advantage for everybody.

Next morning, Charles's mother heard him moving about, and had his breakfast ready to put before him the moment he appeared. His father was not in evidence.

'Where's Dad?' he asked. 'I hope he doesn't expect me to go to work today, because I can't.'

'In the office,' she replied. 'Talking to Vic, I shouldn't wonder. Ask him yourself. I don't know any more than you do what it's all about. You were pretty late getting in last night.'

'Yes. Sorry, Mum – it wasn't my fault. Thanks for leaving the door open and the lights on. We went for a meal, and there was a lot for us to talk about. Charlie wanted to know about the party. She wants to get a new frock for it, and I shall have to get a new suit.' He congratulated himself on having hit on a way of broaching the subject of Charlie and a shopping expedition, without having to lie about what he needed a new suit for.

'I haven't been able to do anything, yet,' she said miserably. 'Your Dad won't listen. That latest bit of scandal about Charlie's father and Jane Hadley has put the tin lid on everything.'

'In that case, Charlie and me'll make our own plans. Hello, Dad. You heard that, I suppose. What's gone wrong this morning? I hope it's nothing you want me for, because I'm not working today. I've got other things to do.'

'If they've got anything to do with that girl of Bellamy's, you can forget 'em,' said Brian, flaring instantly into a temper. 'And her.'

Charles bit his tongue, and went on with his breakfast. 'Don't be daft, Dad. It's settled between me and Charlie. You agreed. Not that you could do much about it now, anyway. I can marry her without your permission as soon as I'm twenty-one.'

'You take that attitude, and you'll get out from under my roof! You're only still a silly kid who doesn't know which side his bread is buttered on. When my time comes, there won't be room with me for bloody young fools who can't see farther than the end of their noses. And don't bank on the fact that you're the only Bridgefoot by name. That sort of twaddle's gone out. There's plenty in the family with a better eye on the main chance than you have – Pansy, for one. She's going round now with Arnold Bailey's son. Vic's as pleased as punch. But what does my son do? Goes doo-lally over a nobody without a penny to her name. So watch it! It won't matter to me whether it's a Bridgefoot or a Gifford or a Bailey, as long as there's some money to go with the name. You'll find you ain't the only pebble on the beach if you go on making such a fool of yourself.'

Charles let the threat pass over him, knowing most of it to be due to temper about something else. But his mother's face had crumpled and he was very tempted to shout back. He helped himself to another slice of bread before answering.

'What's that supposed to mean? That if you had your way I should marry Bailey's daughter and get you a Bridgefoot grandson out of a more acceptable stable? Or are you giving Mum notice that you've got your eye on that brassy bit yourself? I can't see Grandad wearing that!'

He stood up, and went round to comfort his mother. 'Sorry, Mum. I do try not to answer Dad back but it does rile me to be treated as if I'm still in short pants.'

He turned back to face his father. 'Look here, Dad! I'm old enough and strong enough to do a man's work and earn a man's pay, so I think I'm old enough to choose my own friends, and my own wife. As you did. All you'll do by trying to get between me and Charlie, as you did by telling lies to her all last week, is to shove us into bed together without bothering to get married. Like Pansy with her new friends. If that's the way you want it, it's OK by me – only Charlie doesn't happen to be that sort of girl. She won't let me give you that excuse for throwing me out. But I'd go of my own accord today if it weren't for leaving Mum to cope with you. Don't cry, Mum. I'm not going till I'm turned out. Or when it suits me, and I've got a home of my own with Charlie in it. And don't leave any work for me to do next Saturday, or the one after. We've got other plans arranged.'

He sauntered out, feeling far less jaunty than he pretended. It hurt him a lot to leave his mother in tears, because he could see by his father's face that the tirade he had engendered would now fall on Rosemary. Getting the whip hand was all right as far as it went, but using the whip meant causing pain to somebody. But he'd had his say, and it wouldn't do to give in now.

He found his Grandad in the kitchen, and sat down beside him at the kitchen table. Then, to his own dismay, he found that he was crying. It was such a relief to talk to Grandad and Gran. He told them what had upset him. They showed no surprise. Grandad reached for his pipe, and began to fill it.

'It had to come to it sooner or later, my boy,' Grandad said. 'Your Dad's got too big for his boots, lately. Don't take what he says or does too much to heart. It's just the old bull not liking to see the young 'un strong enough to challenge him. You stick to your girl and do the right thing by her. You've got an eye for a winner – just like he had in his day, and me in mine. I'm a lot more worried about him than I am about you. There's something as I don't know about going on and I don't like it, him messing about with Bailey. I can't believe a son of mine wants to see Old Swithinford disappear under Bailey's sort of homes. Vic wouldn't care, but then he ain't a Bridgefoot.'

'Bailey got away with it at Lane's End,' Molly put in.

'It wasn't so bad as it might ha' been. Lane's End lays a goodish way from the church and the middle o' the village.'

'So does Castle Hill,' she clipped back at him. 'That's what he's after now, if Charlie's father can't find the money to buy it. If you want to know what I think, I reckon Brian and Vic are putting money in with Bailey. If I'm right, Brian's got himself into a mess he don't know how to get out of. What he thought was a clever bit o' business has turned out to be a family matter because of Charlie, bless her.'

'Yes, I shouldn't be surprised if you ain't right, me old duck,' George said, looking at her through a cloud of smoke. 'There's been bad blood between Bailey and Bellamy ever since last Christmas. Bailey would get up to any dirty trick to drive Bellamy out. I reckon your Gran's right. Your Dad's nasty 'cos he feels guilty. He's so set on being Lord Muck that it must be turning his brain.' He sighed, puffing out another cloud of St Julien.

'I ain't saying he may not be wise not to have all his eggs in the farming basket. I can't *blame* him, though I don't like it. Only if he is set on investing in business, why don't he put his money in with Choppen and Franks and them? It's the sort of people he's getting so thick with as I can't stomach. And as for Vic . . .' George hesitated, not liking to be disloyal to any of his clan, but he went on.

'I ain't surprised at Vic pushing his way in with the Bailey lot, but I ain't very pleased about it. At least Brian's using his own money. Vic ain't. Half of it's Marjorie's, though I don't suppose she's had any say in it, and most of the rest is still mine. It was me as set him up, and I never have had a penny of interest out of him. He hadn't got nothing but an old tractor and a bit of a lorry when he come courting Marjorie. Not as it makes much difference, as long as Marjorie don't care. Vic can't stand

Bellamy. He's jealous, 'cos for all Vic's brag and bluster, people somehow take to Bellamy better than they do to him. He'd like to see Bob Bellamy have to go. It ain't come to that yet, though.'

Charles was taking it all in. 'Do you mean that if Charlie's Dad could stop at Castle Hill, it would get Dad off some kind of hook?' he said hopefully.

'Don't set your heart on Charlie's father being able to keep Castle Hill,' Molly warned. 'Everybody's saying that there's no chance of that. He just can't raise the money.'

George puffed serenely. 'It wouldn't be the first time everybody's been wrong, though, would it, Mother? A little bird told me a while ago not to get upset about that yet. My little bird ain't often wrong.'

Charles got up to go, suddenly looking very sure of himself again. He went round to kiss his Granny, and on impulse kissed his Grandad as well. He was saying goodbye to his youth, and all three of them knew it. George looked up at him with tears in his eyes, feeling proud enough to burst.

'I'm going on up to Castle Hill now,' Charles said. 'I want to talk to Charlie's father by myself. And then I want to try to see your little bird, Grandad – if she's at home.'

George chuckled. '*She?* Who said it was a hen bird?'

Charles grinned, glad for the tone of the talk to be lightened before he left. 'You did, Grandad. It's one of your sayings. "As a bird is known by its note" – er – so is my Grandad by who it is he tells his troubles to. Well, other than Gran, that is.'

'Dry up, Mother,' George said. 'There ain't no need to waste your tears on Charles. He's all there. Good luck, my boy. Here, tell Charlie from me that I want my first great-grandson called George Francis.'

'Can't be done,' said Charles, laughing. '"George *Robert* Francis" she'll say.'

'Get along with you, do, Father,' Molly said. 'Leading the boy into temptation, that is, saying such things to him!'

'If he were still only a boy, I shouldn't,' George said. 'I don't see nothing wrong with such things between men.'

19

As Sophie had predicted, the leaves were still clinging to the trees in the first weekend of November. Fran and William sat long over breakfast on the Sunday morning, making the most of a weekend that had nothing special in it. Fran remarked that she had been idle too long, and *must* begin on some work. William didn't feel any urge to follow suit. He was enjoying doing nothing, and doing it well. He said so.

'Yes – Ned noticed it,' she said. 'You were asleep in your chair the other day when he brought the logs, and he crept round you so as not to wake you. When he saw me, he winked and said, "As they all'us say, 'Laziness is no good unless it's well follered through.'"'

'"A change is as good as a rest,"' he countered. 'We haven't exactly been doing nothing. We've been pretty well occupied with other people's affairs instead of our own, that's all. We can't do much, can we, till this wedding's over? Then perhaps we may have some time for our own concerns. Which reminds me. What are we going to do about your birthday this year?'

'Nothing much,' she said. 'There's too many other things happening. It isn't a milestone birthday, like last year's was, and we couldn't hope to match that. It turned out to be so very special. I don't want to try.'

He agreed. 'Only a calendar year ago,' he said. 'It's almost incredible to look back and think of all that's happened since then. A lot of it because of your party.'

She nodded. 'I often think Time's a bit like elastic – you can't really say how long it is. It seems to make its own standards. We think we measure it out with clocks, but in fact I think it measures us out by events. Last November we'd only just got to know Bob Bellamy. What a surprise he turned out to be!'

William tossed the ball back. 'And next Saturday as ever is, we shall be in our best bibs and tuckers at his wedding,' he said. 'To a new Jane that neither he nor anybody else knew at all. Perhaps that's the strangest thing.'

'No,' she said. 'I don't agree. If I had to vote on it, I'd give my vote to Beth and Elyot. You could have knocked me down with the proverbial feather when that ramrod of a naval commander stood up and handed Beth into the dance, as if he'd been dancing all his life! It was the dancing that did it.

Daunsinge, signifyng matrimonie.

'But where did he learn to dance? He'd been in the Navy since he was sixteen! I mean – *you* surprised me the night we first danced together, though I did know how much time RAF men spent dancing. Bob Bellamy surprised me too, though the country folk have danced since time immemorial. But naval officers?'

William was enjoying watching her. His eyes twinkled as he set down his cup.

'Haven't you ever heard of Jackie Fisher?'

'Just,' she said. 'Why?'

'He was a sailor who was as crazy about dancing as you are.'

'Good for him. Who was he?'

'A sort of second Nelson. Admiral of the Fleet Lord Jackie Fisher, First Sea Lord, and the man responsible for building us the dreadnoughts that saved our bacon in 1914. Friend of Edward VII when he was Prince of Wales. And as I said, a great dancer.'

'Tell me about him.'

'How much?'

'All there is.'

This was above all what Fran enjoyed about their life together. Their absolute compatibility. She spent a moment thinking about that. Other couples could be very, very happy in a marriage, like Jess and Greg, for example. Crazy about each other, as they still were when they had come to Old Swithinford. But they had never had the absolute content that she and William shared. Jess was too much of a personality in her own right, a sort of 'professional personality', and she knew it. Greg was an artist with an artistic temperament. Fran doubted if Jess had really ever understood quite what that meant. The more of an artist he became, the less she seemed to like him, however much she still loved him. If she did. Fran sometimes wondered. And the more of a business woman she became, the less he seemed to like her. Oh dear! Fran sighed. She loved them both. William hadn't even noticed her moment of abstraction.

'All?' he asked, raising his eyebrows. 'It would take me till next Sunday.'

'Just the bit about the dancing, then. I think that people who love dancing must have some instinct that dancing is symbolic of life in general. Moving to rhythm. As one moves to the rhythms of the seasons, for instance. Making patterns, criss-crossing each other's paths, forming new groups, standing out sometimes, and all "visiting" each other in turn. Country dances symbolize all that, where everybody knows everybody else, in a place like this. But how does it fit the Navy? Tell me about Jackie Fisher. I like the sound of him.'

'Well, he really was crazy about dancing, though to do him justice, he was just as crazy about the British fleet being the best in the world. He used to hold parties on his flagship, even at sea, and make the officers dance with each other – but especially with him. He was also a ruthless disciplinarian. He'd stop a midshipman's leave for refusing to learn to dance.'

'Good for him – though it sounds a bit dubious. What did they do for music?'

William's smile turned into a grin. 'He was a good whistler. Like me. Honestly. If there was no other musician available, he whistled while he danced.

'There was a great do somewhere. Edward VII was there, and his cousin, the Grand Duchess Olga, one of the Romanovs. Jackie asked her to waltz with him, but she said she'd never learned how. So he taught her, there and then. They were both natural dancers – like you and me. Well, not altogether like us. They were only very good friends. He was happily married, and she was married to a brute of a man. He and Olga got so good at waltzing together that once, at a ball on the royal yacht, they were asked to give a demonstration. They danced a Viennese waltz, fast and furious – without touching each other. He was nearly seventy by then. It was so spectacular that the royal guests roared for an encore, but she was puffed out. So he took the floor alone, and did a sailor's hornpipe for them, true nautical fashion, whistling for himself while he danced.'

'Danced without touching each other? A Viennese waltz? How could they? What do you mean?'

'They clasped their hands behind their necks. Jolly difficult, I'd say.'

'Like this?' she asked, suiting action to word.

He was on his feet in a second. 'Exactly, like this.' He took his arms down long enough to pull her to her feet, and began to whistle 'The Merry Widow' waltz. It required concentration, but after a couple of times round the kitchen table, they were managing very well – till William ran out of breath, stopped whistling and took her into his arms to kiss her, over and over again. 'What did I ever do without you?' he said. 'Life with you is such *fun*. I'll bet Jackie Fisher would have loved you.'

'I should probably have loved him,' she said. 'He sounds a bit like you.'

'He was a ferocious disciplinarian. Ruthless, Relentless and Remorseless. Like this.'

He wound his arms round her again and kissed her relentlessly, even when she struggled because she had caught sight of Sophie, in her best Sunday-go-to-meeting outfit, standing by watching them.

Sophie was never quite sure how to deal with such situations. Her mother and Thirzah would have been scandalized at any man seen kissing his wife in broad daylight, 'be they never so married'. And as for fooling about dancing round a kitchen table in the middle of a Sunday morning . . . but then, these two were different. They'd never grown up.

She regarded them now with indulgence hidden by a straight face, as she might have done two boisterous children she felt it her duty to reprimand. Their antics gave her something very precious, though intangible, all the same. Every night, when she rose from her knees having prayed for them along with all the rest near and dear to her, and climbed into her lonely bed, the thought of them together brought back other thoughts of what might have been hers if her man hadn't been killed. They kept alive for her the memory of what it was to love and be loved. She could not have put it into words, but what she meant was that by never allowing her presence to inhibit their childlike insouciance, they somehow included her in their circle of love.

'Hello, Sophie,' said William, over Fran's shoulder. 'What are you doing here on Sunday? I was just giving Fran a history lesson.'

Sophie might think what she liked, but she could hardly allow herself to be seen approving of such frivolity. 'It didn't look much like a *'istory* lesson, to me,' she said. 'If anybody had asked me, I should ha' said as it were more like a couple o' clowns a-practising for a circus.'

Fran laughed aloud. 'So much for Admiral Lord Jackie Fisher, Professor Burbage,' she said. Her tone changed. Why was Sophie there? 'Is anything wrong with Thirzah?' she asked.

'No more'n usual. I called to see 'er on my way 'ome from church 'cos she weren't there. Says she gets short o'breath, walking up that there bit of a 'ill. So there weren't only five of us all told, besides the ringers. Whatever we shall do when the Rector goes, I don't know. We don't care a lot for 'im, I'm bound to say, but 'e's better than nobody. And he goos three weeks today. Tha's really what I come up to see you about – the do for the presentation to 'im. Dan'el told Thirz' as George Bridgefoot's real worried about it, and so am I. "Tha's the same day as 'er birthday," I says to myself, "and I wonder if any o' them is thought about that." So I come round to find out. You see, George asked Dan'el if I'd be responsible for the refreshments, even without Thirz', though I dessay Ida Barker'd 'elp me.'

'We had realized,' Fran told her, 'and decided not to do anything about my birthday. We shall be at Mr Marriner's farewell do.'

Sophie looked very relieved. 'Dan'el says George don't seem 'isself, lately. He's got rheumatiz come in one of 'is 'ips. And I know he's concerned, like, about what's going to 'appen at church. Bridgefoots has been churchwardens, down from father to son, for as long as anybody knows of, and George nat'rally expected Brian would take over when 'e couldn't go on no longer. But Brian ain't been near church for months, nor yet 'is wife. Young Charles 'as never set foot inside it since Robert Fairey's funeral. Then yest'day Sam Curtis was took to 'ospital – not that 'e's done much for this last two year or more. But it's all on George's own shoulders, now, don't you see?'

'Who's Sam Curtis?'

The look on Sophie's face showed Fran what a blunder she had made. 'Surely you know as there 'as to be two churchwardens, even if you don't belong to the church no more,' Sophie told her. 'Sam Curtis is a widderman as used to work for Tom Fairey till Tom sold up. 'E's been people's warden as long as George 'as been Rector's warden, only 'e's been ailing lately. Whoever there'll be to take 'is place, I don't know. Time was when you could all'us rely on folks to do their duty. It'll be the same wi' the ringers, afore long. When we was little, all the boys 'ad a try at bell-ringing, and them as wanted to learn were teached while they was young, like Ned. But it ain't the same now. Who wants to ring church bells? They'd rather stop at 'ome watching their televisions.'

Fran was very much aware of how much all this meant to Sophie, but she had not missed the barb about some folks not doing what was expected of them. She gently countered the charge.

'But Sophie,' she said, 'however willing we might have been to do our duty, as you put it, we shouldn't have been very welcome. They don't have people who live in sin as openly as we do for churchwardens. We were both brought up to be regular churchgoers, as you know very well. But however much we might have wanted to, Mr Marriner wouldn't have allowed us to take communion – unless we "repented" and gave each other up. The church can't have it both ways. If it asks me to choose between it and William, William wins.'

'Ssh, darling,' William said. He could see that Sophie was upset. She hadn't meant them. She couldn't, and didn't, regard them as sinners, however many times they might have broken that seventh commandment. She had meant Brian and Rosemary Bridgefoot, and other old inhabitants who had lately simply drifted away from the congregation.

William was pouring oil on the troubled water. 'We know you didn't mean us,' he said. 'Sit down, and I'll make 'levenses. Maybe we can still help. What's making George so worried about this presentation affair?'

'Well, he booked the old schoolroom for it – bearing in mind, no doubt, 'ow we'd all'us done such things afore, but that's a big bare cold barn of a place and it's the wrong time o' the year for people to turn out, if it's so foggy you can't see your 'and in front o' your face, or freezing cold and slippery underfoot. I can't count more'n a dozen or so who'll be there. It ain't worth all the trouble, lighting the fire and such for no more people than that.'

'Couldn't George have it in his house?' asked Fran.

Sophie looked embarrassed. 'That's what I said, but Dan'el said no. It would be too p'inted, like, if Brian weren't there, and he wouldn't be, 'ccording to Dan'el. Only I promised 'im I wouldn't repeat what 'e said. Things ain't at all what they should be among the Bridgefoots, on account of Brian being so thick wi' the Baileys. I see Joe up at Thirz's this morning, and he said as something 'as 'appened to upset Bailey's applecart and Brian Bridgefoot's and Vic Gifford's as well. Got 'em all in a proper sweat, it 'as, 'ccording to Joe, and it were Daffy Pugh as works for Bailey as told him. And he said when I see you again, I was to tell you as that chap up Danesum ain't well again.'

'I wonder if Beth would hold it in her house,' Fran said. 'There's plenty of room there, and all the church people know her. We could get round Elyot, I think, don't you, William?'

'Quite possible, considering it's Archie's farewell party,' William answered. 'They'll never be great friends, but they do have Beth in common. Let's walk up this afternoon and test the temperature, shall we?'

'Beth'll be at church, playing the organ,' Fran said. 'Could we go to see Mr Petrie first?'

'By car, yes. On foot, no. It gets dark too early, now.'

Sophie cheered up. 'Evensong's at three o'clock, now, 'cos it falls dark so quick. And there won't be no bells, seeing as they rung 'em this morning. It's to be 'oped there's more there than there was this morning. It does seem funny, for me to be there without Thirz'. Tha's another one o' them changes we could ha' done without.'

She left, the blue forget-me-nots in her hat bobbing up and down as she walked.

Fran looked at William, silently asking each other the question they both wanted an answer to.

'I don't see how it could have got out about Bob and the farm,' William said. 'I'd stake my life on Charles Bridgefoot's discretion. But it must be some sort of a leak concerning Castle Hill, I think. We shall have to do a bit of detective work. This bed of intrigue needs a Sherlock Holmes.'

'He wouldn't be any good, here,' she said. 'They would cast him out for being an opium addict. Now Lord Peter Wimsey . . .'

'Let's have a quick lunch, and get on the trail,' he said.

20

Petrie was not expecting them this time, and there was no reception committee of well-spoken children. They found him up and dressed, looking very tired and haggard, though cheerful. There was no sign of Crystal. The large room in which he sat was bleak and bare, though there was a good log fire burning in the grate.

He responded warmly to their visit, and to their polite inquiries. He had, he said, been impressed by Roland's quick appraisal of what he needed to know. He had forced himself to get up and get on with those things that had to be done before he could hope to get a bid for the house.

'I had other unexpected help, too,' he said. 'That house agent you sent – as queer a case of split personality as I've ever met: he's keen as mustard, business-wise, after every penny. But his religious fervour's just as keen, as far as I can judge. It irked him quite sincerely, I think, that he couldn't act for me because he's Bailey's man only just at present.' His thin face broke into a smile, half rueful, half mischievous.

'He proposed to pray for me instead. I told him I was beyond his help, there. I'm afraid I don't take very well to hot-gospellers, even if I am rapidly heading for the next world. When he persisted, I told him I had more need of the other half of a Christian's duty – to love his neighbour as himself. He could witness for the Lord till the cows came home, and it wouldn't do me or the children any good. A willing neighbour, on the other hand, might.

'He took himself off, a bit huffy, to round up the children and pray with them. But the other man who trots after him like a little dog hung back. He asked me what there was he could do to help me. A small, shy and diffident chap, called Joe, who had obviously taken what I said quite seriously. He was reluctant to leave me, and said hesitantly that he'd be back next day to see if there was anything he could do.

'He was as good as his word, too. He found me at work on the house, and offered practical help, though as he has a job in the daytime, and we haven't any light to work by in the evenings, he couldn't do a lot. But another willing pair of hands for half an hour made a lot of difference. Just being willing helped, for one thing.' He paused, as if restraining himself from boring them, though wanting to say more.

Fran helped him out. 'We don't actually know Joe, but we know a lot about him,' she said. 'From everything I hear, he is Noble by name and noble by nature.' She went on to tell him how they knew so much about Joe, and a little of Joe's own troubles in the recent past.

'I've found a real friend in Joe,' Petrie said. 'I need friends.'

'Don't we all?' said William, gently. 'Please count on us.'

'I may be glad to,' Petrie said. 'When the time comes.'

'I'll be back long before that,' William said. 'As it happens, I've got time to spare just at present, though once next weekend's over, Fran has to get down to work. I'm not much good with my hands, but I could fetch and carry.'

'A bit of intelligent conversation would probably work wonders – if you can really spare time for me.' His voice was almost pleading.

The sound of children's voices brought Fran to her feet. 'Do you mind if we slip out before Tanner sees us?' she asked. 'I'd love to see him, but we have another call to make this afternoon that may take a lot of time.'

William rose obediently, and ushered her out.

They drove into the gates of the Old Rectory just as Beth arrived on foot from playing the organ for evensong. The November dusk was already falling, and Elyot had switched on lights outside the door as well as inside to welcome her home again, though she had been gone less than an hour. In the glow of the porch lights, Fran observed her friend with a delighted eye. Nothing would ever make Beth fat, but there was an air of such robust happiness about her now that appeared to reduce her height, and the pallor which only last Easter had been so marked had been replaced by a healthy glow that made her huge dark eyes even more of a feature than they always had been. Ushering them in to welcoming greetings from Elyot, Beth slipped off her winter coat, and acknowledged both Fran and William's glances at her waist with a merry laugh. There was no doubt about it – that willowy figure was beginning to show her pregnancy.

'Stay to tea,' she said. 'I asked Daddy, but he still never comes voluntarily into Elyot's presence without long warning to psych himself up. He still goes hot under his clerical collar, I think, for treating Elyot as a seducer and me as a mad old maid. Or maybe he still feels guilt in case anyone suspects that when he married us, he knew I was already a fallen woman. Anyway, he wouldn't come.'

'Which happens to be lucky,' William said, kissing her, 'because we have been sent by George Bridgefoot and Sophie to discuss arrangements for the presentation to him.'

Elyot had been hovering, kissing Fran and waiting his turn to kiss his wife. He said, 'I don't think your father will ever be able to act normally while he's still here, my love. He just can't come to terms with the fact that you belong to me now instead of him. But we get along very well, considering. Besides, whatever he thinks, he's going to be young A.B.C.'s grandfather. He can't get round that. *And* he knows that our baby was conceived in holy wedlock. That should satisfy him. It could so easily have been otherwise – thanks to William.'

'I'm glad Fran's here to interpret that for herself,' William declared.

'Sit down while I get the tea,' Beth ordered. 'Yes, I will let you come and carry the tray, Elyot.' She smiled towards Fran, and added, 'What the next five months are going to be like, I just don't know. Be prepared up at Benedict's for a command of "Action stations!" at any minute if I happen to get caught out in the rain or produce a loud burp. Talk about an old hen with one chick.' She and Elyot went kitchenwards.

William leaned over and took Fran's hand. 'What is it, my precious?'

'Just thinking of the contrast – it's all too much for me. This beautiful house so full of warmth and comfort and cosiness, and such love and joy, but most of all the pleasure of looking forward oozing like cream over everything. And then what we've just left . . . Peter Petrie's our sort as much as Elyot or Archie or Eric – but what's he got, or got to look forward to? And the children! Why should Beth's baby and Roland's grow up loved and wanted in the lap of luxury, and little Cupid be in an orphanage? Or in a hippy camp with a mother who doesn't want him? It isn't fair! Why does God let it happen?'

'Ssh! You mustn't let Beth hear you. Even Job couldn't find an answer to that sort of question. Keep your mind on Archie and this party of his. That's what we're here for.'

He squeezed her hand, and she nodded. She knew he wouldn't ignore what she said, however much he played it down at the moment. The tea arrived.

English afternoon tea taken with compatible friends, she thought, must be one of the few bits of civilizing ritual left in the twentieth century, though that, too, was dying fast. They enjoyed it while William explained the difficulties Sophie had outlined, and Fran left it to him, knowing how diplomatically it had to be handled.

'Look, William, I want time to think it over, and to talk about it in private with Elyot. And Father. That's only fair to him. I did so hope they'd let him go with a bit of goodwill.'

Now it was Elyot on the alert, not wanting Beth to get distressed. He changed the subject. 'Is Thirzah any better?' he asked. 'Or ever likely to be able to come back to work for us again? Beth declares that she's always been used to working hard and loves doing her own housework, but it's the wrong time for Thirzah to desert us. And what's going to happen after young A.B.C.'s born? We shall have to have help then. Bob Bellamy seems to have appropriated the best domestic help there's ever been round here. What's the score up at Castle Hill, now? What's happened to Jane Hadley? She was, apparently, an absolute treasure, but I can hardly pinch her from my best man, can I? We haven't seen Bob anywhere for ages. Beth's heard lurid tales of them "living in sin" together. Good for old Bob, if it's true. Do you know anything about Bob's plans?'

They sought each other's eyes, and took the plunge to tell. Beth and Elyot listened like children to the fairy-story it all resembled, holding hands.

'Whatever Daddy thinks of Old Swithinford,' said Beth, when the recital was finished, 'I think it's a magic place! Isn't it absolutely wonderful! I wish we could go to the wedding. Bob helped us to have the most wonderful wedding ever – and you two, of course.'

'Yes,' said William, with a wry smile. 'It seems to be our lot in life to get other couples married.'

Fran wished he wouldn't let his own feelings show quite so much, even to friends such as these. She *truly* didn't care. 'I wish everybody could be as happy as we are, or you two, and Bob and Jane,' she said. 'But there's always the other side, to keep a sort of balance, I suppose.' And she launched into telling them about the Petries.

'I shall make it my business to go and see them some time soon,' said Beth. Being the Commander's wife had not stopped the reactions of the parson's daughter.

'What we have told you is all in confidence until after next Saturday, and perhaps after that. Until Jane feels able to make her transformation known.'

'Such good news will break out of its own accord,' Beth said. 'So we shan't have to bite our tongues for long. What was that noise? It sounded like the letter-box.'

Elyot went to look and came back with a letter in his hand, addressed to Beth.

'It's from Daddy,' she said, turning pale, and holding the letter gingerly, as if afraid of it. The lit-up exultation of the last half-hour drained from her as she turned it over. 'Whatever can he have to write to me that he couldn't say? I was talking to him less than three hours ago.'

Elyot took the letter from her, slit the envelope, and handed it back. They all kept silence till she had finished reading it. She sat looking stunned with her hands folded over the letter in her lap, until Elyot went to her and took it from her.

'May I?' he said.

At the sound of his voice she stood up and threw herself into his arms, clinging to him with her face hidden against him. 'Read it out loud,' she said.

Peering over her shoulder, Elyot did as she asked.

My dear child,

The taxi is waiting, and by the time you have opened this, I shall be on my way to Heathrow, where I shall catch my plane to Singapore early tomorrow.

I am simply taking the coward's way out because I cannot face the embarrassment of the official leavetaking and presentation planned. However well intentioned, it would have been false. I know, as well as you do and the faithful of my flock do, how little they will miss me. I have been such a failure here that the only regret I have is in leaving you, my dear child, and those friends I have made of late since you brought me to my senses.

Even had I been well, I should still have been a square peg in a round hole in so truly rural a living as Old Swithinford. For my own sanity, I must go now where what little I can do is needed. I am on my way to join the Church's Mission to Seamen, in Singapore. I will let you know where I am as soon as I am settled. What thanks I give to God that I leave you so safely and so happily in Elyot's care! Perhaps I was sent to Old Swithinford just to do His will in ensuring you such a husband. If I had stayed, we could have become great friends, I think.

My greatest regret is that I shall not have the pleasure of being on hand when my grandchild is born, and I shall, of course, be anxious about you till I hear the news that all is well. I would like to think that you might perhaps give me the chance to come back on a visit to the christening, and receive him (or her) into the church myself. I should like that.

Whatever is left in the cottage is all yours. Do whatever you like with it. It is entirely my fault that you have no happier memories of it as a home.

Forgive me if you can, and never, never doubt my abiding love for you, my loyal, loving daughter.

I shall carry with me always the vision of your happy face in St Saviour's church the day you became Elyot's wife. That you may both remain as happy together always as you were that day is the constant prayer of

Your ever-loving
Father.

The silence in the room as his voice stopped was almost tangible. Nobody moved, except Elyot who closed both arms tighter round Beth's tall, slender form. Then she gently disengaged herself, and tucked an errant strand of hair back into her 'cottage-loaf' topknot.

'Fetch some drinks, Elyot, please,' she said. 'Let's all drink to him. In my opinion, that's the most sensible thing he has ever done since first setting foot in Old Swithinford!'

Mayhap Tomorrow Cometh Not

The stunned village, when the news broke of the Rector's premature and hasty departure, split three ways. His erstwhile small but faithful congregation, excluding George, was dumb with shock that any clergyman could so disgrace his cloth. Sophie acted as one bereaved, and went about her tasks in rather truculent silence. George did his best in Marriner's defence, going out of his way to let it be known that indeed the summons to Singapore had been very sudden and the notice short. The Rector had dutifully consulted the Bishop and George, who had both sent him off with their blessing. (George did not admit to anyone but himself how relieved he was.) In George's camp were the Rector's daughter and her personal friends, who didn't seem at all distressed or disturbed. This fact caused some puzzlement to the third group, who, led by the gossip-mongers, opined that whatever anybody chose to pretend, 'there was more to his going than met the eye.'

Talk passed from mouth to mouth in furtive whispers, and everyone avoided Beth and her friends as if they might have had the plague. Which, as Fran remarked, was an unlooked-for mercy, because it provided such a marvellous screen for their own so uncharacteristically secret doings about Bob and Jane.

Even the weather helped. Saturday morning was foggy, though experienced eyes predicted that it would soon lift. Under its protection, Charles Bridgefoot dressed himself in his new outfit, and covered it up with his old mackintosh. He put only his head into the kitchen at Temperance to tell his mother he didn't know when he would be back. As his parents were no longer on speaking terms with each other, and he had already told them that he and Charlie were going to London for the day, neither of them even bothered to do more than nod to him.

He set off through the fog to meet Charlie, relieved to have got away so easily and excited if a bit apprehensive. He was an untried traveller venturing into unknown social territory.

In the same rather furtive fashion William went to collect the bride-groom. He found Bob ready and waiting, giving last-minute instructions to a couple who were being left to keep their eyes on his house and to feed and care for his domestic animals and the old cat up at the little church. He had not told them where he was going, nor quite how long he would be away. They asked no questions, because they would have done anything for him, since the way he had helped on the day that Arnold Bailey had blown the head off their child's pet kitten.

Fran was surprised at Bob's apparent sang-froid. She looked smart, and Bob's artistic eye surveyed her with appreciation and a twinkle that told her that he had guessed her fears about him. So she told him outright that she had been worried about his state of mind. How come he was so calm and purposeful?

He replied as he could have done only to her. 'I ought to be used enough to the idea,' he said. 'I've dreamt it often enough – only I always used to wake up before the lady became real. Perhaps that's why I used to cry when I woke up, when I was little. The lady in the picture was looking at the man as I've seen you look at William, and I wanted somebody to look at me like that. Sometimes I used to think she did – till I saw you and knew who she was. I had to give up hope, then, but I kept on dreaming it just the same. And Jane came.

'I daren't let myself believe there could be any better ending in reality than there has ever been in my dream. But – well, I've done a lot of thinking. If it had been a bad dream, I should have believed in myself, and waited for it to happen. So I asked myself why I shouldn't believe in a good one. I reckoned that I was as big a fool as most other folks are – they'll believe anything bad as threatens, but they never give good luck a chance. I made up my mind to believe in it. Then I knew it would be all right.'

William was listening, as always surprised by his conventionally 'uneducated' friend's philosophical turn of mind. 'And the auguries for today are propitious?' he said.

Bob grinned. 'Ah, bor, I reckon so, if you mean what I think you mean. Ol' fen tigers like me don't hev no call to carry a dictionary full o' them long words round in our 'eads like you scholards do.'

'If we don't go,' Fran said, 'we shall miss the train, and the dream won't come true.'

In the first-class railway carriage, seated opposite Charlie, who was between her father and Charles, Fran went into her top gear. Charlie was wearing a simple suit of woollen material that showed up every line of her slim figure. She had piled her striking chestnut hair into a plaited crown in which deep gold ribbons to tone with her suit were intertwined. For a split second, Fran felt old, compared with that glowing symbol of youth in flame that Charlie presented to the eye. She watched Charles's face as he reached for Charlie's hand, and saw him close his eyes on the vision. As if he were afraid she wasn't real.

'He's afraid his dream will never come true,' she said to herself. 'It has to, somehow or other. It must. If we all wish hard enough, it will.' She closed her own eyes for a moment and wished so hard that it became nearly a prayer. When she opened them again, she met Charlie's dark lustrous eyes directly upon her. The girl gave her an almost imperceptible nod.

Keyed up as she was herself, Fran understood. Charlie had inherited so much of her father's strange sixth sense that she had known the gist of Fran's thoughts, and was deliberately reassuring her. 'And all shall be well,' quoted Fran to herself silently, and gave herself up to enjoying the present. It was going to be a happy day.

She went up to the Old Rectory the next day to give Beth a detailed account of it, as promised. The sight of Jane on her father's arm, that thin, haggard, set-faced, poverty-stricken proud woman they had previously known, looking so elegant and happy in a long-skirted suit of heavy cream silk, with ruffles of old Brussels lace at her throat, and her sleek bobbed head covered by a Juliet cap of the same materials, pinned there by a jewelled brooch; the dignity and grace of Caxton Hall register office, and of the registrar himself, making the ceremony lack little other than the heart-wrenching tones of the organ; the reception in a private suite in a nearby high-class hotel; and the embrace between Jane and Charlie, long and tremulous, as if they were sealing a long-term pact.

Then the happy wedding breakfast, at which everybody had relaxed, even Charles. Mr Gordon had gone out of his way to make the boy feel one of the family, as it were, admitting to himself that he had not expected the country boy to whom Nick had owed so much in the past to be anything like the handsome, shy but self-contained young man who had been presented to him. While as for Charlie . . . she had simply been herself, Fran said, which was Charlie at her very best. She radiated a happiness that had flowed over them all.

Fran laughed as she described to Beth the scene as Jane's father succumbed to Charlie's charm, wondering how the 'man from the fen' his long-lost daughter had set her heart on could have possibly produced a girl like that as an added bonus to his pleasure.

Fran had almost seen the moment when it had struck him that Charlie was no longer 'just' Bob's daughter. Acting on impulse, he had leaned over, and planted a kiss fair and square, without warning, on the girl's lovely mouth.

Taken absolutely by surprise, Charlie had first reciprocated in a very satisfactory way, and then reacted in her own characteristic fashion.

'*Tiens!*' she said. '*Merci, m'sieur. Mais qu'est-ce-qu'il y a qui se passe?*'

Astounded, he answered her in French. 'Because I have just realized that the most beautiful girl in the world is now my granddaughter. And she speaks French!'

'*Und Deutsche*,' said William, delighted.

'*E Espagnol*,' added Jane.

'Not Arabic?' Gordon asked.

Charlie, blushing delightfully, shook her head. 'But I expect I could learn,' she said. 'I like languages.'

'Then say this after me till you can say it absolutely correctly,' he said. It took her several goes at it before he was satisfied, and he kissed her again.

'What have I been saying?' she asked.

Jane laughed aloud, her pleasure in the incident warming them all. 'I love you, Grandfather Effendi,' she translated.

Fran got up to go, having emptied her budget of details of the wedding. 'So we saw Mr and Mrs Bellamy off to Wales in a hired car, to stay in the Hadley-Gordon cottage where Jane was born, and came home,' she said. 'So that's it.'

'Till Jane and Bob turn up here again and the secret is let out,' Beth replied. 'Just imagine what tales will get about. The mind boggles. Anything and everything but the truth.'

'I can't believe there is any intention of causing real harm. People such as Beryl Bean just can't help gossiping.'

'We should miss a lot of fun without her,' Beth said. 'She only becomes dangerous when she overdoes it.'

'Mm. As Lewis Carroll said about adjectives:

> 'Such adjectives, like pepper
> Give zest to what you write,
> And if you strew them sparsely
> They whet the appetite.
> But if you lay them on too thick
> They spoil the matter quite.'

Beth was still laughing as she waved Fran goodbye.

22

Sophie seemed never to have recovered her spirits after the shock of the Rector's going. Fran did not need reminding that the church was one of the props that upheld Sophie's existence. Benedict's was another, and the remnants of Kezia's family now a poor third.

Fran knew the church to be temporarily troubled, though as far as she could see there was nothing to cause the mood that seemed to have settled over Sophie. Thirzah being ill meant extra for Sophie to do, because she went to see her sister twice every day; but work was the last thing to bother Sophie, especially if it were also duty. Fran did not dare ask if Sophie were getting too tired. She did remark that Hetty was better.

''E were right,' Sophie had replied, nodding sideways in the direction of William's study. 'More fool us for letting 'er get away with it as long as she did. If you ask me, tha's one thing as is wrong wi' Thirz', though. She can't abear to think that anybody can get along without 'er. She's that aggravated 'cos she don't know what's going on up Hen Street as she can 'ardly bear 'er life. She don't get out and about, see, like she used to, so she only knows what Dan'el or me can tell 'er, and that ain't a lot. Even Joe don't go there like he used to, 'cos 'e's so took up with this 'ere preaching, and looking after that gipsy lot up Danesum. I don't know what the world is coming to, that I don't.'

Sophie's tone convinced Fran that she had not got to the bottom of what was wrong. She tried again the next day.

'I thought you'd want to know about last Saturday's wedding,' she said.

'I thought if you wanted me to know, you'd tell me all in your own good time,' Sophie replied, with some acerbity. 'I don't wish 'em no 'arm, but I can't see as what they get up to from now on is any concern o' mine. Things don't work out for many folks like they have done for her.'

Fran, rebuffed, was also shocked. This was not the Sophie she knew.

Sophie had seized a broom, and was attacking the kitchen floor with huge, aimless lunges, one of which caught a very startled sleeping Cat and swept her across the floor. Fran ran to pick up her disgruntled pet, and saw tears dripping from the end of Sophie's nose.

She took charge, putting the cat down and altering the tone of her voice. 'Now stop it, Sophie!' she said. 'I don't know till you tell me what it is you're so upset about, but whatever it is, you needn't take it out on me or on Cat. Sit down, and tell me. Are you worried about Thirzah? Have we offended you in any way? Or what? Come on, now. It's no use pretending that something isn't very wrong. I'm going to call William. You might as well tell him yourself as leave it to me to tell him afterwards. Is it anything that we can help you with? Now just sit still and don't move till I come back.'

By the time she returned with William, Sophie had begun to cry in earnest. They left her to cry while they made tea and sat down beside her.

They expected that when she was ready she would pour out to them whatever grievances she had.

She set down her cup untasted, and began. 'It's all too much to be beared,' she said. 'Nothing and nobody is the same as it used to be. I never thought I should live to see the day when even going to church only made things worse for me. But then, church ain't God's 'ouse no more – well, not like we've all'us knowed it. Seems now as it don't belong to nobody not even us as were born and bred to it, but only to such as don't care nothing for it. It might as well fall down first as last, far as I can see. It's like what Miss used to tell us about rats leaving a ship what was a-going to sink. Folks is leaving the church just like them rats.'

Fran and William were quite at a loss to know what she was talking about. They had been so occupied with Bob and Jane's wedding that they had hardly given a thought to the effect Archie Marriner's sudden desertion might have had on church affairs.

'It's as if the Rector going like 'e did let everything else fall to bits,' Sophie said. 'When you first come 'ere, in the old Rector's time, folks all done their bit. George and Sam had been churchwardens for so long they knowed about doing things right, and so did everybody else, like. We all knowed our places, as you might say. We used to 'ev a vestry meeting about three times a year, and that were that, all fair and square.

'But 'im going off like that, seems we ain't in charge of our own church no more. Last week, the Archdeacon or somebody called a meeting about what's going to 'appen now. It was the first meeting as I ever remember since Mam died when Thirz' didn't have most o' the say – but she weren't there. And a lot as nobody expected to be there was there.

'First this chap tells us we ain't likely to get no new Rector, so till it's settled we shall hev to hev any parson as'll come to take the sacraments, and that mawkin of a lay-reader from Hen Street'll take evensong. Then George said as 'ow 'is 'ip was so bad now, 'e couldn't keep the bell-ringing up, let alone be the leader and teacher like 'e 'as been. 'E said 'e 'oped one o' the others would take over, and if 'is 'ip got better 'e'd all'us stand in for a ringer as couldn't be there. But by that, another one o' the reg'lar ringers stood up and said as they was all agreed it couldn't go on as it 'ad been. It were taking up a lot too much time. What good were it, he said, them ringing for services when only four or five people come? They had settled it atween theirselves as they wouldn't only ring four o' the bells for one service a month, and that only to keep 'em in practice for weddings and such, as they got paid for. They said they relied on George to manage the calling bell still for services.

'After that, it were Mis' Franks's turn – 'er as was the Rector's daughter. She say she were willing to go on playing the organ a bit longer, but she didn't know how she'd manage when 'er baby was born, especially if she couldn't get 'elp in the 'ouse. So come Easter, there won't be no music for 'ymns neither.

'The rural dean had sent a paper for George to read out to us, an' all. It said as 'ow there was a lot of work needed on the tower, and we should 'ave to think about raising a lot more money ourselves for what 'e called our Quoter. I don't know who 'e thinks is going to raise it, seeing as nobody cares whether the church falls down now or not. It'll take more'n a few fêtes and whist-drives and do's as me and Thirz' and Dan and Ida Barker and such can 'elp with to raise thousands o' pounds like they want. But even that weren't the worst.

'George told us as Sam knowed he weren't never coming out of 'ospital no more, and wanted us to get somebody in 'is place straight away. I couldn't see who it could be only Dan, and was expecting George to say so. But before 'e 'ad a chance to open 'is mouth, the Archdeacon said 'e was aware o' the situation and a name had been put for'ard a'ready, a man as 'ad been born and brought up in the village and was able now to do 'is bit for the church. This name 'ad been proposed to 'im, 'e said, by a businessman who was also prepared to be very generous to the restoration fund. And by that, 'e was 'oping we should accept Mr Kenneth Bean as the new warden!

'Well, we was all so thunderstruck, like, that nobody said nothing against it, so it were settled – just like that. Kid got up and made a speech, and Beryl set there a-simpering till I felt as if I should like nothing better than to shove a 'ymn book in 'er gob. It 'ad all been arranged be'ind our backs. We could see that!

'Ah! If Thirz' 'ad been there, she would 'ave upped and asked 'ow it 'ad come as somebody as 'adn't set foot in church for years only at weddings and funerals should be put forr'ard in front of people as 'ad been reg'lar and faithful all their lives – but then, Thirz' weren't there, were she? So that's 'ow it stands, and I don't ever want to goo near the church no more.

'I don't know 'ow me and Dan got back to Thirz's 'ouse, to tell 'er, we was so shook up. But then Dan told us 'ow it's through Bailey as Kid Bean's been made churchwarden. Bailey 'as give Kid a contract to supply all the fittings and such for all the 'ouses 'e builds round 'ere. It'll make Kid into a millionaire, according to Dan'el. But Dan says as what Bailey's after is to get 'is foot in the church and 'is 'and over all the village. Kid Bean's just doing 'is dirty work for 'im.'

Fran and William, appalled, were silent. Sophie's face was working, and she was making strange noises in her throat as if she was choking on words she was trying to hold back.

'And to think,' said Sophie, suddenly breaking into loud, passionate weeping, 'to think that 'Im Above should let it all 'appen, just like 'E let my Jelly get killed! That money as Kid set up the shop with should ha' been our'n, Jelly's and mine, if 'e'd a-lived only six weeks longer! I all'us said bad would become of 'im winning that there dratted premium bond – but who would ha' thought it could ever 'ave come to this? And 'er – Beryl Bean, I mean – lording it over me in church . . .'

That was the last straw. For the first time ever, they witnessed their brave, stolid, reliable, upright and sedate Sophie disintegrate into a defeated woman as distraught and helpless as her sister Hetty in a fit of 'sterricks'. She broke into a storm of loud, wailing sobs, all her habitual control and dignity thrown to the wind.

'I don't want to goo to church never no more!' she said. 'I don't want to live no longer. I want to go and be with my Jelly. What am I got to live for, if I can't look forrard to going to church no more come Sundays and 'oly days? It ain't right. Nothink about it's right.'

She was gasping, sobbing, moaning and howling out protests against everything and everybody, including God Himself. Fran spoke soothingly and laid a hand on Sophie's clasped ones. Sophie shook it off as if it had been a tarantula. Words had no effect on her at all. Fran looked in desperation towards William.

William, pale but purposeful, stood up. 'Doctor?' mouthed Fran. William shook his head. He seized the clean teacloth hanging on the Aga rail, plunged it under the cold tap and turning swiftly struck Sophie a whiplash blow first on one side of her face, and then on the other. The cold water ran down into the front of her dress, and into the mouth she opened to scream, but seemed unable to close again. She held her breath till Fran was almost at terrified screaming point herself.

Then, after what seemed to them both an eternity, Sophie gave a great gasp, drew in a long breath, let it out in a tremendous sigh, and slumped forward on to the table with her face in her hands.

'Genuine hysteria,' said William succinctly. 'Mop her up while I get her some brandy. I doubt if we've heard the whole of it, yet. She's been bottling this up ever since Jelly was killed. She may be exaggerating it a bit, but I guess she understood only too well what was really going on at that church meeting. I think perhaps we ought to get her to lie down. She's absolutely exhausted.'

William raised her head and managed to get a spoonful of brandy down her. She gagged, and coughed and spluttered, but the stimulant worked, and they had to exert a good deal of authority to get her to lie on the sofa in the sitting-room.

'Do drink the rest of the brandy,' Fran said. 'You'll feel better now you've told us.'

Sophie sat up, and her voice, bitter though it still was, was once more her own. 'I reckon Satan 'isself is let loose. And who is there now to stop him ravening like a wild beast among us, I don't know. The Thackerays and the Faireys is all gone and George Bridgefoot's grey 'airs are being brought down with sorrer to the grave. There ain't no more like them – and like the Bible says, "if the salt shall lose its savour, wherewith shall it be salted?" Them as ought to be coming forrard to take their places are all got other things to do – or else they don't believe neither in God nor in 'Is church no more. What does such as Jess and 'er man care about the church? Will that Bellamy and 'is posh new wife ever set foot in it to thank 'Im Above for all 'E's give to them? Does Choppen, as owns 'alf the village, goo near? Not one of 'em.

'And do you two, as my own mother brought up, very near, care whether there's a church 'ere no more or not? Not as I can see! It's 'cos none o' your sort 'as ever done what they ought to ha' done as we are ever come to this! If folks like you had ha' done your duty, there wouldn't ha' been no gaps left for Bailey and 'is imps o' mischief to get through. But you didn't. You left it all to poor old George, and to such as me. And I'm sorry to say it, but it's the truth, all the same. I shouldn't ha' been doing my duty if I 'adn't told you so to your faces. But I've 'ad my say, and I feel better enough to go and get on with my work. That is, if you still want me to. If not, I'll go 'ome. You've only got to tell me.' She stood up, ready to leave.

Fran rose, and went to her, putting an arm round her to lead her back to her seat again. This time Sophie did not shake off the soothing hand.

'Don't be silly, Sophie,' she said. 'We couldn't do without you. And we ought to have seen that you were getting more and more upset, but we were so concerned with Bob's wedding that we overlooked everything else. You know why we haven't taken part in any church affairs. They wouldn't have had us.'

'How do you know? 'Ave you ever tried, just as ordinary worshippers, like? Not above three or four times since you come 'ere, to my recollection. And God knows you two 'ave got enough to be thankful for! But be that as it may, you won't get no dinner if I don't get on with it.'

She gave them a wan smile, and turned towards the sink.

They retired, Fran rather shaken and inclined to tremble. They went towards William's study in the flat – the 'little bit extra at the back' that they had named 'Eeyore's Tail' – as being the most private.

'Whew!' said Fran. 'That was a facer. If she's got it right, it's as if the world has stopped turning on its axis and all the loose bits are flying off into space.'

'You mean the church supplies the centrifugal force that holds the village together? Yes, you've found words to express what Sophie can only feel in her bones. Bailey's a far more dangerous adversary than I had thought. Crafty and clever as well as ruthless. He's been waiting his chance to get in on the inside. Well, thanks to Sophie's common sense and moral courage we have been warned.'

They said no more, and went about their various tasks till lunch-time. Sophie was almost her usual self again. She was comforted that having done what she saw as her duty, it had not robbed her of her dearest friends. She was, if anything, elated, having risked all for the sake of dearly held principles, and won. She was assured, in her own mind, that whether or not they yet knew it, she had enrolled Fran and William in the ranks of the church's allies.

And so, in fact, it proved. It was William who reopened the subject, telling Sophie what he had been thinking.

'Bailey has declared war, and made his first move,' he said. 'Thanks to you, Sophie, we may have been warned in time. None of those you mentioned would want to see Bailey take over from people like the Bridge-foots. We shall have to organize some sort of opposition to him. So cheer up – we are all on your side. You'll have to let us know what he is up to. We'll let the dust settle a bit, and think of something. Look – to begin with, I promise you that Fran and I, and perhaps some more of us, will be at church on Christmas morning, this year. Will that satisfy you for now?'

She handed him a plate of lamb stew salted with thankful tears.

When she took their coffee into the sitting-room after lunch, she was quite her ordinary self again. 'I forgot to tell you,' she said, 'as Bailey 'as give Daffy Pugh the sack. All them houses to be built on Lane's End are sold, and there ain't going to be no more up Castle 'Ill, so Daffy's job 'ere is done for the time being. I know that's the truth, 'cos Joe told me. He's real upset at losing 'is friend Daffy, but per'aps 'e'll stop at 'ome a bit more with our Het now. Oh – and Dr Henderson told Thirz' yest'day as 'e's giving up soon. Retiring, like. Everything's a-changing.'

'Not everything, Sophie,' William said. 'Not Fran and me and you and Ned and Cat and Benedict's. But in any case, it's what the Bible says. "Time and chance happeneth to them all." We don't all believe in yesterday quite as much as the Beatles do.'

23

Beth Franks had stood at the gate of the church after that meeting until all the others had left, her feelings in turmoil. She who was such a recent newcomer had identified herself absolutely with those who until now had upheld the church as solidly as its thirteenth-century pillars. She had seen the pain in Sophie's face, read the despair in George Bridgefoot's limp, noted the heavy tread of Daniel Bates's boots down the path, and watched Ned gaze at the bell sallies, settle his cap resignedly and trudge out into the darkness. It was as if they were all saying goodbye to something they had known and loved and trusted in, but would never be there again.

She felt guilty, though she knew she had no reason to be. It was only how things had turned out, the way the finger of fate had pointed, that made it seem that she had had any influence on what had happened. If she had not left her father unexpectedly and hastily last Easter to get married, he would not have given up the living. She had brought home to him how hopeless his ministry here had been. While there had been a priest-in-charge, however unsuitable, it might have been possible to weather the storm until the tide had turned. But the Rector had cut and run. That was what had really brought about the sad outcome of the meeting she had just left.

She needed to compose herself before going home, because these feelings were not such as she cared to show to Elyot, much as he loved her. Much as she loved him. Her sense of guilt was a very small price to pay for all that she had gained. She felt Elyot's child stir in her womb, and her heart swelled with love, and with overwhelming thanksgiving. Who was she to say that in the long run what happened might not turn out well after all?

That some people had been, and others would be, hurt, there was no denying; but the end was not yet. While there was new life, there was also new hope.

She turned the corner by the lych-gate, close by the Old Rectory, Elyot's large, elegant house – no, *her home* – almost flood-lit by the number of lights he had switched on to guide her back to him. She began to run, wanting to be there and in his arms. How extraordinary it was that at this time last year, she hadn't even met him. It wouldn't be a full calendar year till Fran's birthday on 30 November. Fran and William had foregone any celebration of Fran's birthday this year because it had clashed with the date planned for her father's formal farewell. She had heard no mention of anything being set up since it had become clear that the evening would be free, after all. Yet that evening would be an anniversary for her and Elyot, too – and they owed all their present happiness to Fran and William. Was there still time for them to do anything to repay such an enormous debt? She began to have ideas.

As she greeted her husband she forgot the meeting and began at once to tell him of her plan to repay last year's golden hospitality at Benedict's by having their first social gathering at the Old Rectory on the anniversary of it.

If she had asked Elyot for the moon, he would have climbed to the t'gallant cross-trees on a windjammer going round the Horn in an attempt to reach it for her. She had completely changed his life, and he could still hardly believe it.

'I'll ring Monica tomorrow,' Beth said. 'They may be planning something too.'

Monica said that they had thought of it, but they had all been so occupied with other things that so far they had done nothing about it. It was a lovely idea, and they'd be very happy to go along with it, except for one thing – couldn't it be held at Monastery Farm? She had no babysitters. Beth was disappointed and said so.

'Look,' said Monica. 'It just happens that I can't spare another minute to talk about it now, because Greg will be here at any moment for a long and much overdue business session and I haven't fed the twins yet. Let's join forces. What fun to look forward to! Can you leave it with me for a couple of days? Then I'll be back to you.'

'We would love to have you all here, if we could raise a babysitter you could trust,' said Beth. 'I shall put my thinking-cap on.' That conversation had taken place on the Saturday of Bob and Jane's wedding.

Greg had arrived home to Southside House the night before, having been away for almost a week. He had rung up every night he had been away, but found Jess very cool and distant. Apart from her spurning his sexual advances – which she had been doing more and more ever since they had arrived in Old Swithinford – and putting her work and Eric Choppen's interests before his, he had been very hurt by her suspicion and insinuations of his interest in other women. Much as he had always loved her, and still did, he could not forgive her for her behaviour last New Year's Eve when Monica had so dramatically announced her pregnancy. Jess had made it plain, in front of them all, that she suspected him of being the father of Monica's child; she had not apologized, nor made any move to put things right after Roland had appeared and claimed the paternity.

Things had never been the same between them since. The whole event had curdled the Taliaferro marriage. The bitterness on each side had gone on growing. Jess still avoided having anything whatsoever to do with Monica, and spat like a cat at any mention of the babies. On the other hand, she went out of her way to be 'his' Jess – everywhere except in bed – so long as they avoided any mention of Monica. Which made things very difficult, considering that he was now Monica's business partner.

For the first time in his whole life, his artistic talents had proved to be viable commercial assets as part of Monica's exclusive advertisements in high-class 'glossies' for women. With Monica's elegant designs and the business acumen she had inherited from her father, she had been rising fast as a name in the fashion world when love in the person of Fran's son had caught her out and turned her into a happy housewife and the mother of twins. She had never felt more creative, but she needed a personal representative whom she could trust, and could talk to face to face at frequent intervals. Greg's business sense had never been very acute, but his personal charm made up for any deficiencies in that quarter. So far their joint venture had been very successful, and they were now forging ahead, with great plans to make a bid for the very highest reaches of the fashion world.

His comings and goings to and from home were irregular, and once at home, he had to spend a considerable amount of time with Monica. Jess had disliked the arrangement from the start. She had resented his suddenly coming into his own as a bringer-in of income, because until then she had been the one who had scraped them their meagre living. She was proud of having done so – and then just when *she* had established herself in a secure position financially, he had come by a reasonably lucrative job himself, and moreover one that meant he was no longer at home to do the household chores.

He resented the amount of time and interest she gave to her job, and to her boss, Eric Choppen. Since Monica's babies had been born, Eric had hardly been able to drag himself away from them, and had consequently left more and more responsibility to Jess.

Greg would have expected her to be delighted by Eric's trust in her, but she complained to him bitterly of overwork, and was sarcastic that the reason for it should be Eric's 'obsession' with his grandchildren. She held herself conspicuously aloof from Monastery Farm, though she lived almost within spitting distance of it. As she told Greg, she had no interest whatsoever in the little brats for their own sake – as he had, she said, lip curling with sarcasm. She couldn't 'drool' over them as he did. That hurt him, because they had hoped, vainly, for children of their own. What he couldn't understand was why she should now seem so intent on punishing him. It had never been conclusively proved which of them had to take the blame for their childlessness.

His conscience was not quite so clear towards her now as it had always been before. He had at first hated having to be away from home overnight, but now, enjoying a sense of freedom, he made no special efforts, when all there was to come home to was a charming hostess instead of a loving wife. Just lately, as well, he had found Anne Rushlake there far too often when he did get home, 'keeping Jess company'. Family relationships had deteriorated, too. Jess had always resented Fran having first place in William's life. That Roland was Fran's son therefore complicated matters for Greg with regard to Monica, who could hardly not be classed as 'family' as well, now.

The last three times he had been away, he had been delayed in getting home. This time he had rung home to say he had met an old friend and didn't know what time, if at all, he would be back that night.

Jess had put the telephone down and gone through to where Anne Rushlake was sitting in his chair.

'Missed his train again,' Jess said, flatly. 'Met an old friend.'

Anne smiled. 'I wonder how many times I've heard men telling their wives that!' she said. 'I should have expected Greg to have had a bit more ingenuity.'

Jess topped up Anne's glass, and poured herself a stiff whisky. 'It really does begin to look suspicious, doesn't it?' she said. 'But I can't believe it of Greg. He isn't that sort.'

'All men are that sort,' Anne said. 'They don't all actually get to carrying it through, but they all would if they could, believe me.'

Jess didn't know whether to be glad of Anne's support, or to hate her for her insinuations. Like Fran, Jess had never quite made up her mind about Anne.

She was extraordinarily well-preserved for her age, with a slim, slightly masculine figure, a youthfully clean-cut face and pretty hair. She was very business-like with a somewhat hard, brisk manner. On the other hand, there was a kind of primness about her, especially in her speech, that suggested a Victorian schoolmistress rather than a worldly-wise businesswoman, as did the smell of Dettol she left in her wake. Greg asserted that she put Dettol into the washing-up water, because if ever she did the washing up at Southside House, his cup tasted of Dettol for days afterwards.

Jess wasn't feeling very well-disposed towards her at that particular moment. She spoke with something of a bite in her voice. 'You seem to know a lot about such things,' she said.

'Oh, I do,' Anne answered. 'I do. I spent all the war in a government office, helping to run a seemingly innocuous magazine that in fact carried disguised intelligence. It gave a lot of men very good excuses for not catching trains, and meeting old friends. It was a lot of fun.'

'I suppose,' Jess said, not believing the implied assertion that Anne knew what she did from experience, 'that when they went on such dangerous duties, they took their secretaries with them.'

'They certainly did. There were only three of us, and we had a whale of a time.'

Jess didn't know whether to believe her. Anne had gone home before Greg came in, and began to tell Jess of the man he had met.

'I was with Jon Ashbury,' he said. 'He knew the fellow who begged us to go back and have dinner with him well – had known him for years, a doctor now in a wheelchair. An extraordinary old chap. A wealthy old bachelor living in a great mansion of a house with his valet-nurse-chauffeur and a housekeeper.'

'Fascinating,' said Jess, thinking of what Anne had said. 'Which of Monica's new models did you sell him for his housekeeper?'

There ensued one of the worst rows they had ever had in twenty-five years of marriage.

In consequence, it was a rather subdued and edgy Greg who faced Monica next morning. She noticed, but asked no questions. She hugged him as she always did, sat him down comfortably in an armchair, dumped a baby on him, and lifted her jumper to put the other twin to her nipple.

Greg put the baby he held up to his face to feel the softness of its skin, then tickled the bare bit showing over her nappy till she gurgled and wriggled. He looked at Monica through a mist of tears. No wonder all the great artists had wanted to paint madonnas! Only they hadn't painted real babies. It was, he thought, the most wonderful sight an artist could ever try to reproduce, that of a beautiful young mother breastfeeding a baby. It made sense of everything.

'Will you let me paint you – just like that, Monica?' he said.

'Of course, if you'd like to.'

'Roland wouldn't mind?'

'Why on earth should he? I warn you, though, if it turns out well, Dad would want to buy it.'

'I shouldn't let him – but if it was any good I'd give it to him. I guess every man who considers himself an artist has a secret longing to try that.

It's perhaps the acid test of what sort of an artist he is. I've always wanted to.'

Monica understood at once. With Jess as the Madonna, and the child his own, of course. 'Poor old Greg,' she said.

There was a long silence till she said, 'Here, change babies. This little monster thinks I'm a Jersey cow. Take this nappy and put it over your shoulder, and burp him for me. It'll save time in the long run. Wait till you see my new lot of sketches.'

'Wait till you hear our proposed programme.'

They sat in satisfied anticipation till the feeding was completed and both babies put down.

Greg stooped to kiss both fuzzy heads. 'Some people don't know their luck,' he said.

She looked long and hard at him. 'We do,' she answered. 'But we might never have had it if it hadn't been for you, you know. You saved me.'

He kissed her again, and they prepared to work. Her glowing youth and triumphant motherhood disturbed him, though. He was only just over fifty. Had he got to accept that for him all the physical side of manhood was over? It was still only high noon as far as he was concerned. He was almost green with envy at the thought of Roland coming home tonight to that girl fizzing still with sex appeal. She saw the look, and heard him sigh.

('But I'm not going to be able to save you,' she thought, 'any more than you'll be able to save yourself. You're just too vulnerable to beauty – and I can see that Jess is being a bitch to you.')

'Sit down,' she said. 'Take a look at these.' He did, amazed as always at her skill as a designer. He drew one of the pencil sketches towards him. From his pocket he took a tiny water-colour painter's outfit, and began to fill in around the pencilled lines. In fifteen minutes he had transformed it into a young woman wearing the outfit. She was tall and well made, with strength as well as beauty in every line of her. She had an olive skin just tinted with rose, and large dark eyes, blue-black, under arched brows and long lashes. The outfit she wore was an extremely short mini-skirt which showed the full length of a faultless pair of legs, high-booted in white leather as far as the knees. The fitted white jacket had a cossack collar embroidered in gold, and in her right hand she held white gloves stitched with black and gold. The other hand played idly with the end of a huge, thick plait of dark hair that hung down almost to her waist over her left shoulder.

Greg was hastily washing in a dark greenish background to make the white suit stand out.

'My holy aunt!' said Monica, awed. 'It's an absolute winner! Where are we going to launch it?'

'Bristol as a try-out, then the West End.'

'And who is she, Greg?'

'The model? Calls herself Michelle Stanhope. I booked her provisionally, but I never thought we'd have anything so absolutely made for her as this is. She'll bring the roof down on us.'

'Be careful, Greg.' There was no mistaking her meaning.

'I should be so lucky. Nothing doing, ducky. She's got an 'usband. A great hulking brute of a policeman, who was once in the Guards. And I've got a wife I still love, though I'm not at all sure she still loves me.'

'She'd better make up her mind,' Monica said. 'You're too soft where women are concerned. Could you have painted her like that if she hadn't already made a very strong impression on you? You'd better leave that sketch here. It says a lot more than what a smashing outfit I've designed.'

He didn't argue. He went home and set up an easel with a new canvas on it. Nothing would heal his wounded spirit more than to begin on his 'Madonna and Child'.

24

The Rector's tenancy of the cottage down Spotted Cow Lane ran out at the end of November. When he had left so suddenly, Beth had been told by George Bridgefoot not to worry – to give herself time to make decisions as to what to do with her father's books and furniture, all of which, his note had seemed to indicate, he had assigned to her for ever. Common sense, however, had warned her that he might not end his days in Singapore or any other far-flung outpost of the church, and that there might very well come a time when he would long for England and a few old familiar things around him. She wasn't going to part with those same old familiar things, mostly because of their past associations. That the edifice of her life was now so secure didn't mean that she could dig up and dispose of its foundations wholesale.

She hadn't thought there was any hurry, but after the meeting she knew that things would be different. Kenneth Bean, albeit only Bailey's jackal, would throw his weight about wherever and whenever he could, delighting in his power to deal with such small issues as the tenancy of the Rector's cottage. He would insist that she got it cleared by the date her father had been given. Otherwise, she would be charged a 'reasonable rent'.

Elyot pooh-poohed her concern at the idea. Let her take her own time. Pay whatever rent was asked till it suited her not to, he said. He hardly thought it would land him in the bankruptcy court.

She was grateful to Elyot, and said so. But, having told him by this time all about the meeting and the distress it was causing to the 'old brigade', for their sakes she would not play into Bailey's hands. Even on so small a matter.

Elyot was genuinely surprised at the intensity of her feelings, and inclined to be amused.

'I can see now what people mean by "parochial",' he said. 'It's so unbelievably – *piddling*. Lilliputian. A world of little people with tiny minds fighting each other and causing storms in a thimble about rules and customs going back to the year dot. Quite inexplicable to ordinary people.'

'Very much like HM's ships, I imagine,' she said. 'Except that the Royal Navy is forced to honour its old customs – or else. Am I not right, Commander?'

It was a good analogy, so he gave in. She delighted him with her quick wit and her ability to exchange verbal gunfire with him. He need not have been afraid. She hadn't fought and won her freedom of mind from one man only to surrender it to another, however much she might love him. She could, and did, strike sparks off him all the time – day and night. He drew himself up and saluted her.

'Aye aye, ma'am,' he said. 'You have the ship. Steer whatever course you judge best – as long as you don't let it upset you. What can I do to help?'

'Come over to the cottage with me now, and help me take stock,' she said. 'Then I shall have to find out how to dispose of things we don't want to keep. I daresay Fran will lend us Ned to make bonfires in the garden, but I've lived too long amidst awful poverty to be able to set fire to anything worth saving without a twinge or two of conscience. On the other hand, there's nobody here that one would dare to offer anything to. Such an insult would never be forgiven. The poorer country people are, the prouder they are. That's what poor Daddy would never have understood.'

They strolled across to Spotted Cow Lane, unlocked the door, and went in. Elyot went from room to room, imagining Beth's life there till that momentous Christmas Day when she had walked out on her father and ended up by fainting in his garage. She was sitting on what had been her lonely spinster-of-this-parish couch, crying, when he found her again.

'I don't want to part with things in here,' she said, 'Most of them were my mother's. Or the Pembroke table and Father's rolltop desk, or even his chair. And what about his books?'

Elyot sat down beside her. 'My own feeling is that there is a lot here that you shouldn't even be thinking of getting rid of,' he said. 'Most of it's nice stuff, anyway, far too good to burn. Besides, there's no need to. How many rooms are there in our house that are either empty or just full of junk? Why don't we do what they've done up at Benedict's, and furnish a separate set of rooms? We are going to need help, once A.B.C. arrives – even if Thirzah comes back to do the rough work. We could have a live-in housekeeper. We can make a bonfire of what nobody wants as a gift.'

They went home, and made plans – till the next set of problems confronted them. The rooms at the Old Rectory had to be cleared and prepared, and those at the cottage left spotless.

'No question of just leaving it to Harrods, this time,' Beth said, teasing him.

'Or to Jane Hadley,' he retorted. 'Don't people want work, these days?'

'Jane Hadley is no more,' Beth said. 'She was the last of her kind. Mrs Bellamy will be looking for service herself in future. Nobody can get domestic help now for love or money. Except Fran Catherwood, of course. Honestly, women just have to do their own work, now. Those who used to "do domestic" for other people are old enough to get their pensions and have retired. There aren't any replacements for them. It's a new facet of social history.'

'Well,' said Elyot firmly, 'I'm not going to scrub decks myself either in the Old Rectory or in Spotted Cow Lane. Nor would I allow my wife to, even if she weren't already burdened by young Andrew Beresford Cunningham de ffranksbridge. So what do we do?'

'Find another name for him quick, before he gets too pompously heavy with that one for me to cope with,' she said. 'If you are not careful, I shall take the whole matter into my own hands and call her Mary Read, after the famous female pirate. You are off course, Captain. I want to know what to do here and now.'

'In that case, I suggest a trip up to Benedict's. Fran will know how we ought to set about getting help.'

They left it till next day, which was lucky because Sophie had had time to recollect herself completely. William's promise to take part on the side of the old faithful had been to her what the burning bush was to Moses, or the cross in the sky to Constantine. In that sign, she and the rest could conquer. Just let Kid Bean try any of his tricks on her!

Beth explained their dilemma, and Fran's immediate response was to call in Sophie and Ned.

'That Beryl Bean would be in 'er glory telling everybody 'ow mucky you 'ad left the place if she could find a speck o' dust as big as a bee's knee,' Sophie said scornfully. 'Once the furniture's out, it wouldn't take me more'n a day to make it so as you could eat your dinner off the floor. I daresay Fran could spare me for a day?' Fran knew quite well that whatever she replied would make no difference. Sophie had already got the bit between her teeth.

'We shall have to get some removal people to shift the furniture. We can't do that till we've got the rooms ready at the Old Rectory. They really only want sweeping out and dusting well.'

'I could do that, any day now,' Ned said. 'This weather and these short days, there ain't a lot I can do in the garden, and I'm sure I'm ashamed to come up and take my wages for what little I do, this time o' year. But you don't want no posh furniture pantechnicon for them few things, sure-lie? That new cattle truck o' George Bridgefoot's only needs swilling out with a hose the day afore. Me and Bill Edgeley's moved many a family in his old coal truck, or his hoss-and-cart in days gone by. Flitting ain't much of a job if you know how to set about it right, and me and Bill Edgeley's had plenty o' practice. Afore the war you never see none o' them furniture vans in places like this. That's what neighbours was for. Same as carrying at funerals, and such. As long as one of you's at one end to tell us what to take next, and the other at the other end to tell us where to put the stuff when we get it there, we can flit you in one day, all in daylight, if you see what I mean.'

Both he and Sophie took it for granted that the matter was settled.

'We shall only take out the things we really want to keep,' Beth was telling Ned. 'So we hope Fran might spare you another day to make a fire and burn carpets and rugs and other bits we haven't room for. We don't know how else to get rid of them.'

Fran caught Beth's eye. 'Did you ever go up to see Mr Petrie?' she said apparently changing the subject. Sophie and Ned, feeling no longer needed, excused themselves and left.

'Wouldn't he be offended?' Beth asked.

William answered her. 'He may be a bit embarrassed, but he is in need, and too much of a gentleman not to take kindness in the same way that it's offered. We'd take care not to embarrass him unnecessarily. Elyot, will you stop here and keep my wife company if I take yours for a little jaunt down to see Petrie? It's time I went to inquire again, and Beth can please herself when she's met him and the children whether to offer him anything.'

They left in the late afternoon, and drove down to the house. Petrie had moved his camp bed into the big living-room, where a small fire burned on the hearth. Several of the children sat in front of the fire, on the bare floor, playing jacks with polished stones. They all subsided into embarrassed silence as William and Beth went in. Petrie rose to give Beth his chair and sat down again on his bed.

William made the introductions, asking how he was. He answered that he had felt a good deal better of late, mainly because of what Joe had done to help him in the evenings, doing chores such as sawing up old wood and piling it by the hearth, and so on. 'The children can at least go to bed warm. And they keep me company when Joe can't be here.'

William had sat down beside Petrie on the bed. Jasper rose from the floor, looked Beth up and down rather worriedly, and then climbed up to sit between William and his father.

William laughed, and hugged him. 'You needn't worry, Tanner,' he said. 'This lady isn't instead of your "lovely lady". She's another lovely lady who's one of our friends. She knows all about you.' The child seemed satisfied, but did not give up his proprietorial place at William's side.

William turned back to Petrie. 'You've been getting on well with the house, I see,' he said. 'What's your next move? I hear Dafydd Pugh's been given the push. Maybe it's a good thing you weren't able to involve him.'

'On the contrary, I think. He's involved himself. Since the first time he came here, he's concerned himself with what may happen to Crystal and the children in the course of events. He takes his mission work very seriously. And, strange as it may seem, Crystal listens to him.'

He paused to send the children out, telling them to find Emmy and ask her to bring in their tea.

'Some of them understand too much,' Petrie said, a bit wistfully. 'I have explained to Dafydd what I want done with the house – if we can get a bidder of any sort – and its proceeds. I am helpless to dictate what Crystal shall do, of course. But my guess is that she will go back towards Wales, to join the group I found her with. They'll be in the Elan Valley again sooner or later, and as it happens central Wales is Pugh's home ground. He has offered to stay around for a while to see about selling the house and buying the equipment that would give my family a home base of some sort. Then, in the end, he says he will drive them all down to Wales and establish them on a recognized camping site. It would be some safeguard against them being robbed, or worse, if it was known that there was a man somewhere in the picture when I'm not. Crystal is not to be trusted to stay off drugs, or to care for the children's needs. If she were to make off again with all their child allowance books, for instance, Pugh would see to it that they didn't starve.

'I have to face facts. I can't protect them, once I'm dead. I've looked at it all round, and come to the conclusion that Pugh's influence over Crystal may be the best chance they have. If she just chose to abandon them, they would be taken into care. Probably separated. Money, such as the proceeds of the sale of the house, would be filched by Crystal if by nobody else. That's my real dilemma. Until she proves herself utterly unsuitable, she is their legal guardian. I have come to the reluctant conclusion that a free outdoor life, such as they have been used to with me, would be better than a children's home. It's the two oldest girls who are in the most danger, of course. Emmy is sixteen and Ammy only twelve months younger. And then there's Jasper. My son.'

Nobody interrupted him. It was no time for facile words. They could only let him go on talking. 'I'm uneasy about trusting him to Crystal, even with Pugh in the background. I've had wild dreams of trying to get in touch with my brothers, to tell them of his existence and beg them to take on some sort of guardianship till he is of age. But that's just fantasy, crying for the moon. I know them. So he'll have to take his chance with the rest. There's nobody else to leave him to.'

There was a discreet knock on the door, and a voice from the other side asked, 'May we come in, Daddy?'

'Sure,' answered Petrie.

It was like letting in the tide, Beth thought. Under cover of the noise of eight children and the rattling of mugs of cocoa and plates of slabs of bread and jam, William caught and held Petrie's eye. 'Don't be too sure there's nobody else,' he said. If Petrie heard him over the din, he made no sign.

Beth had sat through the previous conversation in mute misery. William had briefed her what to expect, but she had not been prepared for a man as near to death as Petrie, or for that bevy of children who would soon be fatherless and homeless, and might just as well be motherless. Now that she actually saw them *en masse*, she could hardly believe her eyes or ears. Emmy, tall and slender, barefooted but neat and tidy, had baby Aggie on her arm and a toddler by the other hand. Ammy, not so tall and plumper, carried the tray of mugs and food. Tanner was hanging on to her skirt, and peeping out from behind her like a little faun. Then came identical girl twins, shy and quiet, but utterly composed, while the rear was brought up by a truculent, giggling and pushing Basher.

'Sit down in a ring,' Ammy said. 'And be careful how you take your mug. It's hot.'

The girl's voice was soft, but crisp and clear, used to being obeyed. As cultured as her own, Beth thought.

'Sit down and behave youself, Basher,' said Petrie with authority. The boy sulkily obeyed. Petrie turned to Beth. 'I do apologize for all this,' he said, 'but there is nowhere else in the house warm enough for them to go. Here, Ammy, I'll hold Jade. You get the rest settled.' Jasper had seated himself more or less at his father's feet. Beth noticed the dexterity with which Emmy shifted the baby from one arm to the other, and then sat down herself to feed him the bottle of milk – or whatever it was – that she took out of her thin skirt pocket. Silence reigned as they began to eat. Beth's mind was racing, but all the questions she wanted to ask would have to wait.

'What are Pugh's plans, and where will he go?' William asked, *sotto voce*. He could not believe that Hetty would have him back as an unpaying lodger, whatever Joe might wish.

Petrie's face clouded. 'I wondered when you were going to see the great gaping hole in my scheme,' he said. 'He tells me he has money enough to keep himself fed till the spring – which will be long enough – but not to pay for a room. There are rooms galore here, but no furniture or carpets, rugs or bedclothes. Joe is trying to find a few pieces, and I may be able to help a bit out of my next quarterly allowance, around Christmas. I don't need to tell you what a relief it would be for me to have another adult in the house, till then.' He closed his eyes to prevent the pain and shame in them from being made too obvious.

Beth stood up. 'William,' she said. 'I want to go home, now, please, if Mr Petrie will excuse us. I'm afraid I have a lot of things to see to, urgently. But may I thank you for letting me come, and congratulate you on your beautifully behaved family? What a credit they all are to you!'

She gave him her hand, exactly as she might have done to Elyot last year, or to any other new acquaintance. He stood up, bowed low over it, and bade her goodnight. Before they were out of the front door, they heard him give way to a terrible bout of coughing; and William knew why they had had to make so abrupt a departure. The Beth he handed into his car was drenched in tears she could no longer hold back. He was conscious of feeling envious of her and indeed of all women who had such relief always at their disposal. He felt very much like crying himself.

25

Beth couldn't forget it. Though Mrs Franks now, gently swelling bump to prove it, the slum parson's daughter also stood in her shoes; and behind both of them was the Beth Marriner who had thought only last Christmas Day that she had nothing to live for. Beth the Commander's wife was ashamed to acknowledge the memory of that miserable, ungrateful woman who even then had had so much. She was more ashamed that she had allowed herself to lose all faith in the future.

That was what hurt most since she had left Petrie's house last night. In Peter Petrie she had met a man who truly was in the position that she had only imagined herself to be in; he had nothing but a huge load of anguished responsibility, and for him there was no future and no hope. After telling Elyot all about it in the middle of the night, she had got up full of purpose. To be doing something would be by far the best therapy for her.

What she had witnessed in Petrie's house yesterday was worse than anything she had met even in the East End of London. She couldn't bear to think about it – and yet she wanted to. It was just the same as when she had been a small child and found pictures of the crucifixion in her book of Bible stories. She saw Petrie now as the figure on the cross – having put himself in that torment because of his love for the family of children who were his only because he had tied himself to them with love. Love without hope. A deranged, drug-addicted mother, with no material resources other than what a bureaucratic welfare society was obliged to provide, could not replace what he had given them in such abundance, the gift of himself in an aura of loving, individual care.

How long would it be before Crystal offered those two beautiful oldest girls for sale? That's what Petrie had wanted somebody to understand. The plea had been there in his voice. 'Feed my lambs. Feed my sheep. Feed my lambs.'

He had had no notion of what fertile soil or ground, so well prepared to receive them, his words were falling on. Beth was a Christian steeped in the knowledge and meaning of the New Testament. She could not, and would not, allow his plea to go unanswered. She vowed to herself that somehow she would save Emerald and Amethyst, and let Petrie know they were safe, before he died.

She was not yet ready to divulge her plans even to Elyot – though she looked for no opposition. The coincidence of her visit to the Petrie household with the need to clear her father's home filled her with optimism and faith. Why otherwise should such an opportunity to do so easily what needed to be done be offered to her?

'There's no time like the present,' she told Elyot. 'Let's get a start on moving the furniture and stuff today, if Fran can spare Sophie and Ned at such short notice. If I organize things down at Spotted Cow Lane after I have briefed Sophie here, will you hold the fort for me at this end? I need your help.'

'Eat one round of toast then, before you begin, just to please me.'

She obeyed, anxiously watching the clock.

'Good. Now you can signal "action stations" as soon as you like. Do whatever pleases you, with me and with all my worldly goods. Isn't that what I vowed to you? I meant every word of it.'

'I'm afraid it's the other way round this morning,' she said. 'I'm going to load you with my worldly goods. And it wasn't your worldly goods I wanted. All I wanted was you.' It sounded facetious, but he saw that she was trembling again. 'Hold me, Elyot. I keep thinking that it might just as easily have been you with that awful lung cancer. We've been given so much, I want to repay a tiny bit of it while I have the chance. Do you really mean that you don't mind what I do – in this house, for instance?'

His voice was rough with feeling as he answered her. She unclasped his arms from around her waist, and walked determinedly to the telephone. He went towards the kitchen, content to do the washing-up.

Fran and William both put themselves and their helpers at her disposal. That hurdle was almost too easily cleared. William drove Ned up to consult with George Bridgefoot. The new cattle-truck, spick and span inside and out, was loaned without question. George was only too glad that Beth had understood the need to clear the cottage before her father's legal tenancy ran out. He was glad to avoid all chance of unpleasantness with church affairs on top of what his family was causing.

Beth dialled again. 'Monica,' she said. 'About Fran's birthday. Would you and Roland be prepared to bring the twins out with you and put them down to sleep here if I could guarantee babysitters for them? We do so much want to have Fran's party here. Think what last year's did for Elyot and me.'

'Snap!' said Monica. 'OK, let's share it. Fran is Roland's mother, after all. As far as the twins are concerned, I'd peg them in their sleeping bags on the clothes-line rather than let them spoil it. Can we keep the party a secret till we get it set up? I think there's an idea afloat to get Katie and her children to Benedict's that weekend, but they're big enough to be left with Sophie or Ned.'

'We'll cope,' said Beth, recklessly. 'Who else?'

'Jess and Greg, and Dad. I think that's all, this year. I'd add Mr Bellamy, but I'm told he's still away somewhere. So we'll keep it a family party, shall we? If you don't mind. Let's do it the easy way and get Dad to arrange everything to be brought from the hotel, shall we? He'd love to do his bit, and it would save you a lot of work. We're all a bit short-handed, without Jane Hadley. I wonder what's happened to her?'

Beth rang off quickly. She daren't trust herself, this morning, to lie well.

By the end of that day, she felt that she had been responsible for setting in motion a small miracle. The Old Rectory had been built in the age of domestic service, and there was even a back staircase that led to what had been the servants' quarters. They had all been included in the restoration of the house, including new plumbing and central heating. By early afternoon, they had been refurnished, too. One room had been turned into a small sitting-room, comfortable with carpet, desk and chairs that had previously been rather austerely housed in Archie Marriner's study. Curtains were hung and rugs and pictures in place. Even Sophie had to agree that it was surprising what could be done when folks had a mind to it and used a bit of elbow-grease. But her admiration was reserved for the bedroom that had been set up next to the sitting-room. It was large, and light, and everything from Beth's former bedroom had been transferred to it. The old polished furniture looked absolutely at home there, daintily pretty with white cambric coverlets embroidered by Beth's mother. Old-fashioned in a way Sophie entirely approved of.

At three o'clock in the afternoon, Beth called a halt. Sophie, Ned and Bill Edgeley were being refreshed with cups of tea and sandwiches in the kitchen at the Old Rectory.

'We're very near cleared the cottage, now. One more good load, and then there'll only be the stuff as she wants us to burn,' said Bill.

'Times is changed,' said Sophie. 'When I think 'ow glad Mam would ha' been once with them bits and pieces she's a-going to throw out. We should ha' thought we lived in a palace if we'd 'ad a real rug on the floor, 'stead of one as Mam 'ad pegged 'erself. And real beds, wi' proper mattresses instead o' that ol' iron bedstead and a 'ard flock mattress what all us three gals used to 'ave to sleep together on. Folks hev too much, nowadays. Do, they don't appreciate nothing.'

Beth appeared in the doorway, with Elyot behind her.

'Can you manage to load up once more today?' Beth asked. 'Everything that is left. Sophie, it's time you went home and rested. Fran says that she won't mind if you and Ned spend tomorrow cleaning the cottage. I can't believe how marvellously you have managed it all today.'

Bill Edgeley had stood up, and was fitting his cap snugly over the back of his head. 'It's been a real pleasure, I'm sure,' he said. 'Same as old times.'

After they had gone, Beth went back to the telephone, to do the hardest thing she had tasked herself with that day. She was about to offer charity to a very proud man.

The cattle truck followed Elyot's car down the narrow road to Danesum. Beth had judged the time to a nicety, so that the November dusk had fallen and there were few people out to notice where it went. She asked Bill and Ned to wait in the truck till she told them what to do with what was in it. Elyot, shy and embarrassed, followed her into the house.

Petrie was in bed, coughing dreadfully. Beth sat down on the bed, and thanked him for letting her dump so much unwanted junk on him. He made no pretence at all of how glad he was to accept it. His pride, or what he had left of it, was no match for her loving-kindness.

'I think,' Beth said, cutting short his protestations of gratitude, 'that you will find enough in the van to furnish a bed-sitting-room for Mr Pugh, with plenty of utensils of all kinds from the kitchen for him to make his own meals, if that is what he would prefer. Do what you like with everything there is, bedclothes and such. None of it is any good to us, so what you have no use for, you can put on the fire. Which reminds me – would your two oldest girls like to earn themselves some pocket money, babysitting in our house a week on Saturday? For Mrs Catherwood's twin grandchildren? It's her birthday, and we hope to be able to give her a little celebration at our house. I couldn't help noticing how good they were with the baby and the toddler while I was here. Could you manage without them? If you could, I was going to suggest that they stayed the night at our house, and we'll deliver them back next morning. That is, of course, if they would like to.'

'May I ask them and let you know?' he said. 'Saffie and Topy can see to the smallest ones as well as they can, so that's no problem. It would probably be a great treat for them.'

'How old is Emerald?' she asked.

'In years, just sixteen. There's only about two years between the first four of them – Emmy, Ammy and the twins. I rely on Emmy a lot – too much, I know. She's quite old enough to be a babysitter legally, if that's what is worrying you. She has had to mother the little ones, always. It isn't fair on her, but . . .'

'Ammy still goes to school?'

'Not until now. The powers-that-be have just got round to finding four children of school age here. They haven't been used to school, before – any more than gypsy children are. I've taught them myself to read and write.'

'And have perfect manners,' she said. 'I do hope they'll be willing to help me.'

Elyot had been standing aside, stiff and correct. He suddenly moved closer, and held out his hand to Petrie. 'We're going to want help with our own baby before long,' he said. 'We may as well get our bid in first.'

Beth gaped at him. He had said in one sentence what she had been wondering how she dare try to put into words – and Petrie had got the message. That was the difference between men and women. There had been no exploratory wordage, no offers, no promises; yet everything necessary had been said. The handshake had sealed a mutual trust in each other to make the most of what offered.

'Would they come up and talk to me about babysitting next Saturday?' Beth said, becoming very brisk again. 'Now, what shall we do with the stuff that's in the van?'

She went to the door and called, and Ned and Bill appeared at once, accompanied by Joe Noble.

'Leave it all to us, now, missus,' Bill Edgeley said. 'Joe's here and'll give us a 'and to put everything where it needs to go. You get off 'ome.'

They obeyed the command without question, though Beth wanted to laugh. Elyot wasn't used to being the one taking orders, but she didn't think he had noticed it. He was deep in thought. She was glad that he was as silent on the way home as she was.

What puzzled her most as the week wore on was that no word of any kind leaked from the shop as to the nature or destination of that last trip made by George Bridgefoot's cattle truck.

Beth had purposely asked Sophie to deliver the key of the cottage to the shop next day when the cleaning of it was done. She had no wish to have to hand it over to Kenneth Bean herself.

'What did they do with all the stuff as they didn't want, then?' Beryl asked Sophie. 'We heard as she'd took all the best stuff into their own 'ouse so as to 'ave some o' them old back rooms ready, do her father come back. I shouldn't ha' thought as her husband would ha' wanted his place choked up with all that rubbishy old stuff. Besides, do anybody flit as may, there's all'us loads o' stuff to be got rid of. But there weren't a wisp o' smoke there all day yist'day, no sign o' fires there nor nothing. Where did it all goo to?'

'If I was you, and wanting to find out so bad,' Sophie replied with dignity, 'I should ask somebody what knowed. As it 'appens, I don't. I weren't there.'

'Where was you, then?' said Beryl, suspecting that for the first time ever, she had stung Sophie into telling a lie.

'Same place as Moses was when the light went out,' snapped Sophie. 'In the dark. Same as you are now.' And with that she banged the shop door and strode off, planting her booted feet down as if she squashed a Beryl Bean under her sturdy soles and into the mud with every step she took.

Thanks to the combined discretion of Ned and Bill and Joe, everybody else was forced to remain frustratedly in the company of Moses.

26

All Fran had hoped for at her birthday was to achieve a long-held ambition to have both her children and their families together at Benedict's. For them all to be together under Beth and Elyot's roof was certainly the next best thing, and she appreciated the friendship that had motivated it. It would still be a family party, if not at home. She said so, to William.

'I don't see how you can claim Beth and Elyot to be family,' he said.

'No – only hosts. But all the rest will be family, even Eric. Last year, the family was very thin on the ground, and our guests mostly strangers. But it was what I call a party! This staid family dinner will be quite a different sort of function.'

'I know what you mean,' he said, laughing. 'A party to you means a chance to dance! Are you disappointed?'

'No. There's Christmas to come. Surely there'll be a chance to dance somewhere then. We can't even make any arrangements for a Christmas party ourselves as it is, till Bob and Jane come home and the truth comes out. It's all so *silly*. We couldn't have both the Brian Bridgefoots and the Bellamys – though of course, we should invite both lots and expect Brian to refuse. That would spoil it. All the same, it makes me mad. If we do have a Christmas party, we'll invite who we like.'

She saw that William was taking the matter more seriously than she had intended. 'Might be better not to try anything, this year. Honestly, darling. I get the feeling that the whole structure of the village is in danger. But Sophie's extraordinary outburst the other day made me do a lot of serious thinking. Bailey's aimed his first blow right at its roots. The church. And it isn't a fair contest. He's struck while the troops are demoralized. There's no Rector, George isn't himself, the other churchwarden is dying, and even Thirzah's ill. Besides, Bailey's playing dirty. It's like 1940 all over again in miniature – Sophie and Daniel and the few others of the Home Guard facing up to Hitler's stormtroops with pitchforks!

'I'd hoped that we might never be forced to take sides – but I can't see any option. I promised Sophie, anyway. But what to do, and how to do it? People don't realize what's happening. I'm sure the church means a great deal to a lot who don't attend services, though not to newcomers or young folk open to propaganda. That's where the danger lies. There'll be plenty who think they'd be a lot better off if we became a modernized suburb of Swithinford. More houses mean more people, and more people mean more shops, more trade, more opportunities, better transport services, a new school, all sorts of other new amenities – the lot. They won't see that what Bailey's really after is the rich pickings he'd get from having a financial finger – legal or illegal – in everything. In the line of propaganda he would take, it would all be lumped together as "progress".

'If genuine progress is what people want, that's different again. But how many will see through Bailey, till it's too late? He's another little Hitler. Hitler persuaded too many of the German people that he was just what they had been needing. We decided we could do very well without him, and dug our heels in against him and his propaganda. The odds against us were impossible – but then so they were at Agincourt. It's that sort of odds that makes Brits win or die fighting. We were prepared to fight Hitler with pitchforks and bill-hooks. Luckily, we had a few Spitfires, too —'

'We few, we happy few, we band of brothers,'

Fran began to quote, till she found that her voice didn't want to work. William had been one of Churchill's 'few', yet here he was, whole, hers, still within touch. She felt awed.

He hadn't seemed to notice her interruption. 'We surprised Hitler, but it wasn't really the planes or the pilots who beat him off. It was the British people. They weren't going to give in, whatever the odds. And if we don't want a pocket Hitler to take over our village, he's got to be stopped now. Given a lead, my guess is that the majority of the proper village people would come out fighting. Even chapel people, and those who never go near the church except for weddings and funerals from one year's end to the next. Shaking their fists in Bailey's face.

'As people did who cheered as they watched our dogfights over the Channel. Or even more so later on, when we used to go up to head off doodle-bugs. Our job was to shoot them down before they got over the land, of course, but it was the other dare-devil game we used to play that had people on the beaches cheering instead of rushing screaming to shelter.'

He had forgotten the original cause of his diatribe. He was just remembering.

'We used to fly alongside the doodle-bug till we could get the tip of one wing under one of the flying bomb's, and then gently tip it so as to turn it off course. Not so spectacular as downing it, but a lot more dangerous, and that's what appealed to everybody. It was a lot more subtle, too – maybe it even had Hitler wondering why so many of his secret weapons never reached their targets.

'We may have to use that sort of subtlety against Bailey. We've got to understand his strategy and undermine it. He's set up a fifth column already, people like Brian Bridgefoot and Vic Gifford. He's got a quisling in Kid Bean. His secret weapon is his cheque-book – from Sophie's account, he's already scored a direct hit with it inside the church hierarchy.

'I tell you, he's clever. He's read the map correctly. If he gets the church here under his thumb, he gets the village, and his own way with it. That old church over there is to Old Swithinford what Broadcasting House would have been to Hitler if we'd let him get so far.

'Darling, I'm sorry if you are not going to get your party, but the time for parties is when the danger's over. Next Saturday will give me a chance to hatch up a plot or two with people who know what I'm talking about. We may be able to take Bailey by surprise, as we did Hitler.'

Fran shivered. Her eyes were shining. He instinctively opened his arms, and she fell into them, clinging to him.

'You did that – what you have been telling me? And you're still here,' she said.

'If I had known how much I had to live for, I shouldn't have been half so foolhardy,' he said as he hugged her. 'Think what I might have missed!'

'I'll forget about dancing if you can plan to turn even one of that beastly Bailey's doodle-bugs off course,' she said.

'If we manage even a small victory over him, I promise you a triumphant war-dance, somewhere or other,' he said. 'Where are you off to now?'

'To my study. I must do some work – though in spite of everything, I have managed to get fairly well forward. I think I shall make my Christmas deadline. I haven't heard of you doing much.'

'I didn't intend to put pen to paper until I'd had plenty of time to think and that's what I've been doing. Not thinking to order, or to a timetable – just reading and cogitating and making links that I hadn't made before. Such as noticing at first hand how and why things change. Very valuable education. A village is a world in microcosm. If you don't understand people, you can't understand history. And if you can't understand history, you can't learn from it. We have been given an invidious choice – to watch a man like Bailey change everything overnight, or to take sides in a mini civil war. There's no way we can stand aside and just let things happen, is there? Sit at home in smug comfort saying "I'm all right, Jack" because it doesn't affect us personally? So we let ourselves be drawn in, in order to do what we can to prevent the cohesion of the community from being destroyed to fill Bailey's and Kid Bean's pockets.

'You have to dig a long way down to get to basic rock, which is human nature. That's what Hitler found out. It's all happened before, not once, but many times. About the only thing that never changes is human nature – which in our different ways is the raw material we both work on. Maybe that's why we manage to rub along so well together.'

'Could be, I suppose,' she said, standing on tiptoe to kiss him. 'I've often wondered. Sometimes I've imagined it was an outdated emotion called love.'

She went into her study and sat down at her desk, but she didn't attempt to work. She, too, had a lot to think about – particularly having been reminded to consider human nature. The arrangements that Beth – in cahoots with Monica, as she had been told – had made were very nice and she ought to be grateful. But there was a worrying niggle: two, in fact. Roland's twins, though only three months old, would be there, part of the family gathering. Katie's two children would have to be left behind at Benedict's – with whom? Beth and Monica had both taken it for granted that Sophie would 'oblige'. So she probably would – but she would be wounded to the core. It would mean that she had been demoted in the hierarchy from an important member of the supporting cast to just an 'extra'. Last year, Sophie, Thirzah and Ned had 'seen to everything'. This year, Eric would be sending waiters and waitresses with the food up from the hotel, and all the washing-up, etc., would be taken back there to be done in machines. She saw that in letting such a thing happen she would be helping to break another of those thin threads that were still helping to keep the community whole. At the risk of offending Beth and/or Monica, she couldn't let it happen. Sophie would suffer, and her own relationship with Sophie would be changed. She dared not risk it.

William would understand. She went back to find him, and poured out all her misgivings. The result was that as soon as lunch was over, she set off to visit Beth.

Fran felt she was putting a valued friendship at risk, and had to comfort herself by comparing it with the other friendship she might be in danger of losing, which also included an element that she could only designate as duty. She decided on her way to the Old Rectory that the only honest thing to do was to lay her cards face up on the table, and beg Beth to understand.

Beth understood only too well. After the first moment of disappointment, she showed signs of genuine distress. When she had control of herself, she began profuse apologies and self-recrimination for being, as she said, 'as stupid as her father had been' and for the same reasons. She didn't yet *think* like a countrywoman.

She had wanted to repay Fran and William's kindness, and had simply not thought anything through. Fran's attitude towards Sophie was different from her own towards Thirzah.

She had, if she admitted the truth, always been irritated by Thirzah, first for having shown such a proprietory air over Elyot and his household, and then for being indisposed just when she needed her help. Never once had she been to visit Thirzah, though she was glad to remember that she had asked Sophie or Daniel at church about her most weeks, only to receive very non-committal answers of 'About the same, thanks' – which she suddenly understood was their way of telling her that they knew she had asked only out of politeness.

She was glad Elyot was out, so that she could tell Fran how bad she felt.

'No harm done,' said Fran cheerfully, 'or at least nothing we can't soon put right. Put your coat on, and let's go to see Monica.'

Luckily, Eric was at Monastery Farm when they got there. His presence helped, because he was able to soothe Beth by telling her what awful mistakes he had made because he hadn't understood what he was dealing with. She was lucky, he said, because so far she had done nothing that wasn't 'all in the family'. He understood why Fran was afraid of hurting Sophie's feelings, and suggested that the thing to do, even at this late hour, was to ask Sophie and Ned to stand by in the kitchen of the Old Rectory to set the table, keep the food hot when it was delivered ready cooked from the hotel, serve it up when the guests were ready, and so on. Then they could clear away and wash up, just as if they were in Fran's own kitchen. Did Fran think they would do that?

'They'll be pleased to be asked,' Fran said, very relieved. 'Though you must expect Sophie to grumble, Beth, and for Ned to be shy. Sophie's used to having Thirzah at her side, in my kitchen, for once giving orders to Thirzah instead of taking them. My kitchen's Sophie's domain. Thirzah won't be there, but I'll bet Sophie'll be looking over her shoulder for Thirzah to tell her what to do or not to do, all the same, because she'll be in what is Thirzah's territory. Her invisible presence will be in charge.

'Sophie can't usurp Thirzah's place in the family hierarchy, or her territorial rights, till Thirzah herself has made it quite clear that she is relinquishing them for good. It just isn't done. It causes real distress when the rules are broken. Kid Bean being made a churchwarden over Daniel Bates's head is a case in point. That's one reason I'm treading so carefully round Sophie just at present. She's upset already. And about Thirzah. How ill is she? Might there be the slightest possibility that if we provided a car for her both ways, she could be there in Beth's kitchen to "superintend"? They'd all be happier, if she could.'

'Let's go and ask,' Beth said, jumping up.

'Hang on a minute,' put in Monica. 'Fran, Beth has made arrangements for me to take the twins with me, to be put down between feeds there. But if Sophie and Ned are going to be there as well, who's going to babysit Katie's two? Toddlers aren't so easy to leave in a big house with strangers as babies are.'

Even Fran looked crestfallen. She couldn't have it both ways.

Beth took it up. 'If Katie put them to bed in our house, would they sleep? Would she mind rousing them to take them home to Benedict's at midnight? There are plenty of places we can put them – and I think the babysitters I've set up for the twins would be just as good with toddlers. The Petrie girls – the two oldest.'

'I'll ask Kate,' said Fran. 'They're coming on Friday, so there'll be time for last-minute plans. If Kate thinks it best, we'll leave them at Benedict's with Ned. They know him well enough.' She didn't add how foolishly disappointed she would be not to have them all, just once, together, even asleep. Babies were babies.

'See what you and Elyot have let yourselves in for,' Eric teased Beth.

Beth's answer came pat, quick as a flash. 'Oh,' she said, airily. 'We've already discussed the babysitting problem. We decided we could always appeal to you to help us out. You're hardly ever seen nowadays without at least one baby under your arm, and you'll be out of a job by the time A.B.C.'s born. I expect Monica will give you a good reference as a trustworthy babyminder.'

Fran wondered if anything anybody could have said would have pleased Eric more. It was as if the last link that bound him to the old village's chain of friendship had also been forged this morning.

Fran decreed that for diplomacy's sake she must go home to talk things over with Sophie, and that it would be better for Beth to face Thirzah alone.

Charles's car was standing outside the front door at Benedict's, and William was just seeing Charles and Charlie out. They stopped to greet Fran and explain their hurried visit.

'Dad and Jane came home from their honeymoon yesterday, and went to Effendi in London, to see Nick. But Dad's been away from the farm too long already, so we said we'd go up to London today to see them all and bring Dad back. We'll drop him off in the dark at Castle Hill tomorrow evening and go straight on to Cambridge to drop me, so nobody will be any the wiser,' Charlie said. 'It's jolly well too bad on poor old Charles, having to keep such a secret so long. Jane wants to be here when the cat is let out of the bag, but Effendi wants her for a bit just now to help make the next lot of decisions about Nick. It's tough on Dad – but there's only two or three weeks of term left, and then I'll be home, and Charles will come and help me with the animals if Dad wants to go up to see Jane at weekends. Or so he says.'

The smile Charlie gave Charles would have brought a stone effigy to her assistance.

'I'm counting the days,' Charles said. 'Anything to get away from home, just at present.'

Charlie grimaced at him, and William laughed. 'Kiss her if you must,' he said. 'Don't mind us. We're used to it.'

'One term out of nine gone,' Charles replied. They all understood.

'Give Jane and Bob our love, and tell your Dad we'll be up to see him sometime early next week,' Fran said. She and William stood together to wave the youngsters off.

'They're so *right* for each other,' Fran said.

William nodded. 'Bob thinks so,' he answered. 'He's sure it will all come out right for them in the end. He did foresee difficulties, though. It seems that Charles is having a rough time of it with his father. It won't do him much harm in the long run. I've told him just now that he won't have to wait as long as I did. They are Ferdinand and Miranda – except that it's his father, and not hers, that "their swift business doth uneasy make".'

'Except that it's Miranda herself holding him off,' Fran said. 'Otherwise both their fathers might as well whistle to the wind. "Love laughs at locksmiths."'

'You win,' he said. 'You held me off long enough. But it was worth it. I told Charles so, just before you came home.'

She kissed him and left him, and went for a long consultation with Sophie at the kitchen table.

'If you was to ask me,' Sophie said, 'I should say as once Thirz' knows as she's wanted, she'll be as right as rain come your birthday. If the doctor knowed 'er as well as I do, 'e'd ha' told 'er in the first place to eat as much as ever she could, and stop abed. Then she'd ha' done the hopposite – just to be contrary, like, and 'ave 'er own way. I'm sure as it would do 'er a power o' good to go out somewheer again. Don't, she'll soon be sty-baked. Do that doctor forbid 'er to goo – there wouldn't be nothing nor nobody except 'Im Above as could keep 'er away. But there ain't nobody as dare give a doctor a 'int like that, is there?'

'Except the proverbial little bird,' remarked William hopefully, appearing from behind the door where he had been eavesdropping shamelessly.

27

The first November fog came down over Old Swithinford as Charles drove back from Cambridge after delivering Bob Bellamy home and Charlie back to her college. It blanketed the whole village in thick, dark, cold, grey nothingness, gradually bringing everyday commerce to a slow-down, as if it were a pocket watch lost in a haystack, its spring gradually unwinding. Time was as meaningless in the metaphorical fog as direction or location was in the literal stuff. A general sense of helpless inertia lay over everthing and everybody.

Bob had been back at Castle Hill for two days before anybody caught sight of him and reported his return. During his absence old elements had been removed and new ones introduced into the social life of the community. They had been thrown together, but whether they would prove to be a harmless mixture or a dangerous compound was yet to be discovered.

Bob's unobtrusive return seemed to signal a new turn of events.

The Bridgefoot family was in a state of armed neutrality. Molly was suffering most, as mothers usually do when families fall out. Her main worry, though, was about George. He was no longer the man he had been. His huge physical presence seemed to be reduced in keeping with the slackening of his vigorous personality. His bad hip slowed him down, altered his habitual upright stance and made him limp; the pain of it robbed him of sleep. He had lost his appetite, and with it some of his equable temper. Not that he was bad-tempered – but neither was he the calm, dependable, philosophically optimistic man they were all so used to dealing with. There was a general air of apathy about him that made Molly afraid.

Though she knew that the root cause of it was the friction within the family, she had noticed the rapid deterioration in him after the meeting at the church. She recognized with something like despair a breakdown in him that was more than the physical effects of getting old, and worse than dissension within their family could account for. She could not have put into words what she meant, but she was right all the same. He was losing his grip on everything that so far had made him such a contented man.

As he tossed beside her through long nights, he went over and over again in his mind all the reasons for feeling as he did. He reached by instinct and his intimate knowledge of village tradition the same conclusion as William had from his knowledge of history and the habit of a mind trained to make comparisons.

His village, his community, was not dying; *it was being killed.* Death is one thing, murder another. Death is a natural process that ends life when that life has run its course; murder cuts off the life before its course is fully run. An oak tree by tradition is three hundred years growing, flourishes for three hundred years, takes three hundred years to die and is another three hundred years before it rots away. All the signs were that like the oak, the church, and with it the old community, was reaching the end of its period of flourishing. But it was not being allowed its time to die naturally; instead, it was having poison injected into its roots.

George smarted under the knowledge that the support it had had for generations from the Bridgefoots was now only what he, in his own person, could supply. The continuity of alliance between Bridgefoots as a family and the church was at an end. He was like the last man in a relay race. If he dropped the baton, the race was lost – but he could no longer make the effort to keep running. Not because of his age or physical disability, but because the spirit had gone out of him. It had disappeared during that awful meeting in the church.

With that meeting, 'his' church had lost its autonomy. It had been taken for granted that they would never get another Rector; but even if by a miracle they did, what would there be left to hand over to him? He, George Bridgefoot, could not fight all the new forces unaided. Let Kid Bean ring the calling bell. He wanted to give up, and might even have considered it but for his oft-repeated boast that Bridgefoots never gave up. Besides, he couldn't let down Daniel and Thirzah and the few others whose very lives were bound up with the church as it had been. For their sakes, he had to struggle on.

If only things were easier at home. That would help a lot. He turned over again, to ease his aching hip, and found Molly's arms round his neck.

'It's no use you laying here worrying,' she said. 'You'll only make yourself really ill, and what shall I do, then?'

To his dismay, she burst into tears and sobbed into her pillow. Hip or no hip, he turned himself over to put his arms round her and cuddle her. They were both wide awake by the time she had cried herself out, so she insisted on going down to make a good strong cup of tea.

It was three thirty a.m. The house was a little island in a huge ocean of thick, impenetrable fog. The two of them were absolutely cut off from everybody else. Conditions for the private confidences that even people as long married and as close to each other as they were had never given to each other were ideal. It was almost unbelievable how many of their feelings they had kept from each other.

Each member of the family in turn and their affairs came under their verbal scrutiny: the quarrel at Temperance that had never been made up; the state of war that existed between Brian and Charles; the puzzled rider to that particular state of affairs as to what Charles was up to now that they didn't know; what it could be that kept him so happy and cheerful in spite of everything, including Brian's most pointed barbs at Charlie and her father.

'I hope it isn't because she's letting him sleep with her after all, when they go off together for weekends in London.'

'Could be worse reasons,' George grunted. 'It'll be all Brian's fault if she is. Trying to push Bailey's daughter on him. Good luck to little Charlie for claiming him while she can.'

'George!'

'Well, why not Charles as well as Pansy – or Lucy, come to that. They're young. Like we were once.'

'Not like that, we weren't,' she said.

'Should ha' been, if we'd had the chances they've got now,' he said.

'What did you mean about Pansy?'

He was silent. He hadn't meant to worry her with that. Charles had told him about the sort of parties Pansy said went on among the Bailey set. Drink galore, pot in the fags or even in the cakes, and everybody ending up in bed – or the equivalent – with somebody else. Molly made him tell her all he knew – things that were beyond her belief.

'And Pansy does *that?*'

"Don't be too hard on her, Mother. She hasn't got over young Fairey yet. I don't suppose for a moment that young Bailey would give her a second look if she didn't oblige him that way.'

'Does Marjorie know?'

'Vic must, if she don't. According to Charles, Vic gatecrashes if he can find a good enough excuse to be there when there's a party going on.'

Molly was silent for a few minutes, digesting this bit of information. Then, with all the force of bitterness that through many years of disgruntlement she had held back for the sake of peace, she raised the sluice and let out a flow of words. Most of it was what she had been bottling up against her son-in-law.

'And to think we let our lovely girl throw herself away on a man like him,' she said. 'He wasn't fit for her to wipe her boots on. How she's put up with him, I don't know! Why she ever married him I shall never understand. The way he shows off, the way he brags, the way he takes her down in front of other people, the way he's stopped her doing all the things she used to love doing ... and his awful tempers ... I never thought I should ever hear myself saying it, but I hate him, George. *I hate him.* I can't think of one good thing to say for him. I HATE HIM! I HATE HIM!'

George was shocked, dumbfounded and utterly at a loss to know how to cope. Molly must be quite beside herself to give tongue to such thoughts. That he realized that she was voicing his own feelings – especially just lately – only made it worse. In his agitation, he shook her gently.

'Now stop it, Mother. Do you hear? Stop it! He's our Marjorie's husband, whatever he is. She don't complain a lot, so what's it got to do with us? He's been a good husband to her after his own lights. He's done well by her with regard to money – she's always had whatever she's wanted. So have the twins. He couldn't have been a better father to them. He works hard – when he does work – and it's all for Marjorie's sake. Or for the twins' sake. Getting in with Bailey is only to make more money, for them. He wants to see her dressed better and have posher things in her house than her friends. That's his way of showing how much he loves her. He hopes young Bailey'll marry Pansy – that's what he's after – because he wants what he thinks is best for all of them. And his tempers and rows with Marjorie are very often her fault. When he gets on her nerves she shows him what she thinks of him, and he can't bear that. He's jealous of her because he loves her. He hates it if she gives any attention to anybody or anything except him. Most women would be glad enough to have husbands like that.'

Molly snorted. 'Loves her?' she said. 'He thinks he owns her. Gives her everything she wants? He gives her things she don't want that cost a lot of money, so that other people will notice and wonder how he can afford it. She don't want such vulgar, show-off things. She'd rather have the old, pretty things she treasures till he smashes them in one of his rages. He does it just to spite her, because he can't keep up with her, however much she lowers herself to get down to his level. I know we can't alter it now, but I never stop wishing she'd never married him. You can see she's worried to death half the time. One thing is what's going to happen this Christmas when Poppy comes home. I wonder if Poppy knows what's going on? It was only last Christmas that all the six youngsters spent Boxing Day together up at Temperance while we all went to Marjorie's – remember? We were happy then – and look at us now! Poppy's never been the same since Nick Hadley had his accident, poor boy. I wish he was well enough to come to Charles's birthday.

'Oh, I did so want a party – but nobody else does, not even Charles himself. I wish I knew why. But –' She suddenly sat up in bed. Her cheeks were flushed and her chin stuck out. 'George, listen to me. I want all the family together on his birthday, here, in our home. I don't care if they don't come at Christmas, but I want them all here together on New Year's Eve. If you back me up, we shall get our own way.'

George suddenly tumbled to the real cause of all her distress. She had got it into her head that it was him who wouldn't live to see another New Year. The state she had got herself into was all his fault. He only had a bit of arthritis in his hip – and if he was making a lot of fuss about it, it was because he had hardly ever had anything wrong with him physically in all his life before. All the rest of his grizzling and whatnot could be put down to aggravation and worry, about just such things as she had made such a to-do about. And he had made her believe he was dying! He suddenly let out a chuckle that shook the bed.

'Give us a kiss, my old duck,' he said, smoothing his big hand over her still pretty snow-white hair. 'Don't you worry about me. Remember how when we were first married I used to get blisters on my hands with digging? You used to thread a needle with wool, bust the blister with the needle, and draw the wool through to dry it up. I reckon that's just what you've done tonight! Bust the blister that's been hurting me, and soaked up the soreness I've been making myself such a misery to you about. There's nothing wrong with me only a touch o' the screws, and a lot o' worry about things as I can't alter.

'Now you've said all I've been wanting to say for me, I reckon we shall both feel a lot better. But don't you worry about me, my gel. I ain't going to be the one to leave you for many a long year yet. And about Charles's birthday – we'll do exactly what you say. It's no use trying to talk to Brian or Rosemary. Only you'll have to invite Charlie, won't you?'

'Do you want another cup of something?' she said comfortably. 'Cocoa, this time?'

He watched her out of the bedroom door, remembering times long gone. He heaved himself out of bed and went to the bathroom, surprised to find how much less tense all his leg muscles felt. He looked out of the window, but the fog was too thick for him to see anything. Yet he knew that fog or no fog, the old church still stood there, so very close . . . where it had been all his life when he had needed comfort or solace. He was still its church-warden, and while there was life, there was hope. Kid Bean wouldn't keep him from going up there first thing in the morning, to give thanks for Molly and to pray that all his family would be on better terms with each other than they were now by the time they started another New Year.

'Get into bed, you silly old man,' said Molly, appearing again with two steaming cups on a tray. 'You'll get your death o' cold standing there by that window, and make your hip worse.'

'Not while I've got you to keep me warm,' he said, clambering back into bed and taking his cocoa from her. They sat side by side against their pillows and sipped their hot, sweet drink in soothing, companionable silence. Then he put the light out and she snuggled down with her head on his shoulder. He stroked her face till she slept, by which time he was conscious only of a delicious drowsiness such as he hadn't experienced for weeks – or so it seemed to him. It was at least four hours before the ache in his hip got bad enough to rouse him.

The fog was still there, though it was now broad daylight. He crept out of bed, singing under his breath so as not to wake Molly.

> 'New every morning is the love
> Our waking and uprising prove.'

He wanted to let himself into the church and be back again before Molly missed him.

28

The arrangements for Fran's birthday went along smoothly. Thirzah with great dignity informed Beth that she 'would make the heffort, seeing as she was needed', which set Sophie's mind wholly at rest, even if it was the first time she had ever had to deal with food she hadn't cooked herself, or with professional waiters 'as she couldn't see no need for'.

Emmy and Ammy Petrie had been up to see Beth, to the satisfaction of both sides. The extraordinary thing about the two girls was their poise. Beth saw at once that they had been well briefed as to what they were there for, and how to behave.

Beth treated them as visitors, to their obvious delight. They tried hard not to let their gaze linger too obviously around the room and its furnishings, at the delicate china in which Beth gave them tea, or at the great fireplace piled high with flaming logs.

It gave Beth pleasure when their correct behaviour gave way to curiosity, and she saw how much they were delighting in being treated so courteously in such surroundings. She chatted to them about their charges, if they did consent to babysit on the evening of her dinner party. When she said that of course they would be paid whatever the going rate was, the first note of embarrassment crept in. Daddy had said they ought not to be paid – it was one tiny way they could repay the kindness he had received. Besides, they were looking forward to it so much! They didn't expect to have such pleasure and money too, just for looking after babies, which they had both had to do as soon as they were big enough to lift one.

But Beth was adamant. 'Of course we shall pay you! And you'll stay the night on Saturday, won't you? It's likely to be quite late when our guests leave, and you'll be tired by then. Come with me and let me show you your quarters – always supposing you are still willing to come.'

She led them up the back stairs, and into what she had begun to think of as 'the Marriner Suite'. The girls were speechless with delight.

'Will they be all right at home during the night without you?' Beth asked. 'We'll take you home early next morning, if you are at all worried.'

Emmy made it plain that it had all been fully discussed. 'Mr Pugh will be there in the house once he gets back from preaching,' she said. 'Dad says Mr Noble will sit with him most of the evening. Topy and Saffie can get Dad anything he needs. And they are as used to looking after the boys as we are. The three little ones are no trouble – it's ever only Basher who is difficult.'

They left, shyly, but obviously looking forward to their weekend – which would be to them, Beth reflected, almost like staying a night in a hotel. She rang Fran to report, and Fran, too, began at last really to look forward to her birthday.

The invitation to Jess and Greg had been issued jointly by the Franks's and the Wagstaffes. Greg went off again on the Monday before the party, taking it absolutely for granted that they would go. Jess did a lot of cogitating. She supposed that her loyalty to William enforced her acceptance, but she was, as always, bitterly opposed to having to spend an evening in Monica's company. As it was she could see no way of escape.

Anne went home with her for tea and a chat, as she so often did when Greg was away. Jess brought up the question of Fran's birthday. 'I suppose you've been invited, too?'

Anne shook her head. 'It's family only, isn't it? I don't qualify,' she said. 'Either as family or as a friend of the new Lady de ffranksbridge or of the pseudo Mrs Wagstaffe. I suppose Greg's bubbling over with anticipation?'

'I wouldn't know,' Jess replied. 'I've hardly seen him while he's been at home. He's spent a lot of time up at Monastery Farm, and the rest in his studio. He and Monica have apparently got something special on the go. I wonder what masterpiece he's been creating for her this time? Shall we go and have a butcher's at it in his studio? I know he hasn't finished whatever it is he's doing that's so special.'

'When will he be back?' asked Anne.

Jess shrugged. 'Your guess is as good as mine,' she said. 'Only just in time for Saturday, I think. I don't even know where he's gone – but he'll ring later tonight.'

Anne smiled. 'From the house of another old friend he's just happened to meet?'

Jess's mood turned, chameleon-like, as they went to the studio. She was repelled by Anne's tone and immediately prepared to defend Greg. He was her husband, until lately her uxorious lover. What right had Anne to make such snide references to his supposed infidelity? For the first time, Jess sensed that it gave Anne some sort of satisfaction to dwell on the subject. She resented Anne's attitude, and regarded her so-called friend with suspicion.

The studio door was locked. Jess drowned in fear, and instinctively fought for life. She would not give Anne the least hint of what she was feeling. She wouldn't believe Anne's insinuations. When Greg came back she could soon put things right again between them. In any case, she wasn't going to show her feelings at this moment.

She looked over her shoulder at Anne. 'The lock's jammed,' she said. 'I don't think there is a key to this door, and if there were Greg would be too scatterbrained to use it. I'll find a chisel or something and break it open.'

It took her ten minutes and a good deal of force, during which Anne retired to lounge against the hall sideboard, with a sardonic smile hovering on her face. She knew perfectly well that the door had been locked. She took care not to be too close when at last Jess got it open, and stepped inside.

The smell of oil-paint stung Jess's nostrils. Greg's easel was set up facing the light, and on it was a large canvas. There sat Monica, more or less life-size, her jumper pulled up and her bra pushed down, so that one perfect globe of a breast protruded, its pearly skin highlighted to show its milk-gorged rotundity. Monica's hand covered the aureole, two fingers against the dark patch as she regulated the flow from the nipple into the mouth of the baby attached there. Her other hand clasped the child to her, its rosy cheek and dark hair mirroring Monica's own as she gazed down towards it.

Scattered around the studio were several charcoal sketches from which the portrait had been built up. In spite of herself, Jess's first reaction was a gasp of admiration. Greg, even at his best, had never before produced art of this quality.

Then the knife of jealousy struck home, right into her heart. The portrait had been painted with consummate skill, but that wasn't what made it so outstanding. This was a work of genius, to which hand, head and heart had all contributed. The artist himself was there in every brush-stroke.

Jess's next impulse was one of self-protection. She backed out of the room and pulled the door shut behind her, though the broken lock now didn't hold. Anne could have had no more than a glimpse of the portrait. She should get no more. Jess fought for self-control. She would not give Anne the satisfaction of commenting on it. They went silently back to the sitting-room, where Jess picked up the teapot, and lifted the lid to see if it needed refilling.

'Well, at least that accounts for so much time spent up at Monastery Farm,' Anne said.

Jess answered calmly. 'It explains everything,' she said. 'I expect it's a secret commission from Roland and Monica for a Christmas present to Eric, with a pretty large fee Greg meant as a surprise for me. He wouldn't want me to see it till it was finished – it's not at all the same as the commercial art stuff he normally turns out. I'll bet he's just crazy to get back to it, the moment he is free of whatever it is he's doing now.'

'That may depend on what he doing now.'

'Oh stop it, Anne, for heaven's sake! You haven't lived with an artist husband for more than twenty-five years. I have. I know about artists. Bésides, I love him.'

She went out, leaving Anne with a smile on her lips, and came back with the refilled teapot. The telephone bell rang almost immediately. 'Help yourself,' Jess said, and proceeded to astonish Greg with a loving, cheerful, husband-welcoming voice, put on entirely for Anne's benefit.

Anne listened to the half of the conversation she could hear, which might have been a turtle dove cooing to its mate. Greg was understandably puzzled. He knew Jess too well to believe that they could have got back to such amicable terms for real without an almighty row first.

'All right, darling,' Jess was purring. 'I'll go down early to see if there's anything I can do to help, and we'll expect you when we see you. If you get very late, don't bother to come home to change. Try to be on time for the meal, because that's being sent up from the hotel. You'll ring me again on Friday night with the latest news. Fine. Till then, my darling.'

She kept up her act till Anne had left, and then went back to the studio to look again at that wonderful portrait, bitterness overflowing. So she had been right all along. There had to be something between Greg and Monica, for him to be able to paint her like that.

Her consolation was that it was Fran's precious son who had been hoodwinked into carrying the can. Jess tempered the steel inside herself with the fire of jealousy and the water of tears of tempestuous anger. Monica should not keep her hold on Greg; nor should Anne ever know she had been right. Once Saturday was over, she'd set herself to win her husband back. Her husband. Her one and only, ever, precious lover. He was *hers*. She wanted him back – and she would get him. She had always been able to woo him back to her side before, and she could, and would, again. She began to look forward to his return on Saturday.

Anne was with her again when the phone rang on Friday evening. Jess jumped up to answer it, while Anne watched and listened again to the one-sided conversation.

'York? Yes, I'll hold the line.' Jess's voice was already hardening. Pause.

'Greg? . . . Yes, of course it's me. What are you doing in *York*? . . . The girl on the switchboard told me she had a call for me from York . . . Oh no! Not the old doctor again! Does he live in a hotel? If anybody knows the background noises of a hotel, I do! . . . Yes, of course I'll listen to your story on Saturday when I see you. I shall look forward to it. I know very well what a fine creative artist you are . . . Oh, for God's sake go back to your doctor. Her soup will be getting cold . . . Yes, maybe. If you can get back from Inverness or Swansea on time . . . No, there's nothing wrong with me. I'm fine. 'Night.'

She slammed the phone down, and went back to her chair. She couldn't stop the trembling of her hands, and daren't trust herself to speak.

In the end, it was Anne who broke the awkward silence. 'So you've caught him out. He treats you like a fool because you are one. You let him get round you with a bit of lovey-dovey soft soap every time. How many times now has he missed his train? How many old friends has he met and stayed out with? How many times has Monica actually confirmed where he's been or for how long? He's just a man with a roving eye at the right age for a bit of philandering. You shut your eyes to it because you don't want to see it. It's plain enough to everybody else.'

Jess's fiery temper came to her rescue. Nobody could express contempt in her face better than she could. 'I suppose you are now going to tell me when and where and with what success he has made passes at you,' she said.

Anne laughed. 'I've got more sense,' she said. 'And too much experience. You wouldn't catch me falling for his sort of glycerine charm. It's no use you turning nasty and fuming at me, Jess, just for telling you the truth. If you want my advice –'

'I don't, thanks.'

'OK, don't say I didn't warn you. You and Greg are finished. Washed up. Why don't you just face up to it, and let him go to the devil his own way, while you go yours. Set your cap at money, next time. Now, I'm going home. I'm sorry if I've upset you, but it had to be said. Somebody had to put you wise. Sleep well.' She made for the door.

Jess suddenly came to life again, like an ice maiden melting. Anguish and terror flooded through her. 'Oh Anne, don't leave me!' she cried. 'I can't be here alone all night, now, knowing what he's up to.'

'All right. I'll stay in the house with you, but I don't want to sit here and talk about it all night. There's no point. It's over. I'll make us both another drink, and then I'm going to bed. I advise you to, as well.'

Jess didn't. In the morning Anne reported to Eric by phone that Jess was in bed with a bad cold and a sore throat. 'She'll be all right by this evening, I expect.'

Eric always suspected that Jess's headaches and colds could be induced to serve her own purposes, but he couldn't imagine her letting Fran and William down today. Greg was on his way. He thought no more about it.

29

Though Bob had been back at his farm for almost two weeks, Fran and William had only seen him once. As he had explained, he had really been away too long on his honeymoon, and with two farms to see to, he was going to have to 'work like distraction' to catch up, which he wanted to do before Jane came home. There was still a lot of anxiety about Nick, and they hadn't yet made any plans for Christmas. His return without Jane had caused no gossip but his return as the prospective buyer of Castle Hill had, especially to those who had any inkling of Bailey's plans for it.

On the morning of Fran's birthday, they went down to breakfast and a pile of cards. They represented a whole range of tastes, from the traditional roses-and-verses one from Sophie to the beautiful pen-and-wash sketch of York Minster from Greg and Jess; from illegible scrawls from Kate's two young children to a pressed-flower bookmark handmade by Bob. There were so many that Fran was beginning not to register them properly when she took from its plain envelope a thick gilt-edged card heavily embossed with gold-lettering:

Mr and Mrs Arnold Bailey
request the pleasure of your company on
New Year's Eve
at a housewarming party
for their new home at
Casablanca
Lane's End
Old Swithinford

From 8 p.m.   R.S.V.P.

The envelope was addressed to both of them. They looked at each other blankly.

'What are we going to do about it?' Fran said. 'Why on earth have they invited us?'

'I'd like to bet there's a similar one in Beth and Elyot's post, Eric's, Jess and Greg's, Dr Henderson's, all the Bridgefoots – and everybody else except Bob Bellamy,' he said. 'This is the first shot in Bailey's campaign to take over the village. It's the equivalent of him joining the shooting syndicate Bob told us about, getting his foot in with the *ci-devant* leaders of the community he has to get rid of before he can take over.'

'I shan't go!' Fran said, very firmly. 'I shall have a previous engagement, if it's only with the dentist.'

'If you do go, you will have to find yourself a new escort,' rejoined William. 'I have given my word to Sophie to do my best to confound his politics and frustrate his knavish tricks.'

Fran beamed on him. 'On thee our hopes we fix,' she concluded. 'God save our village.'

She rose, gathering up all her cards and gifts. 'I wonder what the Brian Bridgefoots and the Vic Giffords will do,' she said. 'It's on the same evening as Charles's twenty-first birthday. I expect Brian knew all along. That would account for the decision not to give Charles a party. They would have clashed, and everybody would have had to take sides and form up in battle lines.'

'I think it's rather a pity that we didn't get that same chance to show a bit of a united front at once,' William answered. 'Mm. That may have given me an idea. Let me deal with the invitation. I'll decline for us both. I know you. You would have been so polite it would have convinced him that we were both devastated to miss it.'

He handed her his reply five minutes later, written in his own hand on one of his academic letter-headed cards. 'Professor Burbage and Mrs F. Catherwood thank Mr and Mrs Bailey for their kind invitation, but beg to be excused.'

'That,' said Fran, 'is a put-down so refined that neither of the Baileys will be able to comprehend it.'

Fran had indeed got her birthday wish. At seven o'clock, when she and William knocked on the door of the Old Rectory, she was greeted by her entire family, excluding Jess and Greg: Roland and Monica with a baby each, Kate and Jeremy with Helen and Andrew holding their hands, Eric and Elyot hovering with trays of drinks at the ready, and Beth standing by the piano to strike up 'Happy Birthday'. After half an hour, Kate put her children to bed, and Fran went up to say goodnight to them. Ammy was sitting on their bed, telling a story. They had no eyes for Fran, so she crept out again. Beth really had been inspired to ask the Petrie girls to help. Young as they were, Helen and Andy had sensed their babysitters' competence and experience, and had established immediate rapport with them. Monica had delivered the twins into Ammy's keeping. 'All the baby stuff is in the basket – though you probably won't need anything till you bring them down. Is there anything else you would like?'

Ammy couldn't think that there could be anything anybody could possibly want that hadn't been provided for them. Never before in their whole lives had they been in possession of an unopened box of chocolates each! Left, discreetly labelled, on a tray with bottles of orangeade and canapés.

One glance into the kitchen was simply too much for Fran's composure. Thirzah sat by the side of the Aga looking so much like Queen Victoria that the cork popped before she could greet her. She had to retreat and start afresh. She had never seen Thirzah before without her apron – that was it. Sophie, of course, was wearing her best blue gingham one, and round her neck were the cultured pearls William had brought her from America. They were her equivalent to the royal standard flying over Sandringham. Ned was 'busying himself' clearing flat surfaces for unopened bottles, and generally showing the contingent of waiters and waitresses Eric had provided where to find things. As far as Fran could judge, harmony reigned everywhere.

'Jess and Greg are late,' Beth said. 'I promised Eric that we would be at the table by eight, because of the food being brought ready cooked.'

'Jess was in bed with a bad cold this morning,' Eric said. 'Anne rang up to tell me so, but she assured me that Jess would be fine by tonight.'

'Maybe Greg's late getting back,' Monica put in. 'He rang me to say he might be, because he'd gone up to York. But from what I understood, it had been agreed that Jess should come when she was ready, and he would come straight here if he was late.'

Eric said, 'If I may be allowed to advise you, I wouldn't wait. I would start at eight o'clock without them. They will surely ring up if anything has gone wrong.'

The meal had reached the dessert course before Greg appeared, alone. He was still wearing casual clothes, and looked both tired and strained.

'I only got home about an hour ago,' he apologized to Beth. 'I went home to change because I thought Jess would already be here – but I found her there, not at all well. She had Anne Rushlake with her, and said that at this late hour it would be stupid to change and come out, so she insisted I came alone, just as I was. She sends her apologies, of course.'

His dry tone told Fran that Jess had done no such thing.

'Is she in bed?' asked Beth, all concern. William watched Greg's face as he answered.

'No,' Greg answered reluctantly. 'She and Anne appeared to have been having a bit of an argument, and to speak truth, I guess that's the real reason for her not feeling well enough to bother to change. I walked in on a disagreement about some other invitation both had had by this morning's post. Jess was saying that nothing would drag her there, and Anne that nothing would keep her away. I got my marching orders pretty promptly, and decided I should be a fool to forego a lovely meal I'm in need of and company I like, to be pig-in-the-middle there. So please, here I am.'

They fed him and wined him, and made much of him. He was a man who appreciated creature comforts, and soon cheered up, but it did not escape Fran's notice, or Monica's, that he was drinking much more than usual.

Port and liqueurs were going round the table when the two Petrie girls appeared, each carrying a baby. Monica excused herself and went to feed the babies in the sitting-room. The others remained round the table, though the flow of conversation had been stopped.

Elyot took it up again. 'We got an invitation by this morning's post, too,' he said. 'To the housewarming party of Bailey's new monstrosity. I don't know the man at all, so I suppose Beth must. It isn't my idea of spending a happy New Year's Eve.'

Beth looked absolutely affronted. 'Why on earth should you suppose I know him?' she said. 'I can assure you I don't, and I don't particularly want to, either!' Her vehemence surprised Elyot. 'Avast, shipmate!' he said. 'I only meant that I thought I'd heard you say something about him concerning the church.'

'You did,' said Beth, snapping her mouth with such force that Greg nicknamed her 'the snapping turtle' on the spot.

'He doesn't seem to be a very popular character with my lady wife,' Elyot said. 'I wonder why?'

'Nor with mine, if it comes to that,' William said. Then, becoming quite serious suddenly, 'Nor, in fact, with me. Or anybody else who cares for Old Swithinford and our way of life. He is, I fear, a petty Hitler who has got to be stopped in his tracks before it's too late.'

Beth was the only other besides Fran who knew what he was referring to. 'Go on, William. We're all friends here. Tell them what you mean.'

William outlined succinctly what he had understood from Sophie about the meeting at the church. Everything he reported was corroborated as truth by Beth.

'Those are the facts,' said William. 'I must warn you that I am an historian. Fran once quoted to me something she had read – that an historian is a prophet with his head turned backwards. That's a neat way of saying that you can sometimes guess the future by learning lessons from history. What I make of the facts we are confronted with may be delusions on my part. But I do know a few things about the character of Arnold Bailey from what Bob Bellamy has told me first hand. If you want me to say any more, I will. If you think I'm off my nut, or drunk on Elyot's marvellous port, I'll shut up.'

Beth, dignified and cool, looked round the ring of interested faces. 'I'm the only one among you with a personal interest in the church in its own right,' she said. 'I care about that. I care very much now that the village I've come to love doesn't disappear under suburban houses as part of Swithinford New Town. Elyot and I have very good personal reasons for caring what happens to Bob Bellamy – don't forget he was Elyot's best man at our wedding. Greg, Elyot, Eric – do you think William's exaggerating? None of you belongs to the church, but you know as well as he does that the church is still the nerve-centre of the community, *because there is no other.*

'There's no school for our children to grow up in together and learn the sense of belonging to a community. The Green Dragon's on its last legs, because all the young folk have cars or motor bikes and want the tarted-up pubs in Swithinford with juke-boxes and such things. William's just pointed out to us that if we don't do something soon we shan't have a church much longer. Once upon a time there used to be leaders like the parson and the squire, the doctor and the lawyer. They've all gone. Who's going to hold what's left of this community together if we don't at least try?'

'Bravo Beth,' said Greg, astounded at the fire aflame in this usually calm, self-controlled woman. All the others were left a bit speechless by her clear analysis of the causes of the collapse.

'Why "we", though, my love? Who are "we"? And what right have we to step in and interfere? Look at us. We are all comparative newcomers – compared, for example, with George Bridgefoot or even Kenneth Bean.'

Beth turned on him. 'How dare you say that, Elyot? You are only a "newcomer" because you have chosen not to involve yourself! Your family was here during the Hundred Years' War! Your genetic inheritance – and therefore my baby's – is here. In this village. So are William and Fran's, and because of that, so are Roland's and Katie's and their children's. Greg's wife is one of their family, too. And I am not only now a de ffranksbridge – I am the daughter of the last parson the village ever had or will have if we let Bailey win. Even Eric is allied to us because of Monica. Who are we, Elyot? Collectively, we are the heirs of the old village. If it belongs to anybody, it belongs to us. We simply have to fight for what is ours, and what we've still got, before it's stolen from us right under our noses.'

She sat down suddenly, cheeks aflame and inclined to be embarrassed. She looked pleadingly at William: after all, everything she had said had been in support of his theory.

He spoke gently. 'You are absolutely right, Beth, except for one small detail. Wars may be influenced by wise and courageous officers, but when it comes to it, they are won by the troops – the matelots, the private soldiers, the ground staff. Where is our *masse de manœuvre*, to use Churchill's words?'

Fran stood up. 'In the kitchen. Waiting for orders to dismiss, I imagine. Sit still – I'm going to round them up.'

30

Fran returned almost at once, ushering into the dining-room a muffled-up, hatted and gloved Thirzah, with Sophie, Ned and Daniel following her in a line like ducklings after their mother to the pond. Daniel, bringing up the rear, was looking decidedly sheepish, and was endeavouring to get near enough to Fran to explain in a hoarse whisper that he hadn't expected Thirzah to be so late and though he did know how she was getting home, he thought he had better 'just walk up' to make sure she was all right. Fran guessed that he had been left orders to do exactly that, to make it clear to everybody concerned what a risk his sick wife had taken in agreeing to leave her own fireside to 'oblige' them.

Elyot stood up to greet them, saying rather helplessly, 'We need some more chairs.'

Chairs were brought from the kitchen, and the four rather embarrassed newcomers persuaded to sit down 'to hear what we have been saying about the church'.

Monica went back to her place at Greg's side. Pulling her chair out for her, he whispered, 'Where did the two pre-Raphaelite angels appear from?'

'Beth found them,' she whispered back. 'Why?'

'Keep your eye on them,' he said. 'In another five years, they'll make even Michelle Stanhope look like a free gift, whatever she's wrapped in.'

'Shh,' Beth said. 'Go ahead, William.'

'I know you are all tired,' he began, turning his full charm on to Thirzah, 'so we mustn't keep you long. But we've been talking about all the changes at the church, and where it's all leading. Sophie told Fran and me outright that we weren't doing anything to show we cared what was happening, and that there were a lot of others like us who at least ought to be interested enough to see what's going on under their noses. From what we understood from Sophie, what upset you all most was the way everything was simply taken out of your hands without warning, and more or less handed over to other people who till now haven't had any connection with church affairs. Have I got that much right?' There were mutterings of assent.

'Mr Bates,' said William, appealing, according to convention, to the older of the two men, 'tell us how you feel about what happened at that meeting, and what you think may happen in the future.'

'There won't be no future,' said Thirzah, getting in while Daniel was still rounding up his courage to open his mouth at all in such company and without her permission. 'George Bridgefoot's the only one left to get things done as they should be, and 'e ain't well enough to do nothing properly now. Come Christmas, our church'll only be like that one up Castle Hill. Deserted and derelicted, except for that there lay reader from Hen Street taking one service a month.'

Ned nodded, apparently agreeing in principle with her. 'No Rector, no carol service, no bells,' he said. 'Not like Christmas were once. We used to have a carol service Christmas Eve, and a watchnight service for them as could be there when the children had been put to bed. This year'll be worse than last year. Early communion with no music, took by a parson as we don't know and shall very likely never set eyes on again.'

'But can't the churchwardens organize such things when there's no Rector?' William asked. 'A carol service, for example? Mrs Franks won't have given up playing the organ by then.'

Daniel found his voice at last. 'George would ha' done something o' the sort if he hadn't lost 'eart,' he said. 'Though he couldn't do it all by hisself even if he wanted to. But I don't reckon he could face it, seeing as everybody else is lost 'eart an' all.'

'But isn't there a new churchwarden?'

Fran thought that if William had bellowed an order at them, the four would not have closed ranks and snapped more smartly to attention. They drew together, as it were, standing metaphorically shoulder to shoulder, in the face of the enemy.

'That there Kid Bean!' said Thirzah, voicing his name in a tone of such contempt and loathing that Fran wondered if Thirzah's still-gloved fingers were being crossed under the tablecloth against the devil and all his works. 'A wolf in sheep's clothing if ever I see one.'

'No man can serve two masters,' said Sophie, not to be outdone in applying a knowledge of the Bible. ''E can't be about 'is own business come Christmastime, and His Father's as well, let alone Bailey's into the bargain. If only George was well enough to keep things going, like, there'd be others as would ha' made a heffort for 'is sake. But them as is stopped coming won't start again to watch Kid and Beryl lording it uvver us all.'

'Are you saying that there is still a congregation of proper members of the church, if they took more interest in it?' William asked.

''Course there is!' Sophie was indignant. 'It's only since the old Rector give everything over to that there 'Ector Birch, and we never 'ad no proper parson no more, as folks 'ave stopped coming.'

'Hold your tongue, do!' said Thirzah, red in the face, making signs to her to mind what she was saying in front of Beth.

'I'm only telling the truth. Mis' Franks knows as well as I do as 'er father wasn't cut out to be a country parson. She'd be the first to say so. But there's still a few of us as goes reg'lar and some who come when they can. I reckon there's a lot more as would come, do things was livened up a bit. Time was when folks come from far and wide just to 'ear our bells, and when Miss were alive, our choir used to win prizes. We was proud of our church, in them days.'

'And could be again, if you asked me,' said Ned. 'It ain't the church as is changed, it's the people. But there is folks who still hanker after what it used to be like, and would quite likely start coming again if it was. Folks like the Tibbetts, and the Moulds's and the Wilsons and . . .'.

The four of them vied with each other to round up the backsliders till they amounted to about thirty. William felt he was letting purpose slide into a morass of nostalgia, and cut in rather abruptly.

'That's good – but we can't bring those times back. All we can do – if anything – is to see that Kenneth Bean with Bailey's cheque book behind him doesn't make sure that we lose what's left. The first thing, perhaps, is to show him that a lot of people still care. Get them together for something at Christmas, for instance. Round up a really good-sized congregation for Christmas morning? All you and the Bridgefoots would be there in any case, and some of the others you've mentioned. I've promised Sophie that Fran and I will be there, though if it is only a communion service we shan't be allowed to take the sacrament. We might be able to persuade others of our family and friends to go with us, if they knew why it was so important to be seen there. Jess and Greg – and Mrs Rushlake – and the Commander' – Elyot opened his mouth to protest but the look William gave him acted as well as any gob-stopper – 'and Mrs Franks, of course. Unfortunately, Kate and Jeremy won't be here.'

'But Roland and Monica will, and Monica's father. Don't argue with me, Dad. We've got such a lot to be thankful for since last Christmas.' Eric said no more.

'And Bob and Jane Bellamy,' said Fran, 'and Charlie and Charles . . .' She was aware of the sudden astounded silence.

'Jane *Bellamy?*' It was Monica who had asked. Fran's face flooded with colour and chagrin at having so stupidly and unintentionally let the cat out of the bag. William dared not speak for fear of making things worse.

Sophie came stolidly to Fran's rescue. 'As far as I can see,' she said, 'there ain't many 'ere now as it'll be much of a surprise to. Or make no difference to, and I should ha' thought all of us 'ere knows when to keep our mouths shut if we're asked to. Like me. I knowed a'ready, 'cos I were in the secret of it with Fran from the first.'

('That's one in the eye for Thirzah,' Fran thought, rapidly regaining her composure.)

'We knew too,' said Beth, not disclosing how they had come by the information.

'We wondered,' said Monica. 'That's what made me so quick off the ball. But where is she? Why hasn't she come home with him?'

'I can't say as I'm surprised,' said Ned. 'I were there at work in the garden that day as we had that posh visitor from London up at Benedict's for dinner, and them two were there an' all. I said to myself as there was something going on as I weren't supposed to know about. Then just as I were packing up, Bellamy and Mis' Hadley come outside together for a minute, and didn't know as I was in the shed watching 'em.

'Ah, I says to myself, now I can guess how many beans make five! It ain't allus the easy answer o' four and a little 'un. This one's a case o' "two beans and a bean and a bean-and-a-half and a half a bean". Seems I was right.'

'You were,' said Fran. 'I'm not altogether sorry I let it out, but please don't tell anybody else. You see, young Charles knows already, and he and Charlie went to the wedding in London – but it's being very difficult for him because his father doesn't approve of Charlie. As soon as ever Jane can leave Nick, she'll come home. By Christmas, I think, but Nick isn't out of the wood yet. That's one reason for them keeping everything quiet. And I'm sure you all know that Mr Bailey was hoping to buy Castle Hill and turn Mr Bellamy out so that he could build another estate on it. The wedding helped to stop that happening. What we're doing tonight is trying to stop him building again anywhere else round here. Please don't tell George about the marriage, Mr Bates. Let Charles.'

She looked up at Daniel, pleading, and was abashed. Till that moment when she met Daniel's eyes, she knew that she had never really seen the man behind the name that was always on Sophie's lips. The man across Beth's table from her now was quiet, kind, easygoing and willing to let Thirzah have her way if by doing so he could keep his house at peace. But that clean-cut, weatherbeaten face was that of the man whose principles had made him stand up for Wendy in the face of his wife's domineering anger, and who had offered help when everyone else but Sophie had turned on her; who could, as at that sad time, make his presence felt – just as George had done on another never-to-be-forgotten occasion. He might have been the labourer for George the farmer since they were young together, but they were two of a kind. That was 'equality' of the sort politically minded theorists had never even imagined. Two men of the same yeoman breed. How do you tell one grain of the salt of the earth from another?

Daniel was looking back at her, and his look told her more than his words. 'I'm been keeping George's own secrets for nigh on fifty year, now,' he said. 'It'll be a sad day when I – or any o' mine – can't keep a secret.'

'I think,' said Beth at last, 'that what William has in mind is that if somehow we could arrange something over Christmas and drum up a good congregation, it would give notice that as a village community we're not dead yet. But what sort of thing? We haven't much time, and to try and not succeed would play right into their hands. Could we bring it off?'

The answer came from the most unexpected quarter, Eric. Not just the guest who was there because he was a friend and Monica's father, but the Eric who had once been a Commando officer.

'Yes,' he said. 'But not at Christmas. That would be a mistake. You can't turn the clock back, so don't try. Christmas hasn't got much to do with church, these days. And it's too late. Plans for Christmas Eve were made months ago, for big functions with tickets sold in advance – like ours at the hotel – and for every pub and club in Swithinford. Those who don't go to pubs will go to bed early because they know they'll be roused in the middle of the night to watch pillowcases being emptied. Times have changed. Campaigns against people like Bailey, or the war we were forced into against Hitler, are long-term things that have to be planned strategically from the beginning. It's no use firing the first shot if you haven't got your artillery in place to keep up the barrage. The idea is good, William, but you haven't thought it through well enough. Will a church full of people for just one nostalgic occasion be anything but a gesture of rather hopeless defiance? With the congregation down to five again, the next Sunday?

'You may think I'm a fine one to be offering advice. But maybe I am the outsider who can see the game better than you can. For example: we get quite a lot of people staying at the hotel over weekends who are, in fact, regular churchgoers. They ask at the reception desk what time there are services they can attend. To be quite honest, we haven't thought it worthwhile to suggest Old Swithinford. And yet, of course, that's exactly what we should have been doing, because it's just what people from towns would lap up! If it were made attractive enough. Then there are the tourists. We get a lot, especially from the States. How many people know about the beacon on the tower? Or the frescoes? How many musicians know about the organ?

'Look, my idea when I came here in the first place was to preserve this village as an "olde-worlde" bit of the past. It worked – very largely because I was saved by people like you from making it too "chocolate-boxy", the sort of place that never had existed. The church wasn't part of my plan, being out of my reach in any case, so I never concerned myself with it, till now. But apart from any other consideration, such as friendship or the fact that it is now my home, as a businessman I can't allow Old Swithinford to lose its character. My plans for developing it were, and still are, the direct opposite of Bailey's. I have very good reasons for doing whatever I can to back you, so I hope you'll let me be in on whatever you decide. We need long-term strategy. But tonight we need to think tactically of surprise action in the short term. I can't suggest an alternative to your carol service off the top of my head, but I do say lay off Christmas.'

There was a murmur of appreciation, even from Sophie, followed by another silence.

'When we used to 'ave a watchnight service a-New Year's Eve,' said Thirzah, breaking it a little less portentously than usual, the church would be so full as you could hardly get another one in – and after the blessing we used to stand and wait, so quiet as you could ha' heard a pin drop, till George Bridgefoot's father rung the tenor bell for the first stroke o' midnight. And when he'd got to twelve, there'd be a moment's quiet again, like, to say farewell to the old year and let the new 'un in – and then all the other bells would join in and we'd all turn and wish each other a happy New Year and them bells would still be ringing till everybody had got home safe, however far away they lived. And you could see the lanterns bobbing about as folks walked home, 'cos there weren't no electric street-lights then. Some of us only had jam-jars with candles in 'em. And them as was too old to get to church, or them as 'ad children too young to leave, would all draw their curtains back so as their lights showed out, and set their front doors open to let the New Year in. And they'd be standing against their front doors calling out to each other, and to all of us as we walked past. And the church itself only 'ad 'ile-lamps then, and when you looked back at it the windows would look all soft, like, and the bells sound so j'yful . . .'

'Could we revive that?' asked William. 'Would that be a possibility?'

'Please do,' said Kate, who until then hadn't said a word. 'We shall all be here for the New Year.'

'Won't there be just as many functions arranged for that evening as for Christmas Eve?' asked Greg.

Eric answered, 'Of course there will, but with a difference. On Christmas Eve, people would have to choose between the service and any sort of jollification, because licensing laws treat Christmas Day as a Sunday. No extensions are allowed after midnight. But if anybody wanted to, they could go straight from church on New Year's Eve to a party or a dance that could possibly go on till the early hours of New Year's Day – providing that wasn't on a Sunday. Ordinary pubs can get extensions on New Year's Eve if they want to.'

'I was thinking of the Bailey housewarming,' Greg said.

'I shall be at work,' said Eric shortly.

'We can't leave the twins,' said Roland.

'The doctor will order me to keep my feet up,' said Beth, winking at Elyot.

'We have already declined,' said William, making it plain that he was stating a fact.

'I may be away,' said Greg.

'You can't be, or you won't be here to come to church,' Monica said.

'Bob and Jane won't be invited,' observed Fran.

'What about the Bridgefoots?' asked Beth.

'That scuttles your whole idea, doesn't it?' said Elyot. 'Isn't New Year's Eve Charles Bridgefoot's twenty-first birthday? You mustn't do anything at all behind George's back. He's the Admiral who has got to persuade the . . . Sea Lords to let the action take place at all.'

Daniel was opening his mouth and shutting it again, trying to make up his mind whether or not to intervene.

Sophie was regarding him with impatience. 'Say what you 'ave to say and be done with it,' she said. 'You look like a man driving a pig to market, as'll goo every which way except the one you want it to.'

'Tha's just it,' Daniel said. 'I were trying to drive myself to break my word to George for the first time ever! There's been such ructions up at Glebe and at Temperance about Charles coming up to twenty-one as never was in the Bridgefoot fam'ly afore. Tha's mainly what's wrong wi' George – why he ain't got no 'eart left for nothing else. There ain't a-gooing to be no party, not even a fam'ly one. They're all got invitations for this posh do o' Bailey's, except for Charles hisself. Some of 'em want to go to it, specially Vic Gifford's lot. But George 'as put 'is foot down, and says as they can go wherever they like come evening time, but he's a-going to call a meeting o' the Bridgefoot Farms company at dinnertime on New Year's Eve, and they'd better all be there. I can't tell you no more than that, though I do know what George plans to do. But I reckon as it would do 'im a power o' good to have something else to think about, atween now and then, specially if it was to do with the church. His fam'ly from London'll be 'ere, and once the meetin's over, they'd be free to come to church with 'im and Molly.'

'What a blessing you're here, Mr Bates,' said William. 'Of course we can't do anything at all without George – and I suppose Kid Bean.'

'It won't suit him,' said Ned. 'He's got a invite to Bailey's party. Beryl's running round squawking about it like an old hen with its head off. He'll put a damper on any plans for that night.'

'George can request it,' said Beth authoritatively, 'and as the people's representative Mr Bean would either have to agree or hand his duties over to George, who has been doing both jobs ever since I've been here in any case. I don't think Mr Bean would actually be missed very much. Let's consider other details. Mr Bates, you must know all the men who used to sing in the choir. Could we raise enough to make up a procession? If there are any children who like singing, girls as well as boys, I'll have some choir practices here.'

Thirzah half-raised herself from her chair, and proclaimed, 'Dan'el will be there.'

Fran bit back her giggle by turning to Ned, 'What about the bells? There wouldn't be any point without the full peal. Is there any chance that you could persuade all the ringers to turn out?'

'Ah!' said Ned. 'I shouldn't be surprised. After I've had a word about it with George.'

'So are we all agreed that we test that possibility?' asked William. 'Let me know as soon as you can, and then we'll hand it over to George to be front runner. Then our part will be to get people to attend.'

'It's twenty to midnight, and time we was all 'ome and in bed. Get you off, Dan' el, and see Soph' safe 'ome,' said Thirzah.

Elyot got to his feet again. 'Sit still,' he said. 'I'm going to take you all home by car. As soon as you're ready.'

Eric banged the table for their attention. 'Can I ask just one more question?' he said. 'You seem to have got everything ready to fire the salute to the New Year, except the cannon. Who is going to conduct the service? From what I've understood, Bailey's already made sure the Archdeacon's in his camp. Who's going to be responsible for finding a parson here on the spot at midnight in midwinter?'

They all looked at each other, as William said later, as gormless as the Twelve Wise Men of Gotham who all counted eleven others and declared the twelfth man missing. None of them could see the answer to the problem on which all the rest of the last hour's planning depended.

Sophie caught Thirzah's eye, and Thirzah caught Dan's. They all stood up, feet planted firmly under Elyot's dining table. Thirzah held up a hand gloved in black leather, palm outwards. Mesmerized, the rest all stared at her till silence reigned complete.

'Ask, and ye shall receive,' she said. 'Doubtless the Lord will provide.'

Bob Bellamy had rung Fran on that Saturday morning to wish her a happy birthday, and to tell her that he and Charles and Charlie were off to spend the weekend in London with Jane's father. She asked if Jane would be coming back with them. Not this time, he said, but he hoped in a couple of weeks, so that she was established at Castle Hill in good time for Christmas. She was staying in London till it had been decided what steps were to be taken now with regard to Nick's selective amnesia. Bob said he would let Fran know when they got back.

Physically Nick was getting stronger every day, and to all intents and purposes as intelligent as he had ever been. He retained memory of much of his education without recalling the details of places or people connected with it. His knowledge of English literature and his grasp of Latin and French were unimpaired. His grandfather conversed with him in French, and read Latin with him, most days. He began to teach him German, and found Nick as apt a pupil still as his teachers had previously done. Doctors and psychologists were agreed that his was a most interesting and unusual case – but nobody seemed to have much idea what to do next.

Mr Gordon favoured a personal tutor to coach him for a university place. That had been Nick's ambition. There was no reason why he should not achieve it still. Jane was grateful for the suggestion, but she wanted her son back, not a stranger who might just as well be coming from an orphanage. She insisted on continuing to hope.

He remembered Jane no more than anybody else, but accepted what he was told. He had been introduced to Bob, who was going to marry his mother, as he did his doctors and nurses. Relationships with people were all of the present; the past was lost to him. It was impossible for those trying to help him to put themselves in his place.

Jane pointed out that so far his memory had had little to stimulate it. He hadn't known before his accident that he had a grandfather. While he was in the coma, Jane herself had undergone a metamorphosis. Was her son expected to be able to relate this happy, well-dressed, affluent woman whom he only saw in London with the poverty-stricken village charwoman who had been his mother? He had only ever met Bob about three times, always at functions among many other strangers. Surely the test would come when he was confronted with someone like Charles with whom he had been brought up and who had shared everything with him since the day he first went to school?

Charles understood the situation with his head, but found it extremely difficult to conceive a Nick who did not recognize him. Against the advice of doctors and psychologists alike, Jane wanted to make the experiment of confronting Nick with Charles.

So, while in Old Swithinford that Saturday evening an extraordinary discussion was taking place round the table at the Old Rectory, another problem was being thrashed out after a sumptuous dinner in Belgravia. Charles was on Jane's side, declaring that if she wanted to use him as a guinea-pig, he was willing to take the risk of getting his feelings bruised. He would have enough sense to know that if he was not recognized, it did not mean that Nick was rejecting him. Mr Gordon and Bob were against the whole idea. They thought it too dangerous. It should not be attempted without medical advice and supervision.

Jane was almost reduced to tears of disappointment. She had been so sure that Bob and her father would be on her side, and that it would be Charles who would have to be persuaded.

'Jane, my dearest,' Effendi said soothingly, holding out his hand to her. 'Do you really think that such as we ought to interfere? Think of the risk we might be taking of doing Nick harm.'

'Think of the time that's being wasted while we wait for your expensive psychiatrists to pussy-foot around,' she replied. 'Charles and I both *know* Nick. We know the sort of life he lived before this happened. Has Dr Briegmann any idea of the difference between all this' – her hand indicated everything in their surroundings at that moment – 'and winter on a farm in East Anglia? How can he judge what might jog Nick's memory? What harm could it possibly do Nick to meet Charles?'

Mr Gordon turned to Charlie, who so far had said nothing. 'Charlie, we need an umpire. What do you say?'

'That you're all missing the obvious. You have to combine the two arguments. What you need is a psychiatrist who knew Nick as he was, and is familiar with Old Swithinford into the bargain.'

Mr Gordon looked disappointed, as if he had genuinely expected her to decide the issue. 'My dear,' he said, 'if wishes were horses, beggars would ride.'

'I'm not joking,' she answered. 'What's wrong with Charles's Uncle Alex? I'll bet his reputation as a psychiatrist is as good as Dr Briegmann's, and he knows Nick quite well.' She appealed to Charles, to Jane, to Bob, who were all looking as if they had been struck dumb, to back her.

'Charles?' said Mr Gordon.

Charles nodded, trying to find his voice. 'Dr Alexander Marland,' he said. 'Married to my father's sister. Nick was always in and out of our house when they used to come there after they were married.'

'Charlie – come and kiss me,' I'm beginning to think Charles isn't the only man who can't do without you.'

She leaned over towards him, and obliged. 'How's your Arabic?' he asked. 'Do you remember it?' She did, and proved it. He was delighted with her all over again, told her so, and then turned purposefully back to the business in hand.

It took only a matter of minutes for Effendi to look up Alex, check his credentials and find his private address. 'We may, I think, be up against the question of medical etiquette,' he said. 'I need a personal introduction, not connected with either family, so that I can ask his advice man to man as an acquaintance, with no obligation of medical professionalism attached. William Burbage is the obvious choice.'

Which is why William and Fran were deprived of their usual lazy lie-in on Sunday morning. Mr Gordon had William answering the telephone at eight a.m.; William was talking to Alex by eight-thirty; at nine, Mr Gordon arrived at Alex's home.

He was back at his own flat before eleven a.m. Jane was inclined to be emotional, but her father became his most professional self, and somewhat awe-inspiring to Charlie and Charles.

'I think Dr Marland is exactly the sort of man I would trust to help Nick,' he said. 'Jane, dearest, he has agreed to come round this morning, as I had hoped – but he has warned me that we must not hope for any miracles. I want you and Bob to go and fetch Nick from the clinic. I have already arranged for him to spend the day here. Charles and Charlie are to keep out of the way. When you come back, Jane, go straight to the kitchen – and Bob, you stay with her and help her to prepare coffee or something. You simply must not let Nick know that there is anything afoot concerning him. Send him straight in to me. Tell him I have a friend with me, and suggest that he brings us drinks. Dr Marland wants to observe if there is the very slightest reaction or sign of recognition when Nick meets him. I am also to introduce Dr Marland by name, to see if that means anything to Nick.'

Alex looked up at the thin young man carrying the tray of glasses and bottles. There was no sign of any recognition whatsoever.

'Hello, Nick, my boy,' said his grandfather. 'I'm glad they let you come out at such short notice to see your mother and Bob. This is a friend of mine, Dr Alex Marland.'

The boy set the tray down and took Alex's outstretched hand. 'How do you do, sir,' he said. 'What would you like to drink?'

Effendi excused himself for a moment and went into the kitchen, where he broke the news to Jane and Bob that the experiment had already failed.

'No tears, now,' he ordered Jane. 'It was your idea, and we've tried it; but it's only the first tiny step of a long journey. We now have a wonderful ally in Charles's Uncle Alex. So fetch Charles and Charlie, and explain to them, and then all of you join us for drinks before Alex goes. If there is no remembrance at all of Charles, it does not mean the end of hope. We simply go on waiting.'

'For a miracle?' said Jane, trying to control her face.

Bob took her into his arms, and held her, while Charles and Charlie prepared themselves for what they now knew must be a sad and trying ordeal. Charlie clung to Charles's hand, and they closed in on Effendi as if drawing strength from his cool poise. They all stood waiting for Bob and Jane. His arms were still round her, but his eyes were fixed on a huge plane tree the other side of the street. When he brought his gaze back to the waiting group, he looked round from one to the other separately, and finally down at Jane in his arms.

'Yes,' he said. 'For a miracle. It won't happen yet, my beauty, so don't expect it. You have to wait till the time's right for a miracle, but they can still happen. I know.'

32

There was no miracle waiting for Greg at Southside House. Although he had enjoyed the company at the Old Rectory the night before, he had not been happy. It was the first time in Old Swithinford that he had ever gone anywhere without Jess. He had told them, as instructed, that she had too bad a headache to face the party, but he knew it wasn't the truth. Though they had all pretended sympathy, he knew that they didn't believe it either. Was the rift between him and Jess becoming evident to their friends? That there was a widening rift, he could not deny.

Till now, since the day he had first met Jess, there had never been any woman in his life but her – although he was an adept at flirting. He hadn't wanted anyone but her; she had satisfied him, as a wonderful companion, a loyal wife, and above all, a lover whose passion for him matched his own for her. It had certainly not been the same lately.

As he walked home from the Old Rectory, he wondered if she would be waiting up for him. He hoped so. He felt a desperate need to put right whatever it was between them, now, tonight. For one thing, because he felt pangs of conscience. There had been too many times lately when he could have got home and had chosen not to, preferring the company of other men in pubs, or a bit of fun in mixed company after a fashion show. He knew she had not believed his weak, and sometimes silly excuses, which would never have been necessary if she had been more welcoming, as of old, when he could never get back to her fast enough.

Until he had met Michelle Stanhope.

There were no lights on at Southside House, so he supposed Jess was already in bed. Many were the times she had gone to bed in a huff, pretending to be asleep until he had crept in beside her, whispering endearments and gentle caresses till she had turned towards him as eager to be made love to as he to make love. She was still his Jess, changed very little in looks except that her hair was tinged with white at the temples and her face just a little thinner. He could see her in his mind's eye now, lying awake waiting for him, anxious to make up to him with love for her cool greeting when he had arrived home this evening.

And yet he was lingering out by the gate, reluctant to go in. Why? He tried to find excuses for himself. Perhaps it was because he was fed up with being suspected and even accused of doing things he had not done and had had no intention of doing. And she continually repulsed him. What was she trying to do to him?

There were plenty of other women about these days. Willing women like Michelle Stanhope, who sent him signals he had so far pretended not to understand; who was probably at this very moment in bed with that huge oaf of a policeman whom she had told him was her husband. With those gorgeous long legs bare and that wonderful hair loose, falling over those pert breasts that Monica's design for the close-fitting tunic would show off to such perfection . . .

What would it be like to hold her, to stroke her, to feel the shape of her under his hands, the fullness of bosom and buttock, to watch those huge eyes with their long curling lashes closing with desire as he kissed her . . . In comparison, Jess was old, scrawny, flat as a boy, hard as nails, her eyes blazing with temper rather than love . . . Good God! What was the matter with him? He must have drunk too much of Elyot's good port. He opened the door and went straight upstairs, without switching on the main light. They always left a little alabaster lamp alight in the hall, by whose glow it was easy enough to negotiate the stairs.

He stopped outside the bedroom door, his eye caught in the semi-darkness by a patch of white against the polished natural wood of the door. He switched on the landing light, and saw it for what it was. A notice, as in hotels, hung round the knob, saying in Jess's own bold, scrawling Roman capitals, 'DO NOT DISTURB'.

She must truly have felt ill! Well, of course he would not disturb her. He called softly outside the door, asking if she wanted anything. There was no answer, so he guessed she must be asleep. He would sleep on the divan in his studio.

He went downstairs again on tiptoe. The lock of his studio door was broken, and the door slightly ajar. He stepped inside, and switched on the light. The whole room was in chaos, his easel knocked over, and his *Madonna and Child* lying face downwards on the whiskery raffia matting with which the boarded floor was covered. He rushed towards it, squelching a full tube of vermilion paint flat underfoot in his haste to pick up the painting and discover how much harm had been done to it.

Nothing serious. It had been almost dry, for one thing, and one corner of the falling canvas stretcher had caught and lodged against the leg of the table on which his paints and brushes lay. That had prevented the wet canvas itself from coming into direct contact with the matting.

With shaking hands he stood it on the divan to examine it. He could hardly believe that it was undamaged, because now, with sick revulsion that made him tremble, he realized that this was no accident. It was Jess, his Jess, who had deliberately, and with malice aforethought, taken revenge on him for finding pleasure in something she didn't share, hurting him where she knew she could cause him most suffering. He set up the easel and placed the canvas on it, seating himself down on the divan in front of it.

Any slight guilt he had previously felt towards her lost itself in the face of this proof of what she felt for him. The pain of knowing that she could bring herself to do this to him for the moment swamped every other feeling. He picked a few wisps of loose raffia from the still sticky paint here and there, and sat staring at it till its beauty and his pride at having created it began to counteract the shock.

The pain in his heart oozed away, to be replaced by cold, diamond-hard anger. He covered the painting loosely with its protective cloth again, kicked a few tubes of paint out of his way, and went up the stairs three at a time. The 'DO NOT DISTURB' notice took flight down the steps, and he began to beat on the door with fists clenched into rounded balls of solidified fury.

Little by little, Jess had penned herself into a difficult corner. She was a complex character in a complex situation just at the time in a woman's life when emotions tend to become complex and exaggerated for no good reason. All sorts of feelings that had been building up inside her for a long time had come to a head that week, and she had woken up that Saturday morning with a bad headache, which she guessed had been self-induced.

She had been upset by Greg's phone call telling her he wouldn't be home till late on Saturday and that she might have to start for Fran's party without him. He knew she didn't want to go. Her chagrin was considerably exacerbated by Anne's being there to hear what he said. She was full of resentment in general.

It seemed to her that whatever she did and wherever she turned, circumstances were not to her liking. She was aware that for the past few months she had been getting herself farther and farther out on a limb as far as her family and nearest friends were concerned. She had exactly the same ambivalent feelings towards Fran with regard to William as she had towards Monica with regard to Greg. Till she had come to Old Swithinford, both those men had been exclusively 'hers' – one her husband and the other her brother. She had had to come to terms with Fran's 'possession' of William, but the friendship-cum-business partnership between her husband and her boss's daughter Monica was different. Something she felt she had to keep an eye on, mainly because she was excluded from it.

No one, not even Greg himself, had ever referred again to her behaviour on that evening last year, and her accusation that Greg was the father of Monica's child, but her relationship with them all had been slightly soured by it ever since. Till then, Eric Choppen had also been 'hers': her boss, her friend, her protégé almost, before he was part of the Benedict's circle. Now, because of Monica's babies, he was related-by-marriage to Fran and William. They had become very much closer since they shared grandchildren. That irked her. Then Greg's partnership in Monica's *haute couture* business had meant him being away much more than he had ever been before, just at the same time as Jess was withdrawing herself from her family and friends, and needed him more, not less.

She could see how silly it was to let her resentment cut her off from almost all her circle of friends, and that the longer it went on, the more difficult it would be to put right. She had to correct it before it was too late, and for that reason she had made up her mind in advance to go to Fran's birthday party, putting on an act of enjoying herself if it killed her. She had told Anne of her intention to go and enjoy herself.

Anne showed that she understood the rebuff, and regarded it as offensive. She said, coolly but plainly, that she had honestly believed Jess's assertions that she had never had any intention of attending the party, and had therefore made herself available to keep the injured wife company all day, and if necessary all night too, at Southside House. Of course, she added, if she had misunderstood, she would go back home again, there and then. She would return later to make sure her friend was well enough to set out; and if Jess was not better, she would stay and care for her. The implication was that Greg would not show up at all.

'Bitch,' thought Jess, as she went to lie down, seething at her own stupidity, disliking Anne intensely, and furious with Greg for giving Anne this chance to make her an object of pity. She convinced herself that Anne had to a large extent engineered the situation, and that she had fallen into Anne's trap and allowed herself to be manipulated. In bed, she wept tears of anger and humiliation, made her headache worse, took some painkillers, and fell into exhausted sleep. She did not rouse until Anne appeared again at her bedside with a cup of tea, and the information that it was already well past six o'clock and Greg had not returned.

Anne said, briskly and in a hospital-sisterly manner, that there was now no question of Jess being able to go out. Before waking Jess she had taken it upon herself to prepare a light supper for them both. It would do Jess good now to eat something.

Jess was trapped. She did feel awful, and the one thing she would not do was to appear at the party at anything but her best. So she gave in, and let Anne become the caring neighbour again – though not without considerable resentment.

When Greg appeared, Jess gave him no time for excuses. 'I'm not going,' she said, offering no other explanation.

Her voice, Greg thought, was not only as cold as ice, but as dangerous as splintered glass.

'One of us ought to go,' he said abruptly. 'I'd better go just as I am. What excuse shall I make for you?'

'That I'm going back to bed with the cold and the headache I've had all day.' He hadn't even kissed Jess. He didn't make a habit of kissing women in whose houses he was no more than the lodger.

33

Five hours later, Greg was hammering on the bedroom door.

A flood of misery and anger returned to Jess with consciousness as the noise roused her. The fury in Greg's voice alerted her to the fact that he'd had too much to drink, reviving her seething hostility towards him, which wrecking his studio had done a good deal to assuage. Let him go on banging on a door that she hadn't locked. The notice on the door and his anger at finding his studio violated had robbed him of what powers of logical thought remained to him. He had taken it for granted that he was locked out of her room.

She knew that he didn't carry drink very well, and had relied on him coming home in the rather maudlin state she had often had to deal with after a party. In that state she could always induce him to forget everything but her, and make him hers entirely. What she hadn't bargained for was that he would go anywhere near his studio, and see what she had done there, before coming to find her in bed and letting her seduce him into forgiving her.

She was afraid that she might have gone too far this time. The man pummelling the door wasn't a tipsy lover impatient to get in to her. He was either genuinely, violently drunk, or mad with temper. For the first time ever, she was frightened of him.

She reached silently for her dressing-gown and slipped into it in the dark. Then she sat, tense, miserable, worn out and scared on the side of the bed. The hammering on the door grew louder, and he began to shout.

'Jess! Let me in, you bloody fool. What do you think you're playing at?'

She didn't answer. He hurt his hand with an extra violent thump, and it did not improve his feelings, or his language. He'd teach the silly bitch to indulge in such tantrums about nothing. She was his wife, after all, and he'd make sure she knew she was, if he had to fetch an axe to break the door down to get at her.

Nursing his bruised hand, he began to wonder how Jess had spent her time. She was always liable to overdo emotional reactions. She could have been drinking, which would account for what he had found in his studio, or – his heart missed a beat – was there a more sinister meaning to that notice on the bedroom door?

He was cold-sober in an instant, his volatile temper subdued by fear. He shook the door again, this time by the knob, and it opened at once, making him feel very silly. A wave of relief went through him as he switched on the light, and saw her, to be replaced at once by revulsion mixed with pity and anger.

He had expected either a vengeful virago, a Juno proudly uttering threats against Jupiter himself, or a woeful damsel histrionically wailing like Mariana in the Moated Grange.

'O, I am a-weary, a-weary,
And I wish that I was dead.'

What he beheld was a shivering mouse of middle-aged woman-hood shrunk into the collar of her woollen robe, thin, pale, limp and spiritless, half-drowned in her own tears. He hardly recognized her. The last epithet he would ever before have applied to 'his' Jess was 'pathetic', but that's what this woman was. He had no idea how to cope. He stood there, bemused, feelings chasing each other as swift as his thoughts.

He felt as helpless as she looked. It was the very middle of the night, and he was suddenly desperately tired. He simply could not cope with one of their spectacular rows, which almost always ended passionately in bed – even if he wanted to make it up that way this time. But he didn't. The thought repelled him. This female was not the Jess he had loved so much for the past twenty-five years; nor was he the rather futile artist husband she had mothered as well as wived, and consequently led by the nose, till now.

He was a successful artist. He could be a still better one, if that portrait was anything to go by. Nor was he washed up yet as an attractive man. Michelle Stanhope had made that so evident to him that he hadn't been able to forget it, or her. He was appalled by a glimpse of an uncomfort-able future in which Jess might have good cause to be jealous, if he followed the slippery path he had now started on, and down which his thoughts continued to beckon him. It could lead only to him despising himself far more than he had done in the past when he had so hated having to be dependent on Jess for everything, much as he loved her then, and she him.

Now that he could manage without her, it was her morale that had apparently collapsed. She had got herself into this state only because he had been away longer than she had expected, painted the picture of Monica she had not known about, and spent a pleasant evening among friends without her because she had refused to go. The whole situation was completely irrational. Anger returned.

Jess did not own him, either as a man whose comings and goings she could control by a word, or as an artist who could do only what she allowed him to do. He would have to have it out with her! Make her understand. But not tonight. Let it wait till morning.

He closed the door on her, went downstairs, and made himself some strong black coffee. Then he laced a posset of hot milk and sugar with brandy for Jess, by habit longing to do whatever he could for her. His feelings were in such a muddle that if he had had to face an inquisitor, he could not have said whose fault it all was: whether he had let her down, or she him.

He took the drink up to her, grateful that she had no spirit left in her to fight. He helped her off with her dressing-gown and arranged her pillows for her before leaving to prepare himself for bed. She made no move and said no word as he climbed in beside her, but turned her back on him. His paramount emotion was one of unqualified relief.

He would tell her all about the coming battle between old and new in the morning, as well as make a fresh start with her, though his problem concerning her began to look to him to have as many layers to it as an onion. The toughest one to remove now was his guilty conscience regarding his fantasies about Michelle, but even thoughts of her couldn't keep him awake another minute. Jess was asleep. He stroked her hair gently, felt better, and went to sleep himself.

He woke before it was light, and got up at once. Jess did not appear to have roused, so he crept downstairs to think in peace and make up his mind what line to take. He drank some strong tea, and squared his shoulders against the first task of finding out just how much real harm had been done in the studio. Before inspecting his picture, he set himself to clear up the mess. Apart from a large splodge of red paint on the matting, which he knew could never be wholly expunged, the damage to anything else was minimal. He picked up scattered paper and tidied boards, canvases, brushes, pencils and all the rest of an artist's parapher-nalia in less than ten minutes.

He faced up to unveiling the portrait, which he had decided must have been her main target. He could hardly believe that his hasty estimate of last night could be right, but it was. Apart from one or two whiskers of matting which came away at a touch, and a smudge here and there where thick paint had not been quite dry, there was no damage.

He set it back on the easel, and sat down before it, trying to make some sort of sense of the incident. He had caught an almost exact likeness of Monica – but that in itself could hardly have caused such a fit of fury in Jess. The Monica he had depicted was not a woman with any sort of 'come-hither' look in her eye. Her usually merry, twinkling eyes were cast downwards towards the baby at her breast, and any expression in them was exclusively intense mother-love.

The artist in him felt a starburst of joy. He had succeeded in that where so many other painters had failed. He'd captured the Madonna. Suppose Jess in her anger last night had jabbed a carving knife through the canvas . . . Never, if he had tried for a thousand years, could he have recaptured those eyes again just like that. Following the line of Monica's downward gaze, he studied the breast, and the hand with the fingers round the nipple regulating the flow of milk. He had to admit to himself that it was one of the most sensuous bits of painting he had ever seen, let alone executed himself before. He could see why any woman whose husband had painted *that* should have twinges of jealousy, imagining that he must be very familiar with that bare breast, must have held it between his fingers as the girl's own hand was doing, and felt with his own fingertips its satin-smooth rotundity. If Jess had thought like that, why hadn't she defaced it?

He was overwhelmed by it in its entirety. It had to be a fluke that somehow he had brought it off so very well; but in the growing light of the winter dawn he was acknowledging with awed gratitude the Supreme Creative Spirit he had only been emulating. Since he had been old enough to decide that he had wanted to be an artist, he had known that sometime or other, this was the subject of the work he had wanted most to bear his signature. That it had happened by chance, and with no particular fore-thought, just added to the miracle of it. He wanted to rush upstairs and smother Jess with gratitude and love for restraining herself from damag-ing it. The Jess he loved wouldn't have been able to wreck such beauty, whatever sort of a rage she had been in. It proved to him that she was still 'his' Jess. And that he still loved her.

He stood up, prepared now to go and rouse her with a cup of tea, and put all right between them. On his way to the door, he turned again to take a last look at the portrait, and another revelation hit him. She had not been able to bring herself to destroy the picture of the baby – that icon of the motherhood she had so longed for herself. Moreover, it was a baby that he had created – symbolically if not in flesh and blood. And that, of course, also accounted for the feeling he had put into the work. For twenty-five years he had been wanting to create a child of his own, but it had never been so. Except, now, when all other hope was gone, in paint. He closed his eyes as he felt the same stab of pain that must have pierced Jess when she saw the child he had created – albeit only in paint – at the breast of another woman. No wonder she had been in such despair. Somehow, he would make it up to her. He went back to the kitchen, full of love and sorrow. She was already there, sitting at the breakfast table.

Jess had made a tremendous effort to rid herself of the ravages of last night. She had bathed her eyes and made them up to cover up the last traces of tears. The make-up on her face had been applied very skilfully to counteract the haggard look on her naturally fine-drawn face. Her hair, piled up into its habitual French pleat, had been so arranged that its natural tendency to curl round her temples enhanced the touch of grey there, and though she was attired in her usual ski-pants and a fine lambswool polo-necked jumper, the effect was to make her still slender, boyishly graceful figure slightly more feminine than usual.

He took her whole appearance in with approval and pleasure. She could not make herself young again, and had far too much good sense to try; but this was 'his' Jess, the woman who had held his heart through thick and thin for more than a quarter of a century in those capable, small hands of hers. They were at that moment lifting the teapot, and there was something in the tautness of the curve of her fingers round the handle that set alarm bells ringing in his head. He had been about to go forward and take her in his arms, but she gave all her attention to the tea until the cup was full, and as she passed it to him, he saw the glint of the red light of danger in her eye. So it was going to be war, after all.

He sat down without speaking, disappointed and deflated, hurt terribly and doing his best to choke back rising anger. He wondered which of them would break the silence.

She did. 'What on earth have you been playing at? A nice mess you've left all over the kitchen sink!' she said.

'A nice mess you made of my studio. I've been getting red paint off the floor.'

'You must have put it there. I didn't.'

'The tube was on the floor. I trod on it.'

'So it was you who put it there.'

'Oh, for God's sake, don't be so bloody childish, Jess! It was there and I've cleaned it up. What made you go mad in there, anyway? Even to breaking the lock to get in? Whose idea was that – yours or your precious minder's?'

'Mine. You locked it, so I broke the lock. I wanted to know what you'd got in there that I wasn't supposed to see. In my own house.'

He was amazed at the venom in her voice and walked warily. '*Our* house, Jess. And it wasn't locked against you. It was just a precaution to prevent any accident to my first ever masterpiece, because I knew it would be wet and vulnerable while I was away. I meant to tell you before I left, but Anne was here every time I came in, and I forgot. I'm sorry. What did you expect to find there that you couldn't wait to ask me about when I got home?'

'First things first, Greg. It isn't *our* house. Till now our home, but my house. We live here because of my job, remember? As to what I expected to find, it was what I did find. Something you never intended me to see. A portrait of your doxy suckling your by-blow. Enough to make the cat sick.'

At any other time he would have been amused by the extra twist her archaic choice of words gave to her argument, but the poison she was spitting was already numbing his senses. He lost track of the diatribe that followed.

The sneer on her face sent him into a wilderness of crazy, thorny misery. He was white and trembling, remembering how she had rejected his lovemaking until at one point he had been sure that she must be having an affair with some other man. Then he had put it down to her age, and gone on loving her, her devoted husband, always, her lover whenever she would let him be. Now she was punishing him for what he had not done – but, by God, in future he would! He'd give her plenty to be jealous about. Was that what she wanted?

He was clenching his fists till the injuries he had inflicted on himself last night hurt like toothache. He had to fight for self-control not to lash out and hit her. The code he had been brought up by never allowed a man to strike a woman, whatever the provocation, but she ranted on and on, goading him till he thought he must knock her out to stop her.

Some of what she was saying got through to him. What it all seemed to add up to was that she couldn't take his becoming successful. She didn't like him being away, busy and not as he had been previously, a sort of pedigree lapdog always at her heels, performing tricks at her command.

He was getting angrier and angrier, till he could stand it no longer. To hell with the officer-and-gentleman code that bound his tongue between his teeth so that he couldn't even shout back at her. It didn't exist any longer, except for dear old fogeys like him and William. Women these days laughed at it. It was just what the burn-their-bras-brigade were ridiculing. Yet Jess was expecting him to take all these obscene allegations lying down.

His resistance to breaking the code snapped. He bawled at her across the flow of her speech, asking her just what she had meant by that. Calling Monica his 'doxy suckling his by-blow'.

'Exactly what it implied,' she answered.

'You can't be such a bloody fool! You're out of your silly, bitchy mind. Apart from the insult, you heard Roland admit to being the father of Monica's child. You can't get round that.'

'You mean you can't! It very nearly proves it. The trick such women have always played on unsuspecting husbands. Entice him into your bed the minute you begin to think that you may be pregnant, and who's ever to prove the child isn't his? Roland got what he deserved. I hope his doting mother has worked that out for herself.'

'You goddamned bitch! Are you really saddling me with the paternity of those twins?'

'Oh, not necessarily with both of them. Only with the boy she actually named after you! That's what clinches it, as far as I'm concerned. They're not identical. I think you'd already planted the boy when Roland turned up to Fran's birthday party and took the blame, conveniently giving her another at the same time. Getting far more than he had bargained for, I'll bet. Marvellously romantic escape for her, and you, and everybody – except me.'

He sat down again, tremors like thrills of ice running through his sturdy frame. 'Do you really mean that, Jess?'

She nodded, swallowing tears. She had worked herself up into believing it, and was now suffering herself as much as she was making him suffer.

'Then this is it. We can't go on as we are.'

'I don't want to. If we stay here, I can't go anywhere without having to meet her and her bastard babies. We shall have to move.'

'I didn't mean that. I meant that we can't go on together.'

He was as shocked to hear himself saying that as she was devastated to hear him. Neither had ever contemplated life without the other. Yet neither was prepared to retreat and make for safety. Each felt compelled towards disaster, drawn by some force that had never been there till now, like two strong swimmers who had never been afraid of water because they were so sure of their own strength, yet who were now conscious of an undercurrent they had not encountered before.

Life in Old Swithinford had been magical for Jess till last year. She had proved herself, watched Greg regain his belief in himself, and made a wonderful circle of friends. She had felt that things were too good to last, and had reserved to herself a few characteristic 'rights' to protect herself with if things turned the other way again. Petty jealousies, and strong opinions counter to the general, preserved her peculiar 'Jess-ness'. She still had claws and teeth, though they rarely showed. Or, as William once said of her, it was as if she was hoarding a supply of suicide pills to rattle in the faces of those who loved her, though she had no intention whatsoever of ever taking them. The danger was that some dark night she might swallow them in mistake for harmless aspirins.

From the moment of Monica's arrival, Jess had looked for trouble, though she hadn't known why. She could have kept herself safe enough, in spite of her jealousy, but for the undertow of Anne's persistent harping on evidence building up against her too-attractive husband. She had followed Anne out of her depth, and was drowning in suspicion. She had begun to panic and was losing control of her ability to save herself.

Greg was in much the same state. His metamorphosis had been so spectacular that he had made the very most of it, loving every minute of what Old Swithinford was giving back to him. He knew that Jess was working far too hard, especially as it had coincided with the climacteric period of any woman's life. He, and he alone, was aware of the sore spot that was being rubbed by her advance into middle age. Pity for her and gratitude to her had made him love her more than ever, and his pride in her capabilities had no bounds. Yet her puritanical need to remind herself that life was never all roses had been turned against him. It was as if she was intent on making him compare her with the younger woman he had married, showing him the aggressively efficient middle-aged executive female who had no time for such frills of life as love-making. It had been 'getting at him' far more than he realized, and he had begun to feel that they were now swimming too far apart and in dangerous waters. He, too, was aware of a current that had never bothered him before. Its name was Michelle Stanhope.

Both were frightened. He got up, and began to collect together the things he would need for the trip he had to take the next day. She misread his intention.

'Don't go, yet, Greg. Let's talk. I'm sorry.'

'So am I, but if we can't talk without quarrelling, I had better go now.'

'Where are you going?'

'Away. That's all I know. I shall ring, as usual, of course. Let's leave things to simmer down – till Christmas is over, at least. We both need time to think.'

He found his car keys and prepared to leave. She stood up, and grabbing his jacket, pulled him towards her. He responded, taking her in his arms and giving her his usual hug and a kiss. There was nothing in it to convey to her that she had succeeded in what she had intended – to prevent him from leaving and to persuade him to make up their differences there and then.

She watched him, pride coming to her assistance, as he went into his studio and came out again carrying his precious picture.

'What are you going to do with that?' she asked.

'I don't know, yet. I daren't leave it here.' At the door he stopped, turned and asked the question he had been wanting an answer to all the morning. 'Why didn't you cut it to ribbons while you had the chance last night?'

The eyes she turned up towards him were at their most beautiful, liquid with longing and anguished at the same time. 'Do you really think I could bring myself to destroy your child, even a painting of one, even yours by another woman?'

His heart turned over, partly with grief, partly with rage. If ever a woman had taken unfair advantage of a man's feelings, she had. He slammed the door behind him, and went.

34

For the second Sunday morning in succession, Fran and William had been denied their usual treat of lying late in bed. This morning they had been jumped on at six a.m. by two boisterous youngsters, made to tell stories and provide backs to be ridden, and play endless repetitive finger-games like 'Whoopsie Georgie' that the youngest next generation never seems to tire of. That was part and parcel of the role of grandparents and Fran loved it; but she did sometimes wonder a bit about William, who might not have bargained for it at all. He'd missed the apprentice-ship of being a parent. Nevertheless, he didn't seem to mind.

She rescued a tuft of William's hair from the clutch of little Andrew's fingers, as Kate in her dressing-gown knocked on their door. William heaved Andy off his chest and got out of bed to let Kate take his place.

Returning from the bathroom dressed, he went to the window and drew back the curtains. 'Oh dear, there's a thick fog,' he said.

'Yes,' Kate replied. 'That's what Jerry sent me in to say. He thinks perhaps we ought to skip breakfast and have an early lunch, if that's possible, Mum, so that we can get off home in the middle of the day. After all, we shall see you again at the New Year, and that's only about a month away.'

'Good heavens! Is that all?' said William, turning from the window. 'I think perhaps Jerry's right, Kate. I'm afraid it doesn't look like clearing.'

They compromised with only coffee for the present and decided on a huge breakfast to allow the visitors to get away. It was the happiest sort of family meal with no planning or formality. The result was akin to an indoor picnic of gigantic proportions that included sausages, bacon, steak, kidneys, eggs and tomatoes. William set resolutely about providing fried bread, which both women thought excessive, and unnecessarily fattening.

'Not if it's properly cooked,' he said. 'Kezia taught me how to make proper fried bread.'

'Do you mind if we go now, Mum?' Kate asked, when they'd finished. 'We promised Roland and Monica that we'd call there for a few minutes, and we shall be lucky if we make it home before dusk in this fog.'

Fran and William waved them off half an hour later.

'That's by far the best way of saying goodbye,' William said, as they turned to go in. 'If there is anything that sets me on edge, it's long-drawn-out farewells.'

'Really?' said Fran. 'I seem to remember . . .'

'No you don't,' he said. 'All you are allowed to remember is one stupendous greeting at Heathrow. Quite different. Life didn't exist before that.'

She laughed. 'I hate to see them go, but what Grandfather used to quote is true,' she said. '"Grandchildren please you twice – once when they come and again when they go." Let's go and do the washing-up. Then it can be Sunday again. Just you and me. The old folks at home.'

'I refuse to regard you as an "old folk" however many grandchildren you present me with,' he said. He hung up the tea towel and asked, 'What are we going to do, then, with our gift of a whole Sunday we weren't expecting?'

'Nothing very spectacular, I hope. To tell the truth, I'm tired. It was lovely of Beth and Monica to make me a party, but what with one thing and another, I've found it a bit of a strain.'

He eyed her with some concern. 'Then let's make it a proper Sunday. Let's make up the fire, and go back to bed. Why not? Here we are, just you and me as you said, in our own home, with the day before us, and the fog closing in around us to keep us safe from any other intrusions. Bed's always the best place to put things right again. Come and let me put you to sleep, my sweetheart, and when we wake up we can talk till morning if we need to. From tomorrow morning, you get on with what you must do, and I'll see to all the rest. But today's our own to share. Agreed?'

With his arms around her and his face laid lovingly on the top of her head, she relaxed at once. In bed with William was the only place on earth she wanted to be.

He went to pile the logs on the fire and put the guard round it in case of sparks, and she went to make sure that Cat was in her usual place, guarding the telephone in her study. It occurred to Fran that it might be wise to take the receiver out of its cradle. As she bent down to caress Cat, she heard the squeal of car brakes on the gravel, and stood still, wondering what William would do about answering the door to a visitor. She hadn't long to wait. The front door was opened by the intruder, and she heard Greg's voice calling, asking where they were.

Lucky that they weren't already in bed, she thought, though Greg was the last one to think there was anything wrong about that. The question was, what he could possibly want on a Sunday morning, when time to spend at home was now so precious to him?

They all three met in the hall, which was darkened because of the surrounding fog. Greg was carrying a large canvas, wrapped very loosely in a bit of old sheeting.

They led him into the lighter sitting-room, and both saw at once that he was in some sort of distress. They made him sit down, and William offered him a drink.

'No thanks,' he said, rather wanly. 'I haven't fully recovered from having too much last night, and I've got to drive, in this fog.'

'Going today? In spite of this weather?' asked Fran. 'Must you? What's so urgent – and what can we do for you?'

'Look after this for me,' he said, unwrapping the canvas and standing it up against a chair for them to look at. 'It's caused the worst row that Jess and I have ever had. The sort that ordinary remedies can't cure. If you look at the picture when I've gone you'll probably guess why. But it happens to be the best bit of painting I've ever done in my whole life, and I daren't leave it at home.

'It's happened before, but Jess must have been either drunk or deranged last night. She had me really scared. William, she's your sister, but I have to say I'm beginning to believe she has developed some sort of – let's say mental instability. I know she's my responsibility, and not yours, but it's me that sets her off, so I can't do much. She needs help. She's got a persistent bee in her bonnet about what goes on between me and Monica. It's become an obsession with her. I'm sure I needn't tell you that it's pure imagination. Please look after the picture for me. It isn't finished yet, but the sight of it sends Jess right round the bend. And I can't take any more from her just at present. Do you know what she called that last night? "Your doxy suckling your by-blow." A bloody insult to nearly everybody close to us. So I'm off, and I don't know where, or when I'll be back, so I can't tell you.'

'Hang on a minute, Greg,' said William. 'Give yourself time to think what you're doing. Where's Jess now, how is she and who's looking after her?'

'I left her looking like Lady Macbeth reaching for the dagger,' he said, 'proud as Lucifer and as seductive. All gooey-eyed, wanting me to fall on my knees and put my head in her lap – as she knew damn well I wanted to. If I had done, I'd have had the bread-knife between my shoulders. I had to get out, there and then. Oh, I know I'm exaggerating, but I knew what she was after. She wanted to seduce me into confession, pleading for forgiveness and a fresh start. If I had given a fraction of an inch, I'd have been back to the nonentity I was up in Barra. The no-good easy-lifer she loved to be able to dominate with her ability and forceful personality. But it won't work now – how could it, after painting *that*? Not likely! Nobody's with her, as far as I know – but I dare say her new bosom friend will be round to her soon. She nearly lives there, anyway – Anne Rushlake, I mean. And my guess is that she's at the bottom of all this.'

'What do you suggest we can do?' asked William. 'Are we supposed to know about all this?'

'Bill,' – there was pleading in Greg's voice – 'you're the only one she'll listen to, except for her female Iago. Couldn't you get her to see a doctor? Just keep your eye on her for me. I'll be in touch by phone, with her as well as with you, and I'll come home as soon as ever I can bring myself to face her again. I promise. Now, please let me go!'

Fran could see that he was almost in tears, and held William back from making any more attempts to delay him.

They turned the portrait to the light. 'He's right. It is a masterpiece,' William said, sounding awed.

'And I can see why she went mad,' Fran said. 'I think that even I would be jealous if you had painted that of any other woman but me. He knows how obsessively jealous she is. Why did he provoke her? Why let her see it? What *are* we going to do?'

'We are going to bed – remember? This is our day. Don't panic about Jess. Pride and scorn will uphold her till morning. I'll put Eric's office on my itinerary for tomorrow, and see how she is there. You are not to get yourself upset by this. Greg will quite likely be back by tea time, and I forbid you to worry about anything else but me for the next hour or two.'

She looked up and caught his eye, and actually blushed at what she read there. 'I adore you in that masterful mood,' she said, and escaped up the stairs while he very carefully rewrapped the portrait and found a home for it in the coat-cupboard under the stairs. He wished he could be as sanguine about the whole affair as he had pretended to be.

It was four o'clock when they woke, still languid with warmth and love and sleep, and the foggy dusk was already giving way to the night.

'Stay there,' William said. 'I'll go down and make some tea and put more logs on the fire.' He put the kettle on, and went into Fran's study. He was a little anxious that the phone had been off the hook all the afternoon, and dialled Jess's number. She answered almost immediately, her voice at its lowest, purring, seductive level. He heard the disappointment in it as she recognized him, and guessed that she had been expecting an abject Greg on his way home.

'Why are you ringing?' she asked suspiciously.

'To find out how you are today,' he said, 'considering you weren't well enough to make the party last night. I'm sorry I'm so late getting round to it, but we've had Kate and her family here.' He was incensed by her attitude. He wasn't supposed to know that Greg wasn't there, cossetting her as he usually did. 'Well, as long as you are OK,' he said airily, 'we'll get on with our supper.' He was pretty sure that he caught the sound of a sob as she put the phone down.

So Greg had not gone home, and from Jess's tone he guessed that Anne wasn't present, either. He decided not to tell Fran. A few hours left by herself to think might be the best medicine in the world for Jess.

He took a dainty tea-tray upstairs and climbed back into bed. With her head on his shoulder, once the tea was finished, they began to talk.

'Now listen to me, my darling,' he began, his voice firmer than usual because of the added complication of Jess and Greg, 'I meant what I said. From tomorrow morning, your place is at your desk. I have nothing workwise to do that won't wait, and a lot to do in all sorts of other departments. I'm afraid that in our enthusiasm last night – and probably because Elyot is a connoisseur of wine – we may have bitten off more than we can chew. But having put our hands to the plough, we can't let Sophie, Daniel and Co. down. We've got to go through with this anti-Bailey business, willy-nilly.'

'That means you don't really want to.'

'No it means that it isn't going to be easy. It may make trouble, and in the end we can't win.'

'Oh, darling, why not?'

'Because of what Shakespeare said about everything being subject to time. Time's against us. How does it go?'

'You mean Ulysses talking to Achilles?'

> "For beauty, wit,
>   High birth, vigour of bone, desert in service,
>   Love, friendship, charity, are subjects all
>   To envious and calumniating time."

'Is that the bit you meant?'

He looked down, smiling admiringly at her. 'You never fail,' he said.

'No. Any more than you do on a scrap of history, or a date,' she replied.

'It's history that is warning me now. Nobody ever gets the better of Time. Just think, my sweetheart, if you and I live to be eighty-plus, the grandchildren who were in our bed this morning will be thirty, and Bailey's Lane's End estate a scruffy slum suburb of Swithinford that somebody will be seeking to demolish in order to replace it with twenty-first-century houses made of some material that hasn't been invented yet. Time wins because most people like new things.'

'But it was your idea to do something to stop Bailey taking us all over.'

'Yes, because changes ought to come gradually. Not overnight, as

Bailey wants. And I hate to see good honest people done down to fill somebody else's pocket. George Bridgefoot and such as Dan and Sophie and Thirzah are no match for a man like Bailey. But Bob and good luck have beaten him once. So I join the fray and induce others to help me, partly to put Bailey and Kid Bean back into their proper places within Old Swithinford as a community, and partly because I don't like the underhand way he's going about taking the village over. We still have as much right in it as he has, or any of his new estate residents will have. We have to make him understand that. All we can do is to hope to slow him down by making him realize that it takes all sorts to make a world.'

'Go on. What next?'

'We can't *do* anything without George. If Sophie's right and he has lost heart, my guess is that it is far more likely to be his family troubles than what is happening at the church. That's probably just the last straw. As far as he is concerned, his family and the church are woven together, part of each other, and both part of the village. I intend to go and talk to him tomorrow, and I need your advice.

'His family troubles are all rooted in Charles's love for Charlie Bellamy, whom Brian thinks is not good enough for a Bridgefoot in a place that now contains people like the Baileys. Fran, I want permission to tell George the truth. It would put the heart back into him, as well as taking the almost unbearable pressure off young Charles. What do you think? May I? It would be like playing Father Christmas.'

'Yes. It needn't become common knowledge. Jane would have been home by now, and all of it out in the open if it hadn't been for Nick.'

'Yes, Nick. While you were out the other day seeing Beth, Gordon rang me up. At Charlie's suggestion, Alex Marland has been brought in as consultant with regard to the amnesia. She remembered that Alex knew Nick previously and vice versa. Alex and Nick senior would like me to meet them in Cambridge for a conference about Nick junior. As a sort of arbiter on the outside, not a member of either family or the medical profession. Do you mind if I leave you alone for a day?'

'Of course not. I'm going to be too busy to miss you, anyway.'

'I may do some Christmas shopping, too. Nick Gordon is out of his mind with delight at having two women he adores to buy for – Charlie as well as Jane. He planned to buy both of them a fur coat. I managed to persuade him what desperate embarrassment he would cause Charlie if he did – it's only male hippy students who wear fur coats these days, bought at jumble sales. I suggested a beautiful but serviceable watch instead. But he made me think. Would you like a fur coat from an admirer? It seems to be something every woman wants.'

'Oh darling, don't be so idiotic. If you are thinking of Russian sable so that I could out-do Mrs Bailey, you would bankrupt yourself, and I should hate it, honestly.'

'I expect the Grand Duchess Olga wore sables.'

'I'm not a Grand Duchess. I'm only plain Frances —' she was going to add 'Catherwood', but stopped herself in time, and he appreciated her care for him.

'You're my Princess,' he said. 'And if we are going to get up, it's time we did.'

'Whatever you say, Father Christmas,' she said.

35

According to plan, Fran went to her study, as soon as she had said good morning to Sophie, and William got ready to go out into a slightly less foggy morning. He warned Sophie that he might be very late for lunch. She assured him that whatever time he came home, there would be 'a 'ot dinner a-waiting for 'im' and waved him away with a wide smile. Fran seated herself at her typewriter with a will, pausing only to listen to a strange sound emanating from the kitchen. It was Sophie's voice raised loud in singing.

'Praise God from whom all blessings flow.'

It wasn't often that Sophie sang. Fran understood why she felt it necessary to give tongue this Monday morning. When the hymn changed to

'Through the night of doubt and sorrow
Onward goes the Christian band,'

Fran almost wept. It brought home to her as nothing else could have done the despair that that tiny, ever-dwindling congregation had gone through, feeling themselves abandoned by their shepherd and left vulnerable to attacks from the wolves and jackals in their midst. Then, suddenly, their cry for help had been heard. Something for Sophie to sing about indeed.

William had decided that he ought to see Bob before he went ahead with his plan to revitalize George by telling him all there was to know. He found Bob at work, and they retreated into the warmth of the farmhouse. William told his tale, including a somewhat humorous account of the impromptu conference on Saturday evening. Bob's gentle sense of the ludicrous had always endeared him to Fran, and William was finding it a great ally. When he imitated Thirzah's gloved palm promising Help from Above, Bob's eyes were twinkling like salt sprinkled in a candle-flame. William outlined the plan for the first flank attack on Bailey and his troops on New Year's Eve.

Bob rarely interrupted when listening to a tale. He sat with his head cocked slightly to one side, and paid attention. Fran said he was listening to another voice inside himself at the same time. That way he grasped a situation whole.

'Count us in on everything,' he said. 'Jane and Charlie will both be home then, and you may depend that wherever Charlie is, Charles will be as well. So we'll be at church with the sheep, while the rest are with the goats at the White Elephant's opening night. Couldn't be better.'

'Charles and all the others of his family,' said William tentatively, coming to the most difficult bit of his mission, 'are having a bad time. I'm on my way to see old George.' He launched into his suggestion that he should strengthen his own arm by being allowed to tell George the whole truth, and release Charles from his need to distance himself from his grandfather while keeping such a momentous secret.

William had expected Bob to ask for time to consult Jane, but instead he was silent for about half a minute, before saying confidently, 'Tell him whatever you like. We didn't expect to keep it to ourselves as long as this. I want Jane home, as much as she wants to come, but Nick must come first. As for Charles – I reckon it's been harder for him than anybody.'

William left Bob, as he usually did, marvelling at the man's good sense. He drove straight to the Old Glebe.

He hadn't seen George for more than a week, and was shocked at the sight of him. He seemed to have aged ten years in the time. George's face lit up at the sight of William, and he led the way into the house, leaning heavily on a stick. Molly, it appeared, was out. Things were definitely going William's way so far this morning.

'Is your hip very painful?' he asked, noting the deep lines drawn on George's usually placid face.

George looked scornful. 'Nothing as I should take much notice of in the ordinary way,' he said. 'Sometimes I think it's a good job as it does hurt me, 'cos it takes my mind off other things for a few minutes now and then. Everything as I've ever lived and worked for is falling to bits. Sometimes it don't seem worth bothering to keep going, only I know there'd be worse squabbles without me, and there's Molly to think about. Besides, it ain't in my nature. I always hoped to live long enough to see the next generation o' Bridgefoots before I felt I'd had enough. I don't know now. I don't know.'

'But I *do*,' said William. 'Is that Charles's car that's just driven into the yard? Can we have him in? Let's wait for him. I've brought a bottle of whisky with me. We may have something to celebrate. Hello, Charles.'

'I've only just called to see how Grandad is,' the boy said. 'He's had us all worried, since that meeting at the church the other night.'

'Can you stop for a few minutes? I've just come from Bob Bellamy to tell your Grandad the secret you've been keeping from him for the last six weeks. Shall I tell him, or will you?'

Charles had gone very white, and sat down. 'You,' he said.

Catching sight of the pain crossing George's face, William cursed himself for being so clumsy. He knew what his blundering words had caused George to think, especially as a follow-on to what the old man had been saying when Charles arrived. George had jumped to the conclusion that the news about to be broken was that Charlie was pregnant.

'No, Grandad, no! Don't go off on the wrong tack. There's nothing wrong with me, or Charlie. Oh, tell him, Mr Burbage. You can see by his face what he's thinking.'

So William told him. Charles got up and put his arms round the old man, hugging him as he used to when he was a child and there was pleasure to be doubled by the sharing of it.

'It's been absolute hell, Grandad, keeping it from you, but I had to. But don't you see what a difference it will make to us all, if only Dad will see sense now? He can't despise Charlie, or her father, or kick up such a fuss about me marrying a nobody now, can he? I wish Mrs Bellamy could come home, so that we could tell everybody.'

George hadn't really taken it in yet. William thought that it might be a good idea if Charles went, and left him to go into all the detail.

George, still a bit stunned, looked after Charles with wet eyes in which hope had been renewed. 'If ever a boy deserved his good luck,' he said, 'that one does. But I can't answer for his father. He's as likely to throw a tantrum one way as the other. I don't understand him, though he is my son. But whatever Brian chooses to do, I'm no friend of Bailey's and never shall be. Let's forget Brian, and drink to Bob Bellamy and his new missus, and to my boy and Charlie, and a new start for the Bridgefoot line.'

'Here's Molly coming,' warned William. 'Tell her yourself when I've gone. That's only fair. And as to Bailey . . .' George had given him a wonderful lead, and they were well launched into the plans for New Year's Eve when Molly joined them.

George was able to allay William's doubts that a watchnight service would be possible with so short a time to arrange things and with no direct route to diocesan authority. George explained. The churchwardens, on their own account, could call together any meeting or give permission for the church to be used for any ceremony. If, as had always been the case till now, there was a rector, they consulted with him, and on some matters, had to defer to him. But not in this. George in his own right, and as the Rector's representative, could give permission for a congregation to meet in the church for the purpose of bringing in and ringing in the New Year. Kenneth Bean, as the people's warden, could hardly refuse to go along with a request that came directly from 'the people'. That was the first hurdle cleared. Beth would officiate at the organ – possibly assisted by Greg. There was no reason why lessons should not be read by anybody willing. The gathering could therefore be organized without the aid of a clergyman at all – though obviously it would be of much greater significance if even a lay reader could be present. The lay reader from Hen Street had already arranged a service of his own in his 'tin-topped tabernacle', the 'temporary' church to which Sophie had deep-rooted objection. That was, if anything, good news.

'Thirzah says that doubtless the Lord will provide,' William said.

George gave him a sharp look. 'She may very well be right. Faith can work miracles.'

Duly chided, William turned to the question of the bells.

'Tell Ned to raise a full peal without me if he can,' George said, 'because it depends on how well my hip is when the time comes whether or not I could manage for long enough. But I'll still be there as the leader, and I should like it to be me that strikes the bell for midnight. That'd satisfy me.'

William left feeling satisfied with his morning so far, and went on to see Eric at the hotel, not because he needed Eric's help at present, but because he hoped to find Jess there as well. He was told that Mr Choppen had someone with him, but would be glad if Dr Burbage would wait. He sat in the ante-room to Eric's office, and was unpleasantly surprised when at last the door opened, and there was Eric, showing out his previous visitor, Arnold Bailey.

William had already risen, and had no option but to return Bailey's greeting – though as far as he remembered he had never spoken to the man before, nor been close enough to him to see him properly. He had put together a mental picture via Bob Bellamy, whose views were bound to be prejudiced. Bailey didn't look the part of the villain nearly as much as William had expected. He had no idea what had made him conceive Bailey as a short, fat, florid man in a tweed suit and a pork-pie hat with a loud voice and an East End accent. What he saw bidding good morning was a well-dressed, thickset man who nevertheless was quite average in height. His face was indeed rather fleshy and inclined to be florid, probably due to his love of the fleshpots. He had a head of darkish-blond hair, worn rather too long, and eyes too icily blue to be handsome. While William was correcting his imagined visual image of the man, Bailey turned back to speak again to Eric. His voice was exactly what William had expected, and in that moment, while Bailey had his back to him, William noticed his beautifully shod, size-twelve feet, and his equally enormous, huge, powerful, too white and almost too clean hands.

Everything he had ever known about Bailey came back to William at the sight of those hands. He saw them in his mind's eye holding out the gold cigar-case that he had so deliberately failed to offer to Bob Bellamy at a shoot; he saw them pull the trigger of the gun that had blown a child's kitten to pieces in her sight and in Bob's; and he knew that they belonged to a person who was cruel by nature and ruthless in business.

The anticipation that Eric would introduce them formally and he would be forced to put his own hand into one of Bailey's filled William with such strong revulsion that he felt a spasm of physical nausea. He turned to the window, and took out his handkerchief to wipe the sweat off his palms. There was no doubt about it – his antipathy to the man in the flesh was greater than his dislike of all that the chap had stood for till now. He was steeling himself to be polite when Eric's voice brought him back to normality.

'Hello, William. Sorry to keep you waiting, but Mr Bailey is about to leave. Do come in.' He closed the door and said, 'What's the matter? Sit down and I'll get you a brandy. You look as if you're sickening for something.'

William apologized, swiftly recovering himself. 'Just scared to death,' he said. 'I was afraid that you might introduce me, and that I might have had to shake hands with him. I mean that I should have actually to touch one of those revolting hands of his. They gave me the creeps – honestly, they made me feel physically sick. Have you ever seen any so huge, so cruel-looking, and yet so revoltingly white?'

'Yes,' said Eric. 'Hundreds, mainly on dead Nazis.' He looked at William shrewdly. 'Are you sure you are all right? Or are you really going down with flu and making Bailey into a bogeyman? I think you're just projecting your general dislike of him as an intruder into your rural paradise on to his hands. Did you feel the same way towards me? If you did, you were better at covering your feelings about me than you are about Bailey. But you can't deny that he and I are two of a kind. Businessmen and birds of a feather.'

'Bollocks,' said William, succinctly. 'The first time I ever saw the ogre called Eric Choppen he looked like a spaniel that had just been kicked, and wanting someone to pat his head. If I remember correctly, Jess did. Rather too well.'

Eric laughed. 'And Fran danced with me,' he said. He spread out a pair of strong, bony, brown and rather hairy-backed hands across his desk towards William.

'These are a businessman's hands, all the same,' he said. 'I can strike quite as hard a bargain as any Bailey if I want to.'

Beside them, William's long-fingered, sensitive hands appeared almost effeminate, and were certainly pale in comparison. He glanced across to Eric, eye meeting eye. Then he laid both of his hands into Eric's and felt the strong fingers close over them.

'Yours are the hands of an unsung hero, I guess,' he said. 'I know them to be the hands of a fighter, but they're also the hands of a great lover who's an absolute old softie as a fellow grandfather. But most of all they're the hands of a friend.'

Both men withdrew their hands looking sheepishly embarrassed, but there was warmth in both pairs of eyes, as they made rather a lot of to-do picking up their brandy glasses.

'So what did you want to see me about?' asked Eric.

'Jess. Is she here, and if so, may I have a chat with her?'

'No. She hasn't come in today. I didn't really expect her, after what Greg said last night. Except that I didn't quite believe his story. She had been perfectly well on Friday evening. She rang up this morning, very husky and croaky, and said she was in bed. Why do you ask? Isn't Greg there fussing over her?'

'No. He went off somewhere, ostensibly on business, yesterday morning. According to him, they had just had the mother and father of all rows. I rang her later, and she was so obviously disappointed that I wasn't Greg on his way back to her that she as good as told me to mind my own business and get off the line. I'm always in a bit of a cleft stick between her and Fran, so I haven't told Fran yet. They're fond enough of each other, but not altogether compatible. Jess goes out of her way to rub Fran up the wrong way. If Jess is really ill and Greg hasn't come back, I shall have to go round and see her. Do you know if Anne's seen her this morning?'

'Anne had to take over some of her work,' Eric said. 'I asked her if she'd seen Jess, and got rather a dusty answer. I gathered that there might have been a bit of a cooling off between them – but I had seen that coming. I'd guessed Anne was miffed at not being asked to Fran's party.'

'Surely not! It was a family-only "do". You're sure it wasn't over Greg?'

Eric laughed. 'Not unless Greg has taken leave of his senses altogether,' he said. 'You're putting two and two together and making a baker's dozen!'

'Then what?'

'If you weren't Jess's brother, William . . . and if you didn't have cause to look at the world through quite such rose-coloured glasses, I could perhaps open your eyes a little more. You might see well enough to deduce an incentive from the facts of the case,' Eric said. 'Look at them. Fran is given a birthday party by her family and friends. Her cousin, who was once a surrogate sister, and is now what amounts to a sister-in-law, doesn't turn up to it. Her husband does, full of excuses for her. Next morning, the adoring husband – and he is – bolts, though you say she wants him back. Her new friend – and by the way I have had my doubts about that for some time now – also falls out with her. She probably didn't come to work today because she couldn't face seeing me. Now, there's Fran, Greg, Anne, you and me all in her bad books. Are we all out of step – or is Jess?'

'We've touched on this before, William. You know what I think of Jess – but I worry about her, too. She's one of the cleverest, most practical, forceful and interesting personalities I have ever met – to say nothing of her charm as a woman – but when her feelings are involved she's so volatile that she's dangerous. Like a grenade with the pin out. She's liable to explode and act like a half-witted, over-indulged child. Why? There must be some reason.'

'It was naked jealousy of Fran, for all sorts of imagined reasons, once,' replied William. 'But she got over that ages ago, though as I said, I walk warily.'

'It's still naked jealousy, but who of?'

'Well, I would have guessed Monica if things hadn't turned out as they have. But she must know that there's nothing between her precious Greg and Monica. It isn't as if Greg is that sort of man! He's very attractive to women, I know – but he's her husband, and loves her as much as he ever did. Mostly, when there's nobody else around, she treats him like a rather disreputable old pensioner she can't get rid of. Fran worries herself a lot about him. Once Monica arrived, Jess put her claws out. She and Greg got on too well for Jess's peace of mind. But she kept her sanity till the night Monica told us she was pregnant.'

Eric nodded. 'She lives less than a hundred yards away from our door, but she has never been inside our house once since that night. She has never even seen the twins. What do you make of that? Not even to be polite enough to ask after them. That amounts to more than not just liking babies, William. It amounts to a phobia – we have to face up to the truth about it, William, if we want to stop things from getting worse. It's Monica plus baby or babies that upsets her.'

'Yes,' said William, remembering the portrait that was now under the stairs at Benedict's.

'Well, they'll all be gone from Old Swithinford by the end of January. But eight weeks is too long for Jess in this state and Greg vamoosed.'

'How much has Anne had to do with it?'

'Quite a lot, possibly. Has she tried her luck with you, yet?'

'Good Lord, no! I hope not. If she has, I've never noticed. It would never have occurred to me. What are you getting at?'

'She's man-hungry. You don't notice, because you have no eyes for any woman but Fran. I'm bulletproof for other reasons. But Greg was fair game, and, aim as she might, she couldn't bring him down. What's the line? "Nor hell a fury like a woman spurned." If she can't get him into bed with her, she'll do her damnedest to see that Jess doesn't either. I'd bet my bottom dollar that Anne's been putting the boot in at Greg. Anne isn't particularly subtle. It must have been gall and wormwood to her to watch Beth collaring Elyot.' He grinned, and immediately became very serious again.

'Sorry, William, to bring all this up when you are so full of plans for a fight, and intent on us retaining our solidarity as a group – but I think you'll have to tell Fran so that you can both keep an eye on Jess. Anne will prove a broken reed to her, especially if Greg keeps his distance. In which case, I wouldn't like to take the consequences. I've seen too many men – as hand-picked for their sterling qualities as men as Jess is for hers as a woman – give under pressure applied to their one weak place. So if you're making plans for this coming Christmas, I advise you to keep Monica and Jess apart. And if there's half a chance of enticing Greg back, do it before it's too late.'

'I'll go and see Jess now,' William said. 'And thanks a lot. I've got good reason for believing you're right, but how to deal with it I haven't a clue. When and where did you study psychology?'

'By keeping my eyes open – in the army, in business, and among my friends. I happen to be interested in people. I have to be.'

William used Eric's phone to tell Fran and Sophie to have lunch without him, and went back to Southside House to see Jess.

She was in bed. Her face was swollen with crying, and she had hardly any voice. She made no bones about the fact that while she appreciated his concern for her, she resented his intrusion. She was humiliated that anybody should see her like that, she said, and know it was all because of what Greg had done to her. Even William, who was, she told him, not really her brother any longer, but 'only a puppet Fran kept in her pocket'.

'But what has Greg done?' William asked.

'What all men do, sooner or later. Prefer another woman to the one they're married to. Like you.'

'Now stop it, Jess. You have no proof at all that Greg won't be home by the weekend, or that he is anywhere but on business. You're sending yourself round the bend imagining things, and worrying us all to death over nothing. What have you had to eat today so far?'

'Nothing. I haven't wanted anything since yesterday morning.'

'I'll get you something before I go. I take it Anne will be in to make you a meal tonight?'

He was surprised how little sympathy he had with her, and at his own unwillingness to do more for her. If Jess was ill, instead of being hysterical with outraged pride and insane jealousy, it would be different.

The mention of Anne roused Jess a bit. 'Anne? I haven't seen her since Saturday afternoon,' she said, a note of indignation making her voice stronger. 'I gathered she had a date.' The characteristic curl on Jess's lip convinced him that there was little the matter with her but temper.

'So you've quarrelled with her as well? What *is* the matter with you, Jess? I suppose you wouldn't care to tell me what the real trouble is?'

'You know what it is. I've just told you.'

'And you want everybody to believe you, and let the whole village know that Greg has left you.'

'*No!* That's what I can't bear!'

'Then pull youself together and stop acting like a tragedy queen. You told Eric you'd got flu, and you certainly look like it. Stick to that tale, and stop in bed. I'll find somebody to come and look after you. I'll be round myself as much as I can, but I'm busy and Fran's up to her neck in work.'

He went to make her a pot of tea and a round of toast. She took the chance of washing her face and bathing her eyes. What William thought of her still mattered a lot.

'Now let me give you some brotherly advice,' he said, preparing to leave. 'Lie there and count your blessings – as Kezia always made us do when we thought ourselves hard done by. If I can, I'll call in again on my way back.'

He had just been struck by an idea. Maybe he could engage the Petrie girls to nurse Jess for a few days.

Peter Petrie was up and about, looking, William thought, slightly better. He said so.

'Don't kid yourself,' Petrie said. 'There won't be any miracle to save me. I told you I should probably last till spring, and I'm a little better because day-to-day matters are easier than they were when I first met you. Mostly because of Joe Noble. I don't know what I should have done without him. With his help I've managed to finish a lot more bits in the house. I'm actually beginning to believe I may be able to sell it. But Joe himself is good for me somehow, as the corner of a blanket is to a tired baby – a silent comforter. We sit without speaking, but he's there. Why he does it, I don't know. Sometimes I think it must be because he needs the companionship and the silence himself, too – that perhaps he has something to expiate by doing all he can for me and the children.'

'Could be,' William said, and gave him a brief résumé of Joe's fall from grace by utterly repudiating his only child when she had been seduced by a much older man. Petrie also got a thumbnail sketch of Joe's wife, and of his devotion to his grandchild after he had more or less driven his daughter out.

'He was a simple chap with a good heart, but what happened had made him bitter,' William said. 'Meeting Pugh probably made him feel guilty. So Pugh does the praying, and Joe plays the Good Samaritan. Lucky for you and good for him. What about the arrangement with Pugh?'

'Having him living in the house gives me a sort of security,' Petrie answered. 'And of course there's some comfort in the knowledge that he'll do all he can to sell the house without charge – which was in our bargain – when the time comes. He seems to have had a calming effect on Crystal, so I hope he isn't hankering to get back to Wales too soon. She hasn't seemed quite so wild since he's been here. I think he may be helping her to kick the drugs. I certainly hope so.'

He was silent for a minute or two, and when he turned his face back to William, his calm had been shattered.

'I do my best, William,' he said. 'I try not to think about the future too much. But there isn't a man alive who could face what I have to face without getting down sometimes. Nobody likes the thought of his own imminent demise, for one thing, but in my case it's what will happen afterwards that defeats me and turns me into a moral coward. Will Dafydd Pugh keep his promise to me? Will he get tired of waiting for me to die, and his hiraeth for Wales make him desert before my time comes? Crystal has come to rely on him. What would she do if what money the house makes is left for her to lay out? She'd be back on the drug trail before I was buried – and then what about my family? Would she care enough about them to take them with her wherever she went? All of them?

'She wouldn't want the girls – except to turn them into prostitutes to earn her her drug money. She dislikes them now because she regards them as rivals. I've brought them up too well for them not to see through her, and they were born to be beauties. If only I could live long enough to see Emmy in a job and Ammy at school-leaving age, they could escape Crystal and her lifestyle. Topy and Saffie have no hope. They're twins, and as long as they could stay together, I think they wouldn't be too unhappy in a children's home. That's the best I can hope for those two. That leaves the four boys.

'I haven't much hope for Basher. I can't imagine what genes he's inherited from whoever his father was, but he seems to have been born anti-social. If there are such things as born criminals, I would say he is one. God only knows what will become of him, or where he will end up. He isn't helped by being the only one Crystal really cares about, either.

'Then there's Tanner.'

In the silence that followed, the man's face crumpled, and tears began to creep down his cheeks. William felt too helpless to move or to speak.

'Apart from the colour of his hair, I don't believe he has inherited a single thing from his mother,' Petrie went on. 'He's all mine. My son. What will happen to *him*, William? The other two, Jade and Aggie, are too young to be unhappy for long, but Tanner is only three and a half – and the most intelligent of them all. He's just at the age to suffer the most from losing me and the worst from having nobody else to love him. Besides the fact that Crystal dislikes him because he is so much like me and different from Basher. And I have no choice but to leave him to it. That's what I can't face.'

'You didn't hear from your family then?'

'I didn't expect to. Appealing to them was stupid, but I'm desperate.'

'So desperate that you are asking me to help?' said William softly.

The light of hope in the sick man's eyes hurt William more than his tragic outburst had done.

'I can't promise to do anything more than act as his legal guardian,' said William, 'because I already owe Fran so much. She takes all the moral flak as it is for my sake, so I can't take on too much without her complete agreement. She has four grandchildren, and no doubt more to come. I wouldn't want to intrude Tanner, if you see what I mean. But even without her I can protect him, see to it that he is educated properly, and make sure that wherever he is placed he is cared for and loved. I know Fran well enough to be sure he would always have a home base some-where with us in our extended family, for school holidays and such. I can promise that much. Would that be enough – at least for the present? Legalize it as soon as you like – of course I'll come to put my signature to it, but I would rather not have to bother Fran till after Christmas. Will that do?'

He held out his hand, and for the second time that afternoon found himself clasping two others. This time his own were the strong, brown ones in comparison.

A tap on the door made both sit up and try to look normal. It was

Emmy with her usual entourage of two toddlers, followed by Ammy carrying Aggie.

'Tea?' asked Emmy.

'They haven't stopped talking about their adventure on Saturday evening,' Petrie said. 'It was like a trip to fairyland, according to both of them. They've been having to tell the others every detail, ever since. Including me,' said Petrie. 'I'd forgotten such civilized gatherings existed.'

'And as it happens, that's what I came up for, today,' William said. 'My sister, Mrs Taliaferro, is ill in bed, just worn out with work and worry, and her husband has had to go away on business, so there's nobody to take her a cup of tea and no face for her to see at all unless it's mine. And I'm more than usually occupied. Could you spare one of them – or both – during the middle of the day for the next three or four days? Paid by the day or the hour, as they wish.'

'Both of us,' they said in chorus. 'Topy and Saffie can manage here, if that's all right with Dad.'

William took them both back with him there and then and introduced them to Jess. She made a remarkable recovery as soon as they appeared, William thought sardonically as he left, leaving them to walk back to Danesum. His ''ot meal' was a bit dried up, and Sophie grumbled at him. But for some reason, he had no appetite.

He knew quite well why he wasn't hungry. He was keeping a secret from Fran, and it bothered him as if he had swallowed a sticky-burr or a six-inch nail that would not be digested. There was only one remedy. He would have to tell her, and trust to her own loving-kindness in general and her love for him in particular to agree that he had done the only thing he could have done under the circumstances. He could hardly wait for bedtime to confess.

'It was meant to be,' she said. 'Why was it I found him naked on the side of the road? I couldn't desert him then, and we can't now. Or when the time comes. But his father isn't dead, yet. Tell me about all your visits. You seem to have had a more than usually successful day.'

36

Buoyed up by hope, Sophie was going full-steam ahead towards Christmas, and demanding to know what everybody's plans were so that she could 'get forr'd, like' with anything that involved preparation on her part. For once Fran and William were not at all clear with regard to their plans.

Christmas was a family festival, and Fran loved entertaining; but 'family' meant Jess and Greg, as well as Roland, Monica and their children. Eric's warning not to mix Jess with Monica had been taken seriously.

'Jess and Greg here on Christmas Day, I think,' Fran said, 'and then we could go to Monastery Farm on Boxing Day. But what happens if Greg hasn't turned up again? And what a merry Christmas it would be for us, then! Do you suppose she would play the proud and noble lady suffering grief and humiliation at home in silent solitude, making us miserable thinking about her?'

'You don't sound as if you care very much for any of them just at present, my darling. To tell the truth, neither do I. Whatever we do'll be a comedown after last year, and what I would like most would be to spend Christmas at home, just the two of us.'

She nodded. 'The older you get, the more you agree with what Mary Budd used to say: "families are hell." There's always somebody quarrelling with somebody else. Talk about peace and goodwill – it doesn't seem to apply to families. Now friends, at our age, are quite different. We could have a lovely Christmas with Elyot and Beth, or with Bob and Jane, or with both lots together. But in spite of what I say, I still hanker after Christmas remaining a family festival. I don't want to contribute one iota to the breaking of that custom. And if *we* are faced with family difficulties, think what it'll be like for the Bridgefoots.'

That was a sobering thought. Fran told Sophie that she didn't yet know what the pattern would be, but to prepare as for the hosts of Gideon, just in case.

'Seeing as Christmas Day's on a Wednesday this year,' Sophie said, looking pleased, 'do, that shouldn't cause nobody no trouble. I shall be 'ere Boxing Day if you need me, and then every day till the next Sunday if it 'appens as you do have a lot of guest-es.'

Fran stopped worrying about Christmas, letting her mind wander away after this relic of Middle English pronunciation. Sophie and her sisters always pronounced an 'e' that was no longer there in the spelling of words ending with 'st'. They bought themselves new 'vest-es', or talked of 'lamp-post-es' or 'ghost-es' and so on, just as Chaucer might have done. It had been common all over East Anglia until the war, just as the 'en' plural had been – 'housen' for houses, 'shoon' for shoes. It would die out with Sophie's generation. Any regional accent was now frowned upon by parents, if not by schools, as 'low'. The fashion now was for conformity in everything. That was the kind of change William declared to be inevitable and invincible. She sighed. She wasn't looking forward to Christmas much, this year.

William had been to see Jess, and reported that she appeared to be her normal self again, plus. He couldn't say whether she was putting on an act to make the two Petrie girls adore her more than they did already, or whether the truth was that Greg had been in touch with her and she felt better. In the end, he asked her about Greg.

'Oh, he rang last night, as usual,' she said, coldly and deliberately casual, 'from a hotel somewhere. Says he'll probably be home on Friday.' Her tone of voice indicated that she couldn't care less where he was or if he never came back at all. William was not deceived, but no wiser. Where was Greg likely to be but in a hotel? He had to sleep somewhere.

William said no more. He was becoming heartily sick of his sister and her quick-change range of feelings and moods. He had other things to think about.

One was the meeting with Alex Marland and Nicholas Gordon about Nick. It had been agreed that Jane shouldn't be present, so as to give Alex full rein to speak freely and give his honest opinion without any pulling of punches on her behalf. Mothers can be very unhelpful on such occasions.

Gordon was concerned about the long-term future of his grandson. Alex had carried out a series of tests with Nick's cooperation. He had reported the boy to have an intelligence quotient 'right off the top of the scale', which surprised nobody. He was a quick learner, and had no difficulty in remembering what he learned. Now and then, Alex said, Nick had surprised him. Once he had actually supplied a whole couplet of a poem they were discussing but which didn't appear till a couple of pages further on.

'Such tiny incidents give me hope,' Alex said. 'If they are incipient flashes of memory, it must mean that there is no permanent damage to that part of his brain. It could be that it has only become disconnected, for want of a better analogy. You must remember that I'm not a brain specialist. If anything, I'm more of a mind specialist, which is quite different. I know something about normal patterns of behaviour, and something about what causes them to slip out of gear occasionally. Mr Gordon wants Nick to go to one of the older universities. I see no reason why he shouldn't make the grade. He also cherishes the hope that Nick might follow him into the diplomatic service; again, I see no reason why not, except . . .'

'Well?'

'Except that wonderful palaces in the sky tend to collapse like a house of cards for want of a solid foundation. That's what Nick hasn't got. The foundations of his life have been washed away. That's what's so difficult for us to take in. It's as if he had been born aged nineteen.

'We've deliberately tossed him into learning Arabic because he could not possibly have had any memories of that. He has taken to it like a duck to water. No different from French and German he had known previously. We haven't tapped into memory there. All life is new to him.'

'Does it really matter?' William asked. 'I know how callous that sounds with regard to Jane and his old friends like Charles, but surely it is they who have to learn, not he. They have to learn to accept him as he is now.'

'In his particular case, it may not matter to any tragic degree,' answered Alex. 'But you must allow me to see it from a consultant's standpoint. I want to learn from it, if I can, to help others. It isn't the first case of its kind by a long way, you know. In fact, there were several instances of it after both wars.'

'Alex,' said William slowly, 'are you saying, without giving anybody anything so positive as hope, that you believe there may be just a chance that Nick could regain his memory of the pre-accident years?'

'Yes,' said Alex. 'I can't say I think it's likely, but I have to say I believe it's possible.'

Nicholas Gordon stood up, and was staring down at Alex.

'You are too young to remember,' he said, 'though it's possible that William may. There was a film – just after the war perhaps, certainly a long time ago – about just such a case. It had Ronald Coleman in the chief part, and I think it was called *Random Harvest*. I remember that the hero who had suffered memory loss, fell in love with his own wife, having no idea that he'd ever met her before, and didn't recognize her – until one day the gate of their cottage, which they had lived in previously, squeaked just as it always had done. What odds there are against ever finding the magic "open sesame" in such cases! But it seems that even with the odds at a million to one of ever finding it, there is a chance.'

Alex nodded. 'I know a middle-aged couple who were given a pair of *cloisonné* vases for a wedding present. They put them on the mantelpiece, and one day somebody dropped one of them into the other. It went in, but it wouldn't come out. It had been stuck there for over thirty years when I saw it. Everybody used to try to think up ways of getting it out – it was as intriguing as a Chinese puzzle. Then one day one of my fellow students went home with the couple's son, who was one of our "gang". He stood leaning against the mantelpiece and saw the vases. He said to our friend's mother, "Why do you keep one of these beautiful vases inside the other?" and just lifted it out with his index finger.'

'Let's consider carefully,' said William, 'and put those two cases together. In the first instance, there were already two elements from the past present at one and the same time – the wife and the place. The catalyst, as it were, was a third. The squeaking of the gate had been there alongside the other two many times in the past, and when it happened again, it tipped the balance. The second example is different, but in a queer way adds up to the same thing. The inner vase must have slipped inside the outer one at the only possible place the configuration of the two allowed it to. After all those years, when they were again in exactly that very same position with regard to each other, a finger such as that which put it in was inserted – and out it came. Alex, am I being silly, or would it be an idea to try permutations of people, places and things that Nick might have experienced before? The right person in the right place doing the same thing – eating an orange, making the fire up, pulling a cat's ears – '

'It isn't a good idea if it won't work in practice, William,' said Alex rather sadly. 'The permutations are infinite. We should need eternity to go on trying to find the right one.'

William didn't give up easily. 'You are forgetting the wild card of chance,' he said. 'It was chance that got the *cloisonné* vases apart. Chance that the gate squeaked just when it did. It's like taking a ticket for a lottery, or buying a premium bond. If you haven't bought a ticket or a bond, you can't win. The more tickets or bonds you do hold, the less the odds against you *not* winning. Why don't we at least try? How could we begin?'

Alex was reluctant to go along with anything that would prolong hope that might prove false, but on the other hand he was professionally interested enough to encourage experiment. There was no difficulty about any cost; nor would it interfere in any way with Nick's current progress.

'I suppose,' he said, 'though I am only guessing, that the most logical step would be to return Nick as far as it is possible to surroundings and conditions he was in at the time of the accident. But that's going to be very difficult, isn't it? Wasn't it just at their worst time?'

'No,' answered William. 'Things had begun to look up for Jane and Nick by then. She was working in much happier surroundings, earning a bit more money, and they were living in absolute luxury compared to what they had been used to. She and Nick were occupying one of Eric Choppen's firm's summer cottages, I believe at George Bridgefoot's expense, till Nick completed his A-level exams.'

'Where is the cottage?' Gordon was obviously excited.

'As it happens, on the track that leads up to Castle Hill Farm,' William replied. 'But you can't possibly ask Jane to go back and live there with Nick now! What about Bob?'

'Is the cottage occupied? Would Manor Farms Ltd sell it?'

'I doubt it, but it's empty at present. They're kept mainly for summer letting.'

'I shall offer to hire it for a whole year as a holiday cottage, and move in, if possible, before Christmas. Forget the experiment for a moment – it is still the answer to another problem. Jane wants to get back to Bob, naturally, but doesn't want to leave Nick. She wants Nick, and me, to spend Christmas at Castle Hill with them. I have been resisting it, because they have had no chance so far to be in their own home together. I know Charlie will have to be there, but to have two others as well just wouldn't be fair to them. So I have said no, though Jane is upset about leaving us in London. What could be better than that we are close enough to be with them when they want us – for Christmas dinner, for example – and out of their way when they don't want us? Jane would be near enough to look after us, and we could have our main meals at the hotel. Is the cottage habitable in winter? I'm afraid I'm not exactly used to cold and discomfort.'

'We'll go and see it this afternoon, if Alex gives his permission,' William said. 'I've never been inside one of the firm's cottages, but by all accounts they are fully equipped and centrally heated – the lot. Little palaces, according to Sophie.'

Alex agreed. 'It would provide one stable element of Nick's past – the place,' he said, 'and his mother coming and going would provide a second. God only knows what a third might be. I'm afraid we shall never know. But I think it's worth gambling that far.'

By the evening of the same day, one lot of arrangements for Christmas-time at least had been made. Effendi and Nick would move into the cottage a week before Christmas, giving Eric a chance to get it cleaned, thoroughly warmed, and ready for occupation.

It was the beginning of a period of uneasy calm. Fran remained glued to her typewriter. Sophie reported with grim pleasure that since Thirzah had ventured out as far as the Old Rectory on the night of Fran's birth-day, she had 'felt well enough' to go to church the next day. Sophie's face was a study while telling the tale. 'Then when Mis' Franks called to see 'er to thank 'er,' Sophie said, 'Thirz' told 'er as she 'ad been thinking to 'erself that whatever Dr 'Enderson might say, she'd be a lot better doing a bit o' light work, and 'aving a bit of a walk as far as the Old Rectory every day. So she was going back to work.'

'Mrs Franks will be pleased,' Fran said.

'Ah. So will Thirz', as long as she's choosed to do it of 'er own free will. It's the one thing as the doctor told 'er not to do,' Sophie answered. 'I told you 'ow it would be. I know our Thirz'. And there's another thing. She didn't reckon much to them gals from down Danesum being there a-helping, and being so good at it. She ain't leaving no crack for any o' them to creep into if she can 'elp it. That's what's druv 'er back to work. I never did think there were a lot wrong with 'er. She 'ad to 'ave a hexcuse not to goo up Het's while she couldn't be top-dog at praying. She'll be walking as far as Het's come Christmas, now that Daffy Pugh is gone. You mark my words.'

Greg came home at weekends, but barely left Southside House. Fran offered the invitation for Christmas Day, which was accepted, though without much enthusiasm on Jess's part. The portrait residing still in their coat-cupboard had never been mentioned again.

Beth was enjoying herself training about a dozen girls in a choir, Emmy, Ammy, Topy and Saffie among them, if they didn't all go at the same time. Eric had had notices put up in the hotel about Christmas services at Swithinford and Old Swithinford, not forgetting the special watchnight service. So far, no cleric had been provided by anybody, let alone the Lord, to take the service, but as William said, such help would still be welcome right up to the eleventh hour.

'That,' said Fran, 'is exactly when it will be needed.'

'"Come late, come right," as Mam used to say,' said Sophie. 'Get Christmas over first.'

They did. True to their promise, they turned out for church on Christmas morning, and were welcomed effusively by the new churchwarden, which made Fran wish heartily that they hadn't bothered. The Bridgefoot family's pew had only George and Molly in it, both looking less than happy. Greg and Jess arrived for lunch in a state of armed neutrality that was difficult to deal with. Anne, so Jess said, had gone away to her late husband's family. Fran didn't care where she'd gone, as long as it wasn't to Benedict's. She said so in bed to William. 'As dull a Christmas Day as I ever remember,' she said. 'Except for my present.'

'I'll wear it tomorrow. I didn't want Jess's sneer to spoil it for me today.'

37

Charles was up and out before it was light on the morning of Boxing Day. The weather was crisp and clear and the morning star waning as the pale morning light grew stronger. He was remembering last year's Boxing morning, when a brand new car had been his joint Christmas and birthday present, and he had sneaked out to take it on the road for the first time, before, as he had thought, anyone else would be about.

He'd been wrong about that, and what a difference it had made to his life! He had met Charlie within twenty minutes of driving out, and the world and everything in it had been changed. He was on his way to meet her again now, a year later, at the same place at the same time, but in what different circumstances! And how different the two of them were from what they had been at their first meeting. Last year, he had been only a callow youth, and she had been, quite literally, a schoolgirl home on holiday. In his pocket now was a love-gift for her: not her Christmas present, which she had had yesterday, but a special one saved for today, an engagement ring that so far she knew nothing about. Whatever the season was for other people, for two happy youngsters at least it was a bright and glorious time full of promise, in a world lit for them just at present with good luck and great hopes, and warmed from the inside by love.

Charles felt the clouds of unhappiness at home lift from his shoulders as he drove towards Castle Hill and Charlie. It hadn't seemed much like Christmas at home yesterday. In past years, the whole Bridgefoot clan had always met together for Christmas dinner wherever George and Molly had been living, but yesterday the family had not been complete. The Giffords were absent upon half-hearted excuses from Marjorie, and Alex and Lucy were coming for the New Year instead; but that wasn't what had been wrong about it. He'd missed his twin Gifford cousins, who had always been there before, and last year Nick Hadley had shared their Christmas, too. Nick as he was then, Nick as he had always been. This year, Charles had been the only young one present. But that hadn't been the cause of his restlessness, either. It was the general atmosphere.

With only himself and his parents, they mustered only five against last year's dozen. Though everybody had tried, there had not been much Christmas spirit in evidence, and Charles had watched the clock till it was time for him to go and spend the rest of the day at Castle Hill. Christmas hadn't really started for him till he got there, and that made him feel both sad and guilty. It was Grandad and Granny who were suffering, and none of it was their fault. Or his fault. It was Brian's obdurate objection to Charlie as a future Bridgefoot that had soured the atmosphere, and it was terribly frustrating to him that he and Grandad, who knew the changed circumstances that might make a difference, were still bound by their promise not to disclose anything about affairs at Castle Hill.

Bob had fetched Jane home a week ago, but nobody, it seemed, had been interested enough to notice. The village, immersed in its own Christmas affairs, had given up bothering with Bob Bellamy. There was too much else of interest going on. The nine days' wonder of how Bellamy had managed to cling on to Castle Hill Farm had run its course. In its place were two topics, far more exciting than the doings of a former charwoman and her now brain-damaged son, however sorry they were for the boy.

The favourite topic was the housewarming party on New Year's Eve at Casablanca. Beryl Bean was the pivot of it, not only as the queen of gossipers, but, in this particular case, as the fount of knowledge also, her Ken being involved in the arrangements. Moreover, Mr and Mrs Bean had actually been invited to the party. She, Beryl, was to be a guest at the biggest and most costly party Old Swithinford had ever seen, even in the old squire's time.

At first other women took this information with the usual grain of salt, till she fetched the gilt-edged invitation card and showed it to one of them. After that she had to fetch it so often that in the end she put it in a photo-frame and stood it on the counter.

Beryl had bought a sophisticated cocktail frock too young for her, too tight on her here and there, and which showed a good deal more of her than her previous fellow chapelgoers would have thought seemly. But, then, she wasn't 'chapel', now that Ken was a churchwarden. She was going to be confirmed to the C of E.

Which led naturally to the other topic. Was it true that them from Benedict's and the Old Rectory had refused their invitations? Yes, that Beryl did know to be gospel truth.

Beryl was in her element. She had never in all her life had so much to boast about, so much gossip to disseminate, or so many willing listeners.

Sophie prided herself upon not repeating gossip, though she made her own rules about it. She didn't usually repeat to Fran anything which she could not vouch for as being the absolute truth, but where Beryl was concerned there was an exception to the rule. But for Jelly's death, she would have been Beryl's sister-in-law. There was 'no love lost' between them.

Fran let Sophie talk. As she said to William, it meant that in spite of all that Time and the Bailey types could do, the old village did still exist. The sort of talk that went on in Beryl's shop resembled a strong, regular pulse, showing that the village's lifeblood was still circulating. It had gone on before any other sort of newscasting. Everybody could find out at the press of a knob or the turn of a switch what was happening in London, New York or Tokyo, but they wouldn't see what their neighbours were up to on the screen, and that's really what they wanted to know. As long as Beryl kept up her role as news-dispenser, Bailey could do his worst. The body bucolic would still be alive.

Beryl went on excitedly adding to the details till the day that Ken went home full of the row he had just had with George Bridgefoot. He had met George by chance, according to the version put about later by his wife, and George had told him – not asked him, mind you – about the watchnight service as they was arranging for New Year's Eve. 'Like we all'us used to 'ave once,' George says, 'in the old Rector's time.'

New Year's Eve, the same night as the party! Ken, said Beryl, had told George straight as he'd better go and cancel it, 'cos he wasn't going to agree to no such service, not being able to be in two places at once. He was as much a churchwarden now as George Bridgefoot, and told him so. There wasn't nobody to take the service anyway, was there?

Indignation almost choking her, she went on to relate how George had dared to say that Ken couldn't do nothing to stop it, not nohow, be he never so much the new churchwarden. It had been asked for by the people, a whole lot o' them as wouldn't be going to Bailey's party anyway, and Ken was supposed to be their spokesman and do as they asked. And when Ken asked who had give permission for the service, George said he hadn't been the Rector's warden for forty year without knowing what he could or couldn't do hisself. He didn't have to ask such as Ken. 'It's up to you what you do,' George had said.

'My Ken soon told him as we knowed that, and we should be at the party,' Beryl said, her cheeks red and her manner that of a ruffled old hen. 'Seems George and Molly hadn't been invited, though Brian has, and the Giffords. And do you know what Bridgefoot had the cheek to say to my Ken? He quoted the Bible at him! "No man can serve two masters," he said. "We shall see whether our new churchwarden means to serve God or Mammon, come New Year."'

With excitement passing from mouth to mouth, it was no wonder that Castle Hill was overlooked. So much so indeed that even the arrival of Effendi and Nick to take up residence in Jane's former cottage during the weekend before Christmas had also failed to register. The only bit of news Beryl had to promote on that was that the milkman had told her somebody was there for the holiday, but they didn't want no milk. 'Must be some o' them vegetarians, then, I reckon,' Beryl had commented, and that was all.

Charles had found at Castle Hill on Christmas Day all the warmth and Christmas spirit he had missed at home. It was the first time ever Jane had 'made' Christmas herself, and this time it was in her own home and with few, if any, restrictions on what it cost. The vast room, with its enormous log fire blazing on the wide hearth, looked like a baronial hall. Bob had been responsible for decorations, and the walls and rafters were bright with greenery and berries. Even the huge kissing-bunch of holly and mistletoe had been gathered from the wood they could see from the windows. There would have been no shortage of food or drink in any case, but Effendi had arrived, by taxi, with a pile of hampers from Fortnum and Mason.

There had been much discussion with Alex about preparing Nick for this visit. They had to take him back if the 'random harvest' theory were to be given a chance. But how much was he to be told of the circumstances under which Jane had brought him up?

What would be the effect on this still somewhat frail and bewildered youngster of the knowledge that he was illegitimate, that he had been brought up in dire poverty by his mother who in the eyes of the village people was 'only a charwoman' and 'a bit of a mystery', keeping herself to herself as she had done? They had to take the chance that he did not encounter too many of the wrong sort of people. They had decided that they would not attempt to load Nick with information, but that if or when he asked questions, they should be answered as fully and as truthfully as was compatible with protecting Jane.

Nick had been a bit shy and nervously aware of the strangeness of everything at Castle Hill farm. He had been out of the sheltering walls of the clinic for only a week, and had been just settling down in Effendi's sumptuous flat, when he had been asked to uproot himself again. He was much happier in the cottage, with which both he and Effendi were charmed. Effendi decided that it was the small rooms that gave both of them such a feeling of comfort and safety.

'I like it here,' Nick had said suddenly to his grandfather, as they sat on each side of the fire late on Christmas Eve. 'I feel as if I could study hard if I lived here. When I went into my bedroom a little time ago, I put my hand out to pick up a book from the window-sill as if I expected it to be there. It was a queer sensation. If we come again in the spring, I shall bring some books. I sort of feel as if there ought to be some of my books here.'

It was as good a Christmas present as any of his family could have asked for, a sort of portent that some memories after all might be not dead but only sleeping.

By the time Charles arrived on Christmas Day, Nick had begun to adjust to his surroundings. He remembered having met Charles in London, and the company of two people of his own age did a lot to shelter him.

Effendi had been lavish with Christmas presents, though William had made him think twice about swathing young Charlie in furs, and Jane had refused completely to accept a fur coat, saying that she had to be terribly careful to edge her new status into the village gradually. An expensive fur coat would paint Effendi more like a sugar-daddy than her real father – and then what about Bob's feelings? She had suggested that if they were going on a shopping expedition, there would be no reason why her father should not buy his new step-granddaughter the 'classic' expensive dress that she would never think of buying for herself. They had found exactly what Jane had envisaged that Charlie, at her most feminine, could wear to perfection. It was a plainly cut, very soft angora dress in a shade darker than beige but by no means brown. Nothing to look at without the right girl inside it, Jane had said – but she couldn't think that anybody would look better in it than Charlie. Effendi had insisted on underwear, shoes and tights to match. The dress had a low, round neck, so Bob and Jane bought a Victorian amber choker to go with it, and ear-rings to match. These Jane had offered to let Charles have to give Charlie if he would like to. He had been spared great difficulty by Jane's forethought, and had thereafter searched Cambridge's antique shops till he found an amber-bead bracelet as well.

She was wearing the dress and the choker as she moved to greet him on that Christmas afternoon. He was struck almost dumb by the beauty of her. Jane's instinct had been absolutely right. The tone of the dress made her skin glow under the dusky tan that was habitual to her, and the amber brought out all the chestnut gleams in her thick hair, which she had piled on top of her head in a braided crown as Charles had only seen it done twice before, both times at weddings.

When she came to him to be taken into his arms in front of them all, his senses reeled at the feel of her in that clinging, so soft woollen dress. He had had to pull himself together.

'You look,' he said, pushing her to arms length in order to survey her better, 'just like a brand new conker!'

Everybody laughed. 'That's exactly right, my boy,' said Gordon. 'The nut-brown maid herself.'

He shyly produced his offerings all round, but nobody else would open their presents until Charlie had undone hers. The dark brown eyes grew even darker, and became again the liquid pools with gleams of golden light in them that had drowned all Charles's senses the very first time he had ever looked into them. She picked up the deep amber drop ear-rings and held them out to him.

'Put them on,' she ordered. 'And this.' He stretched the bracelet over her hand. Then she kissed him.

It was over her shoulder, when he opened his eyes again, that he saw Nick's expression. Charles couldn't read it. There was a sort of longing there, and a suggestion of hopeless envy, immediately brought under control. Why on earth should 'old Nick' look like that? Or 'new Nick' either, if it came to that. Jealousy burned through Charles's veins. Nick was not Charlie's brother. He was no relation to her at all – he could be as fond of her as he liked as a step-sister, but nobody had a right to look at his Charlie like that but himself. Certainly not Nick. Once he was completely well, Nick could have the pick of all the beautiful, posh, rich girls in London, considering all the advantages he now had.

Nobody but Charles had been aware of anything out of the way happening. Charles reminded himself that Nick was his friend, even if Nick didn't remember it. The Nick that had been would never have pinched his best friend's girl. He'd been rather funny that way, a bit like William Burbage, stuck with an outmoded notion of what was done and what was not done. Charles decided that he need not worry, but it made him more possessive of Charlie than he had ever felt before.

The only other person it had disturbed was Nick himself. He could not fathom the extraordinary sensation that had swept through him as he had watched Charlie kiss Charles, and registered his response. Why was it that he had felt so envious of *them* – of them, not just of Charles? He had accepted Charlie as his sister, and had liked what he had seen of Charles, whom they had said had been his best friend long ago. He hoped it could be so again, though he doubted whether Charles would ever want anyone else as close to him as it was evident that Charlie was. If only he could remember – things that nobody could tell him, even if they would.

The rest of the day had gone well, but still Charles was glad it was over. This was Boxing Day, their day, his and Charlie's. A day with no family obligations, either, this year; no return visits to make. They could do just as they liked. He had decided that he couldn't take Charlie home to Temperance, and Granny wouldn't be cooking again. Rather than eat cold turkey at the Old Glebe they would have lunch at the hotel, and he had booked a table there in good time. They were invited back to Castle Hill again for supper. That would be nice. It was, after all, Charlie's home.

She was waiting for him at the place where he had practised his first three-point turn last year, sitting on top of the five-barred gate which she had intended to jump Ginger over. No nut-brown maid today, but no be-jeaned undergraduate, either. She was, he noticed, wearing a skirt, which pleased him because they were going to the hotel, and he didn't really like to see women in trousers when they were 'out'. She was neatly shod in brown brogues, which suggested walking. Her hair this morning was back into its springy pony-tail. She wore no jewellery. That, again, pleased him. This morning's Charlie didn't need adornment.

She slid off the gate as his car approached, and was waiting to get in as soon as he pulled into the gateway. The sky hadn't quite got rid of all its dawn glory, and there were still wisps of pink cloud overhead, while the sun was climbing up into banks of grey and bluish-grey stippled with a grey still lighter. Behind the bank of cloud which hid the sun, there was a strip of light that was changing from lemony yellow to turquoise and getting narrower second by second – just letting you know it was still bright behind the cloud. A sort of hopeful dawn, Charles felt. He switched off his engine and took his girl into his arms.

That cars weren't designed for the comfort of courting couples he had long ago found out, though from all he heard from others their secondary use was for sex on the back seat. That didn't appeal to him, any more than he would have thought a cold winter morning the time to try it. On the other hand, cars were not too bad as places to sit together in complete seclusion, to cuddle up, hold hands and kiss – and talk. The little box on wheels in a lonely gateway in a wide and empty expanse of fields was as good a place as any for Charles's purpose this morning.

They began to recall their meeting, looking back on it with laughter and something like disbelief.

'You looked such a goof,' she said, 'all red and stammering, and wanting to run away. I'm glad you didn't.'

'Gosh, so am I! When I think of you then, and then how you looked last night . . .' He stopped to kiss her again, more passionately this time.

'Please don't, Charles,' she said. 'You know why.'

'Sometimes I can't bear it,' he said.

'No, neither can I. But we've got to. Till I've got my degree. Till we're married, in fact.'

He picked her hand up, and kissed it. 'Roll on the day I can put a wedding ring on that finger, then,' he said, kissing her ring finger. 'More than two years more to wait, yet. But just to show you that I'll wait if you will, what about this?'

He took from his pocket the ring-box he had been hiding there from the possible prying eyes of his mother since he had found exactly what he had wanted, six weeks ago. He took the ring from it, and slipped it on to the finger he was holding. It fitted, and he breathed a great sigh. He had told himself that if he had guessed right about the size, it would be a sign to him that it could and would be replaced by a plain gold band one day. He kissed the ring on her finger, and then let go to see if she liked it.

She took one glance at it, and hid her face in his chest. It was, to all intents and purposes, a jewelled daisy – a cluster of small diamonds set in petal-shaped gold mounts around a central gold-enclosed, slightly raised topaz. She took her face away to look at it again, and used his forefinger to count the diamond petals. There were nine. Then she put her head back for him to kiss again, and didn't complain that the kisses were more than those of a casual sweetheart, that time.

'My lambkin,' he said. 'Always?'

'My Charles,' she said. 'Always.'

He felt that it was too dangerous to stop where they were any longer. 'Let's go and have breakfast with Granny and Grandad,' he said. 'Somebody's got to be the first to see it.'

They drove sedately back towards the village, passing the cottage where Nicholas the Elder and Nick the Younger still slept in cosy, contented warmth.

They were made much of at the Old Glebe, and being young and healthy and hungry, sealed their engagement with a huge fried breakfast that gave both the old people great pleasure to see.

'I should love to go up and show Mum,' Charles said. 'But Dad will be there.'

'No, he won't,' said Molly. 'He's gone over to Marjorie's, to see Vic and his new horse. Pansy's been giving him riding lessons, and is taking him out all in his brand new riding gear this morning. I hope it don't give your Dad any daft ideas.'

'I expect he's only gone to laugh,' Charles said. 'You have to learn such things young. Like my future wife did. So that you can fall off your horse when you see an eligible young man with a new car coming.' They went off scuffling with each other like a couple of young puppies, till Charlie broke away and showed him how fleet of foot she could be without the aid of a horse. He was panting when he caught her, and claimed yet another kiss as he opened the car door for her.

'Lovely young couple,' said Molly, wiping a tear away on the corner of the tea towel. 'God bless them both.'

'Amen,' said George. 'She likes her grub. He'll never want for a good meal.'

'Or for anything else he wants, once they've tied the knot,' Molly added.

He nodded. 'As Alex's father said, she's a girl in a million. Still fresh as a daisy.'

He gave Molly a kiss, and went off, forgetting to limp.

38

The young couple left the Old Glebe reluctantly *en route* for Temperance Farm. The assurance that his father would not be there had not altogether satisfied Charles. Life at home had been so difficult just lately that he was not at all sure on which side his mother stood. That she had defied his father on his behalf he knew, but he could also see how unhappy the present state of limited truce between them was making her. He supposed that she still loved his father, even if he found her less exciting after twenty-five years of marriage. Both of them were still only in their forties.

He had a vague notion that this was the pattern marriage as an institution was taking. That it was almost expected of a man in this decade that he should start looking about for something new when the first bloom had worn off his wife and being married to her had become stale through familiarity. He didn't want to think that in twenty-five years' time he would be looking for somebody to replace Charlie or – with panic because of a flash of insight – that in these days when women were so set on 'liberating' themselves, she might be looking for some other man to replace him! As her mother had done?

That was one of the excuses his father was making for his objection to Charlie. Charles felt strongly that it was only an excuse – but why did his father want or need excuses to fall out with anybody? Grandad and Granny hadn't got sick of each other. William and Fran were in their fifties, and seemed as much in love as ever. But he had to admit that both those couples were old-fashioned. His mother was old-fashioned, too. She wanted her marriage to his father to last. That was why she went along with him whenever she could, even against Charles. The real question was whether his father was any happier to be 'in fashion' about this than his mother was to be 'out of fashion'. They called such things 'social patterns' and said that this was the way of life of 'post-war society'. It seemed to him nothing much more than any other change of fashion. As some women 'wouldn't be seen dead' with last year's skirt-length, so some men wouldn't be seen at all with their own wives. It was old-fashioned.

He was on his mother's side. He simply could not make himself believe that he would ever want to change Charlie for another woman just to be like other men, or to have it said that he was 'keeping up with the times'.

He turned to look at her before letting in his clutch. 'Are you sure you don't mind going to see Mum?' he asked.

'Not if that's what you'd like. She really likes me, I think. She only goes along with your Dad. I'd love to see her today if you're sure it won't spoil our day.'

'We shan't know if we don't try,' Charles said. He was feeling full of a confidence that was new to him, since he had put the ring on Charlie's finger. It was a signal to him, as well as to other people, that he was man enough to choose his own wife. He didn't feel so guilty about the situation at home, either, since he had thought it through. His choice of Charlie had very little to do with the situation at home.

He suddenly wanted to do all he could to make it up to his mother. It wasn't her fault that she was over forty, and not so rosy and placid as she used to be when she was happy. She didn't care for the modern fashion with regard to partner-swapping, casual sex, or chasing after the last penny whoever else went without. Mum wanted Dad to be as he used to be.

He felt a sudden pang of pity for his Dad. He had said to Charlie a minute or two ago that they wouldn't know if they didn't try. He guessed his father had had that same idea. If he didn't try the ways of 'modern society', like the Bailey set, how was he to know whether he would like it or not? Perhaps he was disappointed that Rosemary wouldn't try it as well, and go to their sort of entertainments with him. Well, she wouldn't. Of that Charles was absolutely certain. So there was no guessing what might happen next. Poor old Mum. It would please her that he had taken Charlie to tell her the news and show her the ring first.

At Temperance Farm, Rosemary's face lit up at the sight of them. She hadn't so far had a very happy Christmas, and had spent the morning wondering why it was so necessary for Brian to visit his sister, and though she guessed where Charles had gone, she was put out at not being told he was going so early, leaving her all alone.

Charlie let Charles go first, a little uncertain of their reception. But Rosemary had been half-expecting some sort of engagement, if not the public one they had planned. She read her son's face, pushed him out of the way, and went to meet Charlie, putting her arms round the girl's neck, and immediately receiving a hug in return.

'Come in and we'll have a drink to celebrate,' she said. 'And I want to see the ring.'

'Grandad told us Dad wouldn't be here,' Charles said, 'or we wouldn't have come.'

'I shall tell him,' said Rosemary, 'at the right time. It may help him to make up his mind. He's not really a fool. He just can't bear to give in. But he knows he can't run with the hare and hunt with the hounds much longer. It'll be all right in the long run.'

'Do you want us to go before he comes back?'

'Yes – I wouldn't let on anything today. He's always touchy when he's been up to see Vic. I want you to be as happy as you can today. I'll be happy as long as you are, Charles.'

She kissed them both, and stood, smiling determinedly, till they were out of sight.

They had finished their leisurely lunch at the hotel, and there was still a lot of winter afternoon left. Pleasant as it was there, neither of them wanted to return too soon to Castle Hill. It was their special day, and they wanted to spend as much of it together, just the two of them, as they could.

'So what shall we do now?' Charles asked. 'Wander about in the car?'

Charlie looked around her. The sun had come out, a bit weak and pale, but bright and inviting. 'Let's walk,' she said. 'We need some exercise after those two enormous meals. Let's leave the car in the car park, and walk down the lane where that family of hippies live. They say the man's been doing some conversion of the cottages down there.'

'Tell me something I don't know,' Charles teased her. 'I work around here, you know. We've got an odd parcel of land down here. But yes, let's do that.'

They set off briskly, holding hands. The sun's rays were slanting from the west in somewhat lurid glory on the white face of the restored house as it came into view. The rowan tree had been stripped of its berries, but its skeleton still added grace and beauty to the place, just as the old, crooked, unrestored granary showing at the back of it took away some of the raw new whiteness. The sunset's gleams were reflected in the brook, and Charles was as surprised as Charlie at the lonely, dignified beauty and attraction of it all.

They came to the spot where the brambles almost met across the road, and once the other side of it, were in front of the house. In spite of what he had said, Charles had not been as far as this since the Petries had been there. He and Charlie did not want to be seen, but went close enough to get a good look. Attached to the trunk of the rowan tree was a large, hand-painted though professional-looking notice:

FOR SALE

APPLY WITHIN

Vacant possession sometime in the spring.

Charlie drew in her breath, held it, and gazed enraptured. Charles was looking at the notice.

'What would you suppose that can possibly mean?' he said. 'Is it a joke? Whoever's likely to come down as far as this to read it? And what does "sometime in the spring" mean, anyway, supposing anyone were to be interested in buying it? The chap must have put a lot of work into it, but I wouldn't give much for his chances of selling a place as lonely and out-of-the-way as this is. Besides, it's so big.'

Charlie was gazing at it with a faraway look in her eye. 'It's absolutely beautiful,' she said, almost breathlessly. 'He must have put it back again as it was – I mean, it was one big house first, before it was made into cottages, and now he's restored it to one house again. But what sort of people would want to buy it to live in it? Oh Charles, I wish we could! I'm getting messages. It wants us. That's why we came this way today. Don't you see it is the *ideal* place to set up a vet's practice? Only it's far too soon. It'll be gone by the time we want it.'

Charles had realized from other out-of-the-ordinary moments that Charlie had inherited some of her father's strange sixth sense, but he had never before seen her so carried away by it. She stood slightly apart from him, her eyes huge and brilliant as if she were seeing some sort of vision that was hidden from him. The intensity of her feelings, shown in her face, almost frightened him. He moved closer to her, and took her hand.

She clasped it, and brought her gaze back from the future to the present. She squeezed his hand, and cuddled up to him to reassure him, before turning him back to show him what she had been foreseeing as glorious day-dream possibilities.

'Darling, don't you see how it could be meant just for us – in the future? That place at the back – just right to be turned into a small animal surgery. I can't see from here what the field at the back's like, but what I would really like someday is to be able to have farm animals, too. Then to breed special things, like Suffolk Punches, for show, or cows like the continental ones getting popular now – Blonde d'Aquitaines, for example. So that my vet work could tie up with your farming. Wouldn't that be fun? Why are you letting me daydream like this? We would need a lot more land than there is here. So it's hopeless for all sorts of reasons. But I'm still getting vibes from the place. It does want us. I know it does!'

'Now wait a minute. Are you sure it wants *us*? Or only you? I want you, too, but you are making me wait. You can't make this wait, if somebody else, like Arnold Bailey for instance, gets in and buys it to set up a riding school or something. Only, as you say, there isn't enough land with it for that.' She heard him utter an exclamation, as if to himself. The light was failing, but even in the dusk Charlie was aware of the change on Charles's face as well as in his voice. He was taking what she had said seriously.

While Charlie stood gazing and dreaming, Charles stood preoccupied with thought. She heard him say, as if to himself, 'So that's what's at the bottom of it!'

A light came on in the house, and they moved, afraid of being seen. They scrambled back through the gap in the brambles, and once on the far side of the brook, which ran under the road there through a culvert, Charles stopped, and opened his arms to her. She needed no second invitation.

The brook divided the Danesum plot from the arable land beside it. On the arable side, it was fringed with a row of bushes and saplings. Out of sight of the house, now, they remained clasped together, with Charles deep in thought still. She could feel him quivering, but for once it was not just the nearness of her that was causing his excitement. She waited with her head on his chest, listening to the thumping of his heart, and now and then bestowing a butterfly kiss on his chin which for once didn't turn his mouth down to hers. When at last he spoke, it was with a sort of suppressed urgency.

'My lambkin,' he said, 'were you really telling the truth? Is that really what you do want when you're finished at the vet school?'

'Just one of my dreams. Don't take too much notice of me. I don't expect you to work miracles. I'll be satisfied just to be with you. You'll go on farming, and I'll get a job with a vet practice in Swithinford or somewhere. It doesn't do any harm to daydream, though, does it? Just because I'm enough like Dad to feel things doesn't mean that I expect them to come true. Forget it.'

'No, lambkin, I'm not going to forget it. It isn't as impossible as you may think. If all that was stopping it from coming true was the question of more land . . . I told you we owned some land down here. It starts just this side of the Grist brook and runs between this road and the river. It's an odd parcel of land that doesn't belong to either of the farms, but it was the first land my Gran's father ever owned, before he bought Temperance Farm. Dad would have got rid of it before now if he'd had his way, because in these days bits of land a long way from the rest aren't always worthwhile. But Gran didn't want it sold, so it won't be while Grandad's still the boss. But I can see it all now! All sorts of things, just in time. After my birthday five days from now, it might have been too late. Since we were able to tell Grandad the whole truth about everything up at Castle Hill, and he knows that you and I are safe, I think he had more or less decided to announce that he'd give up and let Dad take over from next Lady Day. But he can't. He mustn't! I've got to stop him handing over to Dad. For one thing, it would spoil our chances of your dream ever coming true – but there's much more to it than that. You've made me see what lies behind a lot of things. Come on, my lambkin – it's getting dark and cold, and I'll tell you all I've been thinking back in the car.'

He set off at a pace so fast that she almost had to run to keep up with him, and though he was silent the hand clasping hers told her that his thoughts were moving even faster than his long legs. Once they were cuddled up together in the car, he began to talk.

She was already well aware of the difficulties the Bridgefoot clan were experiencing, and the whole family's puzzlement that his father should be contemplating throwing in his lot with Bailey and his new friends, rather than with the old village which the Bridgefoots as a family exemplified. Strangest of all was his present intimacy with the brother-in-law he had, until so recently, disliked and despised. It was certainly making everybody unhappy.

'But what's been puzzling me all the time is what it was that was holding Dad in Bailey's camp when all hope of them making a fortune out of developing Castle Hill had gone. Poor old Mum thinks Dad's fallen for some woman up there. I still thought it was more likely to be another chance of making money and getting his own back on Grandad for not handing Bridgefoot Farms Ltd over to him. But I couldn't see what sort of bait Bailey was fishing with, because there isn't any other land round here that Bailey can get his claws on to develop. Now I know! I can see through his crafty plan!

'You pressed a button in my memory, this afternoon. When Mum and Dad were having that awful quarrel, Dad wanted an excuse to go and see Uncle Vic. It was the morning they had heard for certain that your Dad was going to buy Castle Hill, and that they'd lost it. Dad was in a terrible state, and Uncle Vic an even worse one. Mum reminded Dad that she was his wife, and should be told what he was up to. He mumbled something about Bailey having a scheme in hand to set up a riding school, which Uncle Vic was keen on because of Pansy. He said they were going to see if they could buy the bit Eric Choppen had at first thought of setting up as a riding school from him, but that was just a blind. I can see now that Bailey's been waiting till he could buy Danesum cheap, when all the work on the house was finished. Grandad was failing so fast that it looked as if he would have to hand over when I was twenty-one. Then Dad would have been boss and had most of the say – I'll bet he'd promised to sell our land to Bailey, however much it would upset Gran. The riding school bit was a blind too. They might have set it up for a year or so with Pansy and three or four horses, but what Bailey had tempted Dad with was buying our land at development price. Within five years from now, all our land here between the river and the road would have been another Bailey estate. Right opposite the hotel too. Then the only thing Manor Farms could have done to stop Bailey spoiling the Hotel and Sports Centre would have been for them to offer Dad even more money to leave it as it is.

'Oh lambkin! My lambkin! Can't you see what you've saved us all from? No wonder you said the house wanted us. I must get to Grandad first thing tomorrow, and tell him all I've just told you. We've got to be ready to stop Dad's game. The whole family's been invited to lunch at Glebe on my birthday and I'm pretty sure Grandad had been planning to call a meeting after lunch, make me legally a partner, and then hand in his own chips and announce his retirement. *And that's what Dad's expecting.* I feel almost sorry for him. But I've had my doubts in this last week whether Grandad would go through with the last bit. But now – if he believes me, he won't.'

'Charles, my darling, don't be too sure you can win. What about all the rest of the family? Money means a lot to the Giffords. They'll be on your Dad's side. And if Pansy thinks she's going to get what she wants, what a disappointment it will be for her. I couldn't bear for you to be disappointed. So don't set your heart on it too much.'

'And do you think I can bear for you to be disappointed, if that house is what you want?' he said, suddenly tightening his arms round her. 'If it will make you happy, I'm going to get it for you, somehow.'

Her response left them both a bit shaken, and they drew away from each other, out of the temptation their dark seclusion offered.

'There's another way I might try,' Charles said, forcing his mind back to matters other than the yielding softness of her breasts under his finger-tips. 'I shall come into some capital next Tuesday – money that Grandad's already settled on me. I don't know exactly how much it is, because I've always thought it would be wrong to ask. But I think I have a good excuse for asking, now. It wouldn't be nearly enough to buy the house, but once I'm legally of age, and a partner in the business, I expect I could get a mortgage. The last thing that Bailey – or Dad, or Uncle Vic – will have ever given a thought to is that somebody else might beat them to it. I shall go up there tomorrow morning to find how much the man wants for it, before even going to see Grandad. I'll buy it for you somehow, my darling, darling lambkin, providing it's good enough for you.'

'It is,' she said. 'I know. It kept telling me all sorts of secrets . . .' She dropped her voice to a whisper, and caressed the ear she was closest to. 'It likes to have children in it. We could make it so happy.'

He was silent, overwhelmed with desire for her, but even more with

Love. He had been afraid that she was so set on her career that Grandad wouldn't be able to wait to see the next generation. Now here she was – 'Would that make you happy?' she said.

Actions speak louder than words. 'There's only one thing that could possibly make me happier than I am,' he said. 'And for that I have to wait for more than two more years. And the poor old house will have to wait, empty, as well. Unless I go and live there by myself. That might be a good idea.'

'I've got a better one,' she said. 'They wouldn't let us get publicly engaged. So why don't we get married, instead? As soon as the house is ready for us?'

'Don't tease me,' he said, hurt. 'Not about that.'

'I'm not!' she said. 'I should have to stop in residence during term-time, but there's no rule about me being married. I could come home for weekends and holidays, the same as I do now.'

The moon in her second quarter had risen above the dark evergreens that shaded their corner of the car park, and a ladder made of moon-beams reached from the car right up into the sky. As Charles recovered from the numbing incredulity of what she had said, he began to climb the ladder, and reached the gates of his heaven when this time there was nothing between the tips of his fingers and her satin skin.

39

By Friday morning Fran had had enough of Christmas. She looked into her study and eyed her typewriter longingly. Her play was very nearly completed and she wanted to get back to it. She heard Sophie arrive, and blessed the fact that Sophie didn't 'go along with there 'ere modern ways'. To Sophie, Christmas Day was 'a 'Oly Day', and Boxing Day 'a Bank 'Oliday', and that was it. After that, things went back to normal, or ought to.

'There ain't no sense in it, as far as I can see,' she said. 'Do Christmas fall in the middle of the week like this year, nothing gets done proper for two whull weeks. But there, nothing ain't like it used to be. I'm sure I give thanks to 'Im Above every night as I can still come to work when I like. Not like them as works in factories, as is locked out for a fortni't. Now, what am I got to do today? Are you going out or is somebody a-coming 'ere?'

That was exactly what Fran was complaining about to herself. They were either entertaining or being entertained every day.

After their less than comfortable Christmas Day with Jess and Greg, they had spent the day with their family at Monastery House, and enjoyed it. The only thing at all surprising there was that Eric had announced his intention of going away from Friday to Saturday. He had had a Christmas card from an old and dear friend who had recently been bereaved and was feeling desperately lonely over Christmas.

'I owe him a lot,' Eric had said, simply. 'It's time I repaid him. It's as good a time as any, just after Christmas and before the New Year. Jess will cope if they need her, but I shall only be away for forty-eight hours.'

It was while they were on their way to Monastery Farm that they had seen and waved to Charles and Charlie. To have had to spend Christmas Day in the light of a love whose candle was so obviously guttering had made Fran miserable, and to catch a glimpse next morning of two such bright faces had uplifted her again. If she had seen them a few hours later, the gloom she was feeling about Jess and Greg might have been reduced, like the stars by daylight, in the glow of their incandescence.

Charles had difficulty in disguising his exultation at home next morning. With only one working day interposed between the Christmas holiday and the weekend, it was a matter of principle on George's part that he expected his labourers to work that day: like Sophie, he thought it wrong for them to expect the break to stretch beyond its official limits. There was nothing waiting urgently to be done on the land, but on farms where there are animals to be attended to, no day is a complete holiday for everybody. Consequently, in theory, everybody, including Charles and his father, were expected to show willing to work this Friday.

Charles saw at once that his father was not dressed for work. He asked if there was anything special he was required to do, and was given a rather grudging negative. Rosemary inquired what he was likely to be doing with regard to meals. 'Home for lunch, but up to Charlie's for tea and supper,' he said. 'They are entertaining the two from Benedict's.'

'We ought to have been having a little celebration party, as well,' she said, but Brian was deliberately not listening. She had tried out the gambit because when she had told him last night about the 'unofficial' engagement, he had not been nearly so nasty about it as she had expected. Common sense bade her not to push her luck.

Charles wanted to slip up to Glebe to see his grandfather without his father's knowledge. He was greatly relieved to hear that Brian had been invited to Casablanca for mid-morning drinks. His mother had also been invited, but had made her apologies on the grounds that she also was expecting visitors, which was not true. There hadn't been much family unity let alone peace and goodwill in the various Bridgefoot households this year.

Charles was sorry for his mother, and after his father had left, he said, 'Don't worry, Mum. It'll perhaps turn out altogether different from what you expect.'

'I'm not worrying,' she said, 'except about your Dad. As long as you're happy, I'm happy. But I don't want to make him more miserable than he is. He doesn't know any longer what he does want. He doesn't even know now what he doesn't want. The nearer your birthday gets, the more worried he is, wondering what Grandad will do.'

'Yes, I know. The business of this service at church on Tuesday night's been like a shot in the arm to Grandad. I'm just going to pop up to see him, now, while he's having his 'levenses, if that's all right with you, Mum.'

'Anything you want to do's all right with me,' she said. 'I'm on your side, especially about Charlie. Off you go.'

He was driving out of the gates of Temperance when he had to wait for three riders to pass. He recognized two of them immediately, his twin Gifford cousins. Pansy he saw fairly frequently, but he had not seen Poppy at all since she had gone up to her university in the north in October. She slid off her horse and came to greet him.

He was seeing her for the very first time as a 'girl', not just 'one of the twins'. They were not identical twins, and had always been different in appearance, but it was quite startling, now. Pansy had filled out, bleached her hair, was very much made-up and was dressed to kill in a complete new riding outfit. Poppy had lost all her puppy-fat, and if anything looked a little too slim. Her naturally dark hair was cut short so that it fitted her rather piquant face like a Juliet cap, with just enough tendency to curl to make her wholly feminine. She was not dressed for riding, except for her hat, which she pulled off to kiss Charles.

'Go on without me,' she called to the other two, 'or you'll be late. I'm going in to say hello to Aunt Rosemary, and then I'll go home again. See you later.'

The man on the third horse gave a growl at his mount that made Charles look up at him. It was Uncle Vic! He, too, was dressed for riding in clothes that were far too obviously new, extremely well tailored and finished off with a pair of handmade boots that almost made Charles whistle. He knew what such things cost, and wondered what Aunt Marjorie had had to say about that! Charles could almost hear Charlie's comments about his seat. He was also, very clearly, extremely nervous. He lifted his crop to Charles as he and Pansy rode away, and while Poppy tied up her horse to the gate and ran in to see his mother, Charles allowed himself a grin at his uncle's expense as he drove off to see his Grandad.

He found he was too late for elevenses and Grandad had gone out to the big barn, Gran said – not to do anything, but to show the men he was there. Charles began to feel that things had been arranged to go his way. He found his grandfather sitting comfortably on a couple of strawfilled sacks, kept there on purpose, sucking his empty pipe (which on principle he never lit anywhere near farm buildings), and sat down beside him to tell him his tale.

He explained the whole situation as he saw it just as he had set it out before Charlie. The old man's silence told Charles that he was both shocked and enormously relieved. He now had the excuse he had been wanting for not being forced to retire and take the back stand that went so much against the grain. 'But we're only postponing it, my boy,' he said. 'The time will come when I shall have to give up, and he'll do what he likes with it then. I shall never give my consent to them fields being sold while your Gran's alive – but money talks louder to your Dad and your Uncle Vic than love does. If Bailey don't get it out of him now, some other developer will offer him a half a million for it.'

'Not,' said Charles slowly and distinctly, 'if by that time it isn't his to sell.'

And out poured all the rest of the dream Charlie had created the previous day. 'I'm going to see how much the man wants for the house as soon as I go from here,' he said. 'If what you are going to give me for my birthday is enough for a deposit on it, I'll get a mortgage as soon as normal business starts again next week, and make sure of Danesum, if I can. Grandad, don't you see? Our land can't be sold without your consent while you are still the boss, and the major shareholder, but you could sell it without Dad's. If you would sell it to me – as agricultural land – as soon as I can raise the money for it, it would kill three birds with one stone. It would make Charlie's dream come true. It would keep the land still Bridgefoot land, so Granny wouldn't be upset. And it would mean it wouldn't be sold for development.

'And there's something else, Grandad. If I can raise enough money to buy Danesum, just the house and the field behind it, before anybody else does, Charlie will marry me in the summer – this year. She'll still go on and finish her course – but Grandad, look what an investment it would be! The more development there is anywhere round here that we can't stop, the more need there'll be for a vet. Then if we can start breeding horses, we could set up livery stables, right opposite the hotel – and look at the custom that could bring. Only I haven't yet got nearly enough money to buy even the house and the Danesum field – but I can do what other people do and borrow it. That's all I need to do straight away.'

George still sat silent, sucking on his empty pipe, and Charles's heart began to sink.

'You'll have to make me some promises, my boy, before I can agree to do much to help you. You did right to come to me and tell me in time. I can see you could very well have got it right. You've got a girl in a million, who's got her head screwed on right. You're a lot better a businessman than your Dad will ever be a'ready, but never let him know I said so. What it boils down to is Bridgefoot pride against money, my boy, and pride is one of the seven deadly sins. But I've got to think about it, all ways round, with Gran, if I'm going to back you. I haven't said I shall, yet.'

'And what have I got to promise, if you do?'

'To keep the Bridgefoot name as clean as I've always tried to do. That's what your Dad don't take into account. You'll have to go along with the times, same as everybody else; but there's a right way and a wrong way to go about everything. I've got to be fair to everybody – your dad, your aunts, and your cousins, as well as you.

'Don't do anything without telling me, even if you have to give up that dream, and don't take a penny of help from Charlie's rich relations. That would be taking advantage, and like as not cause trouble between you and Charlie in the end. Besides, that would hurt me.'

He got up, brushing a few odd straws off himself and shoving his pipe into his pocket. 'Go and have a look at the house, soon as you can, and see if it's worth buying. Make sure the roof tiles are still good. If his asking price is less than £20,000 make an offer a bit lower – £17,000 or £18,000. You could manage that, come Tuesday night, with what you'll come into and what little you've got. If they want more than that, you've got to risk losing it to another buyer till we get a valuer out to see it. Leave it with me now till Tuesday. And God bless you both, my boy.'

Charles left him sitting in the barn, and knew that as soon as he was out of sight, his Grandad would make his way towards the church. He stood still for a moment to clear his vision, and found himself thinking that just as he had somebody he could love and trust to be his adviser, so had Grandad.

Now it was Friday, and Fran had to answer Sophie's question and brief her about the rest of the week. 'Home for lunch today,' she said thankfully. 'Then we are going to Castle Hill for tea and supper. Tomorrow the Commander and Mrs Franks are coming here to lunch. I hate to ask you, but could you possibly come and see to it for us?'

'That don't make no difference to me about it being Sat'day,' Sophie replied. 'It ain't work as I 'ate, it's long 'olidays. Not that it ain't been a good Christmas so far this year, what with you coming to church a-Christmas morning, and then when it come to dinner-time, Thirz' 'ad kept a surprise for me, 'cos in walked our Het and Joe and Wend's little ol' boy. Seems that Thirz' 'ad sent Dan'el up to ask 'em, so now we are all made it up with each other. It were like old times. Mam would ha' been pleased.

'And Joe were in good spirits and full o' that family 'e thinks so much of down Danesum. He can't say good enough about the man. Joe says as 'e's a real gentleman in 'is ways and brings them child'en up beautiful. It's 'er what's brought 'im so low – getting mixed up with a woman like 'er, you may depend. By all accounts, she's a proper Jezebel, all lah-di-dah to speak to, but too lazy to keep 'erself clean. Anyways, when Joe knowed as 'e wouldn't be wanted at 'ome Christmas morning, 'cos after church they was coming to dinner with Thirz', he gets on 'is bike and goes down to see 'ow they are at Danesum, and whether they are 'aving any sort o' Christmas at all. And 'e found the man in bed, coughing bad, Joe said, but somebody 'ad seen to it that all them children 'ad a bit o' Christmas fare – a horange each and some sweets, like. And while 'e was there, them two big gals made the others all sit down in a ring by the side o' their father's bed, and that Daffy Pugh as lives there now come out o' the kitchen with a platter piled up with sausages in one 'and and another piled up with chips in the other. Joe said you would never ha' believed anybody could ha' cooked so many sausages all at one go. And the gals come in with box after box of bought mince pies. I'm sure I enj'yed my own Christmas dinner better for thinking about them sausages! And if I 'ad been asked who it was as 'ad been sure as they'd got something if it was no more than a horange and a bar o' chocolate each, I shouldn't ha' 'ad to look much further than wheer Joe was a-sitting, though I dare'n't ask 'im if I was right 'cos Het would ha' made such a fuss about 'im spending money on folks like them instead of on young Stevie. Not that 'e wants for nothink. Het sp'iles 'im and Joe sp'iles 'im and you should just see the piles o' stuff as Wend sends 'im all the while from America. It ain't right for one child to 'eve so much when them others 'as got so little.

'But I couldn't get them sausages out o' my mind, and when I went to bed last night, I prayed for that Daffy Pugh. I said to myself, what right 'ad I to look down my nose at a man like 'im as was doing just the same as the Lord Jesus hisself done when 'e come among us, feeding the poor and 'ungry. It might ha' been Jesus his very self cooking them sausages, do they 'ad 'ad sausages in them days, which I don't know. I'm often thought about that story of 'Im feeding all them people on two loaves and five small fishes. Surely they didn't eat them fish raw? Was them little fishes sprats, do you reckon? I always used to think they must ha' been, 'cos sprats is the littlest fish I know. We often used to hev sprats for tea when we was little, 'cos they was so cheap and you got a lot for sixpence in them days. But, if they *was* sprats as Jesus was frying for five thousand there must ha' been more'n five of 'em. They'd be easier than any other sort o' fish, 'cos all you 'ave to do is to twist their 'eads off and the innards comes out with it. And if they only 'ad one sprat apiece I reckon the 'eads would ha' filled twelve baskets. But I can't stand 'ere talking, 'cos if you don't soon 'ave your breakfastses you'll be wanting your dinners afore I'm got 'em ready.'

She had been deprived of their company for more than two days, and it was plain that the reconciliation of her family, as well as the prospect of saving the church from the cloven hooves of Bailey and Kid Bean, had wrought a great uplift in her spirits. She was rarely as loquacious as she had been this morning, but Fran would not have interrupted her for anything, though she had stretched Fran's self-control to its very limits, all ways, by the time she had finished.

While Sophie was describing the scene in Peter Petrie's sick room, Fran was glad she wasn't eating her breakfast. Food would not have got by the lump in her throat. She dared not look at William. They, she and William, and Elyot and Beth, and all the rest of their so comfortably smug friends this Christmas should not have left it to a humble little saint like Joe Noble or to the stranger in their midst to think of carrying out so small a kindness. She felt shamed.

William had taken from his inside pocket a pencil, and was doodling on the back of a leaflet. He had drawn nothing but little circles, each with a large black dot in the middle. Fran tried to distract herself by searching for some abstract or symbolic meaning for them, but she could make nothing of them but the closing circle of Petrie's life with its centre of black despair.

Her attention had wandered only for a moment, but Sophie was still in full flight and when Fran picked up the thread again the subject matter was the sprats and her mood changed. She must not let her amusement show. She held her breath lest her mental picture of Jesus in his fish-and-chip shop on the shores of Lake Galilee in the middle of the desert should prove too much for her. Mercifully, Sophie had glanced at the clock, and brought herself back to the present.

'So what shall you be having for your dinner today? Not that there 'alf-bullock as is in the fridge, I 'ope, 'cos there ain't time to cook that properly now. I'll go and do the veg while you finish your breakfastses and cook them lamb chops today.'

Fran glanced William's way. The doodled circles had miraculously turned into sprats, each with a beady black eye fixed on her. There were two sides to everything.

They went up to Castle Hill well in time for tea. Charles had persuaded Charlie to put her hair up again specially for him, and she was wearing her new frock, and all her jewellery. Fran knew at once that something out of the ordinary had happened. The glow on both faces was so bright that it was almost as impossible to look at either of them as it would be to look straight into the midday sun.

If there was a sad note amongst them it was the presence of Nick. He was, as he had always been, a most handsome, cultured boy with a beautifully modulated voice. His manners were as perfect as ever, and he joined in every conversation as though he were perfectly normal. Fran found it difficult herself to remember that as far as Nick was concerned this was the first time he had ever met her; she thought of what Charles must be enduring. He and Nick had been as inseparable as twins since they were five.

When Fran went into the kitchen with Jane, she asked if Nick's presence would alter her plan of rehabilitating herself gradually as Mrs Bellamy. Would it, after all, have to be a grand pantomime transformation scene?

Jane laughed, 'Ask Effendi. We've discussed it with him, and he thinks that we ought to stage it on Tuesday evening at the church. We shall all be there – probably the latest to arrive, so as to make a dramatic entrance. I'm not sure it's wise, but I can't help thinking what fun it will be.'

They went back into the huge room laughing, and Fran reported the conversation to William. He could barely conceal his absolute delight.

'If anything could prang Kid Bean's new kite, that will be it,' he said. 'Do you think we ought to have an ambulance crew standing by?'

'If you could get a parson to stand by it would do more good,' Fran said. 'There isn't one in sight yet.'

Relaxed with Elyot and Beth next day, they went over everything while Sophie was busy in the kitchen, and out of hearing. The sprats came first.

'How amazing!' Beth exclaimed. 'In all the years I've been subjected to Bible studies, and all the times I've heard people trying to find some rational explanation for that particular miracle, I've never heard anybody suggest that the fish might have been raw and need cooking to be edible. Unless, of course, they were dried, like bloaters.'

'Or smoked like kippers,' added Elyot. 'But even kippers need cooking, don't they?'

'It's Mary Budd's teaching,' Fran said. 'Sophie's always telling me how she used to make them "think for themselves". And Mary often gave me examples of how children build on known experience to come to terms with new experience, which is exactly what Sophie was doing. We've lost the art, because we know too much. I feel awful that none of us thought about those children this Christmas. We all left it to Joe and Pugh.'

'You miss the point, my sweetheart,' said William. 'As it was, it gave the children, and Joe and Pugh, a lot of pleasure, and robbed Petrie of nothing. For us to have done it would have robbed him of the last thing he has left – his pride. He's one of the proudest men I know. That's why it's so bloody difficult to help him . . . Help is all right as long as it isn't tainted by "charity" in its modern sense. Remember Bert Perks in *The Railway Children*. Among the poor, anywhere, help can be given and accepted as long as it is just "neighbourliness". That's what Joe offered, and that's what Petrie accepted. If we'd tried to do anything, it would have smacked of charity, and would have hurt more than it helped.'

'Then can't we do anything for him, or them?' asked Beth.

'Behind the scenes,' said William gravely. 'And when the time comes. To ease his mind now that there will be help when it's needed is the best we can do for him. Incidentally, Elyot, he's not a pauper. He does have a very small but regular income. It can't go very far round himself and eight children, though.'

'And they must get child allowance . . .'

'My dear Beth, you've never seen their mother.'

'Nor has any of us except you, darling,' Fran reminded him. 'Petrie told us himself that she hangs on to all their allowance books to finance her periodic disappearances. William is pretty sure she's a drug addict,' she added for Beth and Elyot's information.

'All on the welfare state?' said Elyot.

'It's a grim portent of things to come, I think,' said William. 'Another instance of change being taken for granted too easily. Those who are young parents now were themselves the first batch of "welfare state" children. They grew up with the benefits that Beveridge intended as a boon and a blessing for everybody, to provide peace of mind "from the cradle to the grave", as he put it. But those brought up with it have got used to it, and take it for granted. Child allowance isn't any longer a boon and a blessing to help those in need do their best for their children. It has become their *right* that everybody else should pay them for bringing more and more children into an already over-populated island. And of course, one can't deny that it *is* now their right. It's human nature to demand what is yours by right – so in twenty years from now it will be every man for himself, wanting more and more of his rights until the welfare state collapses. Soon everybody will be on "benefits" of some sort supplied by everybody else's taxes, like the old joke about the Chinese living by taking in each other's washing. I can see Sophie hovering, so I suppose lunch is now ready.'

'Professor Burbage on his soap-box,' said Fran, rather apologetically as they moved into the dining-room and sat down at the table. 'But I see what he means. "Gilbert, thou shouldst be living at this hour. England hath need of thee."'

'I thought that was Milton, not Gilbert,' Beth put in.

'Wordsworth meant Milton, but I meant Gilbert. He foresaw what William's been saying. It's in *The Gondoliers*. Too much of it to quote. Oh, all right. Here's a bit of it:

> 'If you have nothing else to wear
> But cloth of gold and satins rare
> For cloth of gold you cease to care.
> Up goes the price of shoddy.
> In short, whoever you may be,
> To this conclusion you'll agree:
> When everyone is somebody
> Then no one's anybody.'

William stood ready with a bottle wrapped in a napkin in his hands. 'See what I meant?' he said. 'There are times when a bit of ridicule is worth a lot of parliamentary rhetoric.'

'If you're finished with all that gibberish,' said Sophie from the door, 'per'aps you'll let me set this 'ere beef down afore it breaks my arms.'

Friday hadn't been such a good day for everybody as it had for William and Fran and those at Castle Hill. Eric had left early, as he had said he would, after ringing Jess to ask her to stand by for any emergency. There was no emergency, except that the atmosphere between her and Greg was so strained that she was glad of an excuse to leave him alone at Southside House and go to work.

When she had gone, Greg was more uneasy than when she had been there. He could not but blame her for the growing distance between them, but neither could he rid himself of guilt. He poured himself a drink, and sat down with it, inclined to brood over what he began to regard as the ruin of his marriage.

He reviewed the whole course of their relationship over the past twenty-five years. From the moment he had met her, she had been his whole life. He could not possibly sum up his love for her – it was made of an infinite number of things, but the whole was Jess herself, and it was a great deal larger than the sum of its parts. Moreover, it had never changed, not even now. He had always been aware of the cutting edge of her tremendous personality, which had often been turned against him; but there had been a salve that cured every wound, till lately. Whichever one of them had hurt the other, it could always be cured in bed.

He was horrified to realize that he had reached the core of their trouble. Something had gone wrong with their sex life. There had begun to be quarrels that had not been made up in bed – and gradually, for one reason or another, lovemaking between them had become less and less frequent.

He had never yet been unfaithful to her, even really in thought. It had been more negative than that. Because he had wanted her so much, he had begun to stay away when he could have come home, rather than face the hurt of her rejection of him yet again.

He leaned back, and closed his eyes, appalled by two thoughts. One was that this state of affairs couldn't go on much longer. He couldn't bear it. He loved Jess, and still wanted her but not just as a housekeeper. But if she didn't want him, he would soon have to find somebody who did. A vision of Michelle Stanhope rose before him, and he drifted into a day-dream about her. His interest in her was becoming dangerous. She had deliberately turned on her sex-appeal towards him. Michelle would certainly not reject him. Taking a tighter grip on himself, he tried to think of her as a person, not just as a woman whose body caused vibrations of desire in him. He was pretty sure that behind those wonderful eyes there was a scheming brain: one whose objective would be to take the main chance with any man caught in her web, at least till she found out the state of his bank balance.

Greg chuckled to himself. On that score, he was fairly safe from her. She might also have a bit of trouble catching a man with courage enough to challenge that huge six-foot-two, fifteen-stone, rugger-playing type of a husband, who had had both army and police training.

The idea of trying his luck with Michelle wouldn't let him rest. If only Jess would come home now, so that they could talk to each other, he would be able to forget Michelle; but he knew she wouldn't. She would stay away as long as she could, to punish him. So if he was being punished anyway, why not give her something to punish him for? He would write to Michelle, suggesting a meeting to discuss the possibility of her modelling Monica's latest designs, as soon as ever this bloody long-drawn-out Christmas was over.

He got himself some cold lunch, but could not face the long afternoon alone. The most sensible thing would be to go to his studio and work.

Sketches he had made of the two Petrie girls lay on his desk. He picked them up and studied them, chose one, and set up a canvas on his easel. Within five minutes he had forgotten everything but what he was about. Another portrait was in the making, this time a full-length picture of

Emmy Petrie with her long, glorious pre-Raphaelite hair, carrying a baby up over her shoulder. He worked fast, utterly absorbed in it, till it began to get dark.

Then he put the kettle on, made himself some tea, and helped himself to a bit of Christmas cake. Jess would be back in time for supper. He had made himself thoroughly tired, and as soon as he sat down he began to doze. His dreams were full of Michelle Stanhope again. When he roused, there was still no sign of Jess. His pride forbade him to ring her to ask what time she would be home. He went back to his studio, sat down at his desk, and wrote his letter to Michelle. He had to get the letter off somehow today or tomorrow if he was going to be able to set anything up for next Thursday or Friday. He had kept the letter very businesslike, asking her to ring him at the hotel at York for instructions if she were free for a conference there. Then he wrote to a hotel he had not used previously, booking rooms on paper bearing their business letterhead. He pushed both letters deep down into his jacket pocket, and recognized in the gesture his deep-seated unwillingness to go through with what he had planned. It depended on what sort of a mood Jess was in when she came home whether or not he would post them.

He rang her at the hotel, to ask about supper. Could he prepare it for her? She apologized, her voice as sweet as honey, for leaving him so long alone, and asked him if he minded getting his own supper because she couldn't leave just yet. Or he could go and have supper with her at the hotel? Why didn't he do that?

Delighted, he washed and changed and went. She was at her loveliest best, engaged in entertaining a whole tableful of American students who had called there in the hope of finding rooms for the night. He joined them and had a splendid meal, and felt again at peace with the world. He went home ahead of her, to light up and make all warm and cosy for the rest of the evening, though it was already past ten o'clock. She was a long time coming, and he had wandered back to his studio to look again at his afternoon's work when she arrived. She went to find him, and he turned to meet her with arms outstretched. But she took one look at his painting, and he watched her face change from that of his loving, fascinating companion of the evening to the acid-tongued bitch she had been on the night of Fran's party.

'Another picture of your by-blow? With your next little *bonne amie*? Look out you don't get caught for having carnal knowledge with a girl under age!'

She turned and walked away. He thought there never was a woman who could say more with her shoulder muscles than she could.

'Go to bed,' he said. 'I'm going for a walk to post a letter.'

She turned back. 'I'm not interested where you are going, or why,' she said. 'You can go to hell and never come back, for all I care.'

He heard the bedroom door slam, and the key turn in the lock.

40

Arnold Bailey made no bones of the fact that he was a self-made man, and proud of it. As he awaited the arrival of his guests that Friday morning, he smoked a large cigar in the grandly furnished 'lounge' of his new house, with a feeling that both life and luck had been good to him. He was not yet quite fifty, and look what he had achieved already – though he was as yet only on the foothills of his Himalayan-sized ambitions.

He was dressed casually, though with care. That had been one of the secrets of his success – that every time he had wanted to take a step up the social ladder, he had taken note of what was, or was not, worn in the class to which he was aspiring. He could now afford the good-quality clothing that, without shouting loudly, still proclaimed its expensive origin. Unfortunately for him, he had not been quite so careful in restricting his love of the fleshpots, with the result that his figure did not do justice to his clothes. Round his middle was a good deal farther than it should have been for a man who was not much above average height. His generally heavy aspect was not helped by a fleshy, round and rather red face, adorned by a trim, small moustache that, like his receding though thick hair, still bore the tints that had nicknamed him 'Ginger' while he was at school in the Covent Garden area of London where he had been born.

He was more than pleased with his Christmas present to himself and his family, the new house on which he had had to use every bit of influence and the power that ready money gave him to get it finished and ready for habitation in time.

Moving into it had satisfied yet another in the long list of his ambitions. The old sort of 'country gentleman' had largely disappeared after the first war; after the second war, there had been a general levelling out so that there was a chance for everybody to be 'middle-class'; and yet, as he had heard quoted, he was aware that it was still the case that 'some people were more equal than others'. Fate had landed him in the Swithinford area just as it had been designated as a 'new town', and businesswise he had made the most of his opportunities; but it had been gradually borne upon him that Swithinford itself was so middle-class that however much money you had to throw about, somehow you didn't make the grade of being more equal than the rest. The latest generation of 'country gentlemen' who did not still have the advantage of ancestral homes, lived 'out in the sticks', in places like Old Swithinford.

His native wit and his business acumen pulled one way, and his ambition to be a country gentleman the other. He had seen Old Swithinford as a place ripe for development, and he intended to be the man to develop it. His chance had come with the death of young Robert Fairey, the last of a line of one of the old farming families. It had made the boy's father vulnerable to his offer of a very large sum of money for the farm. The four-hundred-year-old house had been a separate transaction, and Bailey had seen his chance of killing two birds with one stone. He had bought it, pulled it down, and built his own country house on the site.

He had made the most of his luck all his life. He had been born to a London couple who had at first been greengrocers, until their dealings with the lorry-drivers who supplied the goods to Covent Garden at unearthly hours of the morning had given them the idea of setting up an all-night café close by. That had proved a success in its own right. When 'Arnie' had left school, he was already well acquainted with greengrocery and with transport. But he had a bachelor uncle in the building trade, and his father, who also had an eye on the main chance, had insisted that he learned the building trade. That had paid off, too, because at the beginning of 1939, he had fallen from a scaffold and injured his back. It had been a slow recovery, leaving him not quite fit enough for active service when war broke out.

Produce from the countryside came up to London and Covent Garden as it always had done, though now every load was documented and regulated for equal distribution; but the lorry-drivers (often the produce-growers themselves), finding their way through bombed and burning streets, were even more glad of what the café offered them. Besides, many of them were not above adding a couple of bags of onions or carrots or other scarce vegetables to their loads on purpose for them to be 'knocked off' while they were having a cup of coffee, to be distributed illegally on the black market. The café as well as the farmers were on to a good thing.

Then the war-machine caught up with Arnie at last, and conscripted him – C3. His skills included knowledge of the building trade, and of transport. He was attached to the RAF regiment, and sent to East Anglia.

The war dragged on, and the longer it continued, the worse grew the rationing and the more money there was to be made out of the black market. It was all very satisfactory.

Then came the time of the V2 rockets – and one scored a direct hit on the café, demolishing it, and Arnie's parents, and his bachelor uncle who happened to be visiting there just at the wrong time for himself, but the right time for Arnie. He found himself the sole heir to insurance and compensation pay-outs, a bank balance far greater than even in his wild-est dreams he had ever conjured up, and his uncle's building business, which had also been very successful when homes were being demolished faster than they could be replaced or repaired.

As soon as he was demobbed, he used his capital to transmute the odd-jobbing builder into a building construction company, and moved his wife far enough away from her home for her origins not to be known, so that she might become 'a lady of leisure' to rid her of any East Anglian accent, Arnie foreseeing that she would be a great asset to him in making the right contacts. He was also conscious that he himself was neither as well spoken or as well educated as he needed to be. He set himself to get education in speech and grammar vicariously through Norah.

By the time Swithinford needed construction companies he was al-ready known as one of the biggest in the region, ready to take the next step and become a fully fledged 'developer'.

In the meantime, Norah had made her presence felt in Swithinford itself, through the WI, the WVS, the Red Cross and anything else in which a well-spoken, reasonably well-educated and very well-to-do woman could make her mark. Their last stroke of luck had been to land on the Lane's End property in Old Swithinford, and with it, a new and modern lifestyle.

Looking around for allies, he hit upon that other jobbing-builder who was also on the rise because of an unexpected legacy, Kenneth Bean. Bailey had found in him just the sort of henchman he wanted, and was prepared to make it well worth Ken's while to keep him informed about anything and everything going on. Nobody could have been in a better position than Kid Bean to do that. He had been born and bred in the village, and as with all country people, he could not only remember what had happened in his own lifetime, but uncover all sorts of skeletons left in family cupboards from generations past. His wife Beryl was at the centre of the present, and he had plans for the future that would, he hoped, give them a much more prominent place in the social scene than they had had so far.

It was with delight Bailey struck Choppen from the list of his rivals, when Choppen's daughter had got herself into that mess with Frances Catherwood's married son. Eric Choppen had apparently lost interest in any further development of the village – indeed, he was against it, rather than for it. Then, via Beryl and Kid, Bailey was let into the secret of

Brian Bridgefoot's chagrin about his son's affair with Bob Bellamy's daughter. Beryl gained every scrap of evidence that she could of the split between George and Brian, and added 'advantages' of her own invention before passing them on to Kid, who added more before recounting them to Bailey. Then there was the revelation that Vic Gifford, whose daughter Pansy his own son was chasing for a bit of sex on the side, also belonged to the Bridgefoot clan. He began to see the pattern. As the church lay at the centre of the village, so the Bridgefoot family lay at the centre of the church, and therefore of its more traditional inhabitants. George and the church were really one and the same thing. His greatest rival was George Bridgefoot, representing all that was past . . .

If he intended to become the new headman of the place, he had to strike the Bridgefoots down. Ken, who understood better than he did, showed him how and where to strike, and in the absence of any rector to stand firm behind George, promised to let him know when the time was ripe. Armed with his cheque-book and the acquaintance of Norah with the Archdeacon's wife through her 'work' with the Red Cross, he won the first round. His toady was firmly ensconced in a seat of power within the church, and the church as it had been was completely demoralized.

He had last begun to feel that even Bob Bellamy could not stand against him and his kind of luck for long, when Kid had told him of his quarrel with George, and the arrangements for the watchnight service. They both laughed heartily at this feeble last flicker of defiance on the part of George and the remnants of the congregation.

'Said the gnat to the elephant, "Who are you pushing?"' sniggered Bailey. 'How many people do they think they are going to get there? Ten at the very most. As the other churchwarden, I suggest you make a lot of fuss about the expense of the heating and lighting, when you get a chance.'

He was a bit put out when the answers to his invitations to people living at such places as Benedict's, the Old Rectory and Monastery Farm came back, couched very formally, all but one declining on the grounds of a 'previous engagement'. It did not occur to him to wonder what the previous engagement could be. 'They think we're not good enough for them,' he said to Norah. 'Just let them wait and see.'

'I did hope the two from Benedict's would come,' she answered. 'The others don't really matter.'

He looked again at the refusals. 'They don't even plead a previous engagement,' he said. 'I'll ask Ken about them.'

Friends of Bellamy's, Ken had said. Thick as thieves. That was something completely beyond the Baileys' understanding. He was fretted by the refusal from Benedict's.

He had set up the mid-morning drinks session mainly to show off his new house to a few chosen people before the great day, but also, if possible, to find out if George Bridgefoot had any allies in his mini-rebellion. Brian Bridgefoot had accepted his invitation to the party, but had added a rider that as it was his son's twenty-first birthday that day, his wife might not be able to get away. The Giffords had accepted *en masse*.

Brian arrived at Casablanca on Friday morning feeling a bit uneasy. His conscience towards both his father and his son had been troubling him rather a lot just lately, especially when George had been so 'downed' by what had happened at the church. He had argued with himself that the old man was so obviously on the downhill slope that he would have no option but to hand over – and he, Brian, would have no guilt about it because it was so plain that his father was not capable of carrying on. Then the old chap had suddenly brightened up, and Brian became worried. He had promised a lot to Bailey, when he should be 'the' Bridgefoot; but as he drove to Casablanca that morning, he was conscious that if after all he might not be able to keep his promises, he wouldn't be so upset as he had imagined. Not as far as Arnold Bailey was concerned, at any rate. He wavered between the nostalgic pull of his roots, and all that a future allied to Bailey offered him in material and financial terms. He would have to play it by ear, at least till after next Tuesday.

He was greeted by Norah effusively with a kiss which he didn't want or return. It came to him that Arnold himself was all right as a business partner, but Norah was the sort of woman he just couldn't stand. That went for most of the rest of their set; he could tolerate the men, but when their flashy women were present as well, something rose in his gorge that he didn't like. He endured more than a kiss from Barbara, the Baileys' twenty-year-old daughter, who flung herself into his arms and hugged him, reeking of horse mixed with French perfume. Unbidden there arose before his mind's eye a vision of Charlie Bellamy.

Then through the window he saw Vic, arriving escorted by Pansy and Darren Bailey, all three on horseback. Revulsion against the whole lot of them churned his stomach. All he wanted was to get away, but having committed himself, he now had no choice but to stay for a short time. Kenneth Bean there, as a guest?

Bailey himself drew the talk round to the church service. Brian resolved to keep what little he knew to himself, but Vic had no inhibitions. He had gathered, he said, that it was really all the doing of William Burbage, though everybody knew he was no churchman. It wasn't the church itself Burbage cared about. It was a lot more likely, Vic thought, that he was just doing it to get his own back on Bailey about Bob

Bellamy. In fact, Vic opined, it was probably Burbage who had lent Bellamy the money to keep Castle Hill out of their hands.

'Are any of the rest of them in the plot?' Arnold asked. 'Will they get any sort of congregation? Who else is likely to be there?' he asked, and decided that he would need to know to a person who attended that service. He called Kid Bean to his side, and issued orders that Mr and Mrs Kenneth Bean, the people's warden and his wife, were to be there in the church on Tuesday to see and report all.

'But we're coming to your party,' said Kid. 'I can't disappoint Beryl now. She's got her frock, and everything.'

Norah took charge. 'You can come when the party starts, then go to church and come back afterwards,' she said. 'The party'll go on till the early hours. You won't miss much.' She took it for granted that that was that, and so did Kid. He left miserably to break the news to Beryl, and Brian took the opportunity of leaving at the same time. He felt a glimmering of hopeful relief. If his conscience got too much for him when the time came, he, too, could attend both functions.

Sophie heard about Beryl's frantic reactions from Olive 'Opkins, and reported them to Fran on Saturday. William was still a bit concerned that the church occasion should go off well.

'I really can't explain why I thought that Thirzah might be right, and that the Lord would look after his own,' he said. 'But it isn't the service that matters – the important thing is to show Bailey that in spite of his machinations, the church is still alive. I wonder how many we shall muster? I've done a rough count of those we know will be there, and I make it about forty, counting Ned's full team of ringers and Beth's choir of eight. That's quite enough to show Bailey that we're not dead yet.'

The telephone rang. 'Beelzebub and the pit!' exclaimed William, in exasperation giving rare voice to one of the medieval oaths that always made Fran laugh. 'Can't I get you to myself even for five minutes? Shall I let it ring?'

'No. Too risky, considering Kate and Jerry and the children are expected tomorrow.'

'See?' he said, getting up to answer the insistent bell.

He came back looking slightly puzzled. 'It's Eric,' he said. 'Full of apologies, but can he come round at once for a few minutes? He has brought his old friend back with him and he thinks there is a special reason why we should see him tonight. Didn't Eric say the old friend had just been bereaved? I hope he hasn't found whoever it is suicidal and daren't leave him, because that may mean he's having to pull out from Tuesday night's arrangements. I've told him to come.'

It was not more than fifteen minutes before they heard Eric's car on the gravel, and William went to pull open the huge front door to him. They returned together, and behind them was another, looming, shadowy figure.

'I'd like you to meet my old friend Nigel Delaprime,' Eric said, presenting him to a rather startled Fran. The stranger moved forward.

As he stood between Eric and William, he overtopped even William by a couple of inches. He was, Fran guessed, getting on for seventy years old, but his back was as straight as a ramrod, and she was instantly aware that never, in all her life, had she ever met an elderly man so handsome or with such an overpowering presence. Far from being a suicidal maniac, the blue eyes that twinkled into hers as he bowed over her hand seemed to bathe her in a glow of comfort and security, though she was not aware of needing any. He straightened up, and she could hardly believe that under the folds of his warm greatcoat was a clerical collar.

William, too, was bereft of words. Eric looked like a magician who had just succeeded in pulling a rabbit out of a hat. 'Perhaps I should have said, 'my old friend *the Reverend* Nigel Delaprime,' he said. 'Very willing to help us out on Tuesday night at church, if we still need him. He will be staying with me at the hotel.'

'Eric,' said Fran severely, 'you told us that you were going to see a friend who had been bereaved. Does Mr Delaprime know what an awful contriver you are?'

'He told you only the truth, my dear lady,' said the clergyman, his deep cultured voice sending shivers down Fran's back. 'I shall leave him to explain when there is more time to spare. But if you want me to help you out on New Year's Eve, we must get permission from someone in authority. My clerical collar doesn't allow me to step without licence into another diocese, or another man's pulpit, you know.'

'But it's already so late, and a Saturday night – and I'm afraid our Archdeacon might not welcome a request from such as we,' said William uncomfortably. 'None of us can pretend to know him, or he us. I hope Eric has been telling you the truth about us!'

'Indeed he has. We have been driving together and talking for six solid hours. I feel as if I know everybody here. So if you are quite sure that I will do, and you haven't in Eric's absence arranged for anyone else to help out, I'll have a word with the Bishop. I know him quite well. He used to be my fag at school. May I use your telephone?'

William led him to Fran's study, to allow him privacy, and came back looking utterly incredulous, and in need of pinching himself to make sure that he wasn't dreaming.

'Thirzah certainly knew what she was talking about,' he said. 'The Lord has provided!'

'And how!' said Fran.

William could never remember her being reduced to using an American-ism for emphasis before.

41

Charles went down to breakfast, wishing he was anywhere but where he was and that it was any day other than his birthday. He was struggling with an overplus of intense emotion, from one extreme end to the other of the whole range open to the human heart.

Molly and George had planned that after lunch there would be a 'meeting' of Bridgefoot Farms Ltd, at which Charles would be given shares from George's own majority holding, and made a junior partner, and at which time he would receive all the rest of the family presents. This plan, like others made for this day in what seemed to be the long-ago past, had been knocked on the head.

For one thing, in spite of all opposition from his father, Charles had got himself engaged to Charlie on Christmas Day. In Molly's eyes that made Charlie already 'one of the family', but she knew only too well that the atmosphere of the gathering would be ruined if Charlie and Brian were present; besides which it would make them thirteen at the table – and that was something Molly dared not risk, considering how ill George had seemed only a week or two ago. It made a good excuse for not inviting Charlie, as she had explained to Charles as well as she could. He hadn't expected Charlie to be invited, so he wasn't upset, but it did colour his attitude to the other matters already on his mind.

George had done a lot of serious thinking since his talk with Charles that day in the barn. In the light of what Charles had said, the pseudo-meeting they had set up after the birthday lunch would perforce have to be held as a genuine meeting of shareholders. There was a lot at stake, and no time to waste.

When Charles had left him, he had strolled across to the church to sit in its cool silence to think things out in the presence of his Great Ad-viser. The more he thought, the more he believed that what Charles had surmised was only too possible.

Having reached his decision, he went home and told Molly all about it. He would have endured torture rather than deprive her of a scrap of the pleasure she was so much looking forward to, but with so short a time to

play with, he had no option. Though disappointed, that in such circumstances the family gathering on Tuesday could not be as happy and
amicable as usual, she made no fuss.

'I know it's hard on you, Mother,' George said, putting his arm round
her and stroking the top of her hair. 'I know you're pulled both ways, like I
am. Brian's your son.'

'No more than he's yours,' she said. 'We've always been in everything together, and I know you wouldn't be telling me all this if you
didn't believe it had to be. I'd begun to think that if you didn't soon
give up the work and worry and let Brian see to things, I should lose
you altogether, but I reckon if you handed the land over to him now,
with all this fear about what he might do on your mind, you'd whittle
yourself into your grave even quicker. You do just what seems best to
you.'

'It'll mean that after lunch we shall have to have a real shareholders'
meeting,' he said. 'Only shareholders there, I mean. We can't let 'em all
hear everything that's said. We shall have to split into two lots, them as
are shareholders and the rest. They can go into the sitting-room, and we'll
stop round the table – me and you, Brian and Rosemary, Marjorie and
Charles. That's all.'

She looked worried. 'Marjorie without Vic?' she asked. 'That'll cause
trouble.'

'Vic ain't a shareholder, no more than Lucy is, or Alex or the twins.'

'Oh dear! I'd forgot that Lucy had no shares,' she said. 'Can't I give her
mine at the same time as you give Charles some of yours? I was keeping
'em for her one day, anyway.'

'She'll get her fair share some day,' he said, 'and she ain't exactly in
want for anything now. You stick to 'em a bit longer. The time will come
when I'm forced to hand over, but unless Brian shapes up a bit better
than he has done just lately, I've got to make sure he can't do just as he
likes with it. It ain't all his fault. It's the way things are, now. I had to wait
till my old Dad had gone afore I got anything except a shilling or two a
week extra for being his horsekeeper, though when he did go I just got
everything, as I expected, 'cos I was the only one. But now that us old
folks live so much longer, sons like Brian are old-age pensioners afore
they ever get anything. But he ain't the only one. We're got to be fair to
'em all now. Daughters as well as sons.'

Charles was unhappy because he knew what he had said had upset his
grandparents, and he was flinching from the thought of the flaming row
there was likely to be with his father. He had noticed that Brian had
grown less irascible and more confident while his grandfather had
seemed to be losing his grip, and guessed that Brian was banking on

George announcing his retirement. He could have led Bailey to believe it was a certainty, as it might have been if he, Charles, had not put his finger into the pie.

He had been worrying what effect disappointment could have on his father, or worse still, on his parents as a couple. They had never been quite the same since that Saturday morning quarrel. Would his mother stand by his Dad if Uncle Vic and Bailey and all the others of his new friends turned against him because he wasn't able to deliver the goods after all? Poor old Dad! Poor old Mum. They'd been such a happy family once. Until Dad had turned against him because of Charlie.

But Charlie! To switch his thoughts to her was to evoke in him other emotions of such hope and wonder that they caused him twinges of exquisite joy almost too strong to be borne. He stopped half-way down the stairs to close his eyes and think that, though this birthday was not going to be the happy day any of them had looked forward to, there was a lot to make up for it. Things that so far only he and Grandad knew, but which they would all have to know by the end of the day. Such unbelievable things!

Last Friday afternoon, he had been to Danesum again, and talked to Mr Pugh, who, acting in lieu of Petrie, had shown him over the house. Though it still needed more doing to it, it was in better shape than Charles had dared to hope, especially, he was relieved to notice, the roof. He had no previous experience of this sort of thing, but he got the impression that Pugh was too surprised at having anybody take any interest in the property so soon to drive as hard a bargain as he might have later. Charles had set out with a good deal of trepidation to conduct his first bit of big business on his own account, and began to worry a little that it seemed to be proving too easy. When it transpired that as a prospective buyer he might be able to raise ready cash – providing that the asking price was not too high – and that there was no urgency on his part for the property to become vacant immediately, Pugh handed him over to Petrie.

The stumbling block to all Petrie's scheme for keeping the family together when he should no longer be there was a catch-22 situation: he couldn't buy the equipment they would need to shelter them until he sold the house, and couldn't vacate the house (voluntarily) till they had the equipment. He needed it to be there, ready and waiting, before the emergency arose. He dared not trust Crystal to deal with it after he was dead, or Pugh, because he didn't trust the influence Crystal might bring to bear on Pugh. Petrie knew how strong it could be – she had had the same effect on him for a short time, aware of her as he had been; but in any case, what did an evangelist like Pugh know about conditions in a hippy camp such as that Crystal would undoubtedly make for? Less still a simple, honest countryman like Joe Noble.

Through the long nights he had lain awake coughing, Petrie had worked it out that Crystal and the family had got to be prepared to leave Danesum quickly, before the welfare people, who were already aware of their irregular existence, interfered. Though Crystal had every right to the legal guardianship of her own children, there was the danger of her drug addiction becoming known. She would not prove a reliable guardian, but as long as the family were all together they would survive in their mother's unpredictable absences till – he dared neither think further, nor plan. He had William's promise to keep an eye on Jasper from afar, and in that he trusted implicitly. Any other hopes of doing more for them grew slenderer as the days passed and he grew weaker. He had begun to resign himself to the fact that he could do no more.

Then, out of the blue on this end-of-the-year morning had appeared the shy, curly-haired blond giant whom Petrie had seen driving about, who said his name was Charles Bridgefoot. A name Petrie had heard, but had never matched to its owner.

Petrie liked the look of him, and when in the preliminary chat Charles had not only mentioned William, but made it clear that he regarded the professor as little lower than the angels, a wisp of optimism drifted across Petrie's vision. He decided to tell his visitor exactly what his own position was.

Charles would have been embarrassed by such confidences from somebody looking death and its consequences so squarely in the face had something Petrie said not reminded him of Charlie's trancelike expression when she had first seen the house and told him that it was sending her messages. He believed now that she must in her fey way have been picking up Petrie's longing for something or someone to come and solve his problems.

Charles was overwhelmed with pity that he strove to hide, but felt empathy with the man whose urgency to sell was as great as his own to buy. He was being forced by circumstances to make a quick decision, just as he had forced Grandad to do. It was all a very strange set of circumstances.

He sat there pondering till the silence between them might have been uncomfortable, though in fact it wasn't. Charles was trying to think what his Grandad would do if he were now in Charles's shoes; and Petrie sat watching him, thinking wistfully that apart from the colour of his curls, Jasper grown up would be just such another. All his family were like

Charles in stature, tall and well made, and Jasper was already showing signs of inheriting those genes. This was as near as he would ever get to seeing his son at twenty-one, so he took his fill of looking at Charles while he could, storing up the image for future sleepless nights. Let the boy speak when he was ready.

Charles did, asking if he might be just as frank with his side of the story as Mr Petrie had been. He spoke of Charlie, of his father's opposition to her and, without giving any detailed reasons, of his need to make his mind up quickly and decisively, and then act at once. Petrie listened like a child to a fairy story to this tale of youth and love and strength and hope. It could be that in his end was this young couple's beginning. And the gossamer thread of their mutual acquaintance with William grew longer and stronger till it reached out to encompass Jasper as well.

'There's a divinity that shapes our ends . . .'

It was all meant to be. He felt soothed.

'So it all depends on your asking price,' the youngster was saying rather wistfully.

Petrie pulled himself back to the present. 'I can't sell for less than £15,000,' he said. 'That's my estimate of what it will cost to buy what I must have, and leave a little bit of cash over till they get used to doing without me.'

'And my absolute top limit is £17,500, according to my Grandad,' Charles replied. 'But I shan't know until next Tuesday how much I may have to borrow. I don't know what my birthday presents will come to, though I do know that I have some money to come that Grandad has already put aside for me when I'm twenty-one. Mr Petrie, we can't do anything, really, till the holiday period is over. But could we make a bargain now, and trust each other till I can get a solicitor here early next week? Would you sell to me for £15,000 down on signature of the contract, and my word that you may stay here till – till – then? If you could, I will give you my word that if I find after Tuesday that I can afford more, I'll pay you more, up to £16,250, splitting the difference between your limit and mine.'

Petrie could hardly believe that he was not already deliriously near death. Charles was almost delirious with hope. He felt sure that, good businessman as Grandad was, his Christianity would have led him to make the same offer. He knew it was not the proper way to do business, but then, the circumstances being what they were . . .

And that was how it had been left. Charles had asked for complete confidentiality, even from Pugh. Petrie gave his word, and after Charles had left, fell peacefully asleep.

Charles had been right about George. When Charles had reported the interview to him later the same day, the old man had been obliged to turn his face away to hide his feelings, but had simply said, gruffly, 'You'll do, my boy. You'll never regret doing a man in trouble a good turn. Just be careful that the solicitor understands, and makes a watertight deal for you – and let me know if you want anything.'

So now, for Charles, the crisis had come, and today he had to face up to telling his father what he had done. Until he had crossed that stile, he felt he could not let Charlie into his wonderful secret, just in case he still had to disappoint her.

He drew a deep breath, and went on down the stairs to breakfast, heaps of birthday cards, and the congratulations, love and good wishes of both his parents. He hugged his mother and shook hands with his father, wishing he didn't feel quite such a traitor to him. He told himself that he was being loyal to the Bridgefoot cause as a whole, and that it was his father, not he, who was stepping out of line. He cheered himself as well as he could by thinking that maybe Grandad was right, and it would all turn out well in the end.

He excused himself as soon as he could, and made for Castle Hill, to be overwhelmed all over again by Charlie, and the love and congratulations showered on him by them all. Charlie had found for him an antique cravat-pin that she assured him she had chosen specially for him to wear at their wedding – whenever it was. It was more than difficult as he held her and kissed her not to tell her everything, but his resolution not to give her a clue of any sort held out. He hated having to leave Charlie on this, his special day, but was sensible enough to understand that it was very necessary for it to be first and foremost a 'family' occasion. He hugged to himself the knowledge that unless things now went terribly wrong, nobody would be able to argue about Charlie being 'family' by this time next year.

Outside the church on his way home he came upon a fleet of cars almost blocking the road, including Grandad's and a florist's van. He was flagged down by William, Fran, Mr Choppen, Mrs Franks and Sophie, besides a tall man in a clergyman's collar, all wanting to offer him their congratulations. Grandad proudly introduced him to the stranger.

'What are you all up to?' he asked.

'Rehearsal,' William told him. 'We're doing things properly tonight, I believe. I suppose you wouldn't like to sing in the choir?'

'Heavens, no!' said Charles hastily. 'Though I used to – Are you really going to have a choir, processing, tonight? Who's going to be in it?'

'Mrs Franks has been doing a Miss Budd and training a few youngsters,' said William. 'And Daniel Bates will lead them, as he always used to. I expect he'll be the only man. That's why I was trying to recruit you.'

'More's the pity,' cut in Sophie. 'Anybody'd think 'Im Above expected women to do most things as men get the credit for – like these 'ere fresh flowers. I come down and see as the Christmas greenery wasn't too wilted, like, and when I get 'ere I find all these 'ere beautiful fresh flowers to be arranged. I don't know who could ha' sent 'em, but I must say as I 'ope it wasn't that Bailey a-trying to save 'is soul with 'is cheque-book agin. Do, I shouldn't hev nothink to do with 'em.'

'You needn't fret yourself about that, Sophie,' George said. 'I do know who sent 'em, and it wasn't me, neither. Charles, my boy, give Sophie a hand inside with 'em, will you?'

Charles obliged, carrying in two long boxes of wonderful hot-house chrysanthemums.

Sophie, to his great astonishment, closed the church door very carefully behind them, leaving the others still standing talking outside.

'We ain't seen no flowers like this 'ere since your Aunt Lucy's wedding,' she said. 'Do, it don't take a lot o' guessing wheer they come from. But I'm glad to get you to meself just a minute, though, 'cos I'm got something as I want you to hev, and I'm been keeping 'em in my purse just in case I should come across you today.'

She fished in her pocket and found her purse, and from it extracted two coins, which she held out to Charles. Terribly embarrassed, he was about to ask her what she wanted him to do with them, when he realized that they were a present that he dared not question. One golden sovereign, and one half-sovereign.

'Tha's just enough gold to make a man's wedding ring,' she said. 'A woman's only takes just the one sovereign. You see, I 'ad a lot of 'em in a old tea-caddy, as my Mam and Dad had saved, till Mis' Catherwood made me put it in the bank after Jelly got killed. But just afore that, Jelly and me was going to get married, and we'd took some out o' the tea-caddy a'ready to 'ave 'em made up into rings. Then they wasn't needed for me and Jelly after all, so why shouldn't you hev 'em now to make you 'appy? And when the time comes and I 'ear as there's going to be another wedding like your Aunt Lucy's in this church, do we keep it going that long, I've still got the sovereign as was going to be my wedding ring as you can hev to make Charlie's with. God di' n't mean 'em to be wasted, I'll be bound. 'Ere, 'elp me to get these flowers unpacked afore the rest o' them outside want to come in.'

She started bustling about, and Charles knew that it was a sign that he must not try to thank her. He had never felt so utterly inadequate in all his life; but his heart sang, even if he couldn't use his voice.

The door opened, and all the rest entered. Charles excused himself, and made a hasty exit, to go home and get dressed for whatever was to come. George soon followed, and after a quick conference, the others left, too. William and Fran were to accompany Eric and the Revd Delaprime back to the hotel for lunch.

Fran acknowledged to herself what a blessing Eric's invitation had been. There really had been too much of this Christmas, what with one thing and another. It was unlike William to let himself get rattled, but she knew that as time had passed he had grown more and more unsure about his part in challenging Bailey by organizing this service tonight. She understood him absolutely. He had merely done what somebody had to do, if only to moderate the breakdown of tradition till it could be assimilated more easily by those to whom it mattered so much; but he had been uneasy about it, partly lest the service should be a flop, and partly because they, as a couple, had long ago ceased to have any full association with the church, for obvious reasons. He felt himself to be an intrusive interloper, pushing himself forward, and he hated it; yet if he had not done anything, nothing would have been done. Fran remembered Sophie singing in her kitchen, and wished she could persuade William to forget everything except the comfort and hope he had given back to such as Sophie and George, and that through them he had kept the heart of the village beating.

He had relaxed a little, once Eric had produced the Revd Nigel, though to tell the truth, it had not been very easy for anyone to relax at Benedict's since Kate and Jeremy and two excited toddlers had arrived on Sunday. She had found herself for the very first time thinking that three days at a time was as much as most grandparents could stand, much as they might love their grandchildren, and even if they had nothing else to worry about.

Then Monica had come to the rescue, though apologetically, not wishing, as she had said, to steal Fran's guests. But it was a wonderful chance for her to invite Kate and her family to spend a day with them, because her father thought it incumbent upon him to stay at the hotel with his friend. Besides, who was going to look after the children while they went to church for the watchnight service, as they wanted to? The babies and Kate's toddlers were all too young to be taken out at midnight, or to be left alone. Wouldn't the most sensible thing be for Kate and Jerry to sleep at Monastery Farm that night, so that the children could all be put to bed there? Then only one of them would have to miss the service to act as babysitter, if they couldn't find anyone else to do it.

Monica had since been to see if Beth could spare any of the Petrie girls, who were practising to sing in the choir. Beth was put in a quandary, but when Emerald Petrie heard that there was absolutely no one else available, she had volunteered. That they would make it up to her, somehow, they told her.

So Kate and her brood had left happily after breakfast this morning to spend the rest of their time with Roland and Monica, to Fran's guilty relief. She had been looking forward to seeing the Revd Nigel again, and had already taken the opportunity to ask Eric more about him when she had happened to meet Eric at Monastery Farm yesterday. Who was he? Had he truly been bereaved, and if so, of whom? Where and how did Eric come into the picture? Fran was intrigued, really wanting to know, and Eric, in confidence, told her all.

Nigel had been the padre of Eric's regiment throughout the war. He had been with them at Dunkirk, and in the desert, and on D-Day. When Eric had been selected for special duties (his euphemism for Commando exercises, as Fran knew), Nigel had elected to accompany them – on secret missions and daredevil raids, and wherever danger was greatest. He had never failed them, Eric said. His wonderful physique had added brute strength when they had needed it, and his robust faith and practical ministrations in the face of danger, suffering and gruesome death had kept their morale high when nothing else could.

Fran was quite prepared to believe every word that Eric uttered; the feeling she had at once been aware of in the Revd Nigel's presence was that of marvellous calm.

'I used to think of him,' Eric said, 'as the dog who looked after the Darling family in *Peter Pan*. A huge, clever, brave, sweet-tempered, pedigree St Bernard, always with help at hand, or round his neck. And wherever he went, his batman went with him, a little Cockney chap called Tommy Trossell – a sort of tough mongrel terrier, wiry and thin but brave as a lion. And the funny thing about it was that they both seemed to be immune to danger, and came through the lot without a scratch. When it was all over, Tommy hadn't got a home left to go to, and Nigel wasn't married – I never have known why – so the obvious thing was for Tommy to go on looking after "his Guv'nor". Nigel always referred to Tommy as "my man Thomas".

'I owe him a lot. About a month ago, Tommy had a heart attack, and died. I offered to go to Nigel, then, but he assured me that he was all right. Then last week I got a phone call. He was looking after a little church in Wales and had had a dreadfully lonely Christmas. You know the rest.'

'He's wonderful, Eric! If anything could put the seal of quality on our watchnight service, you've provided it. It's as if he has been sent to us on purpose.'

'You're right about him being top quality in every way. I don't know, because he's not the sort of man you ask questions about himself. You just thank your lucky stars that you crossed his path, or he crossed yours. I hope he'll stay a while now he's here, if they don't need him back in Wales.'

She hoped so, too. His calming influence was what they all needed.

The Bridgefoot family had assembled, and lunch had passed off in an amicable atmosphere of goodwill. Charles had been glad that there were so many of them, because it meant that conversation was general, and he wasn't the centre of attention all the time. Aunt Lucy's baby, Georgina, was old enough to sit in her high chair at the table, and caused a lot of welcome amusement and distraction.

George rose. 'I ain't much of a hand at making speeches,' he said, 'but this is one as I've been looking forward to making. The first of the next generation of Bridgefoots is twenty-one today. So, before I say anything else, I want to wish him long life and happiness. Your glasses are all filled – so here's to you, Charles, my boy.'

They stood, and drank. George did not sit down again, but allowed Charles time to thank them, for that and all the wonderful presents he had been given.

Then George went on again.

'And though he is only twenty-one, he's already showed how much of a Bridgefoot he is, by following in his grandfather's and his father's footsteps. As soon as I'd met my Molly, I didn't bother looking about for anybody else. I married her while I had the chance. Come Brian's time, he found Rosemary and he didn't waste any time before making her our daughter-in-law either, for which we are forever grateful to him, and to God for our good luck in getting her. Now Charles has gone and done the same. He's got himself engaged to be married to a girl who is one of the most beautiful I've ever set eyes on, besides being clever enough to get herself into Cambridge University, and into the bargain a girl as fit to be a farmer's wife as he could have found in five counties. So let's drink again to Charles and Charlie. I wish she was here. Good luck and happiness to them both.'

As they stood up this time, Charles looked towards his father, and noticed how reluctantly he rose to drink the toast. Charles had been gloating at his Grandad's cleverness in reminding Brian that he had chosen his wife where he liked and when he liked. Brian hadn't responded as heartily as either his father or his son would have wished. Charles felt a tweak of anger towards him, and it strengthened his resolution to get his own back later, when the time for his speech came. He was

265

getting up to thank them now, again, but caught his grandfather's eye and subsided, to let his grandfather hold the floor.

'And we still have another toast to drink before I turn my attention to more serious business. You all know that when we sold the Pightle to Eric Choppen, we got a developer's price for turning a poor old woman out of her home. It couldn't be helped, and we had no choice in the end; but I never felt as if I had any right to my share of that money, so I made it all over to my grandchildren – £10,000 apiece for all them as we'd already got, to be handed over to them as they reached twenty-one, and the rest put away to do the same for any more as we may be blest with yet through Lucy and Alex. So Charles is the first one to get his, and here it is my boy, a cheque for your £10,000. With special love from me and Gran.

'That's got nothing at all to do with the business side of Bridgefoot Farms Ltd, though, so in a minute, I shall be asking all them as ain't shareholders in the firm to leave us as are to a private meeting, at which we shall make Charles a partner.

'If all of you help to clear the table now, and take the dirty crocks out to the kitchen, you can leave 'em there to be washed up afterwards, because I want all the shareholders here, and that means Mother, and Marjorie, and Rosemary, as well as Brian and Charles and me. The rest of you can go and talk to each other in the sitting-room. We shan't be any longer than we can help.'

Lucy picked Georgina out of her high chair, and led the way. Marjorie, flushed, was looking appealingly at her father as Vic didn't move, but he refused to catch her eye. It was Poppy who saw what was happening, and said, 'Come on, Dad. Load yourself up and put the plates and things in the kitchen. Then you go and talk to Uncle Alex while I do the washing up. Are you going to help me, Pansy?'

Only the shareholders were left, sitting uncomfortably looking at each other. George stood up, and eyed each of them in turn.

'Now,' he said, 'we'll get this over as quick as we can, and be as business-like as we know how. I've done a lot of thinking in this last few weeks, and I know what I'm going to say and do. But before I say anything else, I want to remind you all of something. Bridgefoot Farms Ltd is a family business, run like any other business. We all take our share in the profits according to the size of our holdings, paying rent ac-cordinglie, as well. Me as well as the rest of you. *But the land is still mine.* I hold the title deeds for the land, and because I'm the biggest shareholder, I'm the boss. It's a heavy old responsibility to me, and sometimes lately I've felt like giving it up and just being a sleeping partner – but I can't. I can't because I've got to be fair to you all, including Lucy.

'And there's other things to think about, as well. I don't like what's happening round here. I don't like seeing Tom Fairey's farm turned into that estate as Bailey's built there. But for the grace of God, Castle Hill 'd have gone the same way. The more land the developers get to develop round here, the more they'll want. But while I'm above ground, they shan't put a single house on Bridgefoot land! That's why I'm reminding you as it is still mine. And while I'm alive, not a foot of it will ever be for sale.

'So we must do the best we can, and try to please as many of us as is possible. It ain't going to be easy. I like things as they are, but Brian wants to modernize everything. I'm content with what I make farming, but Brian wants to gamble on other things. I don't blame him – I'm only saying that I can't go along with him. We shan't be able to hold development off for ever, and Old Swithinford is bound to be part of Swithinford New Town before the end of the century. All we can do I reckon, is to slow it down, and try to make sure it's no worse than it need be. What happens at the end of the century won't matter a lot to me and Mother, but while we're still here we don't want it all to be changed.

'So what am I got to do to please you all? I reckon this is going to be the crucial year, so it's the wrong time for me to give up now. My idea is to leave everything as it is till Michaelmas, apart from me giving Charles some of my shares in the firm, and we'll think again then, in the light of what happens between now and then. We might have to break the firm up, and the farms. Let Brian run one his way, and me run the other bit my way. I should keep the Old Glebe, and that bit of land as belonged to Mother's folks as she don't want to part with. Brian could run Temperance and the rest just as he liked, only he couldn't sell it. I'm going to make a fifth of my shares over to Charles today. He could go along with which of us he chooses. Marjorie can please herself whether she leaves her holding in with one of us, or has its value out in money to help Vic pay his rent. Rosemary the same. Mother will stay in with me whatever fool's thing I do, I know. Now I've said my piece, and you've all got till Michaelmas to think over what'll be best to do then.'

Brian was heard to mutter.

'Speak up, my son,' said George. 'I ain't so young as I was. What did you say? Sounded like "Bloody old fool" to me.'

'It was,' said Brian, very red in the face.

Charles saw his mother smile. He was quite stunned by what his grandfather was proposing to give him, but he wasn't missing the finer points of George's strategy. He had relaxed as soon as George had said he wanted to keep the land that had been in Gran's family. Grandad was playing his game for him, wily old fellow that he was. He had already scotched any chance of another estate down Danesum Lane twice over.

Charles was content to let matters rest there. And as long as Grandad was alive he would be able to rent the fields Charlie would want when the time came. He would have to get up and thank Grandad in a minute – and break the rest of his news to the others.

Rosemary, raising her voice in the uneasy silence after George stopped, said, 'You've got one thing wrong, Grandad. I'm no keener on Brian's new ideas than you are. I don't want him to handle my little lot for me. I should like Charles to have it, now, today, to add to his. If you can give your shares away to Charles, so can I. I've never been allowed any say before, so Brian won't miss my support, one way or the other. I'd rather be out of it altogether.'

'Marjorie, what about you?' George asked anxiously. He didn't need telling why Rosemary didn't want to be counted in with Brian.

'I don't want to answer till I've thought about it. I have my two girls to consider. And I won't be made to take sides between Dad and Brian.'

'You haven't got to decide till September, anyway,' George said. 'So cheer up, my girl. Let's leave it there, and go back to remembering it's Charles's birthday. Fetch all the others in again. Ain't it nearly cup-of-tea time, Mother?'

Brian was looking like a thundercloud, and when the others came back, there was an excited buzz of everybody telling everybody else. Molly did her best to restore the party feeling by getting tea and producing a huge iced cake for Charles to cut while they all sang 'Happy Birthday' to him.

Brian and Vic drifted together, definitely put out. Vic's loud voice could be heard above the others. Charles listened, lowering his eyelid to George.

'It's William Burbage as is behind all this silly business of this do at the church tonight, set up for no other reason only to spoil Arnie and Norah's party,' he was saying. 'That's because he sides with Bellamy about everything. Arnie and me think as it was him and her what put the money up for Bellamy to buy his farm. It's a pity as young Charles has got hisself mixed up with the Bellamy lot.'

'Ssh!' hissed Rosemary and Marjorie at him in chorus.

It was George's turn to droop his eyelid to Charles. Charles laughed. His heart suddenly felt as light as a feather, and he had lost all inhibitions about saying what he now had to tell them.

First he thanked them for coming. Then he thanked them again individually for their presents, making much of his mother and his father. Then he turned to his grandmother and grandfather.

'I can't find words to thank them for what they've done for me,' he said, as if he had been making speeches all his life. 'You all know what it amounts to in money – but none of you know yet how they have made a dream come true for me. You see yesterday I bought a house, for Charlie and me to live in after we're married next summer, as soon as she's finished her first year's exams.'

Brian was glaring at him as if he might have gone mad, obviously believing that he was teasing them as revenge for Charlie not being asked to his lunch party. Vic was sniggering, whispering to Pansy, and a flush of anger mounted in Charles's face as he guessed the nature of the innuendo. He gave his mother a conspiratorial smile, as if to hint to the others that she had been in the secret all along. She hid her mouth with her handkerchief, determined not to let her son down now in this open challenge to his father.

Charles was struggling a bit, but determined not to break down. He looked directly at Brian. 'If you are interested enough to want to know where my house is, I'll tell you. It's at the bottom end of Danesum Lane – the four old cottages that have been turned back into one big house again. I was keeping it all a secret, because Charlie doesn't know that I've actually bought it, yet; but I wanted Grandad and Gran to know just how much they've done for us.

'They both love Charlie – you heard what Grandad said. They love her for herself, as I hope you all will in time. Not because she'll be my wife, or because she's a good vet, which she will be, or because some of you may change your mind when you know that her new step-grandfather is who and what he is, and her new stepmother as much of a lady as Mrs Catherwood or Mrs Franks. If you don't believe me – and I can see some of you don't, or perhaps don't want to – ask Uncle Alex. He knows.'

Charles sat down very suddenly, and Rosemary rushed to hug him and hide his anxious face. She hadn't heard what he had been saying, after his first announcement had stunned her, but she knew that she had watched him take on his father in a fair and open contest, and that his youthful, simple directness had won the fight. She had never been so proud of him in all his life before.

Then hubbub broke loose. Uncle Alex and Aunt Lucy were there, congratulating him; Aunt Marjorie was crying openly, clinging to her mother; Poppy was kissing Charles with tears running down her face, and Pansy, all smart and cool, was holding out her hand to him. Grandad stood like a benign presence, silent; but Vic got up, and was making moves as if to get ready to leave, mumbling something that sounded like 'Bloody young fool. Who does he expect to believe such a load of old cod!'

Only Brian never moved. He sat sagged forward, like a puppet whose controlling strings have broken.

'Are you ready, Marge?' said Vic. 'Come on, get your things together, all of you. I told Arnie we'd be there early, in case he needed any help.'

Marjorie kissed her mother and turned to face her husband. 'You and Pansy go on, then. I want to hear more about Charles's house and what's happened to Charlie's father. He'll run me and Poppy home in good time to get ready for the Bailey party. You go on when you're ready, and I'll bring Poppy in my car. I hate being early at parties, anyway.'

'Wait a minute, Vic!' said George, his voice booming over them all, loud and full of command. 'Before any of you go, I want another little say. Charles, my boy, it hasn't been the birthday party for you that it might have been, though I think you've got plenty to be happy about, all the same. So have Mother and me. We've had all our family together once again, and that's worth a lot to us. You never know when it may be the last time, so thank you all for making the effort to come.

'Before you go, though . . . There's been one or two things said here this afternoon that I've got to put right. One thing is that I know you can believe what Charles has been telling you. Bob Bellamy married Jane Hadley a couple of months ago, but she's only just come home to him because of young Nick. He's having the best treatment love and money can get him. As Charles said, Alex is one of his doctors.

'The other thing I've got to say is that I don't like William Burbage being run down in my hearing, and in my house *I won't have it* – which brings me round to this service as is being held tonight. You all know as well as I do that William and Fran are no churchgoers, and why. That's their business. What William has done in setting up this meeting in the church tonight has been done more than anything else for my sake, and for all them as I stand for – folks as belong here, and who were here in the days afore money could buy everything, even so-called churchmen. It can't buy love, and it won't buy God. I've been hoping till the last minute that the Bridgefoot pew would be full, like it used to be, tonight. I can see as it won't be, but Mother and I will be there, and Lucy and Alex . . .'

'And me,' said Charles.

' . . . and Charles. The rest of you will no doubt please yourself where you'd rather be. I dare say none of you will want to leave Bailey's party just at midnight when the fun is at its height to come to church. I just want to tell you that us who will be there'll be praying for all of you who ain't. You don't need me to tell you which lot of us'll feel best tomorrow morning. That's all. A Happy New Year to you, all of you.' He sat down.

Vic went, taking Pansy with him. Molly surveyed those who were left. 'Why don't we all have another nice cup of tea, now?' she said.

They needed something to do. Rosemary and Poppy went to help her make the tea. Alex and Lucy, sitting beside Charles, engaged him in excited questions about his house and his and Charlie's plans. George sat back in his fireside chair, and turned his face away from the rest. Marjorie was trying to act normally, but her gaze went again and again to where Brian sat at the table, silent and immobile as a dummy. He was looking down at his plate, on which a slice of birthday cake still lay 'chimbled' into crumbs.

She went to him. 'Come on, Bri. None of us can be happy, with you like this. What can I do to help? Which of us, or them, has upset you so?'

'Thanks Marje. All of 'em. None of 'em. I dunno. Me. I wish I could just go somewhere and be by myself till Michaelmas.'

'So where are you going, tonight? I shall have to go to Bailey's party, but if I can I'm going to slip out when Kid Bean does, sit with Dad and Mother in church, and then go back again, to keep Vic happy. Why don't you do the same?'

He shook his head. 'I can't think. I don't know what I shall do till I've thought through all that's been said this afternoon. I'm going home to Temperance now. Tell 'em where I've gone.'

She kissed him, still wiping away tears that were not all for the brother she loved so much. By the time the fresh tea was brought in, Brian had gone. Nobody remarked upon his going. Georgina was demanding attention, and Alex and Lucy were preparing to put her to bed, at the hotel, where her babysitter would be Lucy's babyminder, brought down with them on purpose and booked in at the hotel for the night. There were still five hours to go till they re-assembled at the church.

It was by common if unspoken agreement that they all went their own way till suppertime. Rosemary's conscience was troubling her about Brian, though she knew she had done right.

Charles prepared himself to drive his Aunt Marjorie and Poppy home, and told his mother that he was then going straight on to Castle Hill to tell Charlie what all the rest of them now knew.

'See you in church, Grandad,' he said, as he kissed his grandmother again and again, wishing he dared to kiss his Grandad, too.

The old couple were left alone.

42

Fran and William, having spent their first evening alone with each other for what seemed to them like a month, were reluctant to bring it to an end. Towards 10.30 p.m. William began to look at his watch.

'Sit still,' Fran said to him. 'We don't have to be there for another hour. It'll be cold in the church, after this.' She indicated the glowing logs on the hearth, and Cat stretched out on her side on the hearthrug with her creamy belly towards it and her head, resting on one chocolate-dipped paw, tilted sleepily but provocatively upward.

'You're a minx,' Fran said to her. 'If you were a woman instead of a cat, I wouldn't allow you to look at my man like that!'

William laughed, got up and bent down to rub Cat's tummy, making her curl up with pleasure. 'She's the only other female that interests me at all,' he said. 'Shall we have hot drinks before we set out?' He went to make them, coming back in a few minutes with steaming hot chocolate. He gave Fran hers, and steadied himself down to sit at her feet with his head against her knee.

'I don't really want this old year to die,' he said. 'It's been the first whole year we've been together – er – night as well as day. I've treasured every minute of it, even the bad bits.'

'There weren't any very bad bits for us,' she said.

'No, because whatever happens now and however sad it makes us for the moment, it's cured as soon as we can be together again, just the two of us, like now. I hate every evening like this to end. But we've got to get ready to go out, instead of—' he looked up at her, and smiled his mischievously enchanting smile that still turned her heart over. 'I'd rather go to bed,' he said. 'That would seem to me to be the very best way of seeing the old year out.'

'Or the new year in?' she said. 'What's the difference?'

'Is that a promise? Or does it depend what sort of a mood we're in when we get home? I may be in the very depths of despair by then, if this all turns out to be a terrible fiasco.'

'In which case, it'll be my job to cheer you up somehow.'

'Or we may of course, be over the moon,' he said. 'In which case . . .' He pulled her up out of her chair, and folded his arms round her. 'Just let me tell you once more in the old year that I love you more and more with every day that passes, and with every night that falls. Every new year means more time to look forward to spending with you – I hope for at least another twenty-five more at least. We shall only be in our eighties, even then. What worries me is the thought of all the years we wasted.'

'Remember Lot's wife,' she said, laughing. 'We always swore we wouldn't look back.'

'What would you have if you could wish for something special in the New Year?' he said.

She eyed him quizzically. 'Christmas is over and my birthday doesn't come round again till November,' she said. 'There's no more excuse for presents. But if you want a really serious answer, it would be that we can go on just as we are. Like tonight. Just more of the same. What about you?'

'I'll settle for that, too,' he said. 'Well, 99.9 per cent. You know what I want to make it 100 per cent, but that's too much to hope for. I feel the missing bit, though, on occasions such as tonight.'

She wouldn't let him spell it out. 'Come on,' she said. 'It's time we went to get ready. How are we going – in the car or on foot?'

He went to the window and pulled back the curtains. 'Come and look!' he said.

The evening was fine, crisp, still and clear, with the temperature a degree or two above zero. The moon, only a day or two past the full, had risen high, and the stars were brilliant in an almost cloudless sky.

'It will probably freeze before morning,' he said, 'but who wants an internal combustion engine on such a night as this? "Let's stroll down to the village, 'neath the magical moon above . . ." he sang, parodying the song which seemed to have become their theme tune.

'"Just singing hymns together . . ."?'

'Mm. "When we ought to be making love"? That's a new variation on the old theme. Go and put your coat on. It's lucky mine's already down here.'

Another variation was to be found at Castle Hill. Charles had got there just as the rest of them were sitting down to supper, and had had no chance to get Charlie to himself till the meal was over. It was still only nine o'clock.

Bob went out to see that all in the yard was secure, and came in again beaming. 'Come out and look at the sky,' he said. 'It makes you glad you don't live in a big town, a night like this does. You wouldn't be able to see the stars there for the street lights and the advertisements. But from here I only know of one place where you could see it better still, and that's from my old fen. There's even more sky to see, there.'

They all went out, and looked their fill. 'Do you mind if we go for a walk before setting off for church?' Charles asked.

'Not as long as you're back in time,' Jane said. 'You'll have to drive your own car back, but we'd rather hoped Charlie would come with us.'

'Will there be room?' she asked.

'I think so,' said Effendi. 'We'll use my car.'

Charlie yielded. This was the first time her father and Jane were going to appear in public together, and they needed all the support they could muster.

Bob and Jane stood, still looking at the starry sky, as the young folk went out. Charlie turned, as if to speak to them, and Charles politely waited. Then she dodged him, and was gone, fleet of foot, running away from him up the hill towards the little church. Bob raised his voice as Charles stretched his long legs to go after her.

'The key's under the ivy on the left side of the porch,' he called.

Charles made no effort to overtake her till they were close to the church porch. Then he caught her up and seized her, swinging her off her feet and sitting down with her on his lap on the stone bench in the moonlight, just as Bob had once sat in the sunlight holding a frozen, starving Jane.

Charles was trembling. 'Oh, Charlie!' he said and buried his face in her neck.

He'd get the key and take her into the church to tell her his news. They weren't safe against their love for each other, sitting here alone in the moonlight. Thank God, he thought as he set her on her feet and went to fumble for the key among the ivy, that what he had to tell her meant that there would be only another six or seven months of this agony of waiting. He didn't think he could have held out against his physical need of her for another two years. Not even for Grandad's sake.

He took Charlie's hand, and they opened the church door and went inside and sat down in the same pew as they had sat last Easter at Beth and Elyot's wedding. It was cold in there, but they didn't feel it as he unfolded to her the story of his visit to Petrie, and told her what had happened during the meeting at lunchtime today. If it was musty in the old church from want of fresh air, they didn't notice. If anyone had asked them, they would have sworn that it still smelled of bluebells and oxlips. Reverently, they made their way out, locked the door and prepared to join the rest of the party.

Jane knew the secret of dressing well without show. She had brushed her short, thick, bushy bobbed hair till it gleamed in the moon's rays, and she wore no hat; but her long, slim figure was shown to perfection in a tweed cape over a close-fitting suit, the cape's collar standing up behind her head and showing off her clean-cut, handsome profile. Charlie hoped she would have legs and feet like Jane when she was as old. She climbed into the back seat of Effendi's Daimler with her father and Nick, who was very quiet, leaving the front passenger seat for Jane.

At the hotel, the Revd Nigel was locked in a chess game with Sir Rupert Marland in the executive suite that Eric kept empty for himself or his partners, or any very special guests. They were watched with interest by Lady Marland, and Alex and Lucy, who had joined Alex's parents for dinner.

The hotel was full of guests spending the New Year's holiday where country air, good food and sports facilities were all readily available, and tickets for a New Year's Eve dinner and dance had been sold out long ago. Eric was concerned only in the overall success of the hotel, because the new manager and manageress had everything now at their fingertips; even Jess was not required to do anything but be on hand during the day in case of emergency, and for the normal run of business which would start again on Thursday.

Eric had learned from the two previous Christmases that many of his holiday guests were middle-aged or even older, past the time of life for making family Christmases, and choosing instead to have everything done for them in a friendly hotel.

Notices about church services in Swithinford were posted up as a matter of course, but he had gone out of his way this year to make sure that the watchnight service in Old Swithinford had been advertised well. Then he had become personally involved because of the Revd Nigel's arrival, and had started recruiting a congregation from among his hotel guests.

The Marlands had fallen for the village and the church at the wedding of their son to Lucy Bridgefoot, and having heard about the service, had decided on the spot without telling anybody but their son and daughter-in-law to book into the hotel over the New Year. Their presence in the hotel had persuaded some people that the watchnight service in a real village might be a new experience, and made others think they too would enjoy a bit of welcome nostalgia. When the news spread that the handsome, stately old priest with the twinkling eye was going to be the cleric involved, their numbers grew again. Neither of the chess contestants was willing to abandon the game unfinished, though the minutes were relentlessly ticking away. Eric was the one who was getting agitated that they wouldn't be dragged from it in time to avoid giving William a heart attack.

Greg had spent the day alone, after Jess had set out for work. Since their last quarrel, they had existed in a state of icy politeness towards each other, middle-aged spouses living under the same roof and eating the same meals, watching the same TV programmes at news-time, and filling the gaps between with their own private pursuits. Greg was still sleeping in his studio – though he was not quite sure why. Jess hadn't locked her door against him after that first time, as far as he knew, but he hadn't dared to try to find out. He was not sure in his own mind whether his cowardice was caused by fear, or by guilt: fear of her continued rejection, or guilt that he had posted his letter to Michelle Stanhope. So far, there had been no reply. There would be no post tomorrow, being a Bank Holiday, and as time passed he wished more and more that he hadn't flared into the temper that had caused him to do anything so silly; yet all the same he was excited at the thought of what it might lead to.

Jess had had to go to work on Monday, so he had spent the day alone, and before evening he had begun to miss her. When Tuesday brought no reply to his letter, he felt a bit like a prisoner whose execution had been postponed. In spite of the face Jess was putting on their situation, it could be that it was only a battle of wills as to which of them would give in first, as it had sometimes been in years gone by after disagreements not nearly virulent enough to be called quarrels. Perhaps one more day would bring them closer, especially as they would have to appear together in church that evening. After she had left for work on Tuesday morning, he felt lonely and miserable. He considered going across the yard for a drink at mid-morning with Monica and Roland, till he saw Kate and Jeremy arrive with a car full of child-paraphernalia, and guessed that they were spending the whole day there. He was in no mood to play Uncle Greg to Kate's boisterous couple of kids.

Benedict's then? No. He couldn't bear to be in that loving couple's company again so soon. Christmas Day had been as much as he could endure, and it wasn't fair on them.

He went to his studio, set up his easel, and began to work on his portrait of Emmy Petrie. He became more and more absorbed as his brushes obeyed his fingers, and his fingers symbolized his thoughts. There was no doubt about it: just by chance he had discovered his true metier. He was a good painter, but as a portrait painter he was a fine artist. His mind ran forward. Who could he get to sit for him? He ought to try his skill on a man – but somehow he didn't want to, yet. Michelle? God, no! He didn't mind painting her as a model, all posed and unnatural, but without those clothes there would be nothing there to paint! He was after something much more than just a good likeness. Jess, of course; he would love to catch that inner fire in her that he loved so much, even when it scorched him, but at present that was out of the question. She wouldn't sit for him, and if she did, he couldn't do justice to her. He couldn't paint her as he had painted Monica or the Petrie girl. He knew he couldn't: but why? Because he couldn't put a baby into the picture. He knew now why he had never even tried to paint her, all the time she had been 'his' Jess. He had been waiting till he could paint her as he had painted Monica, with a child. That could never be, now.

He had better not let her see this picture again. He packed up, stood the canvas with its face to the wall, washed his brushes and consulted his watch. It was nearly five o'clock, and she would be home soon. He made up the fire, put the kettle on, washed and shaved and put on a suit. He found himself humming as he waited for her, and was glad that tomorrow was a Bank Holiday with no post. Going to church together tonight might be exactly the thing to put things right. He could always ring Michelle to say that Monica had changed the plans.

Jess came in looking less tired than she had done lately, and took in at once her husband's appearance, heard him singing, saw that he had made preparations for her homecoming, and told herself that she was a bitch and that there was no need to take her misery, jealousy or even her silly pique out on Greg – it was just that he was always there, like the whipping-boy of old, when she felt the need to lash somebody, as she did more and more all the time. She did her best to control these terrible feelings, but they were there, inside her, and every now and then something happened to turn her permanent feeling of nausea against life into an attack of helpless vomiting, like a plate of fat pork offered to a seasick sailor.

But there had been no fat pork about today at the hotel, and the nausea of the Christmas period was wearing off. There was little work for her to do. Anne had returned to work yesterday, tight-lipped about her family Christmas, but with a nimble, caustic tongue and a triumphant look in her eye.

In her own low state, Jess didn't care for this new, rather brash and jaunty Anne at all. She had been quite pleased when Eric had sought Anne out, and given to her tasks which Jess would have felt it necessary to do herself. As a result, she had spent the day more as Eric's guest than his PA.

She had excused herself from the lunch with Fran and William, but had succumbed to an invitation from the Marlands, and after Fran and William had left again, she had joined the group consisting of Eric, Nigel, Sir Rupert and his wife. In so civilized a setting, she had begun to feel much more like herself again, especially after a delightful conversation with Nigel. When tea was over and he and Sir Rupert went off to fight a battle on a chessboard, she had gone home much more at peace with herself and everybody else than she had been for a long time.

'I've had tea,' she said, in her ordinary voice, without the cold and jagged edge to it that had so often cut Greg lately. 'I couldn't help it, under the circumstances.' And to his surprise and delight, she sat down beside him and told him about her day, while he drank the tea he had made and ate a toasted tea-cake he had prepared for her. They'd have supper later, she said, and actually dropped a casual kiss on him as she went up to have a leisurely bath. She came down again in her dressing-gown, smelling of L'Aimant, and cooked a mixed grill for them both. Home became home for Greg, the place where he wanted to be.

Then at around seven-thirty, there came a tap on the door, which opened uninvited to admit Anne. Jess looked up, surprised and none too pleased, though giving Anne a polite welcome. To Greg her entrance at that juncture was like a blow. He was affronted by this rude invasion of his home, and found it difficult to be polite, though he was on his feet almost before she had closed the door behind herself.

He knew that in her presence the fragile peace he and Jess had been making with each other was in danger. The finely sculpted porcelain they had been repairing was left unfinished, laid down too quickly, before the glue had set. The slightest jolt would smash it into fragments again. He was sure that Anne had been partly responsible for the undermining of his relationship with Jess, though he didn't know how or why. He didn't like Anne, and he didn't trust her.

She was talking excitedly to Jess, and barely acknowledged his greeting. 'I thought you'd like to see me in my new party frock, bought specially for tonight,' she said. 'I haven't worn anything like this for donkeys' years, but I couldn't resist it when I found it in the sales.' She took off a fur stole, threw it over a chair, and paraded her party self for them.

She was a mature woman, and the dress, smart as it was, was too young and too modern for her. Her tall, rather angular figure was draped in a closefitting 'simple' black dress of the kind that usually costs a fortune, but did nothing for her. Or if it did anything, what it did was wrong. It had a low square neck that showed a good deal of her rather bony corsage, and long tight sleeves. The dress was of ballerina length, and, in deference to the prevailing fashion, she wore the ubiquitous knee-high boots. There was something so incongruous about them that they jarred on Greg's vision in the same way that a knife scraping a saucepan set his teeth on edge.

He liked her even less tonight than he ever had before. Both women saw the pained look that wrinkled his brow, and read his thoughts. Jess immediately bristled in defence of her friend.

'It's absolutely fabulous, Anne,' she said. 'Though I don't know how anybody manages to dance in those boots!'

'Oh, it won't be your classy sort of dancing,' Anne said. 'These boots are all the rage for – just jogging up and down as close to your partner as you can possibly get. The general effect is very much like the pre-war time, as far as I am concerned, even though the music is different.'

'Very suitable for tonight's sort of party, I imagine,' said Greg, unwisely.

Anne 'looked daggers' at him. 'It'll be something the like of which this place has never seen before, you bet,' she said, crudely.

'You're welcome to it,' Greg retorted, though taking the sting out of his reply with a charming smile. 'I'm just glad I haven't got to endure it. Enjoy yourself.'

'Oh, I shall, I shall,' Anne said, giving him a sideways glance to prove what she meant. The sort that used once to be termed the 'glad-eye'. Then she turned from him to Jess. 'I still think you were mad to turn an invitation like this down, Jess,' she said, 'even if it is too low and common for Greg. Think of us singing "Auld Lang Syne" at midnight while you ring out the old and ring in the new with Sophie Wainwright and Co. I must go – I mustn't keep my partner waiting. Happy New Year.' She threw the stole around her shoulders again, and went.

As he turned back from seeing Anne out, he caught sight of Jess's face, tense, scornful, angry, distraught. Anne had managed to shatter their mended relationship, reducing it to ugly shards of earthenware which neither of them felt were worth the effort of picking up, let alone ever making anything pleasant out of them again.

He spoke gently, though, not able to bear the pain he read in Jess's face. 'How long will it take you to dress?' he asked. 'I promised I'd be there fairly early, to make the last arrangements with Beth and to set William's mind at rest that we did intend to be there.'

Jess reached for her cigarettes, and lit one slowly and deliberately. 'You go on,' she said. 'I'll come when I feel like it, if I come at all. You go and wallow in false nostalgia for what you never had. I prefer not to be involved in false attempts to get yesterday back. Only fools attempt the impossible. Nobody will miss me if I don't come. I'm just the odd one out round here, now.'

He went to her, trying to keep his loving sympathy for her floating above the rising waves of anger inside him, but she pushed him away.

'Oh, for God's sake go and leave me alone,' she said.

He did.

43

The church windows glowed softly with a gentle light that blended with the moonlight, the old glass mellowing the electric lighting that never really penetrated it. The silhouette of the ancient building was softened by the shadows of the bare elm branches surrounding the churchyard. Raw as Greg's feelings were, the sight soothed him. He stood by the gate, and let the peace of it run over him. This was beauty that didn't depend on temperament.

If anything drew him towards religion it was that in its buildings and ritual reposed remnants of all that was best of humanity. It represented what men through the ages had tried to give back to whatever elemental force they believed had first created them and given them the means by which to sustain body, mind and spirit.

Those strong, upright pillars in this old church supported a roof that sheltered space saturated with wonderful music and glorious language and where, as the greatest poet of this century had said, 'prayer had been valid' for at least five hundred years. What must the aggregate of that prayer amount to? He was not given much to prayer himself, but when sitting at that organ he marvelled that such sound could possibly be made by fingers as profane as his own. Up there on the organ stool he felt a continuity with the past that was almost prayer in itself; and looking from there down into the nave, he was sometimes awed by the feeling that in that spot a residue of Good had collected, as the breezes of autumn will collect leaves together. Perhaps that was what others called God. He hoped that he would get a chance to play that organ once at least tonight, because if there did happen to be a letter in the post for him next morning, he knew now that nothing would prevent him from following it up, and that after that he would never be able to bring himself to touch the keys of a church organ again. He needed love – and it was clear that Jess no longer loved him. He could not live at all without love and beauty, and she was destroying both, and him with them. But tonight he had not yet committed himself to anybody else, and couldn't decide whether he was the guilty one or the innocent sufferer. He was just a straw blown on the wind of eternity, helpless in the face of circumstances greater than his will or purpose.

The footsteps he heard approaching were those of Fran and William.

'Where's Jess?' Fran asked, but needed no answer as she felt the tremors running through him as she kissed him. So they had had another row, and he was here alone, waiting for them. They said no more, but he guessed that they understood, and was glad of their presence beside him.

The ringers were assembled, and had raised their bells. They stood in a ring beside the bright sallies, talking in low tones, and Greg looked towards them, imprinting the scene on his mind for transfer to canvas 'some day' – if after tonight he ever painted again. Everywhere he looked there were things he wanted to stay at home and paint – such as Fran as she looked in that soft dark moleskin and that white, cossack-like hat, wholesome, happy, voluptuous even. Life and Love personified; all that he was missing. Or that leonine old head of George Bridgefoot, standing in his pew with the white wand at the end of it, denoting the church-warden. Why hadn't he painted George while there had been time? So far, only Molly was in the pew beside George, but others from the village were beginning to drift in – he saw them now all as individuals he should have recorded for posterity before this great threat of exile had ever hung over him.

The pews were certainly filling up, and William was visibly relaxing. He asked Fran where she would like to sit. 'In our own pew,' she answered – and, realizing what she had said, let her laugh ring round the building. As if they had a pew they could call their own! What she had meant was that on the few special occasions they had been there together, they had always sat in the one where they had first stood together to watch Lucy Bridgefoot married, and had followed the responses holding hands, as if they were also being married. It was 'their' pew. In some way, the church had claimed them for its own that day.

Then Beth and Elyot arrived. Elyot sat down with Fran, and Beth and Greg moved off together to the organ, arranged things, and came back. Beth said that she was going to wait in the vestry for her choir to assemble, because they were actually going to process behind the priest tonight, as in days of old. She had managed to raise eight youthful and willing singers, who would be led by Daniel Bates in the surplice he had never expected to wear again. In fact, so great had been the zeal of Thirzah and Sophie to make sure that it was ready for him that they had washed, starched and ironed every surplice they could find, which meant there were enough of each size for all Beth's singers, and some left over.

That was lucky. The vestry door opened, and Ned Merriman put his head in. Seeing nobody there but Beth and Greg, he sidled in to say that he'd just heard as there was going to be a proper choir tonight, and if they'd known both him and Peter Tabrum would have liked to be singing in it like they used to be, seeing as they wouldn't be needed as ringers till that part of the service was over. Beth was overjoyed and sent them off to find surplices from the snowy row hanging on their hooks.

'Three men, after all,' she exulted. 'What a pity I didn't think to ask! There might have been more.' Her eye took in Greg, and she said, slowly but with absolute conviction, 'You can't fool me, Greg. I guess you got your musical education at a choir school, so your voice was trained first. Find yourself a surplice – you're not new to wearing one, I know. You're going to be in that choir tonight, if only to keep Daniel from drowning the rest. Please!'

He gave in easily, because he had no will of his own. It must be like this to drown, he thought, to give up struggling and relive your life over again in the last few minutes of it.

Arrayed in a surplice for the first time since he had joined the forces at the beginning of the war, he obeyed Beth's order to go and start playing the organ voluntaries now. When they were ready for the service to begin, she would change places with him.

He left by the side door, and went in again by the little door in the chancel, and sat down to begin to play. The church hushed. Fran knew at once whose touch it was and simply wanted to sit and listen, but new arrivals kept attracting her attention. Sir Rupert and Lady Marland, Alex and Lucy. Doubt as to where they should sit: Lucy insisting that she and Alex joined George and Molly in the Bridgefoot pew, the others falling into the pew behind. An empty pew across the aisle bore the other white wand.

Twenty or more complete strangers, though Fran remembered seeing one or two of their faces in the hotel this afternoon. If they kept on coming, the church would be full. She stole a glance at William, and reached for his hand. She felt that she wouldn't rather be anywhere else in the whole world than where she was at this minute.

More arrivals. Rosemary Bridgefoot, slipping in beside Lucy, but no Brian. She was gathering everything, having gone into her overdrive gear as soon as Greg had played his first note. She saw, and felt, George's sorrow that his daughter-in-law was alone.

Kid and Beryl Bean. She could almost hear the surly, unpleasant surprise registering itself in Kenneth's mind as he took in the size of the congregation, while at the same time watching Beryl making the most of her entrance.

Her fair and rather lifeless hair had been set professionally into girlish ringlets, and huge costume-jewellery ear-rings dangled from her ears, almost touching her shoulders. She was wearing a short, white fur evening cape, below which 'the' party frock was visible for the rest of its flowing, full, orange-coloured length. From the way she had cockled down the aisle, Fran guessed that below the beaded chiffon was a pair of very high stiletto-heeled sandals. Beryl would not dare to remove her wrap, Fran thought. She doubted if that sort of dress had much in the way of straps.

It was William's turn to grip Fran's hand, to stop her gasp of incredulity from breaking loose, because he knew the signs. He dared not catch her eye, till the vision before them had, at Ken's command, sunk to its knees. Fran kept her eyes down, and William allowed his own to meet Elyot's. Under the cover of the pew's wooden front, he freed his hand from Fran's and made the 'thumbs-up' sign. The church was nearly full, now, and still they came. Fran controlled herself, and gave her attention back to the latecomers.

Well! Joe Noble and Hetty, making straight for Sophie and Thirzah, where they sat together. Fran's heart soared, for if anything could have made the evening perfect for Sophie, that was it.

Eric and Nigel, both straight into the vestry. Then Eric out again, to stride down to where Roland and Monica were keeping a seat for him near to the front. How splendidly Eric had played his part in all this – not to 'take the mickey' out of his rival developer, but to place himself fairly and squarely behind those who were his friends.

It was almost time for the service to begin. In the last few minutes, Fran noticed George turning again and again to watch the door. Someone he had hoped would be there had not come. She couldn't bear him to be disappointed, but there was nothing she could do. Of his Bridgefoot blood, only Lucy was there. William, too, had noticed, and it was with another squeeze of her hand that he drew her attention to the latest comers, Bob and Jane, Jane's father, Charlie, Charles and Nick – in that order. Charles saw them into the last wholly empty pew, and then made his way down the aisle to George's. Alex and Lucy stood up to let him pass them to sit next to his grandfather.

Now the vestry door was open, and the touch on the organ keys had changed. Nigel stepped out, such a splendid sight in his own right that, as Fran told William afterwards, she thought that God must have lent them an archangel for the evening. From the back of the church his rich voice announced the number of a hymn, and a chord from Beth brought them to their feet.

> 'All people that on earth do dwell,
> Sing to the Lord with cheerful voice,'

sang the surpliced choir as they followed Nigel down the aisle.

Fran gave up any attempt to sing herself as she recognized first Ned and then Greg in the choir. The indigenous congregation, heartened beyond belief at the sight and the sound, joined in with a will. Before the procession reached the chancel steps, the west door opened again to let in Marjorie and Poppy Gifford, who followed the side aisle down to slip in beside the Marlands behind the Bridgefoot pew. In the middle of the hymn, George turned, and hugged them both across the divide between them.

And then came Jess, who crept in like a frightened mouse, and sat, alone, right at the very back.

It was over all too soon. At ten minutes to midnight, Nigel announced the last hymn. George moved, before Beth began to play, and went down the centre aisle to take the sally of the tenor bell into his hands. He was joined by the other ringers except for the two in the choir, who would have plenty of time while he tolled the hour. When all was ready, Nigel announced that after the hymn, he would pronounce the blessing, and asked them then to remain standing, silent, till the stroke of midnight. During the last verse, the choir processed again back to the door of the vestry, leaving that noble figure standing alone. The silence was so intense that Fran imagined it thickening, as if Time past, five hundred years of it at least, was being poured back into the church like milk into a saucepan, to gather to itself the last few seconds of the year and blend them with eternity. The tears started to slip down her face and, turning her head, she was glad to see how many others of both sexes were affected in the same way. Behind them, George raised his arms.

Dong! sang the tenor bell – dong! Three! Four! Five! Six! Seven! Eight! Nine! Ten! Eleven! Twelve! The sound throbbed away till it died.

'There she goo,' said a hearty country voice from somewhere, and then the clamour of the whole peal of eight rang over them in exuberant welcome to new Time. William turned to clasp and kiss Fran before the pewed order broke, and the occupants began to mingle, villagers and strangers alike wishing each other a happy new year, shaking hands with friends, kissing and hugging all those especially dear to them.

Fran looked for Greg, and then for Jess, but could see neither, and she had other duties to perform. She must not let the party from Castle Hill go before she had introduced Jane as Mrs Bellamy to as many people as she could.

Fran found Sophie and her two sisters at her side. Sophie was 'too full for words', as she said afterwards, her spotless handkerchief being very much in evidence, especially when William bent and kissed her as he wished her the traditional greeting. Fran had a conscious desire to kiss Joe Noble, but was able to restrain herself, and had to be contented with shaking his hand. Daniel let go of William's at last, saying, 'Thenks, sir, thenks. Thenks from all on us,' over and over again.

They began to wander, a few at a time, out to the waiting fleet of cars.

Kid and Beryl Bean, having arrived almost last, had had every intention of being first away, so as not to miss any more of the high spot of the party than they could help. But they had not been the last, and found their car boxed in by a huge, brand new, gleaming Daimler. They stood, furiously impatient, for its owner to come and move it to let them out. Beryl's shoes were hurting her, and Kenneth was not at all happy at the thought of reporting to Bailey what he had witnessed. As the minutes went by, and the bells still clamoured deafeningly above them, Beryl began to complain about well-off folk coming to spy on country bumpkins just for fun, expecting 'em all to be too soft in the head to complain if they couldn't get their cars out to go about their business. Who did they think they were, sticking a car that size outside a little country church at midnight? She was all for going back into the church and asking whoever it was to come and let them out to their 'other engagement'.

'I shouldn't, if I was you,' Kid said. 'There's nobody round here with a car like that as I know of. P'raps it's the BBC, come to take pictures for television.'

She had no choice but to endure her pinched toes till a large group of people came down the church path chattering: Bob Bellamy and his daughter, with a posh woman and a very well-dressed older man, Charles Bridgefoot and – wasn't that Jane Hadley's son what had had the accident and wasn't right in his head now? That accounted for it, Beryl whispered to Kid. One of the doctors must have brought him out of the 'sylum for Christmas to study him, and that's who it was stopping in that cottage.

The next moment she was staring at them all as if they were exhibits from Mars. That smart woman was Jane Hadley, done up so's nobody would hardly recognize her! Well, so she was back again, was she?

The posh, older man unlocked the car. 'You drive us home, Bob my boy,' he said. 'You'll find your way quicker than I shall by night. Come on, Charlie, kiss that fiancée of yours goodnight, and come and cuddle me in the back seat instead. There's room for you and me and Nick.' He saw the situation with regard to the car, raised his bowler hat to Beryl, apologized and opened the car door for Charlie to get in.

Fran, William and Elyot all came down the path together. Elyot hurried towards the Daimler.

'Don't go, Bob,' he called. 'Beth and I had set our hearts on you all coming to drink the New Year in with us. We've got a lot to celebrate, what with our own wedding and yours to Jane. You're blocking the road, you know, with that battlewagon. Drive her round to our place. You as well, Charles. Eric's got to take Sir Rupert back to finish a game of chess with the Reverend. I'll just collect Beth, and be with you to let you in in a minute.'

'Well! Did you ever?' was all Beryl could find to say, as Bob manoeuvred the car out of their way. 'So he's married her! None too soon, mind you, seeing as she lived with 'im all last summer. But I shouldn't have thought them at the Old Rectory would have wanted to be so thick with such as them, would you? We all'us knowed she wasn't what she made herself out to be. But I wonder who that great black car belonged to?'

'Didn't you hear young Nick call him "Grandfather"? That's who he is – her father.'

'Ah! That accounts for that sort of car, then, and where Bellamy got his money from. That's a funeral car, that is! They're all'us better off than most other folks, undertakers is. And to think we never knowed all them year as she lived here that she were a undertaker's daughter!'

If Kid was worried about what he had to tell, the new year opened with splendid prospects for Beryl.

The Old Rectory was set a long way back from the road, which took a sharp bend round the corner of the large, tree-enclosed churchyard. Between the porticoed door and the road lay a large area that had once been all velvet lawn and flower beds, but since the restoration had been paved, though grass and flowerbeds still flanked each side of it, and shrubs in tubs and urns in front of the house, between the elegant windows, softened its large expanse of wall. The moon was shining full upon it, showing up and reflecting its gleaming whiteness against the dark trees and the bulk of the church behind it, from which the bells were still sending out their medieval greeting to the wide East Anglian space of earth and sky.

At the wrought-iron gates, the party of friends stopped to admire the picture it made, waiting for Beth to catch them up. 'Need we go inside till they've stopped?' asked Charlie. 'I mean, you don't often get both together, do you?'

'Just look at those stars!' Jane said, in an almost awestruck voice.

'And listen to those bells!' added Fran.

> 'A rainbow *and* a cuckoo, Lord!
> How great and good the times are now!'

quoted Fran. 'Stars *and* bells!'

Beth had arrived. 'Don't let's go in then, for a few minutes, unless anyone is cold,' she said.

'I'm not,' said Jane, cuddling close to Bob.

'Nor me,' said Fran.

'How could you be?' asked Charlie, admiringly. 'You look just like a Russian princess in a fairy tale.'

'More like a duchess, I think,' William said. 'Duchesses are solid and real, even in fairy tales. Moonlit princesses turn themselves back into moonbeams when their bewitched lovers try to touch them.'

'The only other place I've seen stars like those is in the desert,' Effendi said.

'Or the quarterdeck of a ship at sea,' countered Elyot.

'I ought to go,' said Charles. 'I think Grandad may want us all together just for a minute or two before bedtime. It's been such a wonderful evening for him, even though Dad didn't show up. Would you mind if I left you? And if you are still here, may I come back when I've been to see Grandad? It's only five minutes away.'

'Just walk in, if we've brought ourselves to leave all this,' Elyot said. Charles kissed Charlie, and left.

The bells rang down, and the last gave one extra ring, which hummed away into the distance, and silence fell. Elyot and Beth stood together under the portico. 'Say when you want me to open up,' he said.

Nobody moved. It was as if they were all held in the spell of the moon's magic. Then William crossed the smooth paved yard, and saluted Elyot. 'Permission to use your quarterdeck, sir?' he asked, but did not wait for a reply. Instead, he began to whistle, and then to dance. He went round the yard alone till he came to where Fran was, and opened his arms to her. The tune changed to the waltz from *The Merry Widow*, and she understood. Here was a quarter-deck, she was his Duchess Olga, and he was a man who when happy had an overpowering need to dance. He had not broken his step before she was dancing too.

The rest stood spellbound, watching them as they circled the forecourt and came to the end of the tune. Then Bob joined in the whistling, and turning to thank him, William dropped his hold on Fran, and clasped his hands behind his neck. Fran's arms rose instantly to the same position and still they moved as one. Eye to eye, toe to toe, they obeyed with mutual instinct the impulse of the rhythm, whirling and twirling and side-stepping at will till, as if at a command, they drew towards the middle of their dancing floor and he took her in his arms to finish the tune with a swirling flourish. Then he bent his head and kissed her, a long, unhurried, unabashed lover's kiss. Their spellbound spectators broke into applause, and the dancers moved towards their hosts on the steps.

Effendi said, as if in awe. 'They are two of the Enchanted Ones. Those who, as Menander said, are beloved of the Gods, and *die* young.'

Charles sought out Beth as the others moved into the house, and excused himself. 'I had to come back to fetch my car,' he said, 'but Mum needs me to do something for her.'

To Charlie he whispered that Aunt Marjorie was upset, and he might have to take her home. The kiss he gave her was a good imitation of William's. 'Our turn next,' he said. 'This year. I can't believe it.'

He didn't know yet why he was wanted at the Old Glebe. He had opened the door, and spoken to Grandad who said that Aunt Lucy and Uncle Alex had gone straight to the hotel to make sure Georgina was all right, and would soon be back, but he would be glad if Charles wasn't going away again because they might need him and his car. When he'd asked why, Grandad had said, 'Sh!' with his finger to his lips, and told him that Gran and his mother were in the kitchen, but he had nodded his head sideways towards Aunt Marjorie, who was sitting in Gran's chair crying, with Poppy on the arm of it trying to soothe her.

Charles hoped that he wasn't going to be asked to fetch a very drunk Uncle Vic home, but if so he didn't see why there was much cause to hurry. So he had stopped to watch William and Fran dancing in the moonlight before going back. Things had not improved in his absence.

Instead of the happy family rejoicing he had expected, he found Grandad doing his best to cope with five distraught women. The centre of it all appeared to be Aunt Marjorie, who was very uncharacteristically not only sobbing, but behaving quite hysterically.

'No!' she was saying. 'I won't! I want to stop here. I'm never going back to him. I can't! Mum, don't send me home! Let me stop here. Dad, let me stop here.'

She was clinging round her mother's neck, drenched with tears. Poppy was still trying to soothe her, stroking her hands and wiping her tears away, as well as her own. All Molly had gathered was that for some reason her elder daughter was refusing to go home. She supposed that it was because Vic had been too drunk to accompany her to church and that she was ashamed of him. She might also be afraid that by this time he would be drunker still, and violent when he got home. Molly was upset for George's sake, because she didn't want anything to spoil his pleasure tonight, and neither did she want Alex to see Marjorie in such a state.

Rosemary was upset, but Charles was relieved to see that his mother had herself well in hand. This was his new-type Mum, attempting to take control even of Grandad, who was looking absolutely bewildered and altogether 'done up'.

'Ah, there you are, Charles. I'm glad you're here to help me. Sit down, Dad. And you, Mum. Poppy, fetch a face cloth and a towel and wash your mother's face.'

Poppy obeyed her, and the moment she was out of the room, Rosemary said sharply, 'Now, Marjorie. What's this all about? If you don't want Poppy to hear, out with it quick. What's Vic done this time? What's he smashed now that has upset you like this?'

'Only everything between us for ever,' Marjorie answered, reacting much more sensibly to a bit of stringency than to all the loving sympathy. 'I'm leaving him. I can't and I won't go back to that pig of a man ever again.'

George had heard that remark three or four times on previous occasions. He tried to restore some sanity into the scene tonight. 'I suppose he was drunk when you came away, and made a scene,' George said. 'I was afraid that might happen – but you don't want everybody to know, do you? It's happened before, and he isn't the only husband that'll be a bit worse for wear after that party. It won't do any good for you to run away so that he has to face you when he is cold sober tomorrow. If he finds you there waiting to give him aspirins for his headache, he'll be sorry, and say so. If he has to come here to fetch you, he'll smash everything in sight, and that I won't put up with. Now, my girl, I ain't taking his side. I'm just telling you not to make bad worse. Pull yourself together, and go home.'

'If you turn us out,' said Marjorie, 'we shall go to the hotel and get a room there for the night.'

'You could come home with me,' Rosemary said. 'Only do tell us what happened, Marge. As Dad says, it wouldn't be the first time you've seen Vic drunk. Was he drunk enough to be violent to you there?'

Marjorie shook her head speechless.

'Oh, for heaven's sake, Mum,' said Poppy, who had come back into the room. 'They'll know sooner or later. If you won't tell 'em, I will. We went to look for Dad to tell him we were leaving to come to church. There was an awful crush, and most of 'em were the worse for wear. Dad wasn't in sight by the bar, but there were people everywhere, upstairs as well as down, so we went different ways to find him. I met Pansy, just disappearing into a bedroom with that awful Darren Bailey – you don't have to be told what Pansy gets up to with her boyfriends. She was as drunk as he was, so I left 'em to it, and went to find Mum.

'I found her outside one of the bedrooms, looking white and sick. The door of the room was open, and there he was – Dad, I mean. In bed with some woman. To put it bluntly, Grandad, that's what the second half of the party was for. Pansy had warned me what to expect, but I didn't let on because I thought all of us except her would be away before midnight and I guessed they wouldn't be drunk enough for that before then.

'Don't look at me like that, Grandad. I know what I'm talking about, and you know what Pansy is. That's what parties are like nowadays. Why I won't go to any.'

She stopped, and went to her mother, who was making a great effort to calm herself.

'I saw him, Mum. I saw what you saw, and I never want to see him again. Is it any wonder that Mum doesn't want to see him again tonight, or tomorrow morning? Find him clambering into bed with her? She means what she says, this time, and so do I. I can soon go back to college, but if you love Mum, you'll have to take care of her. Dad and Pansy won't.'

'Can I go home with you, Rosy? It would save Alex knowing, if we went now,' said Marjorie.

Charles was feeling sick. To come from where he had been, to this! And there was still a question somebody had got to ask. 'Was Dad drunk?' he forced himself to say, at last.

Aunt Marjorie looked bewildered. 'Bri? I – I don't know. I didn't see him, drunk or sober, anywhere. I didn't know he had decided to go to the party. He hadn't made his mind up when I left here this afternoon. Do you know, Rosy?'

'I didn't go back to Temperance when he did. I knew I wasn't going to any party, so I stayed here with Mum and Dad and Lucy and Alex till they went. Then I just popped home to put a warmer suit on, but he'd gone out by then. He must have been there, somewhere, Marge. He wasn't at church.'

'We'd better go before Lucy and Alex come in,' Rosemary said. 'Poppy, there's plenty of room for you as well. Things'll look a lot better in the morning. They always do. And don't be miserable. Think what a triumph you had over Bailey tonight at church. Quite likely it'll make Vic think – and Brian. They both found out this afternoon that if they want to be in the swim as modern men, they must expect their wives to be modern women, and have some say in things. You've got the whip hand, Marge. Just use tonight to let Vic know that you have. Come on, Charles. I shan't be at all surprised if we find your Dad at home and in bed. You see, I know him. Whatever he is, he's still a Bridgefoot when it comes to the crunch. He was in a right old mess this afternoon, not knowing whether to let his father down or lose face with Bailey and Vic. Ten to one he decided not to show up anywhere. He probably went somewhere for a drink, and then home to bed.'

But he was not in bed. Marjorie and Poppy were quite certain that he could not have been at Casablanca. They began to get worried. At one thirty, Rosemary had an idea. 'Go and see if his car's here, Charles. He may be playing a trick on us, and is hiding till he can creep in without waking me.'

Charles found him, lying half in and half out of the back seat of his car, still inside the dark garage. He was barely conscious, groaning with pain and very cold, having lain there for more than eight hours unable to move. Alex, summoned hastily, pronounced his trouble to be no more than a slipped disc, which he had apparently sustained while snatching hastily but awkwardly at a crate of wine intended for the celebration of his son's birthday, but completely forgotten in the heat of the afternoon's meeting. George and Molly were soon there, too.

They got Brian into his own bed, dosed him with whisky against the cold and aspirin against the pain, and left Rosemary very happily fussing over him as she would have done Charles, who allowed himself to catch his Grandad's eye.

There was a decided look of wicked triumph in it as they went downstairs together.

'That should stop his capers for a bit, my boy, I reckon. Thank God it's nothing worse than a slipped disc.'

'How long will he have to stop in bed, Uncle Alex?'

'About two weeks. It'll be a lot longer before he can drive a car, or lift anything.'

'Let's kill the fatted calf,' George said. '"For this my son was lost, and is found again," unless I miss my mark. I should be even more thankful if I could think the same about Vic. Come on, we'd better be getting back to the Old Glebe.'

He was a long time saying his goodbyes to Marjorie. 'Take your time to think things over,' he said to her, visiting her in the bedroom where Rosemary had put her to bed, too. 'Whatever you decide, me and Mother'll be behind you. But it's no use meeting trouble halfway. If I were you, I should wait a little while and see what happens to Vic now. He won't be half such a fool if he hasn't got Brian to compete with. That's been half his trouble.'

She hugged him, saying nothing. He kissed her, and left. She was soon asleep.

Not so Poppy. Her heart had turned over when she saw Nick as they went out of the church, and she had caught up with him to greet him. He had politely but completely ignored her.

She had been told everything – except the fact that he had no memory. Well, she told herself that it was hardly to be expected that he would now want any more to do with Vic Gifford's daughter, when he had all the girls in London to choose from. Their friendship had only been a school-

291

girl's dream, after all. Very dear to her, but too fragile to last. She was sad remembering.

William lay on his back, staring at the ceiling, warm, relaxed and happy. He was living the whole evening over again in his mind, lingering longest on their impromptu performance in the moonlit forecourt. The light of the setting moon was now mellow, and by it he could see Fran lying beside him, though it had turned much colder since midnight. What a wonderful woman she was, this love of his! He could hear her breathing, and smell the perfume she wore mingling with her own particular personal scent, by which, he thought, he would be able to track her if he were blind and deaf. Only one of his senses remained unsatisfied. He turned on to his side, and gathered her on to his shoulder, running his fingers over her face, down her arms and then along the whole smooth length of her.

'Tired, my darling?' he asked.

'Of course. Aren't you, after all that dancing?'

'Yes, gloriously so, your highness. But not too tired, I hope?'

'Too tired for what?'

'For you to keep your promise. It was a promise, wasn't it?'

She reached out to him. 'Aye aye sir,' she said. 'It was a promise.'

'Poor old Jacky Fisher,' he said. 'His Olga was only a duchess. Dancing with her never led them home together to this. A Happy New Year to you, my love, my love, my love. My precious, adorable love.'

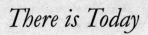

There is Today

44

The weather after the New Year was miserable, dark, raw, grey and inclined to be misty. It did nothing to help to cheer up the dull, flat period after Christmas, when things were expected to return to normal, but this year did so with a difference.

On New Year's Day, there were so many topics to be chewed over that by the end of the week every one of them had been picked as clean as the Christmas turkey bones. The Bailey camp-followers were deflated by the church's successful challenge and were a bit subdued. Bailey was furious at having been so checkmated, and took it out on his menials. Ken and Beryl were given to understand that as things had turned out, their future was not quite so rosy as they had been led to hope. In consequence, Beryl's tongue had to give pride of place to other items rather than to their part in Bailey's party, which she had been so looking forward to regaling to everybody. Disgruntled, her tongue became more than usually barbed.

There was the matter of Jane Hadley's marriage to Bob Bellamy, for example. To find how high the fen farmer and the village charwoman had leaped up the social ladder while she and Ken had been laboriously climbing only to slip down again was gall and wormwood to her. The story she told was very highly coloured by her surmise of Jane's origin in an undertaker's parlour, and her assumption, so glibly offered that it soon acquired a false patina of truth, that the money which had saved Bob and cheated Mr Bailey and Ken out of a fortune had come from the same grisly source, had all the dubious evidence of oft repeated and translated gospel truth before the week was out.

Brian's mishap had jolted the whole Bridgefoot family back into their usual warm relationship with each other, especially as it had happened as a tailpiece to the meeting in the afternoon, which, fraught as it had been for them all, had cleared the air. The short time that Brian had been missing had frightened them all enough to wipe out a lot of hard feelings.

George had woken up on New Year's Day a much happier man in spite of his and Molly's anxiety about Marjorie. She was never one to create a scene without good cause, and this time she certainly had good cause.

Marjorie had been disgusted from the start by the whole tone of the party, and upset to find how much Vic and Pansy seemed at home in the atmosphere there. Faced with the glimpse of her drunken husband *in flagrante delicto* with another woman and stunned with shock she wanted her family, especially her father. The full flood of her hurt at being so affronted, insulted, shamed and disgraced overwhelmed her when her numbness had worn off, and they were all assembled at the Old Glebe. Her conscious outrage was accompanied by a wave of self-knowledge.

She didn't care about Vic. She had been bottling up a growing dislike of him, combined with resentment as he took her more and more for granted, crediting all his 'success' to his own cleverness without ever a word of acknowledgement as to where his start had come from, or what she, personally, had done to help him through the years. The glimpse of him she had had through the bedroom door had revealed to her the truth that she had been trying to hide from herself, that what she had felt for him lately was more than dislike, and bordered upon hatred. Her feelings towards her husband having been made clear to her, they were almost immediately put into perspective by her desperate anxiety about the brother she did love, especially during the short time that he had been missing. She couldn't have cared less what happened to Vic, as long as Brian was safe.

When her father visited Temperance early next morning to see how Brian was, he went to see her as well, and had a long talk to her in the privacy of her bedroom. He told her that he and Mother had meant what they had said, that whatever she decided they would stand behind her – but he advised caution before action. She ought not to act on injured feelings without taking other things into consideration, such as the effect on the future of the twins. It would be silly, he said, after all these years of putting up with Vic, to leave him in a fit of pique now and let everybody know the reason why. If she did intend to leave him, she owed it to all her family to make the break with as much dignity as possible.

There were other sides to it also. There were all the legal and financial aspects to be gone into. Her father thought she should go home, making Brian's accident the cause of her having stayed away last night; give Vic time to get rid of his hangover and come to terms with his own behaviour, and then have it out with him as calmly as possible, to let him know where he stood. Besides, her father said, she might feel differently, in time. If she didn't, then she would have to make up her mind whether legal separation or divorce was what she ultimately wanted. That surprised her most. She would have expected him to set his face against divorce.

She lay where she was after her father had left her in a strange mixture of moods, reluctant to move, yet impatient to be up and doing.

She was warm, comfortable and safe, in a bed in her brother's house on family territory, territory that of her clan, which for four hundred years at least had been rooted in the village. This was home, and the key of her Kingdom. She couldn't make the effort to leave it, yet. But she had no choice but to emerge from it and face whatever life had to offer.

She forced her mind back to the events of last night, and was at once quite certain that it had been an end to something more than the old year. Once out of bed, she set foot in a new year and a new life. She could be positive about that, because there was no way she could contemplate going back.

She was perfectly calm – so much that she surprised herself. She could only suppose it was the suddenness with which the end had come that had made her behave as theatrically as she had done last night, because this morning she didn't care. In fact, she was glad. She had had enough of life with a man for whom she had no longer any feelings other than dislike and contempt; the man who was her husband, and who in all good faith she had sworn before God to love, honour and obey 'for better for worse, for richer for poorer, in sickness and in health' till death did them part.

She felt very guilty to be contemplating freeing herself by breaking her vows, made in church and before all the family, especially her father, to whom such things meant so much. She wondered how much her parents had guessed, that her father should so unhesitatingly declare that whatever she chose to do they were 'behind her'.

She didn't know even now what her own feelings were with regard to anything else but the overriding one of continuing to 'live with' Vic. As her father had reminded her, there were a lot of other matters to be thought about besides her personal feelings – the farm, the tenancy, her 'home', her children, her future, Vic's future, her children's future and the scandal of a divorce in the Bridgefoot family, where until now such things had been absolutely taboo. Partly because of the rules of the church, in which they had been so strictly brought up, partly because of what the neighbours would say. Now she had to face up to what she was going to do. The truth was that without knowing it she had made the decision long before last night; all she had to do now was to act on it.

It must be all of fifteen years since she had first wished consciously that she had never set eyes on Vic Gifford. Why on earth had she ever married him? So many things became clear with hindsight. The answer was that she had been as determined to find out what sex was all about as any other youngster, and to do that then, in a family like hers, you had to get married first. Her horizons had been very limited, and Vic had seemed so handsome, so very much of a man. All she had thought about was being able to go to bed with him. He had appeared just as anxious to get her into bed, as indeed he was, but it hadn't occurred to her then that he had also regarded her as a 'good catch'. She'd learned better since.

She had very soon found that he was a man with only two interests, sex and money. After her adolescent sexual curiosity and longing had been satisfied, she had become utterly disillusioned by that facet of her marriage. His lust and his technique were more akin to those of the farm bull than to a loving husband. Within a few months she was both dreading it and finding it useful. His demands on her were beyond any connection she had ever made between sex and love, let alone romance. On the other hand, it was not long before she had discovered that when upset or thwarted, he was like a mad bull in his anger, roaring and charging with all his strength and natural ferocity at whoever or whatever was nearest. He had just enough control over himself at such times not to attack her, but one by one her treasured possessions had stood in for her. Then, when the passion of temper had worn itself out, he went into a maudlin phase of self-pity which ended by him telling her that everything he ever did was for her sake, and demanding his marital rights of her there and then.

She had learned that it was the only way to put things right between them, but this morning, the very thought of it made her shudder. Never again. Never again with any man . . . least of all Vic.

The advent of the twins had given her the incentive to keep going, to make the most of the marriage she had entered into, however unsatisfactory she had found it personally. They had by that time, with her father's help, turned a ruined farmhouse into a lovely dwelling, and it became her pride and joy to keep it, and her two lovely little girls, immaculately beautiful. They had begun to make money, and she was able to indulge her taste for antiques, for nice bits of old furniture or china, and to enjoy her hobbies of handwork of all kinds, especially her love of fine needlework. For a time he had been more satisfied, showing off his children as he showed off his new cars or his latest bits of up-to-date machinery; but her failure to produce him the son he wanted had soon wrecked the peace again.

She turned her thoughts towards the twins. It was no wonder that they were not identical, and she had often had reason to thank God that it was so. They could so easily have both been like him. As it was, they were no more alike in personality than they were in looks. Coming up to twenty, now, and going their own ways. If she had needed any proof that they no longer needed her to keep a home together for them, last night had provided it. Pansy would hereafter always be in league with Vic against her, and Poppy had made it clear that she was proposing to cut herself loose from both of them as soon as it was possible. Well, she would be the last to try to get Poppy to change her mind. She was no longer going to be a wife to Vic, and was not much needed as a mother. Her daughters could always come to her if they did need to. So what was left for her? Her home? She hated, to the depths of her soul, the way her house was furnished now, longing for the old bits she had polished with such love and joy in days gone by. They had recently been replaced by repulsively up-to-date and ostentatiously expensive new stuff. All her home was now was a show house for Vic's wealth and 'success'.

Perhaps she could take up her hobbies again, neglected of late years because Vic objected to her doing anything on which she had to concentrate, thereby not giving him the whole of her attention. The little cottage piano on which she had learned to play she had been allowed to take with her when she married, and it had given her much solace in those early days of disillusionment; but that had had to be thrown out to make way for Vic's choice of a heavily upholstered suite with a three-seater chesterfield.

Why, then, wasn't she terribly upset this morning, and in black despair of the future?

Because she was free! She stretched luxuriously, revelling in the thought. She was forty-five, supremely healthy and reasonably intelligent. She had means of her own, and expectations of more, some day. She had a home with her parents if she cared to take refuge there, though she wouldn't for their sakes. She would, on the other hand, always stay close enough to them to be there if or when they needed her. At the Old Glebe, and at Temperance, she was both loved and needed, but above all now she longed to be free. She *was* free. She could sew and knit and crochet and embroider and read and play a piano to her heart's content. Best of all, she need never play the prostitute to a sex-crazed man again as long as she lived. What a glorious beginning to a new year, so to be born again.

Of course, she had to go back to the marital home for the time being, taking her time to decide where to establish herself in a new home all her own. She felt able to cope with anything, this morning. Vic had had his day, and had not been satisfied. Now she held all the cards. It might be uncomfortable for the immediate future, but she wasn't worried.

It was Poppy who was worried. 'Will you be all right, though, Mum? Safe, I mean. He'll be so nasty, and get violent.'

'Don't worry about me, my pet. I'm going back now on my own terms. I ought to have stood up to him years ago, instead of letting myself be treated like a toad under a harrow. I've been giving in for the sake of peace. There's no longer any peace to keep. Even a worm will turn. He's never disgraced me in public before. He won't get away with it this time.'

'Good for you, Mum. You know whose side I'm on.'

'You're a Bridgefoot. So am I, and that's what he's going to find out. Pansy's a Gifford. She'll stick to him. So you needn't worry about either of them.'

Poppy was astounded at her decisive, practical calm. She had always felt angry at seeing her mother so crushed and yielding, so humble and placatory. There wasn't a trace of anything like that about her this morning. She looked, Poppy thought, the same only different. As if she had been laundered: fresh and crisp and clean.

That was, in fact, just how Marjorie felt. Last night she had felt dirty, discarded, tossed aside, crumpled, trodden on, dragged through the mud, stained. Her talk with her father had made her see that Vic's behaviour had stained nobody permanently but himself. Her image could be restored, and this morning, in her own eyes, she had restored it. She had ceased to be a Gifford and had returned to being her true self, a Bridgefoot with her Bridgefoot pride intact.

Pansy was still in bed, sleeping it off, when her mother reached the house that was no longer home to her. Of Vic there was no sign, except for a pile of bills he had opened and looked at, and left by the side of her plate. Those by his own plate were all bills relating to the farm, for which cheques could be drawn on the business account with his signature only. The rest were household and personal bills, to be drawn on their joint current account and needing both signatures. She had always been grateful to her father for persuading her to insist on that arrangement, never more so than now.

Among the bills on her side of the table was one from a tailor for Vic's new riding clothes, and another, startlingly high, for his handmade riding boots. Yesterday, she would have regarded both with horror and anger, but fearing a row would have said nothing. This morning she merely transferred them from one pile to the other, along with one or two more, such as those from the wine merchant and the saddler. He wouldn't get any of them past the accountant as farming expenses.

She washed up the dirty things in the sink, and then went upstairs to change. She had quite a happy time throwing all his clothes and other personal bits and pieces into a heap on the bed in Poppy's room. Then she fetched some oil from the outhouse and made sure the lock of her bedroom door, and the little brass bolt, worked smoothly and silently. It was lunchtime, and she was getting hungry, so she made herself some cold beef sandwiches, and was finishing with a cup of coffee when he came in.

He sat down at his place at the table, and looked round for his meal. She gathered that he was going to pretend that nothing was wrong. Then he caught sight of the bills, and the truth of the situation dawned on him. The balloon went up, as she had known it would, getting more and more inflated till it burst and sank, soggy and distastefully flabby, at her feet.

She moved herself out of his reach, literally withdrawing her skirts, and showing all she felt in her face. 'Don't you dare touch me,' she said. 'Now or ever again.'

She was glad that she had had enough courage to go back and face him. It would keep down the scandal, too.

Nicholas and Nick returned to London. Charles, having Poppy at hand, explained Nick's amnesia to her, and begged her to go up to Castle Hill with him to see them all, but she declined and he had more than enough to do on his own behalf to think any more about Poppy. He was in negotiation with Petrie, making the most of the rest of Charlie's vacation, and sharing Brian's work with his grandfather, extra to his own. Diplomatically they consulted Brian at every turn, and peace reigned at Temperance again, especially between husband and wife. Brian proved to be a much more patient patient than Rosemary could have believed possible. She liked having him dependent on her again, and he revelled in getting the lion's share of her attention. He knew how unhappy he had made himself, as well as his wife and son, by acting on his own initiative without consulting them at all. Though not prepared yet to concede that what he had been considering was wrong or even foolish, he was in no particular hurry to be back in double-harness with Bailey again. The longer he could make his slipped disc an excuse for avoiding both Bailey and Vic, the longer it gave him to make up his mind.

At Benedict's, return to routine was welcomed. Fran had met her Christmas deadline, and proposed to have a bit of a rest from her typewriter. William said that having had what amounted to six months of his sabbatical leave without doing a stroke of real work, it was time he got down to it. Sophie went about looking the picture of content, her only grouse to Fran being that if only they had a real parson at church all the while, like that one as had took the service on New Year's Eve, more people would go to church 'reg'lar'. Fran heard and noted the implied reproof. She and William ought to make an effort once a month, whoever was in the pulpit.

Nigel was still with Eric at the hotel, which meant that nobody saw much of either of them. Once Beryl's post-party budget had been opened, debated and sorted through, it appeared that for a short time nobody was minding anybody's business but their own.

William and Fran had seen nothing of either Jess or Greg. Visiting Monica, Fran learned that Greg had gone off somewhere on the

Thursday morning following New Year's Eve. Monica was not surprised. She said she had asked him to deal with as much as he could towards their next show without consulting her, while she was in the throes of moving house. She knew that he had been excited by her last batch of designs, and was going all out to make sure that they got the right models.

'I just wish he looked a bit happier,' she said. 'What's the matter with Jess, Fran? He's making me feel guilty, as if my giving him a job has upset his life with Jess.'

When Fran told William what Monica had said, he retorted that they were no longer responsible for Jess and Greg, thank goodness. His guess was that Jess was going through one of her periodic spells of jealousy about something, most likely the success Greg was making of the chance Monica had given him. William had always suspected that Jess rather enjoyed her previous role of the devoted wife willing to 'work her fingers to the bone' for the feckless husband she had made him out to be. She was like that. There had been other times similar to this, and no doubt there would be again. But Greg was quite old enough to look after himself. Leave them alone to sort themselves out, he advised. Apart from them, this was a period of lovely calm after the storm.

It was at the hotel in the third week of January that the calm broke. Nigel had to go back to Wales, and Eric proposed to take him. It was a quiet time, businesswise, and a chance for Eric to book himself off for long enough to see Nigel home and help Roland and Monica to move. He could leave everything confidently in Jess's hands. He went to her office on that Monday morning to tell her what he proposed.

He met Anne and stood back to let her pass. She barely acknowledged him, though he noted her flushed cheeks and her jutting chin, as well as the faint odour of Dettol which never failed to amuse him. It was about the only thing left of the subdued, rather dejected widow he had engaged as Jess's assistant.

He paused outside the office door to think. He was fond of Jess, and wished he knew what was causing her present rather depressed mood. As Jess had been gradually losing spirit, Anne had been gaining it. She was dressing differently, looking more animated, putting herself forward much more than she used to. He seemed to remember Greg was fed up with Anne always being there when he was at home. He smiled to himself. At least that meant that Greg had not fallen victim to Anne, though she might possibly have tried her wiles on him.

Eric opened the office door, and went in. Jess stood by the window, and didn't turn at his entrance. Her back was rigid, and he noted one hand clenched into a ball, while with the other she was wiping her eyes.

'Jess! Are you OK?'

She swung round, and he saw that her tears were tears of anger. 'Oh, it's you,' she said. 'Good. I was coming to see you. Which of us do you want to leave, her or me? One of us will have to go.'

'What are you talking about?'

'Anne. She claims that you have been giving her all my work to do lately because I've been incapable of doing it properly, and that if she is going to do the work she wants the job. Is that the truth? Are you so sorry for me that you think I can't do what you pay me for? I would have rather heard it from you direct than from that treacherous bitch!'

Then she sat down suddenly, and cried. True to the personality that never did things by halves, when she cried, it had a lot in common with a tropical storm. He had seen her once before in this tempestuous state, and had known how to deal with her then, but the circumstances had been very different. He could hardly take her into his arms here, in broad daylight, and let her cry it out on his shoulder; nor, when she had cried it out, could he take her home and put her safely into her husband's arms. Her husband was away. He had heard Monica say so. He decided that in the present circumstances, the friend must give way to the employer.

'Go and wash your face,' he ordered, 'and when you are coherent again, I'll see you in my office. I'll expect you in ten minutes.' Then he left her.

When she presented herself at his door, her head was high and her mouth set, though her hands were trembling and her high cheekbones so flushed that she looked as if she had daubed them with rouge.

He had coffee and brandy waiting for her, and was sitting at his desk smoking his pipe, contrary to his own rules. He motioned her to a chair on the other side of his desk, careful to keep it between them.

'Drink that and calm down, and then I'll hear what all this nonsense is about,' he said. 'Is this a personal matter between you and Anne, or is it any of my business?'

'Both.'

'Then you had better start at the beginning, and tell me. Wait a minute, though – would you mind if I ask my friend to come in? He's in the next room, kicking his heels waiting for me. If it's business we may need an arbitrator, and if not his experience in dealing with personal matters is wide. As he is going back to Wales tomorrow, you can speak as freely as you like in front of him. If you prefer, I'll leave. I'm pretty sure that Greg's mixed up in it somehow. There's no other reason for you getting yourself in this state.'

She didn't answer, so he went and fetched Nigel. Then he suggested that they all moved back to his sitting-room, where they wouldn't be disturbed, and could sit in comfortable chairs and discuss whatever the matter was as the friends they were, not as boss and secretary. He picked up the internal telephone.

'Mrs Rushlake? Man the main office, please. I need Mrs Taliaferro with me. Now, Jess, start from this morning, and work backwards.'

'Anne came in to see me, as usual, and I asked her if she was all right, because I hadn't seen her at all over the weekend, though she knew Greg wasn't at home. In fact, as I reminded her, I hadn't seen her at all to talk to since she called in on her way to the party on New Year's Eve. She was very offhand, and said perhaps I might stop to remember how rude Greg had been to her the last time she had called at our house. I reminded her that he had apologized, because he hadn't meant to offend her, but in any case she knew he would be away all the weekend, because I had told her he would be.' Jess gulped, but controlled her face and went on.

'She was – well, to put it bluntly, she made it clear that she had better things to do than hold my hand when my husband wasn't there. Especially as she wasn't wanted when he was. I told her not to be so silly, and changed the subject back to her Christmas holiday. How had she got on with her stepchildren?

'Then she accused me of being nosey, and asking awkward questions. As I was obviously dying to know, she'd tell me. She hadn't been anywhere near her family. She'd spent Christmas in Norwich with her new boyfriend, Frank – Bailey's new clerk of the works. I daresay I wasn't very diplomatic, because I truly was surprised. I laughed, and said "Oh, Anne! I'm sorry I asked, but I had no idea it was as serious as that." And she simply flew at me! I needn't think she was going to be available to keep me company when Greg had left me for his other woman altogether, because she wasn't. If I thought other people didn't know he had left me, or was going to, I was wrong. Everybody who'd had anything to do with us lately could see for themselves, and it was obvious that you were on to it, because I was in such a state that you daren't trust me to do anything properly.

'As soon as she had shown her face last Tuesday morning you'd given her instructions to do what there was to do, letting me off for the day. She was very narked about that, because she'd wanted to slip off early. She and Frank were going to the Bailey do, so she'd hoped to get an hour or two in bed before setting out to a party that was likely to go on into the small hours. But it was the first time and the last, she said, because she had no intention of being anybody's dogsbody. She'd come to work here to help out, but she'd do my work only if she was paid for it, though you needn't be sure of her, because if I hadn't got a man to work for me, she had. Frank what's-his-name had asked her to marry him. Then she heard you coming, and stalked out. You must have met her in the corridor.'

It sounded defiant, but Jess had had a job to continue to the end. Eric knocked out his pipe into an ashtray to give her time to steady herself again. Then he said gently, 'Jess, what is wrong between you and Greg? Would it help to tell somebody?'

'Not you!' she said fiercely. 'You're almost the last one I'd tell. But you know there is! And how it all started.'

'In that case, I'll leave you with a much wiser man than I am,' he said, and got up and went out. Jess burst into a storm of weeping, from which, after a great deal of incoherent babbling, she emerged to find herself facing the huge and handsome clergyman, who in the interval had taken the opportunity of turning his collar parson-way-round. She began to tell him everything. It took her a long time, because she was insistent on dwelling on every little detail; but at last she got round to what had happened on New Year's Eve, and the dreadful quarrel they had had after the service. There had been a letter for Greg next morning, which she was sure was the cause of his leaving there and then and staying away over the next weekend. He had been home for two days last week but had hardly spoken to her, though he had seen Monica before going off again last Friday. She hadn't seen him since.

'Oh dear,' Nigel said, pouring her out another glass of Eric's brandy. 'There are times when I think I'm lucky never to have tried marriage. From all you've told me, I gather that the real trouble is that you love each other too much. You're both so possessive of each other that you make mountains out of molehills. If my guess is right, he's far more unhappy than you are, if he is with another woman, even in her bed. It takes two to quarrel, you know. So I wonder why you've been trying so hard to persuade me that the fault is all yours? No, don't answer. Just think about it. I don't imagine that you've been getting much sleep lately?'

She shook her head, meaning he was right. 'As to your so-called friend, I think that she, too, is in some degree to be pitied. It's as plain as a pikestaff to me that ever since she met you and your husband, she's been aware that you have had a very precious thing called love, which I guess she has never wholly experienced. She had a foolish but very human desire to spoil for you what she could never have, as a child will break another child's toy because he wants it himself. Let us pray that her Frank may make her happy, so that when your Greg comes home to you you'll find you have a husband and a friend as well.

'Now, how are you going to react to your husband if he is doing what you suspect? Show him the door, and be miserable all the rest of your life? Just to punish him for being human? Why do that? Or am I mistaken in thinking that you have some reason for making him do what he didn't intend to? So that by secretly taking the ultimate blame on yourself, you could expiate some wrong you have done him? You've sat here making charges of cruelty and neglect and even adultery against him, but it doesn't take a clairvoyant to see how much you still love him – as much as he still loves you, I guess, whatever he happens to be up to just at present. Your marriage has already lasted for well over twenty-five years, probably because you are so compatible. If you still love him, you will forgive him anything, even a bit of adultery. If he loves you as I think he must, he'll forgive you everything. Are you going to give him the chance?'

She didn't reply, but went on crying, though more quietly.

'Drink your brandy. Now, am I to regard what has passed between us as if it were a confession, or may I tell Eric? Because I think that before anything else happens, you must be given a chance to come to terms with yourself. You can't do that while you are in this state. Or while you are frantically filling your empty hours seeing to Eric's business, and being confronted every day by your erstwhile friend bolstering herself at your expense. Eric must insist that you take some time off. Go away for a couple of weeks. Be alone with yourself. It's surprising how much you find out about yourself when you are your own only companion. It has taken me till these last three months to find that out. So don't go to friends – go somewhere alone.'

'I'd rather stay at home.' Her voice was husky and low.

'Of course. In case Greg comes back. I hoped you'd say that. Try it – as long there is someone you can to turn to if you find you can't endure it all alone. Eric, for example. You could trust him with your life – as many men have done already. May I tell him, and ask him to stand by if it becomes necessary?'

She nodded, and he held out his hand. She put hers into it, and he clasped it with both his.

'May the God of Love go with you,' he said. She didn't want to let go because she felt so safe in contact with him; but Eric was tapping on the door and asking if he might come in. He took in the situation at a glance, and went straight to them, taking her from Nigel into his own arms and sitting down with her cradled against his shoulder.

'It's your turn to make yourself scarce,' he said to his friend. 'This isn't the first time I've taken Jess home in this state. You can tell me as much as I need to know this afternoon on the way to Wales.'

They set off on the six-hour journey after a very early lunch, and in the seclusion of the car they discussed the problem of Jess. Eric was able to fill Nigel in with a lot of details Jess had left out, but Nigel disclosed one that Eric didn't know about – Greg's portrait of Monica and the baby. Eric took a long time to answer. Then he said, 'I don't wonder that envy is included in the list of the seven deadly sins, if Jess is anything to go by. There's a lot of difference between jealousy and envy. Jess has always been accused of "having a jealous streak". I'm not so sure. Till now she's never had the least reason to be jealous of Greg, yet it's plain that something's eating at her like a cancer. If it isn't love she's short of, what is it? The only thing I can think of is children. It looks as if the lack of children must be his fault. She taunts him about having to paint the child he hasn't given her, to punish him. Nothing hits a man harder than to be told he's only half a man in that respect. I don't know which one of them to be sorrier for, if that is the case.'

'I think you may be right. But if she's harbouring envy till it turns to spite against Greg every time any woman produces a baby, she's just building herself a torture chamber. I've suggested she takes a holiday, if you can spare her. And don't fuss over her, or let anybody else, if you can persuade them not to. The only person who can sort her out is herself. I think she'll realize how stupid she is being. But I hope her Greg will soon come back to her. Where do you stand in the picture?'

'I'm as happy now as I've ever been. I've sort of fitted in, here. I like women's company, but I don't hanker after any of them. Why should that surprise you? You never married.'

'Because the only woman I ever wanted was married when I met her. I didn't get over it for twenty years. Then the war came, and at least I wasn't lonely after that. Now I am. My man Thomas can't be replaced any quicker than a wife can. But you're the luckier of the two of us. You've got a lot of wonderful friends in Old Swithinford.'

'That's exactly what I meant,' said Eric.

45

From Worcester, Eric rang William, giving him only the briefest outline of Jess's latest 'indisposition'.

'Useful word,' William commented. 'What is she indisposed to go along with this time? You sound like a secret agent. Tell me the truth – is she ill, or just throwing another fit of temperament? In other words, do I have to leave my writing before I've properly started on it to go and look after her, do I ring Danesum and ask the Pre-Raphaelite maidens to do their angels-of-mercy act again, or would the easiest thing be to get the BBC to broadcast an SOS message for Greg?'

Eric laughed. 'Sorry, William. You're too quick on the uptake.' He explained briefly what had happened.

His voice changed, and William noted it. 'I can't in all conscience just disappear without alerting somebody. Nigel says she ought to be stopped in her tracks now, and made to do what only she can do, which is to sort herself out. So I'm not asking you to go and coddle her. Quite the reverse. Leave her alone to find out what the root of the problem is. I agreed that we should at least give that a try, but my courage has failed me. She just possibly might do something dramatically silly. Could you find an excuse for giving her a call tonight? Monica knows Nigel's number, and if anything should be wrong, I'll be back the day after tomorrow. I ought to have consulted you before leaving, but it all blew up so suddenly. Actually, I think Nigel's treatment may be right, but she isn't my sister. She is yours, and you may feel differently. I do apologize.'

'I sometimes wish she wasn't mine,' said William. 'Her trouble is that she has had to hold the fort for so long that she can't believe the siege is over. Or to put it in Sophie's language, if she can't be first horse she won't pull at all. She still can't face the fact that as far as I am concerned, Fran's first horse. As Jess has always been to Greg. I have no idea what's up between them, but I must say that at the moment he has all my sympathy. I think Nigel's right, too, but I don't think I dare tell Fran. She wouldn't be capable of giving the experiment time to work. She'd be over to Southside House to be used as either a sponge or a punch-ball, and for once I don't propose to allow it. But I'll ring or go round myself before bedtime. So thanks – and don't worry.'

He cursed silently as he put the phone down. He wanted to get on with his own work. There was a chance for Fran to let up a bit, and he wanted her to enjoy it. He considered that they had done enough, during the last six months, of minding other people's business and neglecting their own. Playing the Good Samaritan was all very fine, but they did have private lives, too.

He knew Jess's moods only a little less well than Greg did – but there was the rub. If Greg was playing with fire, and set a conflagration going, it would be himself and Fran who were forced to deal with the casualties. Maybe he had better warn Fran, but not till he had to. He managed to have a word with Jess while Fran was having her bath, his excuse being that he needed Greg to do a sketch for him – which happened to be true. Jess was cool and distant; she was not expecting Greg home till after the weekend, but was taking time off to rest while there was a chance in this least busy period of the year. She'd be OK by herself, thank you. Glad of a bit of peace and quiet. William hardened his heart and did not invite her up to Benedict's for Sunday.

After two more days, it was Sophie who told Fran that Jess was not at work, so she supposed she might have flu. She had heard it from Joe, who had got it from Daffy Pugh, who had heard it from Frank Chessman, who had been told by Mis' Rushlake, who was having to do all Jess's work extra, specially as Mr Choppen was taking time off as well. But then, they must know that, seeing as Roland and Monica were moving out of Choppen's house. 'Them children should ha' been brought up here wheer they rightly belong,' she said.

Secretly Fran agreed with her. She, too, was feeling the need of a bit of peace and quiet, and was a little aggrieved that having done all they had done to help stabilize things with regard to the position of the older inhabitants in the village for the time being, it should be her son pulling the plug out, upsetting the frail balance of family and friendly relationships, already tangled a bit by business being interwoven with friendship.

Sophie, having had her say, was inclined to be optimistic. 'So come a week a-Monday, and they're gone, we can all settle down till February filldyke's over, and March manyweathers comes in like a lion, as the saying is. But afore you know wheer you are it's gone out like a lamb, and it's spring again. Miss Budd used to tell us child'en that God meant us to do like the 'edge'ogs do, stop at 'ome and sleep and rest in the bad months so as to be ready for spring. For once, this year, I can't see nothing ahead to stop us. Well, nothing as is cluss to us at 'ome 'ere, I mean. Me and Thirz' and Het 'ave all made it up with each other, and that's a blessing as I can't never give thanks enough for. Het and Joe seem to be getting along well together again – which reminds me. Joe told me as that man down Danesum don't get no better in 'isself, like, but seems a lot brighter all the same. And Joe said he's 'inted once or twice as he'd like to see 'im' – she nodded her head sideways towards William's study, where he was now spending a lot of his time – 'but I told Joe as 'e'd started a-working on 'is new book and don't want disturbing no more than can be 'elped. There ain't no more news as I *know* of, though there's all'us rumours, even though Beryl ain't been 'erself since that do a-New Year. Seems to have got 'er comb cut a bit, some'ow. Brian Bridgefoot's up and about again, though 'e can't do a lot, and stops at 'ome most o' the time. Marge spends a good deal of 'er time with 'im. They always was very close. If I could believe Beryl, which I can't, I'd repeat what she's 'inting at, which is that Marge would rather be at Temperance with 'er brother than stop at 'ome with 'er 'usband. Seems 'er and Vic ain't getting on 'cos Marge don't like Pansy being so thick wi' young Bailey, and Vic does. According to Beryl, them two young'uns are too thick, if you know what I mean, so no wonder Marge don't like it. But then, Beryl 'as got to 'ave 'er knife into somebody, specially when she's aggravated. Olive 'Opkins told me 'ow put out she is to find out as all 'er tales about Jane 'Adley's – I mean Mis' Bellamy's – father being a hundertaker was all lies. She 'ates to be proved wrong, and don't want to 'ave to believe as 'e's really a posh gover'ment man rich enough to buy the whull village if 'e wanted to, which as far as I know he don't.'

Fran understood quite well that she was really being asked to tell William about Petrie.

William at once said that he'd work better for a break, so if she was going to Monastery Farm this afternoon, he'd go to Danesum.

He was glad he had made that decision. He could see at once that Joe's report was true. Petrie was going downhill, all too clearly wearing the look of a man with the hand of death upon him. William found it very hard to take, as if he were losing a friend of long standing. As indeed, he thought, it might have been if Fate had allowed it.

Petrie had gone into a long bout of terrible coughing, which William could only sit and watch, suffering and thinking. But it was over at last, and the sick man, having got his breath back, apologized, turned a cheerful face to him and disclosed the good news.

The house was sold, the deal signed, the cheque due on signature handed over, and Dafydd was already undertaking the task of making inquiries with regard to buying all that Petrie had set his heart on for the family to start their new life with. William's head was full of questions that he was too polite to ask, as well as those he feared to ask but needed to know the answers to.

Petrie read his mind. 'Let me put you right into the picture,' he said, 'though for the moment, in confidence. You are worrying yourself needlessly about me, personally. There's no need. Part of the bargain is that we needn't vacate the house till I'm dead. The purchaser is young Charles Bridgefoot. He offered you as a referee had I needed one, so I gather you know him well. That was enough for me. He is his own best referee, but with your name always ready on his tongue I would have trusted him with anything anyway.'

William absorbed his surprise without letting it show. 'Charles doesn't need my name to back him,' he said. 'Round here "Bridgefoot" is synonymous with integrity. And as for money, there's plenty on his side and more – much more – on the side of the girl he's engaged to.'

'It's for her he's so anxious to get it,' Petrie said. 'She sounds very unusual. He says she knows the old house wants them. I'd like to meet her. It's nice to think that I'll be leaving a bit of happiness here behind me to make my efforts worthwhile.'

William made a mental resolution to arrange that meeting, if it were ever possible. If there were time: that's what it amounted to. Petrie's eyes had filled with tears. 'I lie here imagining things,' he said, 'at night when I can't sleep. I like to think that Tanner will be as good a specimen as young Bridgefoot is, one day, and be as much in love. That's something I missed. You didn't. You don't have to tell me.'

William was quick to answer. 'But you have a son. I haven't.' The silence from the bed was eloquent.

'I will do as much as is possible for Tanner,' William said. 'I told Fran I had made myself his legal guardian subject to his mother's agreement. Trust me to do my best. That's all I can promise.'

'It's enough.'

'Tell me about the other children,' William said. 'Are they aware of what is going to happen?'

'Emmy and Ammy must be, I think. They may have tried to explain to Topy and Saffie. The others are too young to understand. There's no sense in making them miserable before they need be. When the stuff is bought and is here, they will have to be told what it means. I hope to be well enough to refresh the girls' memory of camping life. They were used to it, before we came here. None of them is old enough to drive, and Crystal's never learned. But Pugh has found a camping site, a permanent one, somewhere close to Aberystwyth which is within easy distance of his home. If Crystal behaves herself well enough for the council not to interfere, they could stay there and those of school age could go to school.

'I find myself praying, William, though I don't know what to. I can't bear to think of them losing touch with each other. The welfare people would have had to split them, on the grounds of age and sex. They would all be put in different homes, except perhaps the twins, and might never see each other again. Thank God – or whatever – that Crystal has chosen to stay here so long. While she is in evidence, her guardianship, such as it is, may keep them together. I rely on Pugh and his belief in his Lord to do the rest. She may listen to him.'

He began to cough again, and William stood up and held out his hand.

'I'll see you again, soon,' he said. It would, he feared, have to be very soon. He judged that he could leave his next visit till after Roland's removal, and there was nothing else to think about. Perhaps he could get Charles and Charlie to go with him.

He saw so little of Fran during the next ten days that he began to tease her about feeling neglected and asking her if she was proposing to leave him for Eric and the twins. He stayed resolutely in his study, and was surprised, as well as very pleased, at the progress he made with his work. Sophie tended him in Fran's absence as she might have done a baby left in her charge, doing everything for him, as he told Fran, except put him to bed. Only she could do that.

By the time Roland and Monica were safely settled in their new home, and Eric back at Monastery Farm alone, William had had long enough without Fran constantly near for him to pity Eric. He packed away his work on the day Fran came back wholly to him, declaring that they were now about to have a little honeymoon of doing nothing but be with each other. The weather had remained dry, but February came in dull and cold, and above all dark. He went out of his way to make sure that when Fran came in on the last day that she had been required to help, Benedict's was a blaze of light and warmth. He had got her back to himself again, and was at peace with the world. They shut out all thought of others, and spent the evening in mutual content.

Next morning, they woke to heavy, solid rain. 'So it's going to be a black February, not a white one,' Fran said, watching the cold, steady downpour from their bed. 'What a good thing we got the move finished just in time. We shall have to get up, because of Sophie, but we can just please ourselves what we do all day.'

> 'Let it rain! Who cares?
> I've got my leman upstairs,'

William misquoted, pulling her towards him.

The bedside telephone shrilled.

'Damnation!' he said, reaching for it while kissing the tip of her nose.

She listened. 'I can't hear a word you're saying,' he said. '*Who* is it from? Did you say you don't know? Look, unless you stop crying and speak so that I can hear, you're wasting time and money. Now, Jess, blow your nose and start all over again. An anonymous letter? Look, I'm still in bed. I'll be round as soon as ever I can. Yes, if you want her, I'm sure she'll come as well. Give us an hour.' He hung up.

'Damnation it is,' said Fran, getting out of bed. 'There goes our nice quiet time. We might have expected something, but I didn't expect it from that quarter. I thought she had decided she could do without us, since Christmas. But at least it sounds like something a bit out of the ordinary. Fancy her asking for me! Did she say anything about Greg?'

'Yes, I kept catching his name among the wails. Though I don't know what it has to do with him. The state she was in sounded genuine enough, and so did her appeal for you to go with me. My guess is that she has had enough of her own company, and any letter that wasn't from Greg would have caused this if it was only the milkman's bill. Let's get our breakfast over quick, and go.'

Fran left a note for Sophie, and they set out into the downpour.

They found Jess in her kitchen, still in her dressing-gown, her face pinched and her nose red with crying, her eyes sunk back into her head, and her long hair screwed into a bun at the back of her neck, showing all the grey that was normally made into such an attractive feature. She was standing by the kitchen dresser, supporting herself by leaning on it, and staring down at the letter lying before her.

She turned, not to William but to Fran, though it was William who took her and led her firmly to a chair. Fran picked up the letter, and put it on the table before Jess. Neither was going to look at it till invited to do so, though the one glance Fran had got showed her that it was certainly not the milkman's bill, nor from any other person willing to identify himself.

'Read it,' croaked Jess, pushing it towards them.

It was a square piece of paper, suggesting to both newcomers at once that it was a sheet of A4 from which a printed letterhead had been cut off. The letter was inscribed in a childlike script without capitals or punctuation:

wouldn't you like to know where he is that loving liar of a husband of yours. how many times now has he told you he has been visiting the doctor up in yorkshire i wonder and how long will it be before he goes again and never come back at all not long now some friend some doctor but a good bedside manner all the same. you ask him if you ever see him again but if he is a liar you are a fool believing all he tells you doctors are not all old and they are not all men neither. she calls herself michelle stanhope but her real name is ella morley why don't you let her husband know what she is up to with yours he will be glad to know who to look out for one dark night and i am glad it won't be me if he ever catches them at it he'll kill him he knows how to when he's got his dander up and if he does that mr tolliver of yours will be sorry he ever got anything of his up i write as a friend who knows a lot more than you do about these goings on and i warn you that if you want to save your precious husband's life you had better act quick.

if you don't believe me ask tolliver to show you the picture he painted of her in a skirt so short he might as well not have bothered but its all the same to him he knows well enough what's underneath her skirt i'll bet he likes a bit of young blood because she must be every bit of twenty year younger than you.

i don't like to know of such goings on and i am wrighting to her husband as well and i shall give him your name and address. you see i have known him since he was born and i kno as i speak the truth when i say as he has killed men before now and got away with it so i am warning you beware.

Before they had finished reading it, Jess was moaning. Fran went to her, and Jess stood up, put her arms round Fran's neck, and clung. Fran looked over Jess's shoulder at William, who still had the letter in his hand.

'Burn the filthy thing, and forget it!' Fran said. 'It's only from some nutter who has taken a scunner at you for no reason. None of it's true, anyway.'

Jess became rigid in Fran's arms, and when she spoke, it was as if she were spitting out a mouthful of bitter aloes.

'That's where you're wrong. It's probably all true. I haven't seen Greg for three weeks and I have no idea where he is, except that to keep me quiet he rings nearly every night, and about a week ago the switchboard in a hotel had to ask me to hold the line for a call from York. That girl on the switchboard didn't know what she'd done! I wonder how many other marriages she has broken that way!'

Fran knew by William's calm, deliberately controlled manner that in fact he was having difficulty in listening to Jess with sympathy, and losing patience with her because he knew that whatever the outcome was, in the end it would be himself and Fran who would have to deal with it.

'I think it's a matter for the police,' he said. 'Anybody capable of sending an anonymous letter is beneath contempt, but of course there's always the chance that the sender is mentally unbalanced or drunk or drugged. Or just plain vindictive. But as Jess has just pointed out, such things may have disastrous results. And when, as in this case, they contain allegations against people specified by name, they are probably actionable. Have you ever had any before?'

Jess shook her head, but disengaged herself from Fran looking stubborn.

'I don't want any investigations made. I don't want anybody else to know about it. At least till I've seen Greg again and got the truth out of him. Things have been going wrong between us for a long time, now. It's been awful . . . you know it has! Ever since – ever since . . .' She began to show signs of going into a fit of hysterics.

William looked grim. 'I suggest you go and get dressed, while Fran and I make you some breakfast. Then we'll decide what's best to be done. We'll talk when you feel a bit calmer. I won't believe your accusations against Greg without a bit more proof than there is in this letter.'

Seeing the resolve on his face, Jess gave in, and went. Fran put the kettle on, and began to clear the table up.

'Leave that, sweetheart. We need to talk while she's out of the way. Other people may be involved, and you know what Jess is. What do you suggest we do?'

'Get her to tell us what she actually knows, rather than what she only suspects, first. Then pack her things and take her home with us. We daren't leave her here by herself. We shall have to try to find Greg, shan't we? Sorry, my darling, but blood is thicker than water when it comes to the crunch. She's our responsibility next to Greg's. For our own sakes we shall have to look after her. Ssh. Here she is.'

Jess had certainly wrought a change in her appearance. They made her eat a round of toast, and then sat round the kitchen table for a conference.

'Now, Jess,' William said. 'Are you sure you're not making a mountain of misery out of a molehill of nonsense? The world's full of beautiful women. Greg sees them as he would see any other beautiful thing – a flower or a sunset or a Greek vase. You can't keep him under lock and key. What makes you think there's even a whisker of truth in any of it?'

Jess heard him with an air of despair that was now turning rapidly to anger. There was plenty, she said, to be told, and she began to tell it. They heard all about the recent quarrels, the locking of doors, the discovery of portraits of other women, his excuses when he couldn't get home, her evidence that when he rang her 'from a call box' or 'from a friend's house' he was really in a hotel or a restaurant – and so on, and so on. Everything, in fact, except her rejection of his advances and her attack on his studio, and with no mention of Anne's part in making her suspicious.

'So: let's do a bit of detective work on the letter. Does this woman – Michelle Stanhope or Ella Morley or whoever she is – actually exist? The only way to find that out is to ask Monica.'

'No!' blazed Jess. 'I won't let her know anything about it.'

'Let's look for a bit of internal evidence as to who might have written it,' Fran said, practically. 'Whoever it is is neither so simple nor so uneducated as we are expected to believe. It's jolly difficult to write without punctuation when you are used to putting it in. I know. And all those little i's and deliberate grammatical mistakes don't fool me. Here and there apostrophes have slipped into the right place out of sheer habit, like that in "he'll" for "he will" and the possessive apostrophe in "husband's". "Wrighting" is spelled wrong on purpose – but how many people that truly couldn't spell "writing" correctly would say "I have known him"?'

'And that silly bit about her husband being a killer,' William added. 'That could be said of Greg himself, or me, or any man who was in the war. It's designed to frighten you on Greg's behalf, to stop you from throwing the letter on the fire straight away. It must be somebody who knows how much you love him.'

'It did frighten me!' said Jess. 'I did love him and I'm still frightened. Do something, William!'

Fran thought she had never seen William look so exasperated before. 'How can I, if you won't let me? We don't know where Greg is. The letter was posted in York, by somebody I guess who had heard Greg's name spoken but never seen it written down, because it's addressed to you as Mrs Tolliver. How did they know the address, though? It seems to me that the only person who could possibly help us in any way is Monica. But why bother? What was the purpose of the letter, anyway? You're not thinking of ringing up this murderous husband, I hope? I'll do what I can to track Greg down, but . . .'

'Oh, you fools, don't you see?' Jess stood up and screamed at him. 'It's as plain as a pikestaff to me! There's only one person who could have sent it – Greg himself. It's his devious, underhand way of letting me know he's left me. Too much of a coward to face me with it openly. I would never have believed that he could be so cruel – or so *common*. I think that that's what hurts me most. To think that I've been coddling and working all these years for a man who could do that to me in the end! It makes me feel like a trollop.

'Do you think I'm going to let anybody else know about this letter – least of all that smug little cat so self-satisfied with herself and her litter of kittens? It's all her fault that he's ever set eyes on Bitchella Morehope, or whatever her name really is. Don't tell me that Greg sees *her* as a Greek vase. He sees her for what she is – a glamour-puss with sex to sell, and, as he says, one twenty years younger than I am. You can't tell me anything I don't know about him in that field! I'll find a way to pay him back, don't you worry. As you said, William, anybody capable of sending a letter like that is beneath contempt – but not beyond revenge.'

She shook and gasped with furious anger, resisting all attempts on Fran's part to soothe her. William didn't try.

'Go and help her pack some things,' he said to Fran. 'She's coming back to Benedict's with us, now, whatever she says or does. Did you hear that, Jess? No protests, or I phone for a doctor and get the police.'

'I had made up my mind what to do before this letter came. I'm going to disappear. Let him find the cage empty when he doesn't get a reply to this and comes back to find out why. I'm all packed, and ready, all ready to go. So, you've made my plan perfect. I'll hide at Benedict's, where I can keep my eye on everything, including him when he comes. Nobody but you and Sophie need know where I am. Sophie will keep a Wagstaffe secret rather than have yet another scandal in the family.'

'She may,' said William coldly, angry at her sneer at Sophie's loyalty to them. 'But I'm not prepared to perjure myself and betray all my friends with anything so stupid. We shall be the first people everybody will ask – even the police. How long do you think you can go missing without somebody getting the police in, and quizzing us?'

'I've thought of that. I shall write Eric a sweet little note thanking him for giving me the break, and telling him I'm making the most of it by going to stay with some friends. If you two won't play, I shall know that I haven't got any friends.'

She was showing agitation, her face drained of all colour and her red eyes flicking from side to side like a trapped animal looking for a way of escape. She picked up the letter and made as if to tear it up, then smoothed it again with clawlike hands and folded it, once and twice and again and again, till she held the tight little wad clenched tight in her palm.

'Get your things,' said William, curtly.

She sped up the stairs and he stopped Fran from following her. 'If she is going right round the bend, she'd better do it where I can deal with it,' he said. 'I'm sorry, Fran, but I don't see what else we can do.'

'Neither can I. It may be that Greg will come looking for her. I hope so.'

'I shan't stir another step until I have your word of honour that if he does, both of you will swear you don't know where I am,' said Jess, from the bottom of the stairs. William went forward to relieve her of two heavy suitcases. 'I waited upstairs till I saw Eric leave,' she said, 'and wrote him the note while I was waiting. We'll post it on the way.'

She made a final round of the house, securing all the doors and windows.

'We'll play it her way for a few days,' William whispered. 'I'm sure we can trust Eric to keep his eye on what's happening, and he'll be able to get all the gen from Monica. We can just lie doggo and let him get Greg back by hook or by crook.'

It suddenly seemed too ludicrous to Fran to make much of a tragedy out of it.

'And the wicked wolf in the sheepfold shall bring back the lost sheep rejoicing?' she said. 'I only hope you may be right.' But for once there was no answering twinkle in William's eye.

46

As a retreat, Benedict's was ideally situated. Though it lay no more than half a mile from the church, it stood back from the Swithinford road, surrounded by its extensive garden, which until the old squire's death had formed only part of its 'estate'. Between the house and the road lay a meadow, known to all the indigenous as the 'front cluss', across which an avenue of tall, mature trees led to the gravelled front court and the porticoed front door. Fran had hesitated a little about adding the cost of the cluss to that of the house and the extensive restoration, but had succumbed to William's urging, though their renewed acquaintance was then no more than a few weeks and three meetings old. He had said that the house and the field belonged to each other, and one without the other was incomplete.

She had never ceased to be grateful. There were several self-set but fast-growing trees in the hedgerow bordering the cluss, and the old trees on each side of the avenue were so large and stately that they almost met and made a tunnel of shade in high summer. There was a slight curve in the drive about halfway between the road and the house, so that from the road the trees hid the house completely. It was a never-ending surprise and a never-ending delight to sweep round that bend and find the long, low house in its clothing of Suffolk pink wash waiting for you, with its adornment of white paint and the big black door hiding itself in the shadows of the porch and pediment above it. Even in winter when the trees were bare the inhabitants of Benedict's could escape the scrutiny of outsiders with the very minimum of care.

Jess was put to bed and made to stay there for a couple of days, under the pretext of having been sent home from the hotel before she gave everybody else the flu, especially as Greg was having to stay away to do all the business while Monica got settled into her new home. Sophie accepted the story without question, and at Fran's request stayed away from the 'invalid' in case she caught the virus. But Jess had no intention of remaining a prisoner in her bedroom, and though she still had puffy eyelids with dark hollows beneath them, insisted on getting up, so Fran had no option but to take Sophie into their confidence.

As Jess had surmised, she was as safe with a secret as the Tower of London, but it amused Fran a bit that she aligned herself with Greg, and not, after all, with the Wagstaffe concerned. When poverty had driven Jess and Greg back to take shelter with the family Sophie found Jess 'too sweet by 'alf' (which she interpreted as being patronizing), while Greg's childlike, insouciant charm had made her his champion for ever.

Fran decreed that William was to go back to his study, forget Jess was there and get on with his work. She and Sophie would cope with Jess. He seemed quite prepared to agree to that arrangement, showing uncharacteristic toughness towards their enforced visitor.

He even surprised himself, when Fran gently pointed out to him that he was being unusually unsympathetic towards Jess, by having to admit that she was right. He ought to have got used to having to sort out Jess and her life; he'd been doing it for the last forty years – except for the war years when inevitably they had been out of touch, and the last couple of years since they had all been in Old Swithinford. Perhaps his irritation with her at present was because he had got out of the habit of regarding her as his responsibility. He could, and did, observe her more objectively now than he had done in the past, and he was less willing to give her his time and his attention because time had become so much more precious to him, and he had somebody else to give all his attention to.

Taking himself to task for his lack of feeling about her at this present juncture, he came up with some surprising conclusions about himself.

He had been forced against his inclination to give Jess his promise not to tell Greg that they knew of her whereabouts. He hated that sort of conspiracy, but he could not and would not break his word once given. It was his refusal to break the promise he had sworn so long ago to Janice, his legal wife, that kept him still in his detested role of Fran's 'live-in lover' or, as he sometimes bitterly referred to himself, 'only her lodger'. If he couldn't bring himself to break a promise for Fran's sake, he couldn't imagine himself doing it for Jess. Did it matter, one way or the other? His answer was a very direct affirmative – because it involved his image of himself, as well as his relationship with Eric and Greg.

He suddenly saw, with amazing clarity, one of the social problems that any small enclosed community had always had, and still did. Relatives and friends overlapped. The criss-crossed bloodlines tangled with the strands of friendship to make up a strong cord out of the same people, the whole being an unbroken loop that could be made into an infinite variety of patterns like the string between two pairs of hands playing cat's cradle. There must always have been terrible clashes of loyalty because of it, such as the ties now between himself and Fran and the Choppen family, or between the Bridgefoots and the Bellamys. It was in such cases that custom and tradition took over. Family quarrels and even village feuds were always resolved somehow, provided outsiders didn't interfere. Left long enough, some other crisis, like the next hold in cat's cradle, took over and changed the pattern of the string. Then it was that they found that 'blood was thicker than water' or that 'friends were closer than brothers'. The rules of conduct had been sifted and settled, generation after generation. They all knew the rules, and could judge to a nicety when to apply them. In the end, they had no option but to settle any dispute by making it up with each other, or both parties suffered. It was the age-old remedy of 'the hair of the dog that bit you' put into practice.

His difficulty at present was the conflict between his blood tie to Jess and his friendship with Greg. He had grown to love Greg as a friend recently far more than he had ever been aggravated by him in the past as a brother-in-law who seemed always to be letting Jess down. Now, for the first time, he was wholly on Greg's side. It had to be because Jess had traduced Greg – as he suspected she was doing now. But since she loved her husband to distraction, as it was obvious he loved her, why? That was the question William put to himself, and could find no answer to. He could only hope, philosophically, that when the crisis came, he or some-body else would be able to produce some amulet or the hair of the dog whose bite was still festering inside Jess.

He felt considerably better for having worked out what was the matter with himself, and several days passed in which nothing whatsoever unto-ward happened. He was able to get a lot of work done; Fran was quite happy to keep in touch with friends by phone, making his work her excuse for not going out; and Jess, being waited on and treated like royalty, told Fran – and even Sophie – a lot of her troubles until she had talked a great deal of bitterness out of herself. She began to read, and actually laughed and joked with Sophie about their mutual childhood memories. She was certainly a great deal calmer than she had been for a long time, and both Fran and William were congratulating themselves that if or when Greg was traced or turned up, there would be some rational explanation and a willingness on both sides to bridge the gap between them.

William wondered how long Eric's patience with either would hold out. He had not, apparently, put a term to the length of Jess's 'break', and as a businessman he might be being forced to rely too much on Anne Rushlake. William shored himself up against such fears by remembering that Eric did not care very much for Anne.

He went to visit Eric. William was grateful to Eric for taking it for granted that he did not know where or how Jess was. The more William saw of Eric, the better he liked him. As he drove past the church on his way home, he saw George Bridgefoot letting himself in with the huge key that was now necessary, the church having to be locked against intruders and thieves for the first time in its history. For a minute or two he envied the old man the comfort the church was to him, not as a refuge but as somewhere to express gratitude for the good things of life, like friends. When he reached home he found a Jess who seemed almost back to her normal self, and relaxed, thinking that perhaps after all it had only been a storm in a teacup. He should have known better.

47

Although the days were lengthening perceptibly, dusk still fell early. Sophie went round the house drawing curtains and switching on lights. As she said often to Fran when bidding her goodnight before setting out for her own cosy little cottage, there was a lot to be said for winter evenings when you had a home of your own to go to where there was nothing else to do and you could stop 'hived in' till morning.

William thought how right she was as he rounded the bend in the drive and saw the lights of Benedict's welcoming him home. He did not propose to go back to work tonight, so after supper he could just laze in front of the fire with Fran – and Jess, of course, at present, though to do her justice she usually retired early with a book and left them together for the bit of the day they liked best.

She helped Fran wash up after supper, and at about nine o'clock excused herself and went to bed with a book. William got up from his armchair and went to sit on the hearthrug at Fran's feet, with his head against her knee. They had no need for words. The warmth, the isolation and the content in each other's company was all they asked.

It was almost ten o'clock when the unmistakeable sound of car tyres on the gravel brought William to his feet in one agile movement. At that time of night it could only mean some sort of emergency. He looked down at Fran, who pushed an indignant Cat from her knee and sat up, lifting her eyebrows in inquiry.

'Stay where you are,' he said. 'I'll go.' She heard him unbolt the great front door, and the next moment his voice. 'Greg, my dear fellow! Do come in.'

Fran was on her feet in an instant, for two reasons. One was to fling herself at Greg and give him a hug of welcome, the other to signal frantically to William with her eyebrows to keep his voice down.

William led Greg to his own armchair, and went to get him a drink.

Fran looked Greg over, and said, 'You look just about all in. Where have you come from?'

He gave her a half-smile, and said wearily, 'In the first place, from York. Just now, from home – Southside House – if that is still my home. I'm not sure.'

'What do you mean?' Fran asked.

'I don't know whether I've got a home any longer, or a wife. I've been ringing every night for a week, without getting an answer. When I found she wasn't at home tonight, I went straight up to the hotel to see if she was working late. Eric wasn't there, so I rang his home and he told me that she had been a bit off-colour and he had insisted on her having a short break from work. Said he'd had a note from her to say she was going away to stay with friends. That's all he knew. So of course I came here, to see if you knew anything, though I had gathered from her that since Christmas for some reason she wasn't anxious to keep closely in touch with you. That's why I haven't rung you before now. I've been driving all day, not stopping to eat, and worrying myself into a frazzle. I'm just about all in. But I half expected something like this, all the same.'

Fran noted with enormous relief that so far he had asked no direct questions that had forced them to lie, and that by giving her something to do, to go and get him a meal, he had staved off the moment of truth. She left him to William and went to see what she could find for him to eat where he was. When she took it to him, he was talking to William. She guessed instinctively that after food, his greatest need was to talk, not to question. He wanted to tell somebody his side of the story. She asked what the trouble was.

'I don't know what's the matter, Fran. I don't know anything, except that I can't take much more. She's never been quite the same since we came back from Scotland. First of all I thought it was all simply jealousy of you – and perhaps reaction to all those years of struggle and poverty, and her age. But it didn't change a lot even after luck seemed to turn our way. She was jolly nasty to you, and she turned against me as well. That's what I can't understand.

'After she went to work for Eric it got worse. I got it into my head that she had fallen for him – or he for her – and that I was in the way. The old story. The good-for-nothing husband her principles wouldn't allow her to reject, even though a man with all that Eric had to offer was standing waiting. How could I complain? She certainly didn't owe me much! When I couldn't stand my jealousy of Eric any longer, I confessed it to Monica. She swore that there was absolutely nothing between her father and Jess, and I believed her. But now I'm back where I was before, so I'm asking you. Is Eric at the bottom of all this? Has he whipped her away from me to a little love-nest somewhere? *Does* he know where she is?'

'No,' answered William, with absolute conviction. 'I went to see him this very afternoon, and he's as worried as you are. It seems that she staged a tantrum in his office just as he was about to take some time off himself, quarrelled with Anne Rushlake, slammed in her notice to him, and then went to pieces.

'So he took her home, and ordered her to take time off, stop at home and rest till he got back, and till she felt better. He showed me the note she wrote him, saying she was going to stay with friends. His greatest concern, like ours, was where you were, how much your whereabouts had to do with her throwing this fit, and how to get in touch with you. Monica didn't seem to be much help, even if Jess would have allowed her to be consulted.'

Fran decided to let William do as much of the talking as he was prepared to. The last thing they must do was to contradict each other.

'But I've been ringing her every night – even after there was never any answer. Did you see her before she disappeared?' asked Greg. 'Surely you must have known what was happening?'

'Yes,' said William truthfully. 'We got a garbled telephone call one morning early, just after you'd been home the last time, and of course we rushed over to Southside House. It was pretty hair-raising. She was already packed, and ready to take off. We couldn't stop her.'

'Finish your supper,' cut in Fran, sensing danger. 'I'm going to make you some hot, strong coffee, and William, give him some brandy to go with it. I think we owe it to him to hear his side of the story before we tell him anything Jess told us.'

They let him talk. He filled in all the gaps Jess had left. He reminded them of her behaviour on the evening Monica had revealed her pregnancy, and her refusal to believe that Roland, and not he, was responsible for her condition. He told them of her constant bitchiness towards him, and his growing suspicion that she deliberately had Anne there every time he came home, to prevent them from ever being alone long enough to put things right between them. Then as Monica's pregnancy had advanced, and he had been made her partner, he had been forced to be away from home a lot more.

For the first time, Fran thought, he began to hedge his words a bit, and look guilty.

'She didn't give me much encouragement to come home to my *wife*,' he said, emphasizing the word. 'What was I to think? With all that has happened to us since we came back here, I've been a different man, especially because I didn't have to feel so hang-dog about not contributing my share towards keeping us going. I feel better in health and better in spirit – if anything, younger and more of a man than I had been for years. You'd have expected Jess to be pleased. But all I got from her, more and more, was the cold shoulder. I know some of it's my fault. But when I was two hundred miles away, after three days' hard work, there wasn't much to tempt me to leave a comfortable hotel to drive home just to listen to a couple of catty women discussing their work for that bloody hotel all the evening, and then find that instead of a wife I had only a housekeeper! Look, Fran, there never has been a marriage happier than ours was once. However hard up we were, we could make up for it in bed. I simply couldn't believe that this new, cold creature was my Jess. I tried hard to be patient, but it's just got worse and worse. There could only be one explanation – another man. Who can it be but Eric?'

William shook his head, and Greg went on. 'It came to a head the weekend of Fran's birthday,' he said. 'I'd been consoling myself with painting – real painting – and I set about that portrait of Monica with one of the twins. I couldn't believe I had done it! Well, you know what happened to that. Is it still here?'

'Of course it is,' Fran soothed him. 'In the safest place we could find for it – right at the back of the cupboard under the stairs. It'll be there whenever you want to finish it.'

'I doubt if I ever shall, now,' he said. 'I'm no good at anything without Jess.'

He hid his face in his hands, and they could do nothing but wait. But he lifted his head, and went on, telling all that had happened that night. 'She's still the only woman in the world for me. So what am I to do, Fran? What can I do?'

William and Fran looked at each other in the silence broken only by Greg's misery, both filled with the hollow emptiness of helplessness against Fate that is the essence of tragedy. When at last Greg sat up, Fran led them back to the facts of the matter.

'William told you we went to see Jess when she called us that morning,' she said. 'We found her nearly crazed with grief and jealousy, accusing you of all the things you have just been accusing her of, and more. You see, you hadn't been home when she had expected you, and that morning she had got an anonymous letter telling her where you were, and what you were doing with one of your new models – a married woman named Michelle Stanhope. She was beside herself, absolutely shattered. We couldn't do anything with her.'

'So it seems to be a case of the pot and the kettle calling each other black, without a shred of real proof on either side,' said William. 'I haven't the faintest notion of how to begin to help them to think of each other as all bright and shiny and clean again. You've got yourselves into it, and I'm afraid only you can get yourselves out. Which means that one of you has to make the first move.'

'That's what I had intended to do, but now . . .' Greg sat up, white-faced and very tense. 'An *anonymous* letter?' he said. 'Telling her about Michelle? Who could have sent it?'

Fran stared at him with sinking heart. Guilt was written all over him.

She said, quite brutally, 'She thinks *you* did. She thinks you wanted her to know the truth. That's why she couldn't face being at home if or when you did turn up again.'

Greg was on his feet now, every other emotion submerged by anger. 'She really thinks I am cad enough to put my hand to a filthy anonymous letter? She hates me that much? Then there isn't any hope. I might as well get in the car and go straight back to York. There are other willing women besides Michelle, and Jess can't think any worse of me than she already does. Or you, either, apparently.'

'Or you of Jess, just as apparently. You're wrong about her, as it happens. She's never cared a bean for any other man but you.'

'Nor I for any other woman but her! She knows that.'

'So what about this Michelle, Greg?' This was William, calm, gentle, but purposeful. 'I take it from your attitude that the accusation made in the letter is true?'

It was his kind, sympathetic tone that broke Greg's defences. Greg turned towards him, staggering with fatigue and emotion, and would have fallen but for William's ready arm. William lowered him back into the chair, but Greg would not let go of his hand. Here was another male. One who knew what love was, who had himself had many years in a sexual desert, who might possibly understand and excuse or even forgive where no woman could be expected to. Fran could hardly bear the appeal in Greg's sensitive face as he gazed up into William's.

'Can I tell you what happened? She's physically the most beautiful woman I have ever seen. Just to look at her, to watch her move, is wonderful. Enough to fetch any man to her feet. She's as gorgeous as Helen of Troy – and as dangerous. Or perhaps Delilah. She knew my weak spot.' He went on to explain how Michelle had got under his skin. 'While Jess still loved me, and I still loved her as much as ever, I was immune. Over this last Christmas, I found that my immunity was wearing thin. Every time Jess sneered at me, or made it quite clear that she wouldn't have me anywhere near her, I thought of Michelle's huge eyes and that gorgeous wealth of hair, and those legs . . . I'd already got a letter written asking her to come up to York and discuss terms for the show with me – which I expected her to interpret as an invitation. I carried it about in my pocket for days, not really knowing whether I wanted to post it or not. After that last row, I went out and posted it, and followed it up myself as soon as I could get away.'

'And Michelle came.' Fran's voice was flat.

'Don't look at me like that, Fran! I feel bad enough as it is. And I came tonight to confess to Jess, and tell her what a fool I'd been, and that she now had every reason to want to be released from me, and all the evidence necessary – if that is what she wants. I haven't any right to expect anything else. God knows what I shall do without her. I'm everything she's ever thought me, but not the cad you seem to think I am, Fran. I came to confess, and to see Monica, because I shall have to clear out altogether, obviously, especially if Eric is involved. I wanted to get it over.'

Fran was struggling against a desire to go and throw her arms round him to comfort him. William, looking calm still but grave, released himself and pulled up a chair close beside Greg. 'I don't think we've yet heard it all, have we?' he said. 'And if you didn't write that letter, who did? Not that I thought for a moment that it was you,' he added hastily.

'By the time Michelle arrived, I was already regretting everything,' Greg answered. 'In fact, when she began to make it quite clear what she'd come for, I pretended to be surprised, and told her a lot about Jess. But the evening was long, and we had a pleasant meal together and because I was in distress anyway I drank far too much and – well, maybe I am a cad after all to say so, but to tell the truth, she very nearly raped me. I left the hotel next morning, and I haven't seen her since, though of course I'm having to keep in touch because of the business link and the bargain I'd made with her about the show. Till I can hand over to Monica. Then I'll disappear.'

'So who wrote that letter?'

'Does it really matter? I'm washed up, anyway.'

'Yes, I think it does. Who was there in that hotel who could possibly recognize you?'

'Nobody that I know of. Of course I suppose it's always possible that the receptionist may be a nutter who thinks it her business to report if she suspects anything – I did give my own home address for my room, and Michelle's correct one for hers. If that is the receptionist's hobby, I guess she doesn't have a lot of spare time on her hands, though, nowadays.'

'She wouldn't have a job, after the first such letter, either,' William said drily. 'Besides, how would she know about the woman's husband's previous record as a killer? You're not using your head. There are two people besides yourself who could possibly have sent it – Michelle or her husband. Or much more likely, the two of them in cahoots. It was a set-up! If Jess had been silly enough to ring the husband, as the letter suggested, she would have got the lady herself, with all the details, and a threat of blackmail – to stop you from being murdered by a jealous husband, or of her blowing the gaff to Monica and losing you your job, or of exposure to all the fashion-model agencies that you regularly raped their models, or God knows what. You had told her enough about Jess to let her know that any threat of exposure of your behaviour in this area would have been silenced with money. My guess is that they've been playing that game every time an innocent like you appeared on the scene. As you said, this Michelle doesn't make a fortune modelling.

'So for a start, take yourself out of your own doghouse. You may be a bit of a soft-hearted fool, but you're neither a Casanova nor a cad. You wouldn't have been so easily gulled if you hadn't been such an innocent where harpies like her are concerned.

'How much Jess will believe, and how she will take it that you have in very fact slept with another woman, I can't answer. She's as proud as Lucifer and as volatile as quicksilver, besides being mad with anger and heartbroken with jealousy just at present. You can hardly expect her to act rationally – but I think you can be sure of one or two things. She'll never stop loving you, whatever she may say, so for God's sake don't do anything silly to give her any more ammunition against you. I think I can give you my word that she'll never tell anybody else, for her own sake. My guess is that when she's had time to recover from the shock, you'll find the door of Southside House on the latch. Always supposing that you want to open it and get in.'

'Haven't I told you so? Do you really mean you think she may forgive me?'

'She isn't a fool, Greg,' said Fran, urgently. 'You know that better than we do. Her trouble is that she's too much of a woman. Her emotions are stronger than her reason. She acts on instinct, and only thinks afterwards. It's a very feminine failing, after all. I agree with William. Give her time to get over the worst of it. Then come back and make a clean breast of it, and ask for another chance. I can't see you being either disappointed or cast out.'

He was very quiet. Then, reluctantly, he said, 'I know you both believe what you say. I want to believe you, but . . . her nastiness towards me started long before I'd ever seen Michelle, or even before I had to stay away overnight sometimes. Why does she hate Monica so much? How does anything you've said account for her attitude to my painting? It can't be because my masterpiece happened to be a portrait of Monica, if she is now heartbroken because of the letter about Michelle. And in any case, we nearly had a repeat performance because I started on another painting of the oldest Petrie girl. She's harbouring some other grudge against me that you don't know about and I can't tell you what I suspect it may be, for her sake, because it isn't anything anybody can help to put right. All I can promise is that I will do my best to make her forget it. May I ring you, from wherever I am, to keep in touch with what's happening? Till we know, one way or the other, whether or not she'll ever see me again?'

'Of course,' said William speaking for them both. Relief that they had got away with their deception of him was almost palpable in the air between them.

'So what are you going to do now, tonight, I mean?' asked Fran. 'Go back to Southside House?'

'Oh, Fran! I couldn't. I was hoping perhaps you'd allow me to stop here. Can't I?'

That was Fran's worst moment of panic. She saw that William was as stumped as she was, and didn't know what to say or do. She was struggling to invent a convincing lie about there being no beds made up when Greg solved their problem himself.

'It's already well past one o'clock, and I don't want to hang around in the morning, so I shall get off as early as I can. Couldn't I make the fire up and stay here in this chair till I can let myself out when it begins to get light? I don't suppose I shall sleep much, wherever I am.'

Fran gave him a soothing hot drink, some extra cushions and a blanket. She kissed him warmly and assured him again of their love and their help. William ostentatiously removed the tray of bottles, and Greg laughed, looking like himself for the first time. They said goodnight to him, and went to bed.

'Whew!' Fran exclaimed once the light had been put out. 'I don't want to go through that again. It's a good job Jess went to bed early, and has started sleeping soundly again. Why did you take the drinks away so blatantly? I've never seen you so inhospitable before, and never felt myself more so, considering that he knows perfectly well how many beds we always keep ready for just such unexpected visitors.'

'I was afraid he might help himself to another brandy to lull himself off to sleep, and still be there when Sophie drew the curtains in the morning,' he said. 'That would put the cat among the pigeons, for Jess to find him here. As it is, I think he's liable not to wake early of his own accord if he does get off to sleep and I shall have to be prepared to get up early and go to wake him, and see to it that he has some breakfast before he leaves.'

He set the alarm, and lay down again; but the strain of the evening had been too much for them. They tossed and turned, but couldn't get to sleep. They began to discuss things in whispers, until after about an hour William suggested that he should go and make them another hot chocolate drink to soothe them both to sleep.

Fearful of waking the armchair guest, he switched no lights on, but crept down the stairs on bare feet as silently as Cat might have done, helped by the glow of the tiny decorative lamp always left on in the hall to show that the house was occupied. He was back almost at once, without the promised drinks.

He climbed back into bed, and took Fran into his arms. She sat up, afraid, imagining what terrible revelation he had to disclose. 'What's . . .' she began, but his arms warned her to keep quiet.

'Ssh!' he whispered. 'I peeped into the sitting-room. He was asleep all right, in front of the fire, on the hearthrug – with Jess in his arms. I think – er, I can only guess from the tiny glimpse I got – that they had – er – been making it up!'

The flood of relief was too much for Fran. They pulled up the covers right over their heads, buried their faces in each other to stifle any sound, and laughed till at last they drowsed into sleep, too worn out to bother about what the morning might bring.

48

William's last waking thought had been that there was no need now to wake early, so he had reached out and switched off the alarm. Fran's had been that they had both forgotten that it was Saturday tomorrow, with no Sophie to worry about.

They were therefore surprised to be startled into wakefulness in the early dawn by the slamming of the front door and the noise of car doors and engine revvings on the gravel.

Fran clutched William and listened. 'That's Greg leaving,' she said. 'In a jolly nasty temper, too, from the sound of it! You must have been seeing things last night.'

'I certainly wasn't,' he said, rousing himself to think. 'They must have been quarrelling again this morning. Oh, hell! I'm sick to death of them! In fact, I think I've had just about enough of other people's difficulties to last me a lifetime. Now, I suppose, we have to hurry down and stop Jess from committing suicide. What line are we going to take with her? Do we tell her that he was here, and let her pretend surprise? Do I tell her brutally what I saw, and make her explain? What is it all to do with you and me? All I want is to be left alone with you for a day or two, but I never have a chance. I know one thing though: before I have to go back to work again, I'm going to hire a cottage somewhere in the most isolated spot I can find, and take you there for at least a month where nobody – *but nobody* – knows us.'

'The trouble is that we ask for it,' she said. 'We can't blame anybody but ourselves. It's like being at the middle of a spider's web. It seems to me that wherever the web is touched, we get the vibrations.'

'That's a good analogy,' he said, seriously, though preparing to get out of bed. 'I was thinking about it only the other day. Every thread of a web is connected to every other. It's constructed like that on purpose. The trouble is that we came back into it just at the wrong time. It isn't strong enough to withstand the pressures, now. I don't know why we try to save it, because in the end we shan't be able to. It won't exist for much longer, and nobody but the few old folks left will know or care what's happened to it. Good thing, too, probably, for those born since the war. Our trouble is that we weren't. So we rush out to try to help other people, as our grandparents would have done, and get ourselves entangled in the web for somebody else to come and finish off. Like now. There's so many strands of obligation wrapped round us just at present that we couldn't escape if we were really desperate to – and I am, well very nearly. I'm a fool.'

She laughed. 'A jaundiced one, too, this morning. Not at all my usual wise Solomon. Do you remember what Jim in *Huckleberry Finn* said about Solomon? That he couldn't have been as wise as all that, to burden himself with three hundred wives and about a thousand concubines. A wise man, Jim said, wouldn't have chosen to live in the middle of all that "blim-blamming". Where do you suppose Jess is, and what is she doing? Which one of us had better go and find out?'

'Both, I think. And we'd better be dressed, in case there is any emergency. You go and look in her bedroom while I go downstairs. Listen! She's getting her coat on – to clear off before we're up, I'll bet. I heard the door of the cupboard under the stairs creak, I'm sure. Stay up here at the window, and keep a watch on the front gate.'

Fran went to the window. The weather had cleared during the night, and the dawn in the east was wonderful to see. Important as it was to watch for Jess, she simply had to run to look at it out of the landing window. It was as glorious as she had expected, but her view of it was somewhat blurred by billows of smoke rising from a huge bonfire of garden rubbish on the edge of the spinney. Ned had been grumbling for weeks that he couldn't have a bonfire, and had, no doubt, taken advantage of the first fine morning with a bit of breeze to it, Saturday though it might be. Ned himself was not in evidence, so she surmised that he had dashed down to make and light the bonfire and gone back home to his breakfast. She was just turning away to go back to her look-out post when a cloud of thick smoke drifting away revealed Jess standing over the bonfire. She was wearing neither coat nor hat, but frenziedly pushing a large canvas right into the heart of the fire.

Fran screamed for William, who heard her from the kitchen and rushed back to her. He reached the landing just in time to see Jess give the picture a last vicious shove into the flame, and he let go of Fran to run to its rescue. At the same moment, Jess took flight towards the house, running like a hare towards the back door. Fran stood as if paralysed, knowing that the picture would soon be going up in flames. But before it could catch, the door of the garden shed opened, and Ned appeared brandishing a long-tined pitchfork. He neatly tucked the tines of it under the edge of one of the stretchers, and lifted the whole canvas bodily out of the flames. As far as Fran could see from that distance, no part of it had actually caught fire. Ned threw down his fork and brushed the picture over with his bare hands. Then he took it into the garden shed, and shut the door behind himself.

Fran's reaction was so strong that for a moment she wondered if her legs were going to support her, and clung to the window-sill. She was trembling, and crying with relief. Then Jess emerged from behind the yew hedge, still running, just as William made the same sort of speed down the same path in the opposite direction. Jess's shock at seeing him gave him a moment's advantage, and he grabbed her and held on to her while she fought him, beating and scratching him about the head and face. He made no attempt to stop her, simply holding her tightly until with a swift movement he slipped his arms down under her bottom and heaved her into a fireman's lift position over his shoulder. She gave in, and hung there limply as he turned back with her towards the house. Fran moved, and was in the kitchen by the time he set his burden down on a kitchen chair and, still panting with the effort, turned, locked the kitchen door and put the key into his pocket.

Fran's instinct was to rush to Jess to try to comfort her, but the look William gave her stopped her. 'Put the kettle on,' he said curtly, not taking his eyes off Jess. Fran obeyed.

'Now, Jess,' he said, his voice firm and crisp. 'If you are proposing to throw a fit of hysterics, I warn you that I am used to dealing with them. I shall unhesitatingly slap you hard in the face with a wet towel, as Greg should have done months ago. On the other hand, if you are now prepared to stop being Lady Macbeth and Othello combined, and tell us what this nonsensical drama is all about, I'm prepared to listen, and even to sympathize to some extent. But you will remember that you are in Fran's house and our home. If you want us to help you, start at the beginning and we'll do all we can; but this is your last chance. The other alternative is for me to send for a doctor, who will in turn send for a psychiatrist. A woman capable of destroying a man like Greg, and a great work of art, in nothing but a fit of selfish pique, is a danger to society and should be restrained. If necessary, I shall see to it that she is, even though she is my sister. *Look at me, Jess!'*

His raised voice cut through the air like a whiplash, and Jess cringed, but looked straight back at him for the first time.

'I mean every word I have said,' he went on in a slightly gentler tone. 'So which is it to be?'

In the long silence that followed, Fran made tea and set a strong cup before both the contestants. William was still holding Jess's eyes, and she was now staring belligerently back at him, her chin jutting and her cheeks flushed. Her eyes, Fran noticed, were still brilliant but less wild, and her clasped hands had begun to tremble. As Fran passed behind her to pick up her own cup of tea, she smoothed a wild lock of Jess's hair and, finding no rebuff, stooped to kiss the top of her head. Then she sat down at the table, too, and said gently, 'Drink your tea, Jess. Then start by telling us what happened last night. We did keep our promise, you know. We didn't let on by word or deed that you were upstairs in bed.'

Jess turned to look at Fran, breaking William's cruel visual dominance over her at last. 'I wasn't upstairs in bed,' she said. 'I was hanging over the banisters just outside the door – which you had very conveniently left open. I heard every word.'

'Then you know as much as we can tell you,' William said, taking control again, but in a far less domineering fashion. 'Are we allowed to ask what you made of our conversation with Greg? And what your reaction was to what he told us?'

'What do you expect? I learned that my husband has been sleeping with another woman. Just as I suspected.'

'Careful, Jess,' William warned. '"Been sleeping" is not what he confessed to. It happened once, and once only – under very strange circumstances. I admit that you have a right to be hurt, but surely it isn't beyond forgiveness? And if you heard every word, as you claim, you will also have heard the truth, that you drove him to it. You know what he suspects – that you no longer love him. But he still loves you. Is it worth breaking such a marriage for? One single night's slip when he was probably set up in any case, and drunk into the bargain? The real trouble is your insane jealousy.'

'But I did forgive him. Last night. I came down and told him so.' Her head came up, proud and unashamed. 'If you must know, we made love on your hearthrug. That shows you how much I forgave him that night with Michelle whatever-her-name-is.'

Fran could hold her tongue no longer. 'So what on earth went wrong this morning? Why did he go? Where has he gone? And why did you burn his picture?'

Jess clamped her lips together, as if to say she had told them all she intended to; but William forced her to look back at him.

'Because it was a portrait of Monica? That's the point at which your possessive jealousy of him got the better of you and turned into this kind of madness. You know perfectly well that his interest in Monica has never been more than that of a friend who happens also to be a fellow artist. Now, he's more like an extra grandfather to her children.'

Fran noticed her wince on the word, but William didn't appear to see the significance, and charged on. 'However you try, you can't make him the guilty party with regard to Monica, either.'

Jess suddenly let out a wail of utter despair, awful to hear after her show of defiance, and frightening to behold. Fran remembered Sophie, sitting in the very same chair but in a very different state of *extremis*, only such a short time ago.

William looked at Fran in puzzlement. What had he said, to cause Jess to change like that?

Fran got up and ran to put her arms round Jess. 'So that's what it is!' she said. 'It isn't other women at all – it's their children you're so jealous of. And against Greg because you never had the chance to stop working to have any? Or because he didn't want any? Oh, my dear Jess! None of us has had enough sense to think of that. And now it's too late, you just can't forgive him for it.'

'Wrong again. What it's too late for is for him to forgive me. I can't ask him to. That's why he must go, and find somebody who can still give him the children I've deprived him of! You see, William's right. However hard I try, I can't make him the guilty one. But he doesn't know, and I can't bring myself to tell him. All he knows is that it isn't his fault we didn't have any. I didn't know he was sure of that, till this morning. He'd never told me before that he'd made quite sure it wasn't him who couldn't have any. He said that if it had been him at fault, he would have told me, and suggested that either he set me free, or that we applied for an adoption. But it wasn't him, so he kept quiet. Not that that made much difference, because in the conditions we were living in at the time, no adoption society would have looked at us.

'I raged at him this morning for not telling me before. And I told him to go and find somebody else, because although it's too late for me, it isn't for him. It's hardly ever too late for men! I told him I never wanted to see him again, once too often. He went.

'And I love him so! That's why I daren't tell him the truth. He could never have forgiven me. I had to make him think I was upset because he hadn't told me the truth.'

William had stretched his hand right across the table to her, and she clasped it in both her own, put her head down on it, and moaned. Fran watched in an agony of sympathy, not knowing which of them to comfort. It was all too close to home for William himself, apart from his sorrow for Jess. Fran knew very well that the tears now trickling down William's cheeks unchecked were mostly for Jess and Greg, but partly also for himself and her, for the children their love for each other might have produced if they had found each other in time. That was Fate – and tragedy. She was consumed by the pity and the terror of it for them all. He looked up, and read her face, and put out his other hand to her – and smiled.

She drew a deep breath, and willed herself not to shed tears. Instead, she sat down between them and, taking Jess's hand as soon as William let go to find his handkerchief, she said, 'So tell us what the real truth is, Jess, and let us judge what Greg might do.'

William, startled, gave her hand an encouraging squeeze. He heard Eric's voice in his head, saying that Jess had a sore place somewhere that just wouldn't heal and that maybe she needed drastic surgery. They had found the sore place: maybe Fran was about to apply the knife. Perhaps Jess had to tell somebody the secret she had kept so long, to let out the bitter acid of guilt that was eating away her common sense. Why it was that such a loving and passionate coupling had never produced children.

Jess took her time, mopping herself up and finishing her now cold tea; but both her listeners were aware of a change in her. She was marshalling her facts, and approaching her agonizing task with cool, calm courage. Just as the Jess of pre-Swithinford days would have approached any serious crisis.

'We met early on in the war. It was love at first sight, quite literally, and we didn't fool about wasting time when we had only four days of leave left. We got married on the next 72-hour leave we could make coincide, and had a three-day honeymoon. We didn't bother with any of the contraceptive devices that were available to us then. That's half the trouble still – how can you think of such things when you love and want each other as much as we've always done?

'When he'd gone back, I found that I was pregnant. I wasn't in Monica's lucky position. I had to think hard and act for the best, as I saw it.

'I was in the Wrens. When it was known, I should be discharged. Greg was in France with the BEF, and at any minute there might be a telegram. Mum had died, and Dad had been killed. There was only William – and he was flying Spitfires. One wouldn't have offered very good odds on his chances of surviving even to the next day. There was nobody.

'I wanted Greg's child as I had never wanted anything before, but I couldn't risk it. I told myself that we *would* both survive, we'd simply got to, and that there would be plenty of time for as many babies as we liked once the war was over. So I never told Greg. I just went to a back street abortionist instead.'

Fran could hardly bear to listen. She had had two babies. Still had them, in fact. The thought that she might have deliberately destroyed either of them made her feel physically sick, although in Jess's plight, she might easily have taken the same way out. But supposing the baby had been William's child . . . ? She shivered. What's done may be past recall, but that isn't the end. Some things can never be past regret.

Jess was talking again. 'We did both survive, by a miracle, I suppose, and I soon found a job. It wasn't nearly so easy for an unemployed artist or an unknown poet, and musicians seemed to be ten a penny. But Grandfather died, and the legacy I had was like a promise from heaven. We were still alive and young and in love and we didn't care a damn about the future. Something was bound to turn up for us. We went through the capital, footloose and free – as Sophie would say, "like a hot knife through butter" – till I had to become the breadwinner again. We talked about the children we wanted, but it didn't seem the right time till we had a little more security to offer them. So I went to a clinic and got fixed up. No use relying on Greg for that. Financially, things were going from bad to worse for us. Greg simply couldn't get work, and began to lose heart, and stopped trying. Then once when we were discussing it, he confessed that he thought he lacked motivation – that perhaps if we risked it and had a baby, it might push him into making a fresh start and more effort. So we stopped taking any precautions at all, but nothing happened. Not for want of trying, either.

'Well, I had all the proof needed to show that I wasn't the infertile one, but I couldn't bring myself to tell Greg that I knew it had to be him. Or how. He began to suggest, ever so gently and kindly, that perhaps I ought to consult a gynaecologist to find out why I couldn't conceive. To please him, I did.

'Of course, the gynaecologist knew at once what had happened. It was all too common in wartime. He told me that though I might conceive, indeed, had probably done so many times, there was no chance that I could ever carry the child. The abortionist had made such a mess of me anyway that if by a miracle I did carry it long enough for it to be born at all, it might not be normal, and the chances of trouble for me were more than should be risked at my age. I was getting on for forty by then.

'I went home nearly mad with despair, but nothing could induce me to tell Greg the awful truth. I relied on the half-truth that's so hard to deny. The consultant *had* said there was no reason why I shouldn't conceive – and that's what I told Greg. We simply had to go on trying and hoping. What I didn't know, until that awful time when Monica announced her pregnancy and I couldn't bear it, was what I had been doing to him all those years. We had such an awful row when we got home that night. I accused him of being the father of Monica's baby – to hurt him, I suppose, as much as I was being hurt.

'He swore he wasn't, of course, and asked me why I thought he could give her babies when he couldn't give me one? And all I did was to get nastier and nastier to him. When the twins were born – not identical – I taunted him about having to have a bit of help from Roland to make a success of it. I envied any woman with children so much, and there was Monica with two under my nose all the time, and my man showing how much he wished they were his. I know he couldn't help it. Babies are beautiful things. But I began to hate him for it. He always went to see her, and them, as soon as he got home, and I got so that I didn't want him to come. I can see now that I was really only punishing myself, as somebody has since told me, though I didn't believe him.

'Now I know that after I had been to the consultant, Greg went, too, to make sure it wasn't his fault. He was about as fertile as any man could be – but he hadn't told me because he didn't want me to know that it had to be my fault. He just took the blame, because he loved me so much. That hurt me most of all. I felt I hated him for showing me up to be what I am. To myself if to nobody else.'

'But there wasn't any blame,' William said. 'It was nobody's fault. Just Fate.'

Jess nodded. 'Yes, that's what made me feel so awful this morning. He had taken the "blame", and I'd let him. Not only had he not got what he wanted – I suppose what every man really wants – but he had put up with all my taunts of him as well, just because he loved me so much.'

'So you told him the real truth, this morning, and he couldn't take it, I suppose,' William said.

Jess shook her head. 'No – I still couldn't let him know how I had deceived him. When we made love last night, he begged and pleaded for forgiveness. I knew it was I who should be asking him to forgive me. I did tell him how much I still loved him, honestly I did. I wanted us to be like we used to be, but I knew we couldn't until I had told him the truth.

'I was screwing up my courage to tell him and risk everything, when he began to talk about that picture. He said he had always wanted to paint a madonna and child, but he had wanted the mother to be me. The last twist of the knife.'

She went quiet, white and still, almost as if she had suddenly died.

'And?' prompted William.

'I lost control of myself again. I told him that if he wanted to come back to me, he had to destroy that picture and never attempt another like it. He just picked up his coat, and slammed himself out. For ever, I expect, now. He might have forgiven me everything else, but he'll never forgive me for burning that picture. He'd put his whole heart into it. And all his love for me, even though it was Monica's face he'd painted. And I burnt it.'

William caught her as she began to sway, and carried her to bed.

She came round almost immediately, to find Fran bathing her face.

'Where's William?' she asked, a glance showing her where she was, and a moment's reflection reminding her why.

'Phoning,' answered Fran. Jess sat up, pushing Fran's hand and the cold sponge away, and reaching for the towel that lay on the bed.

'Not for a doctor, I hope,' Jess said, in a perfectly normal, Jess-like voice. 'Don't drown me, Fran! If William isn't panicking for a doctor, why has he left you to act like an old hen trying to persuade a duckling she's hatched to come out of the pond? I'd much rather have a cup of tea, and I don't want a doctor. I'm all right. At least, I shall be if I don't die of pneumonia. You never do things by halves, do you, Fran?'

'Neither do you. I'll make you some tea as soon as ever William gets here to look after you.'

'I don't need looking after. I'm OK.'

Fran gave her the sponge and the bowl. 'I suppose you wouldn't like to bathe my face while I faint, would you? It's hardly been "Silent night, peaceful night", for us, or a case of joy coming in the morning. We sit up with Greg half the night, find a madwoman on our hands in the morning, sit through a Greek tragedy, after which you pass out and scare us both out of our wits! Then you open your eyes looking as if you have just had a shot of adrenaline, while I'm likely to keel over with weariness and worry. Are you sure you're all right? This isn't just another mad reaction?

'You're a pest, Jess,' she added. 'A beautiful, engaging, horrible, bitchy chameleon. You haven't really changed a bit.'

Jess looked round for somewhere to set down the bowl of cold water. Fran took it from her, and she put up her arms round Fran's neck.

'Neither, thank goodness, have you – or where should I be now? I'm truly sorry, Fran. For everything. But you're wrong that I haven't changed. Chameleons do change. I've changed this morning.'

She held her head on one side, listening. 'Fran, if William isn't getting a doctor, who is he phoning?'

'Monica. We thought the chances were that Greg would go straight to her to tell her that she couldn't rely on him any longer, and hoped we might just be in time to catch him before he left, and get him back here. To deal with his responsibilities, if nothing else. We really were scared, you know. Here's William, now.'

He crept in, expecting to find another harrowing situation. His surprise at seeing the cousins both sitting on the side of the bed with their arms round each other reduced him almost to doubting his own sanity.

'Well?' said Fran, rather sharply. She was reaching the end of her resources.

'Too late. He'd been there, but had left again twenty minutes or more before I rang. He wouldn't say where he was going, or when he would be back, if ever. He had already told them the outline of what had happened. I promised to let them know any developments. Monica's very miffed. I don't wonder. She has a lot of business tied up in his hands. He can't just walk out on her and disappear like that. He won't, anyway. He's hurt and he's furious but he's still Greg. One night with a modern Delilah is more likely to make him see sense than to blind him and make him pull the temple down on us all. Even on you, Jess. People don't change overnight, like that.'

'Some do,' said Jess. 'When there's a good enough reason. When I came round just now, I was in my right mind. Too late, I know. I can't expect him ever to forgive me for burning his picture. But for that, I'm sure he would have understood what was the matter with me – what I told you. There's no excuse for me destroying him heart *and* soul. He might have come back to me to have his heart mended, but his soul was in that picture. However much he's suffering, I shall suffer with him. But at least I'm sane again.'

In spite of herself, her voice broke on a sob. 'You don't understand, do you? Shall I tell you? When I came out of that faint, I felt different. Like coming round from an anaesthetic, and knowing that an operation you've been dreading is over. I felt light, as if I might levitate, and float off the bed. It was a lovely feeling, and I haven't quite lost it yet, although I can remember everything else as well now. I do know why I felt like that, though. What I have been dreading for twenty years has happened. I've got rid of something – that awful secret I'd had to carry for so many years, getting heavier and heavier all the time. Starting to turn malignant, like a cancer. Now it's out. I'd had to learn to live with it, to bear it and the pain of it. That's what changed me so much. Now that I can start to live without it, I shall at least be more like my real self, and more able to cope with it. Except that I shan't have much left to live for, without Greg. He still doesn't know what was the matter with me, and if he never knows now the knowledge can't hurt him, though the one thing I now want more than anything else in the world is to be able to tell him everything. He can't think any worse of me than he does. If I hadn't been such a fool this morning, I think everything would have been all right again.

'What's happened has probably saved me – but not *us*. That's bloody Fate again. I told you I heard every word last night. You told him where his picture was – otherwise I should have had no idea where to find it.'

William sat down on the other side of her. 'If you'll promise to stop crying, and pull yourself together, I think I can prove that Fate was on your side. It will take me a few minutes, but you'll lose all my sympathy if I come back and find you raving again. Will you give me your word?'

She nodded, and reached for Fran's hand. They sat in silence, neither daring to speak, until they heard William's footsteps on the stairs again.

He came in sideways, holding the canvas towards him, and when he was able to, turned it towards her. The worst damage it had suffered was a light burn mark on the back, and black smoke-smudges on the front.

'God was watching,' Fran said, 'only we usually call him Ned. He rescued it.' Jess's face had lit up with hope so blatant that it was agony for the other two to watch.

'It's an omen,' she said. 'Leave it with me. I'll be down in half an hour, and then, if you'll let me, I want to go home.'

They didn't argue. In fact, both of them could hardly have wished for anything more than to have their home to themselves. Jess explained that all she wanted was to get herself back to normality as fast as possible. She would ring Eric and tell him that she had returned and would be back to work in a week's time, unless he needed her urgently before then. She told William and Fran that her need now was to restore Southside House into a real home again, to fill it from room to room and crevice to crevice with herself and Greg, even if he never set foot in it again.

'But he will,' she said. 'He doesn't know I tried to burn his picture. He thinks you have still got it safe. One day, he'll come back to find it, and you'll have to tell him where it is. Hanging in his home, where it should be.

'William, would an art restorer be able to get those smoke marks off?'

'I wouldn't risk the work of any other hand on it but Greg's if I were you,' William said. 'He'll be able to deal with them himself better than anybody else could.'

'I'm not so sure about that,' said Fran. 'Will you let me try an experiment? I'm just going to try Kezia's tip with new bread to clean smoke marks off.'

In ten minutes, only the burn mark on the back was left as witness to the morning's drama.

'It's a good omen,' William said. 'I'll get it framed.'

Jess agreed, and repeated that she wanted to go home. Fran, ever practical, went to pack her some provisions. Almost standing on her head in the chest freezer, she allowed herself a bit of private amusement. Whatever the crisis, it seemed to her that it couldn't be got over without food. Even the holiest of sacraments of the Christian church couldn't get along without bread and wine, which was food, whatever sort of symbolism you might attach to it.

49

Sunday. Blessed Sunday. No need to get up a minute sooner than they wanted to, and nobody but themselves to please. While William went down to make the tea, Fran lay with Cat stretched out beside her with her head in the crook of Fran's elbow, and listened to the sound of the calling-bell for the eight o'clock communion service at the church.

She tickled Cat under her chin, and made her open her startling blue eyes.

'Cat,' she said, 'aren't there times when you're glad you're only a spoilt animal with no obligations to anybody or anything? Because if you aren't, you jolly well ought to be!'

Cat yawned, and closed her mouth again, pursing her lips so that the whiskery area round it stood out and the fine whiskers for a moment pointed forward. Then she wriggled her head sideways to be able to look up at Fran, opened her mouth again to emit the sound Fran loved best, neither a mew nor a purr, but a satisfied comment composed of both. When she shut her mouth again this time, she left the very tip of her pink tongue showing.

'You are a shameless hussy!' Fran said, accepting the invitation to rub the furry belly Cat offered by turning herself on to her back and dangling two helpless-looking little seal-tipped forepaws on to her own chest. 'If you weren't a true-bred Siamese, I should suspect you of being a re-incarnation of some practised French courtesan of the eighteenth century. You know all the tricks. A hanger-on, relying on your own beauty to get you everything your heart desires, including our complete subjection to your wiles. You're a sybarite – and I adore you. You have no obligations to anybody, have you? Just think of poor old George Bridgefoot with his aching hip this morning, feeling absolutely obliged to go to ring that bell. And that miserable-looking curate from Swithinford, having to go through the performance twice. But he does his duty. He fulfils his obligations – to people like Sophie and Thirzah and Daniel and the rest, who are all trudging through this cold morning to a colder church because of their obligations to custom. And to 'Im Above, of course. And Beth will be there, down on her knees giving thanks for the bump on her tummy – because she is a parson's daughter and feels obliged to set a good example. I hope she remembers her obligation to Elyot for it, as well! Are you listening to me? I could go on a long time, yet. Think about Bob Bellamy – whatever he'd rather be doing on a cold morning like this, he's obliged to be out of bed by six to start looking after his animals – he can't have Charlie's horse and a yard full of bullocks in bed with him, as I feel obliged to have you. Or a dog the size of Bonzo. And I'd like to bet Jane feels obliged to be up and waiting with his breakfast already cooked when he comes in. Life, Cat, is full of obligations for everybody except such pampered creatures as you. Obligations are the coin in which we humans pay for the pleasures of having relatives and friends. No – William's obligations will not run to going back downstairs again with you. You will find your plates already replenished if you deign to go and look by yourself. Move over.'

She gave Cat a shove, and sat up to take her cup of tea from William.

'I've rung Jess,' he said. 'She's fine. She's quite sure that she can cope, now. I think she means it.' He lay down again, and Cat strolled on to his chest.

'No you don't,' said Fran, pushing her off the bed. 'That's my place, and the one thing I am not obliged to do is to give it up to you.'

'Where,' she said, having settled her head on his shoulder, 'do you suppose Greg is? Ought we not to try and find him?'

'He's a man who can take care of himself if he has to, and certainly no coward. He has been putting up with a lot of flak from Jess just because of the soft side of him. But I'm afraid she may have roused the tough man in him, now, though. He left us mad with temper, and from what she told me, Monica couldn't have helped him a lot. What would you expect him to do?'

'Go and punch somebody's head.' Fran said. 'Most men would want to.'

'Yes. Those two have been taking each other far too much for granted for too long. This has shaken both of them up.

'My real guess is that she wrote that letter. It actually suggested that Jess should ring her husband. Why? To let him know what he already knows, that she's bored by her life with him, and after a more interesting and better-off man.'

'But you told an entirely different story yesterday,' protested Fran indignantly. 'You said it was a set-up by both of them, a game that they played regularly.'

'Sweetheart, do we want a completely broken man on our conscience and a broken-hearted woman on our doorstep for the rest of our lives? I certainly don't! Greg was already despising himself so much that all the perfumes of Arabia wouldn't have sweetened the foul smell of his unfaithfulness to Jess. He couldn't have faced life at all, after making love to Jess again and remembering all she meant to him. I couldn't let him go despising himself to that extent – he would have done something tragically silly! He's that sort of man. I had to think up something that would put the blame on somebody other than him. I don't know which I feel the most sorry for. But I'm not sorry that it's all blown up and burst at last. To tell the truth, I've had just about enough of the Taliaferros. Kiss me . . . I must get up and get to work before he comes back and Jess calls on me to avenge her honour with pistols at dawn on the croquet lawn, either against her adoring husband or the other woman's murderous one.'

Fran pulled herself away and looked down on him. She was reminded of the Cheshire Cat as his spate of words wiped out his irritation bit by bit until only his face with a rueful smile on it was left showing.

'Oh, how romantic,' she said. 'A duel! Back we go to the eighteenth century again. May the best man win,' she said. 'I know who I should put my money on.

> 'Thrice armed is he who knows his quarrel just.
> But four times he who gets his blow in fust.'

At bedtime William announced his intention of getting off very early with the picture, and doing a few other oddments in Cambridge while he was there. Would Fran like to go with him?

She declined. She said she ought to be there when Sophie came, to explain Jess's sudden return home without letting on about Greg's visit. There was also the question of what they should tell Ned, who had not been taken into their confidence about Jess staying there at all. She had been very careful to keep out of his way and his sight. But what was he to make of Saturday morning's little episode? He would notice as soon as he went into the shed that the picture he had rescued had disappeared.

'Least said, soonest mended, I think,' said Fran. 'If there is one person in this place who knows how to mind his own business – even better than Sophie does – it's Ned.'

That decided, William took the picture, and went.

Sophie arrived so full of gossip herself that Fran had to make a decided effort to get in first with her information that Jess had felt so much better about everything yesterday that she had made up her mind to go home. She had asked that they still kept it dark that she had been there at all. Fran would not lie to Sophie, who understood and asked no questions. She pursed her mouth disapprovingly, and said, 'That's only like she all'us has been. Up and down like a see-saw. What upset 'er in the first place? I 'ope it don't mean as she's fell out with 'er 'usband. She's been very funny with 'im, often, in front of other folk as well as me. But 'e's so goodnatured with 'er, I'm often thought she didn't know 'ow lucky she was. But then, all marriages ain't made in 'eaven, like you and 'im, and some never get made at all, like me and Jelly. And there's some as never ought to ha' been made.'

'Jess and Greg love each other,' Fran said, on sure ground with that. 'So if it was because they'd had a tiff, I'm sure it will soon be put right.'

'Not like some,' said Sophie darkly.

'Why don't you tell me?' asked Fran. 'Instead of throwing out hints. Who's been gossiping, and what have you heard?'

She said it very lightly, as if asking Sophie to share a joke with her. Sophie hesitated. She loved telling tales to as good a listener as Fran was, but was loth to repeat things she could not vouch for in every respect. As Fran had hoped, Sophie sat down, and began at the beginning, 'going round the sun to meet the moon', as she would herself have said of any other long-winded tale-teller.

'There were a good few again at church yist'day morning,' she said. 'Olive 'Opkins was there. She's a funny sort o' woman, Olive is. Like a pea in a porridge – neither good nor 'arm, as the saying goes. She were just the same when she were a child, never could get things right. And I know, seeing 'ow she's just my age and I went right through Miss's school side by side with 'er. She's all'us been inoffensy, except for one thing. She never 'as been able to get things straight enough in 'er own 'ead for anybody else to speak after 'er. Olive loves to gossip, but never gets anything she 'ears right. Beryl Bean loves to talk about other folks and don't know the truth from her own lies. Olive never means no 'arm, but whatever she 'eard she told Beryl, and then it got blowed up like a poor old cow with the bloat, besides being twisted into lies like liquorice. I don't *know* as Beryl means 'arm, either, but she causes enough. Anyway, Olive's lost her job with Beryl Bean, but what I'm telling you come to me through Olive, so believe it or not as you like.'

She dropped her voice. 'It's to do with the Giffords. Seems there's real trouble atween Vic and Marge. That's why she spends so much time up at Temperance. And becos' of it, Brian won't have no more to do with neither Vic nor Bailey and that's sp'iled some o' Bailey's big plans so as 'e's heving to draw 'is 'orns in a bit. He's set back till 'e can get 'is 'ands on another bit o' land big enough to develop like Lane's End.

'So Beryl's lost 'er lodger and Ken's got to go out odd-jobbing again so Beryl's 'aving to cut her coat accordin' to 'er cloth and all. And the fust thing she does is to sack Olive 'Opkins.

'"Well," I says, "from what I can see you won't 'ave no trouble getting another. Everybody's calling out for folks to work in their 'ouses, since that Jane 'Adley as were glad to take all the work she could get turned out to be a lady and married him at Castle Hill. She's likely one as wants 'elp 'erself, now."

'Then Olive sort of turned 'er nose up, and said that if she did 'ave to lower 'erself to go back to doing 'ousework, *she*'d be partickerlar who it was she worked for. "Are you 'itting at me?" I says, but she coloured up like a beetroot and I knowed as she were only repeating what Beryl 'ad said. But she could see it 'ad ruffled my feathers, so she clumb down and said it were too far to go up to Castle 'Ill even if she were wanted. She said she didn't intend to be nobody's skivvy. "It's them who are never 'ad nothink theirselves as treat you like muck, though," she says. "Like that Mis' Bailey." Then she said that she'd been up to Temperance Farm to see if Rosemary needed a daily 'elp. But she never got nothing for 'er pains, 'cos when she got there Marge were there, and so was George and Molly, and Brian was a-shouting as he was going to kill somebody when young Charles opened the door to 'er and told 'er to go away, 'cos it wasn't convenient for anybody to see 'er just then.

'Then this morning, Dan'el 'ad 'eard it all by the time 'e come in to 'is breakfast. It's all over the place as Marge 'as left 'er 'usband and Brian 'as tried to kill Vic Gifford. Bailey's sacked that man as took Daffy's place, and Pansy Gifford's going to live with Bailey's son in the show-'ouse as 'e's 'ad till now. The man's going to live with Mis' Rushlake in the School'ouse. Whatever Miss would ha' said I daren't think, though she says as her and him was married while they was away at Christmas. But fancy Marge Bridgefoot leaving 'er 'usband – though Olive did say as she wasn't quite sure whether it weren't Brian as 'ad left Rosemary. Tha's 'ow she is. You can't speak after 'er.

'Quite likely there ain't a grain o' wheat in 'er whull bushel o' chaff. Shall I do out that room as Jess 'as 'ad, or do you reckon she's likely to be coming back?'

'I haven't a clue,' said Fran. 'Perhaps we ought to ask Olive 'Opkins.'

When Sophie had left her, Fran was torn between amusement and anxiety about the Bridgefoot family. Had she but known it, she had good cause for the latter.

After Vic's first rantings and ravings, excuses and maudlin pleadings, to all of which Marjorie had turned a deaf ear and a stony heart, had come a period of sulks that she found hardest of all to ignore. She refused to do anything for him but see that there was food in the house and clean clothes when he needed them. Apart from that, she went her own way.

She had her own car, and after she had finished what she thought of as housekeeping, rather than wifely duties, she did as she liked, which often meant spending the day at Temperance, or going wherever her fancy took her. For the first time in her life, she spent lavishly on whatever she fancied, drawing on their joint account at the bank. She went round looking in antique shops, treating herself to bits and pieces of beautiful old china as near as she could find to those that had been victims of Vic's temper over all the years of her marriage. These she usually left wrapped, and deposited at Temperance 'till Vic should come to his senses'. Her one twinge of conscience was towards Pansy, who was aware of the atmosphere in the house and didn't like it at all, mostly because it affected her own pleasure.

She had always played up to her father, being the one who could get anything out of him, though she had known all the time that it was their mother they depended on. Pansy was her father's daughter, wilful and headstrong, lively and bold in company, and much more sexually precocious than her sister Poppy. She had been well aware when exploring the mysteries of her first adolescent love affair with the son of a neighbouring farmer that her father was satisfied with her choice. She had had no intention whatsoever of accepting him as a husband – she had already seen much bigger game in the distance.

But it hadn't stopped her from sleeping with him when the chance arose. It had been Poppy who had carried her secret, and borne the burden of her sister's guilt. Then Robert had died of leukaemia, and within the family it had been a secret no longer. Then, to her surprise, it had been her father who had raised the roof, and done everything in his power to prevent the thing he dreaded most of all, which was that the neighbours should know what his Pansy had been up to. Sexual misdemeanour was still the sin of all sins as far as neighbours were concerned. Marjorie, remembering the reason she had ever married Vic in the first place, was shocked and distressed, but stood firmly behind her daughter, though she acquiesced in Pansy's exile till the chance of any scandal had passed.

She had come back a very different girl. There was one way she could get almost anything she wanted, and since Robert was dead, what did it matter? Darren Bailey was at hand, and more than willing.

She found to her amazement that her father was no longer against her. He had observed that in matters of that kind, there was now a different set of values abroad. If she could get away with that sort of behaviour, so could he. Far from throwing a fit at the gossip she was creating by her part in the goings-on of the new-rich, modern, rather vulgar set, he encouraged her, and made it plain that he would like to be part of it, too. Rather amused, she had introduced him, and he had been invited to the party. The Gifford family had been broken cleanly into two.

Pansy was no fool, and knew that financially and socially within the village, her mother held all the cards. Uncle Brian was disengaging himself. Charles's girl had turned out to be the winner he had always wanted for his son; the Bridgefoot family was closing up again, with only her father and herself left outside on the fringe.

She felt guilty. It was she who had got him into this mess, but she could not get him out again. She felt bound to stick to him. She sensed that the Baileys were turning cold towards him, and felt terribly sorry for him. She cared no more for Darren Bailey than she would have done for any other healthy young man willing to give her a good time. He had not mentioned marriage, but he had pleaded for cohabitation on a more or less permanent basis.

She was not able to sum up her mother's feelings about that as easily as she could those of her cruder and simpler father, but she could hardly believe that her mother, or her grandparents, would allow the present discord at home to go on much longer, or that it would end in any kind of separation; but if it did, her father would come off decidedly the worse in every way, especially with regard to money – and that was the key to membership of his new 'club'. She and she only could make him secure there, by becoming, to all intents and purposes, Darren's wife and a member of the Bailey family. She announced her intention of leaving home and moving in with Darren Bailey. She was not to know that by doing so she was bringing to a head much more than the change in her own immediate future.

Vic had been outraged by Marjorie withdrawing her person from him, because in his primitive book a husband had inalienable rights over his wife's body which nothing but physical distance could deny him. That she had withdrawn from any contact with him had hurt his pride unbearably, but there were two consolations. One was that it was such a private matter that nobody was ever likely to find out and be able to scorn him for it. The other was that he was not going without sex. The woman who had been so willing at the party was equally available at any time, anywhere – or, at least, had been until the last weekend, when she had suddenly thrown him over for a newcomer.

After nearly a week, he was desperate. Hadn't he got a wife, whose duty it was to satisfy his sexual demands? He would show her that locking her bedroom door against him was no good. He watched his opportunity on Saturday afternoon. She was about to do the washing-up, and went to fetch his cup from the arm of his chair. He caught her round the waist, and pulled her down on to his knee.

She was almost petrified with horror as she realized his intention, caught off her guard against him, and knowing herself to be no match at all for his six-foot odd of burly physical strength. She fought him tooth and nail, scratching and clawing his face and pulling his hair, biting his arms and kicking with all her strength, though his grip on her prevented her from reaching the right place.

Her denial of him had turned him into a frenzied animal with swollen, blood-suffused face and reddened eyes like those of an elephant in must. He tore off her clothes, pushed her up the stairs in front of him, tried to break down her locked door with his foot, but in the end raped her on the bed he had been occupying since the night of the party. She fought him till she had no more strength, and was forced to submit to his rage, his lust and his weight. Then it was over, and she began to sob.

When her strength even to cry gave out, she began to feel a terrible nausea. Thankfully, she saw that he had fallen asleep. She was filled with such murderous hatred that she longed to fetch the poker and bash his head in, but her strength had gone, and the nausea was overcoming all else. She vomited before she got to the bathroom, and that was the last straw. She had never felt so soiled in her life before, not even when as her father's land-girl in the war she had spent a whole day mucking out the pigs. The only thing she could think of was to get herself clean again. She had to wash him and everything he stood for from her person and her life. The desire to get into a bath of water as hot as she could bear it and scrub herself all over with a stiff brush was imperative. Every square inch of her that his flesh had ever come into contact with had to be sanitized. She ran bath after bath till the hot water tank was empty, washing her hair and scrubbing herself all over till she looked like a boiled lobster. She poured bathsalts and toilet-water into the bath, empty-ing bottles with abandon lest any scent of him should ever remain on her. Then she towelled herself till she was almost raw, and covered all her self-inflicted abrasions with scented body lotion. The horror at last began to wear off, and having locked the door, she lay supine till reason returned to her.

She had to get away before he roused, or the whole performance would be repeated. She forced herself to get dressed quickly, packed her overnight things and crept out of her bedroom, locking the door after herself and going down the stairs in her stockinged feet. She stood for a moment in the middle of 'her' kitchen, thinking that she would never set foot in it again. Then desire to retaliate in some way hit her, and she began to think again. The truth was like a stream of cooling water after the hell of her ordeal.

She was, and would always be, a Bridgefoot. That house and the land were only Gifford's by courtesy of her father. She was a Gifford only in name. She would claim what she considered to be her rights as ruthlessly as Vic had taken what he considered to be his, but she could make no plans at this moment. All she wanted was to get away before Vic roused and found her gone. She headed for her brother at Temperance, too distressed yet to face her father and mother at the Old Glebe.

Only Brian and Rosemary were there when she arrived, and she poured out her story in a few graphic sentences. Rosemary sat beside her, holding her hand. Brian sat white and tense at the table, his fists clenching and unclenching, but otherwise showing little of his feelings. Then he stood up.

'Where's Charles?' he asked of Rosemary.

'Helping with the yard work,' she said. 'It's his Saturday to help.'

Brian went to the door and yelled at the top of his voice for his son. When the boy came, Brian sent him to fetch his grandparents, telling them that they must come at once.

'Tell them Aunt Marge has been assaulted by Vic, and is here. We have a lot of serious decisions to make, and need them both. If I could get my hands on him, I'd kill him!' He went inside and banged the door, leaving Charles on the step facing a startled-looking Olive Hopkins. He took it upon himself to explain to her that she had better come back another time.

The warmth of being in the midst of her family had already put a lot of heart back into Marge, as had Brian's swift action. By the time her parents came in, she was able to greet them calmly, and let Brian relate what had happened. Rosemary produced cups of hot, strong tea.

George took a sip, and looked round the table at which they were all sitting. 'We're all here,' he said. 'All of us that matters, that is. Now, my gel, I know you went back to him after New Year's Eve because I advised you to. I was doing what I thought was best – giving him enough rope to hang himself properly. It looks as if he's done it. I've been expecting something to blow up ever since, as Mother knows, though I didn't expect anything half so bad for you as this.'

Molly nodded, and spoke directly to Marge. 'I've always suspected what sort of a man he was,' she said. 'Men like him ought to be castrated. I should like to get at him myself with a rusty saw! But look here, my pet, I dare say that in the last twenty odd years there's been many a time before when you wished he had been. You've got to forget what happened today. Tell yourself it was only one more time, and the last ever. Then put it out of your mind.'

'I fought him,' Marge said, her mother's understanding and frank speaking putting yet more heart into her. 'I scratched him and bit him and pulled his hair, but he was too strong for me.'

'You should have throwed pepper in his eyes. That would have stopped him.'

In spite of herself, a wan smile lit Marjorie's face. 'I don't keep a carton of pepper up my bra, as a rule, Mam,' she said.

'Pity,' said Molly calmly. 'Many a girl did when my mother was a gel. Well, in her pocket if not in her corsets. Pepper come loose from the grocer in a screw o' paper then. A face full o' pepper'll take a man's mind off nearly anything, and I've never heard of anybody managing that job very well with both parties sneezing their heads off. There! Now you're all laughing, and that's what I hoped. The past's over and we've got to think forr'ard. Your Dad's done a lot of his thinking already.'

It was George's turn. Marge, he said, wouldn't want to go back to Vic, and needn't, ever again. There was a home for her at the Old Glebe. 'Or here,' put in Brian. But, George went on, they had to look at the matter from a business point of view as well as from Marge's personal one, and do the very best for her they could money-wise. Vic had legal rights both as Marjorie's husband and a tenant of Bridgefoot Farms Ltd. The farmhouse and about seventy acres, he, George, had bought outright and given to Marge and Vic as a wedding present. By any reckoning, half of that was now Vic's. But all the other land he farmed had been added, field by field since, as it came up for sale. That belonged to Bridgefoot Farms Ltd and all the hold Vic had on that land was his tenancy rights, if he wanted to keep it and go on farming it. But Marge owned half the house, and half the 'home farm'. If she wanted to sell, he couldn't stop her. He'd get half the money, but wouldn't have a house unless he bought Marge out. With her holdings in the firm she'd be comfortably off if not rich. So it was really up to her to say what she wanted to do.

'I very much doubt whether he'd have enough capital to buy it and run it, the way he's been throwing money about lately,' Brian said. 'But of course his rich friends may very well come to his rescue. What's the matter, Marge?'

'I don't care if he has to sleep rough,' she said. 'But haven't you all forgotten Pansy and Poppy? I must have a home of my own for them to come to!'

'Isn't Pansy going to shack up with young Bailey?' Charles asked.

'And how long do you think that's going to last? Besides, I want a home of my own. My own roof over my own head, where any family or friends can come and go as they like, except Vic. I'll get a court injunction against him if he ever sets foot on my doorway.'

Brian was speaking again, slow, deliberate, and sincere, as if Vic had broken a witch's spell, and turned him back to his old self again.

'We mustn't do anything in a hurry, but we mustn't hang about,' he said. 'Will you let me deal with Vic, face to face? I've had an idea. I can't put it forward till I've seen him. In the meantime, where do you want to be, Marge? What about Aunt Esther's flat? I can soon move my things out. Then Rosemary and I can look after you, and Poppy can come as often as she can, and Charles and I can see that Vic doesn't bother you. We've got to find out where you want to buy a home of your own, and what it's going to cost. You've had enough for one day. It's time you put Marge to bed, Rosy. There's always tomorrow.'

'Not always, not for everybody, there ain't,' George said, getting to his feet. 'But Brian's right. We've done as much as we can today. And there's just one more thing I want to say. *This is a family matter.* It'll soon be common knowledge that Marge has left Vic, but nobody need know why. We want our Marge to be able to hold her head up high again, like she used to. Vic won't tell, and if none of you do, it can't get about. Not even Charlie, Charles. OK? That's all, then. God bless you all.'

Marjorie was the Bridgefoot Fran knew least, but after Sophie had left for home, and William had not returned, Fran sat thinking with Cat on her knee, and felt sad that yet another family in the circle of her friends was in trouble again. Instead of the peaceful old age a man like George should have been enjoying, there seemed always to be something to worry him. She supposed it was the other side of the coin of success, of having made money, and of course, of the changing social conditions. Old people didn't adjust easily to such major changes.

William was much later than she had expected him to be, but he would have rung her if there had been anything wrong. She was prepared to sit and think. She sifted through the bits of gossip Sophie had passed on to her, wondering how much truth there was in any of them. She dismissed a lot of it, though as Kezia would have said, 'there's no smoke without fire'. The bit that stuck in her mind most was the passing reference to Anne having declared herself married to Frank whatever-his-name-was. If that were true, maybe Eric's summing up of her as 'man-hungry' had been correct. Mary Budd, Fran's old friend who had left everything she owned including the Schoolhouse to her favourite niece, could not have known, or even suspected, much that Anne had chosen to keep hidden from her. Fran had accepted Anne as a friend on Mary's recommendation, but she had reservations now.

William came in carrying the picture, explaining that he had waited for it, taking himself off to see Monica to fill the time. That had been a very lucky decision, because he had learned a lot about Greg's movements. Greg had, in fact, been staying with Monica and Roland for the past two days, and had only gone off again that morning. William and Monica had exchanged what they knew so far, except that he had not given Jess's confidences away. As he and Fran had suspected, Greg had driven madly back to York to see if he could pick up any clues from the hotel register of anyone else who could possibly have written the letter. Without result, of course, but it had given him something to do till he got rid of some of his anger and fear.

Then he had come to his senses a bit, and felt that he had to go and explain the position to Monica, because the last time he had seen her she had not been particularly sympathetic and he wondered if he had blotted his copybook with her as well for good and all. She had been sorry, she told William, but it really had been the wrong time for him to complicate matters by being such a stupid ass. She had more than enough to do just then with trying to get a house straight and coping with two six-month-old babies, as it was. Twins were great when you could just bath and feed them and put them down to sleep, but very different when they blew mashed vegetables all over you and rubbed it all over their faces while hanging sideways out of their high chairs, and vying with each other to demonstrate the power of their lungs. She had needed Greg more than she had ever done before just when he had let her down.

But this second time she had been able to give Greg much more of her time, and more sympathy. She had learned a lot from it, too. She had been mad with Jess because of her silly suspicions, and for avoiding her so pointedly. It was all so ridiculous that she hadn't been able to believe a woman like Jess could be so silly as to be jealous of her. Greg was old enough to be her father, and she had always thought of him like that, a charming extra uncle she could tell her troubles to. But she had tried to see him through Michelle Stanhope's eyes, and had succeeded.

What could any woman want more than a man like Greg? A handsome, well-bred gentleman of the old school with a heart as big as the Albert Hall and brain and talent to match – while as for charm and sex-appeal! As if age mattered. She could now see quite well why Jess had been so jealous. A few years ago, a man like Greg would have had to be 'a bounder' or 'a cad' to make advances to a younger woman, especially if he was already married, and Greg was neither. Now, she said, it was women who made the advances. Society didn't condemn such behaviour any longer, and women were hell-bent on taking over every privilege that had once been the prerogative of men. It was the innocents, like Greg, who had to be protected from such women, not the other way round any longer. Sex now was a king who could do no wrong, and it was almost treason even to suggest there should be any limit to it. Why should she, a modern young woman, be so much against the trend of her own generation? Because, she said, she was the product of a true-love marriage, and herself wouldn't be satisfied with anything else.

'It's society's fault, not Greg's,' she had said, 'but he's taking the blame, because that's the code he was brought up in. You must never blame the woman. According to you, Jess still loves him as much as ever. His trouble is that he won't, not can't, believe that. So he's got to be made to. We are on his side as far as not blaming him too much about that wretched Stanhope woman, but we're on Jess's side too. If there's anything we can do to get them back together, we'll do it.'

William said he had expressed his own opinion that a bit of time would work more wonders than deliberate interference at present. Jess had rid herself of her hatred of Greg by trying to burn his picture, had repented and gone back home wanting him with all her heart. Monica was sure that Greg's longing to go back to Jess was nearly breaking his heart.

'I said,' said William, 'that in my opinion nothing could be better in the long run than that they should both have to endure that state of affairs a bit longer. The "absence-making-the-heart-grow-fonder" principle. Jess had her home and her work, and us to keep an eye on her. But Greg had no anchor anywhere. Wasn't he the one in danger of doing something silly?

'Monica said that she had absolutely loaded him with work on purpose, setting up future clothes shows, for which she would simply have to get down to it and make some rough sketches so as to make him believe she was in earnest. It would also mean that he would have to come back to see her at pretty regular intervals. "We'll give him hospitality, and keep our eye on his activities," she said.

'So we have left it that she will report every time she sees Greg, and the moment she thinks his conscience will let him go near Jess again, she'll let us know, and we must do the rest.'

Fran smiled at him, her head slightly tilted to one side – a very characteristic pose when she was teasing him. 'The Gunpowder Plot and the Babington Plot and every other conspiracy rolled into one,' she said. 'And you love it!'

'No I don't,' he replied, rather indignantly. 'I don't really want to be bothered with any of it any longer. But I have to give Time what help I can. That's the secret of all successful plotting. Mind you, if he just walked in to Southside House tonight and she gave him the look you've just given me, they'd be in bed together within five minutes. Hussy!'

'You haven't shown me the picture yet,' she said.

He took off the brown paper, and stood the picture up against the piano stool. They both drew in a breath, and held it. It was incredible what a frame could do to enhance a picture already so beautiful. The expensive gilt 'swept' frame was exactly right for it, and the effect was breathtaking. Fran let out her breath, almost in awe. William knew why. What Greg had seen, and caught for ever on canvas, was Love in all its aspects, Love triumphant over all. William sat down on the arm of Fran's chair and pulled her towards him, his face on top of her head.

'We needn't worry,' he said. 'Time has a better ally than ever I could be. If ever there was a talisman, that's it.'

50

William took the picture to Jess the next morning, and helped her to hang it. She wanted to go back to work, but Eric insisted that she took the rest of the week off. He had had some new ideas, he said, and would be in touch.

'Hoping Greg will turn up before he has the responsibility of her again, I expect,' Fran said.

'I'd rather Greg didn't,' William told her. 'Whenever he does, we shall have to stand by, and at the moment I want some time for myself, at home, before I forget all the ideas I had when I had to knock off working to deal with Jess.'

Fran resolved that he should get his wish if she could do anything to ensure it. She told Sophie so when they were both in the kitchen making coffee. 'So we'll do everything we can to help him,' she said, 'like taking his coffee to him now instead of letting him come out and have it with us.'

Sophie looked offended. ''E'd only got to ask,' she said. 'Do, I should ha' took it to 'im wherever 'e was, and willing.'

Fran laughed. 'That's what I meant,' she said. 'We've got to get in first, and forestall him. He loves his coffeetime with us in the kitchen. We won't let him waste his own time, or ours, for a week or two. So off you go to take his to him now.'

When Sophie came back, the two of them sat at the table for their usual morning talk, tête-à-tête.

'Seems Olive 'Opkins got something right for once in 'er life,' Sophie began. 'Marge Bridgefoot 'as left 'er 'usband, for good. She run away

Sat'day afternoon, and is never going back no more. And I know that's the truth, 'cos George 'isself told Dan'el, and 'e told us. She's up at Temperance with Brian and Rosemary now, till she gets over it a bit, and can start looking about for a 'ome of 'er own. George told Dan'el as it were no secret, seeing as 'ow folks would soon find out. They might as well know the truth straight off, he said, as 'ear it all wrong from Beryl Bean. There ain't much as George don't tell Dan'el, though Dan never breathes a word unless George tells 'im 'e can. He said Marge would like to live close to, but there's a lot to be done, like, about the farm and the money and such afore she can think about finding somewhere. As far as I know, there ain't none for sale now, since Mr Choppen and them bought all the cottages and all the big 'ouses are done up and lived in.'

Fran was amused that Eric had been promoted from 'that there Choppen' to 'Mr Choppen'. She wanted to keep the conversation going and Sophie needed no more encouragement.

'What happened, then? Why did she leave him?'

'That I wasn't told, and I shan't ask.'

'Is her husband still living on his farm by himself, then?'

'It ain't *'is* farm, and never 'as been,' Sophie replied. 'Seems 'e can lay claim to 'alf o' what George give 'em for a wedding present. That don't seem right to me – but there, Marge did vow in the sight of God to take 'um for better for worse. Must ha' been something a lot worse, if you ask me, to make George agree to 'er breaking 'er vows, but I dessay we shall never know what.'

She stood up, tall, stern and disapproving. 'Sich gooin's on!' she said. 'I don't know what the world's a-coming to, that I don't.' She stalked away, more in sorrow than in anger, as Fran could see. In spite of her own anomalous position in all such discussions, she could not help but share Sophie's feelings.

That was on Wednesday, and the peace and quiet William had asked for lasted for the next two days. On Friday evening, Monica rang with a report about Greg.

Of the four suggestions she had made for venues at which to show their autumn collection, he had deliberately chosen to go straight back to York. He could make no decisions until he had seen Michelle again, he said. (Fran's heart sank: it was more than possible that she would tell him she was pregnant by him. What good would their talisman be, then?) He had told Monica and Roland about the anonymous letter, and his feeling that he had to find out who wrote it, to use what he discovered as a touchstone to decide what he was in honour bound to do.

As Michelle had not turned up to the meeting at the hotel, he had driven boldly out to the little town in Derbyshire where she lived. He had called at the town's police station to ask for directions, and found himself face-to-face with the station sergeant. They had recognized each other at once, and Sergeant Morley had addressed Greg by name – both feeling and looking utter idiots, according to Greg himself, Monica said, taken back by the coincidence.

Greg said he had recovered first, and told the sergeant that he had come to see and talk to both Miss Michelle Stanhope and her husband, if possible. The giant had invited Greg into the interview room, where he had asked Greg to sit down and state his business, telling Greg before he began to understand that Mrs Morley and Miss Stanhope didn't really have much to do with each other, and advised Greg to take a lot of what Miss Michelle Stanhope said with a pinch of salt – as he did.

Such a nice, solid, gentle giant, Greg said, that he hated to have to say what he must. He told his story bluntly, omitting any mention of the letter.

'You're not telling me anything as I didn't know about before, you know,' Sergeant Morley said. 'Though you're the first one 'as has ever had the guts to come to tell me about it afterwards. So what is it you want? If you want me to divorce her so as you can marry her, I don't know what to say. She hasn't had any use for me since she got into this modelling job, except to frighten other men into doing as she wants. I know that. She's after a fool with more money than a policeman earns, and to mix with folks of your sort.

'I can't say as I don't love her, because after a fashion I do. I did when I married her. I used to think I should kill every other fellow who even looked at her, and every man does – but when you must you can get used to anything.'

Greg said he had taken a real liking to the man, and was completely out of his depth what to do next.

'You don't look much like a killer, big as you are,' he had said.

'I'm no murderer, if that's what you mean. But I've been in the army, trained to kill. Why did you say that?'

'Because of what the letter said about you having killed men before.'

'What letter?'

Monica had enjoyed telling her tale so far, but the rest wasn't so easy. She said Greg had become distressed at this point, because when Greg told Morley about the letter, and of his suspicion that he or his wife or both of them had written it, a great change had come over the other man. He had gone into a deadly cold rage, and Greg wondered if he had misjudged his adversary after all. There had been a few very nasty minutes. But the policeman did control himself, and Greg heard him growl, 'I'll kill the lying bitch with my own hands! I never thought she'd go that far. It would lose me my job if nothing else. Where is it? Show me it.'

But of course Greg hadn't got the letter. He hadn't even seen it. He had to explain that it had been sent to his wife, and added that it looked as if it would break his marriage and lose him his job, as well.

Morley had demanded to know all the details, and Greg had told the truth, very much as he had to Fran and William, and Morley pulled himself together. A young constable had knocked on the door, and was told the sergeant wouldn't be a minute.

'I'll get it out of the bloody bitch if she did write it,' he said. 'And if she did try to shop me like that, I'll do for her if I have to drop her one dark night. I'm done with her for good. A night or two in bed with another man I've had to put up with for years, but taking my character away I will not put up with. If you're a sensible man, you'll clear off back to your wife and make her see reason. I'll deal with mine!'

'And according to Greg,' said Monica, 'he just showed him out as if he had truly been a stranger calling to ask for directions! But you can see what an awful dilemma it's left poor old Greg in! He daren't come away now till he's seen Michelle and warned her. If she swears she didn't write the letter, and begs Greg to protect her, what on earth can he do?'

'Go to the police,' said William, with a good deal of irony. 'Only Greg could get himself into such a mess. He isn't fit to be let out by himself. And Jess is like a charge of gunpowder ready to be touched off by a falling star. I'm very fond of them, so don't get me wrong, but I could happily strangle both of them at present. There's nothing we can do till we hear more.'

He put the receiver down, only for it to ring again almost at once.

'Eric,' he said. 'Coming down now for a drink and a bit of a consultation about Jess.'

Fran was frankly glad. Though they shared practically everything, William had always had a tendency to keep his deepest worries to himself. She knew all the signs that in fact he was in deep distress about Jess and Greg. To have a male friend to talk to was probably what he needed most.

Fran's keen eye soon picked out that Eric was not as bright and cheerful as he had been the last time she had seen him to talk to.

'Relax, Eric,' she said. 'I can't deal with two of you so strung up that you're out of tune. I suppose the Jess–Greg crisis is at the bottom of it? You probably know as much as we do.' Well, all except Jess's private, guilty secret.

He nodded. 'They're both such complex characters,' he said. 'I'm not sure I understand either of them, let alone both. Jess is a beautiful firework that has to be handled with care – and I wouldn't put up with it in an employee if she wasn't such an asset and I wasn't so fond of her. But it's getting serious, work-wise.

'I've seen Jess,' he said. 'She looks remarkably calm, and is desperate to get back to work, which I'm sure would be good for her. But there are all sorts of complications. Anne Rushlake had to take over from her that morning when all this blew up. I need them both, but I can see that in future I have to keep them apart. Especially if Jess is going to be without Greg, while Anne has got herself married. That's really why I've come to consult you. What chance is there, in your opinion, of Greg coming back to Jess? He's got himself into a mess. What I don't know is if he has enough guts to get himself out of it, and come back to face the fury Jess can be.'

William answered slowly, picking his words. 'He is, as you said, a complex character. I didn't really know him till they came back from Barra, and was inclined to despise him as a dilettante who lived off Jess. I was wrong. For one thing, he's a great artist, waiting to become greater – though only Jess can make him try. We have only ever seen the artist. Monica's seen the potential man of business. None of us but Jess knew the soldier – but they didn't give DSO's away for nothing. Even in wartime.'

'You mean Greg won a DSO?' Fran almost squeaked.

'Didn't you know? Well, that proves my point. He wouldn't talk about it.'

Fran had been watching Eric's face, and read every expression. 'Any more than Eric talks about his,' she said, wickedly.

'You win,' said Eric. 'But for heaven's sake don't tell anybody else! I wonder what Elyot Franks is keeping under his hat. Or you, William. DFC, I suppose.'

William shook his head. 'No. Wrong. All I got out of the RAF was a lot of excitement and a wife like Michelle Stanhope.'

The bitterness in his voice made Eric turn towards him in surprise, and Fran in anger. He saw both, and immediately apologized. 'Oh, for Heaven's sake! I'm not grudging anybody their decorations. I was only thinking what fools all men can be. For twenty-five years Greg and Jess have had the greatest prize of all, and are in danger of losing it over a woman like this Michelle. I had twenty years in the wilderness because I snatched at something I thought was a prize – and still can't claim the real one because I have the other.'

'And I,' said Eric softly, looking straight at William, 'was given one, as you have been. And it was taken from me, for ever. What have you to grumble about?'

William sat down, ashamed, abashed and very contrite. Fran ignored him.

'Sorry, William,' Eric said. 'May we get back to Jess? I take it that both of you believe Greg will be back soon? Good. In that case, I propose some changes. My business is doing extremely well. That the hotel got off to such a good start was due in large measure to Jess, but it will almost run itself now, under the management we've got. Jess is redundant there, but not to me as MD of the whole outfit. Anne knows her job well, and has the languages at her command, but she does rub other women up the wrong way.

'I propose that she and Jess should no longer work under the same roof. If Jess becomes my PA and general personnel officer, she can do it better from the main office at Monastery Farm. As such, she will be top female executive. Anne can stay on as she is at the hotel, doing what she is doing now – but she'll still be second fiddle to Jess. If Jess works from the main office, I'll give her a special, very plush one there, where she only has to cross the yard to get to it. Then she'll barely be out of sight when Greg's at home, and there will be no excuse whatsoever for Anne to intrude on their personal lives.'

'*Deus ex machina,*' said Fran softly.

'You think so? I hope so. For everybody but myself. To put it in a nutshell, I'm bloody lonely. I haven't had to go home to an empty house, till now, when there's just me again. I hate the silence. I have more sense than to intrude too much on Monica and Roland. I have thought of going back into the hotel, but that thought makes me shudder. I have got a home, even if there's nobody in it and I have more real friends now than I have ever had in my life before, except for the sort one makes in wartime – but again, I can't and won't rely on them. Cupid's been almost too busy around here in the last couple of years . . . but his arrows just glance off me, perhaps because I wear a suit of armour.

'Incidentally, Fran. I also have a domestic problem. I need help in the house. I don't mind doing housework, but I can't do the housekeeping – all the sort of things you leave to Sophie. Somebody to see the fire is alight when I get home and that there are clean towels in the bathroom.'

She suggested that Olive Hopkins might do.

At the following weekend, Jess paid an unexpected visit to Benedict's, choosing a time when she could be fairly sure that Sophie would not be there. She was looking much better, though either angry or excited, if her bright eyes and flushed cheeks were anything to go by. She began by saying that she had come straight from seeing Eric, who had asked her to meet him in the main block of offices, which lay in the same complex of buildings as Monastery Farm and Southside House.

She proceeded to tell them what they already knew of his proposal for a new set of arrangements but her suppressed excitement could hardly be caused by that alone. There was a glow about her that had not been visible for a long time.

'Out with it, Jess,' William said. 'Tell us what you really came to tell us. News of Greg?'

'A letter from him.' She took it out of her handbag, made as if to pull it from its envelope, changed her mind and shoved it back, held it caressingly between her hands, hesitated, coloured like a sixteen-year-old, and replaced it in her bag.

'Sorry,' she said. 'I'd love you to read it, honestly, but I can't bear to let you. It's a love letter, the same sort as those he used to write to me while they were waiting on the south coast for D-Day. Pages and pages of it because now, like then, he has no real hope of ever seeing me again. So he just goes on and on telling me how much he loves me, what a wasted life his was until he met me, and how wonderful it has been ever since, until he messed it all up. And that just as it was over thirty years ago, if he doesn't ever come back to me, he'll still go on loving me from wherever he is, heaven or hell. This time, though, he says, it will be just as much a death to live without me as it would if he had been blown to bits then. The difference is that then neither of us had any choice. This time the choice of whether he comes back or not is all mine. He takes all the blame.

'And that's the bit I can't take, because it isn't his fault. The blame is nearly all mine.

'I got the letter yesterday. I read it through and through again and again, and lived through that wartime separation all over again, minute by minute. I was on duty the night before D-day, and of course we all had to know it was on ... Somehow I managed to carry on doing what I was supposed to do, though I wasn't really there at all. I was with Greg, wherever he was, part of him, willing him to take me with him whatever happened to him. I wouldn't have cared that night if he had had a dozen other women, as long as he came back safe and whole to me in the end. So why should I care now? I don't care. I want him back, as much as I did then. Except ... that he placed his entire faith in me, and I let him down. I destroyed his child. If he does come back, I'm going to tell him before I let him decide to stop with me. I've got to. He says he'll never feel clean again until he knows I've forgiven him and forgotten. Neither shall I till he knows. I must tell him. I must.'

She broke into a storm of uncontrolled weeping and William moved to make her sit down, but she threw herself into Fran's arms, and clung there.

'Go away,' Fran mouthed at William, who needed no second bidding.

Fran held her, and simply let her cry. Jess was now surrendering the last vestiges of her pride. All those years she had clung to her story, making herself half-believe what she had led Greg to think. Once she had brought herself to admit it, not only to herself, but to them, there was only one more person to tell. Fran could have staked her life that when he knew, there was no question of Greg not forgiving her. The difficulty Jess had was in forgiving herself. She'd tried to exorcize her guilt by punishing herself, but it hadn't worked. She had still carried the guilt.

Perhaps these tears were washing it away at last. Greg's letter had made her come to terms with it.

In fact, the tears were soon over, and Jess pulled away, giving Fran a smile through which a lot of restored hope and courage was shining. Fran responded in kind. 'Go and wash your face,' she said, 'and I'll get William back. Then we'll try to decide on the best strategy.'

It was taken as read that it was now only a matter of time before Greg did return, but as William pointed out, he was hardly likely to take the risk until he had been given some idea of how he was likely to be received. Or before he was able to clear matters up altogether with that woman and her husband. If he wanted to 'feel clean' again, he had to wash the whole unsavoury event right out of his hair, and Jess had to give him time to do so. He added, a bit tersely, Fran thought, that it would do more good than harm to both of them to let their lacerated feelings have time to heal a bit before engaging in any sort of passionate reconciliation. (He had had many more years of experience than Fran had in dealing with Jess's over-emotional character, and had found there wasn't much to choose between her and Greg in that respect.)

'I must write to him,' Jess said. 'Ought I to tell him everything, before he commits himself to coming back to me?'

'Don't be so daft,' William exclaimed, looking so incensed that both women laughed. 'You can't undo things of that sort in writing. Greg, you notice, hasn't attempted to. He has had enough sense to be entirely positive. An abject woman crawling to his feet in sackcloth and ashes is the last thing he'd want to come home to. And the same thing goes for telephone calls, so don't try that, either. Just send him a line or two saying that when he's ready to come home, he'll find you ready to welcome him. That will be enough. Let him get within sight of you and the sound of your voice – even more importantly, perhaps, within arms' length of you, before you spoil everything by turning a happy reunion into a death-bed confessional. I know you! And women are supposed to be the sensitive ones who know best how to handle such things,' he said, scornful, for the moment, of the whole female sex. It made Fran laugh, and even Jess had the grace to admit that in this case, he was probably right.

William drew her close to him. 'I know I am,' he said. 'And another thing – don't expect him tomorrow. It will take him a week to get his courage up. There's really no hurry, is there? He won't be going away again the next day, so you'll have time together to calm down. We shall be here if you need us, but don't involve anybody else but your two selves if you can possibly avoid it. A bit of common sense and a good dose of love should put things right, I think.'

William's stock as a counsellor rose considerably in Fran's book. It was a very much more down-to-earth Jess who went home.

William actually got down to some work in the next few days. With Jess off his mind, he got on well, and Fran rejoiced to hear him whistling again in the early mornings as he hadn't done since the turn of the year. Sunday came round again, and they both half-expected a telephone call from a happily reunited couple. It was about three oclock in the afternoon when the bell rang.

'You take it,' Fran said, weak at the knees now that the crunch had come. But she could tell at once by the tone of his voice that it was not the call they had been expecting.

'Who's there, besides you?' he asked.

'Yes, I'll come straight away.' He put the phone down. 'Emmy Petrie,' he said. 'Her father's haemorrhaging and she and her sister are alone there with him. I'll go. Will you phone old Henderson? Tell him everything, and persuade him that he must turn out.'

He left five minutes later, and all Fran could do was stay put at the end of the phone. It was far worse than being in the thick of things. Men went into action, and women waited. Like Jess before D-Day, even though she had been on duty as a Wren officer.

'For men must work, and women must weep'? Fran was a bit cynical about that, actually. Women had mostly worked hard enough as well, if they'd never got the credit for it. It was quite time they had a bit more say in things – but she did wish that they wouldn't be quite so aggressive with their feminist demands. She couldn't see much sense, or improvement, in the sexes declaring war on each other. All females couldn't be queen bees. Women hadn't been completely downtrodden, even in the working-class world, though some feminists now wanted to make out that they had, and that all men were only drones. Men were still very useful, like William this afternoon – especially if both lots would agree to be equal partners. There were all sorts of ways of going about things and, after all, hadn't it always been wrily acknowledged, even by the lordly males of the nineteenth century, that 'the hand that rocks the cradle is the hand that rules the world'?

Not now, though. There were women like Crystal, who claimed the same rights of sexual freedom as men had arrogated in the past, and the same right not to rock a cradle. Not that there were many quite like Crystal, thank goodness. Fran did wish she had some idea what was happening down at Danesum.

5 I

It was already dusk when William tapped on the door and walked in, turning right towards the room he knew Petrie occupied. He was met in the doorway by Emmy, the feeble light of a naked electric bulb hanging in the hallway making her look ethereal in the gloom. Her thick mass of auburn hair was parted in the middle, and hung down her back in one thick plait, pulled back from a white face in which her naturally fair skin shone pale like thin skimmed milk. Her brown eyes seemed to take up half her face, so agonized were they, and at the sight of him she clasped her hands together in a gesture of such relief that it went straight to his heart. He saw at once that the front of her thin frock was blood-spattered, and that she had been trying to wipe the blood off. His first thoughts were for her, not the man he could hear breathing so hoarsely in the next room. He put both arms round her, and held her, pulling her head on to his shoulder.

'My dear girl,' he said. 'You did absolutely right to ring me. I've asked Mrs Catherwood to send the doctor, but we must do all we can before he gets here. Are you all alone?'

'Ammy's here,' she said, 'but so are Jade and Aggie. We couldn't let them see, so I sent her with them into the kitchen. She can keep them quiet there, and give them food and drinks. It's awful. I think he's going to die.'

So did William. He hoped that the doctor would arrive in time. 'Do you want to go back in with me?' She shrank away, as if in horror, and said, 'May I go and get myself clean, and then tell Ammy you're here? Then I'll come back, if you need me.'

'Don't come if I don't call you,' he said. 'I'll be here when the doctor comes.'

It took him a lot of courage to open the door and enter the sick man's room.

He lay high on his pillow, sitting up hunched against it as much as he could, with his face turned away and his eyes shut. The pillow and the top of the coverlet, as well as his clothing, were soaked with blood and sputum, horrible to see. William went round and squatted at eye level by the bed, taking the thin, flaccid hand in his own.

'Peter,' he said. 'Can you open your eyes? It's William.'

Sheer disbelief showed in the eyes half-opened to see if what he had heard was true. The hand clasping William's exerted a feeble pressure. 'William,' he said. 'Call me John. Real name.'

'Don't try to talk. The doctor will be here soon. Is there anything I can do before he comes?'

There was a bout of coughing before he got an answer. 'Clean me up a bit.'

William stripped off his coat, went to the door and called for Emmy, asking for a bowl of warm water, some cloths and towels, and if possible some sort of clean clothes and sheets. The poor girl looked anguished, and abashed. 'I've already used all the towels, and there aren't any other sheets and things,' she said.

'Where's your mother?'

'Gone out for a ride in the new Dormobile with Mr Pugh and the others.'

'Ring Mrs Catherwood. Tell her I want pyjamas, towels, hot-water bottles, sheets and blankets. Oh, and my old dressing-gown, and a bottle of brandy.'

'The telephone's in there.'

'Use Pugh's. Tell Ammy on your way to get the water.'

Petrie had begun to cough again, so William held him and got blood-spattered himself.

Ammy called from the door, and he told her to set the bowl down there. He would get it when he could – but to his surprise, the door opened, and Joe Noble came in. He picked up the bowl, taking in the scene at a glance, and with a large handkerchief from his pocket, he began to bathe Petrie's face.

'Wheer are all the others?' Joe whispered.

'Out with Pugh in the new van.'

'Best if they don't come back awhile,' said Joe. 'But 'ere's a car coming now.'

It was Fran, loaded with things she could get her hands on quickest.

'Don't come in,' William called. 'Drop everything on the floor. We'll get them. Joe's with me. Get off home and keep chasing old Henderson.'

She didn't hesitate, breathing a prayer of thankfulness for Joe. He and William had got their patient washed, dried, clothed in William's pyjamas, and lying in clean sheets under old but warm blankets surrounded by towels to prevent him from soiling his bed again, before they heard the doctor's car.

The look of relief and comfort on the invalid's face was like that of a child whose ear-ache had suddenly stopped.

'Thanks,' he whispered. 'I never expected to feel so clean and comfortable again. I expect it's the result of all that medical training. I just wanted to die clean.'

Ambulance men followed the doctor in, and within twenty minutes Petrie was on his way to hospital in Cambridge with Joe beside him, and William following in his own car. He and Joe were asked to wait while the preliminaries were completed. William found a public telephone box and rang Fran. It might be hours yet before they could get home.

'I'm worried about those two girls. They've had a terrible day, and if the others are late getting back they're there alone with two babies. I'll ring from here as soon as I know anything, but I'd be more comfortable if you'd ask them to let you know when their mother gets back.'

'A fat lot of good she'll be to them!' said Fran indignantly.

'We can't do more. It isn't interfering just to inquire. Nor charity. Just loving-kindness. Go to bed if it gets very late, my darling. I shall need a long hot bath, and a warm bed, but – I'm afraid this is the end.' He rang off quickly.

It was more than two hours before William and Joe were told that they might just look in on the patient before leaving the hospital. He had been put into a small side ward, of the kind kept for those for whom little could be done, though oxygen cylinders and other apparatus were all there at the ready.

Petrie was breathing much more easily, and had been made as comfortable as was possible. Joe went to the side of the bed, held Petrie's hand for a moment, and then retired to the foot of the bed, where he knelt down and prayed silently, face on clasped hands.

Petrie beckoned William near. 'This is it,' he said, very low. 'A month, or only a few days. I know and they know, and they know I know. They'll do a full examination tomorrow. Bad luck. I needed just a few weeks longer . . . So please, William . . .'

'You mustn't talk.'

'Yes, I must. It may be my only chance. The children. Do what you can.'

'Trust me, John.'

'I do. Absolutely. Take that key. It's to the drawer in the table in my room. I've left an envelope addressed to you. There's a letter for you, and one to the local magistrates if you should need it. Some money – so that you'll have a bit in hand to bury me decently if you want to. I don't care.

Some certificates. She won't ask for them, but they might be useful. She doesn't care for any of them except Basher. He's like her – rejects everything and everybody, me especially. She hates Tanner, because he's my son and obeys rules. He'll suffer most. I wish – I wish I knew they could all keep in touch with each other. The only thing they've ever had enough of is love.' Silent tears trickled down his face.

'I think Emmy and Ammy know, and the twins may guess. I intended to tell them myself, but I've left it too late, unless . . .'

'What are you asking me to do?'

'If I'm still alive on Friday, bring them all four to see me, if they'll let you.'

'I'll do my level best. And I'll come again myself tomorrow evening.'

He took the other man's thin hand, and held it. 'I promise, John – I'll keep my eye on them all for as long as I can. And about Tanner – I've already promised you. If I can get his mother to agree, I'll see to it that he gets a good education. That's your chief worry, isn't it?'

Joe stood up. 'I reckon we ought to be going, sir,' he said. 'He's had enough for now.'

'Thanks, Joe – for everything,' said Petrie 'And goodbye.'

'Goodnight, sir,' said Joe. 'Not goodbye though, just yet. I'll see you again.'

William turned at the door, and Petrie beckoned him back.

'I forgot. Will you let Charles Bridgefoot know? He's kept his bargain not to turn us out. But he has plans of his own to make now, I must keep my part of the bargain.'

William left soft-footed and silent.

For once, it was Fran who told Sophie the latest news next morning. She had heard it all from William as soon as they were both awake, including William's account of the rock Joe had been to him last night.

'They were too late to go back to Danesum,' Fran said, 'so William took Joe home to Hen Street, and promised that he would go to see that all was well there this morning. I had checked that Mr Pugh and the rest were all safely back, so those two girls weren't alone.'

'Did 'e say how bad the man was?'

'Yes. I'm afraid he's dying.'

Sophie clasped her hands together in her lap, lowered her head, and closed her eyes.

Fran's prayers for him were no less heartfelt, even if she didn't follow Sophie's ritual attitude for praying. When Sophie looked up, two pairs of sorrowful eyes met.

'What will 'appen to all them poor child'en?'

'Their mother's still alive.'

'She won't look after 'em. Joe don't say much, especially anything as is bad about folks, since 'e got religion again from that Daffy Pugh,' Sophie said. 'But he do say as 'e can't make 'er out at all. She don't have no more to do with them child'en than you or me does. The man's 'ad to be both father and mother to 'em. She don't take no more notice o' Joe than if 'e were a straw blowing across the field, but she talks to Pugh. Joe says Daffy would ha' went back to Wales a long while ago if 'e 'adn't 'ave 'ad 'opes of 'elping 'er to a better sort of life, as you might say. But Joe says 'e he don't think she'll ever care enough for them child'en to look after 'em properly. They'll be no better than horphans, once 'e's gone, poor things.'

Fran didn't answer. She couldn't give William's or Petrie's confidences away, even to Sophie. Sophie was following her own line of thought.

'Not that it's anything new for families o' child'en to be left like that,' she said. 'In times gone by, there weren't nobody to look after them as fathers got killed at work, like my own did when a bull gored 'im to death, only what their mother could earn. And then sometimes she would be took from 'em as well, like 'appened in that Spanish 'flu as were so bad just after the First War. But you see, in them days there was big fam'lies for 'em to spread out among, like, so they was kep' with their own kith and kin. It ain't like that no more.

'Them poor young things down Danesum ain't got nobody.'

'Except Joe. And William to do his best. But their father isn't dead, yet.'

'And their heavenly Father, as the Bible says, don't let even a sparrer fall to the ground without 'Im knowing. Despair for 'em yet I will not, but pray for 'em I shall.'

Fran always felt better after talking to Sophie.

William had left early, to report to Danesum and to seek out Charles Bridgefoot, as he had promised.

He found three of the four girls busy in their bare kitchen, making porridge. All looked wan and tired, and showed traces of recent tears. William's heart was wrung for them afresh – waking to grief is one of its worst trials. They were so glad to see him that he felt utterly inadequate.

'How is Dad?' Emmy asked, while the other two paused, tense, in what they were doing, to hear his answer. Petrie had said that he wanted to tell them the worst himself, but William guessed that the girls were already more than half aware how matters stood.

'I left him after midnight, feeling a great deal more comfortable, and in good hands,' he said. 'More than that, at this stage, I don't know. They are carrying out X-rays, and so on, today. Is there any chance I may speak to your mother?'

They all looked embarrassed. 'I'm afraid she's still asleep. She may not wake up for hours, yet. I've just sent Basher across to see if she needs anything. He's the only one she will let try to wake her,' Emmy said. William didn't pursue the matter. She had probably got a fix somewhere yesterday.

'Mr Pugh then?'

'I'm afraid he isn't here either. They went out yesterday to test the new Dormobile – which isn't quite new – and Mr Pugh said it needed a lot of adjusting. Dad had told us that it was bought to take us all back to a camp in Wales, now that this house is sold. So Mr Pugh's taken it back to the garage this morning. I think he is anxious to go home to Wales, but he wanted to leave everything ready for us to move before he went. Of course he didn't know Daddy was going to be so much worse. When he comes out of hospital, he may not be able to drive us all that way.'

'No, I'm sure he won't,' William said gravely. 'When I leave here, I am going to see Mr Bridgefoot, who has bought the house, to see what arrangements we can make with him. You may not have to leave just because you have the means to, yet. How are you managing? Have you any money to buy food, and so on?'

She shook her head. 'Daddy had to keep money locked up, because Basher stole it, for Mummy. I think it is in the drawer in his room, but it's locked, and I can't find the key.'

There arose from the next room sounds of wailings and infant cries, mixed with shouts and yells and bangings, and Topy's voice trying to control one and soothe other small children.

'I expect they're all hungry,' Emmy said. 'May we let them have their breakfast, Mr Burbage?'

William felt like a felon, that he had given no thought to the needs of the youngest.

'Of course. Do forgive me. How are they?'

'Jade and Aggie are easy to manage. Tanner is being very difficult. He wants to go in to Daddy's room to see him all the time, and won't be made to believe that Daddy isn't there. He's never like this in the ordinary way, but then . . . He hates cars, because he's always travel-sick. He was yesterday, and so ill we put him to bed straight away. He wanted Daddy this morning, but we don't know what to tell him.'

'Let them come in,' said William. He could see at a glance that Tanner was in a state of extreme agitation. Catching sight of William, he ran at him, clinging and crying, and demanding to be taken to 'Daddy's woom' to see him. He fought Ammy like a little tiger as she tried to wash his face and make him blow his nose, yelling 'Daddy! I want my Daddy! Where's my Daddy?' All the same, he seemed to find some comfort in William's male presence, and at last let Ammy dry him till he could seek the shelter of standing between William's knees and snuffling into his shirt-front. William was in a dilemma. His desire to do his utmost to comfort the child was checked by the realities he was up against. He held the little boy within the circle of his arms, but common sense told him that at this stage he must not allow the child to form any special bonding with him as a father-substitute. That would only result in Jasper being hurt twice, until any of them knew for certain what was going to happen.

So William talked to Tanner, persuading him to eat the porridge Ammy was trying to give him where he stood, and told him that Daddy was being looked after in a place where they were going to try to make him better, doing his best to palliate the little boy's grief without telling him lies or giving him false hopes. Gradually the sobbing ceased, and Tanner took a few spoonfuls of food.

'I'm going into your father's room now, if I may?' he said, looking at Emmy for permission. 'I have the key to the drawer. Your father told me to look there for an envelope addressed to me. Will you come with me?'

She understood, at once, and picking Tanner up, said, 'Look, if you are good and quiet, now, you can come with me and Dr Burbage, and see that we've got the bed ready for Daddy to come back to when he can.'

It quieted the child and they went to the desolate little room to find the bulky envelope. William slit it open, and looked quickly over the contents. As Petrie had told him, one smaller envelope contained a fairly large sum of money, mainly in notes of not less than twenty pounds. He slipped it back before Emmy saw it, and took his own wallet out of his pocket instead. He gave the girl ten pounds in small notes, and told her to go shopping for anything they needed. 'Take the little ones with you, and buy them some sweets, and yourselves some treats for once,' he said. 'There's a lot of money in here, but I must read the letter your father has written before I know what to do with it. Don't worry – that ten pounds is only a loan, for the moment.'

He left them, very sad at heart, and drove away to find a secluded place in which to peruse the rest of the envelope's contents before going to see Charles, or having to face Fran with details he knew would distress her terribly, especially about Tanner.

The most obvious solution to the problem, that they should take Jasper into their own home and keep him, was the most impossible when looked at from close quarters. Fran had already got four grandchildren who were not his – always a subject to be dealt with in kid gloves, even now. Could they possibly risk disturbing the status quo at Benedict's by introducing a small and very disturbed child, even if that would be fair to him?

William knew that he had to harden his own heart against any such suggestion. Against Fran. 'Cupid' would only have to rush into Fran's arms and call her his 'lovely lady' for her to sweep away any arguments he might bring against her – but there was still the one that he hated having to bring up. He was not her legal husband; therefore they would not be able to adopt the child legally, even if their age was not already against them. If they were able only to keep him by right of Crystal's permission, as it were, they could be making themselves potential victims of black-mail by a drug addict. Most of all they had to think about the child himself. Until now, he had been at home among other young children. Whatever the conditions, would he not be better, at least for the time being, among his brothers and sisters? Yes, said William's reason. No, said his heart – hadn't his father been his main source of love? Who would now protect him from Basher? It simply could not be thought of, and in any case, there were more urgent problems to be dealt with at this very moment.

He pulled up the car before he reached the main road, and opened Petrie's letter to him. It only reiterated what they had agreed verbally, and listed the other documents enclosed with it. One was a letter to the chairman of the local magistrates, drawing their attention to the fact that Jasper was his child, registered as such, and begging that if they were ever involved in any decisions with regard to the boy's future, they would consult his friend, Professor William Burbage, etc. William breathed a sigh of relief when he remembered that only very recently, Elyot had been made a Justice of the Peace. He had an ally in the right place. His gloom began to lift a little.

The money, Petrie explained, was the extra cash balance on the agree-ment he had made with Charles regarding the price of the house. He was to ask Charles about it, if he cared to, because he, Petrie, did not feel able to give Charles's financial secrets away. But it was undoubtedly his to do as he liked with. He dared not leave any sum worth having in Crystal's hands. Would William take it, keep it and dole it out to Emmy as needed, until the move to Wales took place? Then he was to give Dafydd Pugh one hundred pounds for the journey and any essentials the family needed to set up camp before Pugh left them.

He is a strange man, [Petrie had written] but basically, I think, an honest one. He believes with natural Welsh fervour what he preaches, and tries hard to put what he preaches into practice. But he is also a young man, full of Welsh passion. The sooner he is out of reach of Crystal's spider's web, the better it will be for him. Though he will be the nearest succour in geographical distance my children will have, I hesitate to leave him with any obligation to visit them oftener than is absolutely necessary, especially for anything to do with money, which Crystal would wheedle out of him by hook or by crook. He would be no match for her at all. Whereas, if it were Joe, I could trust him to do his duty to his neighbour first, last, and always. I have nothing to leave him but my blessing and my thanks.

My main reason for arranging for this move for them all is to keep them all together for the next couple of years or so. Emmy and Ammy are both very responsible girls, and the twins are so close to them in age that if the two oldest choose to leave and go their own way as nature bids them, the twins will want to stay together, and will take over the care of the three smallest for as long as they can. I am not God. I cannot forecast what will happen – I can only do my best. Please may I suggest that you keep the rest – invest it if there's anything worth bothering about left over when everything is settled, acting as banker for them until it is used up? I think you will find that Crystal has means of her own.

I ask much of you, William, in the name of the friendship that might have been ours had the threads of our lives crossed earlier, and for the remnants of which I can only once more express my thanks, and leave to you and your beautiful Fran the memory and the love of

John Petrie Voss-Dering

With blurred eyes William looked at the rest of the contents of the large envelope: a letter addressed to each of the four oldest girls; a fatter envelope marked 'My mother's miniature Bible and the only thing kept by me when she died: for Jasper on attaining his majority'; then there was the envelope containing the money, which William didn't stop to count; and another brown envelope containing several certificates. Petrie's own birth certificate, from which William learned that he was indeed John Petrie Voss-Dering, son of Capt. Desmond Voss-Dering, and his wife Venetia Petronella, of a London address, and that he was now just over forty-three years old. Tanner's birth certificate: John Jasper Garnett, mother entered as Crystal Garnett, of No Fixed Abode, father John Petrie Voss-Dering, also N.F.A. Jasper not yet three and a half years, and of course, by inference, illegitimate. No certificate for Jade, but another for Agate Hugh, registered in Swithinford, N.F.A. (father unnamed). So Aggie was still only seven months old. Burdened with this knowledge,

William drove on to seek Charles Bridgefoot. He had been so occupied with Greg and Jess, and then with Petrie, that he had forgotten that the Bridgefoots had also had a bad time since that wonderful New Year's Eve. He approached the gates of Temperance Farm, to ask where he could find Charles with a good deal of trepidation. Sorrow and trouble were in the air like an infection.

There was not as much sorrow and trouble in the Bridgefoot household at Temperance Farm as might have been expected, all things considered. It had been a wise move to let it be known at once that Marjorie had left her husband, because as it left little room for speculation, gossip was short-lived.

She was occupying the self-contained flat at Temperance that had been arranged for Rosemary's old aunt, and though quietly licking her wounds when alone, was calm and determined in general company. Nothing would or could make her go back. Nobody tried to persuade her to, and the pleasure of being with Brian and Rosemary, who were so compatible and loving, did nothing but remind her how sweet life might still be, in comparison with what it had been. They cosseted her, and she did her best to help without letting her presence in their home get in the way of their reconciliation with each other which had followed Brian's accident.

She saw one or other of her parents, if not both of them, on most days, and found them wholly supportive, too. She had, in effect, returned to the bosom of her family, and was very happy to be there. Poppy wrote her long letters, which gave her much more pleasure than they had done in the past, because she had always previously had to share them with Vic, and listen to his constant carping about Poppy being so silly as to prefer education to some practical way of making use of her country upbringing, like Pansy. Poppy wrote much more freely to her mother now, telling her about her studies and her growing interest in them. She had never written much about her social life, and Marjorie had surmised that it was because Poppy knew how her innocent pleasures would be scorned compared with Pansy's more robust ones, especially by Pansy herself. They had grown apart in the last couple of years, though until they had left school no twin sisters could have been closer.

They had nothing to share, now. Marjorie was worried about Pansy, because it went against the grain to see a daughter of hers so bold and forward in distributing her favours; but she had anxious moments about Poppy too, whom she thought too reserved and retiring. The air of wistfulness she detected in Poppy's letters lately could hardly be wondered at. She was cut off from the others at a time when the family had come apart at the seams. Though the Gifford family had come cleanly into two halves, Poppy still loved her father, and Pansy her mother. She had to be fair to them.

Pansy and Marjorie communicated by telephone once a week at a set time to ensure a connection. Pansy's social life was as hectic as Poppy's appeared uneventful. One had to catch Pansy, as one would a fly, at the still moment when she had settled. Marjorie supposed that Vic must be a bit lonely, and made veiled inquiries.

'Dad?' said Pansy, a bit tartly. '*He*'s all right. Enjoying himself thoroughly, now that he's got used to you not being there. You know how he's always hated being by himself or going into a house with nobody else there. He just makes sure it never happens. I'm having to act as your "stand-in".' She carried on with an air of grievance that left Marjorie in no doubt that Pansy had been wanting the chance to make her feelings known. She hinted that her mother had timed her exit just too soon, before the show house had been refurbished as planned for her and Darren Bailey to live in, thereby selfishly leaving Pansy trapped at home. She made it clear, however, that she was still leaving home as soon as the house was ready. She hoped that by that time Mum would have had enough of being a lodger and be back to see to Dad and free her.

'The trouble is that I can't move an inch without Dad,' she said. 'He insists on going wherever I go. He's out with me and Darren all the time. Actually, the practice in riding is doing him a lot of good. He's becoming quite a horseman, in his way. I suppose that's a good thing. They are considering that riding-school and livery stables idea again, the one that Grandad squashed by vetoing the use of the land opposite the hotel that Charles can apparently do what *he* likes with. There was some talk of Choppen setting one up and there wasn't enough trade for two so close together. Darren's father still seems all for it, but Dad's hesitating and won't give any answer. I suppose it's to do with money. Must run, now. Bye, Mum. See you.'

Marjorie regaled this to Brian and Rosy.

'I wish she'd tell me something I didn't already know, for once,' she said. '"Something to do with money" indeed! She's not a fool, and neither are the Baileys, father or son. Nor Vic, where money's involved. So what it boils down to is that all of them think I am. Let 'em think. It all depends on me, and I shall do just as I like when I like, as far as the law lets me. I'm in no hurry to do anything as long as you don't mind keeping me here a bit longer.'

Brian was happier than he had been for a very long time. He had a very strong bond with this sister, who was only thirteen months younger than himself, and he had always regretted her 'throwing herself away' on a man like Vic, whom he despised and disliked. Just lately, when he had had long intimate talks with her, he had understood how little life had offered Marjorie when she had been at marriageable age. While he had been helpless on his back after the mishap of New Year's Eve, both of them had solved a lot of their own problems by listening to themselves talking to each other. Marjorie had wondered, and asked, how and why Brian had ever got in so thick with Bailey, and gone along with anything in which Vic was concerned.

He had defended himself with some reason on his side. He told her that it had all really begun when the disastrous fire had left them the biggest farmers in the village. Farming was going downhill, even where the land was farmed properly, but their father was such an old stick-in-the-mud . . . he had become very restless.

'There was us and Tom Fairey and Jack Bartrum and a tenant farmer up at Castle Hill. The Manor Farms syndicate had all the rest, and went round buying every other scrap they could lay their hands on. Did any-body imagine they would go on *farming* it? I was pretty sure that Choppen was a developer-in-disguise, waiting his chance.'

He had thought he must be right when Robert Fairey died and Bailey got in quick on Lane's End. Old Swithinford, he guessed, had been scheduled for development, and somebody on the planning committee had taken a large back-hander to let Bailey into the know. If development was inevitable, he had seen that they would be sitting pretty between two developers outbidding each other. If they were willing to pay the sort of price they had paid Tom Fairey, moneywise things looked very bright. The Bridgefoots could all be millionaires overnight, and retire on the proceeds of their land; or, as Brian saw clearly, make even more money by investing in one or other of the development firms. When Castle Hill seemed ripe for plucking, and both he and Bailey had personal reasons for hoping to see the back of Bob Bellamy, he had decided to make a move. Bailey had offered him the chance to invest a bit of his own money in the development of Castle Hill. Brian had smiled, ruefully, at his sister. 'I had guessed wrong, all the way along,' he had said.

That was true. He had been aware for some time now that he had fallen between two stools. Choppen had bought up the village not to cover it with measley dwellings, but to use its rural charm for a very different though equally lucrative venture. His interest was as much in keeping the Bailey type of developer out as George Bridgefoot's or that of people like the Benedict's set was.

All last autumn he had been very uneasy, because he had got himself far deeper in with the Bailey lot than he had meant to. He had truly expected the love affair between Charles and Charlie Bellamy to fizzle out, especially when she went up to Cambridge, but again he had been wrong. To be 'off hooks' with his son was almost more than he could bear, sometimes, but there was no turning Charles. 'I honestly don't have anything against the girl herself – or her father, if it comes to that. The trouble has been that I couldn't be in both camps at once. The more I saw of the Baileys the less I liked them – especially as I seemed to have set myself up with Vic and Kid Bean as working partners as well as the Baileys themselves. When Rosemary turned on me, that was almost the last straw. I lost my temper and vowed I wouldn't give in to please anybody. Then to top it up, if they didn't set up that business at church on New Year's Eve. Whatever I did would be wrong. The more all my feelings went along with Dad and the church lot, the more I wriggled on Bailey's hook because I couldn't get out without going back on everything I'd promised. In the end, I had made up my mind to play Jack o' both sides, and do what you did, only I intended to go back to the party after church. I never got the chance. It was decided for me.'

Marjorie said nothing. She knew that their father had rubbed it in pretty well already. She had heard him telling Brian that he had had a Partner that night who'd be a lot more use to him for the rest of his life than ever Bailey would have been. She did, however, describe in greater detail to him than she had done to the rest just what she had seen and heard at the party, including her awful exposure of Vic. She had cried, then, softly and silently, and the sight had almost torn Brian apart. It had been his obstinacy in believing that his own ideas must be the right ones that had led to all the misery within their formerly so close family. Now it was up to him to do anything he could to repay them for the way they had accepted him back and cared for him and his interests while he was laid up.

He was infuriated at the knowledge that Vic could legally claim half of the house and land that George had given Marjorie as a wedding present. Vic had no claim on anything else except as a tenant of Bridgefoot Farms Ltd. It was at this point that he had been struck by an idea.

Marjorie had a small income from her shares in the farm, but she would need capital. Vic had no other home but where they had lived and farmed. He would have to be coerced into buying Marjorie out. The property in question was only seventy acres of land with a house on it, situated on the far side of Swithinford. Its size was ideal for the livery stable project Pansy had mentioned. Brian knew very well which side he was on now that he was one of the Bridgefoot family again, and could see that they were being offered a way out.

If Bailey's interest were to be diverted from Old Swithinford now, he might let their village alone in future. His former association with Bailey could even prove to be of profit to them as well, in the long run. There were other fields, bought to enhance Vic's holding, which were not, and never had been, what they meant by 'Bridgefoot land', though owned by the firm. They were neither agriculturally nor environmentally important. As a candidate for development purposes, they were far more suitable than anything around Old Swithinford. Brian had no qualms about pushing Bailey in that direction, if he could ever persuade his father to sell those other fields.

He had gone to see Vic as soon as he had been allowed to drive, told Vic what he thought of him, and set out the choices open to him with regard to Marjorie, adding that the family solicitor had already been briefed to look after her interests. Though Vic had shouted and blustered, Brian gathered that Vic was in no financial position to buy Marjorie out without help. What it meant was that she had Vic over a barrel. She had plenty of evidence for a divorce, and could no doubt claim maintenance if she so wished. (Brian was well aware that she had no such wish, to be in any way dependent on Vic. All she wanted was to be detached from him utterly and for ever.)

Brian was looking forward to getting back to work, but in the meantime he was gradually settling himself back into his old place within the family and therefore within the village. Two aspects of that were still gnawing at him. He had, for the sake of his re-established relationship with his son, to make peace with Charlie and her family. That they should have turned out to be who and what they were made it more difficult. And he was sadly lacking in the matter of friends of his own generation, or with similar interests. Those of his own standing with whom he had been brought up were all gone now – the Thackeray brothers, Tom Fairey, even Vic. He had been offered the hand of friendship by all those who had been drawn together round Benedict's. In his 'big-headedness' he had regarded their overtures of friendship towards him as 'patronizing', and had resented and spurned them. Now it was too late – they would not want any association with an ex-Baileyite. The bitterest pill of all to swallow with regard to that was that Bob Bellamy, now his only farming equal and contemporary, was as firmly established inside that group as he felt himself to be excluded. He had not seen or spoken to any of them since before Christmas, and was rather dreading the time when he did.

He was sitting chatting to Rosemary and Marjorie, sharing their late ''levenses', when he saw William's car drive into the yard.

William had driven towards Temperance with a very sad heart. As he guided the car through the big open gates of the farmyard, he saw Charles making his way towards the house, and tooted his hooter to draw his attention. Charles paused, straightened up, recognized him and held up his hand.

William opened his car door and called to him. 'I need to talk to you, Charles. Come and sit here with me for a few minutes if you can spare them.'

'OK. Let me swill the mud off my boots.'

William watched him perform the task with interest. It must be six weeks since he had last seen the younger man, and what a difference they had made. Sensitive by nature and accustomed professionally to reading and assessing the moods of the young by their faces and their expressions, William registered what it was. Gone was the rather strained expression of feverish emotion trying to hide anxiety, and in its place was one of such calm, assured, unhurried purpose that William almost laughed aloud. It was as though the mantle of George had in reality fallen upon the figure of his grandson. They both gave off an aura of tranquillity, which said as loudly as if they had spoken,

> God's in his heaven,
> All's right with the world.

That's what security of all kinds had done for Charles, William thought. He had plenty to be pleased about. It delighted William that he did not bother to hide his joy, or play down his good fortune out of either false modesty or superstitious fear. Not that he had any need to fear nemesis, William thought, as he pushed open the passenger door to admit him. Nemesis only followed hubris, of which there was no sign in this youngster's bearing. William hated to have to say a word that would dull the sparkle of the cornflower blue eyes, but he told, as simply as he could, what he had come for.

Charles was silent, looking out into the yard. Then he said, 'Life isn't fair, is it? A man like that! I liked him so much. Are you sure he's dying? Can I do anything now to help? Could I go to see him in hospital? Is there anything he needs?'

'Which do you want me to answer first? Yes, he knows he is dying. That's why he asked me to come and see you myself. He liked you, too. He said that you had kept your part of the bargain, so he must now keep his. I was to tell you that.'

Charles flushed. 'We had a verbal bargain – that I would give him a bit more than he asked for the house, if I found after my birthday that I could afford it. I could, so I did.'

'I think, then, that that is what I have here now in my possession, holding it as banker for his family after all his debts have been settled. What was his part of the bargain?'

'To get out of the house by the spring, so that I could do what I needed to it in time to marry Charlie this summer. But I didn't want it to be like this! I would never have turned them out. I must try to see him and tell him so. Even if it had meant I had to wait another whole year for Charlie. What can I do to help him? He's so – such a gentleman.'

'He was born one, by nature.'

'Yes – I knew Petrie wasn't his real name, of course. He had to sign the sale agreements in his proper name. But I should never have told anyone. What are his plans, now?'

William explained. 'I think that all we can possibly do is make sure that they go as soon as possible so that he can be assured that they are there safe before he dies. I guess we have about two more weeks. That would give him more comfort than anything else, I believe. Are you quite sure that all your house purchase agreements with him are watertight?'

'Grandad put a young man from our family's firm of solicitors on to it, and he has certainly made everything as legally safe as possible. His one worry is that either Pugh or Miss Garnett might claim squatters' rights. Do you think there's any danger?'

'Not from Pugh. He can't wait to get back to Wales. I think I must try to see to it that Crystal doesn't get hold of a key to the house, or is ever let inside by anybody else – at least while this crisis lasts.'

'Come in and have a drink, William. I need one.'

Neither of them noticed the use, for the very first time, of William's Christian name by the boy who until then had been embarrassed by the age difference or by awe of William's academic standing. The closing-up of the distance between them had been as easy as sliding a sword into its own scabbard.

William accepted the invitation, feeling in need of some sort of uplift himself, though being with Charles had made him feel a good deal less depressed. Petrie had once said to him that it would please him to think that his efforts to restore the house would be rewarded by him being able to leave some love in it. He thought that a visit to hospital from Charles might soothe the dying man on that score. He said so as they went towards the kitchen door, but qualified it by saying that he was intending to ring the hospital tonight to ask permission for all the four oldest girls to go on Friday afternoon.

The three seated at the table looked up as William followed Charles in. Brian stood up, embarrassed and not knowing quite what line to take. William turned first to greet Rosemary, and then Marjorie, whom he did not know at all. Marjorie's presence was a godsend to Brian. He had time to note that William was being his charming self to her, and Charles and Rosemary's ease with the visitor, before he had to do anything himself. By the time William's 'Hello, Brian' accompanied by a hand held out towards him was over, it was Brian who was calling to Charles to get the whisky bottle out.

Charles told them all the news about Mr Petrie, and William answered all the sympathetic questioning.

'It's rather a facer for me,' Charles said. 'We had said "sometime in the spring", but with a thing like this you can't start planning as if you know what will happen when. William says that Petrie had meant to move out anyway as soon as ever possible, because he knows I have a lot to do to it before any part of it is fit for us to live in. There's time, though, now, for us to get part of it habitable and furnished for a summer wedding. When, Dad? I suppose, like all other farmers, between haytime and harvest – but we shall have to wait till Charlie's exam results are out. I can't believe any of it, yet.'

Rosemary was looking wistful. She would be only the bridegroom's mother at this wedding, with very little say in anything.

'I hope it will be a real wedding – a proper one, I mean,' she said.

Charles swung round on her, not quite sure of her tone. 'What do you mean by that? Are you afraid that we shall have to sneak off to a register office to make sure the baby's born in wedlock, as Grandad would say?' he teased. 'Come off it, Mum! You know perfectly well it will be a real wedding, and Monique O'Dell can start as soon as she likes to make a pure white bridal gown this time. Only for heaven's sake, don't any of you let on to Charlie that I said so! She doesn't know anything at all about this yet, and was as prepared as I was to have to wait a bit longer if it had to be. She probably wouldn't marry me after all if she knew I'd been shooting my mouth off like that.'

He was highly embarrassed, now, and they all sought to help him out by chattering on.

'Do you really think it will be a village wedding, here in Old Swithinford church? Like Lucy's?' asked his aunt.

'Very much like Aunt Lucy's, I imagine,' said the still embarrassed groom. 'Why shouldn't it be? Charlie's a farmer's daughter, spinster of this parish, just as Aunt Lucy was, isn't she?'

'Her stepmother's posh family won't want it in St Margaret's, Westminster, with the reception at the Savoy, or anything like that?' said Rosemary.

Charles was beginning to look harassed. He had yet to learn that two women with the scent of a wedding in their nostrils are like terriers straining on a leash, and as difficult to restrain.

'I said that as far as I can guess, I imagine it will be as much like Aunt Lucy's as one pea is to another,' he said, catching sight of William grinning from ear to ear. 'You had better start thinking about keeping the Glebe Barn clear, Dad,' he said, deciding that it was easier to go along with them and give them plenty to think about than to upset them at this point.

'OK. Let's all raise our glasses to it,' said Brian. The mention of the barn had seemed to satisfy both women and set their hearts at rest.

'I hope they do ask Monique O'Dell to make all the clothes,' Rosemary said. 'I've never seen anything so lovely as Lucy's wedding, even if it wasn't a white one.'

'Or according to Sophie, quoting Mrs Hopkins,' William said, 'there never had been a wedding there that they remembered where all the women's frocks had clashed together so well.'

'I hope Mr Taliaferro'll be there, and that him and Mrs Franks can agree which of them should be at the organ.'

A sudden restraint fell on them which told William a great deal. So Greg's absence from home had been noted. He strove to pass it off as of no consequence.

'I don't think you need bother about those two squabbling on the organ stool,' he said, laughing. 'Have you forgotten what happened on New Year's Eve already? They're two very accomplished musicians who like working in tandem.'

It was Charles who eventually broke the silence, in a voice suddenly gone very flat.

'It can't possibly be like Aunt Lucy's was,' he said. 'Robert won't be there. Who'll be my best man? Nick, of course – especially as he's Charlie's stepbrother now. But it won't be the same, with him not remembering anything. You catch yourself talking to him about things you expect him to know, and then suddenly you dry up because of the look on his face. He'll be a perfect best man, of course, only not *my* Nick. I don't want anything to spoil it, but there it is. I can't have Robert, and I can't have the real Nick.'

William was surprised at the feeling in Brian's voice, and the expression of sympathy on his face as he said, 'Don't get upset about what you can't change. There's always a thistle or two in any harvest. It will still be Nick. Be thankful he's alive at all.'

Charles got up and went out.

'He's right, though,' Marjorie said. 'It can't be quite like Lucy's. She had a whole raft of bridesmaids to choose from. As far as I know, Charlie's got no girl relations.'

'The twins are still Charles's cousins,' said Rosemary.

'Use your head, Rosy. Poppy might be acceptable, but can you see Bob Bellamy letting Pansy, living with Darren Bailey, follow his daughter down the aisle? Even if she would? Don't let anybody suggest her as a bridesmaid on my account. Poppy's different. If Charlie wants her, I shall be pleased.'

William left them still happily planning. He had to turn his mind back to less pleasant things. On the spur of the moment, he headed the car, not towards home, but towards the hotel. He wasn't ready to face Fran yet with the story of his visit to Danesum this morning, and little Cupid's distress. Her heart was too soft, sometimes. A few minutes with Eric would help a lot.

52

It was a good move, as it happened. He found Eric alone in his office, relaxed and ready to chat. William told him about the Petries and his own involvement with them.

'You get involved little by little,' he said, 'and then find you're in it up to your chin. I knew from the start that Petrie was going to die: what I didn't know was how much I was going to care. It's those children that have got under my skin now. Especially the little boy Fran found wandering last autumn, and who was in such a hell of a state this morning. She's going to be terribly upset about him. I don't know how much to tell her. Neither of us is at our best, after the harrowing time we've had with Jess.'

'Why not give Fran a ring and tell her you're having a quick lunch with me here?' Eric replied sensibly. 'Then we can talk at leisure.'

For once, William was glad of an excuse to stay away from home for a bit longer. He wanted to leave his call to the hospital as late as he dared, to be sure that the examinations were finished and Petrie was back in his bed, before he asked for permission for the girls to visit there on Friday. Fran quite understood his desire for a bit of male company, though she had enough sense not to say so, and told him that he was with absolutely the right person to find out what Jess's state of mind was, and whether or not there had been any more moves towards a solution of the mess Greg had got himself into. All of which was very soothing to William. Some women would have made much more fuss.

They ate the lunch Eric ordered up in the little ante-room to his office, where they could talk in private, and Eric could indulge in an after-lunch pipe.

'I've had a pretty busy few days since I saw you at the end of last week,' he said, puffing between words to get his pipe going well. 'I went to see Jess – and, incidentally, saw that picture of Monica Greg painted, as well. I've offered her whatever she cares to ask for it, but she says it's Greg's and she can't sell it, though if she could there isn't enough money in Old Swithinford to get it out of her.'

'What is the latest score?'

'I don't wholly understand either Jess or Greg. Did you know that he had written to Jess?'

'Yes. She came up and told us. Acting about eighteen, emotionally, like a romantic miss with her first love-letter. We advised her to reply briefly that she wanted him home as much as he wanted to come. As she said, she had to reply, but that's where both Fran and I saw danger. Jess simply can't do things within reason. If she had got going with her pen without our douche of cold water on her ardour, she would have written him a passionate love-letter forty pages long that would have convinced him that he was the biggest cad since George IV and caused him to be pressed to death under the weight of his own guilt. Love at any distance greater than arms' length is more than either of those two can deal with. However they've managed to survive as long as this without sight of each other is a mystery to me.'

Eric laughed. 'You've certainly got Jess's measure,' he said. 'Whatever he's done, she's already forgiven him ten times over. She's a different woman now from the one she was before all this blew up, but if he keeps her waiting much longer, my guess is that she'll go into reverse again. So, to prevent another terrible explosion, I've done my best to keep her occupied morning, noon and night, reorganizing the admin offices down at Manor Farms Ltd's headquarters.

'So now, unless she wants to, there'll be no need for her ever to go near the hotel or Anne Rushlake – or whatever her new name is – again. She's a very efficient woman too, in her own way.

'The others don't like her as they did Jess. It's so easy to get close to Jess. I wish Greg would come back. She and Greg both need lovers. Neither can get along without a lover-relationship. That's what caused all this hoo-ha in the first place, isn't it? It would be good for me, too, to have them so close by. Less than a hundred yards away, always with a welcome, for a drink and a chat.

'With only Jess there I daren't risk an evening tête-à-tête with her. She might misunderstand my motives – and it could be dangerous.

'Sex is like fire – a good servant but a bad master. One shouldn't play with either. It doesn't do to let one or the other get out of hand. Being celibate doesn't really worry me, but I'm not prepared to run risks. William, I ought not to be talking to you like this, for all sorts of reasons. Forgive me. Jess is your sister, and I meant no disrespect to her. Nor to hurt you personally. You've been in the same boat.'

'I didn't have memories or any hope,' said William, a bit huskily. 'But my God, was I lonely! I didn't risk close friendships lest they be misunderstood –

'Celibacy didn't worry me all that much, until after I'd met Fran again. That was the really bloody time. But I think you're wise. Come and see us instead. Meanwhile, how do things stand about Greg?'

'Monica's heard from him. He's working hard on the business side, and she says he seems very hopeful that with every day that passes the danger of any comeback from his – er – night of indiscretion grows less. So far he hasn't mentioned coming home. She thinks he's scared, much as he wants to. Putting off the acid test of whether Jess will have him back, whatever she may have written.'

'Then somebody has to help him, before, as you say, Jess goes bashing into reverse gear again. We can't – we're already in too deep. I think perhaps it's up to Monica. Couldn't she invent some reason why he simply has to come to see her, soon? Once he's in the vicinity, one of us can get him to take his courage in both hands and simply walk into Southside House, before letting Jess know he's around. Then it'll be up to the gods – but I don't think there would be any need to call on them for help once those two middle-aged fatheads are within reach of each other. We just have to manoeuvre them together!'

'I'm not exactly cut out for a part in such operatic intrigue,' Eric said, rather dubiously. 'But I think you may be right. For one thing, all this is interfering with my business, and I can't let it go on a lot longer. I'll explain to Monica. She'll be glad enough to play one of the gods. She's fond of Greg, if not of Jess.'

William eyed his friend with amusement. 'You don't like women very much at all, just at present, do you,' he said.

'Only yours,' answered Eric promptly. 'She's a one-off.'

'Then do your bit like a soldier to get Greg back to the front line. Set it up with Monica, and then get out of the way that weekend. We'll keep out of it, too – we'll arrange to go out or have guests so that if rung up by either Romeo or Juliet in suicidal mood, we are simply not available to visit or be visited. I daren't declare that if I were not pretty sure we shall be neither wanted nor needed. Shall we make the Saturday or Sunday after next *der Tag*?'

'Easier for me on Sunday,' Eric said. 'But in this case, Saturday's the

382

best bet. I can legitimately be too busy on a Saturday. That's the plot laid.' He paused, tapped out his pipe, and sat back. 'May I change the subject? I had a visit from George Bridgefoot this morning, wanting to hire that cottage on the way up to Castle Hill on a year's lease. For his elder daughter, who's left her husband and wants to come back to live here once the legal formalities are over. She's got her eye on Dr Henderson's house, when it becomes vacant, George says. But old Henderson keeps havering about retiring. That cottage would do for Mrs Gifford in the interim. She sounds a sensible sort. Do you know her?'

'I met her for the first time this morning, to talk to. There's something Fran-like about her, though it's only a reflection of a reflection of a reflection, if you see what I mean. I expect that's why I felt I knew her and liked her.'

'That's a recommendation for her, I must say,' said Eric. 'It's a pity I can't help. But I've let that cottage already to Bob Bellamy's father-in-law for a whole year from Easter. I can't run back on him, because they're having a bit of bother with Nick. He's started digging his heels in, and says that he won't go near any university while he's brain-damaged. He says he will go on studying, but they've got to give him more time. He also declares that he feels more at home in that cottage than anywhere else.

'Bob and Gordon are all for letting him try anything even if it means him living there alone or missing a trip abroad with his grandfather. Jane's against it. She says he wasn't brought up to be a rich dilettante lay-about, and the only condition she'll agree to him having his own way is if he works at least half-time somewhere. Bob will have him some days doing odd jobs on the farm, and I've offered a waiter's job.

'Bob's another lucky one. Jane's got a lot of grit. We still miss her – I'm afraid Mrs Hopkins is a very poor substitute. Some women only have to be in a room for ten minutes to leave it feeling like home. Like Fran. You've got a home, William. Go away! Go to it.'

'I will, as soon as I can. May I use your telephone to ring the hospital? I may have to go back to Danesum and I'm more than halfway there.'

He was surprised to be told, without any difficulty at all, the results of their examination. He had expected only the bland, off-putting formula reply that most hospitals use to casual inquirers but got a full report and an invitation to a consultation with the doctors next day.

'Mr Voss-Dering named you as his next of kin, Dr Burbage. He would be very grateful if you would agree to come.' William was barely capable of a reply. He felt in some extraordinarily way honoured.

What he was told was much as he had feared. There was nothing to be done except to try a major operation, which might have been possible had the patient been stronger. The element of risk was considerable. That was why he had been asked to be present at the consultation tomorrow.

William agreed to be there and made his plea to be allowed to take the girls on Friday. Not all at once, they said. Two at a time. He was satisfied with that, and went back to Danesum, glad to be able to offer the older girls even such a little hope, and a chance for them to see their father.

'I don't see how we can all go,' Emerald said. 'One of us will have to stay here with the little ones.'

'Won't your mother be here? Just for once? Or Mr Pugh?'

The girl coloured and shook her head. 'He'll be out all day. He's getting everything ready for us all to move to Wales. We were only waiting till Daddy was well enough to make the journey, in any case.'

Ammy, who had so far said little, was more forthright. 'Mr Pugh won't ever look after the little ones,' she said. 'He says he can't cope. It didn't matter, because we are almost always here, and when Daddy possibly could look after them, he would. And he doesn't get on with Tanner. He says Daddy spoils Tanner. He likes Basher, though, which is a good thing.'

William suddenly saw red. How dare that sanctimonious bastard pass judgement on Petrie, and take out his prejudice on a three-year-old child? Or see Basher only as a possible convert?

'Be ready for me to pick all four of you up, at about one o'clock,' he said. 'Mrs Catherwood and I will find someone to look after the youngest ones, here or at home, till we get back. Tell Mr Pugh to keep Basher. He owes your father that much.'

He didn't relish telling Fran anything about the day he had had, especially his pledge of her help on Friday, but he couldn't wait to get home all the same.

'Wait a minute, sweetheart,' he said, as she came to meet him. 'Let me go and have a quick bath, and I'll tell you all there is to know. I'm not fit to touch you at present.' Not till he had got rid of his rage, he thought, his anger against the unfairness of life, as well as his sudden fury of distaste against Pugh.

While he was steaming himself and doing his best to subdue his misery and frustration at being able to do so little, and his anger that Pugh would do even less, he heard the telephone ring.

When he went down Fran had taken tea into their beautiful, warm, glowing sitting-room, and was waiting to welcome him as she usually did, standing in his arms with her head on his chest. When he lowered his head to kiss her, she felt the tears on his face.

'Has it been so awful?' she asked. He could only nod and, sitting down, pulled her on to his knee.

'Who rang?' he said, the comfort of having her close giving him strength again.

'Oh, that Mr Pugh from Danesum. You are not to give looking after the little ones on Friday another thought. Of course he will take care of them while you are at the hospital. Now tell me what it's all about.'

It was a relief to talk. To tell her everything.

'I let all of it get on top of me, my darling,' he said.

She kissed him, and smoothed his mop of wavy white hair back from the furrows still wrinkling his forehead.

'Tell me exactly what the plans are for Friday, and everything you now know about Petrie.'

'John,' he corrected her. 'John Voss-Dering. I want to remember him as John mainly because he wants me to. I think perhaps he feels it is a kind of talisman for me to hand on to Jasper in due course.'

He told her again with every detail added except one, which was of little Cupid's terrible distress, and then joined in her laughter at the 'plot', in which she had to take part by agreeing that neither of them should be available if things didn't go as the peacemakers planned.

She sat in thought for a minute or two, and then said, 'I think it's time we invited Bob and Jane up here again, especially if this problem about Nick is really worrying them. They probably need to talk to somebody right outside the family. Let's invite them to lunch for that Saturday, making it clear that we hope they'll stop and have supper with us, too. Sophie will do the lunch and prepare the supper – it must still be a treat for Jane not to have to bother about meals. If we are pledged to give them our whole attention that day, we can let it be known – to Jess, for instance, if we see her, and everybody else via Sophie – without giving it away who it is we are expecting.'

She told Sophie next morning where William was going, and why. It was Sophie who had asked, delicately, as William was getting ready to leave, if there was anything the sick man was likely to need that they could send him. 'I mean,' said Sophie, 'is he got a change o' pyjamas, like? William's got plenty as 'e could spare, if they was never seen again. Joe 'ad thought about it, but didn't like to say, 'cos 'is own wouldn't ha' fitted, 'im being such a short man. I'm only ever seen that Petrie once, but Joe says 'e's quite as tall as William, only not so well covered. Shall I go and see what I can find?'

'Yes – and thank you for thinking about it,' William said. 'If he needs anything else, Joe can take it on Saturday. Joe means a lot to him. I can go at any time.'

When Fran sat down later with Sophie, the subject arose between them again. Sophie, it appeared, knew almost as much about things as Fran did, having had a long conversation with Joe.

'Joe says as 'e, the man, I mean, 'as been planning for a long while for them all to goo,' she said. ''E 'oped 'e would be able to goo to Wales with 'em, and see 'em all settled in them tents and things as 'e's bought with what young Charles paid 'im for the 'ouse. And Joe says as 'e wants them now to goo without 'im, while Daffy Pugh is still there to drive 'em all that way and being a Welshman 'll know the way, like. Then soon as ever 'e's out of 'ospital, 'e'll go after 'em and make sure they're all right.'

'I'm afraid he will never come out of hospital alive, Sophie. We mustn't have any false hopes about that.'

Sophie gave a great sigh, as if she were relinquishing her last hope. 'If prayers could ha' saved 'im, for them child'en's sake, they would ha' done,' she said. 'Me and Joe and Thirz' and Dan 'as prayed for 'im every day and night since 'e were took so bad. But we can't change God's will, and we must abide by it. It is to be 'oped that Daffy Pugh gets 'em there all safe and sound. Have you thought what you want me to get for Sat'day next week when them from Castle 'Ill is coming for two meals?'

Fran knew that she was being asked why the visit should be such a long one. She was not going to tell Sophie the real reason, but was sure of a sympathetic hearer for their worry about Nick, which would be public knowledge soon enough. She impressed on Sophie that she was speaking in confidence, and repeated what Eric had said about Nick's desire to stay in the cottage, and go to work if he had to.

'That ain't no secret,' Sophie said. 'Olive 'Opkins was in the know and she'd talk the 'ind leg off a donkey if she's got anybody to talk to and a breath o' news as nobody else ain't 'eard. You 'ev to feel sorry for 'er living with a man like Ben 'Opkins as never opens 'is mouth to 'er day or night. Struck dumb, some folks say, like Zachariah in the Bible. You see, 'e were caught poaching on land as used to belong to old Bartrum, as were such a nasty old man 'e'd hev the law on anybody. Ben 'ad to 'ave a lawyer to get 'im off, and the lawyer told 'im to keep 'is mouth shut and never say a word as might be turned against 'im. So 'e never said nothink in court that day only 'is name, and never 'as said a word as 'e 'asn't 'ad to ever since. Mind you, there's them as say any man as lived with Olive would be the same, 'cos 'owever 'ard 'e tried, 'e wouldn't ha' got a word in edgeways. They're like Jack Sprat and 'is wife. They say Bailey's like a mad bull about Charles Bridgefoot getting in front of 'im with Danesum.

'Lucky for that poor man as he didn't get his 'ooks on 'im. Beryl's 'ad plenty to say, though never a word o' sympathy for them poor horphans. "What can a man such as 'im expect," she says. "Serves such folk right as don't do nothing only get children and leave 'em for other folks to bring up out o' the rates."

Sophie, having let herself go, was red-cheeked with indignation. She had no need of a Zachariah Hopkins. The facts loosened her tongue.

'Make us some more tea, and let's talk about the menu for our guests next Saturday week,' Fran said.

<h1 style="text-align:center">53</h1>

The consultation was brief, and straight to the point, kept so by the patient's own medical knowledge and the great penumbra of matters unknown to the doctors.

One thing was very clear to William – that the few days in hospital, with food and care and treatment, had made a decided improvement in the immediate condition of the sick man. It was this that the consultants had seized upon; if he continued to improve, to get enough strength back to withstand the shock of the operation, there was a chance that his life might be prolonged. As anxious to end the present discussion as they were, he asked for another twenty-four hours to make up his mind.

'Now, William,' he said, briskly, once the white coats had disappeared. 'Let me set it before you. I won't ask your advice, because that wouldn't be fair to you. I accept their word – which as you heard, merely offers a dubious chance of giving me a bit of extra time. For myself alone, I wouldn't even consider it. In the end there is no real option, and I would prefer to die here, now, in comfort, without more fuss. But there's my family.

'Perhaps I made the wrong decision in trying to arrange their future for them. Perhaps I should have left it to chance. When I made the decision, I had no idea that I could have left them round here, with anybody at all, like you for example, to care a tinker's cuss what happened to them. It seemed almost a miracle that Fate had sent me Pugh. I'd counted on living long enough to see them settled there, especially after another miracle sent Charles Bridgefoot to buy the house and give me the money I needed.

'It seemed to me that the sooner I moved them, the better. If this had not happened just when it did, we should all have been gone within a couple of weeks. Pugh's crazy to get home to his chapel roots, and it seemed sensible for us to make use of each other. For one thing, as an extra driver on so long a journey with all those children. But what now?

'A few more days here, and I should be well enough to go with them – carry it all out as I had planned. But this chance of the operation that may possibly prolong my life has another aspect. Money. It matters. Think, William, the longer I live, the longer my annuity goes on. If I die now, it stops, and they have nothing immediate to rely on but what you have in your wallet. On the other hand, while I still continue to breathe, I can assure them of food and shelter, and such things as camping fees, though I have paid a good deal already, in advance. I can prolong that time of security for them by accepting the chance of this operation, even if it's only for a few weeks. Crystal gets child allowance for all but Emmy, and Ammy's will cease when she reaches school-leaving age, soon. It's paid, of course, to Crystal.'

William did not interrupt him, or offer any comment. Petrie rested silent for a few minutes, grateful for the time to think.

'Emmy is the child of the student with whom Crystal first dropped out of the university. I imagine there's good blood and high intelligence there; and Ammy, only thirteen months younger, is so much like Emmy that I guess she's his too, conceived before he left and born after. Of the twins, I have no notion – but they're nice girls too, probably with the same sort of parentage. It is easy to forget now that "hippies" have become synonymous with "yobos" how middle-class a lot of the original "flower people" were: youngsters disillusioned by post-war Britain and the aftermath of Hiroshima and Nagasaki, determined to take power over their own lives into their own hands instead of leaving it to the politicians and scientists and academics they accuse of making such a mess of "their" world. Crystal's an extreme example – the product, like me, of an upper-class "service" home, too suddenly set free. In her case, with no social conscience to act as any sort of brake.'

He was talking easily, comfortably, without doing more than clear his throat now and then. William had to keep reminding himself that this was not just an enjoyable discussion after dinner at high table. Every now and then he opened his mouth to make a comment, caught himself in time, and watched the twinkle in Petrie's eye show how much he understood.

'Have you ever met anyone completely amoral? Without an inkling of what is right or wrong, without a shred of social conscience? Take my word for it, William, they do exist, and somehow they can get away with doing just as they like. Decent human beings have consciences, otherwise I should have let them all die on the mountain road. My conscience relieved her of any obligations, even to her progeny. I can't help wondering who fathered Basher. He's the only one she has any feeling for, probably because he's like her. He has the stubborn rebelliousness against all authority – especially mine – that she avers is "freedom".

'She must have been practising some form of contraception, to account for the five-year gap between Basher and Jasper. My mistake, William, my great mistake, the one I'm paying the price for now. He's more than a social responsibility. He's my son.'

One long, thin hand crept out over the coverlet, and William reached for it, and held it, willing his own strength into it.

'I must stay alive every day I can, for his sake. So I shall accept the challenge of the operation,' he said. 'Tomorrow, when I see Emmy and Ammy, I shall tell them *why* it is I leave Jasper to them as a special charge. They may have put two and two together long ago, or even believe I am their father, too. They know the youngest two aren't mine.

'I worry less about the babies. They aren't old enough to remember what happens now. Crystal will claim the four youngest as long as she can draw child allowance for them, but they won't benefit by a penny of it. Then there's Basher. But for the girls, leaving Jasper with him would be like leaving a thoroughbred puppy caged with a hyena. The girls will protect him for as long as I can go on supplying them with the absolute necessities of life. You see why every day I can live will help.

'Go home, William. I've made my mind up. I'll tell the medics here tomorrow that they can experiment on me to their heart's content as long as they keep me breathing for as long as possible. Jasper will get older day by day, and more and more used to not having me around. He's at such a vulnerable age for this to happen.'

'I'll talk to the girls as well, when they've seen you tomorrow,' William said. 'I can say the things you'll find too difficult. They'll have to understand why you have no legal rights and Crystal does – even over Emmy till she comes of age. They know already why you made arrangements for the move to Wales and I'll make sure they believe that a reversed charge phone call to me would set some sort of help in motion in any sort of emergency. You have my word for that.

'And there's another hope. This has been a long winter, and because I'm on leave, I promised myself that after Easter I'd take Fran away for a complete break. By absolute chance, Jane Bellamy's father has a cottage in Wales that I'm going to rent for a month. Only a short distance by car from where they'll be. We'll go and visit them, take them out, and when we come back we'll be able to report to you all the details you'll want to know.'

'If I'm still alive after Easter.'

William didn't answer. He got up to go, suddenly remembering that he had messages.

'Joe's concerned about your comfort here. He tipped Sophie off to remind us that you would need clean clothes, and that his wouldn't fit you, but mine would. So she and Fran made up a case of them for you. Joe's coming himself to see you on Saturday. That made me think to ask if you had any cash, to buy yourself a newspaper or whatever. Don't argue with me, John – I haven't argued with you once, have I?

'Look, I'm aware that there's no sense in leaving money in your locker, so I shall only leave a few shillings there. But I slipped in the tiny safety-razor that went through my RAF days with me. Made specially. Under the razor-blades you'll find a little hidey-hole with a couple of treasury notes in it, quite safe from discovery unless you know where to look. We were looking death straight in the eye, too, in those days. We never knew where we might have to bale out, and what we might need. Do take it. See you tomorrow.'

William's unusual quietness next morning indicated how much he was dreading his afternoon's task. He went to his study immediately after breakfast and, asking no questions, Fran went to hers, intending to work; but stone walls or physical distance had long since failed to prevent them from communicating feelings to each other, and by coffee-time Fran could bear her feeling of unease no longer. She had to find out and share whatever it was that was so distressing William. She made her way to his study, and went in.

He was sitting in his office chair before a pile of papers on his desk, pen in hand – but he was looking blankly somewhere beyond any immediate horizon of space or time, grieving. Of that she was aware before he heard her and turned his head. She was beside him then and, setting her coffee-cup down on his desk, pulled his head towards her, letting him rest it against her while she laid her face on top of his hair. His arms reached round her waist, but neither spoke. It was if she could absorb his thoughts through the contact of their bodies.

When the tension began to leave him, she said, 'Who is it you are grieving for, my darling? Just Petrie, or Mac as well?'

'How did you know? Both. For another friend lost. I know now why I felt so drawn towards Petrie from the moment I saw and talked to him. He was the one man since Mac was killed that I think could ever have filled his place, though I didn't realize it until I dreamed about Mac again last night. No, not my nightmare of his fall – just about being with him.'

'I know,' she said. 'You talked in your sleep. I was ready to wake you if you had showed signs of it turning into the nightmare.'

'No, it was a lovely dream, until I woke, and found myself without him. It made me think about John – Petrie. Mac only left an awful vacuum. He wasn't married, and I was too young to realize that he might have left other responsibilities that only a real friend could shoulder. I grieved only for myself. But John's different. If he had lived, he could almost have become Castor to my Pollux. Things are different now. I do have a lot of other men friends, but still I miss Mac, partly because there's nothing left of him, if you see what I mean. That's why John Petrie's different, as I am different now. I have you, and he has eight – no, only seven – children. Six plus one, the special one. This afternoon I have to share his grief, and theirs. He has to explain to the four oldest exactly what their situation is. And I have to fill in the difficult bits for him, once they have seen him. I can hardly bear face it alone. Will you help, Fran?'

'Do you need ask? What do you want me to do?'

'Let me bring them back here. I've promised that I'll explain their own history to them – everything. And why he has agreed to have this operation for their sakes. That will be the worst bit of all.

'Those girls are such a tribute to him. I've never heard one of them complain about anything. But until now, they've been lucky in spite of everything, because they have had him. As he said to me, "All they've ever had enough of is love." But they have to do without him, now, whichever way it goes. Then they'll be alone – as alone as I was without Mac.

'No! No, my darling. There's absolutely nothing we can do, except be on call. Not while their mother is alive, and stays out of the police's hands. *That*'s what I have to explain to them. If you'll just stand by, I'll be able to manage – but without you, now, I just can't cope. I'm only half a man, when it comes to things like this. God, what did I ever do without you!'

Into the charged silence that followed, the telephone bell crashed and shrilled. Fran reached for the handset, and listened.

'Of course you can,' she said. 'He's here, now.' She cupped her hand over the mouthpiece, and said, 'It's the oldest Petrie girl, very upset, and asking to speak to you.'

She sat down, and watched the effort William had to make to sound his normal self. His replies were soothing and calm, and, though she could see from his face how disturbed he was, deliberately firm.

'Yes, I think you must. Just as Mr Pugh says. Trust me, Emmy – I do believe that it would be best for you all. Yes, at one thirty, then. No, tell Mr Pugh that I can't say what time you will be back. We agreed that you should be in my care for this afternoon, and the others in his. We must stick to that arrangement for your father's sake. Yes, as early as possible. Before dark. Certainly in time for you to put Tanner to bed. Go and get ready now, before anything else happens. Goodbye till I pick you up.'

He slammed the receiver down, stood up and began to swear. He cursed with a vocabulary and vituperation that Fran had never even suspected him capable of, but along with her surprise came a feeling of great relief, as if he were letting gas out from a distended stomach. She felt it herself, and knew that for him it was providing even greater easement. The target of his anger appeared to be Dafydd Pugh.

When, at last, his invective ran out, he sat down heavily in his chair and looked towards her, smiling a slight, lop-sided smile that was both triumphant and apologetic. Then he stood up again, turning towards her, and she met him halfway. They simply stood, clinging to each other, while she waited for him to explain.

As soon as he could control his voice he told her. Little Tanner had been very difficult, having somehow picked up, in the way that small children do, that he was being left behind that afternoon while his sisters went out. He had first thrown himself into a temper, shouting and screaming and throwing things, and then started crying uncontrollably, until he had made himself sick. All attempts by his sisters to distract and soothe him had failed, and they had been almost at their wits' end when Pugh had appeared, with their mother in tow.

Crystal had, Emmy said, gone straight to the child and slapped him, not once, but repeatedly, as hard as she could, forbidding his sisters to interfere, till she had reduced him to a sobbing, vomiting heap. Then Pugh had picked him up, stood him on his feet and held him upright, shouting at him to stand up, stop yelling and listen.

The terrified child had turned his head and bitten Pugh's hand. Basher and Crystal had laughed aloud, and the man had retaliated by striking Tanner so hard that he fell over and just lay there – either fainting or unconscious. Ammy had rushed to pick him up, but Pugh had shoved her aside, and ordered them all to leave the boy to him. Emmy hadn't said what happened next, till Pugh told them that he was going to tell them something they'd better listen to.

With their mother's consent, he said, in the absence of the man they called father, he would be acting *in loco parentis*, and they must all obey him, from that moment and until he had seen them settled in their new home in Wales. He warned them that his rule would apply especially to Tanner, whose trouble was that he had been spoilt. He needed discipline such as they had seen him apply. There should be no more spoiling of the child by sparing of the rod.

Emmy, said William, had sobbed out that she had tried to stand up to

Pugh, declaring that she couldn't and wouldn't leave Tanner this afternoon in that state, and didn't mind staying at home to look after him.

'He wouldn't listen,' she said. 'He told us we had to go, and suggested that Mummy should give Tanner a dose of the medicine she had got ready for the long journey if he was carsick. It would stop him vomiting again when he came round, and probably send him to sleep as well.' Then Tanner had come round, and Crystal had made him swallow something – Emmy didn't know what. Pugh laid Tanner on the hearthrug, just as he was. Emmy had asked permission to wash his face and cover him up, but he'd been too drowsy to know by then. He was very pale, and had gone to sleep almost at once.

Then Pugh had calmed down, and said it would be silly to wake him, because he'd be upset again if he saw them leave. So they must get away before he roused. They were to walk to the end of the road, and meet William there.

'I had to let you know,' she had said. 'Though if he knows I've told you he'll be furious with me. I think he's gone mad. What ought we to do?'

'You heard what I told her,' William said to Fran. 'What else can they do? I can't let John down, but they mustn't say a word to him about it. I don't suppose he injured Tanner physically, though God knows what psychological damage he may have done. Those travel-sickness preparations do contain a soporific, so if they gave him an adult dose, he may very well sleep till I get the girls back to him. I'll make sure I see him – Tanner – before I leave, and that he's all right. I think, after all, that I'd better take them straight home. If I need you, I'll phone and ask you to meet me there. Try not to worry. We only have a very distressed girl's account to go on. It may not be half so bad as she made it sound.'

That was all very well, but Fran wanted to know more, and he wanted her feminine counsel and advice. He had to tell her what he had been withholding from her about little Jasper's reaction to his father's absence.

'Yes, I know, my sweetheart,' he said. 'It's our helplessness that's so hard to bear, isn't it? Now you know why I had to curse as I did. It was the only thing I could do.'

The clock was relentless, and he had to leave. In the doorway, he paused, and said, 'I wish I had Eric or Bob Bellamy with me. Either of them would break that bloody preacher's neck first, and do the explaining afterwards. I told you I was only half a man But I can only handle this my way.'

From the shadow of the hall behind them, Sophie's tearful voice spoke. 'I 'eard all that,' she said, 'and I can't say as I'm surprised. I never did take to that Daffy, for all 'is praying. As if God would take notice o' the dog as could yap loudest. I'll stop 'ere with Fran, and be ready to go down there with 'er if needs be. I reckon our prayers'll do more for 'em all than 'is'n will.'

Several times during the hours that followed, William envied Sophie her unshakeable faith. It was as harrowing an afternoon as he had ever spent.

The four girls whom he found waiting for him at the end of the lane, he hardly recognized to start with, mainly because they were properly dressed against the weather in new duffle-coats, with hoods pulled up against the wind and their usually bare legs not only stockinged, but shod in new, sensibly stout shoes. He guessed, as he afterwards discovered correctly, that Petrie had spent money on them to set them up against the cold weather of Wales.

He got out of the car and opened the back door to Ammy and the twins, indicating that he wanted the oldest, Emmy, to sit beside him. He had hopes of talking to her on the journey about what to expect at the hospital. It was only when, after thanking him politely if huskily, she threw back the hood of her coat, that he realized quite what he had let himself in for. The white, wan face, of which eyes reddened and swollen with weeping seemed the larger half, was not that of the self-possessed, sensible girl he knew as his sick friend's housekeeper, nurse and companion; it was that of a frightened waif, worse than orphaned, who had that morning seen a corner lifted of the dark veil covering a horrid future. Stealing a quick glance at the other three now huddled in the back seat, he also saw that of the four of them, she was the most in control of herself. The others were still a mass of tears, still heaving great sobs and snuffling under their enveloping hoods, the twins clinging to each other and Ammy huddled into the corner, trembling violently. Emmy, fighting back her own tears, told him that they had not dared to make a fuss in front of their mother or Pugh, but once they had got out of sight of the house it had got the better of all of them.

'I'm so sorry,' Emmy kept saying, 'but you see, once we had started to cry, we simply couldn't stop. Thinking what Jasper will do if he wakes up and we aren't there . . . There isn't anything to give him to eat. None of us has had anything – the last lot of food we had bought has run out, and I was going shopping this morning with the money Dad put into my letter from him. There was no sugar to put on Tanner's porridge, and he wouldn't eat it. That's how it all started.' She gulped again – and with sickening understanding William saw that they hadn't got such a thing as one single handkerchief among them all.

He had switched on the ignition, but turned it off again at once. There was no way he could proceed straight to the hospital as planned. Nor, said a sudden shaft of common sense, could he remain where he was, out on the highway – a middle-aged man with what must appear to any chance passer-by as a car-load of young female passengers all displaying very obvious signs of fear and distress.

He should have had enough sense to bring Fran with him – but then, he hadn't expected any such complications as this. He felt in his pocket for his own handkerchief, and then, with a surge of relief great enough to be pleasure, reached across in front of Emmy to open the glove compartment and take from it a box of man-size tissues. The girl at his side knelt up in her seat and distributed them, while William groped in his numbed mind for the next sensible thing to do. That box of tissues seemed to him like an omen. He had, above all, to think and act practically.

He had to give the children time to recover a bit before their father saw them, or willy-nilly the truth would come out, and there was no guessing what the end result of that might be. He longed to turn back to Benedict's, but for one thing it would take too much time, and for another, the sort of sympathy that Fran and Sophie would offer would be more likely to do more harm than good at this juncture. No – he must deal with it alone. He had put his hand to the plough. So what next? Food. His stunned faculties had began to function again.

The hotel was only a couple of hundred yards away. He drove swiftly into the same shaded corner of the car park where Charles and Charlie had sat on Boxing Day, and told the girls that he was going to find some food for them to eat on the way.

He asked the receptionist brusquely if Mr Choppen was in his office, and being told that he was, made his way up there two stairs at a time. Eric must be told nothing except that he had four hungry children whom he was taking to see their father in hospital. It would be better for the whole affair to be kept quiet, for everybody's sake.

Eric issued orders, and within ten minutes William was on his way again with packets of sandwiches and bottles of coke and pop. The girls fell on the food and began to lose the anguish in their eyes. Once into the outskirts of Cambridge, he stopped at a public lavatory and sent them in to bathe their faces and tidy their hair. They certainly looked very much more presentable when they returned, and even found a few weak smiles.

In the car park at the hospital, he told them as much as he dared. They could only go into the ward two at a time, and he would wait outside with the other two. They would not be allowed to stay long.

'You will find your father looking very much better than when you last saw him,' he said. 'But he won't be able to talk much. Listen to what he tells you, but don't tell him of Mr Pugh's behaviour. It would only worry him to no purpose. Just tell him how much Jasper is missing him, and leave it at that. He will see that you have been crying – but so do most people visiting those they love in hospital. That won't surprise him. I shall be just down the corridor in the waiting-room, but it is you he wants to see today. He has made arrangements for you all according to what he believed to be best. There, that's the bell for visiting time. I'll tell you everything else I know on our way back. Don't worry – I'm going all the way home with you. Off you go. I think you will only have less than an hour with him altogether.'

He put out both hands, one to each of the two oldest girls. He watched them set their chins firm, hold up their heads and walk away. He wished that they were his daughters; he couldn't believe that if they had been, they would have been any better brought up than these two had been, though by a man no nearer to them in blood than he was himself.

He sat down with the other two to wait, engaging their interest in things going on around them, his professional skill as a teacher coming to his aid. The twins were so much alike that he still didn't know which was which when the time came for them to change over with their older sisters.

Caught in the homeward rush of cars, it took them a long time to clear the traffic of Cambridge. As he reached the turning towards Danesum, it was almost five o'clock on a dull, cloudy evening in which the dusk seemed to be falling early. He had had no chance to add anything, yet, to what Petrie had been able to tell them himself, but he had sensed their anxiety to get home, and had taken a quick decision to postpone his talk with them. They had already been through more than enough trauma for one day, and so, in fact, had he. He felt absolutely drained.

They had been very quiet after leaving the ward, using the unwonted luxury of his box of tissues to wipe away the silent tears that persisted in creeping down their white faces.

The twins held hands, and William, inclined to look for a gleam of comfort wherever he could, saw clearly that as long as those two could remain together, they would perhaps suffer less than the others. The silence in the car encouraged him to think. He wanted a rest from other people's troubles, though, either *en bloc* as a community under threat, or as individuals he was fond of. How he had come to get himself so deeply involved with this family of vagrants, whose affairs were now pulling at his heartstrings so strongly, he didn't know. It had just happened that way. That would soon be over, however, resolve itself how sadly it might. Then he would take Fran away, and have her to himself in peace somewhere out of the hive of glass their village had become.

A feeble light in the kitchen of the Danesum house was all that welcomed the girls home, but the moment he brought the car to a standstill, they scrambled out and went rushing round to the back door. Only Emerald waited for him, to accompany him in, trying in her way to express the gratitude the others had neglected to show. It was still darkly twilight, and the two of them stood at the front door, expecting to be let in that way – till around the corner of the house came back the other three, all calling distractedly for their sister, all crying and clamouring and exclaiming in a desperate gabble from which the only word William could decipher was 'gone'.

'What do you mean?' asked Emmy, grabbing her sister and shaking her. 'Who's gone? Where?'

'All of them! Everything! The new Dormobile and the trailer, and all the stuff we had packed in it.'

'Mummy? Mr Pugh?' The truth was beginning to sink in. 'Gone without us? They can't have. They wouldn't!' But she ran, shepherding the other three in front of her, back round the corner, to where, at lunchtime, the loaded vehicles had stood.

It was as if they had completely forgotten William's presence. He had not yet accepted what they had said. He was trying to think what explanation there could be for the hysterical commotion he now had to deal with. Well, he had better go and look for himself. Wearily, he realized that he was too tired and worn out to accept the possibility of further trouble. He would have to phone Fran, and ask her to come, if anything else was wrong.

Then the front door opened, and by the naked electric bulb in the hall, he saw silhouetted in the doorway the short, spare frame of Joe Noble.

'Mr Burbage, sir!' he said. 'Thank God you're here! They've took every mortal thing, and done a moonlight flit – Pugh, and her, and all the littl'uns, gone as clean as a whistle. Come in, sir, and see for yourself!'

54

William never could recall afterwards what happened in those first few minutes of shock.

There were only impressions crowding upon each other, some vague, some in vivid psychedelic Technicolor. Of the house, always bare and ill-lit, now stark, frigid and freezing cold; of an enormous relief that that sturdy little figure which was Joe Noble was there in his sight, and of a ridiculous desire to repeat what Joe had just said to him in reverse; of the twins, holding hands, retreating towards the back of the house in a prolonged though subdued wail; of his own first need to open the door into the room Petrie had occupied, in order to reach a telephone and make contact as fast as he could with Fran.

The room was empty except for the old bedstead, on which a thin sagging striped mattress still rested. One glance told him that the telephone was gone. Then Emerald came in, with two letters, holding herself upright and rigid, still too stunned to react with anything other than her usual acceptance of her responsibility for all the rest of the family; but the sight of the empty bed undid her, and as William sank down on the mattress in his own mental and emotional confusion, she went to him and sat down close beside him. It was her stony face that awoke William to the vast consequences of their discovery, and of his own part in the trauma of the present moment, as well as all the future consequences of it. None of it was his fault, nor in point of fact of his own seeking, but there it was, waiting to be dealt with as Mount Everest had been waiting to be climbed. He took Emerald's hand, and she collapsed up against him, dry-eyed but suddenly limp. She still clutched the two letters in her hand.

Just inside the door of the room was Joe, with Ammy clinging to him. He was looking towards William as if waiting for orders. 'Mr Burbage, sir,' he said, 'what shall we do?'

His voice recalled William to sense and the need to do something. 'Make sure first, I suppose,' he said, gently disengaging himself from Emerald and standing up. 'How long have you been here? Are you sure they've actually gone? All of them? Have you looked upstairs? The babies may be in bed and asleep. The vehicles have gone – you're sure? Emmy, would you and Ammy go and look?'

He wanted to talk to Joe, man to man.

'They've gone all right, sir. I reckon it was all planned. You see, Davvy asked me if I could get a hour off from work this afternoon to help him. They'd never unpacked any of the new stuff, 'cos Mr Petrie kept saying the sooner he could get them all moved, the better. Then when he was took bad, it seemed as if Davvy hisself couldn't wait to be gone. He's told me again and again lately as Wales was calling him, like, to go back there, and once he said if they didn't all go soon, he'd go anyway by hisself and leave them to get there as well as they could without his help.

'To tell you the truth, sir, I thought he knowed as he was getting too thick, like, with the woman whatever her name is, and was worried 'cos she was always hanging round him. But I was worried about him – Mr Petrie, I mean, 'cos anybody could see he wasn't going to be well enough to do that long drive all by hisself with all them children to look after. So I thought if I could do my bit to help get the last few things packed like, it might be best for Davvy as well as everybody else to make sure things was all ready for 'em to get off as soon as he was out of hospital. Or even if he never come out.

'So I left off work early today and only just called in at home to tell Het where I should be and that I might be late, and then I come straight on here. As soon as I see the new van and trailer had gone, and Davvy's own car still standing there by itself, I knowed what had happened. I see how he had took me in, and planned it all so as I should be here when them gels found they'd been left behind. A man like him, to do a thing like that! I were so took aback I didn't know which way to turn. Till you come.'

Yes. William followed his reasoning, and saw that he was right. Of course it had been planned. Everything fell into place. Pugh's 'helpful' phone call that he would 'look after' the little ones. The 'lucky chance' that there had been to hand some 'medicine' to drug the smaller children into docility, and a trumped-up reason for administering a large dose at the crucial time to the one who might have caused trouble before he had got the girls out of the way.

And the letters, which so far they hadn't opened, more or less proved that it had been a carefully laid plot.

Further speculation was useless. He had to decide what to do next. The first thing to be done was to get himself and the four girls back to where Fran was. Sophie had said that she would still be there. What a blessing that was! The girls came back, miserably shaking their heads.

He said to Emerald, 'Go and find the twins, then, and look after them. Tell them that I'm taking you all home with me, so get what you may need for tonight. You can't stop here alone. When we know for certain where we all stand it will be time to make other arrangements. But there's room for you all at Benedict's for the time being, so don't worry. Let's be off as quick as we can.' They obeyed him, simply, like automatons. He felt like one, too, though natural wit was gradually coming back to his aid.

As soon as they were out of sight, he turned to Joe. 'Joe, can you drive a car? Have you got a licence?'

'Yes, I'm been driving anything and everything where I work since I first started there. I'm never had a car o' my own, but I've druv one for years and years.'

'Good. Take this' – he gave him some money from his wallet – 'and get Pugh's car filled up with petrol and bring it back to Benedict's. We don't know what we may need. I must get the girls there before any of them collapses on me from shock and distress. They've already had more than enough for one day – a lot this morning that you haven't heard yet. I'd be glad of your help a bit longer, till we see what we ought to do. For one thing, you know Pugh better than anybody else.'

Joe settled his cap on his head, nodding his willing agreement. 'What about these 'ere?' he said, picking up the letters. 'There's one for you and one for me.'

'Let them wait. I don't suppose they'll be much help. It's a question of what to do first.'

Joe handed him the letters, and went. William took them, called his flock and shepherded them out to his car. They were dry-eyed, though their white faces showed fear of the present and blank terror of the great unknown wastes of their future.

The wave of anger that swept through William at the sight of them was like a shot of adrenaline to him. The ability to think and cope came back with a rush. He went back inside the house, switched off the lights, asking Emerald about the keys. All she could do was to shake her head in a gesture of utter helplessness and incomprehension that he found harder to bear than sobs or hysterics. The keys were not where they should be, but she didn't care. He concluded that she – and indeed perhaps all of them – had mercifully reached the cut-off point with reality. Nature has her own way of dealing with situations otherwise unbearable. Never mind the keys. Get them away.

An hour later, they had been welcomed, warmed, fed, washed and tucked up, two to a bed in bedrooms next to each other, with the doors left open. Sophie had insisted on that. 'Now leave 'em by theirselves,' she had said to Fran, who was inclined to fuss. 'It'll be when they wake up again as they'll need us, not now. They'll be asleep in five minutes. They're too wore out to care about nothing else, poor things.' She was right, of course.

William had had a shower and a large whisky, at Fran's insistence, by the time Joe returned. Sophie put food for four on the kitchen table, and made Joe sit down with them. When they had eaten she cleared away and sat down again, taking it absolutely for granted that she and Joe were as much part of the decisions to be made as William and Fran were.

'What about them letters?' Joe asked. 'Ha'n't we ought to see what they say?'

William nodded. They might as well start from what there was to be known – though his mind had already raced forward to the first and worst task staring them in the face. Somebody had to tell Petrie. William shrank from the task, and wondered if, like so many other unpleasant tasks, it could be handed over to the police. He put it aside for the moment, till they could see more clearly where they stood.

He opened his letter, which as he had guessed, was from Crystal. He spread it out where he and Fran could both read the large, flowing, educated hand and its curt, decisive phraseology.

Dear Mr Burbage,

I assume that you have been told that this house has been sold over the heads of myself and the children. I was not consulted at any point.

I understand that Petrie was intending to remove them, or perhaps I should write 'us', to Wales. Therefore, in his absence, which I am informed may be permanent, I propose to take advantage of the arrangements he has made. I must point out to you that he has no claim whatsoever upon me or any of the children I have taken with me. However, since he has chosen to involve you, and you have consented to be involved, I shall expect you to continue to share his responsibility for those old enough to be left behind. I cannot and do not intend to try to cope with the four who are quite accustomed to looking after themselves. Perhaps you will be good enough to inform him of my decision. I have no doubt whatsoever that he would wish me to make use of all that he has provided for the future comfort of the younger ones, since they have no other resources.

Yours sincerely
Crystal Garnett

It was as unbelievable in its coldness, and as incomprehensible in its lack of any other feeling, as a communication from another planet might have been; and yet, as William recognized immediately, it was absolutely in keeping with everything Petrie had ever said about the woman who had written it. She was as amoral as a dead halibut.

He looked across at Joe, who was having difficulty in seeing or believing what Pugh's letter conveyed. Joe passed the letter across the table to him, asking him to read it aloud.

This, too, was well written, in a clear legible hand, by a man who was no stranger to the use of language, though the tone and style could hardly have been more different from the woman's.

Dear Joe,

As the Lord is my witness, I write this only after much prayer and soul-searching, and in grievous trouble of spirit. I have told you how I have felt for some time that the Lord was recalling me to continue His work in my own native country of Wales, now that I have no gainful employment to keep me here.

But I believe that it was the Lord's will that led me here, to this house and these people. He first led me to you, so that together we could try to save these souls. Otherwise, I am sure, He would surely have sent me home once I had done my part in selling this house. Since then, I have been pulled both ways. But I feel that I am chosen to do His work in helping to save the woman, Crystal, from the snares of the Evil One, and to bring her into the fold. I pray that I shall be able to do so.

Since I have been with her, talked to her and prayed with her, she is no longer dependent upon drink or drugs. She depends on me. It so happens that many of her former friends are in mid-Wales, which is my home. I shall therefore be able to continue to see and pray with her, and do all I can for her in her new home. I truly believe that in agreeing to aid her in her plan to leave secretly and without warning, I am obeying the Lord's command. He has chosen me to be His instrument to help her to a new start in a better life. She has explained to me the temptations of the flesh which lie ahead for girls in such places as their father has chosen for them to live in, and for that reason she will not now take them there. She is prepared, with my help, to take and care for those young enough to be trained up in the way of God. We do not feel able to accept responsibility for the moral welfare of Petrie's four teenage daughters, for whom she says she has no legal responsibility.

We are hopeful that through you, and through his acquaintance with Prof. Burbage, their father will have made other and better provision for them elsewhere.

I trust that as I have been called to do my duty towards her and the youngest, you will do yours towards him and the others.

Watch and pray.
Your brother in Christ,
Dafydd Islwyn Pugh

Joe's hand had curled itself into a fist, which in the silence that followed the cessation of William's voice he brought down with a crash on to the table. Sophie looked up into his expressive face, and was the first to speak.

'Now then, Joe,' she said. 'Don't take on. If you ask me, I should say as it's all for the best. I ain't saying as 'e ain't done well by you but you don't need such as 'im, now. I never did trust 'im – too much say and too little do for my liking. All wind and water like the barber's cat, preach what he might. They're all alike, such as 'im as'll talk the 'ind leg off the donkey, and then leave it to starve with nothing to eat but fancy words.

You're done your best, Joe, and we're all proud of you, that we are. You hev just showed 'im up for what 'e is.'

William was astounded at her intuition. Of all those Pugh's defection might injure, simple-hearted Joe would be hurt most. He had put his trust in a broken reed. Preacher and saver of souls though he had claimed to be, Pugh had committed the one sin that Joe had been most aware of, because of his own daughter's fall from grace, which had been the cause of him losing his Christian faith in the first place. It was clear that Joe took it for granted that Pugh had succumbed to the wiles of the modern Jezebel.

'Liar! Hypocrite!' exploded Joe. 'With that poor man laying at death's door, to do such a thing as this to 'im. And then to call it the Lord's will!'

'We mustn't judge him too harshly,' Fran said, afraid for Joe. 'Perhaps he meant that he felt himself in danger, and wanted to go before it was too late. Some of it sounds very sincere. That awful woman hoodwinked him and used him, but you mustn't read into it that he's been sleeping with her. He may want to, because when all is said and done he is only a man, and she probably held out the promise of it to keep him because she needed him to get her back to Wales and the sort of men she is used to, who will keep her in money for drugs and drink. She let him think he had "saved" her and that she was turning over a new leaf because of him, to serve her own purpose. He's devoted his whole life to bringing sinners like her to repentance. Can you wonder that he'll do anything she asks? He thinks she's his greatest success! He's only a silly man who happens to have a gift of words, and believes what he wants to believe. No match for a woman like her, but that only makes him a weak man, not necessarily a bad one. He may still be a good one.'

Sophie snorted. 'A good man? Doing what he done to that poor little child this very morning? And going along with her, a-leaving them four gals upstairs to charity? Don't you tell me as such as 'im is a good man! 'E might ha' been, like Adam, if the woman hadn't tempted 'im.'

'What did he do this morning?' Joe asked puzzled. He was told.

'There's nothing too bad for him,' Sophie said. 'And bad will become of 'im.'

'We're wasting precious time,' William said, for once irritated with Sophie and Fran. 'He'll find out soon enough. Leave him to heaven. We've got other things to think about.'

Fran saw the need to intervene again. 'But she told Pugh, or let him think, Joe, that the four girls were not hers,' she said. 'They are. They're all hers by other men, all except little Jasper. He is Petrie's. I wonder why she bothered to take him with her, especially as Pugh doesn't like him.'

'A bargaining counter against Petrie, should he live, and against me, if he doesn't,' said William. 'She's clever. Her letter is meant to warn me in no uncertain terms to keep off the grass. She knows exactly where she stands, and that the police can't interfere with her taking her children where she likes, though I suppose they might in time catch up on her for abandoning the twins. What's worrying me is how we are going to break this news to John – Mr Petrie. Perhaps I ought to go back to see him tonight.'

Fran looked at him anxiously, worried by his manner. This man, letting things get on top of him, was not the William she was used to. She guessed why it was – he was not in control of anything. In spite of endless committee meetings at work and the obstreperousness of young colleagues, he could usually if necessary have the last word. In this, he had no word at all, though the great wheel was running downhill out of his control. She spoke firmly.

'What good would that do? You'll only make things worse. You're already done up, and so is Joe. Besides you can't leave me here by myself, to cope with those girls. They are asleep now but think what may happen if they wake up? We may need a doctor, or even the police. It's nearly nine o'clock now.'

'I shall stop 'ere tonight,' Sophie announced stoutly. 'I shan't leave you by yourself, as you might know. But I reckon as Het'll be heving sterricks if Joe don't soon goo 'ome. Can't you leave telling 'im in 'ospital anything at all till the morning? That's what I say.'

It was a decision William did not feel able to make. It was John's family that had been abducted and abandoned, not his or Sophie's. He asked Joe to stay just a few minutes more, while he rang the hospital.

He was soon back. 'They said he had been so distressed after saying goodbye to the girls this afternoon that they had sedated him, and he's asleep. They're not prepared to disturb him tonight, especially to be told bad news. I think perhaps I shall have to tell the police, and I must certainly let Charles know that the house is empty, and not even locked. I hate to ask you, Joe, but do you think you could face the task of telling Mr Petrie, going early tomorrow instead of the afternoon? I see no reason why you shouldn't make use of Pugh's car. I want to go first thing to consult Elyot Franks – who is a magistrate – and then to see Charles. After that, if you want me or need me, I'll join you at the hospital. I really think that would be best.'

Fran sighed with relief. She could see that he was almost at the end of his resources, suffering for them all, because of his acute sensitivity to every possibility. People like Joe and Sophie, though just as kind, had their feet so firmly planted in the soil that a bit of rough weather didn't shake them. In an emergency, they were like the house built upon rock. But they were all worn out. The best thing for all of them would be to get some rest now, while they could.

*

Sophie had put herself to bed in the flat, and was up and about long before William and Fran, although they, too, woke early. He had roused long before it was fully light, and in the twilight had found Fran already wide-eyed and listening for any movement. All was yet quiet.

He pulled her head on to his shoulder, each strengthened against the anticipated rigours of the coming day by the presence of the other.

'They were just knocked out last night,' he said, meaning their unexpected guests. 'I'll go and make some tea for us, so that you are ready to go to them if they wake.'

'I think I can hear Sophie about already,' she said. 'So you'd better get dressed. We don't know what to expect.'

He had barely had time to get downstairs before Fran heard sounds from the end bedrooms, and creeping down the passage, listened. All four girls were in one bed, and their grief and distress were almost palpable. She stood for a minute or two getting her own courage up before knocking and going to them. The twins were lying clasped in each other's arms, still in bed, and the other two sat on the bed, one each side, tearful themselves but still trying to comfort the younger ones. Though very reluctant to intrude, Fran felt that they all needed reassurance and support. She took her usual practical line – that food was the first essential in any crisis.

'You'll all feel better able to face the day when you've had breakfast,' she said. 'I think if you were all to get up and dressed, and come down, you would be able to help us to decide what to do next. Will you do that? You will find towels and things in the bathroom.'

She didn't stop for any of them to try to speak, leaving her suggestion hanging in the air almost as an order. It obliged the youngsters to pull themselves together and obey her. They were all conscious of Benedict's as their only refuge this morning, and had found Fran's lack of overt sympathy helpful rather than otherwise. There would be plenty of time for tears later.

Sophie had porridge, toast and scrambled eggs waiting for them, having given William and Fran theirs in William's study. With her first spoonful of porridge, Emerald choked, and began to cry.

Fran and William, on the alert, heard Sophie's attempt to comfort her, and went to her rescue. Though hungry, all the others had laid down their spoons, too.

'I'm so sorry,' Emerald sobbed. 'You are so kind, but I can't help thinking about Tanner. What will he do without us?'

'Or Jade, and Aggie?' said Ammy. 'We always looked after them in the mornings. *She* never has done. They hardly know who she is. Why didn't she take us as well? Or why didn't they leave the little ones with us? Where do you think they are? What are they having to eat?'

'When you have eaten your breakfast, we'll tell you what we talked about last night,' Fran said. 'For the moment, you are our guests, and we shall be worried if you don't eat. Besides, you'll feel a lot better if you do. Then try to find something to do. I'm sure Sophie will let you wash up, and help her. Mr Burbage is going out to see about things, but I shall be here all day with you. There, can you eat up your porridge, now?'

'Not till I've 'eated it up again, they can't,' Sophie said, suiting action to word. 'Cold stodgy porridge ain't only fit for pigs. But nice 'ot porridge with cream and brown sugar is good enough for the Queen. It'll only take a minute.'

Fran escaped, to tell William that all was as well as could be expected. Somehow, Sophie had made the girls smile. Even cold porridge could apparently have its uses.

William went first to Temperance Farm, and told his tale, adding that he thought that Charles should provide new locks at once, since it might very well be part of Crystal's scheming to pretend they had gone, only to return and acquire squatter's rights once she could get in with the keys she held and must have taken with her. No Bridgefoot would have thought of that sort of modern skullduggery, and in consequence Charles was more than grateful.

William asked out of politeness about Brian's health and Marjorie's spirits. Brian answered for himself. He still could not lift or carry heavy weights, but otherwise he was now fit for work. As for Marjorie, he was hoping to negotiate with Bailey for him to buy her share of the house and the land that went with it. 'Once Charles is married, and Marjorie and Vic are divorced, there'll be a lot of changes,' he said. 'We're planning to reconstitute Bridgefoot Farms Ltd on a new basis. 'It all looks as if everything may be all for the best. Let us know if there is anything we can do to help that poor family.'

William left them feeling his burden lightened because shared. His next call was to Elyot, but it was Beth he first encountered, and to whom he poured out the story.

'You talk to Elyot,' she said. 'I'm going up to see Fran. Those two oldest know me better than they do her. Besides, a walk will do me good. Elyot thinks I'm the only woman who has ever carried a baby, and that God didn't really know what he was doing letting females take such risks.'

She fetched her coat and stood on tiptoe to kiss Elyot as he helped her on with it. William decided that God had known very well what he was doing with those two and grinned sympathetically at Elyot's anxiety as a prospective though decidedly middle-aged father. Maybe having four almost grown-up girls dumped on you overnight was the easier task, after all.

Elyot wasn't of much immediate help, but said that he would find out what he could. He would go back to Benedict's with William now to see the four Petrie girls for himself, and walk back with Beth.

They settled down to coffee. Sophie was intent on keeping all four girls as occupied as possible, and Emmy and Ammy were only too happy to serve the coffee and see Beth again. She suggested that they should stay in the sitting-room with the four grown-ups, to discuss their situation.

'Of course,' William said, 'we shall know better when Joe gets back, and tells us what John wants us to do. There's the phone. I'll take it in my study.'

It was a very tense and shaken man who returned ten minutes later. Fran read his face, and at once asked the girls to take out the coffee cups and inquire what they could do to help Sophie prepare lunch for two more, because Mr and Mrs Franks would be staying.

Once they had gone, she looked up at William for explanation. Something had obviously gone very wrong.

'That was John,' he said. 'He has discharged himself from the hospital, against all advice, and insists on starting at once in pursuit of Pugh and Crystal – all the way to Wales if need be. In Pugh's car. Joe's frantic, because he says John will never make the journey, but nothing will change his mind. I begged him to wait till I could get there to go with him, but he refused point blank. It would waste two precious hours, he says, and we've wasted too much time already. He is convinced that Jasper is in actual physical danger at the mercy of Crystal and Basher, without his sisters to protect him. He has never said anything like that before, but I'm afraid what happened yesterday morning doesn't make it sound as mad as it might otherwise. He says he has to find them before Pugh leaves them. He and Joe are in the hospital car park, where Joe refused to give him the car keys until he had spoken to me.

'Then Joe grabbed the phone from him, and said that as he could do nothing else to prevent him from setting out, the only thing possible was for him to go as well and share the driving. So somebody has to go and tell Hetty, and Joe's boss, that he won't be back for several days. Then we were cut off.'

'Have they got any money? Won't that stop them?' asked Elyot, practically.

'The car's full of petrol, and I left John twenty pounds on Friday,' William said. 'Joe may have a pound or two in his pocket as well. Ought I to try to catch them? Pugh's car's old, though it isn't bad, but mine's a lot faster. I suppose I could get to Wales almost as soon as they do, if I went now.'

Fran looked appalled, not least by the stupidity of his suggestion.

'And then I suppose Elyot will set off after you, and Eric after Elyot, and Bob after Eric?' she said scathingly. 'Really, darling! "I'm crying because Mr Rabbit cries, and Mr Rabbit cries because the boy cries, and the boy cries because he can't get the goats out of the turnip field." Surely we can think of something more sensible than that!'

'I suppose we could alert the police to look out for the car,' said Beth.

'If anybody knew the number, or even where they were heading for,' said William, ruefully, accepting Fran's point. 'I hadn't thought of that.'

'Perhaps the girls know,' suggested Beth hopefully, going to William's rescue; but that proved to be a vain hope. Nobody knew anything more than that their destination was somewhere north of Aberystwyth.

'So now we know,' said Fran, abrasive because of her worry with regard to the unexpected depth of their involvement, and not helped by the sight of William in a most unusual state of 'flap'. Beth and Elyot looked equally clueless as to what to suggest next. She spoke into the vacuum, filling the silence with the first thing that rose to her tongue, instinctively expecting words to prime the pump of practical thought. 'Perhaps we should now all set out one after the other to tell the king that the sky has fallen on poor little Chicken-Licken Hetty-Letty's head. We all seem to have lost sight of common sense. What can anybody do that is sensible but wait? If we start rushing about like ants in an anthill we shall only make things worse. At least Joe's used his common sense. He knows Petrie as well as anybody does, and is on the spot. Surely it's better for William to be here to deal with any formalities, and help to care for those actually in our house? Petrie knows where he's going and what to expect when he gets there. William would be a Yankee at the court of King Arthur – if he ever found it. It's no good flapping around like a lot of headless geese. Let's have lunch, and then try to *think*.'

Sophie appeared to say that seeing it was only a cold lunch anyway, she had set lunch in the breakfast-room and that she and the girls were having theirs in the kitchen, and what was all this the girls were saying about Joe setting off to Wales without anybody knowing?

'I don't know what we shall do with Het,' she said. 'It'd better be me and Thirz' as tells 'er 'cos without Joe about nobody else could deal with 'er sterricks. Them gels can wash up after dinner, and if William was to take me and Thirz' to see Het, likely 'im being there would 'elp. Thirz' might ask Het to goo to hers till Joe gets back. Them twins could take young Stevie out for walks and such. It would give them something to do.'

There, thought Fran, spoke the voice of common sense. They all needed to be doing something. William said he thought they needn't involve Thirzah until they saw how Hetty was going to take the news, and Sophie didn't argue.

He left her to explain to her sister the reason for their visit, once Hetty had stiffly invited them to sit down. Hetty showed no signs of having hysterics, once she had taken the news in. Very sensibly, she asked questions instead.

Sophie was inclined to resent her simple sister's questioning. She told Hetty sharply that they had told her once. She wasn't deaf, was she?

No, Hetty said, she wasn't. She was asking because she just couldn't believe her ears. It was too good to be true that him, that Daffy who had as good as robbed her of her husband, was gone away for good. And with that, she had sat down and indulged in such a mild and ladylike attack of hysterics that Sophie had only to threaten to send for Thirzah, and it was all over.

Sophie, much mollified, offered to go up and sleep with her till Joe came back. Or would she and Stevie rather go and stop with Thirz' and Dan'el?

Neither the one nor the other, Hetty said. She had got used to being by herself a lot lately, and as long as Joe did come back, she didn't care about a night or two by herself. In fact, she had been wanting to paper their bedroom, and this would be a good chance 'cos she could sleep with Stevie and needn't make the double bed up every night.

'Well!' said Sophie, once seated again beside William in the car. 'Fancy our Het being as sensible as that!'

William hoped that there might be more than that for them to be thankful for, before bedtime. In fact, what news there was was a mixture of good and bad. William was restless, with half an ear turned all day towards the telephone. When it did ring, just after teatime, it was only Beth. He was disappointed, and called Fran to talk to her.

Beth and Elyot had meant what they had said about offering Emerald Petrie a job as Beth's companion-help and the baby's nursemaid. With only Thirzah as a 'daily' to do the rough work, in such a large house, Beth could do with help now. So if homes had to be found for the girls somewhere, they would take Emerald at once – providing she was willing, of course. But what about her sister? Ought those two to be parted, especially now? If not, she and Elyot were quite willing to take them both in, at least until Amethyst left school. Would that help Fran and William? She would leave it to their discretion if or when to tell them.

'But I should love to have them,' Beth said wistfully. 'It would make me feel better to be doing something to help, and we really must have somebody when young A.B.C. arrives. We don't think we could do better.'

Fran could hardly restrain her elation. If two could be absorbed, there was hope for the rest. Miracles were still possible, it seemed. To be positively *wanted* was the best balm that could help to salve the lacerated spirits of those adolescent girls.

The next time the telephone rang, it was an operator asking if William would accept a reverse charge call from Leominster, William agreed at once. He was relieved to hear John's voice. But why Leominster? What was wrong? Too ill to go on?

No, in fact, he was feeling reasonably well. Being out of hospital and active instead of having to lie and worry had been good for him, but the car had let them down. Between Worcester and Leominster, the exhaust pipe had fallen off. On Saturday, miles from anywhere with no mechanics at work if garages were open. No hope of repair till Monday at the earliest, and without enough money to pay for it anyway. They also had to have accommodation while they waited. Would William cable some money, to be picked up at the main post office in Leominster? Take it from what was in his wallet – perhaps £100?

'More,' said William, 'and don't argue with me. You don't know what you may want, yet – you are not to run risks by being cold or going hungry. I can't get it off till Monday morning, though. Post offices here are all closed, too.'

'Soon enough. We can manage till then. The car won't be done till Tuesday. Thanks, William.'

'Don't hang up! John! Listen! The girls are here with us, and you can tell Joe that Hetty's OK. But we're completely in the dark, at this end – where you are, where you're heading for, or anything. It's very wearing, especially for the girls. So do keep in touch. You can reverse all the charges.'

'OK, will do. Must go now, because Joe's waiting outside, and it's raining cats and dogs and blowing a gale from the west. We've got no-where to sleep yet. I wish I knew Tanner was as safe as the others are with you . . .' The line went dead.

William began to curse, out of sheer frustration.

'Don't!' said Fran, sharply. 'You know how I hate swearing.'

'It does me good,' he answered shortly. 'You should have let me go after them. It will come to that in the end.'

When she didn't answer him, he stopped swearing and sulked instead. It was only a measure of his distress, she knew, but she didn't see why it should be visited on her. They said very little more to each other till bedtime. She put the light out and turned towards him in the dark.

Remorseful, he gathered her into his arms. 'Why have you been so cross with me all day?' he asked, stroking her face.

'Me cross with you? I haven't! You've been the touchy one! I thought you were mad at me, because it was me that got us into this mess in the first place. You didn't want me to respond to that first letter. But how could I foresee what it would lead to? I'd feel a lot worse than I do now if I hadn't done anything then, and then we'd found out afterwards what a genuine call for help it was. So I shan't say I'm sorry. As it is, we are doing all we can.'

'Darling, I'm not mad with anybody, least of all you. Just bad-tempered because I'm so miserable and worried. And I don't swear, in the ordinary way. You know I don't. I know how it upsets you, and in any case I deplore it as a habit. I'm sorry.'

She snuggled closer, and turned her face up to meet his placatory kiss. 'We're both touchy,' she said. 'It's like that old nursery-tale again. The goats have got into the turnip field and Jasper cries, so Emerald cries, so Petrie cries, and so it goes on. Then I cry, because I love you, and you swear because I cry, and because Petrie grieves, and back it all goes to where it started, with me finding Jasper. People who don't care don't get hurt, so they don't pass the hurt on. The more you love, the worse you get hurt – but I'd rather have it this way, wouldn't you?'

He didn't need to reply. They were at one again. Instead, he went back to his preoccupation with Petrie's awful plight.

'I might have known that old car would let them down. I should have insisted on going myself in my car and letting him take the one chance he had of getting better.'

'No, my darling. He has no chance. We must face up to it. That's really what's the matter with us. We know the score, and we can't take it. But at least we should know better than to take it out on each other. I suppose even love can have two sides to it. If it wells up and overflows because it can't get away, there's a flood. Let's look on the bright side. Hetty isn't kicking up a shindy, and Beth wants to give Emmy a job and house Ammy. So stop worrying and go to sleep.

"'Sleep that knits up the ravell'd sleave of care".'

'That dratted man knew everything,' she said, and William actually chuckled.

5 5

Being already 'there' at Benedict's, Sophie had no trouble with her conscience about being 'at work' next day, although it was Sunday. When Fran and William went downstairs, she'd already given the girls breakfast, and was organizing them into helping her.

'I thought,' she said, 'seeing as how there'll be a lot to get dinner for today, as they could 'elp me do the veg and such, and then goo with me to church, if you tell 'em to. Then after dinner, I shall have to walk up to Hen Street and make sure as Het's all right, and if any of 'em want to come with me, they're welcome. Else it'll be a long day for 'em, poor things.'

William and Fran, who had been undecided how much to tell them of last night's news, felt that they were less tense on this second morning, as if for the moment the resilience of youth was disguising their grief and suspending their anxiety enough to allow them to take what pleasure they could from such an unexpected adventure.

William's news that he had spoken to their father last night, albeit in a bit of difficulty with the car, relaxed them even more. As Fran remarked afterwards, they must have felt till then as if they had been walking weightless in space. To know where their father was and what he was doing set their feet on the earth again.

They had not known Sophie before, except by sight, but they appeared to find her solid presence and company more comfortable than Fran's or William's. Fran decided that they had better take the two eldest aside and tell them of Beth's offer, in case they should meet her at church.

It was received with a mixture of pleasure and gratitude, in which there was still a large element of doubt. 'It would be wonderful,' Emmy said, 'especially as Mrs Franks would let Ammy stay with me as well at first. But won't Daddy and the little ones need me, if . . .'

That 'if' was the unexploded land-mine. If what? Not just one 'if', but a great bomb made of 'ifs', which might go off at any moment.

William felt that for the first time he could fully understand, with his heart as much as his head, why a dying man who while living had managed to create such 'wholeness' out of lost scraps of humanity should have made such strange plans as he had for them after his death.

He realized that Petrie's hope had been to preserve for them as long as possible the bond he had himself forged for them. He was putting his trust in the children themselves, integrated as they were into a firm family unit. Considering under what extraordinary circumstances that solidarity had been achieved, he had probably seen that it was most likely to continue under circumstances which, however unusual, were at least those they were used to, and understood.

Left to well-meaning but necessarily detached bureaucracy, the old-fashioned roots of affectionate responsibility for each other with which he had bound them together would have been torn up and left to wither in the arid atmosphere of 'welfare' which cared for bodies and minds, but not for spirits. What, in essence, Petrie had done was to recreate by the force of his personality and determination the same sort of tribal ties of kinship or communal responsibility that, for instance, the Bridgefoots or Sophie's family, the Wainwrights, still displayed.

William the historian as well as William the man found much to think about in all that, especially in the present social conditions of over-population, a growing ethnic minority and the restlessness of contemporary youth that would rather be anywhere than 'home' or 'bound' by any permanent ties. Beth's offer and Sophie's ready sympathy had shown clearly that there were people who still understood that 'welfare' meant more than the immediate necessities of food and shelter. If there were more like Beth, he personally wouldn't have quite such a heavy load on his one pair of neighbourly shoulders.

'It's really all too soon to try to take any decisions yet,' he announced to the two girls. They were glad he had not pressed them, while he needed to talk it through with Fran first.

Sophie, bustling the girls out of hearing upstairs with orders to make their beds, also wanted to give William the benefit of her thoughts.

'They ought to stop 'ere all together for a few more days, till they get over it a bit,' she said, reprovingly, as if she half-suspected William of seeking an excuse not to do what she clearly considered to be no more than his Christian duty. She was doing what was in her power to help, and her tone made it clear. 'Though I do hev' to say as there's one thing as I can't put up with if they are going to be 'ere and under my feet in my kitchen for long, and that's them houtlandish names. I can do with "Emmy", if it comes to that, 'cos I went to school with Joe's sister Em'ly as died, but 'eathen names like Hammy and Toapy and Saffy I cannot abide.'

'Neither can I, if I tell the truth,' Fran answered, overhearing. 'But their names are about all they've got left to call their own. We can't take them away from them, just because we don't like them, can we?

'What you call "outlandish names" are only short for their real ones. Their mother went in for the names of precious stones. I'm sure you've known Beryls and Rubys and Pearls before. These girls' real names are Emerald, and Amethyst, and Topaz, and Sapphire. All jewels.'

'Beryl Bean ain't no jewel, whatever she's called,' Sophie said, deftly turning the subject, and not willing to admit defeat. She raised her voice to send it upstairs, putting into it an edge of command. 'Now then, togethers, do you 'urry up. Don't, we shall all be late for church.'

Fran and William, left in a blessed interval of normal Sunday morning quiet, looked more closely at their situation. Both took it for granted that for the immediate future they had to continue to house and feed the abandoned waifs; but what of the longer term? How much was it possible for them to do?

As Fran pointed out, Sophie had so far been wonderful, but she was, after all, a middle-aged spinster not at all used to having young and disturbed people around her. She would probably decide to go home to sleep tonight, even if she didn't feel obliged to go to support Hetty in Joe's longer-than-expected absence. The breakdown of the car meant that if the two men could not leave Leominster till Tuesday, they could hardly be expected back till Thursday or even Friday.

'And what's going to happen then?' William asked. 'Petrie will have to return to hospital –'

'If they'll have him. He discharged himself,' Fran reminded him.

'And in any case, his plans are all in ruins. I can't see any way out for him but to hand the whole family over to the welfare people . . . Don't look at me like that, Fran. *We* can't do anything about it.'

He crossed the room to stand, a bit irresolute but unusually stern of face, in front of her. She was not going to like what it was he was forced to put fairly and squarely into words, and they both knew it.

'Beth and Elyot may save the two oldest girls, and Petrie has always foreseen that for some reason Crystal will stick to Basher, but that still leaves *five* others! When he is dead, they will have no parents and no home. Charles has begun already to put things in hand to take over his house and make plans for his wedding, but even suppose he – suppose they – were prepared to sacrifice everything for the time being, five such young children couldn't be left in a place like Danesum alone. Wouldn't be allowed to. They'd just be scooped up into care.'

He paused. 'And to keep them all here would be out of question. You must see that, Fran. Look, I'm an old academic, not used to children. You've already got a family, and work that you love. I know quite well what you think now that you want to do, but it just isn't on. That's why it's up to me, here and now, to prevent you from getting any such stupid idea into your head. In this case, you must let your head, and mine, rule your heart. Darling' – he was pleading, now – 'however unhappy it may make you at present, the alternative would be infinitely worse. I won't consider the possibility. I simply *will not let you* wreck our lives, and believe me, that's what it would mean. You can't!'

He sat down suddenly at her feet, and laid his head against her knee. She knew, of course, that he was right, but . . . how could they make such a brutal decision, on such selfish grounds? Her mind flew away, as it always did in such moments of stress, seeking abstractions by which to hold off the moment of truth from which she had no other means of escape.

He was waiting for her answer, and there was only one answer. She bent down and kissed the top of his head, and held it closer to her, while, limp with relief, he buried his face in her skirt.

'You're right,' she said, 'and I know you are. But can't we play it by ear till we know a bit more? We'll do what we must, but let's take it a day at a time. The gods may find a way out for us. Let's trust them.'

They sat in silence, while he regained his equilibrium. He felt as if he had been looking into the crater of a volcano, but instead he now looked up into Fran's face, sad but serene. He was more than grateful to her that she had not put up the fight he had so feared. It was this type of situation that made him feel so acutely the insecurity of his position as 'only her live-in lover' or 'a lodger who slept in her bed'. Not a husband with any other hold on her, or on Benedict's, but love. She was as aware as he was that any reminder of that spelt danger for them both.

To avoid any further probing at the moment, she plunged into telling him of her conversation with Sophie about names. He was immediately attentive.

'You know, I think she may have hit on something useful, all the same,' he said, getting up. 'The last thing they need in their new lives is to have to carry the past with them – always to be "that gang of hippies". It would help to start them off again with names that make people think of them as people in their own right.'

She would have agreed with anything he said, rather than take one step herself nearer to the abyss of a quarrel with him, so they greeted the returning churchgoers with their decision, and as William had predicted, there were no objections, except from Sophie, who whispered to Fran as they put lunch on the table, 'I 'ope as I shall remember them there names proper. I'm never 'eard of anybody called Samphire afore. I thought that was somethink you ate, what grows on sea walls. Mam used to boil it with salt and put vingedar on it, like you do beetroot.'

Fran caught William's eye, and felt the weight of the long day ahead of them suddenly lighten again. At her suggestion, they all squeezed in round the kitchen table to eat lunch, and made conversation general. Fran asked Emerald if they had seen Beth at church.

Yes, Emerald said, and Beth had suggested that perhaps they, meaning herself and Ammy – sorry, Amethyst – might like to walk up to the Old Rectory this afternoon and see her. She had accepted, and hoped Fran didn't mind – but she had thought afterwards that perhaps they ought not to leave the twins alone.

'They can come to 'En Street with me to see Het,' said Sophie. 'And then they can come back 'ere by theirselves, 'cos I shall stop with Het as long as she wants me, and then goo 'ome till bedtime. There'll be nothing for me to do 'ere, tonight.'

William gave her a smile that she understood meant that if she didn't come again till morning, it would be soon enough. The worst was over, except for the endless waiting for news.

It was almost a pleasure to watch the youngsters finding a hearty appetite. It would be during the evening that time would hang heavy, listening all the time for the telephone bell. William had been dreading it, too, and as soon as the two groups had set out, in opposite directions, he told Fran of an idea he had had to make the evening hours less strain.

'Let's light them a fire in the sitting-room of the flat, and let them have it as their quarters, to do as they like in. They can move into the bedrooms there, and make all the drinks and snacks they like in that kitchen. They can still have their main meal of the day in here, and help Sophie. They're better kept occupied. But they can have the TV set in there, and radios. Something they've never had before. Maybe they'd enjoy reading if we just left books or magazines lying about? Is that a good idea? To leave them by themselves?'

She laughed aloud, and the gloomy shadows retreated a bit further into the far corners of the day.

'You mean you want us to be left to ourselves a bit!' she said. 'Shame on you, Professor. You can't hoodwink intelligent students like me as easy as all that. But you know it's a splendid idea – for us all. I've been dreading having to entertain them.'

'There won't be any more phonecalls, not till Tuesday evening unless there's another emergency,' he said. 'I'll tell them so, and disconnect the flat's phone.'

So Sunday passed, after all, much more comfortably than could have been expected, and Monday morning ushered in the new week.

56

It was a week in the second half of February, the dark time of the year; a black February, with rain and blustery winds, with dark mornings and early dusks. A dull February, without a lot happening that was new, especially after all the fireworks there had been around the New Year.

There were still no hopeful signs with regard to a new incumbent, though the congregation at church had risen slightly in number. George was 'more like hisself again', going about his churchwarden's duties singing hymns, and not letting his new co-warden's attempts to raise petty issues put him out. He treated Ken rather as he would have done a little stray mongrel yapping at his heels – often simply ignoring him, sometimes metaphorically patting his head, and occasionally slapping him down.

Bailey was lying low, licking his wounds and keeping in the shadows until he should be able to reinstate his claim to being the newcomer destined to haul Old Swithinford into the twentieth century by his up-to-date ideas and his astuteness, to say nothing of the money he had already made. He was finding it rather more difficult than he had expected, and was having to cultivate the acquaintance of farmers and smallholders farther afield, such as Vic Gifford, on the far side of Swithinford. He was rather regretting his haste to build his own new house where it was, now that his grandiose schemes, starting with Castle Hill, had fallen through. So far, it seemed to be in a social no man's land, which was not at all what he had intended.

Lane's End Estate was going ahead whenever the weather would let it, and a few houses on it were already occupied – but so far there was little mixing between the old inhabitants and the new, who did their shopping in Swithinford. Bailey had envisaged a merging of the old village, Hen Street, and his new estates, which in turn would have expanded to a larger suburb requiring shopping centres, garages, new schools and so on. All of which projects he had confidently expected to fall into his hands. For the time being, such high hopes had had to be 'put on the back burner'.

Life was dull in Beryl Bean's shop, though there would be more custom, and therefore more people to exchange gossip with, once spring-cleaning fever began to spread. In the ordinary course of events, such outsiders as Petrie and his family of 'ragamuffins' were not worth her attention, but in time of famine, even crumbs are welcome.

Then events began to tumble over each other, and the dullness which had drugged everybody into a state of comatose hibernation blew up like a bottle of homemade wine, disclosing dramatically the effect of slow fermentation, very much as Hitler's blitzkrieg had exploded the peace of the phoney war in May 1940. The departure of Pugh and Crystal on a Friday afternoon preceding a particularly wet and generally 'unpromising' weekend, which had kept people at home rather than at the bar of the Green Dragon, had delayed the effervescence a bit, but the presence of the Petrie girls with Sophie at church had reminded someone else that William had been seen taking Sophie to visit her sister Hetty in Hen Street on Saturday afternoon. That was queer, wasn't it? The cork of the bottle was beginning to rise with the pressure of curiosity. Thirzah's truthful answers to probing questions after church on Sunday meant that by Monday the mixture was bubbling over.

Sophie arrived a little late and a bit put-out on Monday morning, having encountered Olive 'Opkins while shopping for the enlarged household at Benedict's. Olive had seen no reason why she should not inquire about Hetty's health, 'seeing as Sophie had been took by car to see her on Sat'day'. Beryl had been so sorry for poor Het.

'So I went straight into the shop,' Sophie said, 'to find out what it were as she 'ad been guessing and 'inting at. She said they was all so sorry to 'ear what 'ad 'appened, and asked if Het were very upset yest'day, or if she 'ad seen it coming. "Upset?" I says. "Not as far as I know. What about? If it 'adn't a-been Sunday, I should 'ave 'elped her strip the bedroom wall, what she intends to get papered while Joe's away." "Ah!" she says. "So you don't deny as Joe is away! There's no smoke without fire as a rule." And as I stand 'ere, if she didn't go on to say as it's all over the place as Joe 'as left Hetty for that woman up at Danesum, and 'ad gone off with 'er to Wales! I'm sure as I were so flabbergasted as I didn't know what to say to shut 'er up.

'"And how come," she says, "as them gels from Danesum are up at Benedict's then? Are them two took 'em in to be looked after there till the police find Joe and their mother?"

'Well, I told 'er the truth – but that's the last thing folks want to believe. I should ha' thought everybody would know Joe better than that.'

Fran sought out William, to warn him to be prepared to ward off even police inquiries if tales of abandoned children got about. She found him in his study, making effort to disguise from her his anxious restlessness. Was there anything she didn't know about, she asked? What was it he was keeping from her?

His mood was evasive. He reminded her that though Petrie's affairs were uppermost, she mustn't forget that they had foolishly undertaken to be part of the intrigue designed to restore Greg to Jess, set up for this coming Saturday. He thought they should abandon it, in which case he'd have to tell Eric and she'd have to cancel Bob and Jane's visit.

To his surprise, she rebelled. She agreed that on the surface, their plan to reunite Jess and Greg did look like comic opera – but it hadn't been at all comic when they had had to deal first with one and then the other of that unhappy couple. A couple who were, in case he had forgotten, *their own*, and therefore had the prior claim to their time and attention. In her opinion, what they had done already might have prevented comic opera from becoming tragedy. They couldn't pull out at this crucial point.

Besides, how did he know what might have happened, one way or the other, by Saturday?

'We've got to go through with both. All right, maybe we were stupid to get ourselves loaded with either. But then, as Sophie would say, "Donkeys go best loaded."' Having had her say, she gave him her usual smile but for once got little in return. She felt 'narked' by it all.

'I'll cope with one if you cope with the other. Who is it that is always telling me not to run to meet trouble? I'm optimistic about Greg and Jess. Don't let this other business spoil it. However much misery you put yourself through won't prevent Petrie dying. You said *we* had to accept it. You as well.'

Neither wanted to make things worse by wrangling with the other, so they left it, but it hadn't done much to cure William's unease. It crossed his mind that he was showing his age at last. Must be, if he could allow Fran to irritate him.

For her part, she was aware that all she had done was to make matters worse. She found Sophie waiting for her, to ask her about one of those small domestic matters she had testily told William she would cope with. Sophie was about to load the washing machine with the weekly wash. Had 'them gels' anything as ought to go in?

Fran was staggered by the size of the problem posed. It was something she hadn't given even a glancing thought to. They had brought nothing with them except one little hold-all. Had they got a change of underclothes or nightwear? Four girls of their age might be in desperate need of clean knickers, if nothing else. In any case, they had been wearing the same things since Friday morning, unwashed unless they had been 'dabbing things out' overnight. Distasteful as it was, she would have to ask, and then deal with it.

She found Emerald, and was appalled by what she learned. They had in the past made do with a common pool of underclothing, mostly obtained from jumble sales. They had done all the washing since they could first remember. Since being settled in Danesum, they had had a second-hand washing machine. But everything, including the washing machine in which their spare clothes were waiting to be washed, had been taken. She hadn't liked to worry Fran about it, or the 'other problem', till she had to.

Fran went back and told Sophie, glad of anybody to share her distress with. 'It isn't any good me offering them anything of mine,' she said. 'Mine would be miles too big.'

'Nor mine,' said Sophie, sadly. It was fortunate that she had her back to Fran, whose face registered her reaction. She wouldn't be surprised if Sophie still wore egg-timer-shaped laced corsets with long-sleeved home-knitted 'vestes' and fleecy-lined navy-blue bloomers.

'Them two oldest are tall and thin like Mis' Franks,' Sophie said. 'I wonder if she's got any old things she could give 'em to be going on with?'

'What a good idea,' Fran said, thinking what an excuse that would make for consulting Beth. Beth couldn't, just at present, get into some of her clothes. 'And Monica's cast-offs would fit the twins. I know she's got plenty that she still can't get into. I'll go and phone both straight away.'

Beth promised to look out some things and said she would bring them up, because she was anxious to talk to Fran. She and Elyot had been impressed all over again by the two oldest Petries, and were prepared to relieve Fran and William at once, if it would help. Fran said she guessed that William would want to ask their father, and consider the other two. The fact remained, however, that they might have to be parted before long, and to meet with Beth might ease a final separation later.

'Do come up, Beth,' she said. 'William and I need you if they don't. Things seem to be getting us down.'

Then Fran sat by the phone, flat and depressed. What had she just admitted to Beth? That something was getting between her and William. They were both letting it get under their skin. Why? She had been hurt by his attitude to her this morning, and had been stung into retaliating. But what had he said or done to hurt her? Could it be that she didn't like his preoccupation with Petrie, and felt excluded? *Jealous*, in fact? She was horrified that it might be so, and went back over any possible cause. He had said that under other circumstances he might have found in Petrie another special friend, another Castor to his Pollux. That could explain why he was now so much in distress. This Castor was being ripped from him, too, though when Mac had been killed, he hadn't had her. Didn't that make a difference? Guilt flooded over her. She was acting like Jess!

She knew better. Men needed other men as much as women needed other women. He was suffering, and she was making it worse for him, not better. She had to be the strong one – as women were so often called upon to be when men needed mothers, not wives. She was ashamed that she had allowed him and his mood to throw her out of her normal gear.

She dialled Monica. They settled down for a chat, which made Fran feel a lot better. Monica's brisk, common-sensical grasp of the situation heartened Fran immensely.

Underclothes? Drawers full of them that she never expected to be able to get into again – and outdoor clothes, too, if any fitted or could be made to fit. 'Have you forgotten that clothes are my business? No problem!' Besides, said Monica, new clothes had a psychological effect on women in trouble – and what awful depths of despair those poor kids must be enduring! Their need for clothing could be looked on as a godsend, if the want could be supplied. Which of course it could be, without putting the recipients under any further obligation.

'So why don't we make an event of it for them? Can it wait till tomorrow? I've arranged to come over to see Dad, and was hoping that I'd be able to call in to see you. I'll bring my two over to tea. Couldn't Beth come as well, with her contributions? We could throw a sort of lingerie party. Honestly, Fran, there is a limit to what tea and sympathy can do, and I expect you reached that last Friday night. If you don't want four permanently damaged egos on your conscience, stop the rot by doing something out-of-the-way before it's too late. We could have an all-female get-together such as those girls have never dreamed of. Shall I bring Dad up to keep Grandfather William company? How is he?'

Fran told her. Oppressed and depressed.

Monica became instantly concerned. 'In that case, Dad might help,' she said. 'He's had a lot of experience, but his motto is and always has been that you're no good to anybody else if you don't look to yourself first. William is too sensitive to cope alone with this sort of thing. We'll shut him up in his study with Dad and Elyot and a bottle, while we indulge in a clothes binge. There'll be plenty of nursemaids around. I'll bet one of the hardest things for those kids to bear is not having babies and toddlers clinging to them.'

Monica's good humour and practical solution won Fran over, and induced her, if still a little dubiously, to begin to set up the 'lingerie party'. Her hesitation was caused only by a suspicion that Sophie would disapprove, and either decline to help at all, or indulge in one of her rare, dignified sulks, thinking festivity at such a time highly inappropriate. She was wrong.

'I'm caught them poor gels crying many's the time when I ain't told you,' Sophie said, 'them not wanting you to know, like. It's bound to get worse for 'em every day, waiting and waiting. But a bit o' pleasure never done nobody no 'arm. Don't the Bible tell us so? "A merry 'eart doeth good like a medicine." And in time o' trouble it gives folk something else to think about, like getting a funeral tea for the fam'ly used to in days gone by. So what shall we give 'em for tea tomorrow? Ham sandwiches and salmon sandwiches and scones and them cream buns as I make as 'e's so fond of, and a chocolate cake by my special receipt and some shortbread biscuits?'

'That would be far too much,' Fran protested.

Sophie caught her eye. 'Not with three men in the 'ouse, it won't,' Sophie answered. 'They never grow out o' being like little old boys at a schooltreat, old as they may be. You mark my words.'

Fran found herself laughing, in spite of her misgivings. 'All right. Have it your own way,' she said.

It turned out as well as Monica had predicted. Fran told the Petries in the morning that they were having guests to tea, who they were and that they were invited to 'join the ladies'. It would be better than staying cooped up in the flat, though she hoped they were enjoying 'playing house' there.

The response was another surprise. Yes, it was wonderful, and such fun – but that only made what might happen to them at any minute more frightening to think about.

Fran understood. The realization of what it meant to be so completely abandoned was only just beginning to sink in. Emerald told her that they had talked about their situation while they had been alone in the flat. She had told them that her own case was different from theirs because of her age, and she must get herself a job as soon as she could, even if it meant leaving them. So of course she would accept what Mrs Franks was offering. Make sure of it while she had the chance. And it was almost too good to be true that Amethyst could go with her, at least for a little while. By then, Emerald said, the twins had begun to cry, and it had been awful. She had promised them that she would ask the Professor – or Daddy if she ever saw or spoke to him again – to try to make sure that they were not parted from each other. 'And we'll come and see you,' she had said, 'wherever you are, as often as we can.'

'If only we knew where the little ones are,' the twins had said, speaking for them all. 'We miss them so much.' Fran left her, rather abruptly. Emerald told her sisters that if they were asked to help wait on the other guests, they had to show just how well they could behave.

Then Sophie called them, saying that she needed as many pairs of hands as there were to spare, considering all them things she had got to cook. And keep them busy she did, till they had forgotten much of their sorrow in learning cooking skills they had never before had a chance to try. It was lunchtime almost before they knew it, and after lunch Fran explained that the party really and truly was for them – so they were free now to go and have baths and make their lovely hair as pretty as they could.

They came down again, rosy and clean and shy, the two oldest with their thick hair plaited up round their heads, and the twins with plaits over their shoulders, bound in old country fashion with brushings wound tightly round the ends. Demurely and politely they answered Beth and Elyot's greetings, and stood back again into the corner of the sitting-room, wondering why Mr Franks had left a suitcase in the hall. Did it mean they were going away? Had they changed their minds about the job, after all?

Then Mr Choppen's car arrived, and their ears picked up a sound so familiar that tears sprang unbidden: two babies were yelling their heads off.

'Oh, for heaven's sake!' Monica said, coming in with one baby on her arm and the other in a carrycot. 'I'm sorry to disrupt the peace like this, but we woke them up to feed them before they were ready and I expect the little brats will grizzle all the afternoon in consequence. Put all those bags in the middle of the floor, Dad, till I can say hello to everybody. See what you've got coming to you, Beth! No, Dad, I'll see to everything – you escape and find the rest of the men. Here, somebody, hold this one while I get the other out. Don't have twins, Beth. You'll find you haven't got enough arms. Or laps, for that matter.'

Fran took the hint that Monica was throwing out so plainly. She relieved her of Annette, now fair-haired and inclined to be curly, who stopped whining at once, poked her finger into her grandmother's eye, and gurgled. Little William, much larger and still abundantly dark, was determined to show off the full power of his lungs. Monica picked him out of the cot and offered him vaguely round. 'Who wants?' she said. 'I've had enough of him for one day! I don't think he likes my face.'

Amethyst got there first, and took the baby with such yearning in her face that for a moment Monica almost forgot her act. She took Annette from Fran, and plonked her into Sapphire's arms, then pushed Amethyst with little William into a chair. Topaz immediately knelt in front, cuddling the baby's bare feet and blowing on to his toes. The yelling stopped.

Sophie hovered, and all eight females began to indulge themselves in one of those baby-worshipping rituals men find so completely inexplicable.

The three secluded in William's study remarked on the phenomenon, and while Eric and Elyot lit their pipes, the topic uppermost in William's mind was soon under discussion. He set the details before them, and asked, seriously, whose responsibility, in their opinion, those children were. Not Emerald, but the other seven. Their legal guardian was still alive, though completely irresponsible. What he wanted really to know was whether, as in Amethyst's case, either Crystal or the welfare service could interfere with such ideal arrangements as Elyot and Beth were offering. It worried him, William said, that people – the ordinary man in the street – had no idea when it came to it what rules were made in their name. Elyot said he had, as a new magistrate, begun to look into it, but it was a very long, complicated and obfuscated process, this 'care' business, as far as he could see.

'Look at it this way,' William went on. 'If anybody stole a baby, the charge brought would be of "taking it without the parent's consent". So was the reverse true – that if a parent, such as Crystal, didn't care a brass farthing where her children were as long as she didn't have to look after them, and would give consent to anything, there could be no charge to bring? Take the case of Amethyst. Could anybody interfere with her being allowed to stay with her sister in Elyot's home, if that's what all of them wanted?'

None of them knew; but presumably, Elyot said, the ultimate fate of such children was in the hands of the social services. The welfare state.

'Then – forgive me for saying so, William, – but ought you not to have just sent for the police, and let them deal with the whole situation?'

'That's my dilemma,' said William. 'Who was it who said that if he had a choice between betraying his country or betraying his friend, he would betray his country? I made a promise to their father that I would do my best to see that they were not split up. There didn't appear to be any reason why I should have to be involved. How could he possibly guess that he would crack up just at the crucial time, or that Crystal would do what she did? He trusted Pugh. We don't know yet how far that trust was justified. He didn't trust bureaucracy.'

'Perhaps he – and you – may be mistaken about that,' Elyot suggested. 'Neither you nor he seem prepared to give it a chance.'

'If you had promised a dying friend, would you risk it till you were forced to? Besides, I'm a historian. I try to see things in perspective. We've lived through a social revolution since 1948, when all of us consented to what we believed was a wonderful concept. We forgot how things were bound to go on changing. The wheel goes on turning – that's what "revolution" means. We didn't foresee that the great umbrella of "safety from want" would rob future generations of their individual social consciences. We'd provided care for old folks or orphaned children. Women were freed from the responsibilities of their old parents to take jobs. Why shouldn't they? We can leave the state – meaning politicians and bureaucrats – to look after those who can't look after themselves. So our consciences, in theory, should be easy. Till you are the one with the problem. Then you find out how impossible it is for an "institutionalized" service to deal with the increase in the workload. Population has increased. All it can do is provide what seems best for the greatest number in any category.

'But there's the rub! How and on what criteria is it possible to put people into categories? As Fran would no doubt quote, "We differ from each other like the stars in glory." You can't legislate for tens of millions on an individual basis. Petrie's family aren't just a litter of state piglets.

They are Emerald and Amethyst, Sapphire and Topaz, Jasper and Jade and Agate. And Basher. Their only "fault" is that they were ever born at all.

'Can you imagine Sophie putting her mother into a home? This community, small as it was, used to look after its own. Still does, often.'

William stopped almost in mid-sentence, looking apologetically at his guests. 'Sorry,' he said with a rueful little smile. 'I didn't mean to give you a lecture, but it has got a lot off my chest.'

'Stay on your soapbox, Professor,' said Eric. 'I can't answer for Elyot, but I don't often get a chance to hear a lecture. If I understand you right, the wheel's being forced to keep turning. So what happens when it's gone full circle?'

'Who knows? That's where policy makers and politicians fail. They can't be fortune-tellers. It depends on what other wheels are revolving at the same time. Look at this village. In my fifty years we've had one revolution and half another. When I was a boy, there was still one local landlord – a member of the aristocracy owning most of the land, and living on the rents he drew from it. Elyot's ancestor. Then there was the squire – my own step-grandfather, who was really only a successful yeoman farmer. He had bailiffs to run his farms for him. The other yeoman farmers who owned their own land employed labourers, but they worked on it themselves as well – Bridgefoots and Thackerays. There were a few real peasants who owned land worked entirely by the family. All the rest were farm labourers.

'Now, only fifty years later? No aristocrat, no squire, and the number of "labourers" you could count on the fingers of one hand. Farming has become an *industry*, now. It doesn't need "labourers". They have to be skilled workers, with knowledge of machinery and chemicals and God-knows-what else, who happen to work on land instead of in garages or factories. They don't want to live in "tied" cottages – they live in council houses until they can buy one on an estate, and become middle-class home-owners. Like us – except that we do up old houses to suit ourselves. We still try to cling to the past ideal of "rural England."

'Who are we to say that others shouldn't have what they think is the best, now? Sociologists will probably put us in a new category designated "die-hards", those who won't let go of the past. Maybe we few die-hards have managed to save the centre of the village, and there's always a chance that the seeds of old ways will lie dormant till they have a chance to germinate again, but apart from the little green belt round the church, the rest will be under housing estates.

'Why on earth are you letting me rant on like this? All I wanted was a bit of sympathy and advice in my dilemma of how I can avoid betraying a friend who has put his trust in me. I can't for once see round it. And Fran wonders why I'm "moody". Don't you, sweetheart?'

She had put her head round the door, and heard the last bit of his tirade. She gave him a wicked smile in return, having come to ask them to join the 'Christmas party' in the sitting-room. He came, rather sheepishly ushering in his two patient listeners. It did indeed look a bit like Christmas.

Food was piled high on every flat surface, and each of the girls was clutching a plastic bag filled to overflowing with garments they kept feeling surreptitiously to make sure they were still real and still there. Monica's twins, satiated with attention and tit-bits, were more than half asleep again, one across Emerald's shoulder, the other under Sapphire's arm, though both girls were happily also handing round plates, as if a baby was a sort of natural appendage that hindered nothing.

Fran and Monica kept on exchanging messages with their eyes as to the success of their venture. Sophie had been right, too. There was soon nothing left but a few sandwiches.

'May I get you another cup of tea, Commander?' asked Emerald, deftly shifting young William from one arm to the other.

'No, thank you. Come and talk to me instead.' He beckoned Beth over to join them. 'May we expect you and Amethyst to come to us before the weekend? Say Friday if your father agrees?'

Emerald blushed and fidgeted with the baby's toes. 'We'd love to – if he allows us to leave the twins without us so soon. They're younger than us. The weekend would be rather long and lonely for them to have to start being without us.'

'Wait a minute,' said Monica, having heard Emerald's answer. 'I've had an idea. I've got a mountain of work to do, and no help. Why don't they come and visit me for the weekend? I should be glad of their help, honestly. Would you like that Topaz? Sapphire? Is it OK with you, Fran? William? That's fixed, then. Dad can bring them – I believe he said he was coming on Saturday.'

The party began to break up. Sophie retired to the kitchen and the girls, having reluctantly handed back the babies, went to help her wash up. Beth and Elyot made their farewells.

'Now,' said Monica, when the door had closed behind them. 'I hope I didn't jump the gun with my invitation to the twins, but I didn't have a chance to tell you earlier. Greg's on our plates again. He rang up last night. He's more or less extricated himself from the York business, and wants to go home, it seems more-or-less at Jess's suggestion. But you know Greg – his guilt is overpowering his common sense, and courage is deserting him. He daren't bank on anything – and I'm not sure I blame him, when I think what Jess can be like. Anyway, he won't risk a proper welcome. He proposes to leave York very early Saturday morning and come to see me first, which suits me.

'But then he said that he might have nowhere to go on Saturday night if Jess kicked him out, so would it be all right if he came back to sleep at our house? Naturally, I couldn't let on that a trap had been set to keep him at Southside House. I had to invent an excuse on the spur of the moment, so I said I was having other visitors and all my beds would be full. So they will, now. He'll have to stop in the house with Jess, or leave for the hotel and "never see her more" – the lovely, silly idiot that he is. He's a darling, and I love him. I hope what's happened has taught Jess a lesson. Silly bitch.'

She looked lovingly over towards William and her father, companionably chatting, as unlikely a pair of ambassadors for Venus as one could imagine.

'Angels do come in some funny guises, sometimes, don't they?' Monica said.

Fran followed her look and her thoughts. 'Have we ever told you the true identity of our personal and particular Aphrodite?' she asked. Monica shook her head, and Fran leaned towards her. 'Sophie,' she whispered. 'Honestly. Beat that if you can!'

57

It was past eight o'clock before the telephone call came. Petrie (only William ever really thought of him as anything but 'Petrie') was ringing from a bed-and-breakfast farmhouse outside the town of Kington. He was coughing a bit, but to William's anxious inquiries said that as far as he was concerned all was well. He wished he could say the same about the weather, which was really bad. Rain and blustery winds, rivers overflowing their banks, minor roads blocked by floods. Not the sort of conditions for a trip like this in which time was important.

After hanging about Leominster for two days, as soon as they had got the car back they had set off, but it was such a filthy wet and dark night that they had given up at Kington. They would set out early next morning in the hope of reaching the camp-site on the coast between Aberystwyth and Borth sometime that day. What was the position at William's end?

William reported all well – even with Hetty, up to the present. The girls were still at Benedict's but . . . and there followed the information of Beth's offer to the oldest two, and a request for permission to go ahead and accept it. *Of course*, Petrie said. How could William possibly doubt it? There was great relief in his voice, as if in some way he regarded it as a good omen. William assured him that for the time being the twins would continue to be based on Benedict's, but they, too, had been invited out for the weekend. The only sensible thing to do with them at the moment was to go on from day to day, until John himself was back and within reach.

The tone of voice immediately changed again. 'That's something I can't be sure will ever happen,' he said. 'I've no idea what I'm going to find when or if I track the others down. There are local reports of ferocious gales along the west coast and whole caravan sites being swept away or flooded out – I'm having nightmares about the boys. Thank God I bought that nearly new Dormobile. They'll be fairly safe in that if they are where I hope they are, on the site I booked for them. Crystal doesn't drive, so they'll have to stay put where Pugh leaves them.

'I'm worried about Joe, though. I can't keep him here with me much longer, but he refuses point blank to leave me. If we make Aberystwyth tomorrow, I want to send him home without me. Or if, as he says, I can't manage without the car, from Aber I could put him on a train, especially if you'll cable me some more money, to the PO in Aber. No, of course I still need him – I can't think what on earth I should have done without him – but fair's fair. We didn't expect it to turn out as it has. When I find out anything worth telling you, I'll be in touch again. And William, I'm expecting that when I do find the rest of my family, my only resource will be to hand them over to the welfare people, and then find the nearest hospital that will take me in. So I release you absolutely from any promise or obligation to me about the others. Thanks again for everything. Bye.'

He had rung off before William could stop him. There was nothing to be done but go on waiting, though the focus of the worry had been transferred from Benedict's to Wales, which, according to the news next morning, Wednesday, was experiencing the most appalling weather conditions for years. William went out early to send off the money 'by telegram', in his anxiety heaping one worry on top of another till there was such a pile that it must soon topple over.

Back at Benedict's it wasn't a lot better. They, too, had listened to the news, and heard reports of the weather in Wales. The girls knew what camplife could be in such weather, even with such an experienced camper as Daddy in charge. They wept secretly for Tanner and Jade and Aggie, every now and then in their despair giving Fran or Sophie a glimpse of details of a way of living neither of them had ever imagined before.

Sophie prayed silently all the time, and aloud if called upon for on-the-spot comfort. Fran wished she had even that resource to turn to. For once William was leaning on her, instead of the other way round.

When he came in, he expressed aloud, to Sophie as well as to Fran, his concern for Joe. Was it possible that Joe's job might be endangered if he stayed away too long? Hetty's fortitude might not hold out much longer either. Fran saw where all this was leading, but held her tongue. She took herself away rather than argue with him. But around mid-morning, William went to her in her study. He simply could not stand the inactivity, he declared, of sitting about at home doing nothing.

If she agreed, he'd set out straight away to find and help Petrie, and then bring Joe home. Just what she had feared. Acting almost out of habit, she got up from her office chair and tucked her arms round his waist under his jacket, laying her head on his chest. He closed his arms round her, and put his face on the top of her head. He knew that Fran didn't believe for a moment that he considered Joe a simpleton. He was probably as capable as William himself of making a trip from Taranto to Helsinki if he was called upon to try. It was that William himself could not stand the strain of just hanging about giving rein to his imagination. He wanted to be doing, even something as unreasonable, expensive and possibly dangerous as he was proposing. She had enough sense not to put into words what both already knew.

'Can you be back by Saturday?' she asked. 'Apart from the Greg business, and Bob and Jane coming, the girls are leaving and I should be by myself all Sunday. Not that I mind in the ordinary way – and of course I shan't try to stop you if you really think you ought to go. Could you make it there and back in two days?'

He looked at the clock – eleven forty-five. 'Two and a half days, if I got off immediately after a fairly early lunch. If you're sure you wouldn't mind, I'll just go and look at some road maps, and calculate distance and time.'

She hoped that concentrating his mind on something else would restore a bit of his usual common sense. She smiled wryly, remembering her rather scornful reference to the old nursery tale she had certainly never expected anybody to put into practice. William put his head in again to say he still hadn't decided, but as he was going to get the car filled up with petrol he would call and have a word with Eric. Nigel Delaprime, whom Eric had driven back after the New Year, was holding the fort at one of the 'mother churches' in Kilvert country. Eric could probably offer some good advice about short cuts or diversions.

Fran felt a good deal happier. It wasn't like William to get himself into such a tizzy, but if anybody could talk him out of it, Eric was the man.

Besides, Eric wouldn't want to run the risk of William not getting back to help deal with Jess if things went wrong in 'the Southside House Plot'. She began to get worried, however, when the rest of them had all finished their lunch, and he had not returned. Sophie disappeared upstairs with piles of clean laundry, and Fran sat alone at the kitchen table when he came in.

'Darling, you have been a long time,' she said. 'It'll be dusk before you get away, at this rate.'

He sat down rather heavily, his face serious, though at the same time less tense than it had been when he went out. 'Leave my lunch where it is for a few minutes,' he said. 'I'm not going anywhere, so don't worry about the time. Eric says I'd have to use main roads all the way, and if the going's as bad in Wales as they say it is, even some of them may be flooded by now. I couldn't get back by Saturday. Besides . . .'

'Something's the matter,' she said, instantly afraid. 'What is it? Greg?'

'No – no one as close to us as that,' he said. 'But there has been a bad accident. It doesn't seem to be a good time to be taking foolhardy risks, and I don't want to leave you. We're all safer at home in our own beds, I think.'

'You're stalling – tell me quick. What's happened, and who to? Not Joe?'

She looked so horrified that he was round the table and holding her (almost before she had drawn another breath), cursing himself for not being direct with his bit of bad news and frightening her.

'No, no my love, Joe's all right, as far as I know. It's Vic Gifford – had a very bad fall from his horse. It happened while I was with Eric, and I don't know any details. They took him to hospital unconscious. Somebody who had been following the hunt too far behind to see it happen brought the tale to the hotel while I was there. He thought it might be a really serious injury. But you know how tales get stretched from minute to minute. Vic's probably only concussed. It just made me feel that all I wanted to do was to get home to you and stay here.'

'Praise be for that!' she said, letting her true feelings show. 'I feel the same. Anything could happen this week! I'd rather not let you out of my sight even while you eat your dinner, in case you choke on a chicken bone. I suppose one should say "poor old Vic" but with things as they are at present I'm afraid I just don't care whether it's his collar-bone or his leg that's broken, except that it will mean trouble for the Bridgefoots. They can hardly press on with their plans if he is seriously hurt. It might even mean Marjorie feeling she ought to go back to look after him.'

William had finished his lunch when Sophie went through the kitchen on her way to the scullery, still called that though in modern terms it would be the 'utility room'. They heard her talking to Ned.

'Listen,' Fran said. 'Ned's telling her about Vic Gifford. He's heard the details, and it sounds bad.'

She was right. Ned came in to tell them what he knew. He never wasted words when he had bad news to tell.

Vic had been out on his horse a lot lately, with Pansy and young Bailey teaching him. Not that you could teach Vic anything, because in his own estimation he already knew it all. When Pansy had told Vic this morning that they were going to follow the hunt, he had said he would go with them. Pansy said no, he wasn't ready for that yet, and they wanted to go without him. But he wouldn't be said nay. So they set off together, but he soon got left behind.

'The hunt went over his way, and they was all a-galloping in full cry along by the side of a hedge with Vic and a few others trying to keep up. Seems Vic let the horse have its head, not wanting to be seen at the tail end, or else it got away with him. They say as the horse had been used to hunting, and got excited. Anyway, as far as I can make out, they was all going 'ell for leather when them in front swerved off to the left, and Vic wasn't prepared for it. The horse followed the others, and turned as well – but Vic didn't. He went straight on, over the horse's head and right into a big tree trunk. They took him to hospital, but he were dead anyway. Broke his neck.'

Sophie had sat down, overcome. 'Oh dear-Oh-dear,' she said, over and over again. 'Oh-dear-Oh-dear! Whatever will 'appen next! Oh-dear-Oh-dear. It never did seem right for such as Marge Bridgefoot to be gettin' a divorce, but she won't 'ave to now. She'll be a widder instead.'

Fran, exasperated, looked as if she would like to slap Sophie hard. Her recent emancipation could only be skin-deep. Death, it seemed, was nothing to Sophie compared with the disgrace of divorce.

Ned, putting on his cap, sensed the sudden tension, and tried to smooth it away. 'Ah, it's a bad job,' he said. 'But it could have happened to somebody as would ha' been missed a lot more. Not that 'e's ever done me no harm and I can't say as I ever really knowed him. But 'e were like that. As soon as he'd married Marge Bridgefoot, 'e got a swelled head, and such as me weren't good enough for him, though he were nothing and nobody till then.'

'You 'adn't ought speak ill o' the dead, whatever you may think, Ned Merriman,' said Sophie severely.

'I should be telling a lie if I said anything different from what I thought. I ain't speaking ill of the dead – I'm telling the truth about him as I knowed him when he were alive. Being dead don't alter that, does it?

He got what he asked for, I reckon. If he'd been content with marrying Marge and being a farmer as were doing well, he'd still ha' been alive now. But not him. He had to be a gentleman. Even Marge wasn't good enough for 'im. Folks won't forget that.'

Sophie let it go without further argument. 'Poor Marge,' she said. 'You're right about that, Ned. She never did ought to ha' married Vic Gifford. But there, if we all done right all the while, none on us would never do wrong. That's too much to 'ope for. It's a sad old world for us all, sooner or later.' Ned left, rather hastily.

Fran regretted her momentary irritation with Sophie. It was sudden death that had been too much for her. Jelly's sudden death had robbed her of a husband, Ned's only son had been drowned. As Sophie said, most people had sad memories to cope with. Even Fran herself.

The gloomy day closed in, and wore wearily to its end. To be in the safety of her own bed with William lying beside her seemed to Fran to be all she ever wanted out of life again.

58

Thursday morning presented Fran with a problem of etiquette she had never before encountered. It was necessary in some way to acknowledge Vic Gifford's death in a letter of condolence – but in the present circumstances, to whom? Finding it impossible to decide, she suggested that it would give William something to do if he were to go and call on George and Molly.

He found the whole family in shock but facing a similar dilemma, too honest to pretend to mourn a man whom they had never cared for and of late had positively disliked and openly disowned. His rape of his wife they had never disclosed, his flagrant adultery which was common knowledge being accepted as a good enough reason for Marjorie leaving him and considering filing a petition for divorce.

'We don't know what to do,' Molly said. 'There'll have to be an inquest, so that'll give us a bit more time to make up our mind about the funeral. We've got to think about Pansy and Poppy. He's their father, when all is said and done. We shall all have to go to the funeral for their sakes. We should be cried shame on, if we didn't.'

A car drew up at the door. 'Ah! Here comes Brian. I hoped he'd come up this morning. It was all so sudden yesterday that we couldn't think straight.'

'How is she, this morning, my boy?' asked George anxiously, almost before Brian had got inside. There was no need to ask who she was. William acknowledged Brian, and stood up to go. This was no time for intrusion.

'Sit down, William,' George said. 'Hear what Brian has to say. It's Marge, you see, as we're worried about. She's acting very queer. We don't care about you knowing.' He looked back at his son.

Brian shook his head. 'Still the same. Hard as nails and cold as charity,' he said. 'Neither a tear nor a word to show any feeling. All she'll say is that she wants no more to do with him dead than she did alive.'

He turned to William. 'I don't wonder – but it leaves me in the soup. Somebody's got to see to things. They both made wills when they were married, and have never changed them since. Identical wills. Each left everything to the other, and the executors were the survivor, and me. That was Dad's doing, I think – he was making sure that somebody would look after Marge's interests, even then. But nobody expected this. She don't want a say in anything, so it's all up to me.'

'That don't sound like Marjorie,' Molly said, inclined to be tearful. 'She's usually so sensible.'

'P'raps not, Mother,' said George, for once impatient with her. 'It sounds like Vic's wife, who put up with his goings-on till she couldn't stand it no longer.'

'What about the twins?'

'Pansy rang up, in a terrible state. She was there, on the spot, when it happened. I expected her to break Marge down, but she listened as cool as a cucumber. Told Pansy she couldn't make out what she was saying if she didn't pull herself together and stop crying. I think Pansy wanted her to go home, 'cos I heard Marge say, "No, I'm not coming anywhere near. You can come here if you like, but don't bring Darren." As I said, hard as nails.

'I had to ring the college and break the news to Poppy. Marge said to tell Poppy she couldn't speak to her. So it was Rosy who comforted Poppy as well as she could, and Poppy said she'd get home to her mother soon as ever possible. "Tell Mum I'll be with her at the funeral," she said. So I did. Marge only laughed, and said, "She may think so, but she won't. The two o' them can follow the coffin together, if they want to. I shan't be there." And, Dad, she means it. I can't budge her.'

William insisted on excusing himself, but George followed him outside. 'You can see what we're up against,' he said. 'For myself, I don't care a mite, but I don't want Molly and the others upset. To tell you the truth, I feel the same as Marge. I pay my last respects to all as I've got any respect for, but that don't include him. If I ever did have any for Vic, he lost it for what he did to my gel that night she run away. If you knowed what we know, you'd feel the same. She don't want him buried here. I'll see to it that he ain't. Let 'em take him back to where he were born. He were ashamed of his own family, after he begun to get such a swelled head, but there's four brothers and two sisters still alive, all with grown-up families o' their own. They'll be there in full black, like crows behind a plough. Folks such as them love a good funeral, and when it's one o' their own as has got his name in the paper by killing hisself, wild 'osses wouldn't keep 'em away. And that's what's worrying Molly – she don't want to cause no more talk than she can help. But there'll be talk enough, whichever way. I shall do whatever Molly wants me to, but I shan't try to make Marge do anything she don't want. Not even for Molly's sake.'

'Fran asked me to give you her love especially,' William said.

That brought a smile to George's rugged old face. 'Give her mine back, and look after her. If you ever treat her like Vic did Marge, I'll break your neck myself.'

William daren't inquire what it was that might cause him such a dire end. He was still wondering what it was the Bridgefoot family had kept hidden when he reached home.

Sophie had been news-gathering overnight at the one place other than a Bridgefoot household likely to know the whole truth – Thirzah's house.

'When Dan 'ad gone back to the farm,' Sophie said, 'me and Thirz' 'ad a bit of a talk between ourselves, like. If Dan knows what it were as made Marge leave Vic so sudden when she did, 'e's never said – but we reckon there must ha' been more than what went on at that party. Something as the Bridgefoots won't never tell nobody.'

Something with sexual connotations, then, Fran thought. Something more shocking than his adultery, because everybody knew about that, though Sophie would never let any allusion to it 'pass her lips'. Well, there were worse things. She said so to William, when he told her what George had said.

'Homosexuality? Rape?' Fran asked. 'Poor Marge! At least she had enough guts to escape. But it makes you wonder how many other men there are like Vic – and how many wives in the past put up with it and said nothing. If they complained, they got no sympathy. It was always the wife's fault if a marriage went wrong on grounds connected with sex. More power to Marge's elbow. That's one change I'll go along with all the way.'

'Are you warning me?' he said, lifting one eyebrow for the first time in a week.

'You just try it and see,' she answered.

'I shall regard that as a positive invitation,' he said, 'if ever you deny me my marital rights as your husband.' The eyebrow came down again, and the light went out of his eyes. 'If ever you have the chance, that is.'

Under the raillery, there was always that hint of bitterness. Fran wondered now and then if he had any idea how much it hurt her. And yet perhaps it was the grain of sand that caused the pearl of great price their oyster shell contained to go on getting bigger.

George was, for once, wrong in his estimate of the talk Vic's death would occasion. Sophie remarked on it. 'Beryl's keeping very quiet,' she said. 'Got her orders from Kid, I shouldn't wonder. They were thick with Vic through the Baileys. But there's a good many like 'er as don't feel they belong to the village no more. Them as live in the council 'ouses and in Hen Street mainly. They're in with the new lot, like Vic Gifford was. Ned was telling me 'ow the men down the Green Dragon were saying so last night. They never 'ave liked Vic much, but they wouldn't ha' said so till lately, him being George's son-in-law. Them as 'ave all'us lived 'ere, and their fathers afore 'em, can't abide new folks taking things over, let alone folks as do belong, like Kid Bean, going against us. Vic won't be missed a lot. But when it comes down to it, 'e were still one o' George's fam'ly, say what you may.'

Vic's death had at least broken into the interminable waiting of that week. There were no phone calls. William was getting himself into such a state that Fran began to worry about the effect it was having on him. It was no good her telling him that none of it was his business, because whatever she said didn't change his conviction that he had to take all the responsibility. Especially for the four children still under their roof.

It was difficult to get them to be optimistic, or to look forward, because the only bit of the future really settled was that on Saturday Emerald was to go into the employ of Beth and Elyot, causing the first break from each other the girls had ever known.

Nevertheless, they were young, they had some new and pretty things to wear, and they were not going far. For the twins to be having a weekend's holiday was an adventure in itself. When Friday went by, too, without news, William was almost in despair. What news did come now could hardly be good news. The chances were that all they would learn would be that the younger children were in a children's home, and Petrie where their chance of ever seeing him again was nil. William said that it would be better for everybody that the girls would not be at Benedict's when Joe came back alone.

Time inexorably drew Saturday slowly on, and there had still been no word when Eric picked up the twins, while Emerald and Amethyst sadly and shyly said goodbye and left to walk to the Old Rectory. Sophie was in tears. During the past week, she had grown very fond of those poor orphans. She had wished they were her daughters.

The house seemed terribly empty, after they had gone, though with all the preparation for the guests from Castle Hill there was plenty for Fran and Sophie to do. William was at a loose end, and disappeared. His cast-down mood was beginning to worry Fran seriously. She left Sophie to her own devices, and went to look for him.

They were now caught between two separate causes for concern, without being able to forecast the outcome of either.

Fran found William standing staring out of one of the sitting-room windows, hands in pockets, the picture of dejection. He turned at her entrance, showing her a face from which the mask of control had for the moment slipped. For once it was he who was in need of moral support, not she. She led him to his chair and herself sat on the arm of it. She drew his head towards her, and held him while he tucked his arms round her, saying nothing. She was silent, too. What good were ordinary words, everyday words, commonplace words? They might swab the wound, even cleanse it, but they didn't go deep enough to heal. That's why even the most illiterate of folk turned to verse, however banal, in the stress of deep emotion. Poetry was the shorthand that conveyed emotion swiftly, when it was needed.

She turned his face up, and kissed it, quoting the first appropriate lines that came to her mind. 'Remember Boethius, my darling,' she said.

> 'O strong of heart, go where the road
> Of ancient honour climbs.
> Bow not your craven shoulders.
> Earth conquered gives the stars.'

Silent still, he clung closer, but she knew that she had got through to him. She left him only in answer to Sophie's call for help. Time was passing and visitors were expected.

59

Greg was later than Monica had expected him to be, partly because the nearer he got to Cambridge, the slower he drove. He had had Jess's letter, but there had been something about it that had puzzled him. It was not the answer to his own humble plea for forgiveness that he had hoped for. It was neither Jess as she had been lately, deliberately and bitchily withdrawing from him, nor was it a positive welcome to reconciliation. It was cool and kind, but hedged with reservations. Its hesitant tone, balanced, as it seemed to him, on a razor's edge of non-commitment, had hurt him almost as much as it had comforted him. It was not the sort of letter that might have been expected from 'his' Jess, who normally did nothing by halves. So why had she chosen to answer his loving letter in this half-hearted fashion? He could only conclude that she wanted to forgive him, but still found herself unable to do it with her whole heart. In which case . . . ?

He argued to himself, as Fran had done to him on her own behalf in the past, that half a loaf was better than no bread at all; but Fran at that stage had never known what it was to have a whole loaf from which you could cut slice after slice without it ever growing smaller. He had. He didn't think himself capable of being within sight and sound of the woman who had so utterly satisfied him since the moment he had first met her, and be content with only crumbs. That was the trouble. He wouldn't be in this present mess if Jess hadn't starved him. Could that possibly be the reason for her reservations now – that she had already given so much that she had no more to give?

Fran had suggested to him once, in the very early stages of the rift between him and Jess, that it might be something to do with Jess's age, referring, of course, to the menopause – the 'change' – now so openly discussed. Good God, had that been meant literally – that at the cessation of ovulation a woman could change from what she had been to someone quite different? That his scintillating, fascinating, beautiful, passionate, full-blooded lover could 'change' and become as unlike what she had been as a poppy pressed between the pages of a Bible is unlike the same flower fresh-picked? It couldn't be! It wasn't possible!

Yet that was how Jess had seemed lately, recognizable as herself but lacking that extraordinary vitality that had made her such a sexually satisfying partner, as well as his only love. No, Love.

That was when fear struck. There might be another, too-terrible-to-contemplate reason which, because of her love for him, she had kept and was keeping from him. She could be ill – terminally ill, perhaps with cancer. It would be just like her to shield him from the hurt of knowing, weaning him away from her so that when she left him for ever he would be to some degree inured to the loss of her.

He trod on the accelerator, cursing himself for wasting so much time. He could have been there by now – and he still had to call and see Monica. She was the last person to ask about Jess, so he would have to wait now till he got to Southside House. When, of course, he still might find Jess perfectly well and interested in everything else but him. He slowed down again, and in a very troubled state of mind drew up outside Monica's new home.

Eric had already arrived with the Petrie twins, and Monica greeted him by berating him for being so late. She had been expecting him for the last two hours. She needed a really long, businesslike session with him, which was no longer possible now. Her day, as well as her accommodation, was booked to its limits. However, she insisted that he stay to lunch before he went on. Reluctantly yet gratefully, he accepted.

Reprieve, or only stay of execution? In his present state of mental and emotional confusion, he simply couldn't judge. It was almost two o'clock before he could bring himself to set off again for Old Swithinford. Bare trees, bare gardens, bare streets. Nothing at all, anywhere. The entire village, no doubt, was subdued by the news of Vic Gifford's death, which he had heard about over lunch. There were no lights showing in Southside House as he approached it. What could he possibly hope for in so dead a place on such a dead day as this? Only the death of all his hopes. Steeling himself against all eventualities, he forced himself out of his car, opened the front door and stepped tentatively inside.

She had heard the car, and the opening of the door. She stood in the doorway of the big, lavish, up-to-the-minute 'kitchen-diner'. One glance at her told him that at any rate she was not dying – she looked better than when he had last seen her. Her sprite-like face first registered joy absolute, with eyes brilliant as dewdrops on a sunny spring morning. Then a red flush raced up her cheeks till it suffused her whole face and neck, replaced the next instant by frail, tissue-paper whiteness. She put out a hand on either side of herself to hang on to the doorjambs, but he was there and had caught her before her legs gave way.

Jess was in his arms again. That was the only thing his mind would register. He picked her up bodily and held her where he could reach her face to kiss her closed eyelids. Then he nudged open the door with his elbow, and carried her inside. 'His' fireside chair still stood where it always had, so he went to it and sat down with her on his knees. Then he began to kiss her properly, hungrily, while he still could, before she came round and told him to go again, this time for ever. He murmured endearments made precious by more than twenty-five years of usage, crooning them into her hair, her neck, her still-firm rounded little breasts – and back to her mouth again. He began to be uneasy that her swoon of surprise was lasting rather a long time, but while it lasted she was still his – though he'd have to do something if she didn't come round soon. He kissed her left eye, willing it to open, his own closed momentarily in something akin to prayer.

Her right eyelid lifted a fraction, revealing an eye as alive as a flame.

'You forgot "bomb-baby",' she said, her lovely deep voice catching on a gurgle halfway between laughter and tears. A charge of hope shot through him, revitalizing him.

'But the whole darned world's no longer upside down,' he said, kissing her again, this time getting the sort of response he had been used to, and had begun to think that he might never experience again.

He looked around him. An upright fireside chair is no place to mend such lacerated love in. He turned her face towards him, to make her look at him. 'Jess,' he said, struggling to keep desire down and temper it with caution as well as contrition, 'Jess, my darling, are the nightingales really singing for us again?'

She kissed him. His heart leapt. 'Then what are we waiting for? Let's go to bed!'

'No!' she said, struggling to free herself from his arms. 'No! Not till all the bomb damage has been cleared away. If that's possible. If it ever can be.'

His hope was flattened, and he was thrown off balance as if by bomb-blast. He felt as if life was being sucked from him. She loved him, she wanted him – but she was Jess, and Jess couldn't forgive him.

'The damage I've caused?' he managed to say, after what seemed like eternity.

'No, the damage I've done, the bomb you don't yet know about. What damage have you ever done, except love me too much? That's what I couldn't – still can't – take any longer. All the love I don't deserve. All the years you've gone on loving me when . . . ' She couldn't go on.

He was still holding her on his knees, and felt the tremors running through her as she hid her face in her hands.

'What are you talking about, my darling? What can you possibly have ever done to equal what I've done to you?'

'That's what I'm trying to tell you. We can't take anything for granted, till you know . . . '

She was sobbing quietly now, and his heart was turning over with anguish: in utter bewilderment, but with love overpowering. It was love entire, the thing that made her the woman to match the man in him, more than just his lover. She was his daughter, and his mother, his priestess and his goddess, his queen and his slave, his Muse perhaps, now, more than ever before.

He put her away from him, and stood up. 'I don't know what you're talking about,' he said. '*And I don't want to know*. You are you and I am I, and that's all that matters. Tell me afterwards if you must – but let's go and listen to the nightingales in Berkeley Square first. Darling, it's been so long.'

Everything else could wait.

They slept, woke, made love again and slept again, and woke again to find that the dark had fallen. Then they still lay, arms entwined, till Jess began to feel the darkness round them deep enough to be her friend. She could confess so much better if she didn't have to watch his face. He, too, was afraid of breaking the magic spell of their reunion, but he had to let her tell him. Besides, he was still not feeling as secure as he wanted to.

'Am I really home again? For ever?'

He heard the tears in her voice, though she held them back. 'I don't know,' she said. 'You may not want to be, when you know what I'm going to tell you. You've got to know, whether you want to hear it or not.'

He was sobbing on her breast long before she reached the end of her story. She sat up, holding him to her, cradling him as if he had been the baby that was never born. He was agonized by love and pity for her, for the hope she told him of, never lost, but month by month destroyed. For her guilt that she had never told him the truth, causing her such pain now; that she had deceived him by not admitting that she knew all along whose fault it was.

He interrupted. 'Fault? My darling girl, how can you call that *fault*? Would you have said it was my *fault* if I'd been killed on D-Day? I would have been a war casualty. So were you. I'm glad you didn't tell me, at that time. I think I should have deserted and been shot, rather than leave you, if I'd known . . . You did the only thing possible. It wasn't your fault that our baby was a war casualty too.'

He turned on his back, to take in properly what he had just said. 'Our baby. *My baby!*'

'Oh, don't,' she wailed. 'I can't bear it.'

He turned back, and grabbed her, almost suffocating her by his unexpected response. In the semi-darkness she couldn't read his face, but his embrace and his voice were those of elation.

'You don't understand, do you, my darling, what you have just done! Not *to* me, but *for* me. Why do you think I've always regarded myself as such a hopeless failure? In those terrible days up in Barra, watching you gradually giving up hope, always being disappointed? Oh, I went and had sperm counts and all the rest – you never knew, and they said I was OK – but the proof was there. I didn't give you the baby you wanted. A man doesn't feel he is a man till he's fathered a child. That's where I failed, and all the rest followed. For all my creative ability, I couldn't make a child. But I did! I did! As you proved yourself by conceiving it. Oh, don't you see, my precious? Somewhere up in that gorgeous heaven out there, so full of stars tonight, there's a little soul waiting to be born again – the one that could have been ours. Is still ours, if we can think about it like that. He can be born again in making me the artist I can be, now. The artist who painted that portrait of Monica.'

'I tried to destroy that, too. Fate wouldn't let me do it twice.'

Her voice was low, and full of tears again, as she began to talk, easily now, though full of poignant sorrow. She told him of the many times she had, in fact, conceived, as the gynaecologist had told her she might, only to lose it again after one week, two weeks, once, even, after nearly two months. Of the despairing days in Barra, when missed periods didn't any longer mean hope, but meant despair, because they told of time running out on her. Of her fear of losing him, once he drew the same conclusion. Of her resolution that as she had robbed him, she had to set him free to find another woman who could make up to him for her failure. It wasn't too late for him. That was when she had engineered their move back to England, where, at least, she would still have William to care for, and to care for her, if she succeeded in pushing him into the arms of some younger, still fertile woman.

Only to find that it was William who had the other woman! And that is where the true bitterness had set in – not really about anything in particular, but everything. There were babies everywhere. And then he had to go and paint one – or at least, a mother with one. Creating the baby he had always wanted but giving it, his painted child, to another woman. As she had planned, of course – but she had never faced up to what it would mean to her till she had seen that picture.

That had been the last straw. She had known perfectly well that the baby was Roland's – but symbolically it was everything she had lost. So she had sent him away. Into the arms of Michelle Stanhope.

That was when the abscess of her own self-hatred had burst. She had tried to burn his picture, and then, in her lonely agony, had confessed everything to William and Fran. From that very minute, she had felt better. She had even dared let herself hope that he might come back. That lovely parson who had taken the New Year's Eve service and to whom she had talked without telling him any details, but who seemed to understand all the same, had said that if she could forgive a little bit of unimportant adultery, the Greg he had met that night at the church would forgive her *anything*.

'Greg, was he right? Is that what you've been saying? Even though I tried to destroy your painted child as well.'

'Promise me that you will never mention the name of Michelle Stanhope again,' he said.

'Greg, poor woman. It wasn't her fault. It was mine. I forgive her everything.'

'Oh, you do, do you? Well, I don't want ever to have to think about her again. An Amazonian Lady Macbeth, full of avaricious scheming and contempt for other people. One day I'll tell you, but not yet. Not tonight. I only want to think about us. Jess, can I?'

Actions speak louder than words.

It was past seven o'clock when, both bathed and dressed, they made their way downstairs at last, restored in every sense.

'Go and sit down,' he said. 'I'll make us a cup of tea. Then if we're hungry we'll find something to eat later, even if we have to go to the hotel for it. I'm not hungry for anything now that I'm home again with you in sight and within my reach.'

The sitting-room fire had burnt so low that she had a job to rekindle it, but she had got it going again to a good glow by blowing it by the time he brought in the tray. She was standing, flushed from her exertions, in front of the mantelpiece and under his picture.

He set the tray down, and stared unbelievingly at it. His masterpiece was there, undamaged, displayed and loved.

The tea was ignored while she stood beside him to let him take it in afresh. He was overawed by it.

'Do you know, my darling, I think I painted our lost baby's little spirit into that,' he said, in a tone of reverence. 'He wanted to come back to us, and he has done. We've got him. He'll never let us part again, or leave us. He's here to inspire me to greater and greater things. Do you believe me?'

'Yes,' she said, 'absolutely.'

Only a symbol – but symbols don't grow up and leave home. Or have to go to war.

60

Several times during the next hour Fran thanked whatever gods she had any faith in that of all their friends it was Bob and Jane they were expecting. There was something about Bob that had a different sort of effect on William from that of his other friends; perhaps it was Bob's deep, unsophisticated streak of natural philosophy, very much like George Bridgefoot's. George was a committed Christian, Bob an undisguised pagan, yet they had a great deal in common. One believed in miracles, the other in magic. In Fran's estimation, there was little difference. Both believed entirely in powers greater than themselves, by whatever name they called those powers. She thought that she must fall somewhere between the two of them: if asked, she described herself as 'a religious heathen'. They were both able to accept the ups and downs of life with more equanimity than most folks. They could, and did, as Kipling so succinctly put it,

> meet with Triumph and Disaster
> And treat those two impostors just the same.

Both of them had certainly met those two impostors. If William would only open up to Bob today, he would find support.

Then there was Sophie: not quite her usual, unruffled self, reminded of Jelly's sudden death by what had happened to Vic Gifford and sad because she was missing the girls to whose plight her own lonely, loving spirit had responded in such full measure; perhaps worried by Joe's continued absence and silence, fearing that Hetty's surprising fortitude could not be expected to last out much longer; and keeping a very concerned eye on William, for whom her love and respect were so intermingled that Fran occasionally teased him that in Sophie's theology he ranked only just below the Holy Ghost.

Altogether, thought Fran, as she watched Sophie preparing coffee and William a tray of drinks, things this morning could have been a lot worse. When the visitors arrived, the depression lifted even more. Sophie smiled as Jane chatted to her, and as she watched William shake hands with Bob, she almost saw his shoulders straighten.

There was a lot of news to catch up on, between them. The first item on their agenda, naturally, was Nick. Bob sat back, his eyes drinking in every detail of the room, and let Jane do the talking.

As she said, they already knew that Nick had thrown a bit of a spanner into the works. Bob had taken it in his stride. She was the one who was worried.

'I know Nick better than they do,' she said. 'He's always had a streak of determination that looks like stubborn obstinacy. Now, when he's offered everything any young man could possibly want, his refusal to accept seems like rebellion and crass ingratitude.'

She supposed there might be a reason for it that they didn't understand. If there was any chance that his yen to live in Old Swithinford and the cottage had any remote bearing on the past he didn't remember, ought they not to grasp the tiny sliver of hope and cling to it? He said that he felt strange in London. Lost. Looking for something he couldn't find. They couldn't put themselves in his place. He could learn from them what they knew about his former lives by asking questions. It was the things nobody else could know about that troubled him. If he knew the question, he would also know the answer. Or, put the other way round, he would know the answer, if only he could find the question. There were things about himself he felt he had to know, had to find out. Once or twice while staying in the cottage last summer, he said, he had experienced such strange sensations that he had almost felt the questions he wanted answering hovering about in his mind like ghosts that vanished again before they could be identified. For a split second, one of them had been there in church on New Year's Eve. He only ever felt them near him in Old Swithinford. Wasn't that to be expected? Grandfather was wonderful, but if he, Nick, didn't understand himself what 'it' was, how could anybody else know, and help him to find out?

'So we've agreed to let him have his own way,' she said. 'Alex Marland's all for it, as a last throw. Effendi doesn't mind. He's retiring this summer anyway, and had plans to travel with Nick, but he'll be just as happy being a farmer's boy. The only thing I'm really worried about is that Nick can only remember a rich and pampered life in convalescent luxury. That's why I'll only agree to his coming back to the cottage if he works – and I mean works – for his living. He's had it too soft, lately.'

Bob interrupted her rather excited recital in a slow, lazy voice, as if what he was about to say had little if any import at all.

'It's no good having fits too fast over a thing like this, my duck,' he said. 'Give it time. Let the boy alone, and let time sort him out. So far, he's been proggled and pumped by doctors and psychiatrists as don't know what they're looking for, and chivvied from pillar to post by other folks who love him and want to help. It only hazes him more. Seems to me as that bit of his memory lays in his mind like a seed as won't sprout. Perhaps it never will. Some seeds never do. In the old days when corn were sowed broadcast by hand, they used to take that chance into account, and sow four grains for everyone as they expected to harvest.

> One for the mouse, one for the crow,
> One to rot, and one to grow.

'Things happen as they will. Dousing Nick with a hose pipe'll do more harm than good, if all he needs is a spring shower. If it were left to me, I'd wait for the shower. Sooner or later, that's bound to come, though if the seed's rotted by then it still won't sprout. He's been too well looked after for any mouse or crow to get at it. So I ain't worrying. I'm just waiting for the harvest. Now Jane, my pretty, no tears today. I know it ain't up to me to go against all them London doctors and I might still be wrong. But seeing as he's made his own mind up anyway, I dare say what I think. He'll be all right.'

Once they were all seated at the table, Fran said, 'Bob, why didn't you say all that before?'

'To tell you the truth, because I wasn't so sure about it myself till just now. Being in that room makes me able to trust myself. I do still miss that picture, Fran. I wish I could paint one good enough to put there, but I know I can't. Why don't you get Greg to do you one?'

William and Fran looked at each other, wondering how much they dared say.

'He never saw the original, you know,' Fran said. 'William did, of course, but he doesn't remember it any better than I do.'

'I remember it well enough. It was just a portrait of the two who lived here then, and their dog, out under a tree with the house in the background. What Greg ought to do is paint you and William dressed like they were in the picture. I could draw him a sketch to show him near enough what it was like.'

'It's a wonderful idea, Bob, and if ever the conditions are right, we'll carry it through.'

'What conditions, William?' asked Jane.

William looked at Fran, asking her pardon in advance. 'There are two,' he said, 'both imponderable at present. Greg can't be asked if he isn't here. I'm afraid it's touch and go between him and Jess. And I wouldn't agree to it unless – until – I had been able to put a wedding ring on Fran's finger.'

Bob looked completely satisfied with that answer. Jane asked what he had meant about Jess and Greg. He indicated that he would tell her all, when Sophie's sharp ears were safe in the kitchen.

'Tell us about the plans for Charlie's wedding,' said Fran. 'We can't help knowing the Bridgefoot end of it, because of William's involvement with the man who has done up Danesum. To think of a lovely young couple like Charles and Charlie living there and loving Danesum. What's happening to them softens what has happened there. How much have you heard?'

Not a word apparently. The Petrie tragedy had been played down as much as the Gifford one. Fran sadly realized why. It was a sign of another marker reached in the separation of the village that had been one and indivisible, into two. The old and the new. Ancient and modern. The modern consisted of the council housing, Hen Street and the Lane's End Estate. Those who lived there were not the same sort as those who had lived in the little tied cottages Eric had bought and now let as holiday homes. They were the new generation of artisans, all considering themselves 'middle-class', a meaningless term if ever there was one, since no one would be bold enough to call himself 'top-class', and no one was allowed to be 'working-class' except in politicians' terminology. Middle-class really meant 'equal and all alike', the goal being 'to keep up with the Jones's' next door. Those who made it were concerned only to stay there; those who didn't dropped out, and nobody cared about them. Petrie's troubles hadn't touched them. Nor indeed those of Vic, who was as ordinary as everybody else. Even Beryl's acid tongue had been neutralized, because Ken had risen to be middle-class. The circulation of gossip was slowing down. If interest in one's fellow men no longer trills along the wires of communication, there is no dance of blood along the arteries and the community is dead. Perhaps, like a worm, if cut in two each part could grow whole again.

'How do you feel about this early wedding, Bob?' asked William.

'I was worried at first when Charles appeared on the scene. I didn't want any youngster like him to suffer what I had had to with Charlie's mother. He gave Charlie his heart to play with, and I was afraid all she would do would be to laugh at him, and break it. But that day as Robert Fairey died, he came to her for comfort. I sent him to find her in the tackroom, and I watched for them coming back. They were holding hands, and both had been crying. She was carrying a bunch of oxlips as I'd picked and he'd took to her, and I could see and hear and smell spring everywhere all round us. I got that message clear enough. Whatever happened in the meantime, come summer she'd love him as much as he loved her. And I was right. They were meant to be together, now and always.'

'Lucky for them,' said William. 'We four all had to wait till summer was nearly over.'

'What about Jess and Greg?' asked Jane.

'Spring, but in wartime.'

'So what's gone wrong now?'

This time, it was left to Fran to tell the story.

Then William said, 'So if your sixth sense is worrying you about me being on edge today, Bob, now you know why. I'm nearly out of my mind about John Petrie and all those children, and about Joe Noble. He ought to have been back home by Thursday, but we haven't heard a word. I feel responsible to his wife as well as him. I ought never to have let him go. I should have gone myself. But there was this business with Jess and Greg, and she is my sister. Which one ought I to have put first? It's the old dilemma. If your children are upstairs asleep and you find an outbreak of fire on the stairs, what do you do? Try to get to the children, or put the fire out? We left Jess to herself and tried to help the children. If she hasn't blown her anger up again, Greg may be safe, but it won't be our doing. And we couldn't rescue the Danesum family. They were doomed, anyway.'

'Don't give up hope for Jess and Greg till you know,' said Fran. 'And remember that four out of eight of the children are safe if not happy. Let's go and sit down in the sitting-room. Sophie's probably put our coffee in there by now.'

'I'm going to take Bob down to look at Danesum, from a historical point of view,' William said. 'It'll do me good to go there again looking forward instead of backwards. And Bob's such a good listener.'

61

Fran and Sophie had agreed that after such a large and rather late lunch, they wouldn't need anything more than a cup of tea at teatime, but would have an early 'farmhouse-style' cold supper. Sophie would leave a tray with all the tea things ready for Fran to serve, and 'pop down to see Thirz' for a hower'. Even Daniel was getting anxious about what Het might do if Joe didn't soon get in touch. 'What with one thing and another,' Sophie reported him as saying, 'I reckon it's a rum ol' do.' Fran couldn't have agreed with him more.

The men came back just as she was making the tea, and Bob was full of his first real visit to Danesum and the barrows William had explained to him, as well as his conviction that Charles had done the right thing in snapping it up. He knew just what Charlie had meant about it 'calling them'. He'd had the same feeling himself.

William went into the kitchen to Fran, on the excuse of carrying the tray for her. She saw at once that his spirits had risen.

'We drove round by Monastery Farm on the way back,' he said, 'just to see if there were any signs of what might be going on at Southside House. Greg's there, at any rate. His car's standing outside, but I couldn't see any lights anywhere.'

Fran's face lit up as she turned towards him. 'Gone to bed!' she said. 'Want to bet?'

He set the tray down hastily, so as to be able to put his arms round her. 'No, not yet. It's too soon to take anything for granted, but I think it looks hopeful. As long as Greg's there with Jess, anything may happen.' He kissed her, and picked up the tray again.

Sophie came back much more cheerful as well, and brought them up to date with the 'Vic Gifford affair'. Inquest next Monday, but as the verdict was bound to be 'accidental death', the burial had been arranged for next Thursday.

'Not 'ere, though. Dan says George can't find nowhere 'ere to put 'im with the Bridgefoots, so it'd be better for 'im to go where 'e was born, among 'is own. I said as that would mean none of us could go and pay our last respects, but Dan said George had thought about that, and was 'iring a special bus for anybody as wanted to go. Tha's something I'm never 'eard the like of afore, and it don't seem right to us. But Thirz' thinks as we ought to go, bus or no bus, seeing as Dan's worked for the Bridgefoots all 'is life and 'is father afore 'im. Besides, as she says, it ain't for Vic 'isself we should be going, but for the sakes of them 'e's left behind.' And because old-fashioned village ways demanded it, thought Fran. Even by bus.

They had finished supper and gone back replete to drink coffee and port in the sitting-room when Sophie, white-faced and flustered, opened the door without knocking, and blundered in.

'Come quick,' she said to William. 'It's Joe!' Fran followed William into the kitchen.

Joe stood just inside the door, hardly recognizable as the man they knew. He was ready to drop with weariness, his eyes red-rimmed and glittering with lack of sleep. He was also filthy, and in his arms he carried a bundle wrapped in a blanket, which was also filthy and stank the kitchen out with the stench of stale vomit. Sophie pulled up a chair for him, William went for the brandy bottle and Fran reached for the bundle.

'No,' said Joe, sitting down with the bundle still on his knees. 'He ain't fit for you to touch. He's been sick most o' the way, and he were bad afore we ever started. Besides, 'e's very near unconscious now, and I reckon as it 'ould be best to let 'im sleep while he will. 'Cos we shall hev to clean him up afore we can do anything else with him.'

'Who?' said Fran, reaching to pull the blanket back in spite of Joe's effort to prevent her. There was no mistaking the coppery head of Tanner, filthy as it was. 'Oh Joe!' she cried. 'You've found them! And he's still alive, whatever sort of state he's in.'

'Ah,' said Joe wearily. 'He's alive, if only just. So are the other two as are still asleep in the van. Cried theirselves to sleep, they did, 'cos I couldn't do no more than look after this one and keep driving on when I could put him down again for a few minutes. He's been sick all the way.'

Fran could see that William had reached the end of his tether, and was likely to become another casualty if he had time to stop and ask Joe about Petrie. She began to issue orders.

'William, go and tell Bob and Jane what's happened. Ask them to go and investigate who or what is still in the van, whatever Joe means by that.'

'The Dormobile,' Joe said. 'If they're still asleep, tell 'em not to wake 'em. There's enough to do with this one first as it is.'

'All right, William – do as Joe says. Sophie, go and run a bath for Joe in the flat, while I get one ready to bath Tanner in the main bathroom upstairs. Then come and help me, if you can face it.'

'No, let me,' said Jane from the doorway. 'Bob's gone out to the van. He'll cope.'

'Yes, that makes sense,' Fran answered. 'William, Joe'll need your help. He's all in – he's dropping with exhaustion.'

It took no more than five minutes to prepare the two baths. 'Give him to me,' Fran said.

Joe shook his head. 'He ain't fit for you to touch,' he said. 'You've got no idea. You'd throw your hearts up. Let me carry him up and strip him. Have you got an old sack or something I can put his clothes in? Ned can burn 'em in the morning. I can't be in no worse mess than I am a'ready, well all my top clo'es, that is. So you might as well let me finish the job.'

He stood up, staggering with weariness and the weight of the child in his arms, and Fran and Jane followed him upstairs holding handkerchiefs to their noses.

'Stop outside the door,' Joe said. 'I'll call you when it's fit for you to come in. Don't get upset if he starts to cry – though I don't reckon he's got strength enough left for that.'

When he let them in, the offending garments had been tied inside a plastic dustbin bag, and Joe was holding up the still unconscious child in the water, having given him a first good swilling down. Fran got her arms round the little boy first, and both women knelt by the bath.

They kept the bathwater at body temperature so as not to rouse him, while Fran held him, and Jane sponged. They had changed the water twice before Jasper began to show any signs of consciousness. The third lot of water was scented with Fran's latest expensive eau-de-toilette, and she lifted him out on to a warm towel on Jane's lap. The coppery hair had sprung back into its curls, and his soft skin was slightly pink now from the warmth of the water and the friction of the towel.

He opened his eyes, his face crumpling and ready to cry. Jane was rocking and soothing him, but his glance had fallen on Fran. 'Lovely lady,' he said and, closing his eyes again, sank back into Jane's warm embrace. 'Isn't he beautiful,' she said, wistfully.

They wrapped the child in blankets, and laid him on Fran's bed. 'Jane,' Fran said, 'please leave him to me now, and go and tell William I want him. We must see to Joe next, and then listen to what he has to tell us. I'll be down as soon as William and I have decided what to do with Jasper.'

Jane went, and William came. Fran could tell from his face, which bore tear-streaks down it still, that he had already asked Joe what he wanted most to know, and that the answer had not been good. She sat down on the bed, masking the sleeping child, and held out her arms to him. 'John?' she asked.

He nodded. 'Dead,' he said. When he raised his face from her shoulder, he added, 'That's all I know, yet. Just that he's dead.'

She moved, so that he could see what was behind her. 'But Cupid isn't,' she said. 'They rescued him. What shall we do with him, for the present, I mean? We can't leave him up here alone, in case he wakes. Will you carry him down? Let's lay him on the settee in the flat. If we left the door open, we should hear him if he did wake and cry. We must give Joe some attention, next.'

William lifted the child up carefully, and Fran followed him downstairs.

Joe was sitting at the kitchen table, drowned in a dressing-gown a foot too long for him, wearily sipping soup.

'I didn't think 'e ought to 'ave no more than that till 'e comes to hisself a bit,' Sophie said, addressing them over Joe's head as if his ordeal had robbed him of all his senses and turned him into a dumb animal. ''E couldn't ha' put 'is trowsis and jacket on again as they was, so I'm done what I could to sponge 'em. They'll soon dry on the Aga rail. Do, they'll be all right for him to go home in, but they'll still need to be cleaned afore 'e can wear 'em again. And Mis' Bellamy and him are both gone to see to them others.'

'Which others?' asked Fran, sitting down weakly by Joe's side.

It was William who answered her. 'Jade and the baby, Aggie,' he said. 'Not Crystal, or Basher.'

Bob appeared at the kitchen door. 'Them littlest ones are still fast asleep, wore out with crying, like Joe says, I don't doubt. They're both filthy, and the baby wants changing, but Jane says it would be better not to disturb 'em till we're ready to deal with 'em in here. They can't be left by theirselves, though, so I've come for a pail of hot water with some disinfectant in it and some cloths and a scrubbing brush an' such. We'll clean the van up a bit while we wait. It ain't all that bad.'

Sophie was already fetching him the things he had asked for. 'Shall we bring 'em in, when they rouse?' Bob asked.

'Of course,' Fran said. 'They'll have to be bathed, as well, but if they'll sleep a little longer, it will give us a chance to hear what Joe has to tell us.'

Joe pushed his soup bowl away, and began. He had refused to come home and leave Petrie, because he was sure that he wasn't fit to manage alone. So they had gone on in such weather as he had never known before – high winds, floods everywhere in the valleys, and snow on high ground, with gale force gusts so bad that sometimes he could hardly hold the car on the road. By Thursday they'd got close to the place near Aberystwyth, where Petrie had arranged for them to go. The site had had to be abandoned. All the camp manager said was that such as had transport had made for other places further inland. Petrie was sure that Dafydd wouldn't have left them till he had found them a safe place somewhere else.

So they'd gone to a police station to find out where they could have gone to. There were three camping-sites within a radius of twenty miles, but because the weather was getting worse all the time, all three were by now likely to be overcrowded with refugees from those on the coast.

'He – Mr Petrie I mean – said as we hadn't no choice but to go on looking for 'em while he still could, 'cos things were a lot worse than he'd ever expected 'em to be. He wouldn't stop for nothing, so all we 'ad to eat was whatever we could get as we went. I could see as I daren't let him drive, though he wanted to. It were getting dark and the wind blowed harder than ever. He weren't strong enough to hold the car against shufts o' wind like that. We got to one o' the camps and I stopped. He clawed out of the van afore I could get my door open, and rushed about in the rain looking for the big new van. I couldn't stop him. He soon got wet through, and I was fit to drop myself with tiredness, but on we had to go. There were still one more site to visit, and when we got there, well after midnight, there it was.

'I druv up as close to it as I could get that old car, and he got out to look and listen. There wasn't a sound from the inside of it, so after prowling round it in the rain he said as he had a spare set o' keys to it and he was going to let hisself in. And there were them three littlest child'en, fast asleep, locked in all by theirselves. So we set down to wait, expecting her to come back, but she didn't. He was wet through and cold and in such a rage as I thought he'd die there and then; but I were too tired to think. All I wanted were a cup of hot tea and somewhere to lay down for a nap. So I found the kettle and I made a pot o' tea, and got him to hev a cup. Then I just set down and went off.

'But while I were asleep, he went out and prowled round looking for her and that big old boy they call Basher. It were still bucketing down with rain, and he must ha' been gone a long while, 'cos when I woke up and found as he weren't there it were beginning to get light, and by that time I were getting frit, I tell you straight, for him and for myself. As far as I could see, them children hadn't none of 'em moved a muscle, and I begun to think as I should be found by the police in a van as didn't belong to me with three child'en all dead. But he come back at last, soaked to the skin and nearly done for. He were so short o' breath he could hardly speak, and all he said was for me not to waste time – just go and fetch the police. I went out to the old car and started her up, but she'd got set in the mud, and I couldn't get a grip no-how. The wheels just kep' spinning round, and the engine roared and kicked up such a row as woke the folks in the next caravan. And after a long while the man in it got dressed, and come out and asked me what I thought I was playing at. I told him the truth, and where I was going if I could get the car to move. He turned out to be a good sort o' bloke, and said as he wanted to go in and speak to Mr Petrie. I had to give up, so I went back, and heard what he said.

'It appeared as him and his wife had seen 'em arrive on Saturday, and noticed as their mother was leaving them littl'uns too much by their-selves, or with only the biggest old boy to look after 'em. So by that they had kep' a eye on 'em, though not liking to be seen to interfere. He said they'd spoke to the mother, and she'd seemed clart enough to know what she was doing. Well, as I know, she was, as long as she was doing what suited her. But a-Tuesday, he said, the biggest boy had been real excited, like, and had gone and talked to his missus in their caravan. She had quizzed him a bit, and he'd told her a lot. The man as had druv 'em there wasn't nothing to do with them. When he'd got 'em there and parked the van, he'd left 'em and gone, 'cos he lived not very far away. Then his mother had gone round the camp to see if there was anybody else she knowed there and who had she found but *his* very own father, as he had never seen afore. The bloke said his missus thought it had been planned. Anyway, it wasn't long afore this chap as Basher said was his father had brought his car round and took the trailer and all as was in it away to where he was camped over the other side as was higher and drier.

'That's when this next-door chap had started to be real oneasy, 'cos though she were about during the daytime, she'd left the ol' boy in charge when it got dark and went off with the man. Come Wednesday night, she took the biggest boy with her, but though they kept a sharp look-out they didn't see the littl'uns go. He said he felt sure they'd been locked in and left. His missus told him he were a fool – did he think any woman in her right mind would leave three such littl'uns locked in by theirselves on a night like that? But he couldn't rest when the wind got so bad as it did, so afore settling down for the night hisself, he'd gone out to listen and see if they was all right. He couldn't hear nothing. It was all as still and silent as the grave, he said, so he'd thought as his wife was right, and their mother had took 'em after all. But it was him as had been right, and his missus wrong, and now he knowed for sure he was going to report their mother if she ever done it again. Mr Petrie told him he needn't bother. He knowed her, and I was on my way to do just what he's said.

'The man went home, and I made Mr Petrie take some of his wet things off. He were shivering and coughing, but said he'd be all right till the child'en had woke up. We couldn't wake 'em, no 'ow. Then at last he says to me, "Joe," he says, "they weren't meant to come round. She must ha' *drugged* 'em." And he went over to where Tanner laid. He'd been sick all the way there, and he'd been sick again that night afore we got there, so he were in a terrible mess. He looked down at him and said, "This one's my own son, Joe. I can't and I shan't leave 'im here. There'll come a time when she'll overdose 'em, and kill 'em all, and then set fire to the van or something to pretend as it were a haccident. I've been making up my mind. This is my son, and this is my van, and I'm taking 'em both and the other two. If you're well enough to drive it back to Cambridge, I can hand them over to the police there as well as I can here. But it'll depend on you, 'cos I ain't going to be well enough to drive."

'"I'm had a good rest," I said, "and a bit of a sleep. There's nothing I should like better than to get off home, if we can get this van out. What about Pugh's car?" "Leave it where it is," he said. "I'll write to him, soon as I'm back in hospital." So we got ready to set off home there and then. I didn't have a bit o' trouble moving that new van, 'cos it had been parked on a proper hard standing place, d'yer see. But I told him as I shouldn't start unless he agreed to get all the rest of them wet things off and lay down. "I shall get in it with him," he said, meaning Tanner. "That'll get me warm." That's how I shall remember him – how he looked that minute. Smiling down on that little old boy. It were like watching a angel smile.'

Joe put his hands up to his face, and they waited in awed silence for him to go on. 'We found a new sleeping-bag as hadn't been used, and sponged the littl'un down as well as we could, and there were plenty o' room for both of 'em in it. I knowed as he were thin, but undressed he were nothing but a skeleton. I dried his vest and pants, thin old things as they were, against the hot air o' the van's heater, so as he could put 'em on again afore we had to stop for petrol or anything. And when the child'en did begin to rouse at last, he got dressed as far as he could so he could look after 'em and I could keep at the wheel. It weren't them as I were worried about, by then. It was him. I could see him getting worse, and coughing all the while. When he started to sweat, and breathe hard, I knowed what were the matter. My old Dad died o' pneumonia. But we were on a lonely old road and I thought my best plan would be to get him back to hospital here, where they knowed about him. We was just this side o' Worcester when he asked me to stop, 'cos he'd started spitting blood. We both knowed then as he'd never get back here no more.

'"Make for Leamington fast as you can," he said, "straight to the hospital, and leave me there. There ain't much time and I'm thinking about the children. Don't take no notice o' speed limits, now."

'I tread on that accelerator, and I hadn't gone above ten mile afore there were a police car a-flagging me down. I stopped, glad enough to see the police, and told 'em why I was in such a hurry. They took a look at him, and told me to drive on a bit to a caff about a mile farther on. So I did, and we took the kids out and got 'em into the caff with me, while they done what they could for him. Next thing I knowed, there were a ambulance come up with its lights flashing and its two-tone going full blast. They soon had him in it and off it went, and then they come and questioned me proper. After they'd done, they helped me to get the children back into the van. They asked me how far I still had to come, and I said it wouldn't take me much more than a hower and a half, and that we was expected home, though I knowed it were only me as was. So they told me to wait while they done some phoning. When the chief one come back, he said, "Sorry mate. DOA."

'"DOA?" I says. "What does that mean?"

'"Dead on arrival," he says.' There was another long pause before Joe at last went on.

'I told him everything I could, like, but the child'en had begun to cry and I said if he didn't let me get off quick I should never get 'em home. And I told him that if he did, I could stake my life they'd be looked after properly once I'd got back safe. I had to give him a reference, so I give your name and address, Mr Burbage sir. I hope I done right, and you don't mind. He rung the police at Cambridge, and they knowed of you, so he believed me and let me come.

'I'd found some stuff in a bottle in the front o' the car, as said on it as it were for travel sickness, and that it made folks sleepy if they took too much. So I give all three o' them a good dose. It's worked for the two youngest, but Tanner were too far gone a'ready. I laid him on the front bench aside o' me, but I had to stop about every ten minutes for him to be sick – or the other end – till he passed out. Then I laid him down again, and got here as fast as I could.'

Jane had crept back in, and had heard the last part of Joe's story. The kitchen, stilled into silence, overflowed with sadness.

It was Joe who broke the silence. 'How's the little chap now?' he said.

Fran went to look. 'Sleeping like a lamb,' she answered. 'I expect it was whatever he'd been given that upset him, as well as his usual travel sickness. By the time you got him here, he'd probably got rid of most of it. Now he's just worn out.'

'Then I'd better be getting off home,' Joe said.

'Yes, off you get,' said Sophie. 'I'll get your clo'es for you, and you can put 'em on in the bathroom. I dare say somebody'll take you in a car.'

She picked his garments from the Aga rail, and stood for a moment looking as if she had been hit over the head. 'Lawks!' she said. 'It's a good job as somebody 'as thought about it. We're got three children 'ere as ain't got a rag o' clo'es between 'em! Go on, Joe – get yourself dressed as quick as you can. I'm a-going 'ome with you, 'cos there's drawers and drawers full o' child'en's clo'es up at your place as Wend's sent for Stevie and he's never had on. And we shall want 'em, now, tonight, not when Het's finished heving sterricks at the sight o' you. I'll come with you.' She was divesting herself of her apron as she spoke.

'Can I take the van, sir?' Joe asked. 'Then I can change my things, and bring Soph' back, and whatever they can find as'll be any good. Besides, I reckon you may need me again, yet, like if the police come asking questions.'

Fran was astounded by the practical common sense both of them were displaying. It seemed to set her back on a more even keel. It roused William out of his lethargy, too.

'I'll ring the Cambridge police, Joe. Please tell Hetty how grateful we should be for some clothing,' he said.

'We shall have to get the other two out of the Dormobile if Joe's going to take it,' Jane said. 'It's time they got some attention, and we ought to let Bob off his vigil with them. They'll need a lot of cleaning up, and they must be getting hungry. You look after Tanner, Fran, and leave the others to me and Bob.'

'What a blessing it is you're here,' said Fran. 'Will you be able to manage?'

Jane laughed. 'Really, Fran! Bob's a farmer, and you aren't the only woman who has ever changed a baby's dirty nappy before, you know.'

Fran felt bewildered, out of her depth. Her mind was in chaos, but then could there ever have been a more chaotic evening? It was as if darkness was brooding over the face of the deep, so that the earth, as well as her mind, was without form and void. But in the beginning order had come out of chaos, as she supposed it must again. She glanced at the clock, feeling that it must already be midnight – but even time was playing tricks. It was not yet two hours since Joe had arrived. Plenty of time yet for whatever else had to be done.

Her mind cleared. What had been causing her to feel so confused was that however unobtrusively he did it, in the ordinary way it was William who made the decisions. Tonight too distressed to take anything in his normal stride he was leaving it to her.

With more time than she had thought on her side, she could cope – if she had to. But why was she panicking, with all these other capable folk there, each in his or her way doing the right thing without thinking about it? It wasn't all resting on her shoulders, even if William wasn't carrying as much of the load as he usually did. She leaned forward and kissed Jane, remembering that what they had in common was the experience of having to cope alone with babies when neither had a man around to rely on. 'You know where to find anything you need,' she said to Jane, and turned her attention back to William.

He was still sitting at the kitchen table, inert and pale, trying to come to terms with the finality of his friend's death. He must, of course, have been expecting it, must have told himself many times to be prepared for it, and yet still he was finding it too much to accept. Perhaps, Fran thought, it had been Joe's voice and the simple unadorned telling of his tale straight from his heart that had made it so poignant and hard to bear.

She reached her hand across the table, and William put his out to clasp and hold on to it. The kitchen door had closed behind Joe and Sophie, and on the other side of it there were noises of muffled voices and the unaccustomed sound of a baby feebly grizzling. Then footsteps up the stairs. Bob and Jane with Jade and Agate. How strange it all was! Fran heard the Dormobile draw away, and still they sat, hands clasped across the table, communicating without words.

She squeezed the hand she held and he looked up at her.

'It would have been just the same if you had been there,' she said. 'You couldn't have done anything that Joe didn't do. Except, perhaps, make it harder for John. He would have known how much more you understood what it all meant to him than Joe did, and would have been trying to spare your feelings. He didn't die without a friend beside him. That's what's worrying you, isn't it?'

He nodded, still not trusting himself to speak. Then he said, 'That among other things. Wondering what to do next. Like having to tell the four girls . . .'

She had forgotten that. 'Oh, not tonight!' she exclaimed. 'What good will it do to give them even one more night of grieving that they can be spared? Besides, how could we keep them away if they knew their little brothers were here? Leave them till tomorrow morning. We can't tell them what's going to happen to the boys till we know. They'd be out of their minds with worry. And, darling, we have to think of those little ones too, especially Tanner. What a terrible week he must have had!

'If he catches sight of Emmy and Ammy, he'll think he's going home again – only be torn from them again, and put among complete strangers. We can't let that happen. I know I'm right. If they are to be parted again – for good – they really shouldn't meet. Can't we hide him, for the time being, anyway? Joe and Sophie won't say a word if we ask them not to. Nobody but us need know anything.'

'But that means that we have to make decisions too quickly, perhaps tonight. Decisions we have no right to make, especially until I can think clearly. John had been trying to find a solution for a long time, ever since he diagnosed his own condition – and then in the end death defeated him. But even so, he stood a better chance than we do of saving them. We have no claim to them, nor responsibility for them, under the law. Except for Emerald, everything John foresaw and feared could happen to them now will. And I – we are quite helpless to prevent it. Damn! Who on earth can that be?' The telephone was ringing.

She ignored it. 'Speak for yourself,' she said. 'The law? In this case all that means is their mother. I'm not giving in to her without a fight. Possession's nine-tenths of the law – and they're here, *in our possession*.' She had to stop, to listen to the one-sided conversation.

'William Burbage speaking. Yes, Joseph Noble, of Swithinford Bridges. Peter Petrie. That's what he called himself, but it wasn't his real name. Yes, as it happens, I do. It was John Petrie Voss-Dering. Last fixed abode, Addenbrooke's Hospital, where he was until eight days ago. Yes, lung cancer. I suppose they will still have all the records of his medical history. No, he discharged himself. There was very little hope, as they will tell you. Yes, plenty of corroboration. I understand. I shall be here all day tomorrow. No, as far as I know, they were not his, nor their mother his wife. Hippies? I suppose you could say so. Modern-day travellers, certainly. He was a vagrant, but not a hippy. He bought some ruined cottages to restore, and she squatted on his property.' After another pause William's voice was terse as he replied, 'I happen to be a historian, as you know. I am interested in the site as a possible Viking grave place. I got to know him, and I liked him. Very well, tomorrow morning. Good night.'

He sat down. 'Police. They may not bother about an inquest. What's one idle layabout more or less to them? They know of the existence of the three children who were with Joe, but didn't seem particularly interested, and I was as cagey as I dared be. I imagine they'll try to find Crystal, if they can. She's quite sharp enough to keep one step ahead of them. My guess is that the police of Cambridgeshire and Worcestershire and Dyfed will all try to push responsibility for them on to each other. But they can't just do nothing, my darling. In the end, they're bound to win. I don't want you to get hurt, or I wouldn't have bothered to prevaricate at all.

'We've had this all out before. We can't keep them permanently. They may be, as you say, in our possession at this moment, but they could never be ours by law. Apart from any other reason – you force me to say it, or you know I wouldn't – this is an "immoral household" as far as the social services are concerned. We shouldn't be regarded as suitable applicants, even as foster-parents. Oh, sweetheart, don't cry! I can't bear it. Not tonight. Ssh! Here's Joe and Sophie back.'

They came in loaded with bags of clothing of all sorts and sizes, and another bag filled with expensive toys, some of them still in their boxes.

'How kind of Hetty,' Fran exclaimed.

'How daft o' Wend', if you ask me,' Sophie sniffed. 'And I don't care if Joe does 'ear me say it. Got more money than sense.'

Joe nodded agreement. 'I'm been trying to get Het to send all this here stuff to the Red Cross or the Salvation Army,' he said, ''cos Steve can't only wear one lot o' clothes at a time. But all she'd say was that you never knowed when you might want something as you'd throwed away. And for once, Het were right.' He and Sophie both glowed with satisfaction at being able to 'do their bit' to help.

'Sort some out for the two little ones,' Fran said to Sophie, 'or else ask Mrs Bellamy to take what she needs. I'm going to put Tanner into these lovely warm pyjamas and this dressing gown. And those rabbit slippers if they'll fit him. Oh! A teddy-bear – just the right size, too! Most teddies are too big. I don't suppose Tanner's ever had one at all before.'

Her barrage of talk was deliberate, to give William time to recover. 'Come and help me,' she said to him. 'Sophie, could you heat some milk for the baby's bottle? I hope he's got one.'

'I got it filled in the caff, but he didn't wake enough to want it,' Joe said.

'The police have rung,' William told him, 'and will be coming round in the morning. They may come to see you as well. You must get home to bed, now. Take the van back, and drop Sophie home on the way. We shall need her help more in the morning. Oh I forgot. Of course, it will be Sunday. Never mind, we'll cope somehow.'

The look Sophie turned on him made him feel like the child he used to be when he had forgotten to learn the collect for the day. 'I shall be 'ere, Sunday or no Sunday, till it's church-time,' she said.

They said goodnight, and left. Fran and William took the clothing Fran had selected, and went into the flat to Tanner.

'Is there any need to rouse him at all?' asked William.

She put down the clothes and went to him. 'We couldn't leave him here by himself, could we? We shall have to decide what we're going to do with them all for the night.'

'Put them all in one bedroom, and take turns to sit with them?' he asked.

She didn't answer, but sat down by Jasper and stroked his glowing curls, now damp again with perspiration. He opened his eyes, creasing his face into a puzzled frown. Fran shushed William, and waited. The little boy might not remember anything, having had such a terrible trauma, and it would be easier for them all if he didn't. He sat up, looking all round the unfamiliar room, and then towards Fran and William. It was clear that he found their presence comforting.

Then he scrambled off the settee, as naked as he had been when Fran had first encountered him. 'Wee,' he said, taking her hand and looking desperately up at her.

She swept him up in her arms, and rushed him to the lavatory. By the time they came back, he was trotting by her side. He still wore the frown of concentration that had so intrigued Fran when she had found him trying to find his way into Basher's too big shorts. His trust in her, she thought, was as absolute now as it had been then.

'I fought – I *th*ought – that I was in the car, and being sick,' he said. 'And I was cold and I was sick. I wanted my Daddy, but he'd gone away. But I fink Mr Noble helped me. I keeped on being sick all over my new coat that Daddy had bought me.'

'I've got some new clothes for you here,' said Fran. 'Will you let me help you to put them on?'

The pyjamas were brand new, white, warm and fleecy, with ribbed blue collar and cuffs at wrist and ankle. They engaged his interest at once. There were little blue teddy-bears printed all over them, and once they had negotiated his way into them, he gave each teddy-bear a detailed inspection. 'I fink they're vewy nice,' he announced. 'F – *th*ank you.'

'Let's put this on, then,' Fran suggested, holding up a blue dressing-gown that had been worn and washed, but still fitted if it was a fraction short. She sat him back on the settee, and he co-operated, still intrigued by the little blue teddies on his cosy pyjamas. She wriggled the slippers on to his feet, glad to find that they, too, were not a bad fit. The fronts of them had rabbits' heads, with long white ears and big eyes, and very perky whiskers. They had never before been worn.

He stuck out his legs in front of him, and tried to come to terms with the incredible.

'I's got – *I've* got bunny-wabbits on my toes,' he said. 'Weal bunny-wabbits.'

Fran was expecting that every moment he would come out of his dream and start to ask for his father, or say he wanted to go home. So far, this had been almost too easy to be true.

'Are you hungry?' she asked.

He shook his head. 'I'd wather have my teddy-bears and my bunny-wabbits,' he said. He sat looking at his legs and feet, as if mesmerized by them.

Fran said softly to William, 'I think the journey home must have been so traumatic that when he passed out it was nature's way of making him forget everything,' she said. 'He will remember, in time, of course, but he's not connecting, yet. It all seems like a dream to him, the bad bits as well as this good bit. Let's hope this only wears off slowly.'

'If you'll have a nice warm drink of milk to please me,' she said, 'I've got something else for you. Will you drink it if I get it?'

For the first time, he looked really troubled. He slithered off the settee, and grabbed her hand. 'Don't go away, lovely lady,' he said. 'Let Dr William fetch it for me.'

So he knew who they were! William went, and using the milk that Sophie had heated, he made Tanner a cup of the sweet chocolate he loved so much himself. Fran sat down and took the child on to her lap. He put his head against her, and began to yawn again. 'Can I keep my bunny-wabbits on if I go to sleep again?' he asked. 'Where am I going to sleep? I don't want to go back in the Dormobile. It makes me be sick. I fink Daddy was there, but I 'spect it made him sick 'cos when I waked up he had gone and Mr Noble was there. And I sicked and sicked. Where is he?'

'Mr Noble? He's gone home. No, you won't have to go back in the van again – ever. Look, Dr William's brought your drink. When you've had it, we are going to find you somewhere nice and warm and cuddly to sleep tonight.'

He drank the chocolate, beginning to drowse again. 'I wish my Daddy was here,' he said. 'I want to show him my bunny-wabbits.' Fran hastily produced the teddy bear, fearing that the time for tears had arrived. 'Show them to Teddy,' she said. 'He's come to keep you company.'

Tanner was immediately diverted from thoughts of his father. Fran was relieved but surprised. She concluded that the child normally so keenly intelligent and articulate for his age must have regressed physically and mentally almost to early toddler stage during that week of such misery. He reached out his arms for the teddy bear, hugged it to him, and allowed the warmth and comfort of her arms round him, brimmed over now by ownership of a new toy, to anaesthetize him. His eyelids drooped, and he slid almost instantly back into the deep, healing sleep from which they had roused him.

William squatted in front of Fran, his face showing her what he was feeling. 'I don't want to part with him, any more than you do,' he said. 'But we must. Fate's against us.'

'Not altogether,' she said. 'I've been thinking. We've already got so much that we mustn't ask for more. We can't have everything. The way to keep Love is to share it. We've always known that, so why aren't we acting on it now? He's Tanner to his family, but he'll always be Cupid to us – and Cupid has a job to do. *We* don't need his services, but maybe somebody else does. Jess and Greg, for instance? Today of all days? Oh William, my darling, I want to risk it. I want to make John's last throw of the dice win a fortune for us all. Will you let me try? Will you come with me to take him up to Southside House now? If they don't want to keep him we can bring him back, or they can in the morning, and he'll never know. Please, darling. *Please.*'

'Wrap him up well,' said the professor, no longer the hesitant man not able to get beyond grieving for his friend and too angry at his own helplessness to act. 'We mustn't be long about it, though. Bob may be wanting to get home to his animals, and we have two other children to see to who may be more trouble than Cupid is. I'll go and see what the position is with them. If all's well, I'll go straight and get the car.'

He went back to the sitting-room. The moment he opened the door, he smelt the smell that he had come to associate with freshly bathed and well-powdered babies.

There they were, Bob and Jane, one on each side of the fire, each holding a baby. In William's own chair, Bob was playing 'Hi! to the market' with a giggling Jade. Not that William would have recognized in this child the solemn, shy toddler that he had only ever seen peeping out from behind Amethyst's skirts, or seated on the floor being fed by another of his sisters. This child, dressed in a sleepsuit, was astride Bob's knee, one little fist in each of Bob's large brown ones. Bob had not heard William come in, and Jane, looking up from the baby she held, put her finger to her lips.

'Ready?' said Bob to the child.

> 'Hi! to the market,
> Gee! to the fair.
> What shall we buy
> When Baby gets there?
> A ha'penny loaf
> And a penny bun,
> Then – homeagainhomeagainhomeagainhomeagainhomeagain,
> Market's done!'

The 'homeagain' line had been accompanied, as for generations past, with

461

a galloping, jolting ride on Bob's knee, and 'Market's done' by the toddler being thrown up and caught again.

''Gain,' said Jade, giggling. 'More 'gain.'

There can be no sound more infectious than a toddler's excited laugh. All three adults joined in. 'Caught me at it again, William,' Bob said. 'Idling, as usual.'

'I wish this one was as easy to please,' said Jane, hushing the flushed baby she was rocking, in her arms. 'He must be hungry, but I can't persuade him to take anything, either from his bottle or a spoon. By the look of him, I'd say he's cutting a back tooth, and his mouth's hurting. But he'll never sleep if we can't get something down him. There's one thing to be said for both of these – they don't seem to mind strangers. I think we had as much fun bathing them as they had. Where do you propose to put them down to sleep?'

'I'm afraid we haven't got round to thinking about that, yet,' William said. 'Do you want to get off home? I'm sorry if all this has kept you – I know Bob has his animals to think about. But actually I'd come to ask you if you could hold the fort here for another half hour or so. Fran's decided that she can't cope with all three here tonight, so we are going to see if Jess will give Tanner a bed.'

'We're in no hurry, as far as I know,' Bob said, looking interrogation at Jane.

'That's all right with me too,' she said. 'I was going to volunteer to stay the night, if Fran needed me. Bob can't because of all the animals, inside and out. But he's quite willing for me to.'

'I think she'd probably be very glad if you would,' William said. 'But it may depend on whether or not we can park Tanner.'

'Take your time,' said Bob, preparing himself for another ride to market. William slipped out, wishing Fran could see. Then he put his head back in to say, 'Help yourself, Bob. You know where the drinks are, in the breakfast-room.'

'Ah, I'll tell him – when he brings the barrow back,' said Bob, without looking up.

William smiled. He knew how completely at home Bob must feel to have used that old fenland put-down to anybody foolish enough to hand out a completely unnecessary injunction.

'All right, mate. Hold on tight,' said Bob to Aggie. 'Here we go. "Hi to the market . . ."'

62

They drew up outside Southside House, William using the slight downward incline towards the door to coast silently up to it, switching off his lights as he did so. There were lights in the sitting-room, kitchen and hall. He crept silently to listen under the sitting-room window. It wouldn't take much eavesdropping to discover the mood inside.

When all he could distinguish was a low, soft murmur of voices, he felt emboldened enough to find a chink in the curtains, and peep. Jess was in her armchair, though it had been pulled out slightly so as to face the fireplace more directly. By her side, sitting on a low leather pouffe, his head resting on the arm of her chair where her left hand was gently caressing it, was Greg, catching her hand now and then to kiss it. They were not looking at each other, though. Was that significant? While William was trying to make up his mind, he tried to visualize the part of the room not visible to him from his Peeping Tom position, and remembered what it was that was holding the gaze of both. Greg's 'Madonna' hung above the mantelpiece. Well, if he needed a good omen . . .

He waited for no more. He had to lift the sleeping child from Fran before she could get out of the car.

'It's up to you, now,' he whispered. 'I'm sure everything's fine between them, but I'd make a mess of this. I'll stay in the hall with him. Just call, if you want me to bring him in. Good luck, my darling.' He kissed her, giving her back the courage she had begun to feel seeping away.

She daren't allow herself to hesitate now. She tapped lightly on the door before opening it.

'May I come in? I know Greg's here, because of his car, so if I'm intruding, say so and I'll go away again. But – well, we need your help. No, Greg, don't get up. I'll come to you. Welcome home! We thought perhaps things must be all right, or we shouldn't have come. And we've brought you a "welcome back" present – if you want it. We think you may like it. So shut your eyes, both of you, and stay just as you are while I get William to bring it in. It's a bit large and rather heavy.'

They obeyed, partly because nothing could spoil this wonderful first evening for them, and partly because both were silently acknowledging their debt to Fran and William, without whose help they might never have found this promising new lease of love.

'All right, William. Come in,' Fran called. He came, and she signalled silently for him to lay his burden down on Jess's lap. Then, fearing to look, Fran threw herself into his arms.

She heard gasps, and muffled exclamations. She heard Greg say, in a low but passionate whisper, as he moved to kneel with his arms round Jess and the child, 'I told you.' When she did dare to look, Jess had peeled back the wrapping blanket and revealed Jasper's angelic face with its halo of curls. Greg laid his head down against the teddy bear still clutched in the sleeping child's arms.

The tableau held until Greg raised his head, and said, 'What does it mean, William?'

This was the crunch. Sitting down, William, calm and very serious, began to explain. 'So you see what a risk it all is,' he said. 'He's not ours to give you, even if you want to keep him. We may be giving you hope that can't be fulfilled, or offering you something you don't want. It is Fran's idea, and she felt so strongly about it that I had to let her try. She just wouldn't be put off. So forgive us, one way or the other. Only you two can decide.

'If Fran was right, and you want to keep him, we'll fight with you till the last ditch and the last penny, for his father's sake and for his sake as well as for yours. If you decide you don't want him, or can't face the risk, or the trouble, I'll either take him back now or fetch him first thing in the morning, before the police arrive to collect them all. Jess knows all about the family. But it would help us if you could keep him just for tonight, because we've still got the other two, younger than Jasper, to deal with ourselves. We decided we daren't let his sisters see them, or vice versa, until we know something. It would make things so much harder for them all.'

Jess spoke, for the first time. 'Go away, please,' she said.

Jade had finally had enough of riding to market, and said he was hungry. Jane was having a good deal of trouble with Aggie, so Bob took Jade to the kitchen, cleaned the saucepan William had emptied, and looked for more milk in the fridge. That had given him an idea, so he had found some bread as well, and made Jade a basin of bread and milk, feeding the toddler with a spoon and age-old nursery tricks to keep him opening his mouth for the next spoonful.

'One for you,' – in went the spoon – 'One for me' – mimed towards his own mouth – 'And one for little Moses' – as into Jade's mouth went the well-filled spoon. It never failed.

When Jade could eat no more and was showing signs of sleepiness, Bob took him up to the bathroom, found there a clean nappy from a pack of them bought by Petrie before starting back, changed him and wrapped him in a travelling rug filched from Fran's study. Then he carried him back into the sitting-room. By which time Jane was nearly at her wits' end.

Aggie, who was about eight months old, was distinctly feverish, over-tired and very fractious. He grizzled continually, every now and then pulling up his knees and screaming till the red patch on his left cheek and ear was lost among the rest of his scarlet face. Jane knew the signs of colic well enough, as well as those of feverish teething, but she couldn't do anything about either. His colic wouldn't be better till she could get something down him. His mouth was too sore for that. He had worked himself into a frenzy in which she could hardly hold him, beating her with his little closed fists if she offered anything near his mouth. All she could do was hold him and do her best to soothe him by rocking and singing to him till the next bout of colic set him screaming again. She had tried every way she could to soothe his sore mouth. Then Bob came back carrying his sleepy, satisfied charge, and took in at a glance the cause of her distress.

He went straight across to her, saying, 'Here, you take this one. He'll be asleep in two ticks. Sit down and cuddle him. I'll take the other.'

'Oh Bob, I just don't know what to do with him! I expect his stomach's upset, with all that dope he's been given. It will only get worse till we can get something into it to soothe the pain. I've tried every trick I know.'

He laid Jade on her lap and took the doubled-up yelling baby himself. 'Where's his bottle?' he asked.

'It's no use trying that,' she said. 'You can't get it near his mouth, let alone in it. And I've tried feeding him like you feed a calf, with your fingers.'

Bob took the bottle all the same, and disappeared kitchenwards with Aggie under his arm, the bottle in his hand and a determined twinkle in his eye. Jane sat back, glad to be relieved, and enjoyed singing 'Bye, baby Bunting' to Jade till his eyes would stay open no longer.

Bob came back, lowering himself into William's chair with Aggie, no longer yelling, in the crook of his arm. The baby was sucking noisily at a bottle still half-filled with sugared water, as Jane could see. After a few minutes, Bob removed the bottle, and sat the child up for a burp. The grizzling began again immediately. Fascinated, Jane watched as Bob held the bottle close to the child's lips again. Agate stopped grizzling, and smiled a very watery smile. Bob rubbed the teat across his lips. This produced another, broader smile, and an opened mouth into which Bob quickly popped the teat again. Jane could hardly believe her eyes.

Neither spoke till the sound of air being sucked warned Bob to remove the bottle from the baby's mouth. Aggie's eyes had turned upwards, and his long lashes had come down. Bob dropped the empty bottle on to the floor, and settled himself comfortably so as not to disturb his charge till he was fully and soundly asleep.

'Well, that beats me!' Jane said. 'What did you put in his bottle?'

'B'iled water, with sugar in it and . . .'

'And what else? A bit of fenland magic that you know about and I don't?'

'Not as I know of, my beauty. Only a drop or two o' whisky.'

She sat back and laughed and laughed. He watched in delight and a content that even she had never given him before. He was there in his dream-room, with her, and that made everything, but everything, right with his world. They looked across at each other, unable to move because each held a sleeping child, and sent caresses to each other with their eyes. It was all so comfortable that he soon began to doze as well, and drifted off into a dream which was more than half reality.

He roused himself and said sleepily to her across the wide hearth and the glowing fire, 'You know, my pretty, I reckon if these were a couple of kittens as their mother had abandoned, we should take 'em home with us and look after 'em.'

'Well, then, why don't we?' she said.

So the long day came to a close with Jane staying and Bob going home. He would be back in the morning to fetch her and their new 'kittens', intending to spend the rest of the night, if it took him that long, finding disused antique cradles and cots that his sentimental soul had refused to part with. He cleaned and polished till it was nearly daylight, sad because the next day was Sunday and they would have to wait to go out and buy new mattresses and covers.

He had to keep reminding himself that it might only be for a few days . . . and yet in the dream he had himself interrupted, he had been surrounded by a lot of grandchildren, among whom he had recognized both Jade and Agate. All of them young and healthy little animals, not very different from the kittens and puppies or piglets that constantly gave him such pleasure.

William went to bed so exhausted, physically, mentally and spiritually, that he couldn't sleep. He tossed and turned and finally woke Fran deliberately because he needed to talk. They couldn't believe that the problem of the children was solved, even for the time being. Only fools believed in such miracles. It had to be an ignis fatuus, a devil's trick to get them into an even worse mess. Bob and Jane would get over it if the law stepped in and took the children away from them – but would Jess and Greg? Why on earth had he been stupid enough to interfere? Yes, he knew it was because Fran had had some sort of intuition about it, but she did sometimes let her imagination run away with her. In real life things like that just didn't happen. He must be prepared to hold his own against the police tomorrow, and prevent them from acting before they knew the entire story.

Then they had to break the news to Emerald and Amethyst. That couldn't be put off. He thought they ought to go up to the Old Rectory together well before church-time, to make sure that Beth would be there. She must have had previous experience in such things. Then there were the twins, at Monica's house. And who was there but himself to see about the burial of John?

Fran let him pour it all out, listening and soothing him until at last he relaxed and slept. There were only two hours left to dawn. She left him asleep and went downstairs early, before Jane came down with her new 'kittens', to ring Monica, whose babies woke as early as everybody else's did. She didn't want William to hear.

Monica was bright and cheerful. As far as she was concerned, the Petrie twins could stay with her for ever. They were so experienced in looking after babies – it had given them all a wonderful weekend. Her Dad was still there. He'd got on so well with the two girls that she thought she could leave the telling of their father's death to him. Not a word about their little brothers, she promised.

Sophie arrived, and Fran couldn't wait to tell her the incredible news of Bob and Jane being willing to look after the two youngest children as long as it was necessary – to keep them, indeed, if that was what was needed. William came down, drawn and pale, refused Sophie's offer of a fried breakfast, and listened abstractedly while Fran told Sophie where Jasper was, and how he had been welcomed at Southside House.

'Ah! so 'e's back ag'in, is 'e?' Sophie said in a tone of great satisfaction. 'That'll shut Olive 'Opkins up. It's to be 'oped she ain't making a bid to take over Beryl Bean's job. Beryl's been too quiet over this Vic Gifford affair for it to be 'ealthy.'

'If only the law and the welfare people would let well alone for a little while,' Fran said.

'Tha's too much to be 'oped for, seeing as folks nowadays won't even look after their own. There has to be somebody to look after them as can't look after theirselves. It don't surprise me as Bellamy's willing. Countryfolk like him don't forget what used to be. We shall 'ave to wait and see. It's all in the 'ands of 'Im Above, and we must do what we can ourselves, and then abide by 'Is will.'

Suiting action to word, she set about doing all she could to help Jane, who had just appeared with both her new charges.

William and Fran left them, to set off on their sad mission to the Old Rectory.

They were more than glad of Beth's presence during the next half-hour.

Most of the few worshippers had already left when they reached the church on their way home, but Fran saw George Bridgefoot coming down the path to the gate. She hadn't spoken to him since the news of Vic's death had broken. She asked William to wait till she had a word with George. He said that he daren't, because he wanted to talk to Joe, if he could, before the police arrived. She let him go.

George had his troubles too. As she went to meet him, she knew why she wanted to see him so much this morning. George was last to leave because he had stopped behind to share his troubles privately with Some-body who would understand. Everybody else took their troubles to George, but he passed them on to broader shoulders than his own. And that's exactly what she was trying to do. As soon as he bent to kiss her, he saw her troubled face and took her hand.

'Come back into church where we can sit down,' he said. 'Then tell me what's the matter.' It didn't really take her long, and she felt enormously better for it. She told him so.

He nodded. 'I always come and sit here when I'm in trouble,' he said.

'Yes, but you are a practising Christian and I'm not. Not any longer.'

'Ah, but what does being a Christian mean? Doing all what you and William have been doing for that poor family don't seem to me all that far off being a Christian. What did He say? *"Inasmuch as you do it unto them, you do it unto Me."'*

'Sometimes I wish I had the same belief as you have,' she said, a bit wistfully.

'Haven't you? It don't matter what you call yourself, or what other folks call you. In the end it's all one. Putting a bit of love and a bit o' thought for other people into your own life's what most religion's all about. So don't you let me hear you say again that you and William don't believe in God. God is Love. And you two know Him well enough. Get back to William now. And don't think I come to church as often as I do just to grizzle for help. There's many a time I come 'cos I'm got so much to be thankful for. Folks forget that part of it too often. From what you told me, I think as there may be a good chance yet as things'll turn out better than you expect.'

She almost ran the rest of the way home, to be there to find out if he would be right when the immediate issues had to be decided.

She found that Bob had already been to collect his new family, but while Jane had still been there Greg had put in a hasty appearance to ask for some daytime clothes for Tanner. They had sorted the clothes supplied by Hetty into sizes as needed. Sophie had gone straight home. Joe came as soon as William got there. Fran found them sitting at the kitchen table together, William with a glass of whisky and Joe with a glass of beer. The police had not yet arrived.

William asked Joe if he would be in trouble about his job, having taken what amounted to French leave for a whole week. Joe seemed unconcerned. 'I'm worked there since the day I left school,' he said, 'and I ain't had more'n a month off all told. I reckon as I could do without them quite as well as they could without me, now. So if they up-end theirselves about it, I shall tell 'em they can keep their job and I'll find another. And I shan't be able to go about with Davvy no more, now, even if I wanted to. I'm disapp'inted in 'im, though, in any case. Preaching's all very well, but I can't understand him letting that woman persuade him to go off behind the back of a man as were in such straits. Nor him walking off and leaving her like he did with all them little children in such a place that night as they got there. I could go on doing my bit if I had a car. Whose is the van, b'rights?'

'It was Mr Petrie's,' William assured him. 'He bought it with what Charles Bridgefoot paid him for the house – and there must be a bit left over, somewhere. There wasn't a will among the papers he left in my charge, and if he hasn't made one everything, including the van, will go to his next of kin. Those brothers of his who wouldn't own him. I suppose he never mentioned a will to you, Joe?'

'No, he never, but come to think about it –' He paused, trying to recall. 'When we was hung up in Leominster, and 'e was so upset 'cos we couldn't get on, he kept whittling about time going by 'cos he said there was something he ought to have done as he hadn't, 'cos he'd waited till he'd seen as they were all settled in Wales, and now he reckoned he might have left it too late. And next day, he sent me to the garage by myself, 'cos he said as how he was going to try to find a lawyer. What do you reckon he wanted with a lawyer, sir?'

'Heaven only knows,' answered William. 'But I'm glad you told me that. I may be able to find out. Ah, here are the police.'

The police officer turned out to be the local sergeant from Swithinford, who needed only at this stage to check Joe's statement and check on William as well as to satisfy the Worcestershire police as to the identity of the corpse in the hospital mortuary. The local police had followed

William's suggestion to check with the hospital at Cambridge, making an inquest unnecessary. There was, however, the question of burial. Had they any knowledge as to who was the next of kin, if it wasn't William, who had been named as such at Addenbrooke's?

William had made up his mind that honesty was the best policy, and told the bare facts, without elaboration. Then he asked advice as to what needed to be done with regard to the children. The policeman was not much help. He wasn't even sure what the next move was, or which police force would be responsible for making it. But there was a corpse in Worcester that had to be disposed of. His attitude was that it was a matter of no great moment as long as somebody did, or did not, claim it. The officer's tone touched William on a spot still very sore. It was the academic who replied coldly that he had no knowledge of the whereabouts of any next of kin. 'But as far as I am concerned personally,' he said, 'the fact that he chose to live an unorthodox life does not mean that he was not a man before he became a corpse. A man with friends, of whom I happen to be one. If you will supply me with the necessary facts, I will arrange for burial or cremation with the authorities in Worcester, making myself financially responsible if need be. Will that be all?'

Icily if politely seen out, the police officer left. It was Sunday morning, and he had done dutifully all that had been required of him. If the silly idiot he had just left had money to throw about giving a hippy good-for-nothing a posh funeral, let him.

Fran felt limp with relief to see him go. She was proud of her William. He came back from seeing the policeman out looking rather rueful, however.

'He didn't ask about the children,' Fran almost crowed.

'No, but they will – somebody will, sooner or later. I shall arrange for the funeral on Thursday or Friday if I can,' he said, 'and I shall go. Will you come with me, Joe?'

'Yes, sir. And if I get the sack for taking another day off, I will. If ever a man earned my respect, he did, a sight more than Vic Gifford did from any o' them as'll be following him to the grave this week.'

He got up, holding his cap, not quite knowing how to take his leave. Fran stood up, put her hands on his shoulders, and kissed him. 'He was a man, Joe,' she said, 'in all the things that matter. And so are you. Thank you.'

Joe was taken by surprise, obviously delighted, but very sheepish. Women in his experience didn't act like that, but he knew that she had meant it. William was holding out his hand, and Joe took it, the short stocky man and the tall thin one clasping each other's with a warmth of much more than courtesy or gratitude. Each was richer by a friend.

After he'd gone, Fran and William talked, over a rather sketchy lunch, about all the issues involved. Some, William said, they simply had to defer till after he'd been to Worcester, whenever, according to what a recommended undertaker decided. He was quite sure that John wouldn't have wished a penny spent on a funeral that wasn't absolutely essential. It was John's wishes, not his own pocket, that he would go on.

'And about the children?' Fran persisted.

'I have no more idea than you have,' he said, 'except that I guess it is one of those tricky matters they will all shelve as long as they can. The longer it goes on, the worse it will get, because both the children and their unofficial foster-parents will feel it more if they are taken away in the end. For the time being, my guess is that they will have to find Crystal before they can do anything, and until then we can all put in a plea that they are being well cared for. No doubt if she isn't found they will be able to trace her, if they want to go to the trouble, by checking where she cashes her family allowance books. Perhaps, in the meantime, there may be some way Greg and Bob can file applications for fostering or adoption. One slight thing gives me hope. There were a lot of evacuees never claimed after the war, and where their foster-parents were happy to keep them, bureaucracy turned a blind eye. But we live by bureaucracy, now. We can only hope.'

He helped her to clear away the lunch and wash up.

'Do you know, my darling, that this is the first time for more than a week that we have had our house to ourselves and time for each other? I need you close to me. Let's forget everything else.'

63

William woke early next morning, and lay reviewing the past week and the week to come. He turned to look at Fran, who opened her eyes and smiled. She always did that, if he happened to be awake first. Always greeted him, and the day, with a smile. He felt heartened and strengthened by it this morning, and got up to face whatever the week might bring.

It brought the post, first, and a long legal envelope post-marked Worcester. Enclosed in it was another sealed envelope, and a covering letter. The letter explained that the solicitor concerned had acted for John Petrie Voss-Dering in the matter of a very hastily made last will and testament, and was now carrying out instructions for it to be sent, sealed but with a letter attached, to him.

He detached the letter. It was from John, his scrawled signature at the bottom of a sheet of letter-headed paper on which the rest of the letter was typed intimating that he had dictated it and left it to be typed up later because of the haste he had been in. All it said was that the sealed envelope contained a will that John had felt constrained to make while he still could, though he had had no time to ask permission first for what he had done. If by a miracle he was given the chance, he intended to change it so as not to leave them such a difficult task; but if not, he begged forgiveness for taking friendship so much for granted. In which case, William was to open it.

Well, John was dead. There was no reason for William to delay.

The will could not have been shorter. After the usual declaration that it was his last will and testament, there were two sentences. The first appointed William and Joe to be his executors and joint trustees. The second left everything of which he died possessed to them, to be used at their discretion for the benefit of the eight minors named below. They would find any assets he had in an account (number given) at Barclays Bank in Swithinford. Then his signature, and those of two witnesses from the solicitor's staff.

William was unable to think about its provisions. He could only think about the man who had made it, and his feelings overcame him. When Fran appeared, he was glad to hide his face against her, and then go away by himself while she read it.

At eight thirty, he dialled the police in Worcester, then the recommended undertaker, and fixed John's burial for noon on Friday – as it happened, the very same that Brian had fixed for the funeral of Vic in the churchyard of his native village.

William longed only for the rest of this day and the next three to be quiet and uneventful, with nobody there but Fran, nowhere to go but into his study, nothing to do but to sit with Fran in the evenings listening to music till the time came to lie beside her in bed. That's all he asked of the gods, and to his great content and comfort, that's all he got.

By eleven thirty on Friday, the old part of the village was practically deserted. The bus had long since departed, leaving many dwellings empty. Elyot and Beth, afraid that the knowledge they had of their father's funeral that day would be too much for Emerald and Amethyst, had taken them out shopping, ostensibly to help Beth with her last purchases for the baby's advent, an outing planned, they lied, before any of last week's events had occurred. Jess and a skeleton staff were at work in the offices of Manor Farms Ltd, and Greg was having the time of his life looking after a rapidly recovering Tanner, who had never been given so much attention before. As he was still inclined to be a bit listless, Greg sat him on the corner of the settee with his teddy bear (which he insisted on calling his Daddy-bear), told him stories and made sketch after sketch of him for future reference.

The Bridgefoots as a whole had hoped that at the last minute Marjorie would relent, and not add embarrassment to the rest of their feelings. Poppy had been home with her mother for several days, and had seen Pansy. They had been able to indulge in grief together, which had helped Poppy thereafter to maintain a subdued but not unduly miserable front to her mother, who seemed largely unaffected. However, on this morning of her father's funeral, Poppy had got up early, and had had to be comforted against the day's events by Aunt Rosemary, her mother not being in evidence. As they sat down to breakfast, all dressed discreetly in garments suitably dark for a funeral, Rosemary, noticing Marge's absence, whispered a hope that at the last minute she had changed her mind. She warned them all, especially Poppy, to make no comment if it proved to be so. Nevertheless, when the door from the flat opened, they all turned involuntarily towards it, and just as quickly looked down at their plates again. One glimpse of Marjorie was enough to inform them that if she did intend to swell the numbers at her husband's funeral, it would not be in the guise of a mourner.

She looked striking, among the soberly clad family, in a woollen suit of deep rust-red, with a smart tunic top over a cream silk blouse. She was healthily robust, in spite of the fact that her hair had turned almost white. The clear skin that had always been one of her best features had lost its rather sallow look, and made-up lightly looked fresh and blooming again.

She looked her forty-five years, but no more. The large calm eyes that had been so attractive when she was a girl had lost much of their appeal during the last difficult years, but Brian noticed this morning that they showed more than anything else how much she had changed lately. The quality of serenity she had inherited from her father showed in her eyes again. She looked directly across at Brian as she joined them at the breakfast table, willing him to understand why she had taken such trouble with her appearance this morning. It was intended as a signal to them all that she had deliberately chosen to begin afresh from today.

Not that she had been miserable, or difficult, as a sojourner under Brian and Rosemary's hospitable roof. She had been a pleasant guest or tenant, or whatever she was, in the self-contained flat. Always around if Rosy wanted help, always at hand if Brian needed another pair of hands outside, always good for a long chat or discussion, but then withdrawing.

Rosy, who had always been fond of her, worried that she spent too much time by herself in that flat, and told her so. Marjorie replied that that was what was doing her so much good – the peace! Being able to please herself what she did and when she did it.

'I'm sort of finding out about myself again,' she had said. 'I'd got so afraid of rows that I'd stopped trying to hold my own at all. If I wasn't doing exactly what he wanted, I was wrong. But he didn't know what he did want, and I got so I daren't do anything. That's what suited him, I suppose – if I was doing anything to please myself I wasn't giving him all my attention. Once the girls had gone, it was hell. He wouldn't let me read, or knit, or crochet, or do a bit of sewing – if I picked up a book he'd throw himself into one of his tempers, or turn on the TV to some daft programme so loud that I couldn't hear myself think, and then shout at me over the top of the rest of the noise – I don't know how I stood it as long as I did. But I'd married him, and we were brought up to think that if we'd made our bed we'd got to lie on it. Not like it is now.

'But that night of Bailey's party, something in me just gave. I knew I couldn't go on like that any longer. Not that I should have left him, because of disgracing Dad and Mam, if it hadn't been for you know what. But I had to, then. You saved me, letting me come home again. So don't worry about me, Rosy. Bless you all the same.'

It was Poppy who dared to say that morning, when the silence of surprise grew rather long, 'If you are not coming with us, Mum,' she said, 'why are you all dressed up like that? You can't come to a funeral in a red suit!'

'Oh? Why not? If I wanted to grieve, I could do it just as well in a red suit as a black one.'

'But Mum! You're his wife!'

'No, pet, I'm not. I'm his widow. There's a lot of difference. And I'm not a hypocrite. I can't be seen to mourn for him, whatever I'm wearing, so you needn't worry. I'm not coming. But I didn't want to sit here by myself and think nasty thoughts about him, either, so I dressed to make myself feel cheerful. I shall come round to Dad's to see you all off, and then if I feel like it, I'll take myself to Cambridge to buy the materials I need to start making a huge embroidered bedspread, that I've been wanting to make for years. I'm sorry if it's going to upset any of you that I'm not going to the funeral, but I did tell you, and I shan't go back on what I said. There'll be plenty of Bridgefoots there without me. And plenty of Giffords and Baileys. I shan't be missed.'

They were all now staring at her, uncertain whether she was putting on an act or telling the truth. Brian began to wonder if she was going to break down after all, letting go of all the feeling she had been bottling up.

She read his anxious look and took off her new persona for their peace of mind, becoming at once the 'Marge' they all knew.

She bent down and kissed Poppy, and sat down to her breakfast saying, 'Don't look like that, Brian. I haven't gone round the bend yet, and I'm not likely to – but you must understand, all the same. I meant every word of what I just said, and that's why I can't go just to be seen there today. If you stopped to think, you wouldn't really want me to. The whole Bailey lot'll be there. All those women that I know he's been to bed with, and who know I know – including the one I actually saw him with. Do you really want to put me through that humiliation just because of what folks will say? Dad doesn't. I've talked to him about it. If anybody notices I'm not there, they'll know exactly why. It'll be Vic's reputation that will suffer, not mine. Dad's not going to pretend Vic's been an ideal husband any more than I am.

'And Poppy my love, as for you and Pansy, it would have been just the same for you in the future as far as I'm concerned if he hadn't been killed. You know I was going to get a divorce. I should have been his ex-wife instead of his widow, that's all. In the long run, it'll probably be easier for you. You can go on loving his memory and forget the rest.'

Only Brian was in a position to know how right she was. He had been very shocked by a letter he'd had from Bailey that very morning. Bailey, afraid of missing a trick, had played his cards even before Vic had been buried. He wanted to get his hands on Vic's land, and ignoring all niceties had flagrantly made use of his acquaintanceship with Brian as a lever to get his bid in first, suggesting that Brian could either come in with the project or take a hefty commission for acting as intermediary. He wanted the Gifford house and farm, and, if Brian could persuade George to part with it, some of the other land as well, to develop.

Brian had been too disgusted to mention it to anybody before the funeral was over, but he was sensible of what it could mean to Marjorie. She would in future be a woman of very comfortable independent means. He was glad for her sake, and for his own. He wanted no more to do with Bailey, and Vic's death had got him very nicely out of the awkward snare he had walked into. He found himself admiring his sister for taking such an honest stand as she was this morning, even though it made him ashamed of himself.

The rest of them left Marjorie at the Old Glebe. She told them not to worry if she was not there when they returned, because she wasn't at all sure where she would be, or how long it would take her to find what she wanted in Cambridge. Still very calm, she kissed a tearful Poppy, and sent her love to Pansy, and watched them leave in a fleet of cars, before going back inside the house again.

She made herself a cup of coffee, sat down, and began to think. She had stuck to her guns, and she felt like a Bridgefoot again, the only Bridgefoot for the time being in a house crammed with the ghosts of dead Bridgefoots. Those of her family who had lived and died there for generations, and whose presence around her now she began to feel. She sat in her father's chair, which had been her grandfather's, and took stock of her own position. She was, she realized, at the meeting place of her past and her future. The interim time of 'settling-down' was now over. It was time she made firm decisions.

Her mother and father wanted her to make her home here, with them. It wouldn't do. This was the nerve centre of all the Bridgefoot activities. If she were always there, it would be taken for granted that she would take over all responsibility for the ageing couple. The others would gradually let that happen, partly because she would relieve them of their share of responsibility, and partly because they would resent her always being there when they came. Once it became 'her' home, it would never be again wholly 'their home' on equal footing. Their family unity had been their strength; and she was not going to be the reason for spoiling that unity. After all, it was she who had let them down, by marrying a man so alien to everything they stood for, as Vic had turned out to be.

Then there were her two children. She didn't feel as happy as she would have liked about either of them. Pansy was more Gifford than Bridgefoot, but something warned her that in the long run it would be Pansy who would need her most, though Poppy needed her most now. She had to have a home of her own to which either of them could come, and not be overwhelmed by other Bridgefoots if they didn't want to be.

She wouldn't mind living alone, especially if the rest of the family were round about. With them visiting her, and her visiting them, she wouldn't be lonely, would she? She didn't know, because that was something she had never yet tried.

For what she had just envisaged to be practicable, her home would have to be here, in Old Swithinford. But where? There were no houses for sale. The cottage down Spotted Cow Lane was still empty, but she knew that her father had by no means yet given up hope of them getting a new Rector. She supposed she could buy one of the better kind of estate houses at Lane's End, but the thought absolutely revolted her. A Bridgefoot, there? On Tom Fairey's land? Next door, more or less, to the Baileys? Amongst people who were frightened at cows, and were horrified to find where their morning pint of milk originated?

Another thought obtruded itself. She wasn't a Bridgefoot by name. She was Mrs Gifford.

She began to think about him, though she didn't want to.

It was nearly midday. The grave would now be opened ready for him, the clergyman waiting at the church gate, the long line of dark-clad mourners following that huge coffin . . . and she still couldn't care. She had felt a lot more when her old dog died.

She thought of Vic sitting with her family at that very kitchen table, discussing her sister Lucy's wedding arrangements – and his sniggering remarks that had so infuriated her father that day. She had been so ashamed of him! It was from then that she had really begun to hate and despise him. Her memory of him on that occasion was now so clear as to be eerie. She could see him so clearly in her mind's eye. The silence became suddenly oppressive. She jumped up, snatched the cape that completed her elegant ensemble, and ran out of the house. There was nobody in sight, and she had no special objective in view, but she wanted to get away from her memories now, at least for the next few minutes, just until they had buried him. She ran towards the churchyard, and throwing her cape closely round her shoulders, she sat down on the stone-slab top of a Bridgefoot grave so old that its lettering had been effaced by wind and weather, and let herself cry. Not for Vic. She cried for herself, and her life that could have been, should have been, would have been so much happier if she had never married at all. If she had remained a Bridgefoot all her life.

It was then that the idea struck her. She would *not* carry the name of that man for a day longer than it took for her to change it. She would become Marjorie Bridgefoot again.

The past was gone for ever, was behind her, and a new future was stretching peacefully before.

The clock above her struck, slowly, twelve times. It was like an omen, a portent of the significance of the decision she had just made. If the morning of her life had turned cloudy and stormy, there was still perhaps a sunny afternoon to come, and a calm evening full of peace. She stood up, preparing to go – and saw a man coming up the church path towards her.

It was Eric Choppen. He had been to see Jess in her new office to make sure that she was coping all right with half her staff gone to Gifford's funeral. No need to worry, she had assured him; she was close enough to pop home at lunch-time and see that they didn't starve.

He was passing the church on his way back to the hotel and his own lunch when he caught sight of a strange woman – at least, one he didn't know by sight – sitting on a gravestone close to the gate, crying.

He was driving slowly, and in passing took in her very smart appearance, as well as her white hair and apparently good health. So what was she doing there, crying? He was intrigued.

He sat for a few minutes, wondering, and waiting in case an escort was somewhere out of sight round the back of the church. He didn't want to find himself accused of accosting a lone female. But why was she crying? He could hardly drive on without asking if she needed help.

He was within two feet of her before she looked up, and both got a surprise. She might be crying – but he had rarely seen a woman in tears whose eyes were less pathetic, or one less in need of male assistance. Moreover, he recognized her at once – he had seen her at church on New Year's Eve, and several times since in the company of one or other of the Bridgefoots. She needed no swearing with regard to parentage, bearing as much resemblance to George as a middle-aged woman could to an elderly man. It took a lot to make Eric unsure of himself, but at that instant he felt an absolute fool.

She knew him at once, too, for though she had never been introduced to him, there were very few things that went on in Old Swithinford now in which he did not have a finger. She was very conscious of the tears on her face, and wiped them hastily away before standing up, also feeling very silly.

'I beg your pardon,' Eric said hastily. 'I was passing and saw you sitting there alone and was afraid you might be in need of help. I'm Eric Choppen, from Monastery Farm. and you must be . . .' He stopped, out of his depth again. He had been going to say 'Mrs Gifford', but bit it back. She couldn't be. Some of his own staff had been given leave to go to Vic Gifford's funeral, which was scheduled for midday today.

She saw his dilemma, and came to his rescue. 'How very kind of you, Mr Choppen. I'm Marjorie Bridgefoot – George's daughter and Brian's sister. I don't think we've ever actually met before.' They shook hands, both wondering how they were going to get out of their extraordinary predicament. Eric raked vague memories of George's family over. Who could this one be but Mrs Gifford? But she wasn't dressed for a funeral. Then his memory dredged up a rumour that Vic Gifford's wife was filing a petition for divorce. What disconcerting bit of marital history had he inadvertently stepped into?

She was following the procession of his thoughts by watching his face.

She looked him straight in the eye, and he could have sworn that hers held a cynical twinkle.

'And you are too polite to ask me what I'm doing sitting on a gravestone crying instead of dropping tears on my late husband's coffin,' she said. 'So I'll tell you. I was rejoicing, and giving thanks that I am no longer Mrs Gifford. Just before you appeared, I had become Marjorie Bridgefoot again, by my own decree. So please don't let me keep you any longer. Honestly, I'm quite all right. They left me by myself at Glebe because I refused to go to the funeral, and I think the ghosts of my ancestors must have chased me up here, because I truly don't know why I came. I'll go back now, and get myself a drink. I need one.'

'Then let me take you up to the hotel and give you one,' he said. 'Whatever you say, it must be a very traumatic time for you, and I think you oughtn't to be left alone.'

She laughed, a ringing laugh that reminded him immediately of George, so heartily guileless was it. 'Really, Mr Choppen! I haven't got much of a reputation left, and if I hadn't happened to have been born a Bridgefoot, I should have none at all. I'm a wicked woman who left her husband and was considering washing dirty linen in public by getting a divorce, and actually defying all custom by refusing to pretend to mourn the dear departed. But there is a difference between a remorseful widow seen weeping on a gravestone, and a scarlet hussy taking lunch in public with another man while the funeral of her lawful wedded husband is taking place. I don't think even my father would approve of that, however much on my side he may be. But thank you, all the same.'

He smiled his slow, rarely seen but infectious smile. He detested hypocrites, and it was quite clear that whatever else she might be, she was no hypocrite. He liked her, in the same way that he had taken at once to Bob Bellamy.

'I see your point,' he said. 'In which case it's up to me to better my suggestion. You must have some lunch somewhere, and I'm starving. Would your reputation be very stained by having lunch with me in my house? I could smuggle you in without anyone being the wiser, and a telephone call will bring two lunches up from the hotel within ten minutes. During which time I could find you that drink you confessed to needing.'

'It's risky,' she said. 'I was born in this village, and I'm afraid you are a marked man already. Somebody is sure to have seen us here.'

'Want to bet? Everybody has either gone to your dear departed's funeral, or is out for the day. The only possible eyewitnesses are Greg and Jess Taliaferro – and I could swear that neither of those would recognize you in that colour even if you know them intimately. Let's go!'

In his sitting-room, she took the drink he offered and had to clear the top of an occasional table to find space to set it down. While he went to the telephone, she straightened cushions, picked up old newspapers dropped by a sleepy reader, and in general restored a bit of order.

When he came back to invite her to come to eat, he noticed and she apologized.

'I expect it's the female touch that does it,' he said. 'I do clear up, now and again, but it isn't the same.'

They sat down to eat completely at ease with each other. Eric wondered what it was that made for such instantaneous companionship, and hit on it at once. Engaging female as she was, she had never once given him an arch glance, never drooped her eyelashes at him, never looked coy or helpless; never by word or gesture played Eve to his Adam. Her interest in him was as a man, not as a male. She hadn't got even as far as that in her thinking about him, though she was aware of how pleasurable it was to have a bit of fresh company.

She was soon telling him about her present difficulty in finding herself a new home within the bosom of her family without being relentlessly clasped to it all the time. Above all other considerations, she said, she wanted and needed to feel free to do what she liked when she liked.

He told her he understood, because he had had just the same feelings when his wife had died, and everybody had tried to overwhelm him with kindness. He wanted to be private to allow himself to come to terms both with his grief and with the future. He had made this large house into two, and only occupied half. As she probably knew, until very recently his daughter and her family had lived in the other half. Since they had left, he had found that his phase of needing complete privacy had passed. Could she be sure that in the course of time she might not find, as he was doing now, that any house otherwise completely unoccupied could also be a rather lonely one? He had locked up Monica's side of the house, to avoid the sight of the bare, unfurnished rooms.

They both stopped eating, spoons and forks poised between mouths and plates, and stared at each other.

'Any reason why not?' he asked.

'None – except that it can't possibly be true.'

'Come and look at it.'

She laid down her spoon, and followed him.

'Have you got any furniture?'

'Masses – but it's hideous and I don't want it.' She coloured a bit, but went courageously on. 'I'm not exactly a pauper. I can replace it with the sort I like. And I shouldn't haggle about the rent.'

'I have my son's grand piano in here,' he said. 'I should have to get it into store, because there isn't room for it on my side.'

Her voice was hardly above a whisper. 'A piano?' she said. He pushed open the door to reveal a boudoir grand swathed in a cover.

'Terms,' she said, briskly. 'Leave that piano where it is, and I'll do all the cleaning on your side in exchange for the use of it. I shall need housework to do after being a farmer's wife and daughter all these years.'

'Done,' he said. 'Come and finish your lunch. The ice-cream will have melted.'

64

Fran had been alone that Friday morning, after William and Joe had set off for Worcester. There was nobody about. She presumed, from the fact that even Ned was one of them, that everybody else who had ever had any contact with George Bridgefoot in the past was preparing to line up to climb aboard the bus provided for the funeral, to go and pay their respects to him. Not, she thought cynically, to Vic Gifford. Few of them had liked him, and even fewer had much respect for him.

She felt flat and rather dispirited. She was very tired for one thing, feeling a strong reaction to the keyed-up activity of the last two weeks, besides being anxious about William. She had never before seen him so depressed and quiet as he had been lately, and he had actually confessed to her this morning that if he hadn't been absolutely forced to get up and go, he would have asked her to leave him in bed.

She didn't think he was ill, but she did think that he had stretched himself to the limit emotionally, not only dealing with death but also shouldering the multitudinous problems of the living that his chance acquaintance with Petrie had left with him. None of which had yet reached a solution, even though by the end of last week things had looked a little less chaotic than at first. She thought that perhaps Petrie's will, arriving on his plate out of the blue, had been the last straw. The task he had laid on William, with no aid but that of an unsophisticated countryman like Joe, was so vague as to prove to be quite heavy and difficult. The existing situation with regard to the children was bad enough.

How awful it would be if Cupid had to be taken from Jess and Greg now! It would be her fault if it ended with three hearts being broken instead of two mended. She had let instinct and emotion override all reason. What if, and leaving aside whatever Crystal might do, it simply didn't work out? One simply should not interfere with other people's lives, however good one's intentions.

They hadn't heard a word from Southside House since Sunday when

Greg had fetched Cupid some daytime clothes. How had they been coping? She had completely neglected to consider that Jess had an important full-time job, and that though Greg might be enjoying a second honeymoon at home now, it couldn't be long before he, too, would have to return to work. And the same practical issues had to be thought of with regard to the Bellamy household – Jane had her father and Nick to consider, as well as being a busy farmer's wife with a family wedding in prospect, and at any minute Monica might ring to say that she was bringing Topaz and Sapphire back. Before Petrie's last illness he had been told they must begin to attend school. Where, though, now? No wonder William was preoccupied.

Fran sat at her desk, unable to keep her mind on her work. It wasn't particularly urgent. She wished it was. A rapidly approaching deadline would have kept her nose to the grindstone, instead of which she just sat and stared out of her study window, spring-cleaning the corners of her mind in case she had overlooked any tiny scrap of trouble she had forgotten to worry about.

The latter part of the morning seemed endless. There was no sound in the house, no opening and shutting of doors that told her where William was and what he was doing, no rattle of crockery or banging of brooms against skirting-boards to indicate Sophie's reassuring presence, not even the sight of Ned's wiry figure at work in the garden. She was quite alone. She was, in fact, experiencing exactly the situation she had envisaged and intended when she had taken that momentous decision to come back to East Anglia and restore Benedict's. Peace and quiet in which to work had been her objective, together with – as she had once actually rejoiced in thinking she had achieved – the chance to be herself again with no obligations to anybody else. How could she have been so stupid! She would have gone mad after the first week. Luck had come to her rescue, and she was more than satisfied, even in times like this.

'Cat,' she said to the Siamese cuddled up against her telephone, 'Cat! It was you who changed it all! All those silly ideas disappeared like dew against the sun on that evening when William brought you to me. Do you know that? You are my lucky charm, the djinn in my Aladdin's lamp, the genie who has made so many wishes come true. I need him now. What have I to do to bring him to me this morning to cheer me up? Rub your tummy? Oh, all right.'

At the sound of her voice, Cat had unrolled herself, turned upside down and offered her furry belly to Fran's caressing hand. She turned her head to one side, resting it on the pads of a dark velvety paw. Her violet eyes were half-closed in anticipation, her little red mouth ready to make a tiny mew that would turn to a deep-throated purr of ecstatic satisfaction the instant Fran touched her. Fran obligingly rubbed the creamy fur.

'Genie,' she said to the air, 'are you there? I charge you to order all things well. All present difficulties, today, this week, and in the immediate future. At least by Easter – though that's asking a bit much. Let's say by harvest. And I mean all things, so perhaps you'd better be getting on with it now.'

Cat had turned herself into a ball, scrabbling with all four feet at Fran's hand, when the front door bell rang, and Fran heard Greg's voice calling her. He was standing in the hall, holding Tanner by the hand: a shy Tanner who clutched a little teddy bear against what Fran could see at once was a complete outfit of new clothes that were not, and never had been, intended for Steven.

Greg tried to let go of his hand to salute Fran and take her into his arms, but the child clung on, so Greg picked him up and the hug included all three of them.

When they came apart, Fran led them into the kitchen. She felt that she must have conjured them out of thin air, and was afraid to ask any questions in case she spoilt the magic. By the way Tanner climbed up on to his knee the moment Greg sat down, Fran saw that a bond had already been established that it would be very painful to break. The genie must have been listening.

'Well?' she said at last in a low tone, setting out coffee, milk and biscuits.

'So well that I daren't say so,' Greg replied. 'Too good to hope that it can possibly last. I don't mean as far as Jess and I are concerned – that's as much like heaven again now as it ever was. But heaven and all this too?' He glanced downward at Tanner, who was lying contentedly with his head against Greg's chest, munching a chocolate biscuit.

'We daren't allow ourselves to think, one way or the other,' Greg went on, seriously. 'We have decided to make the most of every minute while we have the chance. He's ours for today, at any rate, and for every day as it comes, until – but we refuse to consider the alternative till we're forced to. Can we speak in riddles? Little pitchers have not only large lugs, we have discovered, but minds like expanding suitcases. Able to take in far more than you think possible.'

Fran understood, and listened while Greg talked in riddles she was able to interpret, telling her all that she had been wanting to know. Jasper had been too inertly biddable at first, dazed and cowed into accepting what happened to him without protest or pleasure. It had been sad to deal with, but his fear had gradually left him, and changed his mood to a sleepy, dream-like state. When roused from it, his first reaction was usually of distress, brought about, they thought, either by too vivid memories of the past or by too much apprehension of the future. Some of the things he had muttered in this semi-conscious state had been strange, almost unnerving, considering their circumstances.

There had been a lot of references to his sisters and his 'Daddy', and about being in the van and the terrible ordeal of that journey which to him must have seemed endless. All quite understandable. But now and again he had mumbled things that to them had deeper meaning, bordering on the supernatural.

'Of course we're strung-up,' Greg said. 'Probably reading far too much into what a very disturbed little boy says. But it's queer, all the same. As if he had some sort of prescience that he was meant to belong to us. Like the time Jess had to rouse him from a deep sleep, and he opened his eyes and said, "Now I've comed back I want to stop with you this time."'

They had, of course, persuaded themselves that he was referring to his mother and Pugh having taken him away from his home, his sisters and his father. But it was very eerie – though as Greg said, if they chose to think of him as the child they had lost and found again, did it matter to anyone but themselves?

Most of his memories were of more recent events, concerned mostly with being sick, being hungry, being very cold and wanting his father. Happily, the worst of these were beginning to fade a little. Care and kindness were distancing him from them, or they had distanced themselves in the same rapid way as a nightmare does when you wake up and find yourself in your own bed.

They'd had difficulty in deciding what he should call them. They daren't tempt fate by letting him think of them as 'Mummy' and 'Daddy', but in any case he hadn't seemed to want to.

'I've got a daddy,' he said. 'I fink he was in the van with me, once, and he cuddled me, but I sicked and sicked, and I went to sleep and when I woke up my Daddy had gone. There was only Mr Noble. And then Dr William bringed me here, and I had "daddy-bear" to cuddle, instead.' He had, it appeared, misheard 'teddy-bear' and substituted 'daddy-bear', which obviously had more meaning for him.

Fran wondered what a child psychologist would make of it all, and said so.

Greg nodded. 'If only we knew enough to help him. This morning when Jess was dressing him, he asked her where "something"-bear was. She thought he meant his teddy-bear, and said they would go and find him. But he said, "No, look, I've got him here, under my 'jamas. I meant the other one. The one who cuddles me, not the one I cuddle." Jess could only think he meant me. I do cuddle him.'

'Yes. Like now,' put in Tanner unexpectedly.

They looked at each other rather stupefied, wondering how much more of their deliberately cryptically phrased conversation he had understood. He added, as if he was explaining to them, 'Little daddy-bear thinks my other Daddy isn't coming back any more. So he says I can be Tollybear's little boy instead.'

Greg lowered his head and kissed the child's curls, hiding his own too-expressive face in them while Fran grew goose-pimples on her arms. She told herself that this was no more than an example of a supremely intelligent child 'trailing clouds of glory'.

She tried to bring them all back to the commonplace. 'I think you'll have to have a mummy-bear as well,' she said (forming the intention of supplying an even smaller teddy-bear at the first opportunity).

He sat up, considering the suggestion gravely. 'No,' he said. 'The Mummy I did have took me away from my Daddy. I didn't like her. I don't want a mummy-bear.'

Fran changed the subject quickly. 'What shall we call you then?' she asked. 'Jasper or Tanner?' He drew his brows together in that frown of concentration Fran remembered so well from her first meeting with him. 'Not Tanner,' he said. 'It 'minds me of Basher. I didn't like him, either. I want the others, though.' The corners of his mouth began to turn down.

'You'll perhaps see them again quite soon,' Fran said comfortingly. 'So shall we call you Jasper?'

The frown deepened. 'My other Daddy – the one who used to live with us – said I had another name, but I've forgotten it.' His brows indicated even deeper concentration. 'I fink it was John. We all had funny names.' Fran was thinking that a new name might be a great help to him in putting the past behind him. He was scrambling off Greg's lap. 'I've 'membered,' he said. 'It was John. When the others weren't there, he used to call me Jonce. I fink he said that was what his mummy used to call him when he was a little boy like me.'

(So 'Jonce' he became. Such things have a way of just happening through their own momentum, as William said, later, 'especially when they are right'.)

'We must go,' Greg told Fran. 'Jess comes over from the office at lunch-time. We mustn't keep her waiting.'

'Let's go, Tollybear,' said Cupid/Jonce. 'I'm hungry, and Jessmin makes lovely fings to eat.' He ran to the door, still hugging his little teddy bear.

'He seems to have settled what he intends to call you,' Fran said, amused.

'And Jess,' Greg said. 'Didn't you hear what he just said? I've always called her "Jessamine" in private, and maybe I've been dropping it quite a lot this week. He must have heard me and taken it in when we thought he was asleep.'

'I think little bear has very sharp ears and a very high intelligence quotient,' she said. 'But it's a good omen to be going on with. Give my love to Jess.'

Her thoughts turned towards Castle Hill. She didn't know how Bob and Jane were faring with their penny-in-the-slot family. There was no reason why she shouldn't ask, in their case.

She reached for the telephone, disturbing Cat again. 'Well,' she said, smoothing the cat's ears as she waited, 'I congratulate you, Cat. Your genie seems to be right on the ball. Hello, Jane.' She explained why she was all alone, and told Jane about Greg's visit.

'We're in the same boat,' Jane said, 'afraid we may lose our two. They're such placid little things, no trouble at all. Jade sits and plays by himself with nothing but a basket full of oddments – tin mugs and clothes-pegs and corks and cotton-reels threaded on a bit of binder-twine and huge nuts and bolts to screw together. Too big for him to swallow, but just right for little hands to manipulate. He just piles them up and knocks them down again, or puts one inside the other, or fills the mugs up with pegs. Bob's idea of toys are those that cost nothing and don't break.

'Aggie crawls about chewing a wooden spoon – though I do have to keep my eye on him in case he clouts the cats with it. He tires himself out chasing cats round and round this big floorspace till he goes to sleep wherever he is, usually with his head on Bonzo. Jade's in danger of being spoilt.

'If we can't keep them, it'll be Bob I shall have to worry about. He loves all baby things. I want to risk having at least one, but Bob's afraid to let me. And I suppose we ought to consider the feelings of Nick and Charlie. But it looks as if we've got two, whatever they think. Bob's afraid they may be too much work for his "highborn" wife, who mustn't be allowed to soil her dainty fingers. So if we are able to keep them, he thinks the gamekeeper's wife might consider coming up as a daily help. She's about the only one who would – come to work for me, I mean. Most of the others would draw the line at lowering themselves to work for a no-better-than-she-should-be undertaker's daughter who used to be a charwoman herself. No, of course I'm only joking! I don't care a bean. Oh, do stop worrying, Fran. I'm on a lucky streak. With everything, except perhaps Nick's injury. Let me know if there's anything new when William gets home.

'And by the way, isn't it time we let all the children meet each other again? This barn of a room has its uses. Why don't we all meet here? We ought to keep the three little ones in touch with each other, surely?

Besides, William said that their father cared about that most of all. None of us would have been involved, but for William's conscience about that. He's rather too well endowed with conscience about promises, I think, but I wouldn't have him any different, and I don't really suppose you would. We're both lucky.'

As Fran sat down to a lonely 'scratch' lunch, she began to ponder deeply that last remark of Jane's, remembering her talk in church with George Bridgefoot. They did have a lot to be thankful for. There had been so much trouble, last year, when each family or each individual had tended to look inward and try to solve its particular problem unaided. It was only when threatened by a mutual enemy that they had turned to each other for help, and become a community again. That was a cheering thought. A real community was a collection of good neighbours.

Their village had been split; but the old bit to which she and William belonged was regaining its solidarity, and in doing so becoming new again. Strangely, it was the newcomers who were acting as cement. Wherever you looked, their strands were becoming more and more entangled with the old, as well as with each other. It was surprising just how compatible all the newcomers had been, especially the men. They had already developed an *esprit de corps*, a new one altogether, not based on anything as definable as age or social standing or shared experience as servicemen in the war. It included people like George and Bob and Joe and Daniel and Ned.

William and Joe would probably just be setting off back from Worcester, each grieving after his own fashion for another man who, though a drop-out hippy, had potentially been a member too. Perhaps what they had in common was that they all retained the vestiges of chivalry, if you translated its virtues into modern terms: largesse (giving, if only of spirit), courtesy (treating others as you would wish them to treat you), gentilesse (integrity?), tendresse (loving-kindness) and valour, the last evident in a willingness to demonstrate all the others without embarrassment. Why otherwise should such a strangely assorted couple as William and Joe be now on their way home from Worcester? Because they were part of a real community, they lived in rhythm with each other. She thought of George at her birthday-party, calling, just as he had heard his father call, the figures of the country dance.

Up the middle, down the sides,
Cross the corner, stan' 'a one side . . .

Thomas Hardy's pattern on the carpet, T. S. Eliot's metaphor of the dance – how right they both were as symbols of a true community! And how lucky, as Jane had said, they were to be part of the pattern of the country dance. Where everybody's path at some time or other met or crossed or joined the path of everybody else.

The telephone ringing again ended her musing. It was Monica. Her father had been wonderful with the twin girls, helping them to come to terms with the death of the man who had been the only father they had ever had. She had left it entirely to him, and from what she gathered from them after he had gone home, he had told them about the aeroplane crash that had left him without a wife and Monica without a mother, feeling very much, he thought, as they did now. And he had let them cry, Monica said, hanging round his neck, and with his arms around them.

'You still have no real idea what an old softie he truly is under his stickleback's camouflage.'

He had taken a very practical view of the situation, too. It might save a lot of unwanted complications if they appeared as soon as possible on a school register somewhere – Amethyst in Swithinford, and, if Fran and William agreed, Topaz and Sapphire at the comprehensive just round the corner from where they were now. Her Dad had said that it would be so much kinder to them not to shuttle them to and fro, and she truly didn't mind keeping them. The cost of keeping them? Monica sounded affronted. It might not be for long – and neither she nor Roland was exactly penniless yet. Besides, if absolutely necessary, there was Dad – only she had promised him she wouldn't say so. 'And us,' Fran said, 'as long as you don't tell anybody.'

They left it like that, pro tem.

All right. So it was only a temporary measure; but the dance hadn't come to an end yet.

William came in no later and less worn-out that Fran had expected him to be. He looked tired, but less tense than when he had set out, and less on edge than he had been since the time Petrie had first been taken to hospital. They had supper, and went to the sitting room with William still rather silent and even a bit glum. She had learned long ago that when he didn't want to tell her things, it was no use asking questions. He sat down in his chair, and stretched his long legs out before the fire. Home. She took her seat across the hearth from him, and let him call the tune. When he was ready, he would confide in her, not simply tell her. She kept a loving eye on him, waiting to see if physical weariness would induce sleep. He closed his eyes, and she kept quiet, but he was restless and when she looked up from her book, she found his eyes fixed on her, soaking the picture of her in, drawing her attention wholly back to him.

She replied with a smile that reciprocated the messages his eyes were conveying. She knew quite well what he was thinking, which was what a long day it had been for them without sight or sound or touch of each other. Without speaking, he got up and went to sit on the floor at her feet, with his head resting against her knee. She took the hint. He wanted her to do the talking.

She began with Greg's visit, and though he made no comments, she felt his interest gradually warming to what she was saying. 'After Monica rang, I just sat and thought about Eric,' she said, 'and what a lot we all owe to him. If he hadn't come just when he did, there would have been nothing much left by now. The village we remembered was on its way out. It had got too old and too tired to make much effort to stay alive. Like some old people get, with their minds atrophied for lack of stimula-tion, and their bodies immobile because it's too much effort to move, just sitting and waiting for the pearly gates to open. The old Rector who was here when we first came was very much like that, and the church was declining, going with him. The rest of the village was on its way to the same end when Eric arrived. If he hadn't come when he did, in ten more years it would have been suffocated by little villas and semis and blocks of flats. Eric saved us from that, even if that wasn't his intention. His plans, much as we hated them, gave us time to recover, so that when Bailey descended on us we had spirit enough left in us to fight. My guess is that Eric is as glad as anybody that it worked out like that. He's thrown his lot in with us. He's given people like the Bridgefoots a chance to grow new shoots, if you see what I'm getting at.

'Of course he's had some lucky breaks and he's changed a lot him-self. Look how well he gets on with all of us. Nice man. I like him such a lot.'

'So do I,' William said. 'I remember thinking at first that he was nothing but an efficient machine for making money, remote controlled, because he gave the impression that there was no living man inside him. It's so easy to make too hasty judgements. Take a man like John that Joe and I watched buried today. All that intelligence, all that potential, come to an end like that! Dead at forty-three with nothing to show for it. A completely wasted life – or was it? How many of the rest of us have saved seven children? Not only from actual want, but from loveless neglect, and from falling into lives of dependence on alcohol or drugs or crime or all three. That's what John did. It was Joe who said that. I learned a lot from him today.

'Joe made me feel so guilty. I saw the set-up at Danesum from such a different perspective. He made me see it through his eyes, especially Pugh's part in it. Pugh the evangelist got through Joe's bitterness over Wendy and found the real Joe again. Joe couldn't have thought more highly of him. He worshipped him, and became his complete, very humble disciple. Pugh could preach, but all Joe could do was to pray, and encourage his neighbour to do the same. From what Joe said, Pugh was quite an orator. Joe didn't feel he was pulling his weight until they hit on the household at Danesum. That was the point at which I began to see how different it could look from different points of view.

'Take me – I know about the hippy culture. I deal with potential Johns and Crystals a lot of my time. They were completely out of Joe's ken. He thought Crystal was a prostitute who earned a living for them all when they got destitute, obliging John with her services in return for him keeping his eye on the kids while she was away "at work". When Pugh asked him to pray for them, he thought he had plenty to pray for, but he did it. Pugh put it to Joe that the Lord had set them a task, which was to save them all, particularly Crystal, because she, like Eve in the Garden of Eden, was the cause of all the evil. One does forget how primitive such evangelists can be! A Welsh evangelist set down in Cromwell's own country, where Puritan beliefs still linger. As if you didn't know that!'

He smiled his wicked lop-sided smile at her for the first time in two weeks or more. The smile she returned was anything but puritanical.

'Pugh had split their labours between the two of them – he would save Crystal, while Joe did his best for the man and the children. It didn't take Joe long to see that their worst sin was their poverty. Then when John was taken ill, he asked Joe to forget the praying and just be a friend. Joe said he had got so fond of them all that he would have done anything for them, Pugh or no Pugh. All of them except Crystal, that is. She completely ignored his presence, though Pugh spent a lot of time with her in her studio, preaching to her and praying with her, Joe believed. Does make the mind boggle a bit, doesn't it?' said William, answering the look on Fran's face. 'I think John tried to warn Joe that Crystal simply had no sense of right and wrong. It must have been difficult to get over to a man like Joe.'

'Like trying to teach a Chinaman the thirty-nine articles in Greek,' Fran said.

'Maybe, though it appears John had some success. Joe said he could see how easy it would be for her to make any man do what she wanted. John had told him that she had seduced him, and that he was Tanner's father. It had been as good as an insurance policy for her. She knew John wouldn't abandon his own child, and that after Tanner was born he would be tied to looking after all the others as well. Uncomplicated as he is, Joe had seen right through her,' William said.

'He knew John's plans as well as I did, and when John was taken seriously ill, he was ahead of me. He watched Crystal pretty closely, it seems. He told me he thought that she had been "knocked sideways" by the possibility of John dying, and leaving her to cope with eight children, without him or his money. Joe plucked up courage to warn Pugh to be careful, but Pugh "took him up very short, and ordered him to keep out of it". "Said he knowed what he was doing, which was the Lord's will, to save Crystal from the error of her ways. He thanked God for the chance of bringing such a deep-dyed sinner to repentance at last."'

William rose suddenly, and stood looking down at Fran. 'Whereas I, my sweetheart, passed by on the other side, and left Joe to play the Good Samaritan. That's why he insisted on going to Wales with John. He expected to find Crystal had played some dirty trick.'

William sat down again, very glad to be sharing his feelings with her.

'Joe said he had asked himself a lot of questions that he could only see one answer to. If it was God's word that Crystal was after, why couldn't he give it to her as well as Pugh? Because he was a labouring man getting on for sixty who had a wife, and Pugh was a young, good-looking man without a woman.

'Joe was right, you know, my darling. John and I took Pugh at face value, and trusted him. We thought he was an ordinary fellow with a pronounced kink, but otherwise trustworthy. So he was – but once Pugh had lost his hold on him, down-to-earth Joe had seen that with all his preaching and praying, he was only a man with all a man's natural instincts. John had put all the arrangements into his hands, so that when he was rushed to hospital everything stood ready and waiting.

'Joe told me that he sensed danger there and then. He had worked it out that if John died, none of the stuff would be Crystal's. Pugh had begun to be very funny, all the time saying he must get home to Wales. Joe thought – and still thinks – he wanted to get away from Crystal before it was too late to save himself. With John not there and him alone with her, she wouldn't have much trouble in persuading Pugh into what Joe called "sin" with her. Joe's opinion is that Pugh gave in and agreed to help her steal all the stuff and abandon the girls as the lesser of the two sins. He says he thinks it was Pugh who insisted on taking the small children – as protection for himself against her . . .'

William was silent for a moment or two, before saying, half to himself, 'We couldn't be expected to understand a man like that, though Joe did. He told me he had considered telling me of his suspicion, but decided it wasn't "in his place to warn a professor". Besides, he hadn't then lost all his faith in Pugh, and didn't right up to the day when he had gone to help Pugh at Pugh's own request and found them all gone. His idol then had more than feet of clay. He could find no good word for Pugh except that he had not yielded to Crystal's female wiles, and had walked away from her into the storm rather than spend the night in the van with her.

'Can you see why I feel so bad?' William asked Fran. 'Surely I ought to have been as much aware of Crystal as an unworldly chap like Joe? Especially with an odd-ball such as Pugh. But I also believed John's own prognosis of his condition. He'd got it wrong, and that was what played into Crystal's hands.

'I told Joe then about John's will, and that we, he and I, had been trusted with everything – which included all that Crystal had pinched. He accepted the responsibility very calmly, and we decided that we must wait and see what happens to the children before doing anything else.'

'What do you think will happen to them?' Fran asked.

'Darling, you know I can't answer that,' he said. 'But I've been trying to find out. The police will be looking for Crystal. When children are lost or completely abandoned, the local authority is obliged to take them immediately into care, but as these are being well looked after, no doubt they'll follow proper procedure. It is barely a week since John died, and until he did they could hardly be regarded as abandoned.

'Jess and Greg are too old to be considered as adoptive parents in the ordinary way – but we may possibly get round that. I'm hopeful, anyway. John had had himself registered as Jasper's natural father, and even if a child is illegitimate, the natural father can get some say in a case of adoption; and he'd transferred the guardianship of Jasper to me in the event of his death, as you know. I don't suppose that would give me any chance of custody against Crystal if she were to fight for him but I don't think she will. She won't care, and she won't dare. She knows that I shouldn't hesitate to expose her as a drug addict if I had to. Incidentally, I told Joe all that. We shall keep the money in case we do have to fight a legal battle for custody of Tanner. If I could get it, maybe I could get special consideration given to Greg and Jess as my relatives, or I could keep the legal custody myself and board him out with them, as it were, for ever. Bob and Jane are also above the normal age limit for adoption, but they are obviously such ideal candidates that we ought to be able to make a special case for them for adoptive or foster-parents as they wish. Which leaves the twins. Roland and Monica are disqualified on the same grounds as we are; but we can't go much farther without their mother and the help of the local magistrates. Any potential adopters have to file applications as soon as possible.

'Elyot thinks that as long as the welfare officer is satisfied that they are being well cared for, they will be regarded as being "under protection" by him for three months. Time to let us all settle down again. All very complicated, but I suppose necessary. Such awful things can and do happen to children. A case like this, with people actually queuing up to take them, must be very rare indeed, I think. Even though some of us are regarded as immoral according to the law, most of us rank otherwise as respectable citizens. And we're all in it together. We shan't be fighting anything but regulations, to which even the law allows exceptions occasionally.'

Fran leaned over and kissed him. The worst was over, now he had got it off his chest.

'That's a nice thought,' she said. 'That by dying, John has welded our friends even closer to us.'

He sat silent, looking up at her. 'That's as good an epitaph as he would ever have wished,' he said. 'What he didn't achieve living, he did by dying.'

'Like Hardy's white cat,' she said.

> 'By the merely taking hence
> Of his insignificance –'

'Yes,' said William. 'He was a good man.'

65

On Monday morning, Sophie was a bit tight-lipped with regard to Vic's funeral. She was eager to hear all that Fran could tell her of Petrie's, though it transpired that on Sunday she had seen Joe and heard all he was prepared to tell her. In the end, Fran had to ask her about Gifford's. The trouble was that Sophie's loyalty to the Bridgefoots was at war with her conditioned reflexes with regard to what was right and proper. She couldn't excuse Marge's absence from her husband's funeral, whatever trouble between them there might have been.

'It ain't like Marge,' she said. 'I'm knowed her since she were born, and I should never 'ave thought it of 'er, none of it. Not that there's many as know about the other, yet. There'll be plenty said when folks do know, though, you may depend upon it.'

Fran was all ears. Sophie was bursting with some other bit of news she had been asked not to repeat. Fran knew all the rules of the game by this time, and was prepared to play. If Fran asked, she would reply as truthfully as she could, and then excuse herself that she had not 'repeated' anything; she had merely answered questions.

'What other?' Fran asked innocently.

Sophie coloured, still struggling with her conscience.

'What else has Marjorie done? Did she go somewhere else, instead of to the funeral?'

493

'Must ha' done, else 'e 'ad arranged to see 'er while all the others was out o' the way. That don't matter, as far as I know. All I know is as it were fixed a'Friday as she's going to live in 'is 'ouse, soon as ever she can get 'er things moved. And I know it's the truth, 'cos George told Dan'el Friday night, and Dan told Thirz' and Thirz' told us all yist'day when she had us all to dinner.'

'You all went to dinner with Thirzah yesterday? How nice for you. I hope Joe's got over his long trip.'

Fran was deliberately delaying the disclosure of whatever it was Sophie knew that she didn't, well aware that the longer she held off the tit-bit of news, the greater the pressure on Sophie to tell it would be. It wasn't that Fran desperately wanted to know, though she was interested. It was part of the ritual, like the long-drawn-out chord that tells the dancers to be ready to step into the dance.

'So who was it that Marge was making arrangements with while Vic was being buried, and whose home she is going to share?'

Sophie stopped sweeping, and turned to face Fran. 'I never said "'ome". I said "'ouse". That Eric Choppen's.'

As Fran said later, telling William, she could have been knocked down with the proverbial feather. It took her only a split second to stabilize the information, with the undertones and overtones that Sophie had managed to convey. There was no escaping Sophie's disapproval. The implication of her last remark was very clear.

'I wasn't aware they even knew each other,' Fran said, casually, 'though I had expected that Mr Choppen might get round to letting the other half of his house now that Monica's left it empty. Seems very sensible on both sides, to me.'

Sophie sniffed. 'She could ha' waited a bit longer, and not give people the chance they've been waiting for to run 'er and 'er fam'ly down. She was all right up at Temperance with Brian and Rosemary. Monastery Farm may be made into two 'ouses, but you know as well as I do you can get from one side to the other without going outside.'

Fran knew whom Sophie meant by 'people'. The Beans and the Bridgefoots were now, irrevocably, in opposite camps.

'Really, Sophie! I know you're not overfond of Mr Choppen, but you're the last person who ought to get upset about Marge finding herself a roof over her own head. And besides, you said that William and I could both live here, so long as there was a bolt between his flat and my house. I really can't see why Eric and Marjorie should be anything but landlord and tenant.'

'It was the way she done it,' Sophie said. 'On the very day as her husband was buried! She used to be such a good, God-fearing sort o' girl once, as never put 'erself forr'ard, like. Marge were just a hordinary village gel as married a hordinary village man, and nobody expected 'em to go on as they 'ave done lately. Going against all the respectable old wayses.'

Fran was irritated with Sophie, but did her best not to let it show. The reunion of Kezia's family into a whole again had probably reinforced this nostalgic return to Victorian village morality. She said, gently, 'We don't know all the story, yet, Sophie. Maybe we never shall – but it isn't like you to think ill of anyone. In the end, most of us do what circumstances force us to do. You said yourself that Vic Gifford was no angel. Let's give Marjorie a chance, and hope that she'll be happy in her new home.' They left it at that, and parted to their respective jobs.

Fran learned from Monica that the rumour was true, and that her father was pleased to have got so compatible a tenant. Whatever anybody else said, Fran thought it an excellent arrangement.

She would have been very surprised to know that the person most inclined to 'up-end' himself about it was Charles. Charles was feeling distinctly disgruntled.

He had been absolutely 'on top of the world' at the start of the new year – not only on top of it, but at the centre of it, with everything, but everything, going his way. Only ten weeks later, his interest rating had dropped so low that he began to wonder if he had dreamt it all, and if his plans were moonshine. From the heights of optimism he had been plunged almost to despair by events not directly concerning him.

What with his father's accident, Bailey's party, Aunt Marge and Uncle Vic, things at home weren't concentrated much on him or his affairs. Besides, whatever happened, a farm has to be looked after, and he was having to do far more than his fair share of that, which he didn't really mind except that it disrupted his normal routine of visits to Charlie. There was, after all, a house to be got ready before the wedding that had to be arranged.

It hadn't helped that in the very same week that Uncle Vic had managed to break his neck, Petrie had died and Joe Noble had brought back three very small children to be cared for, two of whom looked likely to remain as permanent residents of Castle Hill Farm.

When he rang Charlie to say he could meet her, she was too busy to meet him. After a few hurried words, she said, 'Must go, darling, honestly. See you on Sunday. Jane's arranging some do about our wedding there, and needs me. You'll fetch me, won't you?' and hung up.

Being very young, and desperately in love, he sulked. He hadn't got over it by the weekend.

The 'do' Charlie had mentioned was the gathering that had grown from Jane's remark to Fran that they ought to let all the Petrie children see each other soon, and had offered to set up the meeting at Castle Hill.

When the two women got down to discussing the arrangements for it, it had mushroomed into something quite other than Jane had first envisaged. She had not lived in a village for twenty years, albeit as an outsider, without learning how it worked, apart from what Bob told her.

The wedding of Bob's daughter to a Bridgefoot would be 'the' wedding of the year. Her own changed status both as Mrs Bellamy and the daughter of a wealthy man who could foot the bill for whatever kind of wedding it was could be a source of trouble. Charles was the only male Bridgefoot that would be getting married for a very long time. Fran suggested, ever so gently, that his mother and grandmother would very much appreciate being consulted. Especially if, as Fran hoped and had been led to think George expected, it was to be a 'village wedding'.

Jane was vexed with herself that she had not made clear to everybody that that was what had been intended from the beginning. And of course Rosemary and Molly must be in on all the arrangements! Then she had added that they couldn't very well have all the children there, in a strange place among strangers, by themselves. All those who were at present caring for the children individually, which meant Elyot and Beth, Jess and Greg, and Monica would have to be invited even if Roland couldn't make it. Fran and William as well, naturally.

'And if Monica's going to be there, we might as well kill as many birds with one stone as possible, and talk clothes with her. So we shall have to ask Charles if he can fetch Charlie home for the weekend. It will almost be like a house-warming party for me and Bob.'

Brian had been invited as well, but had had to refuse. Charles had pointedly asked him if it was deliberate, but Brian had replied that he had already promised Aunt Marge to help her move the few bits she did want to keep to Monastery Farm, and added that he hoped Charles had enough sense not to make an issue out of it. So on Sunday afternoon, Charles set off, still disgruntled and touchy, with his (very nervous) mother. Though they were well on time, Charles recognized William's car there before them, and wondered what on earth the Benedict's lot had to do with plans for his wedding. It didn't need a committee, did it?

Jane welcomed Rosemary at the front door. Charlie, with a baby in her arms, stood behind her, and leaned across to give Charles a kiss. If he had not already been 'fed up' he would have seen both the apology and the love in her eyes; but he was in no mood to see anything but difficulty.

She read his mood, and transferred the baby so that he could really get close to her, kissing him again. 'Bear up,' she whispered. 'You don't know yet what you're in for! But we'll escape when the business part's over.'

She pushed the door into the big room open, and led his mother in. Rosemary gasped, though he had told her about that extraordinary room; but so did he, at the number and variety of people it contained. Fran and William were standing in a circle in the middle of the room talking with the Taliaferros and the Franks. At their feet, sitting on the carpet, was a knot made up of the two oldest Petrie girls, tearfully smothering little Jasper with hugs and kisses. Next minute, the door opened again to let in Monica and her father, and not only Monica's twins, but the Petrie twins as well. They stood, bashfully amazed, taking everything in, till Topaz, awed but unbelieving, ejaculated '*Jade!*' and rushed to take him from Bob's arms, while Charlie handed Agate over to Saffie. Then they caught sight of the group on the floor, and the grown-ups all moved tactfully away, to leave the moment of complete reunion unobserved.

After the first few overwrought minutes, Jane approached them and said, 'I've put a fire in the other little sitting-room for you. Would you like to go in there and be by yourselves?'

'We shan't want my two, either, when the business starts,' declared Monica. 'When those others have got over seeing each other again, they'll look after mine as well. Then we can talk.'

'Wedding before tea,' Jane said. 'Petrie problems after tea, in case those not directly involved in the second item on the agenda want to go home. I think we're all here, now.'

They sat down. Charles and Charlie, next to each other, held hands. Bob made to take his own chair, and was at once swamped with cats, who had felt themselves displaced since the advent of Jade and Aggie, with Ali and Baba claiming pride of place on his chest. Bonzo lay with his head across Bob's foot.

'When's this wedding likely to be?' Bob asked. 'After hay and before harvest, I suppose, seeing as both sides are farmers. I reckon Charles's father'll want him back from his honeymoon before harvest. No later than the middle o' July. Depends whether they're planning a honeymoon, and if so how long for.'

'Are they?' Jane asked Rosemary, one mother to the other.

Charlie giggled, and Charles said, 'Don't mind us. We're only the couple getting married.'

Formality retreated. 'Well, are you?' William inquired. 'If the date of the wedding depends on it, you'd better make up your minds, hadn't you?'

'I'd rather hoped we might just go home to our own house,' Charles said, a bit bashfully.

Jane looked at Charlie, inquiringly.

'I haven't had time to tell Charles,' she said, answering the look. 'We've hardly seen each other for three weeks. You tell him.'

'Effendi wants to give you your honeymoon as his wedding present,' Jane said. 'Up to a month on the continent. He's disappointed that Nick won't go with him, and thinks that to send you two would be the next best thing.'

Charlie looked around the circle in some embarrassment. Rosemary was almost showing what she was thinking. The Bridgefoots couldn't do the wedding, but surely the honeymoon would be at Bridgefoot expense? Bob knew that Gordon's offer was being made not in ignorance, but out of sheer love for them all.

William felt it was up to him to pour oil on the potentially troubled waters. 'It would give Charlie a marvellous chance to brush up her languages,' he said. 'But I'm pretty sure some of us would feel the same. A house isn't a home till you've made it one. So may I make a suggestion? Wedding presents are things to be kept. Why don't you settle to go "home" till harvest's over, and then take Effendi's offer for a lovely holiday just before Charlie goes up again for the Michaelmas term?'

'Speaking of which,' Charlie said, amidst general approval, 'can the bride have a bit of say in the date? It's all very well for Charles and Dad to agree on "between hay and harvest"; which could be almost anytime depending on the weather. In this case the bride has to decree "not till exams are over and the results out". Sometime in June.'

'It sounds lovely. May we think about it? But it does settle the date. The Saturday before May Week.'

'Next item . . .'

And they continued until Jane, interrupting firmly, said, 'It's time we broke off for tea. Fetch all the children in, and I'd like willing hands of both sexes to fetch and carry for the next few minutes. If Monica isn't in a hurry, I think the whole question of wedding garments would be better just left to us women. After tea.'

A total of nine willing and able females, excluding Beth who was not allowed to help, soon made short work of clearing up after a sumptuous farmhouse tea. The days were lengthening now that it was March, and they had taken tea early on purpose. Jane suggested that Bob took all the men up to the church to walk down their tea, and Emerald and Amethyst all the babies back to the smaller sitting-room. Then the women went into the question of the wedding garments.

'What about bridesmaids. How many?' asked Monica.

'This is where we run into difficulty,' Jane said. 'Charlie has no female relatives and no friends around here.'

'There's Charles's cousins,' Fran suggested, thinking Rosemary would be too shy to put her spoke in.

But she did. 'Poppy if you really want her, Charlie. But not Pansy. Her mother asked me specially to tell you so. She wouldn't accept, and wouldn't come without that Darren. Charles wouldn't want him, any more than the rest of us would. Charles is in a bit of difficulty, too. He wants Nick for his best man, but not any other friends except Robert, who'll be there . . . lying in his grave just outside the church door.' She looked at Charlie for support.

Charlie nodded. 'Sorry, Monica, but that's how it is. It looks like the bride and one bridesmaid – Poppy.'

There was nothing anybody could do. They couldn't create bridesmaids out of thin air, or bring Robert back. 'Here are the men back,' said Monica.

'Do you need me and Charles any longer?' Charlie asked. 'May we go? Oh, I forgot. Charles must wait for his Mum.'

'I wanted to take Charlie down to Danesum, now that it is really ours, just to get some ideas,' said Charles.

'Off you go, then,' said Eric. 'Monica mustn't be much longer because of the babies. I'm taking her back to Cambridge and can drop your Mum off.'

'If we are going, we might as well all go together,' Beth said. 'It's been lovely.'

They called the children, and goodbyes were said happily, on the promise that they should see each other again soon.

'Need you go for a little while?' Bob asked William and Fran. 'Can't you stop a bit longer?'

William looked at Fran, who had heard, and with wrinkled brow was studying Bob's face.

'No – we're in no hurry,' she said.

The two men went outside to see the others off.

'Something's worrying Bob,' said Jane.

'Yes, I know,' said Fran. 'That's why I agreed to stay.'

Bob and William came back. 'Can you manage without me, my duck?' Bob asked. Both women laughed. 'I want to show William something,' he said.

'Let's get the babies into bed,' Jane said, and the two women departed up to the bathroom.

'Come with me, William,' Bob said. William followed him to the smaller room the children had been using. A very pretty little room, warm and cosy, made handsome by a few beautiful old pieces, one of them being the eighteenth-century gaming table that had been used for Elyot and Beth's wedding up in the little church on the hill. On top of it stood a beautifully carved Bible-box. Bob went to it and lifted out of it a canvas-wrapped parcel, and put it on William's lap.

'I reckon it's about time we had a look at this,' he said.

William knew what it was. The mysterious parcel Bob had found, along with the lost church registers, in the dangerous bell-chamber of the condemned tower of St Saviour's church. Beth's father, the then Rector, had not encouraged either William's legitimate desire to do a bit of academic research on the church, nor Bob's layman's interest in trying to solve an unresolved historical riddle with the aid of his sixth sense, which Archie Marriner had seemed to think was either a gift from the devil or country bumpkin hokum entangled with remnants of paganism. William had submitted to Archie's diktat, hoping that he would be able to overcome the Rector's doubts by making it official academic research. Bob had passed over to the Rector the missing registers; but had kept to himself – except for William – his discovery of this strange sealed package. William had persuaded Bob to keep it dark till he could find a way round 'difficulties', which really meant his academic conscience. And so it had been left.

But Marriner had gone, and no other Rector had been found. The church stood in a small field that presumably was Church Commissioners' property, and which in turn was surrounded on three sides by what would soon now be Bob's own land. Not a soul but Bob and William were aware of the existence of whatever it was wrapped and sewn into that canvas cover, round which Bob himself had taped oilskin.

Bob produced a shutknife and ripped off the oilskin. Then he passed the knife to William, and waited. Bob had no doubt whatsoever that the academic historian in William would win.

Slowly and very carefully, William began to unpick the thick linen threads. There were three layers of canvas before its contents were revealed to be a thick, leatherbound book looking very much like yet another church register. William sat in awed silence barely daring to open it. He looked up at Bob, only to find that Bob, though his burly physical presence was there just as large as ever, was no longer with him. There was a faraway look in Bob's eye, and a troubled expression on his face. William waited a moment, found his courage, and lifted the leather cover.

A quick glance told him that the faded Roman-hand was in the form of a personal diary requiring secrecy. He would not be surprised to find more difficulties in reading it than a page or two of introductory and scholarly Latin. His gasp of delighted surprise brought Bob's wandering attention back to him.

'William,' Bob said, 'can I leave you to enjoy it by yourself, and tell Jane and Fran I'll be back as soon as I can? I've got to go and find Charlie and Charles. I think I know where they are and interfering or not, somebody's got to do something. Them old ghosts up in the church want you to find out what's in that book, but them down Danesum want me there, now. Before it's too late.'

He didn't wait for William to answer. William decided to pack up his treasure, and go to deal with two anxious women. Neither of them was surprised when he told them why Bob had gone. They both knew him too well to question, and both had seen that he had been disturbed.

'It's Charles Bob's worrying about,' Jane said. 'And I've started to worry as well.'

'What about, and why?' asked Fran, sympathetically.

'Nick. Charles has asked him to be best man, and of course Nick has agreed. But Bob can see right through Charles. He doesn't want this Nick, the one who is Charlie's step-brother now and would have had to be asked anyway. He wants his old friend Nick, the one who remembers all they used to do together before Nick became an affluent suave townee. I think only Bob really understands how Charles feels, and what it means to him. Bob won't give up hope. I'm afraid I have done. And if Charles has shown his feelings today, I guess Bob knows why. He's afraid Charles will take it out on Charlie.'

'Charles is certainly in a funny mood,' remarked William. 'I think we could all feel it.'

'And what else is worrying you, Jane?' asked Fran.

Jane's strong face was very troubled. 'The bridesmaid bit,' she said. 'The decision that there should only be one bridesmaid – Poppy Gifford. Can't you see what it will mean? When Charles and Charlie come down the aisle as man and wife, who'll be following them? Nick with Poppy on his arm. Poor, poor Poppy!'

Fran and William were silent, both awaiting explanation. Jane told them how Nick had fallen in love with Poppy Gifford.

'When it turned out as it did, I began to pin my hopes of Nick's memory returning when he met Charles again. Nothing happened. There was only one person left, the one who had caused him the most anguish he had ever shown about his poor start in life: Poppy Gifford. When she came into church on New Year's Eve, I was almost choking with hope. She went to him, and spoke to him. Fran, I watched it. He was sweet and polite to her, but she meant no more to him than any of the rest of us. I gave up all hope, then, but I saw her face. She was terribly hurt – and in that moment all her hopes died, too. She loves him still, and will never love anybody else in the same way, any more than Charlie would if she lost Charles. How can we possibly put her through such torture as to have to come down the church aisle with him, with Greg still playing the "Wedding March"? And there's nothing we can do to prevent it. She won't let Charles down, or Charlie, or show her feelings. Nobody knows them,

I imagine, but me – and now you. I haven't even told Bob – though you don't always have to tell him things. Don't say a word about it, will you? We can't expect Fate to go on being kind to us. We can only accept and make the most of it. I'm the last one who ought to grumble.'

'Don't worry, either,' said William. 'It never does very much good anyway.'

66

Charlie had known from the first moment she had got into the passenger seat of Charles's car that something was very wrong. As she turned towards him expecting to be kissed, he didn't even look at her. She sank back into the seat, glad that it was dark and he could not see her hurt face, or she his hard one. Then he missed his gear, found it with a muttered growl, and drove off down the rutted old road he knew so well about twice as fast as he ever normally took it.

When they were nearly to the end of the unmade road, she told herself that something she didn't yet know about must be upsetting him, and that he was nerving himself to tell her some bad news. It was no use her getting upset, as well. She leaned her head against his shoulder, and said, 'Where are we going, darling? And what's the matter? You've been in such a funny mood all the afternoon, though it was all so happy and hopeful and lovely.'

'Lovely?' he growled. 'All that damned interference about what is only our affair and nobody else's? And your new posh grandfather wanting to pay for us as if my family and my grandfather hadn't got two pennies to rub together, and wouldn't give us a ha'penny even if he could? What were all the others doing there? As far as I could see, all they did was to overawe my Mum, so that if she had wanted to say anything, she'd have been too shy. It's a good job Dad wasn't able to come. Choppen there was just about the last straw. So, since I don't seem to have any say in anything, where do you want to go?'

She had heard him out, pulling herself away so that their shoulders were no longer touching, stiffening her chin and gritting her teeth to stop the welling tears from falling. She couldn't answer.

He stopped the car. 'Well?' he asked.

She gathered the skirts of her coat from any contact with him. 'Home, please. You can drop me at the door. You needn't come in. Some of those you dislike so much may still be there. Dad will take me back to Cambridge.'

He let in his clutch and turned the car into the road that led through the village.

'I said "home",' she said.

'I heard you. That's where I'm taking you – unless you want to walk back up to Castle Hill. To the home I thought we were going to share together soon, if they let us, the house I've bought for you, without any help from your precious step-grandfather, the house I thought you wanted. So which "home" are you going to choose?'

She could hear by his voice that he was as near to tears as she was, but she wasn't at all sure whether they were the same kind as hers, tears of shock and disappointment and despair, or of quite a different kind, of fury bred from some recent desire to be rid of her and all she stood for.

'The choice is yours,' she said. 'I don't know what all this is about. If you say "your home" I shall walk back – and you can take this with you.' She pulled off her 'daisy' engagement ring and held it out to him. 'If you say "our home", I may let you put it back on my finger when I know why I've had to take it off. Here. Take it!'

'If you want to get rid of it so bad, throw it out of the window. I guess there's another one waiting for you in Cambridge.'

'Charles! How can you?' She tried again to give it to him, and dropped it on to the floor of the car. Neither made any attempt to pick it up.

He said nothing, but drove at breakneck speed through the village and along the Swithinford Road till they came to the Danesum Lane turning. There he had to slow down a bit, and they travelled in silence till they had negotiated the narrow gap through the encroaching brambles to the gateway of the house. Then he stopped, and switched off the lights. Their eyes soon became used to the darkness. She was crying now, huge, silent, heartbroken tears that she would not wipe away because she would not draw his attention to them or give him the satisfaction of seeing them at all if she could possibly help it.

He had already seen them, and had been instantly reminded of how she had cried in his car that morning he had first met her, and how he had longed to lick those tears off her muddied face then. At the sight of her tears now, his anger left him like the air from a burst tyre, leaving him flat and out of control of the situation . . . except that other feelings rushed in to fill the vacuum. First, absolute despair at what his foolish temper had done. He felt her stiffening herself against him, calling on the great streak of personal independence she possessed, bred into her by her fen tiger origins and nurtured all her life by her exile from home to please the mother who hadn't loved her. He had seen it in action before, when she had left him to go her own way – and had nearly killed him by her absence. What if he had called it up so strongly that she was making up her mind to do without him again? He couldn't live without her now, within four months, at the most, of the wedding which would have made her wholly his, body as well as that marvellous brain and spirit.

The fury against himself now burst into a great rush of love for her, accompanied by such physical desire as he had never felt before, and that was admitting a lot. He turned to her, and reached for her, pulling her towards him with a force that took her by surprise. The strength had gone out of her, and she lay for a moment with her face close to his while he licked off the salty tears and joined his own to them. She knew that it was not yet the end: it was much more like the beginning of a new relationship which, if they were to have a good marriage, had to last them for the rest of their lives – maybe another sixty or seventy years. They simply had to 'have this out', and know where they stood now.

'Let me up,' she said, in a perfectly ordinary voice. 'I must find a handkerchief', and she pulled herself away from him. She took his self-control with her. Physical desire for her, there and then, simply overwhelmed any other emotion. He could not let her take herself out of his arms, out of his reach, out of his touch. He was much the stronger of the two, and she had to yield. He pulled her back to him, smothering her with passionate kisses, holding her so tightly that she could hardly breathe.

The nearness of him, the smell of him, his soft blond curls rubbing against her face, were all too much for her. She felt only the tremendous love for him, the man she had long since decided was her only possible husband. She forgot everything else but that they were together again, and exchanged kiss for kiss with him, holding his curly head to her neck as his mouth travelled down it. Everything between them must be all right again, she thought.

That was the difference between them, now. She was still capable of thinking. He wasn't. Her yielding had overcome the last remnants of his self-control. She realized his intent, and began to struggle, but was powerless against his male strength.

'Let me go! Charles, let me go. Now!'

She was wearing the lovely expensive dress Effendi had given her for Christmas. It was low-cut at the neck, with a trimming of three silk-covered buttons at the front; a soft, sensual yielding material that made it no barrier to him and only seem part of her. He undid the three buttons, while she continued to struggle, more and more urgently pleading with him to stop.

He couldn't. The buttons were undone. He slid his hand down her silky neck, and into the opening he had made, found her bra straps and slid them off her shoulder, and lifted the satin-skinned little breast he now had in his hand up towards his hungry mouth. She lay perfectly still for a split second till his passion had taken him off-guard, and then moved. She heaved herself out of his loosened clutch, grabbed his hair with her left hand and jerked his head up by it, and slapped his face with her right hand, using every ounce of her overwrought, outraged strength. He had violated not only her body, but the understanding between them, and the promise he had made that he would not ask her to indulge in sex or heavy petting during their engagement. It had been difficult for both, but each had had a special reason for accepting the restraint.

She shoved herself away from him as he reeled back from the blow in surprise and humiliation, and squeezed herself into the far corner away from him, pulling the strap back on to her shoulder and doing up the dress buttons with trembling hands. Her eyes blazed with fury, seeming to him twice as large as usual and as frighteningly brilliant as shooting stars.

'You beast,' she spat at him. 'How dare you!'

He had cringed from her and was hanging on to the driving wheel, trying to come to terms still with the sexual urge raging inside him and the anger and humiliation of being rejected. But her words caught him through a crack he had never even suspected could be there. He had seen her angry many times before, and had always been amused by it. It had never before truly pierced him, because she had never meant it. This time she did – and he knew how he knew. From the very first time she had ever sworn at him, on the morning they had met and fallen so helplessly in love, her imprecations had always been in a mixture of at least four foreign languages. This time she had not bothered with any but her native one – and only one, very commonplace word at that. But she had meant it: it conveyed more of her contempt and disgust for him than every other foreign oath she had ever used. It reduced him, in his own eyes, to exactly what she had called him. Yet his anger would still not let him ask her forgiveness. He had to make excuses to himself, if not to her.

'What's so wrong about it? An hour ago, you were going to be my wife in three months' time. Everybody else that I know of goes the whole way within hours of meeting each other, and thinks nothing of it. Everybody knows – like about Pansy and her Darren – but who thinks any the worse of them for it?'

'I do, for one,' she said, icicles in her voice. 'Your mother, and her own mother, for two more. They wouldn't let her be my bridesmaid, even if I had wanted her, which I didn't. But there's no need to bother about that, now.'

'Charlie! Charlie, you can't mean that. You can't.'

'I can and I do – if that is all you want me for! If that's all you think marriage means!'

'But I want you so – and you did let me touch you there, just once before. I've lived on that, remembering the feel of you, and imagining all the rest. It's what every man wants. Why should I be different?'

'Because I'm different. Because I want you as much as you want me – it's probably what every woman wants, too. I remember that other time, as well; I knew after it how much I wanted you, and because what had happened that evening had made it possible, I knew that I dare let myself really love you. *Love you.* To be with you for always, for you to be my husband and the father of my children. But I still had to prove *myself* worthy of you in the eyes of your father and mother. I asked you not to tempt me, and you didn't.

'Oh, I know you agreed. You had your reasons, too. But tonight you chose to treat me as if you knew that at heart I was only the whore my mother is.' She sat up straight, her head held high, and her voice cutting into him like the sharp edges of a hole in an ice-covered pond.

'I am not your whore, and I never shall be. I called you a beast, and you were. Acting like an animal. We both know about animals. Most of them mate only for one reason – to produce young. We used to think human beings a superior species, supposed to care for each other, love each other. Sex and babies as a result of it were the proofs of love. Not now though, not any longer. Sex has got nothing to do with love any more. Not with people like Pansy. So if you want to be a stallion led round on a chain wherever there happens to be a mare in season, go and be one. You won't find me on your round.' The scorn in her voice was rubbing salt into the cuts she had already made.

By this time he had both hands on the steering wheel with his head resting on them, and his shoulders were heaving. He had never in all his life before felt so base, so abashed, so ashamed of himself and so beaten. He couldn't think of anything to say that could make any sort of reparation to her. He hadn't meant any of it to happen. He had just lost his temper, that's all.

If only he could be Robert, dead, and out of it all. If only he could be Nick, not able to remember what had been, all that he had had until a few minutes ago. But he wasn't, he was Charles, who until he had thrown it away had had everything. He didn't understand . . . he didn't understand. How could everything have gone so wrong? He had brought his Charlie out to see the house they had been going to live and be happy in. He'd wanted to ask her which of the bedrooms she wanted to be theirs, so that he could surprise her by having a bathroom built *en suite* out of one of the many spare rooms. He had intended telling her that wherever she chose, it would be there that he would make her truly his wife. In their own bedroom, in their own house. But there stood the house in darkness, as it would for ever now unless Charlie was in it. Somewhere on the floor of this car lay the engagement ring of daisies he had looked so long to find for her – because the daisy was the flower that symbolized her for him. They were both so young, and she and love had come to him with the daisies in springtime. He'd trodden on it, and crushed it, spoilt it.

He felt as if his heart was shrivelling, and that under it was a great hollow that could never again be filled. He was choking, sure that the shock of all that had happened was robbing him of breath. He turned his face her way, longing to look at her, but afraid to open his eyes and see what he had lost. But in the end he did. She was still there. Still Charlie, with her hand held out to him.

'Charles,' she said a soft voice. 'Use my handkerchief.'

He tried to say something that sounded like 'I'm sorry' – but she had moved. She was drying his face. He caught the hand, and held it, and said the only thing that could put everything right again. The only thing that mattered. 'I love you so . . .' he said.

'No more than I do you,' she answered. Arms round each other's necks, they sat in silence, wet faces close together.

'Whatever happened to us?' she said.

'I don't know – oh my darling, never again! Never again!'

'I promise. Not till next time. I expect we shall always quarrel, like we did tonight, just because we love each other so much. That's what makes it so hard for us. Help me look for my ring. I can't bear to see my finger without it. It means I belong to you already.'

'Kiss me, first.'

They were both scrabbling about on the floor feeling around for the ring, when the lights of a car came up behind them, and its engine was shut off.

'Who the devil?' said Charles, standing up and wondering what sort of a picture he made in the other car's headlights, with his face still blubbed and streaked with tears.

'Lights,' said Charlie, still on the floor of the car. 'What a streak of luck! I've found it, Charles. Come and put it back on, quick. I don't care who it is.'

'It's your Dad.' They stood before him, and he needed no other proof than their faces that he had been right to worry about them. But conviction that all was well swept over him.

'Put what back on?' he asked Charlie, pretending to look shocked. 'What have you taken off?'

'Only our engagement ring,' said Charles, taking it from her hand and slipping it back on her finger.

'I knowed something was wrong, and I guessed where you'd be. Come home now.'

'We were going into the house,' Charles protested.

'Not tonight,' said Bob. 'Don't spoil it by going in when you've been quarrelling. It's waiting for you to be happy. Places have feelings for people who love them. That man who got it ready for you and then died left it full of love. You can see that by looking at the children he brought up. Don't spoil his gift to you. I reckon as it must have been him that sent me up here to find you. Come again when you're really happy. Besides, they're waiting for us at home, for supper.'

They followed him in to where Jane, Fran and William sat waiting.

'I found 'em where I expected to, just making up a lovers' tiff,' Bob told the others.

'A bad one,' Charlie said. 'Nobody's fault – or both's. I expect we were both to blame.'

'No,' said William. 'I don't believe that. Human nature was to blame. We're all the same. Something goes wrong for us, and what do we do? Take it out on the one we love best.'

Charles looked unbelieving. 'Do you mean you take it out on each other?'

'Very often,' said Fran. 'I hope we always shall. It's the people who don't care about each other who don't quarrel. Couples who say they've never had a cross word have probably never had a tender one either. "Pass the marmalade" marriages, I call them. That's about the only thing they can ever find to say to each other.'

'Charles,' said Charlie, looking mock serious, 'do you like marmalade very much?'

'No, not particularly. Why?'

'How can we keep people from giving us marmalade holders and spoons for presents? If we don't have any marmalade, we shall have to find other things to say to each other. I dare say we shall think of something.'

'Bob,' said Jane, cocking her head on one side and listening. 'I can hear Aggie grizzling. Pass me those warm nappies over, will you?'

The sound of laughter followed her up the stairs.

67

Spring had arrived, almost overnight. Easter, falling early in April, was only four weeks away. The weather had turned warm and sunny, though March winds were playing their usual unpredictable tricks. Ash buds were blackening, elms reddening, willows yellowing, here and there whitethorn was blossoming and in gardens and parks prunus trees were showing pink even through sharp short snow showers. Primroses peeped out under hedges, daffodils burst open and blackbirds sang and called their warning squawks early and late.

The restlessness of spring was in the earth, in the clouds, in the wind, in the air and in everything else, including animals and people just as it always had been until lately, when man's cleverness had encroached upon the rhythmic prerogatives of nature. Longer evenings drew men out into their gardens; brighter days showed women cobwebs in the corners of their kitchens and set up a spring fever of cleaning. Neither gardening nor spring-cleaning were now strictly necessary just because it was spring. New mechanized implements and household gadgets such as vacuum cleaners meant that gardens could be cultivated whenever conditions were right, and houses no longer needed what old East Anglian women would have called 'foe-ing out' on the first day of March, as in the old days had always been the custom. Yet still the commotion of the spring could be felt in Old Swithinford, especially in the heart of the village, more and more now being casually referred to as 'Church End'.

This was to differentiate it from Lane's End, and the estate of new houses which was the nucleus now of an almost but not quite separate community comprising Bailey's estate and the post-war council houses, the urbanizing effect of so many dwellings close together setting up a kind of gravity which was pulling Hen Street more and more towards it. Church End had been there for many centuries, and still obeyed the rhythms of nature and the customs that went with them; Lane's End was new, full of modern conveniences, inhabited by townees using it only as a dormitory, who were bound by no traditional customs or rules. If there were any guidelines for community life there, they were still only emerging from day to day. None had, as yet, been laid down as tradition.

In Church End the spring was pushing people to 'get on with things'. Charles was one of them. Heartened beyond all expectations by what had occurred on Sunday, he set to work on Monday to find small firms of builders, gardeners, decorators and the like prepared to take on the job of making Danesum ready for his bride. There was plenty of work on the farm, but he was indulgently excused from doing any of the extra work the warmer weather made urgent. He had more than pulled his weight when it had been necessary.

Marjorie had got on with it, too, bringing out of store all her bits and pieces of antique furniture, and adding to them whenever she and Rosemary went to an auction sale, or on shopping sprees between scrubbing and cleaning, sewing and decorating, and in general enjoying themselves up at Monastery Farm. Within two weeks of Vic's funeral, Marge was happily installed in her new quarters, to the satisfaction of the principal characters involved, whatever other people chose to say about it.

The noticeable thing was how little was said, in spite of Sophie's dark prognostications. Fran and William agreed that the reason for it was that Bean & Co, though situated in Church End, belonged wholly to Lane's End. They had thrown their lot in with Bailey and the new.

Bailey had lost no time in making a deal with Brian Bridgefoot for what was now wholly Majorie's house and farm, and was in negotiation with Bridgefoot Farms Ltd for the purchase of other fields if he could secure planning permission for them. Swithinford itself was destined to go on growing, and having been baulked on the Old Swithinford side of the town, Bailey was making the most of the opportunity Vic's death had provided for a foothold on the other side.

Monica reported to Fran that she was a bit worried about Greg, though as yet she couldn't put much pressure on him. He was so happy that she couldn't bear to remind him of his obligations to what was, after all, his business as well as hers. The time would come when she'd have to ask him to set out on his travels again, though he didn't want to leave home and Jess, and had started painting furiously – portrait painting; besides having to care for Jonce (as he was fast becoming to them all), while Jess was at work. Monica could hardly pull the plug out of her father's business, especially while there was still such a great doubt hanging over them all about the Petrie children.

Fran was intrigued by all this, mainly because she, too, was suffering from spring-fever but had nothing particular to work on. Ideas were sprouting in her head, and she was giving them time to grow. She loved this gestation period of her work most of all. It didn't require her to sit at her desk and stare at the keys of her typewriter, or do anything but carry the ideas about with her wherever she went. So she made the most of the spring sunshine, visiting. Especially Beth, who was within a few weeks of full term for her baby. She had been booked into the most exclusive of

Cambridge's maternity homes, much to her own disgust, but to keep Elyot sane. Fran promised that she would be on hand to help whichever of them needed her support most. Best of all was that Greg, accompanied by Jonce, was a frequent visitor at Benedict's, and Jess had lost all her spikiness towards them. She didn't come to Benedict's often, being now far too hard at work and occupied with Jonce in the evenings, but Fran and William were always welcome at Southside House. Family feeling had been restored.

Castle Hill would become Bob's officially on Lady Day – the old traditional date for moving or changing jobs. There was a lovely sense of things being as they should be, and Fran was prepared to make the very most of it. The only thing spoiling it for her was that William was not responding to it quite as much as she thought he ought to be. He was himself as far as she was concerned, listening to her ideas even when he was half-asleep in bed, accompanying her willingly to see Kate and Jeremy, waving her off when she was only going as far as to see Beth, and waiting impatiently for her return; but she was the one person he couldn't fool. She tried to sum up what it was that was different about him, and decided that it fell into two separate categories. Unless he was actively engaged or deep in conversation, he tended to be terribly preoccupied with his own thoughts; and there were other times when he looked so weary and worn and worried that she began to suspect – as always – that either there was some trouble with Janice, his legal wife in America, or that he was ill.

When she couldn't stand it any longer, she asked what was the matter. She knew how dangerous it was, but her own nerves were getting strained, and the last thing she wanted was to leave it till there was one of their now very scarce but just as iconoclastic rows.

She chose their usual 'together-time', in bed on a Sunday morning, to broach the subject. One of her fears was set at rest the moment her question was spoken. If it had been Janice at the core of his abstraction, she would have felt the immediate tensing of every muscle down the whole length of him, instead of which his reaction was to pull himself up, tighten his arms round her, kiss the tip of her nose and laugh.

'Really, my sweetheart! Haven't we got beyond worrying about that, yet? I never give the woman a thought, except to be aggravated every time I look at a bank statement and see that she has the nerve to go on accepting maintenance from me when she lives rolling in wealth with her Jewish politician. I didn't think she worried you any more, my darling, my love . . . I just always wish she didn't exist, and never had done. You know why!'

'She doesn't as far as I am concerned. I just wish you wouldn't harp on our situation! If it isn't that, what is it worrying you?'

'It's been a very tiring year,' he said. 'Far more tiring, in fact, than ordinary work would have been, I think. It's been an absolutely crucial year for us all here in Old Swithinford. Our patch, where we belong. I don't want to give myself more credit than I ought, but I honestly believe that if it hadn't happened to coincide with my year off duty, things would have been very different by now from what they are. I was at liberty to put my finger into all sorts of pies I had no intention of doing at all. It probably turned the scale, just by chance – lucky chance.

'I guess our end of the village is safe for another half-century now from Bailey and his ilk, though of course Time by itself will bring other changes. As long as the centre holds firm now, I believe it will last our time, and still be here when the twenty-first century comes in. I think I cared more than I knew I did. I expect that's why I've found it all so wearing, so tiring. And there's still more to be done.'

She had been listening intently, following his every thought and word. 'I see, my darling. In fact, you've been playing the role you were cut out for. Every tribe has its headman. The village had to have a leader, especially when the church more or less gave up. You've played the squire, one of the old sort of squires who looked after all the rest of the tribe and protected them where he could from rich newcomers. Not one of the sort that thought only of feathering his own nest. If you hadn't picked up the headman's role when you did, who would have done? Bailey, with Brian Bridgefoot and Vic Gifford as his bailiffs and Kid Bean as his agent? A fat lot of chance people like Sophie would have stood against them! Or the Petries, whom you and Joe Noble took under your wings. Then there was all that family worry over Roland, and about Jess and Greg – I don't wonder you're worn out. It's been pretty nearly non-stop. I'm sorry, sweetheart, I didn't realize. Can't you stop now, and take a rest?'

'I need a rest and time to myself now – *now*.'

'Why now, especially?'

'Because I'm so excited I can't wait – and I've got to. If I'm touchy, that's why. It's that book Bob landed me with on Sunday. The sort of thing any historian would give his eyebrows for has just fallen into my lap.'

'We'll go for our holiday as soon as we can. I can't go away till Beth's had her baby. I've promised. But by May all the wedding plans should be in hand and the baby safely born. Get in touch with Effendi to make sure nobody else wants his cottage in May. It would be wonderful.'

'Haven't you forgotten something? The thing worrying me most of all? We can't, and I won't, go away till I know for certain what's going to happen to John's family. I may have to go into battle for the custody of Jonce and do what I can to keep the others where they are, loved and wanted. So there you are – you can stop worrying about me.

'As you are,' he said. 'I know. Now do stop, please. It will only add to my depression if I know I'm upsetting you.' She thought it best not to pursue the subject any further.

It was Sophie who brought the matter of the Schoolhouse to their attention. The old schoolmistress, Mary Budd, had been a figure of hero-worship to Sophie all her life, and when she had died, Sophie had rejoiced that she had left her little home just as it was to her niece, Anne Rushlake, who had come to live in it. But when, at Christmas last year, Sophie had heard that Anne had 'took up with' one of Bailey's employees, and that he had gone to live in the Schoolhouse with her, Sophie regarded it as desecration to a holy temple. What would her beloved 'Miss' have said to such goings-on in her house?

However, it now transpired that Anne and her man had been married at Christmas. The temple of Sophie's idol had not been polluted by a middle-aged affair. Nor had Anne's husband been made redundant by Bailey; he had been given his old job back as Clerk of the Works to Bailey's new venture of setting up the riding and livery stables on Vic Gifford's former farm, and with it one of the six dwellings Bailey had obtained permission to build there.

'So she's a-gooing to live there as well, as is only right and proper, seeing as she is 'is wife after all,' Sophie reported. 'Though she's keeping 'er job at the 'otel. I know that's the truth, 'cos Choppen told Marge, and Marge told her father, so it come to us through Dan'el. And I says to Thirz', "Lawks, Thirz'," I said, "that means as somebody else new'll be coming to live in the School'ouse. Oh dear, 'ooever shall we hev living there now, I wonder? Like as not somebody as'll turn it inside out and put new-fangled windows and such into it so as it won't be Miss Budd's 'ouse as we've knowed it no more."'

She went sorrowfully away, leaving Fran to share her regret about the house. It could hardly be said of either that they regretted the removal of Anne from their midst.

Next day, Sophie announced to William, who was in his study, that 'our Het's Joe' was there and asking to see him. William, who was in bored conscientiousness trying to do a bit to his official research, was thoroughly glad of the diversion. 'Bring him in,' he said.

Joe appeared wearing a rather diffident, slightly embarrassed look, and William saw at a glance that he was not in his 'working clobber'. William held out his hand as to the friend Joe had become, guessing by Joe's attitude that whatever it was he had come to say, it was up to himself to take the lead.

'What can I do for you, Joe?' he asked. 'And what are you doing here on a lovely fine day like this?'

He saw that he had put his finger right on the spot. Joe's usually bright, honest and cheerful face was clouded for a second or two with a flush of anger.

'Looking for a new job,' he answered bluntly.

William was appalled. 'You mean you've been sacked? Because you stayed away too long?'

'No, sir, I ain't been sacked. I'm throwed me job up, after forty odd year. I started working there the day after I left school, and I expected to go on working there till I took my pension, but the new boss was only waiting for an excuse to get rid o' me. He wanted young'uns as was trained mechanics, even if he did have to pay 'em a lot more. Though I could turn my hand to most things, I were still only just "ole Joe" as 'd do anything and everything. Took for granted, like.

'Well, when I started going about with Dafydd Pugh, the boss took again' it, and me. So I asked him what it were to do with him, and he said as I was making a laughing-stock o' him and his business, as well as myself. And he wasn't going to have no more o' this getting off home early. I never had been one to be off home to the minute – I'd all'us stop and finish the job. But you see, if I were going out with Daffy somewhere, I had to be home and washed and changed by the time he wanted to go, so I'd told the boss I should be going home same time as all the others. Didn't he throw hisself about! Good as told me I could have me cards there and then if he couldn't rely on me like he'd all'us done till then. I were upset enough as it were, without that.

'Het were throwing herself about at home, and Thirz' putting her spoke in – and I made my mind up as nobody should stop me from doing what I had set my heart on. I told the boss so and asked if I could leave off work a bit early for a few days to help somebody as needed me more than he did. I said as I'd work overtime other days to make up for it, or else he could dock the time off my wages. I never thought he would, but he did.

'Well, then come that week. Seems that the garage forecourt man went off that Sat'day with the flu, which I didn't know, though if I had it wouldn't ha' made no difference, and the boss said not to worry, come Monday morning Joe'd see to it. Come Monday morning, I'd gone to Wales.

'I knowed what sort of a bust-up there'd be when I did go back, so I were ready for him. I told him as I hadn't been at his beck and call for nigh on fifty year only to be treated now like a little old boy as had played hookey to go fishing, so he needn't bother to threaten me with the sack. So he clumb down, till last Friday night when we had words again.'

'He never thought I meant it, and laughed. He's found out as I did mean it.'

William was really disturbed by this consequence, and felt that it was all his fault.

'So now you haven't got a job. What can I do to help?' asked William, rather helplessly.

'Give me the reference as he won't, for one thing, sir. And if you should happen to hear of anything going, let me know. We shan't starve yet.'

'And how has Hetty taken it all? Sophie hasn't said a word about it.'

'Her and Thirz' don't know nothing about it, so far. It's all muddled up, like, with things as go back years. Het were a pretty little thing when I married her, but silly, like, 'cos her mother had sp'iled her so. Soph' and Thirz' both knowed how she was, but I didn't, until I found as I'd married the whull blooming fam'ly, all three o' the sisters as well as their mother!

'When Het started fetching Thirz' up to stop me doing what I wanted, I knowed the time had come for me to put my foot down. And I did. I told Thirz' to mind her own business and I let Het know who was the boss in our house – me, not Thirz'. Do y'know, Het's been as different as can be, since then. A'most as if she was wanting me to do what I had. So when all this happened last Friday, I went straight home and told Het how things stood. And I said as it was our business and nobody else's, and she'd better keep Thirz' and Soph' out of it. Well, I never would ha' believed the way she took it! She never had no sign of sterricks at all. She said she reckoned as I should soon find another job, and so could she, soon as Stevie were old enough to go to school. Doing housework and such, like both of her sisters did. We talked things over real sensible.

'What it amounts to is that that house we live in in Hen Street is too big, and too posh for us. There's nobody there now as Het wants to neighbour with. It's our'n, all bought and paid for, and if we was to sell it and get a smaller, older place, there'd be a fair bit o' cash to put by with what I'm got a'ready in the Co-op, so we could very like get along for quite a while if I didn't get another job quick. I never thought Het 'd ever agree to such a thing as that, 'cos she's all'us been so proud of living in such a lot posher house than her sisters. But it ain't her, after all, as is making a song and dance about it. It's me. Come this morning, and I ain't got no work to go to, I'm sort of mazed, like. I can't help wondering how long it'll be before Het goes back on what she said. Tha's why, if you see what I mean, sir, I felt as I had to tell somebody. I do hope as I ain't done wrong by Het and Stevie. Whatever Thirz'll say when she knows, I daren't hardly think.'

William felt honoured by Joe's confidence, but humbled and ashamed of his own petulance about the Petrie business dragging on so that he couldn't do what he wanted. He had no right to grumble! What he had to do first was see if there was any way he could possibly help Joe out.

'You did what you thought right, Joe. And I've always thought Hetty would be better to rely more on you and less on Thirzah. If I were you, I would tell Hetty's sisters yourself before they hear about it from anybody else, and then ask their advice, whether you want it or not. They'd be your very best allies. And of course I'll do what I can.

'Have you heard any more at all from Pugh? It may be that, getting about as he does on the spot, he could find out more about Crystal than the police can. You will let me know if you do hear from him, won't you? And now, how am I going to explain your visit here this morning to Sophie? She knows you ought to be at work.'

'Yes, I never thought about that till it were too late,' said Joe miserably.

'Then let me fetch her in, so you can tell her now, and then take her with you and go up and break the news to Thirzah together.'

Fran had gone to visit Beth before Joe had arrived, so William took his orders from Sophie regarding lunch, and went back to his study to await Fran's return and tell her.

He had no idea why Joe's visit should have cheered him up, but it had. As far as he could see, there was nothing he could do to help Joe. Nevertheless, once Sophie and Joe had plodded off, he felt better. He even got on well with writing up a bit of the obscure medieval research in which he was only minimally interested. He felt, without the least obvious cause, suddenly much more optimistic again. When Fran came back, she noticed the change in his mood at once, and asked what had happened to cause it. He told her of Joe's visit, adding that he didn't know at all why Joe's news should have any effect on him other than making him feel guilty.

'I ought to feel worse,' he said. 'We certainly can't employ him, and I don't know of anybody else who is likely to need a full-time man. All the same, for some reason the clouds have lifted. Perhaps it is because I decided that I had to take a chance on fixing our holiday while I could. If absolutely necessary, I could come back for a couple of days to a magistrate's court, or anything of that nature with regard to the children. Lucky for us that nobody else has asked for Plas Uchaf in May.'

'Plas Uchaf? What's that in English? And where is it exactly?'

'I had to ask how to spell it. It means "High Place", and is on top of a rise outside the village of Cregrina, in Powys. Mid-Wales, I suppose you'd call it.'

'No wonder you feel better if we are on our way to another high place. I am glad you have decided we can go then. Beth's baby is due four weeks today. If it's on time, it will leave just a week before the first of May. There'll be a lot to get in to such a short time.'

That sobered him again. There was always the concern about the children's long-term future. She saw his face drop, and put up her hand to it.

'No,' she said. 'Keep smiling. Lady Luck may be watching, ready to smile back at those who smile at her first.'

As if in response to Fran, things began to go right, as when Sophie arrived a few days later, brimming over with excitement and the tidings that Joe and Hetty had let it be known that they were selling their semi in Hen Street and would soon be moving.

'Where to?' asked Fran, unbelieving.

Sophie had no intention of dropping the gem of her news till she was ready.

'It's one o' them lucky chances as happen when you least expect 'em,' she said. 'I remember saying the same to you when Jelly left me all that money. I said to you then, and I'll say it again, as when things go wrong, like Jelly getting killed, we put it down to the will of 'Im Above, as if we're all blaming 'Im for letting it 'appen. But when they go right, like Jelly winning all that money, we only call it good luck. My belief is that 'E means us to be 'appy sometimes, like sometimes things is bad for us. I told Joe to keep 'is 'eart up, 'cos everybody's bound to be up and down, like at some time or other. And I told 'im that nobody ever deserved better from 'Im Above than 'e did 'isself. "You just remember, Joe Noble," I says, "that when God shuts one door, 'E all'us opens another." And that's just what 'E 'as done. Praise be.'

There were times when Fran had an almost insane desire to rush on Sophie and shake words out of her. She thought she would certainly scream if Sophie didn't soon get to the point.

'Sophie,' she said, 'I dare say you did find out how Will's mother is on your way round to where she lives, but for once I don't care. I want to know about Joe and Hetty's house, and if you don't tell me, I'll strangle you with the dishcloth.'

'That won't do you no good, would it? I'm 'eard it said a good many times as dead folks tell no tales.'

William shouted with laughter at Sophie's repartee, and Fran stood up, and threw her arms round Sophie's neck. 'Please, Sophie,' she pleaded.

Sophie sat down suddenly, not knowing whether to laugh or cry.

'Joe and Het are going to live in Miss's little School'ouse,' she said. 'Seems when Joe 'eard it was for sale from me a-Monday, 'e went straight to see that Mr Chessman to ask 'ow much they wanted for it, 'cos whether they could buy it depended on them selling their own 'ouse in 'En Street. Well, it so 'appens that Bailey wants to buy any 'ouses as are up for sale in 'En Street, so as 'e can fill it all in and j'ine it to Lane's End in years to come. So Chessman said 'e'd see to it, and it's all set up, only they've all got to wait to move till the new 'ouse for Anne Rushlake-as-was and 'er new 'usband is ready. In the summer.'

Fran gasped. They had heard the startling news at last, at the cost to Sophie of no more than thirteen dropped aspirates. She began to laugh, and William joined in, while Sophie, looking from one to the other, let her own joy out as well. Between peals, Sophie managed to say, 'And you ain't 'eard all of it yet. Het's been to see if she can hev 'er old job back doing Jess's 'ousework. That littl'un they call Jonce is just the same age as our Stevie, and Het reckons two of 'em 'll be as easy to deal with as one.'

Smile on Lady Luck and she smiles back. Fran's smile was wide enough to encompass the world but rested on Sophie – and William.

68

Monica wanted another wedding conference, ladies only, including Rosemary and Molly, and if Jane didn't mind, Fran as well. Charlie, of course, would have to be there, so a Friday evening would be best. She suggested that all their respective men should be deliberately excluded, and given notice that they were not wanted, so that they could make their own arrangements to spend the evening as they wished.

'It sounds intriguing,' Fran said, when Monica put it to her. 'Why am I invited? Don't tread on any toes. What are you up to?'

'Wait and see. I'm asking for you to be there because I may need a bit of backing.'

'Count me in,' Fran said, 'as long as Jane agrees.'

The six women foregathered at Castle Hill. There was, they all agreed, something very nice in being just females together. 'Like hen chaffinches in winter,' Fran said. Then they gave Monica the floor.

'If I may begin by being Monique O'Dell,' she said, 'I must say you've presented me with a bit of a poser. An order for the wedding of the year, around these parts, with no holds barred about cost – but without the necessary personnel to make a splash. At Lucy's wedding a bride and four bridesmaids, and men to match. A set-up to rejoice the heart of any aspiring couturier. All I've got this time is the bride and one bridesmaid! So I've had to do a lot of thinking, and some research for a different sort of set-up from what everybody is expecting. May I tell you what I've been thinking?

'Lucy's wedding was a village wedding, but the bridegroom's side weren't village people. They were posh London folk, mostly professional people. It had to be an orthodox wedding. This one's different, a real village wedding, a farmer's daughter marrying a farmer, a truly country occasion. So why not go out of the way to make it more so? What I'd like to do is to step back a bit in time. Take the question of transport, for example. Cars, however grand they are, can be a nuisance if they are not really necessary.

'From my point of view, they spoil things. I get terribly annoyed at seeing a beautiful dress crushed into a car – even a Rolls – and messed up by being posed silly ways to please the photographers, and show off the car, not the bride or the dress. You know the sort of thing I mean – pictures of the bride getting into the car, or out of it, hanging on to her father's arm – oh well, you know as well as I do. I'm sure by the time they get into the church half of them have forgotten what they have come for! Photographs are all right, but spare me from modern photographers! A lot of them regard themselves as the Master of Ceremonies. I've had them rearranging a bride's veil after I had put it on, and once one of them actually took the bride's bouquet apart and rearranged it because it wasn't "the right line" for his shot of her in the drawing-room before setting out. If the time comes for my daughter to get married, there will be no official photographers, or you can look out for a headline next day – "BRIDE'S MOTHER SHOOTS PHOTOGRAPHER." Sorry, that's my hobby-horse, and I got carried away. But who, honestly, wants pictures of cars?'

There was a murmur of agreement. 'What are you getting at, Monica?' asked Fran.

'Can't we dispense with cars? What did they do in villages before everybody had one? How did you go to church on your wedding day, Mrs Bridgefoot?'

'Car,' said Molly. 'The first bride ever to do so in Old Swithinford. It was only a two-seater with a dickey and Dad and me and two bridesmaids all had to sit on each other's knees, and a right old squash it was!'

'And how did Mr Bridgefoot get there?'

'From the Old Glebe? Walked, of course. It's only a hop, skip and a jump from there to the church, anyway.'

Monica crowed with delight, grabbing Molly and kissing her. 'There you are then – this time everybody walks, if you agree, at least from the Old Glebe onwards. The bride and her father go last, with the brides-maids in front, right to the chancel.'

'Bridesmaids?' asked Jane, doubtfully, with an eye on Charlie.

'Yes – maids, in the true sense, escorting another maid to a ceremony that officially changes her status. Pretty young girls dressed in their best, scattering innocent flowers for the bride to tread underfoot. The origin of paper confetti. What was thrown at the married couple coming out of church was rice – to symbolize fertility.'

'Go on,' said Jane, still looking dubious. 'What if it rains?'

'In June? Don't be so pessimistic. June's the month of roses. Oodles of rose petals to be strewn at Charlie's feet. A rose wedding, Charlie a white rose, Poppy a deep pink one with a golden centre, and all the others in other varying shades of pink. Doesn't that sound nice?'

'Yes – but what others?' Jane had dared at last to voice the question.

'The pretty maids all in a row? Why, the Petrie girls, of course. Four of them and Poppy makes five, enough for a real show from my point of view. Little Georgina as well if she'll co-operate – and isn't there a little girl that Bob's particularly fond of? The one whose kitten Bailey shot?'

'Patty Barlow?' Jane said.

'Would anyone mind? My quid pro quo is no fee at all for those extra dresses, but permission to use my own photographer, with Greg doing watercolours for the glossy magazines. We should probably set a new fashion. But of course it depends on you all agreeing, especially Charlie. It's her wedding.'

Charlie's feelings were undergoing a good deal of emotional turmoil. Until now, she had given very little thought to her wedding as a social occasion, with herself as 'the bride', so often that simpering creature whose only thought was of herself being the centre of attention, on her 'special' day. She had regarded the ceremony as necessary to join her life permanently to Charles's, and to make herself conventionally part of the Bridgefoot family. By wearing a traditional white wedding dress, she hoped to make it plain to them that she hadn't seduced their son to marry her or allowed him to seduce her.

But Monica had made her think further. The function of the brides-maids was to escort to church a maid who would soon be a maid no longer. That was what this wedding meant – not all the frocks and the reception and the party. Above all, what she wanted was to be Charles's *wife*. There were other things to commend Monica's plan.

With Effendi and his chequebook in the background, and the friends he would want to bring to the wedding; with Charles's equally grand connections in Alex and his titled family, there was a danger of the farmers being swamped.

She didn't want her Dad to feel, as Charles's family might, second-class citizens in their own environment. She wanted her country forebears and Charles's to feel that it was their affair, built on caring and custom, not what money and prestige could do to make it 'the wedding of the season' for miles around. She looked at Jane, before she answered.

Jane had her eyes fixed on Charlie, silently begging her to agree, though for a very different reason. The complete informality of what Monica had been proposing would reduce the strain on Poppy of having to be escorted by a Nick who didn't even remember who she was, and on Charles, who would be only too much aware that his best man couldn't and wouldn't remember their earlier friendship, or the third of their trio, Robert, on whose grave she guessed Charlie's bouquet would eventually rest.

Charlie got the message that Jane liked the idea as much as she did, and said so. Nobody else raised a single objection.

William had invited Bob to spend that Friday evening with him, and intended taking Bob to visit Eric for the first time. He watched Fran go without him, as always conscious of a hollowness inside him caused by irrational fear that she might never come back. He looked at the clock, which told him that he could not expect Bob for at least another hour, and did not know what to do with himself while he waited. It was too short a time to go to his study to start work, but the last thing he wanted was to sit alone and think. For the time being, he had managed to shelve the immediate worry about the Petrie children, and he didn't want to start it up again till he was forced to.

Consequently, it was with genuine pleasure that he recognized the figure on a push-bike wobbling up the tradesmen's entrance through the garden as Joe Noble. There was no one he would rather see. He and Joe had business to do together regarding the sale of the Dormobile, and so on.

William went to the back door to let him in, and took him into the kitchen. They sat down, one each side of the table, Joe hanging his cap over his knee in the way of all countrymen.

'Is it about the van?' William asked. 'I haven't got long to spare just now. I'm waiting for Bob Bellamy, who may arrive at any minute.'

'Don't matter,' said Joe. 'Sophie let on as you were likely to be here by yourself tonight, and that's why I come. So's she – I mean Soph', not Mis' Catherwood – didn't hear all I had to say. Not that Soph's a gossip, 'cos she ain't. But the fewer as knows everything the better, I reckon. I'm had a letter from Dafydd Pugh. I thought you ought to see it soon as you could.'

He handed the long letter to William. It was couched, at least at the beginning, like Pugh's other note to Joe, in a style reminiscent of a Cromwell or a Bunyan. But after the first 'brother-in-Christ' sentences, the ordinary man with a tale to tell took over, which made for much easier reading. Pugh wanted his car, which he had left at Danesum. Would Joe keep his eye on it for him?

He then returned to the Petrie family, and his evangelical style. It had been his wish to turn Crystal from her evil ways and help her to 'see the light'. But it had ended in his giving way to sin himself, in backsliding, hypocrisy, and lust.

'The woman tempted me,' he wrote, 'but as God is my witness, I did not eat of the fruit of sin. I let her persuade me, as Eve persuaded Adam, that I should be doing no wrong, but instead doing God's work to see her and those four children safely to where their protector could take the others to join them when he recovered.'

William looked up from his reading. 'Very much the same as he said in his note,' he remarked. 'You can't help feeling sorry for him. He's a very mixed-up man.'

'I reckon he's knowed all along which way he's most likely to go to hell,' Joe said. 'He's been brought up Welsh chapel, and he's frightened of hell-fire, else he'd be after every woman as come his way. Het's told me that's why she took again' him so. "I could see it in him," she said. "He's got hot eyes, hot as hell-fire they are." And I, I could see what she meant. When he were a-preaching, sometimes, it was as if his eyes were like red-hot coals, like, with feeling. But Het meant they was the same when he looked at a woman, burning for the devil and not for Christ at all. Say what you may, women are quicker at things like that than us men are.'

William agreed and went on reading the letter. As soon as the weather improved, Pugh had gone to the camp, but there was no trace of the van or the trailer, or of Crystal or the children. He said that he felt guilty again then, only in a different way. To save himself from the sin of lust, he had left those four defenceless children in the care of a woman such as he now knew Crystal to be.

'Must ha' been blind, afore, then,' Joe said, bitterly. 'There's none so blind as them as won't see. How did he think she come by them eight children?'

William sympathized with poor Joe's disillusionment, but he wanted to read to the end of the letter.

Pugh had gone on trying to find Crystal, and at last had met Basher, who took him to where she was living now in an old bus with the man she claimed was Basher's father. Crystal had not been at all pleased to see him.

She said that she didn't know what had happened to the van or the children. She'd left them safely asleep and taken Basher with her for a short visit to some friends, and when she got back the van had gone. The man in the next caravan told her it had been driven away by two strangers. He had described a tall thin one so well that she guessed it was Petrie, who must therefore be all right again. She said that if he wanted the children so bad he was welcome to them. She hoped she'd never see the little b*** again. He had tried to reason with her, kneeling down and inviting her to pray with him, but her man put a stop to it. He told Pugh he was wasting his breath – couldn't he see that she was high? She left the bus then, and left him talking to the man.

The man said that she was the same as she always had been. She only did as she liked. He didn't want to keep her and wasn't prepared to own Basher's parentage because nobody could ever be sure anyway. He was afraid of her making off and leaving Basher with him. He hoped somebody was looking for her to find out what had happened to the rest of her children. That's why he was letting her stop with him a bit longer – so that she had an address where she could be found, till either she went or he turned her out. (Pugh said that Joe would find the address at the end of the letter.)

After which Pugh entreated Joe to pray for him, the repentant sinner. It would ease his conscience if Joe could let him know any news of the four girls he had helped Crystal to abandon, and any other news of the Petrie family.

William handed the letter back to Joe, who was looking very grim. 'It caps my behind to think as I should ever have got mixed up with such a man,' he said. 'Took me in proper, he did.'

'Don't be too hard on him, Joe,' William said. 'He truly didn't mean to do anything but good. It isn't him that is bad, it's religion gone crazy, as it so often does. He was strong enough to resist a sex-crazy woman like Crystal, and honest enough to tell you how she nearly broke him down. Besides, in the end he has done a lot of good. What he did for the wrong reasons helped. John went to look for his family and died knowing they were safe in your hands. Now Pugh has put us on to Crystal, and his letter is evidence that she neither wants nor is fit to have her children back. That's a real ray of hope. Then there's what has happened to you.

So much has turned out well for you that you must give him a tiny bit of credit for it. All that remains is for you to get another job.'

'I'm got one for the time being, helping Charles Bridgefoot to make a garden down Danesum. I'm all'us enjoyed gardening. I keep thinking, once we're got moved and all square, I shall set myself up as a jobbing gardener, like. There'd all'us be work for me at harvest-time, seeing as I can turn my hand to mending tractors and such. I ain't worried about a job, yet.' He was putting on his cap to go as Bob arrived.

It was a much lighter-hearted William who set out with Bob to Monastery Farm than he had been for a long time.

69

The change in William's morale was plain to Fran the moment he opened the front door to her. She laughed, and taking herself out of his arms to push him away so as to be able to look him up and down, said, 'I see that Pilgrim's burden has been loosed from off his shoulders. I hope it isn't all because of what Eric has been treating you to from his cellar.'

'No,' he said. 'But I did meet with Mr Noble tonight, and it may be that the Hill Difficulty may not be so hard to climb as we thought.'

They talked until nearly midnight, and went to bed happily optimistic. Easter was only one week away, and the weather next morning seemed determined to show just how beautiful an English spring could be.

'Think,' William reminded Fran, 'what we were doing last Easter! Up to our necks in intrigue . . .'

'Gosh!' she broke in. 'Was all that only one year ago? I wouldn't believe it, except that I know perfectly well what tricks Time plays on us.'

'It's made us a whole year older,' he said, a bit ruefully.

'So what? I don't feel a day older,' she said. 'And you don't look it, now. Last week you began to resemble the sedge withering on the lake, so haggard and so woebegone did you appear. This morning you look as if you could push a bus over.'

'That isn't worthy of you, after all that Keatsian stuff,' he said. 'And who in his right mind would want to push a bus over?'

'It's a sign of the times,' she said. 'Even our language goes on changing, and we have to keep up with it or be thrown with the rest of old-fogeyism into the rubbish bin – sorry, I mean the trashcan, don't I? We belong to the last generation who'll recognize any reference to the Bible or any bit of Eng. Lit. they haven't actually studied for their A-level exams. We show our age that way, you know. Maybe we ought to bring our English up to date, and forget all those old-fashioned poets.'

'Are you trying to depress me again? The day you stop quoting will put me into sackcloth and ashes, because it will mean you are sleeping with your fathers instead of with me. Come back to the present, my sweetheart. We have a lot to do, if we're going to be away for the whole of May. Have you told Sophie, yet, that we are hoping to be away for a whole month?'

'I didn't dare, while you were so depressed,' she said, 'in case it didn't come off after all. We'll tell her this morning, if you're sure. But what about Cat? We've never before both left her for anything more than a week.'

'I'll talk to Ned,' he said. 'He's nearly as daft about her as we are.'

As a consequence, Ned was in the kitchen when Sophie arrived, and it seemed as good a time as any for an all-in conference.

That Sophie's spirits were also high they needed no telling. Seeing Ned sitting at the kitchen table, she understood at once that news of some kind was in the air. She went to fetch her apron, but instead of putting it on in the utility-room as she usually did, she brought it in with her, and proceded to go into the contortions necessary for tying her apron-strings into a bow in the middle of her back as she got her word in first.

'Looks as if we're going to hev a real good do for young Charles's wedding after all,' she said. 'Me and Thirz' had a'most give up 'ope as we should be wanted, this time, seeing as 'ow Mis' Bellamy's father's so well off and thinks so much o' Mr Bellamy's daughter. But we was asked last night to go up to Old Glebe to see Molly and Rosemary Bridgefoot, who told us the Bellamys wanted to share all the wedding arrangements with the Bridgefoots, and 'ow 'appy they was to be let in like that to do their bit. So the do in the barn at night'll all be done their way, same as usual. The posh do for all the folks from London and such'll be at the 'otel, like they was before, but me and Thirz' 'as been asked to do everything in the barn come the evening, just as we should ha' done for a horkey.

'I can't get over it all being such a friendly, 'omely do between them at Castle 'Ill and the Bridgefoots, seeing 'ow nasty things was between 'em not so long ago. I'm glad for George's sake. 'E's 'ad a lot o' trouble, one way or another, this last few year. I 'ope as Marge don't go and upset the applecart now, seeing as the others are all right.' Diverted from their purpose, as she had known they would be, they rose to her bait.

'Marge?' Fran asked. 'How could she upset the applecart? Her Poppy's going to be chief bridesmaid. It all seems very close and friendly.'

'Too friendly with some, by all accounts,' Sophie said. 'Folks are beginning to talk, according to Thirz'. That Olive 'Opkins sees too much now she works down in them offices close to Monastery Farm. But there, I never should ha' mentioned it, and I'll say no more.' She shut her mouth into a determined straight line, as if to seal inside it any words struggling to get out.

Fran had the misfortune to catch William's eye, and found it necessary to turn a gurgle of mirth into a bad bout of coughing. William, knowing her difficulty and secretly rejoicing at the reappearance of this lovable characteristic of hers, which just lately he had missed a lot, patted her back and suggested he should put the kettle on to make coffee for them all. He then turned his face away, and stood over the sink, whistling the first thing that came into his head. It was perhaps unfortunate that what rose to his lips was the tune of 'Here's to the Maiden of Bashful Fifteen'.

Sophie looked at the back of his head with suspicion. 'Miss teached us that song at school,' she said. 'Funny thing for her to teach such as us, see-in' what the words to it were. But there you are, it fits pat enough to what I was saying. "An 'ere's to the widow o' fifty". Only she ain't fifty yet.'

'Who?' Fran managed to ask.

'Why, Marge Bridgefoot, as I were a-talking about,' Sophie said. 'I don't know what you're a-laughing about, 'cos it don't seem to me no laughing matter. But there, you very like know a lot as I don't. So if you want to laugh, laugh and be done with it. I can't see nothing funny meself in her getting herself talked about like that, specially with that Mr Choppen as a lot of folks still can't find a good word for.'

William controlled himself with an effort, and said, 'I wouldn't worry about that yet, Sophie, honestly. I was at Monastery Farm with Eric Choppen last night and he told me how satisfactory Mrs Gifford's tenancy of the other part of the house looked as if it might be. One reason he gave was that he hardly ever saw her. He doesn't know her yet, especially as Poppy has been home with her for a week or more. Will you finish making the coffee, Sophie? Come into my study, Fran. Give us about ten minutes, Sophie. Don't go, Ned – I want to ask Greg about something I need to talk to you about.'

They escaped, shut the study door, threw their arms round each other and had their laugh out.

Fran said, 'We're just in a giggly mood this morning. Anything would make us laugh. As Kezia would say, "two straws and a half". It's a long time since I felt so light-headed.'

'M'm,' William said. 'Praise be. That goes for me, too.'

In the kitchen, Sophie and Ned watched their retreating backs with affectionate bafflement.

'I dunno what's got into them two this morning,' Sophie said to Ned.

'They ain't been like this since just after Christmas. All that business down Danesum was properly getting 'im down. I were saying to Thirz' 'ow unpromising 'e looked. I'm sure we was all getting real worried about 'im.'

'So were I,' Ned agreed. 'Seemed to ha' lost his dossity all at once. I told Bill Edgeley so. "Looks as if he's been ate and spewed up again," I said, "like Jonah when he'd been in the whale's belly for three days." But there ain't nothing wrong with neither of 'em this morning.'

The lovely aroma of coffee met the two culprits as they went back into the kitchen. Sophie had taken the opportunity of warming up some scones and had them ready, oozing with butter, on the table. The smell of them was as appealing to the nose as the taste to the tongue. There was a general feeling of wonderful well-being in the air, body, mind and spirit all uplifted.

'I know as it's early for 'levenses,' Sophie said, 'but it'd ha' been daft to stop work again afore any of us 'ad got properly started, so I thought we might just as well have it now.'

They ate and drank not because they were hungry or thirsty, but because food was there, and the ease and contentment and trust in each other round the table was like salt adding savour. Neither Ned nor Sophie showed the least sign of embarrassment, or inquisitiveness about what the conference had been called for. Their calm patience told its own tale – that they were content to wait till they should be told in Fran and William's good time. The rush and bustle of twentieth-century life stood no chance against the peace of Benedict's kitchen.

When Cat strolled in, and chose Ned's lap to sit on, he pushed his chair back from the table to accommodate her, giving William his chance. There were no problems about leaving Cat. Ned would happily sleep in Eeyore's Tail as he had done once before, and see that both Cat and the house were cared for in William and Fran's absence.

It was clear to Fran that Sophie was weighing the whole situation up before saying what she thought.

'Tha's about the best bit o' news as I'm 'eard for a long while,' she said at last. 'I'm been wondering 'ow and when I could get a bit o' spring-cleaning done, proper spring-cleaning, I mean, not just a hextra turn-out, wi' both o' you 'ere and in and out all the while. It ain't been done proper since them decorators left it afore you come in,' she said. 'I don't suppose as you want me to paper none o' the rooms they done, but I shall do the flat again, as I done meself then, if you can find time to choose the paper as you want. I daresay Ned wouldn't be above giving me a 'and. I shall look forward to doing that, that I shall. And while I'm about it – me and Thirz' wondered if you'd let us use your kitchen and the stove to cook things special for the wedding refreshments. If we could get one or two more to 'elp us, with all the room there is 'ere and all the gadgets as you've got and that there cooker with four ovens, we could make a proper good job of it.'

She took it absolutely for granted that there would be no opposition to her plans. Weren't they all in this village do together?

'Just before the wedding?' Fran said, a rather dubious note in her voice. 'You know you are welcome, or you wouldn't have suggested it, but we shall only just have got home ourselves, and there'll be a great deal to do. We'll be bringing the Revd Delaprime back with us to marry Charles and Charlie.'

'We shan't be in your way, shall we?' Sophie replied. 'Whoever you bring 'ere won't have no call to spend the evening in the kitchen, will 'e? You can all put your feet up in that room as I shall ha' spring-cleaned all ready for you to come back to, and me and Thirz'll see as you don't starve.'

William looked at Ned, and dropped an eyelid at him behind Sophie's back.

'Don't worry, Fran,' he said. 'We can always go up to the hotel with the vicar to get a really well-cooked meal if we have to.'

'Hev the last scone, Ned, afore 'e does,' said Sophie, pretending to ignore William's teasing. 'I'll give 'im well-cooked food, that I will. Just let 'im wait.'

Fran and William went back to his study. 'Did you really need to talk to Greg?' she asked. 'Why don't we walk round now?'

'I believe you're narked at Sophie taking us so much for granted,' he said. 'Don't be. It's really a tremendous compliment.'

They found Greg at work in his studio, just putting the finishing touches to a large portrait of Jess reading to Jonce. Fran caught her breath at the sight of it. There could be no doubt that Greg's true metier as an artist was the portrait.

Greg said it was so satisfying to him that he thought Fran must be right. William, who had been as stunned as Fran by the wet canvas still on the easel, told him bluntly that from now on he should stop messing about with things like bird books and advertisements, and take the bold step into portrait painting.

'I can't let Monica down,' Greg said. 'She not only gave me a chance to earn a decent living – she also inspired me to do my first real portrait. But I have talked to her. You see, I've actually got a commission for a large bit of portrait painting. No, I shan't give you even a hint, because I'm so afraid it might all fall through. But I can't do it in the time limit I've got if I have to go away for the business. I could attempt it if I was based here all the time, and still do all that Monica wants in the way of tossing off watercolour sketches for this wedding, or anything else she wants. To have to hurry my painting would defeat me. Bless her, she's an artist herself, and she understands. We've agreed that she will try to get the present manageress of the shop to take on what I've been doing, at least for a trial run, soon. I suppose what it amounts to is that I can be given extended leave, on condition that I rush to the rescue if there's any trouble, considering that Monica herself can't till the twins are a bit older. I was coming up to tell you this morning, but I came in here and picked up a brush – and that's fatal!'

'Where is Cupid – I mean Jonce?' Fran asked. 'You've caught him absolutely – that little frown of concentration is the essence of him, and what makes him so adorable. And you've caught Jess marvellously, too, looking . . . satisfied at last, I suppose. Oh, Greg, it's so wonderful. And William has a bit of hopeful news for you, too.'

William recounted the contents of Pugh's letter, and told Greg he and Joe were going to put all their cards before the 'authorities' – whoever in the long run they proved to be – as soon as the Bank Holiday break was over. 'Don't raise your hopes too high,' he said, 'though I truly think that there is more chance of you being able to keep Jonce than I dare suggest for any of the others. At any rate, I am going to fight for custody of him if I have to, which will amount to the same thing. Where did you say he was now?'

'I didn't. You didn't give me a chance. Sophie's sister Hetty has called for him to take him for a walk with Stevie – to get them used to each other, she says. I thought he'd be too scared to want to let me out of his sight, but he's used to doing what he's told, or asked to do. I suggested to Hetty that she took them up to the Old Rectory in case there was a chance he could see his sisters. It's funny – strange as the life was that he led before, he seems to have felt a security a lot of children nowadays never experience. It must have been badly shaken, but we seem to have got him in time for it not to have any lasting effects. I think any contact with the rest of his family now must be good for him. His world hasn't fallen completely to pieces. Anyway, he went off without a murmur so long as I assured him that I would be here when he came back.'

'We mustn't stay long,' Fran said. 'William said he had to see you, but I really don't know what about.'

'Nothing really,' William said. 'It was only an excuse to get us both away before we offended Sophie by our unwonted levity. We've been a bit glum, recently!'

They left, Fran deep in thought, particularly about Jess and Greg.

Things that happened to people were meat and drink to her. She was one of the few who really could say with absolute sincerity that they did love the human race, and never got tired of exploring its multitudinous silly faces.

She smiled up at William in apology for her silence. They walked on hand in hand. The touch communicated her thoughts to him. 'They've landed safely now, I think,' he said. 'I did begin to fear they wouldn't make it back to base. *Per ardua ad astra*. Greg's had struggles enough, but I have a feeling he's on his way up to the stars now.'

Benedict's, its warm pink glowing in the spring sunshine, came in sight ahead of them.

'Isn't it lovely?' Fran said, somewhat wistfully. 'I hate leaving it, even to go away with you. This is home. Truly, our lot has fallen in pleasant places.'

'It'll be here when we come back,' he said. 'You don't know yet the glorious feeling of coming home to it, but I do. It's almost worth going away just to get the pleasure of coming back. You don't really mind, do you?'

'Don't be silly,' she said. 'I'd go to Spitzbergen or South Georgia or anywhere else you really wanted me to go, let alone somewhere only as far away as Wales.'

'Gosh! Something smells good!' William said. 'I didn't know how hungry I was!'

70

Fran began to look forward to the first holiday she had ever taken with William, other than an occasional visit to her daughter. William was right in saying that they needed a break. He had always teased her about her tendency to want to be an agony aunt, but he could hardly blame her for getting him in so deeply in the matter of the old village's struggle for continuing existence. Why and how had it happened that they were somehow drawn into everybody else's affairs? Why was it them who always seemed to be in, as Sophie would say, 'at every verse's end'?

She could think of a dozen practical reasons, but she knew it wasn't just because they had the time and the means to put at the disposal of neighbours who had less of both. It went a lot deeper than that. It was because they *belonged* – that had been recognized from the moment Fran had reappeared at Benedict's, before William had really been part of the scene. She had been a link with the past. To the village drowning under the threat of being subsumed into modern Swithinford, she had been as the proverbial straw. The village had clutched at her, especially when William came to her side, and had never let go of them afterwards.

It held them bound by ties which, though tenuous, were very strong, and which they had never made any serious attempt to break. The two of them may have been 'standing aside' for many years, but once back again, they had soon become part of the dance.

> I hold thee by too many bands:
> Thou sayest farewell, and lo!
> I have thee by the hands,
> And will not let thee go.

It was time for Sophie to bring in her coffee, after which she must get off for her morning visit to Beth.

Now that the holiday in Wales was actually in prospect, she was impatient to be gone. The arrangement with Jane's father was that as soon as ever they could decide on a date, all he needed to do was to give one day's notice to 'Olwen', the Welsh farmer's wife who looked after Plas Uchaf, and who would then have it all ready for them, and be there to welcome them.

'When are you and 'im going off for your 'oliday, then?' Sophie asked when she came in. 'Most folks as go on 'oliday start telling everybody where they're going next year and when afore they get their coats off from the last one. Not that I know much about 'olidays. I've never been for one meself, though Het and Joe went to Yarmouth once, and Thirz' had a few days once with Cousin Tilda as went to live in Bungay. So when are you a-going?'

'Not till Mrs Franks has had her baby,' Fran answered. 'I promised her I would be on call if she needed me. She hasn't any family left.'

Sophie was all sympathy at once. 'It's times like that as you want your own,' she said. 'Thirz' still goes up to the Old Rectory and does for 'er, though they won't let 'er do much since she 'ad them bad turns last year. Mind you, the last one frit 'er enough to stop 'er eating quite so much, and old Dr 'Enderson were right – she's been a lot better for it. But she does what she can, and them two gels are all'us willing to 'elp if they can. She says they're such good gels – but then, we know that, don't we, seeing as we 'ad 'em 'ere? I'm sure I 'ope as it all goes well with the baby, and we want it to be a boy to keep the fam'ly name going. It'll most like be the only one, seeing 'ow old they both are.'

Fran thought about that as she walked up to the Old Rectory, and Beth came to greet her. Fran did not feel so sure as Sophie that this would be their one and only child. They had more vigour and *joie de vivre* than a lot of people half their age. Beth showed no sign of apprehension, though she was already two days overdue by the doctor's calculations.

'You're a real friend, Fran,' Beth said, kissing her. 'Standing in for all the anxious female relations I haven't got. I expect they would have been like Thirzah if I had had any, reminding me how old I am, and how difficult birth can be, and giving me hints what to expect – as if I was fifteen and had "got myself into trouble". A very difficult thing to do, I imagine, in spite of the Virgin Mary's example. I guess I know quite as much about the extraordinary ways of nature as Thirzah does, or most women of my age, in actual fact.

'Elyot's a very different cup of tea. I hope you're not letting his he-man-Naval-Commander-unruffled-by-anything-pose fool you. He's as nervous as the proverbial kitten. The bravado is all put on. When they asked him if he wanted to stay with me for the birth, he turned quite green and said, "Yes, of course", as wooden-faced as if he had been saying "Aye aye, sir" to an admiral. I daren't tell him I didn't want him – but we shall see what we shall see.

'I don't suppose he has the faintest idea of what he would be letting himself in for, whereas I, though he doesn't know it, do. I've acted as midwife in East End slum houses where the husband was roaring drunk and I've had to barricade the door to keep him out, and where there wasn't a shilling to put in the gas meter to boil a kettle; or where I've had to tell a terrified young doctor trying to deliver a breech birth what to do next; or where the mother was only fourteen and truly had no idea what was happening to her until I put the baby in her arms.'

Fran was quite flabbergasted. 'Honest, Beth? You've never said a word!'

Beth smiled. 'I didn't think it would suit the image expected of me in Old Swithinford even if Father hadn't been trying to make me into the barmy old maid he feared he had on his hands for the rest of his life. Anyway, I told you to assure you that you needn't worry about me. I'm perfectly well, perfectly healthy, and am assured that everything is as normal as can be. Can I trust you just to keep your eye on Elyot, bless him . . . ? It's him I'm worried about, not myself.'

'Let us know when you set off for Cambridge,' Fran said. 'Day or night. And as soon as we are allowed in, we'll be there to see you and A.B.C. Does Elyot really mean to call your baby after his old admiral if it's a boy? Or are you both pulling our legs? What if it's a girl? What will A.B.C. stand for then?'

'Fran, I honestly don't know! He's reluctant to talk about it – as if choosing a name were taking too much for granted. I don't care which sex it is or what it's called, as long as it's strong and healthy. I'll let Elyot choose, boy or girl.'

'I'm not aware of any female admirals, yet, though no doubt the time will come,' Fran said, laughing. 'But of course ships are always female, and some have female names. You may find yourself with a daughter named Arethusa Bellona Calliope!' She got up, preparing to leave. 'See you tomorrow, if you are still here. If not, good luck,' she said, giving Beth a hug.

'You're a bit out of date, Fran, though I must say I like the idea,' said Elyot from behind her. 'Wrong war for me, I fear! They were all First War cruisers, and I wouldn't have expected a woman to know even their names. I suppose that's the result of living with an historian. It's a nice idea, though – I hadn't thought about naming the baby after *ships*. What would you say, Beth, to a son named Ajax Bellerophon Centurion de ffranksbridge?'

'That if he were half the man his father is, I shouldn't care if he were called Lucifer Beelzebub,' she said. 'We haven't got long to wait, at any rate.'

They stood by the door to watch Fran off. The sight of them made her feel good. Everything made her feel good today, especially William, pretending to be looking at the trees, halfway up the drive where he had been watching and waiting for her.

They had barely finished lunch when the telephone rang. It was Beth.

'It looks as if things may be about to happen,' she said. 'Elyot won't believe me that there's no need to break all speed limits to get to the maternity home, or that it may be tomorrow before the curtain actually goes up. But he's got the car running outside the front door and it may be the easier option to let him get me there while he's still capable. We'll let you know as soon as there's any news.'

Fran had enough sense to keep William busy. If Beth was going to give birth in the next twenty-four hours, and all was well, they could be away on their own holiday in three days' time. It would be sensible to begin to plan. Today was Tuesday. If it was convenient to Gordon they could be away by Friday. She suggested that William should go up this very afternoon to see Nicholas Gordon at the cottage, to set it up. While he was gone, she would make lists of what they wanted to take, and she and Sophie would arrange what was to be done at Benedict's in their absence.

William went off at her bidding, wistfully envying Elyot his day while at the same time being very glad that it was Elyot and not himself who had to endure it.

He found the older of the two Nicks at ease in the sun by the window of the little cottage. Nick the younger had been sent off to work – rather unwillingly, his grandfather said. He had expected to be allowed to enjoy leisure until the Easter holiday was over. Jane had been adamant. Those were the conditions he had agreed to, she said, when he had asked to be allowed to spend the summer in Old Swithinford. Bob wouldn't over-work him. It was just a question of not being able to do as he liked just when he liked and how he liked, as it had been so far since he had come out of the clinic.

'It's still less than a year since I found Jane again, and she and Nick put a new purpose into my life,' Gordon said. 'But that isn't all. When I found myself dropped into the rural countryside of England, only sixty-odd miles from my home in London, I found it as completely foreign to me as many another country the other side of the world. Before I ever came here at all, and had only heard about it from Jane, very briefly, I was not prepared to find anything I should like except perhaps the countryside – and even that was the part of England most people had told me was as uninteresting as it was flat. But I'm proud of myself, William, that in the end I had enough sense to urge Jane to stay with Bob. It was a kind of intuition, I suppose. What I would have missed if I had persuaded her to leave you all and come back to town with me! I love everything about it, here. I hope I shall be wholly accepted as part of the community before long – I know from experience in other "foreign parts" that I mustn't take anything for granted. I simply love messing about on Bob's farm, doing whatever he asks me to do. I don't think I've ever met a girl who is Charlie's equal anywhere else – I only wish she were Jane's child, as well as Nick. And to see Jane so happy with those two babies makes me realize all that I missed when Nick was that age.'

'Babies!' said William, who had been carried away by listening. 'What I came for – or what Fran sent me to do – was to fix up with you our stay in Wales. She wouldn't consider leaving until the Franks's' baby had arrived safely, in case Beth needed her. Elyot took Beth into Cambridge early this afternoon. We ought to know by tomorrow morning that we are free to leave.'

'That's just the sort of thing I meant,' Gordon replied. 'Beth and Elyot could be just "the Franks's who live at the Old Rectory" – would be, if this were part of modern suburbia, but they're not. You've just proved it. All the rest of you are sharing this great event with them. So shall I be, now, till I know the news, wishing and hoping for them like everybody else. Does Jane know that Beth's gone into the maternity home? Will you excuse me a minute while I ring her and tell her?'

William was perfectly happy to wait till the new recruit to country-style living proved that he had learned the drill properly.

'How is Nick?' he asked, when Gordon came to sit down again.

The older man was immediately sobered. 'I don't know the answer,' he said. 'I suppose I have to say "frustrated". He has it in his mind that if he ever does recover his memory, it will be "here" – I think he means in this cottage. He tells me that occasionally he gets very strange feelings here – he goes to find something, a clean shirt, for example, knowing perfectly well where it is and which one he wants, but before he gets to it this strange feeling in his head propels him to look for a shirt of a colour he doesn't possess in an entirely different place. It rather frightens him, and makes him "feel queer" he says. Confused and unsure and slightly dizzy. It worries Jane, and me, a lot. We're afraid that the operation was not perhaps quite so successful as we thought and hoped. We can only go on hoping. Are you coming up to the farm? I'm going up to tea.'

William excused himself, saying he ought to go home in case Fran wanted him to take her in to Cambridge.

'Charlie's hard at work for her exams. They begin immediately after the new term starts,' Effendi said. 'I like to be there to help Jane so that Charlie feels she needn't. I wish I could buy this cottage, and call it "home",' he said. 'The flat in London and the cottage in Wales we could all share. But Manor Farms won't sell. I'm lucky to be able to rent it.'

'It isn't big enough to be a home,' William said. 'Possess your soul in patience. You never know what may turn up.'

'I've already had that sort of experience,' Gordon said, laughing. 'Finding you waiting for me on Cambridge station the very first time I ever came here. I thought "William" was a dumb East Anglian who ran a one-man taxi service. I've long ago discovered that very few East Anglians are "dumb" in any sense of the word.'

Once William reached home, he and Fran used the rest of the daylight to make what preparations they could towards getting away as soon as there was news of Beth. It seemed a long time since she had been taken to the maternity home. At supper-time, William asked Fran if she were not getting a bit worried. No, she said, it was Elyot's fault that it seemed so long already. He had panicked, just as Beth had said he would, and whipped her off long before there was any real need. She could probably have spent the whole day at home. They'd know better next time.

Fran urged William to try to take his mind off it. They were not necessarily involved. They didn't want to seem nosey. They had to be patient till news came.

'If it's born in the middle of the night,' she said, 'the people at the maternity home will send Elyot home to let Beth rest. I doubt if he will wake us up to tell us, though of course he might. Listen, there's the telephone now.' She went to answer it, and came back looking slightly anxious. He looked inquiringly at her.

'No,' she said. 'That was Emerald. She said Elyot came back almost straight away, and told her he was going to sit in his study, and would rather not be disturbed. The maternity home would ring when they thought it was time for him to go back.'

They had rung, Emerald said, about half an hour ago. She thought Elyot must have been in the bathroom or the garage, because he didn't answer it, so she had done. She had taken the message and gone to find him in his study.

'He's there, fast asleep, and they can't wake him. They don't know what to do. I said we would go round straight away.'

William went for their coats at once. 'I wouldn't mind betting the silly idiot passed out when he heard the telephone bell. He's been getting himself into a state for a week now. It wouldn't surprise me if he's had one of his awful migraines all day, and said nothing about it. He's probably overdosed himself with painkillers so as to get rid of it before he had to go back.'

'Or over-fortified himself with brandy,' said Fran. 'Want to bet?' William didn't answer.

'He's still asleep,' Emerald said, opening the door to him. 'I keep thinking of poor Mrs Franks wondering why he hasn't got there yet. Do you think we ought to ring the maternity home?'

'Not yet,' William said. 'Stay here. I'll go.'

He saw at a glance that whether or not Elyot had had a migraine, he'd certainly had a drink or two. By his side stood a glass and an empty ginger-ale bottle. Not being quite as innocent as the girls were, William looked for the brandy bottle. The 'horse's neck' was the RN wardroom's traditional drink.

'Nothing to worry about,' he told the girls. 'Please go and make some strong black coffee. I imagine he hasn't had much sleep these last few nights. He had a glass of brandy, and it has just put him very heavily asleep. Leave him to me.'

They went, and William told Fran what he guessed had happened. 'Of course he's had a drop too much – and who could blame him! I guess the ginger-ale ran out, and he went on to neat brandy till that ran out as well. I found an empty bottle in the coal scuttle. Don't let those two girls see it.'

Fran found it and went to put it in their own car while William wetted a face cloth and slapped Elyot's face with it till he stirred.

Realization hit Elyot like a torpedo. 'Beth?' he said. 'Beth? Why are you here, William? Tell me, Fran – what's happened to Beth?'

'Nothing, as far as we know. That's why we had to wake you up. Go and put your fat head under the cold tap. There's been a message from the maternity home. It's time now for you to go. Beth may need you.'

Elyot was looking very helpless, and very guilty. 'I'm not drunk,' he said, 'but I'm in no fit state to drive. And Fran, I don't think I could face it even if I was there. That's why I had a brandy while I waited. What ought I to do?'

'Be a man,' said Fran, 'and chicken out, as nine men out of every ten do when it comes to the point. If you ask me, as Sophie would say, it was much more sensible when men were allowed to leave the women to get on with it while they got drunk. Go and sober up, and then William will drive you and I'll come with you to hold your hand. Good! Here comes Emerald with that coffee. Thank you. Is there anything for Mr Franks to eat before we go? All right, Elyot, all right! Have you had anything to eat today at all? Then don't be silly. You don't want to be sick all over your son as soon as he's born, do you? Could you make him a sandwich to eat on the way, Amethyst? You have? Splendid. We'll come up and tell you if we have to come back and leave Mr Franks there.'

Elyot was quite sober by the time they reached the maternity home, though very white and tense. He was whisked away, and Fran and William shown into the waiting-room.

'I don't think we can leave him, can we? It's too bad on you, my darling, but it may be a long night still ahead of us,' she said.

'I'm not grumbling, however long the night is. I've got quite my share of luck without envying Elyot his.'

Fran was wrong. In less than fifteen minutes, a pretty little nurse appeared to invite them up to Mrs Franks' room to see the new baby. Born over three hours ago, she said. Mrs Franks had given orders that her husband was not to be rung till the baby had been delivered, unless things went very wrong. In fact, it had been quite a quick and easy labour. Mrs Franks had had a little rest, and was now waiting to see them.

Beth sat up in bed, a long plait of hair lying over her right shoulder, while in the crook of her left arm lay the bundle all the fuss had been about. Elyot sat by her side, his hand clasping hers and his head resting on both, though his eyes never left Beth's face.

'Sit still, Elyot,' Fran said. 'This is no time for courtesy.'

She went round the other side of the bed to kiss Beth, as she did so wishing that Greg could have been there to catch for posterity the halo of glory round Beth – the sort that no woman ever wears more than once in her life, just for an hour or two after giving birth for the first time.

She clung to Fran just for a moment before withdrawing her hand from Elyot and moving the wrap from the baby's face. 'A boy,' she said. 'Eight pounds, and not a bit of trouble.'

She turned to Elyot, holding the bundle out to him. 'Do take him, Elyot. He won't break, I promise you. And he won't disappear into thin air, either. He isn't either a dream or a ghost – he's ours, your son. I want you to hold him before anybody else does, and Fran is dying to get him into her arms, aren't you, Fran?'

Beth leaned over, and put the baby into his dazed father's arms.

Fran peered at him over Elyot's head. 'Hello, young A.B.C.,' she said. 'I'm glad you've turned out to be the right sex. I should have blamed myself for ever if you were doomed to go through life with a name like Arethusa.' Then smiling she asked, like Pooh, 'really wanting to know', 'Are we allowed to know now what his name is going to be?'

Beth, looking at Elyot's head bowed over his son, let her tears of joy brim over. 'I don't know any more than you do,' she said. 'I promised Elyot that if it was a boy, he should call him just what he liked, and I wouldn't interfere.'

Elyot looked up, struggling to find his voice. 'His name,' he said, 'is Ailwyn Hugh.'

Nobody needed telling where the unusual name of Ailwyn came from, though Elyot had never before spoken it. It was the name of the boy whose death in the boat they had shared after being torpedoed had haunted Elyot for so long, till Beth's love had brought balm to his agonized spirit. Hugh was the de ffranksbridge family name.

There was an immeasurable moment of almost sacred silence round the bed. It was a tiny breath of time reft from the vastness of eternity, a still point in the turning world. William instinctively understood with a flash of historical insight that in that split second which had seemed an aeon, the great gap between the war years and the present had been telescoped to nothing.

For Elyot, at any rate, what might have been and what had been pointed only to one end, which was the present. Nothing else mattered.

Three days later, William and Fran set out. The public holiday was over, and work beckoned for everybody else but the two of them.

For Sophie this sort of weather spelled spring-cleaning, and she stood with Ned at the gate to wave goodbye to them with mixed feelings. She hated saying goodbye to anybody who wasn't scheduled to return before nightfall, the inscrutability of the will of 'Im Above being what it was. Their plan to stay away for a whole month made her uneasy; nevertheless, she could barely wait for them to get out of the gate before asking Ned to help her move some heavy furniture in the flat, to let her get on with 'that bit o' wall-papering'.

Charles and his team of labourers had worked wonders at Danesum, especially with the garden. He had persuaded the only firm of local thatchers left in business to rethatch the Old Granary, while Joe had helped him to clean up the mess left inside it by Crystal in her hurried flight. Their joint efforts had turned a derelict eyesore into a rare, beautiful old building that could, as Charlie wished, be used for anything from a summerhouse to a playroom, from a surgery to an infirmary for small sick animals, or, as far as Charles was concerned, anything else she wanted to do with it. Everything he did was for her. He was as busy as the blackbird building its nest in the hedgerow, and as happy as the lark trilling its way upwards into the pale morning sky. He had kept his activities at Danesum a secret from her. If she asked he told her only that he was taking the opportunity of getting on with things while people had a bit of extra time to give him. He hadn't invited her to go and see it, because he couldn't bear to recall what had happened the last time they had been there together. She hadn't asked to be shown for the same reason.

On the Sunday after William and Fran's departure, Charles went up to Castle Hill early in the afternoon. Bob was just coming in from a trip to the wood at Jane's request to cut beech twigs and hazel and willow catkins for her flower arrangements.

'Hello, my boy,' Bob said. 'Did you know the oxlips are out again? I reckon that cold spell held them back, 'cos they're a lot later than they were last year. If I were you, I should knock Charlie off work for the afternoon, and take her down to gather some. And ain't it time you took her back to Danesum? You can take my word for it that it will be all right this time – especially if you take an armful of oxlips with you. I'd go today, if I were you.'

Charles had learned to trust his father-in-law-to-be's intuition about such things. He went into the house only long enough to entice Charlie to go down to the wood with him.

The top branches of the trees were alive again with black bodies as parent rooks cawed and squabbled over titbits of food for their hungry broods among the fading crimson flowers of the elms that were such a feature of the East Anglian landscape. The leaves were just uncurling on the twigs, and through and beyond the mass of brushwood the gently swaying carpet of yellow oxlips stretched. The scent that rose from it was like an intoxicating draught to this particular pair of young lovers.

They stopped and turned and wound their arms round each other, clinging tight with faces touching and breath mingling, remembering.

'They'll always remind me of you,' Charles said. 'The sight of them and the scent of them in the church the day Beth and Elyot Franks were married. I knew I should never be able to see or touch them again without thinking of you, if I lived to be ninety and whoever I'd married. It didn't seem possible then you'd ever dream of being *my* girl.'

'Your wife,' she said. 'But I'd known from the moment you brought the oxlips to me in the tack-room and dropped them in my lap, the day Robert died.'

He kissed her then, and she responded, while they stood ankle-deep in golden flowers. Those oxlip-scented kisses were vows exchanged, pledging quite as much or even more than the words they would utter in church in a few weeks' time. It was a wonderful moment for them, blessed as it was by Nature as much in the full bloom of its youth as they were themselves.

When Charlie at last pulled away from him, he said, 'Let's gather a lot of them and take them down to Danesum. I want you to see what I've been doing there.'

They began to fill their arms with the flowers that grew in such riotous profusion that however many they picked not one would be missed from the multitudes still left swaying like dancers under the canopy of trees.

'Charles,' Charlie said, 'I know we oughtn't to, but they do mean such a lot to us. Can we dig up some roots and get a little wood going for ourselves in front of the old granary at Danesum? Primroses grow best if you split the roots while they're in flower. We shall never have a better chance! I'm sure it's damp enough just round there, under all those old fruit trees. They'd grow and spread like anything. Do say yes.'

As if he could, or would, have denied her anything that day, let alone anything so simple or so easy as that, against the law though it might be.

They spent the whole afternoon in a paradise of their own making. She was overwhelmed at the beauty of the granary with its new thatch topped with traditional patterns, and the layout of the garden he was creating just for her in front of the house, with the rowan-tree at its centre. She insisted on setting their illegally uprooted oxlips in a huge circle round the granary.

'It's a circle of Time enclosing an inner circle of Love,' she explained. 'We must never let there be any gaps in it. If any of them die and break the circle, we can always go and get some more from Dad's wood. We'll make sure cowslips and primroses grow together here anyway, and before we know where we are, they will have cross-pollinated into oxlips just for us.'

'Now come in and see our house,' he said.

Nothing could possibly lend more to that day than their delight in each other, but the place and the time were enchanted. As Charlie said when she kissed him goodnight, however marvellous their wedding day might be, this too was a day to be remembered for ever.

Both Charlie and Poppy were due to return to their universities on Thursday of that week. Poppy was reluctant to go where Nick was, not because there was any difference in her feelings towards him, but because she was now mature enough to take a realistic view of their relationship.

Her emotions had been set in a kind of aspic made of schoolgirl romance. They had not changed at all since she had watched Nick walk away from her on Tom Fairey's strawstack, tears mingling with the raindrops on her face. But she saw the future more clearly, and could not let herself hope. Nick's amnesia was such that he might never remember what she had been to him. And if he did recover the memory of that time, it didn't necessarily mean that he would still feel the same about her. Recovery from amnesia might not be complete, or might only return at intervals; then he would have to deal with two entirely separate lives at the same time, or with two different parts of the same life.

She faced up to the fact that she belonged, if at all, to the wrong part. Their standing with regard to each other socially had been reversed. Her home had been broken up in a way not very likely to commend her to his affluent grandfather, or his social circle, which was now also Nick's. Having viewed the situation from this new, prosaic standpoint, she made firm resolutions to put common sense where misty hopes and fading dreams had always been before. Then she cried herself to sleep, and tried to put Nick and the past behind her.

She had read somewhere that in autumn trees grow a layer of cork between the branch and the leaf that must fall, so that the tree shall not bleed when the leaf does drop. When she left tomorrow to go back to college, the leaf that had been Nick must be allowed to drift gently out of her life. She tried hard to convince herself that she would not suffer too much.

Her mother had noticed that she had avoided Castle Hill, and had asked no questions, but now that her departure was imminent, Marjorie hinted to her that it would be discourteous as well as unhelpful if she didn't make an effort to see Charlie with regard to wedding arrangements before both took their minds from it to concentrate on exams. Poppy said she would go up that very afternoon.

There was no reason why she had to see Nick, but she rather hoped she would. She wanted to see if her new resolution would hold. The acid test would be if she could meet him and talk to him in the same way as he now talked to her, which was as if they were new acquaintances who liked each other well enough but had no great relevance in each other's lives. She was concerned about the gossip linking her mother's name with Eric's, for her own sake and the rest of the Bridgefoot family.

She had observed her mother's attitude toward Eric, and vice versa. If they were dissembling, they were being jolly clever at it. All over Easter, he had hardly been seen at all, being either at work down at the hotel, or with his daughter and grandchildren in Cambridge. At the same time, her mother had been backwards and forwards to her family at the Glebe and Temperance, and on Easter Sunday they had all gathered at her home at Monastery Farm for tea. It was plain to Poppy that the family had nothing against her mother living where she did.

Eric drove into the yard of Monastery Farm just as she was leaving to go up to Castle Hill. He greeted her politely, and asked when she was leaving. She told him next morning.

'It's been nice having you about,' he said. 'It's nice for me to have your mother about, too – just to know there's somebody else the other side of the wall. So far, I've hardly caught sight of her, but I hear her playing the piano now and then, and you can tell her from me that I do notice and appreciate all her little kindnesses to me, like the vase of flowers in the sitting room, and the tray left ready for a cup of tea when I come in hot and tired. Next time you're home, you must both come round and have tea with me.' Then he excused himself and left her thinking that she rather liked him.

She began to walk in the direction of Castle Hill. She had hoped that if she had to meet Nick, it would be with others present, but she could hardly avoid him or his grandfather if she took the direct path past the cottage where they were living, so she branched off on to one of the other overgrown tracks made long ago by people taking the nearest way between their homesteads and the little church. It led her behind the church, and towards the farmyard which lay on the far side of the house.

It was large as such farmyards go, a rectangle of buildings enclosing strawed yards in which bullocks were fed in winter, and where Charlie's horse, Ginger, had a little run of his own leading from his stable when he was not out in the pasture. Newer buildings, facing outwards, housed tractors and all sorts of modern mechanical implements. On the far side of the yard was a large old barn, and next to that, end on to her, was another rectangular enclosure that had once been a stackyard in the days before combine harvesters. There were no beautifully thatched corn-stacks waiting there for the threshing-tackle now. Instead, there was just one huge oblong stack made of square straw bales. From a ladder leaning against the far side of it there came into her view the head and shoulders of a man carrying a long-handled, two-tined pitchfork.

It was Nick. She recognized him at once, but there was no point in her trying to run away, as her first instinct had bade her, because from his high vantage point he must have seen her. She made up her mind to carry out her test of herself. She even smiled at catching him at a disadvantage. The Nick of yesteryear had been forced by poverty to do menial jobs round farmyards for a bit of pocket money, and had been more adept at doing them than ever his two friends were, though both of them were farmers' sons. The new Nick, always so beautifully dressed and 'gentlemanly', was to all those who didn't know his story a suave young-man-about-town not at all the same person as the boy who had perfected those bucolic skills in years past. She saw that in fact he was now having difficulty in keeping his balance on top of the stack. It could be that his sense of balance had been disturbed by the injury he had suffered.

She had been about to call out to him, but decided that any distraction might be dangerous and bit her greeting back. She saw his feet slip yet again, and watched him struggle, with the aid of the pitchfork, to stand up straight again. Then he stumbled towards the ladder, made a grab at it and missed it, knocking it sideways away from the stack. Then he, too, disappeared over the edge in its wake, and out of her sight. She began to run.

He lay at the foot of the stack on the large mound of soft loose straw that always collects round the bottom of a strawstack. The fork had fallen from his hand and had landed safely some yards away, and the ladder, which had also missed him, lay on the ground on the far side of him. As she ran towards him, he was pulling himself up to a sitting position, seemingly unhurt but looking dazed. The straw must have broken his fall. He was probably only bruised and shaken.

She flung herself down beside him, and tried to help him to sit up. Instead, much to her surprise, he pushed her down and hung on to her, twining his arms round her and laying his head on her shoulder. He opened his eyes, but shut them again at once. 'Poppy,' he mumbled. 'Please hang on to me. The whole world's spinning round.'

'What happened?' she asked, holding his head firmly against her shoulder, and shielding his eyes with her hand. (It was all very well telling yourself you didn't really know or care who he was!)

'Hold my head. Keep it still, please Poppy. I went up to throw a couple of bales down to straw the bullock yard with. The bale I stepped on was loose – the baling machine couldn't have knotted it properly. When I trod on it the loose straw slipped under my feet. But I'm not hurt, honestly. I just feel very queer. Don't leave me, will you? Not till I feel better.'

Common sense told her that that was exactly what she ought to do. To yell for help if nothing else – though she doubted very much if anyone would hear her, with the stack and the yard and all the buildings at the back of the house between them. But she couldn't leave him, especially as he had asked her not to, even to go and get help. She just sat still with his head on her shoulder, and without thinking stroked his face. He opened his eyes again and this time stared up at her, looking very puzzled, before closing them again with a sigh that tore at her heart.

He had sighed just like that once before when they had been sitting on a strawstack and he was explaining to her why they mustn't meet again. In spite of herself that memory was too much for her, and tears welled up, slipping down her cheeks and landing on his face. The next time he looked up, the puzzlement in his eyes had gone, and a very different expression had taken its place.

'Don't, sweetheart,' he said. 'Don't cry. I thought it was raining.'

The shock immobilized her, for a split second making her world spin. *Could it possibly be that he was remembering? It had rained, that day.*

He closed his eyes again, cuddling closer and closer to her. She dared not speak or move, lest at this crucial moment she said or did the wrong thing. The silence and the stillness seemed to her interminable. She watched as a little dark cloud hovering over the yard against the blue April sky gathered itself together, and in April fashion wept its childish tears, rain falling from it in silvery streaks through the surrounding sunshine. The shower was sharp and cold, and soaked both of them through before it stopped as suddenly as it had started.

Nick laughed, pushed her down again into the wet straw, and leaning over her kissed her again and again and again.

'We're too wet already for it to make much sense to run for shelter now,' he said. 'It's stopped, and Pansy and Robert can't be much longer. Are you cold? Here, have my pullover. Poppy! What's the matter? What have I said? Why are you looking like that?'

She couldn't answer. She didn't dare. It would be worse than ever if his memory would in future reach only to the time of the accident, and nothing since. His reference to Robert and Pansy might mean that it was only a flash, a streak of lightning that could do more harm than good. She could only sit and hold him tightly, to give him as much stability as she could.

He pulled himself up and away from her, so that now he was looking down on her, and she looking up at him. They held each other's eyes as she watched remembrance of something else cross his troubled face.

'Robert?' he said. 'Didn't Robert die?' The look of horror that crossed his face was almost as clear to read as print. He was remembering carrying Robert's coffin. Was that the way it would happen – a snatch here and a snatch there, if he was indeed at this very moment recovering from his amnesia? Did anybody know what form such things took?

The sun was shining on them again now, and they were getting dry as well as warm. She had nothing to go on as to how to help him, except that she was incapable of doing much. It came to her that perhaps that was the best thing to do – nothing. Just wait, and let what would happen next happen.

What did happen was that he lowered himself down again by her side, leaned over her and kissed her again, and then with a huge sigh settled himself down with his head on her shoulder, and shut his eyes against the strong sun. It was some minutes before she realized that he was in a deep, trance-like sleep. Still she did nothing but lie still and wait. It was another sharp April shower that finally roused him, and he began to ask questions.

She told him as much as she dared, sticking firmly to the present moment as the safest bet.

'I was on my way up to say goodbye,' she said, 'to Charlie and your Mum and you, because I'm off back to college in the morning.'

His face clouded. 'Don't say goodbye, Poppy,' he said. 'I know we had to before, but – haven't things changed?'

'Yes, Nick. You've been very ill for a long time. Things have changed a great deal for us both. You live in a whole new world that doesn't really include me. But I'm so glad it was me who was with you just now, when . . .' She stopped, trying not to show him how much she cared still, whatever she might now say.

'Kiss me again before you go,' he said. 'I guess things have changed for you, too. That's what you're telling me, isn't it? You have a new world that doesn't include me?'

How like the old Nick that was – to expect to be the one to have to efface himself. He had so much to learn. She had to be resolute. 'No,' she said. 'It isn't like that. It's just that we are two entirely different people now, from what we were before your accident. You didn't even know who I was when you first met me again. We don't know whether we even like each other as we are now. We can't go back to where we were. Too many things have happened, as you'll find out now, when you can sort your memory out. Come on, get up. You must forget me and go to tell your mother and your grandfather that . . . That the miracle has happened,' she said.

It didn't seem to her to have as much *éclat* about it as she would have expected of a miracle. Perhaps that was why so many people didn't believe they could still happen. So far, this one had only intensified the pain she thought she had got rid of. She wasn't capable of staying much longer in his company without giving way.

Nick still sat where he was, trying to piece together the two so very different strands of his young life. Frightened, Poppy thought, of both.

'I must go,' she said. 'Won't you come with me up to the house?'

He shook his head. 'I don't want you to go. When shall I see you again?'

'I'll be home again soon,' she said. His memory was becoming clearer every moment now. She mustn't stay. It would only make everything worse for both of them.

'Say goodbye to them all for me,' she said. 'I ought not to intrude when you tell them the wonderful news you have for them all.'

She leaned forward and kissed him, a long, soft, lingering kiss. What the kiss conveyed in feeling was written in her face, and there Nick read it. Neither of them could tell whether it betokened hope and faith in a glorious new life to come, or a complete renunciation of all that had ever been.

No one had foreseen the difficulties the return of Nick's recall of the past would bring.

The rejoicing the miracle had at first caused was considerably tempered by Nick's own attempts to explain to them his confusion. He remembered everything both sides of his spell in the coma, but said it was like beginning a jigsaw with a thousand pieces and no picture to follow.

He told them that evening, when all the family and Charles were present, exactly what had happened that afternoon, and Poppy's part in it. He had to get used to remembering before 'this wedding'.

They could tell how much more it meant to him now than it had done before, and they were overwhelmed. Nick was the coolest of them all. He wouldn't now just be obliging Charles. The rest had enough sense to let the two old friends go out together into the fields, and 'find' each other again.

It was his grandfather who pointed out that the very first step to be taken was to get him back to his doctors in London. He warned them, especially Nick himself, not to count on the 'miracle' being permanent all at once. It was crucial to get the boy back into medical and psychiatric care immediately. Tomorrow. Reluctantly, the others agreed. Nick and Effendi would have to return to London, and come back to the cottage at weekends. At this point Bob intervened, with his usual apologetic air. He said that plan made the best sense, common sense, because it would mix Nick's new life with his old, and let him get used to having both. Till he'd done that, he wouldn't know what he wanted next, and it was no use anybody else trying to tell him. It was his life.

'It's only a bit o' time as he needs, if you ask me,' Bob said. 'I mean, look what's happened to all of us sitting here since that van laid Nick out. We ain't the same people as we were then, any more than he is. None of us. We've all got used to things being different, and so will Nick. The only real difference is that it's happened a bit at a time for us, and all at once for him. So what I think,' he went on, 'is that if *we* don't make a lot o' song and dance about it, other folks won't either. By the time he's got to meet folk as he hasn't remembered till now, they'll have got used to it and won't be badgering him with questions. There's bound to be some other nine days' wonder before then. By the wedding they'll all just remember that he's Jane's son and Charles's best friend again. If we don't make too much of a hormpologe about it, nobody else will. Let it alone. That's usually best where other folks are concerned.'

72

Eric chanced to be in the yard when Poppy reached home. She gave him a wan smile as she passed him. He hung around for a minute or two, in case he might be needed, if she had brought home bad news.

He was obviously not needed, and went into his part of the house feeling unwanted. He didn't know why, but he was uneasy and low in spirits. Spring wasn't winding him up as it was other people all round him. When he tried to sum up all the reasons he could find for not feeling 'full of the joys of spring', he concluded that for the first time for years, he hadn't enough to do to keep himself from being bored. He was missing Monica and his grandchildren a lot. As spring advanced, he had taken to having a very early supper at the hotel before going home to his solitude, but the light evenings had begun to seem very long. And where were all his friends?

Occupied with their own private affairs, of course. William and Fran were away. The two he always felt able to take for granted were out of reach. They had only been gone a week – but it would be another three weeks before they were back. It wasn't only that they were his closest friends, who also now shared grandchildren with him; it was that their presence acted as a centrifugal force, that kept the rest in touch with each other. That's why he was feeling so very much alone now. He could hear voices from the other part of the house, and was unreasonably glad to know that his 'alone-ness' was not total. Then the raised voices ceased, a door slammed, and the sound of a car drawing away informed him that there was now nobody there but himself. He felt irritated that his tenants should have chosen to go out tonight. Besides, it was past nine o'clock already. Where could they be going, setting out as late as this? He was worried, though he didn't know why, and decided not to go to bed till he heard them come back, but they didn't need him. So he went to bed but didn't sleep well, and was still feeling low next morning.

He needed human companionship. If he knew his tenant better, he could have found some excuse to go and speak to her, and break this most morbid feeling of solitary confinement. He could not rid himself of the feeling that something had gone wrong for her last night. She might be in as much need of cheering up as he was himself. Maybe he ought to stay at home, today, just in case.

He was disappointed when he heard the car go out again early. There was no point in spending a lonely day at home, but he lacked his usual energy. He got himself a leisurely breakfast while making up his mind.

It was little more than an hour later, while he was still messing about in his kitchen, that he heard the car return, and almost immediately Marjorie tapped on his door and came in. One glance at her was enough to tell him that his intuition of trouble had been right, and the feeling of being needed restored his own equilibrium instantly. He was almost himself again as he greeted her and pulled out a chair for her to join him at his kitchen table. She was agitated, though she was trying not to show it. She did not sit down, making it plain that she preferred to stand, holding her head deliberately high and thrusting a firm chin forward.

'I saw your car,' she said, 'so I knew you were here. I'm sorry to intrude, but I have to talk to you. Can you spare me a few minutes? I won't keep you a moment longer than necessary.'

She was taut and business-like, but he knew it was only a pose. She needed a friend, not just an acquaintance. He gave her his rare but charming smile, and risked saying what he felt.

'Let me put the kettle on. I expect it's too early for me to offer you any other sort of drink, though if I may say so, you look as if what you need is a large tot of brandy. Is something wrong? You look all in, so do go and sit down. May I put some brandy in your coffee? I wasn't going out this morning, so there's no hurry.'

By the time he followed her into his sitting room, she had drawn back the curtains, tidied the room and was sitting rather primly upright waiting for him.

'Now,' he said, 'tell me what's the matter, and what, if anything, I can do to help. I hope there's no bad news.'

She shook her head. 'No. On the contrary. Good news from Castle Hill. Young Nick fell off a strawstack and as a result regained his lost memory. The thousand-to-one chance everyone has been hoping for has come off.'

'But that's absolutely wonderful!' he said. 'So why was Poppy upset yesterday, and why are you so unhappy this morning?'

She set down her coffee cup, and stood up. He had never noticed before how tall she was, and how easy her carriage. She was very much like her father, as much a daughter of the soil as her father was a son. Marjorie's height was well-balanced by a good covering of sturdy country muscle. 'Comfortable' was the word he had first used of her, and it still applied. With that sleek but waved grey head and a face flushed with agitation, she was quite a striking woman.

'Let me tell you what I came to say,' she said. 'I'm afraid that for all sorts of reasons I can't continue my tenancy here. I shall pay you rent for the whole year according to our agreement, but I shall be moving out, back to my brother at Temperance Farm, probably towards the end of next week. As soon, in fact, as they can get the flat ready for me again, and I can get the rest of my large furniture back into store.'

Eric's normal mask of imperturbability was shaken by the surprise. He was lost for words. Moreover, now that she had said what she had come to say, her control deserted her. She sat down again rather quickly, and much to his distress, began to cry. Instinct told him she did not shed tears easily, and that therefore this was an indication of some deep distress.

'I don't understand,' he said at last, his tone very gentle. 'I must accept your decision, of course – and please allow me to say how sorry I am. I thought it was working well for both of us.'

'So it was. I don't want to give it up. I was just beginning to feel that life was worth living again. But there's no help for it. Fate's just got it in for me and my children, and I can't fight any longer. Everything's gone wrong for me.'

'So why don't you tell me what this is all about? I know what it's like to be in trouble, and need a bit of support. If I don't yet know you very well, I know the rest of your family well enough. Don't think of me as a stranger, or as your landlord. Drink your coffee. As I said, there's no hurry.'

She obeyed him, giving him an appreciative smile as she tasted the brandy in it. They were silent till she'd finished it, and he took the cup from her.

'Well?' he said, invitingly.

'I expect it will all sound very silly to a man,' she said. 'But Poppy's gone back to college this morning in a dreadful state. We had the most awful quarrel last night. That's what I can't bear. She's all I've got left, and I'm all she has. She's being absolutely unreasonable, and blaming me for everything. But I mustn't be angry with her. I've got to help her. She's so young – and so hurt.'

'What about?' He could see she was going to be incoherent, and that he would have to help her sort her own feelings out. She hesitated a minute before letting the truth burst out. 'It's this bloody wedding that's at the bottom of it,' she said. 'It's all anybody can think or talk about, and from the fuss that's being made you'd think it was Prince Charles getting married instead of just Charles Bridgefoot. We all know he's the only male Bridgefoot, and we're all pleased for his sake that things have turned out so well. The trouble is that they haven't turned out well for me and my two girls. We're expected to act as if we haven't any feelings for anybody but the lucky couple. That's what's the matter with Poppy. Like me, she's an unlucky one.'

He remembered her recent marital troubles, and sympathized. When she had recovered enough, he asked her to explain what the new trouble was.

She told him, exactly as Poppy had told her, of what had happened yesterday on the strawstack.

'I told her I was proud of her. She had done right, however bad she felt, because if she had let Nick go on yesterday and make love to her, as Pansy would have done, he would have felt honour-bound to stick to her.'

She paused, and held the handkerchief against her lips to stop their trembling.

'That was when she turned on me, like a wildcat. She said she certainly wasn't very proud of me. It was me that had made her do what she had, and let Nick go. What did I know about right or wrong? How dare I sit there telling her what to do or not to do? I had ruined her life, the way I had behaved towards her father, and the way I was going on now . . . all the scandal . . . and everything. I couldn't believe it. We had the most awful scene. I wonder you didn't hear us. I'm so sorry.'

Eric had been able to follow her so far, but he had now lost the thread. He didn't know what scandal she was referring to, or why any of it had any bearing on her tenancy. He could have sworn she was not the hysterical type. There must be more to it yet.

'Mrs Gifford,' he began. 'I'm sorry, but I . . .'

'Don't you dare call me that!' she interrupted. 'At least that's something I can have my own way about. I'm a Bridgefoot. I wish I'd never been anything else!'

'Then may I call you Marjorie?' he asked soothingly, having come to the conclusion that her grief was such that she was in danger of becoming hysterical after all. 'Perhaps I'm being stupid, but I don't understand. Why should it have any bearing on where you live?'

She looked up, her face scarlet. 'It's this latest scandal. She said she knew now why her father behaved as he did. She'd found out about it being my fault all the time. Told me how miserable they had all been at home because of the rows between me and Vic. How dare I complain about him having a bit on the side when I'd driven him to it by the affair I was having? She had thought I was trying to put things right when I went back to him but it was clear now that all I'd been doing was to get every penny out of him I could, before leaving him for good. Pansy had told her that it was me refusing to sleep with him that had made him like he was. He'd gone to pieces and taken to the bottle – they think he was drunk when he was killed. So both my daughters now regard me as a murderess as well as a whore. Did I think Poppy would drag Nick and his family into that? Hadn't I been trying to get a divorce and marry my fancy-man when their father had set me free by killing himself? And look at the way I had behaved on the day of his funeral! She said she'd stuck up for me as long as I could – but I had showed her just what I was when I came to live here.'

The handkerchief was needed again, before she could go on. 'I can't get over *Poppy* talking to me like that, however hurt she was. She had to hurt somebody else, and it's only human nature to take it out on the person you love most. I did try hard not to care, but she kept on till I couldn't take any more. I made her go with me to tell Mam and Dad all she was accusing me of. Brian and Rosy happened to be there. Brian's always been close to me, and took my side against her. He asked her where she had got all her filthy information from. She said it was all over the village, but

Pansy had told her first when they met at the funeral. I asked Dad if he had heard it. He was marvellous – he always is. Yes, he said, it was going the rounds, with a new bit added every day, but he had more sense than to let it upset him. The only way to kill such lies was to ignore them. Poppy wouldn't listen. She said he was only trying to hush things up so as not to spoil his precious Charles's wedding. Poor kid – she'd got herself into such a state she didn't know any longer what she was saying. Brian tried to persuade me to tell her the truth about why I left her father, but I wouldn't. He's dead, but he's still their father. I didn't want them to know what a beast he was. I asked Poppy what I could do to prove to her that the lies being told about me weren't true, and she said it should be plain enough without her having to tell me. I could go back to live with Brian and Rosy, where they could keep an eye on what I was up to. I couldn't let her go back this morning without making it up with her. So I agreed. I'm all she has, or ever will have if she lets all this turn her into a bitter old maid. We've got to get this wedding over somehow. It's a case of me giving in for the sake of all the rest of my family. I'm sorry to have to involve you, Mr Choppen.'

'Mr Choppen? If you are to be Marjorie to me when we meet in future, I must be Eric to you. I'm very sorry, too, and I still can't see the connection. Look, you're too upset and distressed this morning to make any permanent decisions. Go back to your brother by all means till the wedding is over, but why not leave all your furniture where it is? When it's all died down, you can simply come back. The shock probably threw Poppy yesterday more than people our age can visualize. It's awful to be so young and so vulnerable. And as for this scandal – I shan't ask any questions, but it seems to me to have a ring of personal malice about it. Now let me get you a proper drink. I was depressed this morning, but I was only being sorry for myself because I was lonely. I shall feel lonelier still with you gone. Though I don't see you, I know you are there, especially when I hear the piano. There, that's made you smile. I'd ask, if I dared, the name of the man yours is being coupled with. He has to be unattached if you were planning to marry him. The only candidate I can think of is Nick's grandfather. Was that what Poppy was getting so steamed up about?'

He had been getting her drink as he talked, with his back to her, and when he turned to take it to her, she was blushing. Not the beetroot red of embarrassment, but gently. There was also the beginning of a twinkle in her eye. 'Mr Gordon? I've never even met him! You mean you truly don't know who my "fancy man" is?' she said.

He shook his head. 'I haven't heard a word till you told me just now.'

'That's good. I hope you never do, because I swear there's no truth in any of it. I can't even claim him as a friend. It really is a case of smoke without fire. But I will think again about coming back. Especially when Poppy comes to her senses, as I'm pretty sure she will.' She looked at her watch. 'I'm expected up at Temperance, so I'd better go.' She came towards him, holding out her hand. 'Thank you, Eric,' she said. 'That wasn't the first time you've been kind enough to see me through a difficult morning. I'm glad I know my landlord a bit better than I thought I did.' He saw her out, feeling better himself.

Later that afternoon, she rang him up from Temperance Farm, to tell him that Poppy had made herself ill with self-reproach, and the rest of the family thought it would be a good idea for her to go to see Poppy for the weekend. So she'd be up to pack a case later. She was feeling a great deal better, and was full of apologies for her outburst this morning. He assured her that he felt better too, for her visit, and hoped that when she returned she would come straight back to Monastery Farm, and take up her tenancy again. Nobody else need ever know what had passed between them this morning. He was glad it had all turned out to be no more than a storm in her family's tea-cup.

He didn't see or hear her when she came to pack her case, having by that time opened his door to Greg.

73

Jess was at work, Hetty was in charge of Jonce, and Eric's car had told Greg that he was at home. Eric was pleased to see Greg. They got on well together, though they could not have been much more unlike in looks or personality. Eric had tempered and hardened his naturally reserved self and welded it to his acute business acumen to create the archetypal 'business-man' image most people saw in him. He took trouble to look and dress the part.

Greg's dress, except on special occasions, was casually unconventional, though always tastefully if somewhat artistically eccentric. Where Eric's smooth features rarely betrayed his feelings, Greg had great difficulty in concealing his. The lines in his face and his beautiful eyes gave his thoughts away. His ebullience of spirit was so naturally a part of him that it never grated on Eric's nerves as many of his 'hearty' clients did, and Eric's normal outward imperturbability never for a minute fooled Greg into thinking there was nothing behind the controlled mask but a 'money-grubber'. Maybe they were a good example of extremes meeting. They were certainly very much at home in each other's company.

Greg was quick to pick up that Eric was not quite his usual suave self that day. He had no inhibitions whatsoever in inquiring as to why Eric wasn't at work, and what was the cause of him being so down-hearted. From most people such an inquiry would have brought from Eric a polite reply terse enough to freeze the atmosphere, but as it was, Eric confessed to last night's spell of depression. The unspoken sympathy in Greg's face was solace to Eric. Friends were still at hand.

They chatted about Nick. Both feared that his present recovery might only be a flash in the pan, and foresaw what repercussions a relapse would have on all the wedding plans. Eric said it had already had rather disastrous repercussions, and told Greg of Marjorie's visit, quoting her verbatim when he reached the bit about the current scandal. Greg's face as he listened was a study in which embarrassment, anxiety and amusement were mixed.

'What on earth is there in that to make you laugh?' Eric asked. 'It seemed anything but funny to me!'

'She didn't tell you who the man in the case is, then?'

'No. I half invited her to, but she was as close as an oyster. Made me wonder for a minute if there was something in it after all, in spite of her declaration that he wasn't even a friend.'

'That could soon be remedied,' Greg said.

'You do know who it is, then?'

'I'm afraid so. Do you truly mean you can't guess?'

'I don't waste my time playing such silly games. I only know that whoever he is he's caused a lot of unhappiness already and if I did know I should want to go and bash his face in for robbing me of a good tenant and a splendid housekeeper.'

Greg burst out laughing. 'You might regret it. It's almost too good a story to be true. With Biblical overtones of King David and Uriah's wife.'

'What on earth are you getting at? Stop beating about the bush.'

Greg hesitated no longer. He grinned widely, and said, 'Look in the mirror, old chap.'

He had chosen to be facetious deliberately, but was not at all sure now that it had been wise. He watched as Eric's face went red, turned tensely white, and then suffused with blood again, while his strong hands clenched and unclenched time after time, until at last he had absorbed the shock and got himself wholly back under control.

'Sorry, old fellow,' Greg said. 'Somebody had to tell you, for Marjorie's sake if not for your own, though it was difficult to believe you hadn't heard any of it. The tale, apparently, is getting riper and riper by the hour. Somebody intends to keep up the heat till it causes real harm. It seems to be aimed at the Bridgefoots – any silly tale will do to foul their spotless reputation, wreck their solidarity and spoil the wedding, besides hitting George where it would hurt most, in his pride. Marjorie was a ready-made target, and you're just an innocent victim. That silly Hopkins woman saw you talking to Marjorie in the churchyard the day her husband was buried. That's how it started. Then Marjorie moved in under your roof. It's all so silly – but it isn't only in wartime that careless talk can cost lives.'

'It's damnable,' said Eric, his fists still clenched. 'You know I don't care a tinker's cuss what anybody says about me as long as my conscience is clear and it doesn't affect my business integrity. But for anybody – and it doesn't take much guessing who – deliberately to target a perfectly innocent woman who has already had more than her fair share of trouble really gets my goat! And I made it worse for her, thinking I was giving her help when she needed it. No wonder she wanted to get away from here and me! What can I do now to put it right?'

'I think the answer is nothing,' Greg said. 'But that isn't your way. What do you think?'

'As soon as it's dark, I think I'll go up to Glebe and consult George.'

'Good idea,' said Greg. 'And I must go.' He hesitated before turning back to say, 'I think we're all in it, and I'm a bit afraid of your mood. May I ring George and warn him to expect you? We really can't risk any more misunderstandings.'

'Just as you like,' Eric answered. 'But I'm not likely to do anything silly. Surely you know me better than that by now?'

Greg's warm smile spread comfort over Eric's chafed spirits. It told him how much he 'belonged'. 'Let us know how you get on. We shall be wanting to know.'

The kitchen at the Old Glebe was as warm and welcoming as Eric had found it before. George and Molly sat one each side of the table, neither showing any signs of strain or stress. The whisky bottle and glasses stood ready by George's elbow.

'Come in, my boy, come in,' George said. 'And stop worrying. None of it's your fault. Marge has just rung from her hotel, and Poppy's with her. As long as they've made it up with each other, there's nothing to worry about.'

'I wish I could feel as calm about it as you do,' Eric said.

George took a long time lighting his pipe, and invited Eric to do the same. Molly asked to be excused – she had just remembered something that couldn't wait, she said. George's eyes twinkled.

'She thinks we're going to make a night of it,' he said. 'But it is easier in a case like this to be able to talk man to man. This has been brewing ever since New Year's Eve. Bailey and Kid Bean didn't like being worsted, and it got under their skin properly when Brian backed out. They had got their claws into Vic, but it was Brian they needed to split us Bridgefoots up. While we stick together and stand four-square, there ain't a lot they can do. The only chip they've managed to get off us so far is Pansy, and me and Mother both think she'll be glad enough to creep back to us before long, poor child.'

'But aren't you worried about Marjorie?'

'No, not now. We have been, until she got herself settled in a home of her own again. If you mean about what harm this talk can do her, don't give it another thought. It's all a part of living in a village – or it used to be. Before the days of cars and telephones and wireless and television, all anybody in a place like this had to be interested in was what their neighbours were doing. It were the only real entertainment they had. It often used to get to swearing matches between neighbours and even a good old fist fight afore both lots went down to the pub together, as good friends as ever again. This is different. It's meant to be nasty – but it's only the same animal with a few more hairs on. We're used to it. Them as keeps mad bulls knows best how to deal with 'em, as the saying is. The best thing is to take no notice. We should have got through it all with no harm done if it hadn't been for Poppy. It was just too much for Marge when Poppy turned against her. Else you needn't have knowed about it. Did Marge tell you anything about Vic, and her life with him?'

'No, except to shout at me when I called her Mrs Gifford.'

George nodded, laying his pipe down. 'I reckon that's why Mother went and left us by ourselves,' he said. 'She thinks you ought to know, if Marge is coming back to live in her part of your house. Which we hope she will. She was beginning to get cured because it was just what she had always wanted, and she loved it. You see—'

George told his listener everything, starting from the time he and Molly had been so worried about Marge marrying Vic. The poor old man had difficulty with his voice as he went on to tell Eric about the rape. 'He's dead,' he said. 'You shouldn't speak ill of the dead – but I should be a hypocrite if I said I was sorry. He only got his deserts. If I am upset at all about these silly tales now, it's because I can't tell everybody what I've just told you. And to think he's still getting at her from his grave! We can't even save her good name now without hurting the twins – and her – and the rest of the family, and Charlie's as well. We've got to put up with it till it all dies down and they find somebody else's character to take away. But we did want you to know the truth, in case you felt that you couldn't have her back as a tenant under the circumstances. We shall understand, you know, if you do feel that way.'

Eric had listened without speaking a word, but his hand round his pipe tightened until the stem snapped with a crack, and George, looking into his face, saw that his eyes were full of anger and impotence at the injustice of it all.

'If he were still alive now,' Eric said, low and tense, 'he wouldn't be in an hour's time. He wouldn't have been the first I've had to kill with my bare hands. I could have got away with it, but it's too late for me to take revenge that way, now.'

'Revenge don't do much good as a rule,' George said. 'What I want to know is what she wants to know. Is it possible for you to go on living under the same roof now you both know what everybody is saying about you?'

'Persuade her to come straight back there when she comes home from seeing Poppy. I think you're right. Don't give whoever it is the least satisfaction that they've spoiled anything for anybody. And thank you for telling me. I told her this morning that if she ever came back to take up her tenancy again, we might as well be friends.'

Molly appeared from nowhere. 'She'll find a difference, living in the same house with a gentleman,' she said. 'We shall all be looking forward to this wedding even more now we know this is all out in the open. We didn't want you to be upset by hearing it, but perhaps Poppy has done us all a good turn in the long run.'

Eric got up to leave, though they pressed him to stay. He was still terribly angry that there was nothing he could do to put right the past for a woman who had been treated as Marjorie had. He wanted to get out into the air. He couldn't find words to explain to this good old couple the kind of baresark anger it had roused in him. He clasped George's hand, and took Molly into his arms and kissed her again and again. Then he left abruptly, still without speaking.

'Well!' said Molly, over and over again. 'Well! And to think we didn't want him among us when he first come. Next time Fran Catherwood kisses you, you needn't boast to me about it afterwards. I shall remind you how he kissed me.'

George laughed. 'Two o' the same breed,' he said. 'You can all'us tell a thoroughbred from a carthorse.'

Two days later, when Eric went home, he found Marjorie reinstalled. She came through to tell him she was back, and to report on her visit to Poppy. There was no tension between them, and both tacitly agreed not to mention last week's volcanic eruption.

They soon slipped back again into their previous habits, though Eric went out of his way to make sure that he saw her to speak to at least once every day, and she took to leaving him homemade cakes for his tea more often. It was all very comfortably humdrum.

William and Fran would soon be back.

As he strolled home across the yard towards his own house from Jess and Greg's one evening the lights were still on in Marjorie's half. He certainly welcomed those lighted windows. They made the house seem alive. He was only just beginning to appreciate the value of having neighbours. If they were friends as well, like Jess and Greg, they made a considerable difference to one's state of mind. He concluded that his years in Old Swithinford must have changed him. The Eric Choppen who had first come wouldn't have stood in the dark thinking things like that. He had been covered then by a carapace of hardness grown to prevent him from showing any sign of dependence on anybody but himself.

He opened the shared front door, and went in. Marjorie was playing the piano, and in the belief that she was alone in the house, letting herself enjoy it without any fear of disturbing him. The piece she was playing was Elgar's 'Salut d'Amour'. He recognized it, and stood listening, the melody drawing him towards it. He put down his hat, and without stopping to knock, crept in and went to lean on the piano.

She looked up and across it towards him, understanding his gesture that he didn't want her to stop playing. So she finished the piece, and a long silence fell. She thought he wanted to clear away any remnants of doubt about their previous emotion-fraught interview, and left it to him to begin.

He apologized for interrupting her playing. 'It just happened to be one of my favourite pieces,' he said.

She smiled. 'I thought you had come to complain,' she said.

'No, only to say how sorry I didn't understand what you were saying the other day. I had no idea that what was causing you such embarrassment was that I was the mysterious "other man". I understand now why Poppy thought you should get out, and why you agreed. It was to save my reputation, as well as your own.'

'I hadn't got a shred of reputation left to save. You had, and still have. That's why I can hardly believe you'll let me stay here. Are you sure you want to run the risk?'

'I only want to do what's best for you. Your father thinks if we don't panic the gale of gossip will blow itself out, and in any case I'm not in the least afraid of it. But another option would be to run before it. There's nothing that would take the wind out of the sails of such malicious gossip quicker than for it to dawn on the scandal-mongers that the so-called secret association between us is in fact nothing of the kind, but just an open and above-board acquaintance between good friends.

'There's nothing to prevent that is there? Now or in future. We're both in the same boat, both free, both single again, both without other attachments. Wouldn't it make sense for us to team up?'

The colour had risen in her face, and to cover her embarrassment she put her hands back on the keys and began to play again. It was only her strange reaction that alerted him to the clumsy way he had phrased what he had said. She must have interpreted it as a proposal of marriage, or at least of some sort of sexual liaison. How on earth was he to extricate himself from such a situation? It was the very last thing that he had intended. But how did a man get himself out of a gaffe like that without insulting the woman concerned beyond all hope of forgiveness, let alone one who had been so badly hurt by a man before?

He looked across the piano at her with a sinking heart. There was nothing for it but to explain to her that that was not what he had meant at all. She was still playing a familiar piece from memory, stunned, he thought into silence by the suddenness of his proposal to her. He could see her lips trembling, and tears in her eyes. He had to stop it getting even more out of hand, before it was altogether too late.

'Marjorie,' he said, 'I'm afraid I haven't made myself very clear. What I am offering you is . . .' He got no further. She suddenly brought both hands crashing down on the keys, producing loud jangling discords, and stood up to face him like an animal at bay.

'Oh, Eric, don't! Stop now before you spoil everything. I'm so happy as I am. I know I ought to be grateful and honoured, but I had begun to think my luck had changed and I had found one man who didn't think only in terms of bed! I'm sorry to sound so crude, but I may just as well tell you first as last. The last thing I ever want is a man in my bed again! If only you knew! I thought I was safe with you, but you turn out to be like all other men. I can't believe you were offering me marriage – but even if you were, what were you after? You don't really know me yet, so I suppose it was a bid to get a housekeeper and bedmate cheap – two for the price of one in fact. I was glad to be your housekeeper. I ought to have known it was too good to last.'

She sank down on to the piano stool again, hid her face in her hands, and sobbed. He felt as gauche as a schoolboy found trying to see a girl's knickers, and recoiled in dreadful embarrassment, yet at the same time, as her words sank in, the relief that swept over him was unbelievable. Like the second when you knew that the grenade was a dud and wouldn't now go off. He mopped his face, and went round the piano to sit beside her on the duet stool.

'Listen, this time,' he said, 'and let's get it straight. I knew what a mess I'd made of what I was trying to say, and was trying to apologize. Do you really believe me to be such a cad? I didn't mean anything of the sort. All I was offering you was a friend of the opposite sex to be an escort or social partner if or when you wanted or needed one. We're in the same boat for different reasons. Your experience of marriage was such that you'll never risk it again. Mine was so wonderful that nothing else could ever come up to it. Don't be cross – but I went to see your father, and he told me, man to man, just what you had been through. I thought I was safe in offering you my company and protection as a social escort. Now, will you think about it?'

She was looking at him with huge eyes in which wonder was growing as all sorts of possibilities spread themselves out before her.

'I have thought,' she said. 'After such a shock as that, what we both need is a soothing drink, which as your housekeeper I shall go and get.'

'Tea,' he said. 'Hot and strong with sugar and milk. Come in and drink yours with me. Are friends allowed any show of affection for each other?'

'Good friends are. Why?'

'I want to seal our friendship, that's all.' He pulled her up from the piano stool, holding out both his hands to her. Before letting hers go, he gave them a gentle squeeze, and then held on to them till she looked straight back at him, and smiled.

74

Plas Uchaf was all that William and Fran could have hoped for. What both needed from their holiday was peace and quiet, rest and relaxation. William had not realized quite what the last few weeks had taken out of him, though he did remark rather cynically that he thought he had worked harder during his supposed leave than he would have done routinely 'at work'.

More than anything they enjoyed the chance just to be together to enjoy leisure, and the change of scenery. For the first few days, that was enough, and all went well. Fran was content to do nothing but listen to Olwen's lilting voice telling her the local gossip, though she knew none of the characters involved, which, as she said to William, 'made a nice change'. She thought he looked better and younger every day. She didn't feel in the least neglected when he immersed himself in a book, or took long, restful naps. She found a copy of Kilvert's diary and re-read it with enormous pleasure, keeping a two-and-half-inch Ordnance Survey map of the district beside her. From the windows she identified some of the hills by name, consulted Olwen for pronunciation, and planned walks for when she had stored up enough renewed energy. To sit by the large window and gaze out to the huge trees in the field by the side of the house, in which sheep roamed at will, satisfied her. To fall over sheep in the house when a door had been left open was an amusing new experience. Besides, there were lambs that provided her with inexhaustible entertainment as they gambolled and leapt and chased each other till they discovered they were too far away from 'Mam' and legged it back to her uttering their inimitable gargling 'baas'. They never failed to make Fran laugh. To Olwen sheep were the main source of her family's livelihood, and she enlarged Fran's knowledge considerably by tales of them leaping walls, drowning themselves in brooks, getting lost in snowdrifts, being attacked by birds of prey, getting cast on their backs, or worst of all, wandering away just at the time some other nearby farmer was dipping or shearing or marking, and ending up in the wrong flock. Fran found it almost impossible to believe that Olwen or any of her family should be able to tell one sheep from another, but there was no doubting the indignation that they felt when one of last year's lambs was recognized marked the wrong colour by Gwyn-the-Chapel or Trefor-the-Logs.

It had certainly been a very good idea for them to get away for a while, though of course they had to keep in touch. There was no telephone at Plas Uchaf, which was, Fran thought, a great blessing. Useful invention though it was, she very often swore it was one of the Devil's: a means of disrupting peace, killing thought and nipping in the bud any promise of doing anything creative; the Great Interrupter, from whose mischievous intentions they were for a while blessedly free. Olwen, only just over the hill, had a telephone, and Jane Bellamy knew how to get in touch with them in emergency. There was also a public kiosk only half a mile away, from which conscience drove them to keep in touch with Old Swithinford.

Olwen delivered a request that they should ring Jane, and when they strolled to the kiosk that evening, a tearfully excited Jane gave them the great news about Nick. Fran loved the evening strolls to the kiosk, but resented any obligation to stop what she was doing to go and make calls during the day. William said his own laziness combined with Olwen's cooking called for extra exercise, and undertook to go unaccompanied to make any calls that had to be during 'office hours'. He was still in negotiation with the social services about procedures for adoption and fostering, with solicitors about Petrie's will, and with Joe about selling the Dormobile – none of which could be done in the evening.

'Go before lunch, then,' Fran advised him. 'Sophie would quote Miss Budd to you. She used to make them write out bits of gnomic wisdom every day as handwriting practice. Killing two birds with one stone. Nobody bothers now about the sayings (or the writing), as far as I can observe, but Sophie's full of them:

> 'After dinner, rest a while.
> After supper, walk a mile.'

'Suits me,' William said. He was glad to be able to report that so far things with regard to the children's future looked hopeful rather than otherwise.

They were lucky with the weather. After gales and flood, central Wales in particular was enjoying a long, sunshiny spell of summer.

They had arranged for Greg to go to Benedict's twice a week, to post on to them their separate bits of correspondence that he judged couldn't wait for their return. Twm-the-post delivered these bulky envelopes early, having learned that Plas Uchaf had to be given priority over the rest of his ordinary leisurely round, especially when Mr Hadley-Gordon himself was in residence there.

'Let's go for a long walk tonight,' Fran said, 'after we've rung to see if everything's all right at home. What's that hill up there called? Cefn Wylfa. I know how to pronounce it because Olwen laughed at me. I'll bet Kilvert walked over it many a time. As Sophie would say, we've got our dossity back all at once.'

They came back in the dusk to a meal left for them by Olwen, to sit and read in love-warmed silence till very late by Welsh standards. The best part of any day, William said, was when sunsoaked and happy they could fall into bed together.

And so it seemed set for the rest of their time there, till there came a day when Fran detected that William had tensed up again, and was less exuberantly setting out on the long jaunts she proposed than before. She blamed herself; it was another aspect of the same characteristic that allowed her to forget a quarrel in ten minutes, but took him as many days. They had both been exhausted physically before they had ever come to Wales. After two days there, her batteries were completely recharged, and she had expected him to keep up with her. She should have known that if he overdid climbing hills in the moonlight and making long drives in hot sunshine it would use up the energy he should be storing.

She toned their programme down a bit, exploring the adjacent countryside – but Fran's antennae were very sensitive to anything concerning him, and she was alerted to the fact that the change in him was not physical, or at least, not wholly. He was worrying again about something, which he was choosing to keep to himself.

That in itself hurt and angered her. She thought they had long ago got that particular problem sorted out – that try as he might, he could not hide anxiety or worry from her, and that if he persisted in trying it only made matters worse for both. So why was he doing it now, when they had been so elated and happy till whatever it was had started him worrying again?

The answer, she thought, must be that he had heard some news about the Petrie children, and was doing his best to keep it from her so as not to spoil her holiday. Bless him – but she'd rather know, and share it with him. She didn't say so, because he was fooling himself that he had acted well enough for her not to have detected anything amiss with him. She told herself that she would not ask, and for much of the time, she forgot, and believed that he had as well. Until she came upon him when he wasn't expecting her, and she caught him brooding over whatever it was.

To all intents and purposes, they went on as before. They went to visit Cilmeri, where the last Llewellyn was killed; memories of John enticed them to travel the Mountain Road from Rhyader to Cwmystwyth, a breath-taking journey in every sense.

That evening, she had gone out for a short walk across the lamb-filled field by herself, and returning had found him very unresponsive to her, very low in spirits, and visibly 'in the dumps'. Putting two and two to-gether, she decided it must be a mood engendered by memories of John and whatever it was that he had heard about the children since they had left home. Temper flared in her, and she marched in and demanded to know what was the matter.

'Have you had bad news about Jonce, or any of the others?' she asked. 'It isn't fair to keep it to yourself. I care about them too, you know. So tell me the truth. Is that what is upsetting you, and spoiling your pleasure here?'

He leapt to his feet and went to her. 'There's nothing to tell,' he said. 'As far as I know, nothing on that front is liable to happen for weeks yet. If there is anything at all wrong with me, it is that I'm getting homesick, much as I love it here. If I was looking mournful it was because I was thinking about Benedict's and wanting to get back to start on deciphering Bob's book. Darling, I'm sorry. I just don't have your everlasting cruse of physical energy.'

She accepted his word, but she wasn't satisfied. For one thing, when she had asked him the question outright about the children, and he had jumped up to hold her, she could have sworn that he had not been quick enough to hide his feeling of relief. Backwash from ancient quarrels began to swirl coldly round her feet. He had been expecting another, far more dangerous question. She could not get that idea out of her head, though in the next two days he made heroic efforts to be as he had been earlier in their stay in Wales.

Then came a morning when Olwen announced, unconcernedly, that her husband had said the salmon were running at Aberedw. It was one of the miracles of nature that neither of them had ever seen before, and Fran was ecstatic as she watched the glimmering bodies leap upward and fall back into the spray upstream. She was hungry for the picnic Olwen had packed for them, but unable to drag herself away to eat until there came a pause in the succession of leaping fish. William suggested that they could come again tomorrow if the salmon were still running, so why didn't they go on now and find a new view to look at while they ate?

He didn't bother to turn the car, but continued on the way it was facing, at the junction with the major road turning north, which would lead them back to Cregrina by going round the other two sides of a square. They kept their eyes open for a likely place to picnic. A small and rather inconspicuous fingerpost bore the anything-but-inconspicuous legend Llansaintffraed-in-Elvel, to the west of which the map showed a higher area named Carneddau.

'That looks hopeful,' Fran said. 'I'll bet there'll be a good view from up there.'

She was right. They left the car at the bottom, and walked up. It was wild and open and utterly beautiful. The afternoon sky was clear, and whichever way one turned there were other low hills – low, that is, by Welsh standards, but high enough to be named separately on the map. They ate their tea in peace broken only by birdsong and one or two inquisitive sheep, and afterwards climbed a bit higher. At one point the hill rose more sharply, and Fran said she'd stay where she was till he'd been up to see if it was worthwhile her making that extra bit of effort.

'You must come up,' he called. 'The sun's beginning to set, and I'm pretty sure I can see the outline of the Black Mountains as well as the Brecon Beacons. It's all unbelievably beautiful.' He slid down till he could give her his hand to help her up the last few feet to where he was standing. They identified as many mountains and hills as they could, and then turned westwards to watch the setting sun. He wound his arm round her, and they stood close together while the few clouds there had been broke up into a riot of glory as the huge red ball sank into the hills.

'It's almost as good as Hunstanton,' she said.

'Only almost?'

'Well – it may be more beautiful, but that sunset we watched from Hunstanton pier had something extra about it, if you remember.'

He remembered. She was alluding to the day, not actually so very long ago in time, to them a day when their world shifted on its axis: the day on which, though their 'honour' and the remains of their Victorian morality still kept them from consummating their love, they had pledged themselves by a bit of spontaneous ritual that meant more to both of them than any formal wedding service. William had pulled off her wartime wedding-ring and hurled it into the sea, replacing it with one he had bought that afternoon on the spur of the moment. Magic, as at heart most ritual is, made more meaningful by the place, because they had been standing on the east coast where in defiance of all reason one can watch the sun set into the sea.

It dipped behind a hill, on this evening, and they turned to each other and kissed as they had at Hunstanton. But something was wrong all the same. Fran knew it. She shivered in the cool breeze that was coming with the evening, but the cause of her spasm was fear. So her intuition had been right. It was the old bogey she had thought was dead raising its – no, her head again. He had heard from Janice. She should have been able to detect the signs that once she had known so well. Coldly, clearly, she began to remember how Twm-the-Post came early, before she was up. But not before William was. He had been getting up early on purpose to 'vet' Greg's packages before she could ever see a letter from the USA, or even from closer at hand, that could spell utter disaster for them. How would he handle it, after their last years of such happiness? And how would she?

She did not believe that he would let anything, not even his promise and his sense of honour, sever them now. But Janice was the sort of woman who would use any and every trick in the book to spoil for them what they had created with each other, debasing what she couldn't share. He was probably thinking that he would have to resign his post, or face the sort of contumely that other academics – and the Church – retained for those who 'let their side down'. He must know by now that she would never leave him for all the Janices in existence, whatever happened. But that was when her fear turned to anger.

He was the one who was ashamed, apparently, of their 'unhallowed' status. She had done her best to convince him that once having taken her decision, she never questioned it, or him. He had never done her the honour of believing her wholly, which could only mean one thing. That in spite of all he had said, and done, he had always kept the possibility in mind that they might have to part. He couldn't care as much as she did. Not even now – or he would tell her and prepare her for the worst. Hadn't he said just before they had started out today that he had made an appointment to see Nigel Delaprime somewhere tomorrow and would go by himself? To communicate with Janice behind her back, no doubt.

He was still watching the sunset, with a yearning look on his face that normally would have turned her heart over. But not tonight. It was as if they had been sliced in two by a butcher's cleaver.

'I'm cold,' she said. 'Let's go back to Plas Uchaf.' The word 'home' would not come. The ice settled between them like hoarfrost on the trees, getting thicker through the evening hours and crystallizing towards the early hours of the morning, when they turned their backs on each other and neither spoke. Fran decided that they couldn't possibly be more miserable than they were now, so she might just as well confront him, and know the worst. Besides, she didn't yet know his side of what was happening to them. If he didn't any longer care enough for her to protect her from what Janice could do to them, she still loved him enough not to want to add to his sufferings. Over their stilted conversation at breakfast time, she could no longer bear the pain in his face.

'William,' she said. 'Tell me what's the matter. It is Janice this time, isn't it?'

'Yes,' he said – and no more.

'Then where are you going today?'

'I told you. To meet Nigel Delalprime. I have to get back to Old Swithinford as soon as it is possible for us to go. But I'm afraid he may not be able to go before Saturday, as we had arranged. I wish you didn't always make things worse by guessing half and imagining that there can only be one answer to any problem. Your suspicions, for once, have some foundation, but I'm almost as much in the dark as you are. I must get home as soon as I can to deal with what may happen, not what has happened. I am going to do today exactly what I told you I was going to do. If you spend the day imagining I am sending Janice an air-ticket home, it is you who are off course. I promise to tell you all as soon as I know anything for certain.'

He went to her and held out his arms. She almost collapsed into them, and heard his great exhalation of breath that spoke the volumes of his relief.

'There are times when I wish I didn't love you so much,' he said. 'I can bear anything but your distress. Will you believe me that whatever I do, it will be for your sake?'

'Yes – and whatever you do, *we'll* do. Whatever the consequences. Is that a bargain?'

'As far as it is possible for me to make one,' he said. 'I wish I hadn't got to leave you alone today, but I must. And I must get off, now.'

They simply must try to act normally. Think of something else other than Janice, quick. She did.

'Wait, just another minute. I don't remember you telling me you'd answered our invitation to the wedding. I said I would do it, but you claimed it as your privilege. I knew I ought to have seen to it myself.'

He looked sheepish. 'Sweetheart, I quite forgot. But does it matter? They know quite well we shall be there.'

She could hardly believe she had heard him aright. 'William! Of course it matters! I never thought the day would come when I could accuse you of discourtesy. Leave it with me – I'll do it.'

'No,' he said, 'I said I'd do it, and I will. I'm sorry, sweetheart. I don't often let you down, do I? Please leave it to me. Especially as things are now.'

He went, and she spent a long, long day alone. She began to pack to go home. Home.

The packing had cheered her up. She had envisaged Benedict's and couldn't wait now to see its pink walls again in reality. She thought lovingly of seeing the rooms in Eeyore's Tail repapered from top to bottom by Sophie, and repainted by Ned. And the rest of the spacious old house, their lovely home. She could almost smell the smell of furniture polish that she knew would greet her as soon as William opened the front door, and the roses on the dressing table in their bedroom, mingling their scent with that of clean linen. The silver would catch the sunshine and almost dazzle her with its familiar gleam. And best of all – she closed her eyes at the thought – there would be Cat.

How had they ever brought themselves to leave that purring bundle of ecstatic feline love for as long as a whole month? She imagined the weight of Cat on her chest, and that smooth soft fur under her fingers. She could almost feel the little cold wet muzzle poking itself against her chin, rubbing itself against her face till whiskers got up her nose and made her sneeze – at which Cat always looked indignant, opening her violet eyes wide in injured inquiry as to why her indulgent caresses were being so summarily rejected. The memory made Fran smile, so that she could almost hear the curious little sound, half purr, half mew, that induced her to hug and kiss Cat in spite of the offending whiskers, until a swinging necklace or earring caught the attention of a darting paw, and a game of catch-as-catch-can began that only stopped when Cat had had enough, and turned away yawning to cuddle down, her sinuous but solid little body anchoring Fran to her chair for far longer than she wanted to stay there, unless, of course, by that time William's lap was available for the whole performance to be repeated.

William was later home than she had expected and very quiet; but both refused to return to any matter of contention, and peace reigned, if it wasn't their usual kind. All he told her was that Nigel could not get away till Saturday. So they might just as well do the next day what they had planned, which was to go to watch the salmon leap again, go on to Builth

Wells to buy a suitable present for Olwen, and eat lunch there. They carried out their plan, and after lunch, they shopped in Builth and explored the little town a bit before it was time to find again their special spot on the Rogo, and eat their last Olwen picnic.

By the time they had finished their leisurely feast and packed things back in the car the sun was already turning the west into a blaze of golden glory. To watch it drop below the horizon the last steep hundred yards or so still had to be climbed.

'Let's stay here a little longer,' Fran said. 'It's comfortable and sheltered from the wind. But we'll go up before the sun sets. I couldn't bear to miss it.'

William sat down beside her in the little hollow that was protecting them from the freshening evening breeze. 'It'll be at least another half-hour before we need go up,' he said. 'Which gives me a chance to tell you what I've been keeping from you as long as I could. I truly had no option – so please don't be angry with me for leaving it till now.'

She tried to steel herself against trouble if that's what was to be. But now, whatever it was, she would somehow put it off till after the wedding. She was doing her usual trick of pushing off a moment of unpleasant truth by substituting complete irrelevancies and putting them into words. Just till the first sharp stab of pain had gone, and she could bear to face the dull ache that she would have to learn to bear.

'That's why you forgot to answer our invitation to the wedding, I suppose,' she said. 'Oh, darling, I'm sorry I grumbled about such a silly thing.'

'I haven't forgotten it,' he said. 'I did it today, and I can see by your face that as usual, you are running to meet trouble. Who said it was bad news I had for you? Take a look at this.'

He took from his pocket a snowy white envelope, and dropped it in her lap. She saw that it was addressed in his large firm italic hand to Mr and Mrs R. Bellamy at Castle Hill Farm. She pulled out the card and read

Dr and Mrs William Burbage
thank Mr and Mrs Bellamy for their kind invitation
to the marriage of their daughter Charlotte with Charles Bridgefoot.

She couldn't see to read the rest of it. Her hand was trembling and her head spinning. Her face had turned very pale. She put out a hand to him, unable to speak. He was quick to catch her in his arms as she swayed towards him, still staring down at the card. 'Darling, what does it mean?' she asked, her voice trembling. He sprang to his feet, ready for action. She was simply not the fainting sort of female, but she was as near to fainting now as he had ever seen her. He cursed himself for his clumsiness – in first frightening her and then startling her so crudely. He sank on his knees and gathered her into his arms, steadying her as he held her against him and letting her cling to him till her equilibrium was restored.

As soon as she could, she repeated her question. 'Darling, what does it mean?'

'Exactly what it says, I hope. That's why I couldn't answer it before. But now, if all goes as planned and you agree, I can post it before we leave Wales tomorrow.'

She was still stunned and incredulous. She couldn't take it in, and looked in puzzled fashion up to him for explanation.

'Darling Fran, I'm telling you the truth! Do you think I would play silly jokes on you about *that*? Of all things in the world, the thing I want most? I asked you not to be cross with me, because I honestly have had no other choice.'

'Tell me,' she said.

He breathed a great sigh, pulled her head on to his shoulder, and began. 'I can hardly believe it, either. In the first batch of letters Greg sent on to me, there was a letter from my solicitor informing me that he was investigating a rumour from the USA of an accident in Spain involving Janice. He had tried to ring me at home, but of course had been told I was away and that letters were being forwarded.

'I rang my solicitor. You were very helpful, sweetheart, not wanting to accompany me to the telephone in the daytime! He had been in touch with hers in New York, from whom he had heard that she and her sugar-daddy had been in Granada on holiday when the old man had slipped down the steps of a swimming pool and had had to be taken to hospital, seriously injured. His "wife", who had held him up in the water till help arrived, was suffering from shock herself. Two days later, when I rang him again, he had just heard that Mr Joseph's wife had died suddenly, apparently from an overstrained heart. I simply dared not believe it, but in any case I had no proof that Mr Joseph's dead "wife" was Janice. So they set to work. There was utter confusion – but in the end her passport disclosed that the dead lady was a British citizen: Janice Aurelia Denton, previously Burbage, maiden name Denton.'

William was incapable of sitting still another second. He sprang to his feet, seeming to Fran two inches taller than usual, and flung his arms wide as if getting rid of a load carried long on his shoulders.

'Darling, it had to be her! But I still had to have proof of her death. It could have been misreported. If it was true, then, like Winston Churchill crossing the South African border, I could shout, "I'm William bloody Burbage, and I'm free."

'God, but it has been difficult! Confirmation came the day before yesterday. As I was her legal husband, the death certificate had to be released to me, and I asked for it to be sent straight to the registrar in Builth. I picked it up yesterday. The poor old man has now died, too, so there is bound to be a lot of international to-ing and fro-ing, but as far as any of my advisers can see, they needn't involve me. Do you feel strong enough to come up and watch the sunset with me now? Because I'm afraid there are a couple of questions only you can answer.'

She hadn't really taken any of it in, yet. The significance of it all, especially to him . . . She looked up at him, and read in his face such a power of emotion that it awed her into stillness. They stood facing each other, simply holding hands. The circuit was complete and the current running through it lit up the whole world.

'Quick,' he said, 'or we shall miss the sunset.'

They scrambled up, and faced the splendour of the west, lovelier, they thought, than ever.

'Before the sun touches down, will you answer my questions?' he asked.

'If I can,' she said.

'Then – will you marry me?'

She couldn't answer. Words simply would not come. Instead she turned towards him, and held up her face to be kissed. She was not at all surprised to find his face as wet as her own.

'So what more is there to ask?' she said.

'Can you prove you are as free to marry me at Rhulen Church tomorrow morning as I can that I'm free to marry you? I've got it all set up with Nigel. He'll take your word for it, and accept the evidence afterwards, but I want it to be complete, final, from tomorrow for ever and for ever.'

Her mind raced. Brian's death certificate had been in her bank for more than twenty-five years. But – she opened her handbag, fumbling for the zip-fastener that closed an inside pocket. She never undid or sorted out except in emergency the slim little plastic wallet inside that held her driving licence and such things, even though she transferred it day-by-day from one bag to another. There it still was! The cover of the last war-widow's pension book she had ever used, having had her pension paid directly into a special account at her bank from the time she had ceased to be Brian's widow in anything but name and law.

He heaved a great sigh of satisfaction, and put it into his breast pocket.

'Watch the sun go down on your last day as Frances Catherwood,' he said. 'When it goes down tomorrow, you'll be Frances Burbage. My wife. *My very own legal wife.*'

'And we are going home,' she answered, cuddling up to him, while the sun slid behind the distant hill.

He swept her into his arms and said gloatingly, 'So we are, to spend our honeymoon, as I always told you we should, at Benedict's.'